DARK WHISPERS TRILOGY

THE CHILDREN OF THE GODS SERIES BOOKS 62-64

I. T. LUCAS

Published by Evening Star Press

EveningStarPress.com

ISBN: 978-1-957139-54-8

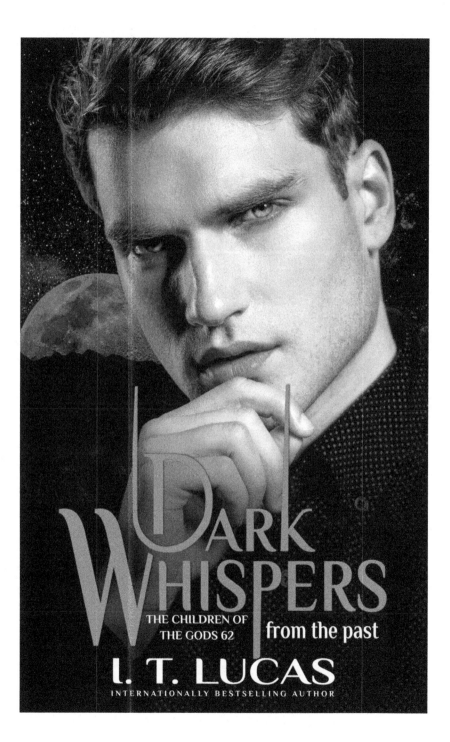

DARK WHISPERS

THE CHILDREN OF
THE GODS 62

from the past

I. T. LUCAS

INTERNATIONALLY BESTSELLING AUTHOR

1

JADE

$\mathcal{T}$he trees were a blur as Jade's booted feet ate up the miles. Propelled by the rage simmering inside her, she ran faster, pushed harder, and let her instincts guide her through the dense forest without colliding with obstacles or stumbling over them.

Leaving her hunting party behind, Jade veered to the right, leaped over a boulder, and dodged a fallen log. Her speed and agility could only be matched by her second-in-command, who was barely keeping up, while the rest would be left to fend for themselves, including her daughter and Kagra's sons.

Their offspring might be pureblooded Kra-ell and possess the most powerful and ruthless of warrior genes, but they didn't have the furnace of rage to push them beyond their comfort zone. Besides, what Igor's offspring failed to realize was that being a powerful Kra-ell was about more than genes. It was about smarts and honing their brains along with their bodies, and it was about honor and following an ancient code of conduct given to the Kra-ell by the Mother of all Life herself.

Exertion usually took the edge off, but today it failed to burn through the rage, fueling it instead. Her lungs gobbling up the mist and her heart pumping blood into her tiring limbs, Jade added a burst of speed and pushed harder.

Not to be outdone, Kagra sped up as well. Her long lean limbs working in perfect synchronization, her dark braid flying behind her like a devil's tail, she was a sight to behold. Watching her protégé blossom into the leader she'd been born to be filled Jade's chest with pride. She wished her daughter could be more like Kagra, but Drova was her father's daughter through and through. Just like Igor, she pissed on the Mother's teaching and ignored even the most basic tenets of the Kra-ell code of honor.

Despite Drova's lowlife murderer of a sire, Jade had had high hopes for her daughter, but even with all she'd invested in teaching and training the girl, it seemed that her nurture could not outdo Igor's nature.

3

Thank the Mother for guiding her to choose Kagra even though her second had been a pain in the ass at times. She wasn't a *yes* female, and she challenged Jade left and right, but she was loyal and honorable, and her mind was strong enough to withstand Igor's influence and retain some of its autonomy.

Kagra had always been a strong-willed, capable female, but during their twenty-two years of captivity, she'd become a force to be reckoned with. In a decade or two, she might match or even surpass Jade's power, but it would do her no good. It would only make her even more desirable to Igor, who wanted his offspring to be born to the strongest females, leaving the other captives to serve his henchmen and produce more of them for his army, so they could raid more Kra-ell tribes, steal their females and slaughter their males.

In a way, the weaker ones had it easier, their susceptibility to Igor's compulsion allowing him to subdue their grief and rage and make them more malleable, but Jade wouldn't have traded places with them for anything, not even her freedom. As long as her anger and grief burned within her heart, she would never stop plotting her revenge.

Although she and Kagra were the two most powerful females in the compound, able to retain some of their free will and autonomous thinking, neither of them would ever be able to break Igor's hold on their minds. They would never get free, and their need for revenge would probably remain an unappeased inferno of fury burning in their guts. But as long as Jade still had breath in her lungs and a mind capable of thinking, she would never abandon hope of one day killing Igor in the most painful and horrific way.

How could the Mother have given such an evil male such an incredible gift?

How could she look upon her children and watch her once proud daughters subjugated and exploited?

Perhaps the devil that the humans believed in was real, and he'd been the one who had bestowed upon Igor the power to bend others to his will. The Mother of all Life was supposed to look after her loyal creations and bestow her gifts upon her most deserving daughters, and very rarely on her most deserving sons as well.

"Slow down," Kagra panted beside her. "You can't outrun your anger."

"I can try." Jade continued at a breakneck speed for several more miles, slowing down only when her legs threatened to give out.

Stretching, she waited for Kagra to catch up.

"You're killing me." Kagra put her hands on her hips. "I'm going to throw up."

"You should thank me for pushing you. What's the only way to get stronger?"

Kagra rolled her eyes. "Train, and train, and then train some more until you can't move, and then do the same thing the next day, over and over again."

"You're lucky that I'm too tired to punch you for that eye-roll." Jade stretched her calves and motioned for Kagra to do the same. "We need to catch a big prey to replenish our reserves. I've burned through everything I had, and I'm starving."

"Let's rest a little first," Kagra said. "I'm thirsty more than hungry." She sniffed the air. "I smell water."

As Kagra beelined for the nearest stream, Jade followed.

Karelia was a beautiful region, densely wooded and rich in water and game, but it didn't make living under Igor's thumb any more tolerable. To have her family and her freedom back, Jade would have traded Karelia for a life of near starvation on barren and desolate land.

CHAPTER 1

Anything would be better than the nightmare she was living in, even death. But since Jade was still in her prime, the end of her life wasn't coming any time soon, and even if taking her own life wasn't dishonorable, the option had been taken away from her along with every other personal liberty and right.

For a Kra-ell, the only way to die honorably was either in battle or in a duel to the death, but Igor had made sure that she could do neither, and he'd also closed every other loophole that could lead to her death or that of her charges.

Sitting on the rocky riverbank, Kagra took off her boots and socks and put her feet in the water. "It's as freezing as usual, but it feels good."

"Summer is coming." Jade sat next to her and started removing her boots as well. "It's getting warmer."

Kagra moved her foot in circles, creating little spirals. "What if you push me in? I might wash up somewhere far away from here, and perhaps Igor's influence wouldn't reach that far?"

"Yeah, and you'll be saved by a frog prince who will kiss you and turn you into an ugly toad."

That got a laugh out of Kagra. "I love it when you take human fairytales and parables and turn them on their heads, but I'm serious. I can't jump into the water with the intention of running away, but if you push me, then it's an accident."

"I can't push you because that would be aiding your escape, which I'm under strong compulsion not to do. Secondly, you might freeze to death before you wash up. And thirdly, if you are not back in the compound within forty-eight hours, he will activate the damn collar." Jade pushed a finger under hers, rubbing it against the chafe marks on her neck.

Most of the time, she managed to forget about the titanium circle around her throat, the symbol that marked her as Igor's slave, but when she ran, the damn thing abraded her skin.

"The remote won't work from that far away," Kagra argued. "Besides, I don't think that there are explosives in the collars. The bands are not thick enough to contain anything. I think Igor just put them on us to torment and humiliate us."

"I'm just glad that they don't have listening devices in them. If I couldn't talk freely with you, I would explode." At first, Jade had thought that the collars contained tracking and listening devices, but after cursing Igor out on multiple occasions and not getting punished for it, she realized that no one was listening. "But I bet that he has location trackers in them in case someone manages to throw off his compulsion." Jade lifted the collar of her shirt and tucked it under the metal. "Not that I can imagine anyone strong enough to do that. If you and I can't break free of his compulsion, no one can. He might have put the trackers in just to make us feel even more helpless, and he succeeded. After twenty-two years of examining every loophole and thinking of every way I could kill him, even at the expense of my own life, I know that there is no way out. We are going to die here, and so will our children."

"Maybe they will come for us," Kagra whispered. "The queen was supposed to send more settlers."

Jade sighed. "No one is coming. And even if they did, they wouldn't know where to look for us."

2

WILLIAM

*A*s William took the stairs to Kian's office two at a time, he was proud of himself for being able to do so without getting winded but at the same time annoyed with himself for being predictably late. He'd planned to arrive at least half an hour early, but as usual, he'd gotten distracted, and now he had less than fifteen minutes left before the meeting to discuss with Kian all the issues that were of no interest to the other participants.

"Good morning." He rushed into the boss's office. "I know that I'm early, but I need to talk to you before the others arrive."

Kian smiled indulgently. "I assume this has to do with your recruitment efforts?"

"Yes." William pulled out a chair next to the conference table and dropped into it.

"How is that going?" Kian asked. "Are the increased incentives attracting better-qualified people?"

William chuckled. "Nearly doubling what we were offering certainly helped attract a higher caliber of candidates, but the qualifications are the lesser problem. The bigger one is finding bioinformaticians who are willing to accept work on a secret project that requires them to live in isolation for several months. They are in such high demand that they can pick and choose, and the good ones are more interested in prestige than money. A secret project they can't talk about or even mention will not help their future career prospects because they can't put it on their résumé."

Kian pursed his lips. "It's only going to last a couple of months, and it's not such a daunting prospect given that the isolated location is Safe Haven, which we've turned into a high-end resort. They can enjoy the beach and the gym, and we even hired a gourmet cook to prepare healthy meals for them."

The gourmet cook and the facilities would be shared with Eleanor's paranormals, but William saw that as an advantage rather than a disadvantage. His team would have only three to five members, and that wasn't enough to keep people from going stir crazy from isolation. And since the paranormal enclave was inside the most secure zone, it wasn't a safety issue either.

William pushed his glasses up his nose. "I hope they don't notice the security measures that can put Area 51 to shame. The so-called resort is guarded better than a top-security prison."

"They won't notice." Kian waved a dismissive hand. "We went to great lengths to keep all of it hidden, and if they see the occasional drone, they will assume it belongs to one of the lodge's guests."

"I hope so." William released a breath. "I lined up several good candidates from Stanford, most of them recent graduates, and I'm meeting with them tomorrow and Wednesday."

"Where?" Kian asked.

The boss didn't like him leaving the village without a Guardian escort, and William braced for a confrontation. None of the other council members were forced to travel with bodyguards, and he saw no reason for being singled out.

"The Bay Area, of course. I meant to tell you last week that I would be flying out tomorrow, but I forgot." He hadn't, but he hoped that it would be too late for Kian to insist on a Guardian escort.

Kian frowned. "Your time is too valuable to waste on traveling to interview prospects. You can use teleconferencing to interview them."

That was an angle William hadn't anticipated, mostly because what Kian was suggesting was absurd. He couldn't choose his team members based on a video call interview. As an immortal, he had extrasensory perception that could only be used in close physical proximity.

"My time is indeed valuable, but so is the information we are trying to decipher with the help of these recruits. I've done most of the groundwork via emails and phone calls, but you know as well as I do that there is no substitute for face-to-face meetings."

Kian lifted a brow. "Are you so desperate that you plan on thralling them into accepting the job?"

William wondered whether the boss was suggesting that he do that or warning him not to do it. Kian could go both ways.

"Thralling humans for our benefit is against clan law, and it's also immoral, but I'm ashamed to admit that the thought has crossed my mind." He sighed. "The reason I want to meet with them in person is that I need to get a sense of who they are as people. Their academic abilities are not the only deciding factor. I'll be spending a lot of time with them over several months, and it's important that I get along with them, and that they get along with each other. If I manage to have a team of three to five bioinformaticians assembled by the end of Wednesday, I'll consider it time very well spent."

Kian regarded him with a smile. "Let me guess. Your nineteen-year-old prodigy refused to come to you for an interview, and you hope to convince her to join your team in person."

That was true, but William wasn't going to apologize for wanting Doctor Kaia Locke on his team. "She's my best candidate, but I would have gone even if her parents weren't an issue."

"What's their problem?"

7

could accidentally bump into a Doomer, and you are not a warrior. Cancel the flight. You're taking the private jet and a Guardian. End of discussion."

Folding his arms over his chest, William glared at Kian. "None of the other council members have to travel with bodyguards." He sounded like a kinder-gartener, but he really didn't want to have a Guardian going with him on the interviews.

"What do you want me to say, that you are more valuable?" Kian leaned back in his chair, but his eyes were still holding William's captive. "I value all the council members tremendously, for their skills and as my closest friends, but if tragedy strikes, they can all be replaced. No one can take your place."

"I'm training Marcel. He's almost as good as me." That was a gross exaggera-tion, but Kian wouldn't know that.

"Almost doesn't cut it, and we both know that Marcel doesn't have that extra something that you have. Shai knows every aspect of the clan business as well and better than I do, but he can't take my place for the same reason. I know in my gut when to make a deal and when not to. Things are rarely clear cut, and I don't base my decisions solely on numbers and charts, just as you don't base yours on calcu-lations alone or rely on tried and tested solutions. You think outside the box."

Regrettably, that was true, but that didn't mean that he should be kept in a cocoon. "I'm not going to show up to meetings with a bodyguard."

"The Guardian can pretend to be your chauffeur."

William snorted. "Do I look like the kind of guy who has a chauffeur?" He flapped his Hawaiian shirt, which was two sizes too big on him. He'd lost about thirty pounds since he'd started training with Ronja and Darlene, but he needed to lose at least thirty more, and it would be a waste of time and energy to shop for new clothes only to do it again in a couple of months.

Kian eyed the shirt with a frown. "Get some new clothes before you go. If you want to impress your candidates, and especially Doctor Kaia Locke and her parents, you can't show up looking like a schlump."

3

KAIA

"Don't cry, sweet pea." Swaying on her feet, Kaia held her baby brother to her chest and rocked him gently. "Whoever decided that babies needed to get six vaccines at twelve months old was a sadistic bastard. They should have spread them out over several months."

Her mother rocked Ryan, who was hiccuping between sniffles. "It's better to get it over with all at once."

Kaia strongly disagreed. When she had children, she wouldn't allow them to be tormented like that.

Poor boys.

Throughout the ordeal the twins had been screaming their little heads off, and when they'd gotten exhausted, they'd switched to pitiful whimpering and casting accusing looks at Kaia and their mother for allowing the nurse to give them ouchies.

"Gilbert should have been here with his sons. I don't want them to associate me with needles. I want Evan, Ryan, and Idina to always think of me as the cool, fun big sister."

Usually the nanny accompanied their mother to doctor visits with the twins, but Idina had come down with a cold and couldn't go to preschool, so the nanny had to stay home with her.

Her mother sighed. "He wanted to be here for them, but he had an important inspection at a job site that he couldn't leave to the supervisor. He had to attend it in person."

Kaia twisted her lips in a grimace. "Yeah, I bet."

It wasn't the first time Gilbert had come up with a convenient excuse to wiggle out of performing his less-than-pleasant fatherly duties, which included changing poopy diapers and wiping little noses. The guy was only forty-eight, but he acted like a throwback to the fifties.

He was a great guy, and he loved Kaia and Cheryl as if they were his own daughters, but he wasn't very helpful with the little ones, leaving all the work of raising them to their mother and the nanny.

It would have been semi-okay if their mother was a stay-at-home mom, but she wasn't. Karen Locke was a sysadmin for a large defense contractor, which was a demanding position with a salary to match. It wasn't fair for her partner to leave all the work of managing the household and taking care of his toddler daughter and twin baby sons to her, and by extension, to Kaia and Cheryl.

Well, mostly to Kaia because Cheryl was still in high school while Kaia was home, exploring her employment options.

She'd had offers from several universities and a dozen or so private research facilities, but she was probably going to accept a position at Stanford so she could keep living at home.

Her mother and Gilbert didn't want her to move out, and she didn't want to do that either. How could she possibly leave her sweet baby brothers, Idina and Cheryl? She would miss them too much.

On the other hand, starting college at fourteen and finishing her doctorate at nineteen, all while living at home, meant that Kaia had missed out on the whole college experience. It would have been nice to try something different instead of doing more of the same for the rest of her life.

She stifled a snort. If her memories of her past life as a mathematician were real and not imagined, she was doing more or less the same thing during two lifetimes, or maybe more. What if she'd been stuck in the same groove throughout her soul's existence? She might have gone through many life cycles, and in each of them, she'd been consumed by the beauty of numbers and the endless patterns they formed. All of creation was based on numbers, and it fascinated her, but there was more to life than research, and she'd learned that lesson in her past life as well as in her current one.

Her previous self had been single, childless, and lonely, while Kaia had a wonderful family and was surrounded by love. Losing her father at a young age had reinforced the lessons learned in her previous life, making her hold on to the people she loved because she could never know how long she would have with them.

Maybe that was why Kaia appreciated her chaotic home life and was in no hurry to leave.

"Come on." Her mother slung the strap of her enormous baby bag over her shoulder. "Let's take the boys home."

By the time they got to the car Evan had fallen asleep, exhausted from all the crying, and Ryan had quieted down but was still sniffling pitifully.

After strapping the twins into their car seats, Kaia got behind the wheel. "I guess we are not stopping by the supermarket on our way home."

Her mother turned to look at the babies in the backseat. "Not with the twins. We can order what we need online and have it delivered."

Kaia grimaced. "They always mess things up, and they drive me nuts with all the messages about approving substitutions. I prefer to drop you off and go by myself. The guy from the secret research project is coming tomorrow, and all we have to serve are Skittles and gummy bears."

"I don't know why you agreed to see him." Her mother folded her arms over her chest. "We've talked about it, and we agreed that you are not going to accept his offer no matter how good it is. You are just wasting his time and ours."

"I'm curious to hear more about the project. What if it's about something so crucial and necessary that I would later beat myself up for not being part of it? Besides, the guy sounds so desperate for me to join that he might present me with an offer that I can't refuse."

That was all true, but there was a third reason for her wanting to meet William, and it had to do with Tony's disappearance. Her mother and Gilbert would freak out if they knew that she was getting involved in that, and her mother wouldn't allow the recruiter anywhere near the house if she suspected that he had anything to do with Tony's fate.

Kaia didn't know whether William had been involved in Tony's case or not, but she was desperate for any clues that could help her find out what happened to her friend.

The thing was that William's offer was very similar to the one Anthony had received a little over a year ago. The highly classified research project had been supposed to take four months, and yet no one had heard from Anthony in over a year. It was a long shot to think that William had been Tony's recruiter as well, but bioinformatics wasn't a huge field, and there weren't that many players outside of academia and major research institutions. William could have heard something, or he might know the people who had hired Anthony.

4

KIAN

"Good morning." Syssi walked over to Kian and leaned to kiss his cheek. "Am I late?"

"You're not." He pulled out a chair for her. "Okidu called to tell me that he's stuck in traffic. He estimates Mia and Toven's time of arrival to be eleven-thirty."

She glanced at William, who was never on time, and then at her watch. "I'm a little late. I didn't want to be the last one to get here, but I didn't want to leave Allegra with Vivian without making sure that she was okay with her, so I waited a few minutes to see how they were getting along. I swear that baby understands every word I say. I told her that Mommy would be back shortly and to play nicely with Aunt Vivian. She smiled and waved bye-bye at me."

"My daughter is a genius."

Syssi sat down with an infectious grin spreading over her face. "I know, right?" She turned to William. "How come you're early?"

"I wanted to talk to Kian about my trip to the Bay Area before the meeting. I'm going tomorrow, and I forgot to tell him about it."

"What's in the Bay Area?"

"I'm meeting with several bioinformaticians, and I hope to have a team assembled by Wednesday."

She arched a brow. "You've been looking for people for months. How did you manage to line up several candidates?"

Looking at Kian, he smiled. "The boss has given me a bigger budget and an attractive location to conduct the research. I've also lowered my standards, and I'm willing to recruit greenhorns fresh out of grad school."

"Doctor Kaia Locke is a greenhorn," Kian said. "And yet she's your best candidate."

William nodded. "She is, and if I get her to join, she can shore up the rest of the team."

"I can't wait to meet her." Syssi tilted her head and looked at Kian from under her lashes. "I also want to see the new and improved Safe Haven. Can we go for a day trip? We can fly in the morning and return the same evening."

"I don't see why not." He took her hand. "Turner and William have designed a security system that is nearly as good as what we have in the village, and the accommodations can rival any high-end resort. I don't mind taking you and Allegra for a visit."

High-end was a bit of an exaggeration since the rooms in the original lodge were small, and the ones in the bungalows were only slightly bigger, but he'd approved high-quality fixtures and furnishings, so the interiors were luxuriously appointed.

"I've seen the brochure." Syssi leaned forward and pulled one from the stack on the conference table. "Emmett's hair and beard are epic. And that gown." Lifting the pamphlet, she laughed. "He looks like a prophet."

"He plays the part." Kian took another pamphlet and handed it to William. "We want to attract people with paranormal talents, and I'm not sure whether Emmett's guru persona is going to attract or repel them. But in either case, he needs it to hide how young he looks."

"The prophet look worked for him very well in the past." Syssi spread out the pamphlet. "I don't see why it wouldn't now."

Kian tapped his fingers on the table. "I'm curious. Would either of you have paid money to participate in a spiritual retreat run by a guy who looks like Moses?"

William laughed. "I probably wouldn't have noticed Emmett's outfit, but I wouldn't have wasted my time on anything with the words spiritual or retreat in it either. Those kinds of things don't interest me."

Syssi shook her head. "I wouldn't have participated no matter how its leader looked. I'm too shy to enjoy communal experiences, especially with people I'm not already friends with."

"You work in a lab full of people." Kian wrapped his arm around her shoulders. "You are also surrounded by people in the village, and I don't see you hiding at home."

"It's different." She waved a hand in dismissal. "I know everyone at the lab, and I'm comfortable with them."

"What about the test subjects?"

She chuckled. "They are usually more nervous than I am, so I have to make an effort to put them at ease. Besides, I have Amanda, the ultimate extrovert, to run interference for me if I need it."

"How is it being back at work?" William asked.

"Challenging." Syssi smiled. "But I'm glad that I decided to return to work. I love being a mother, but that's not all I am. I need to get out of the house, and I need to stimulate my brain. Thankfully, I can take Allegra with me, and she enjoys the change in scenery as well, but it has been only ten days, so it's still an adjustment period." She chuckled. "When Annani took Alena and Orion on a trip to see the Sanctuary and later to Scotland, Amanda and I lost our two best babysitters, so we had to go back to work and hire a nanny."

"I know." William pushed his glasses back. "Roni and I ran the security check on her."

"Right, I forgot about that. Anyway, Eliza is great, and Ingrid did an amazing job converting Amanda's office into a nursery."

Kian shifted in his chair, hiding his discomfort from Syssi. She knew that he was worried about her taking Allegra with her to work, but she thought that he was being overprotective.

William's crew had fortified the security measures at the university to include all the walkways around it, so Kian could see the nanny taking the babies for a walk in their double stroller. Unbeknownst to Amanda and Syssi, there was also a team of Guardians parked near the lab's building, ready to deploy in seconds if needed, but it still made him uneasy having his daughter away from the security of the village.

"I'm looking forward to working in the lab at Safe Haven," William said. "But I'm going to miss my lab here and working side by side with Roni. We make a great team."

Leaning back, Syssi folded her arms over her chest. "I still don't know why you decided to do the research there. It would have been safer to keep the journals here and bring those bioinformaticians to the village. You are going to thrall them to forget everything anyway, so what difference does it make?"

"The journals stay here," Kian said. "I had Okidu photocopy each page and scan them into our secure servers."

Syssi let out a breath. "I know that, and I also know that no one can hack the clan's servers, but someone can attack Safe Haven and steal the information from the computers that are there, or just take the servers with them."

5

WILLIAM

"*I* can answer that," William said. "I worked with Turner to design the security measures, and Safe Haven is now practically impenetrable. We set up concentric perimeter security zones, with the outmost ring starting twenty miles out. We have hidden infrared cameras and sensors installed at all roads leading to Safe Haven, whether paved, gravel, or animal trails. These devices are powered by long-lasting battery packs, and they transmit via the clan satellites directly to the main security room in the village, with a parallel feed going to the security room at Safe Haven. Images of each vehicle's occupants are captured and fed into our proprietary face recognition software and are processed in real time for immediate feedback."

"Wow." Syssi pushed a strand of hair behind her ear. "What if someone is hiding in the trunk?"

William smiled. "We have that covered as well. Infrared cameras scan the vehicles and alert security if they detect hidden occupants. A team of Guardians will intercept the vehicle, stop it, and search it. They will also stop any car whose occupants' faces don't match those that were fed into the system ahead of time. We will have three teams of Guardians with us, so one team is always on duty."

"Is the system already operational?" Syssi asked. "I don't expect any of it to be needed, but the paranormals moved in a week ago, and we are responsible for their safety."

William nodded. "Except for the drones and measures at the lab itself, all the rest is working. The density of the surveillance equipment doubles at every concentric parameter. At ten miles out, the equipment covers all the wooded area regardless of roads or trails. The entire coastline is covered for fifteen miles in each direction, so we are not exposed from the ocean side either. When we assemble the scientific team and start working on the journals, advanced stealth drones with high-power optics and infrared equipment will be monitoring the area around the clock." He chuckled. "Roni hacked into the FAA's servers and instructed them to ignore the drones. We also have battle-grade drones that are ready to deploy on command, and I had one of the noise cannons moved to Safe Haven as well."

He had to admit that the security measures were excessive. It would have been more economical to bring the team to the village, but he saw the merit of having another secure location in case they needed to evacuate the village for whatever reason. Besides, it was good for the Guardians to learn to operate the new systems that he and Turner had designed while the risk of attack was low.

"Wow, my head is spinning." Syssi looked at Kian. "I should have known that your paranoia would kick in big time. Are you expecting a Doomer attack?"

He shrugged. "You never know. The information in those journals is priceless, and since William convinced me that the only way he could get qualified people to work on deciphering them without resorting to thralling or compulsion was to allow them some freedom, I had no choice but to go overboard. Besides, we figured out that it was strategically prudent to have another secure location in case the unthinkable happened, and the village's location was compromised." He looked at William. "Don't forget to power up Armageddon when the team starts working in the lab."

"What's Armageddon?" Syssi asked.

"It's what I nicknamed the lab's security." William took his glasses off, folded them, and put them on the conference table. "The security office, the control center, the servers, the armory, and the lab itself are all located underground, and the entrance is fortified with blast-proof doors. But if the doors are breached, we have a self-destruct button that will detonate underneath the structure and destroy everything inside of it."

Syssi paled. "Are you serious? With the people inside?"

"We have an escape tunnel, but as a last resort, I will blow the place up with everyone inside, including myself, to prevent this technology from falling into the wrong hands."

Shaking her head, Syssi put her hand on Kian's arm. "You should just destroy those journals. I'm starting to agree with the gods on that. Not on the destruction of the Odus, which was barbaric even though they weren't sentient, but the technology to make them. I'm sure that the gods had very compelling reasons for banning the technology. It's not worth the risk."

Kian sighed. "Don't think that I wasn't tempted, but those journals might contain genetic information that could save lives. Along with the code to build the Odus, they might have included the code that's responsible for our fast healing and regenerating. We could transform the world with that knowledge."

"Or destroy it." Syssi let out a breath. "But I get it. That's why I didn't advise against attempting to decipher them. What about the people working on them? How are you protecting the information from being stolen?" She looked at William. "Their minds are not the only way they can copy it and smuggle it out. I'm not a computer expert, and I'm sure that you have it covered, but if you can explain it to me in layman's terms, I would sleep better at night knowing that the information, both the original and the translation, is protected."

Lifting his glasses off the table, William put them back on even though there was no need for anti-glare lenses inside Kian's office. "The Safe Haven lab servers are connected to the village servers via an ultra-secure encrypted link using 512-

bit encryption designed by Roni and me. None of the servers are connected to the internet, and they communicate only via the clan's satellite. All traffic between them requires ongoing authentication. Also, each person working in the lab will be issued a fob key that regenerates a new access code every two hours. Without it, everything they see would be scrambled. None of the information is stored locally on the lab's servers, and all files on the local servers, including cache files, are fully encrypted."

Syssi tapped her fingers on the table. "What about their phones? Will they have to surrender them before entering the lab or before being admitted to Safe Haven?"

"They can bring their phones to their bungalows," William said. "But no phones will be allowed in the lab or the rest of the underground facility. Besides, even if they manage to smuggle one in, it would be useless. The underground and its immediate area will have the same protection as the village, so no electromagnetic signals can be broadcast or received there. Only the clan phones will work. On top of that, all cellular and internet traffic from Safe Haven's general facilities area will be monitored in real time by an AI program designed by Roni and me. If it flags anything, the connection will be severed instantly."

"Wow again." Syssi pretended to wipe the sweat off her brow. "Now I can sleep without worrying about exploding labs. I will just have to contend with nightmares about the end of the world via an army of Odus."

"I will never allow that to happen." Kian took her hand and gave it a gentle squeeze. "Our Allegra will grow up in a world of peace and prosperity."

Syssi didn't look reassured. "You can't make promises like that, Kian. Not everything is under your control."

"Not everything, but with two gods to back me up, a lot is."

6

MIA

*A*s the limo's windows turned opaque, Mia's excitement ratcheted up a notch. It was her first time back in the village since she and Toven had left after her transition.

Orion and Alena had come over to say goodbye before leaving for the goddess's sanctuary, and Geraldine and Cassandra had also visited with their mates, but Mia hadn't seen any of the others in nearly a month, and she missed the sense of community of the village.

"It won't be the same without Annani, Orion, and Alena." She leaned her head against Toven's shoulder. "But I'm glad that Orion is going to Scotland to meet Alena's children. It wouldn't be right for them to get married without doing that first."

"If you say so." He kissed the top of her head. "They are not going to stay there for long, though, and by the time they return, we will be living in the village."

"I'm looking forward to that." She lifted her head and smiled at him. "When they get back, I want to invite them to dinner at our new place. My grandmother will be over the moon."

Toven chuckled. "I can just imagine how anxious she will be about preparing a meal for Annani. In your grandmother's eyes, she is a real god. I'm a broken one."

"That's not true. My grandparents love you."

"And I love them back, but since I don't glow, I'm not a real god."

Toven had lost his glow a long time ago, most likely following the trauma of losing his people, but he was working on getting it back. "You'll find your glow again. I'm sure of it."

"I am too. With you by my side, I feel like a god for the first time in centuries." He smoothed his hand over her arm and leaned to nuzzle her ear. "Especially when you climax and scream, oh god, oh god."

Her cheeks catching fire, she slapped his arm. "I do not."

"Yes, you do."

"Once. I only did that once, you scoundrel."

For the first two weeks after her transition, Toven had been afraid to make love to her, and when he finally had, Mia had screamed his name. She might have added an oh-god or two, but she didn't remember that.

After a month of recuperating, she felt fantastic despite the constant itching and pain of her growing legs. It wasn't as bad as Bridget had warned her it would be, but she had the pain meds the doctor had prescribed to thank for that. Without them, things would have been much more difficult.

"Are you nervous about the meeting?" Toven asked.

"Nope. I'm excited."

Toven had exchanged some emails with Kian and Syssi regarding the terms of Perfect Match's acquisition, and they had teleconferenced with them a few times, but now that Mia was over the first stage of her transition and feeling great, they were going to finalize the terms in a face-to-face meeting.

This time around, though, Mia felt confident, and she wasn't scared of participating. Syssi was going to be there, and the two of them saw eye to eye on things. Also, with both of them being creative people, they had a lot in common and felt a strong affinity toward each other. But Syssi was more business savvy, and Kian was intimidating as heck, so some nervous butterflies were still buzzing around in Mia's belly.

As they entered the tunnel, Okidu looked at her through the rearview mirror. "No need to fret, Mistress Mia. These are just the village's security measures. We are almost there."

"It's okay." Mia smiled at him. "I approve of them wholeheartedly."

Okidu's smile grew even wider. "I am glad, mistress."

It was hard to believe that the butler was not human, and Mia couldn't help but think of him as a middle-aged British man. Then again, the only other cyborgs she'd encountered had been fictional characters in movies and books, and they had been depicted as very human as well, so she had no real reference for how a cyborg should act, and the same went for aliens, which reminded her of what Cassandra had told her about the Kra-ell living in the village.

Lifting her eyes to Toven, she put her hand on his knee. "After the meeting, I want to visit the café."

"Are you hungry?" He gave her a worried look. "I don't know how long the meeting will take, and I don't want you to wait until it is over. I can call Kian and tell him that we are grabbing a sandwich on the way."

"I'll wait until after the meeting. They've been waiting for us long enough."

"It's almost noontime. We had breakfast three hours ago."

"It's okay." She patted his knee. "I mentioned the café because I want to see the Kra-ell girl working there, not because I'm hungry."

He arched a brow. "I can hear your belly rumbling."

Mia laughed. "It does it all the time lately. I need to watch it, or I'll turn into a pumpkin, and you won't be able to keep carrying me around."

Since waking up after her initial transition, she'd been eating like a horse, but it was never enough, and she was hungry all the time.

"There is no chance of that." He leaned down and kissed the tip of her nose. "Your body is using that fuel to continue your transformation. You are no heavier now than you were a month ago."

"Liar." She leaned up and kissed his lips. "But that's okay. You can keep lying to me."

"I'm not lying." He looked genuinely offended.

Mia rolled her eyes. "I had to order new pants that were a size larger than my old ones. I know that I gained a few pounds, and I'm okay with that. I no longer have to worry about the strain the extra weight would put on my heart." She took a deep breath. "One of the best things about my transition is the peace of mind knowing that I'm not going to collapse all of a sudden. I feel drunk on the tranquility."

"It's the pain meds." Toven winked. "And the extra something special I give you every night, and I'm not talking about earth-shattering orgasms."

"You aren't?" She feigned innocence. "I thought that was your best godly expression."

He tightened his arm around her. "Well, if you insist. I'm sure that they have a therapeutic effect as well."

7

KIAN

"Hello, everyone." Mia waved her hand as Toven carried her into the office. "There is no elevator in your building." She cast a glance at Kian that was part apologetic and part accusatory.

"My apologies." Kian rushed to pull out a chair for her. "It was an unforgivable oversight on my part. I should have held the meeting in my office in the underground complex, which is easily accessible."

He was surprised that Syssi hadn't thought of that, but then she'd been preoccupied with returning to work, hiring a nanny to look after Allegra and Evie at the lab, and finding a new babysitter for their daughter in the village for special occasions like today's meeting.

"That's okay." Toven set Mia on the chair. "I'll go back down and bring the wheelchair up, but if you want to make it up to Mia for the oversight, you can order lunch. She is hungry."

"I'm okay." Mia's cheeks pinked in embarrassment. "I can wait until after the meeting."

"I'll have lunch delivered." Kian pulled out his phone.

"Who are you going to call?" Syssi asked. "The café doesn't deliver, and Callie's place is not open yet."

"I'm texting Wendy. She can send Aliya over with our order."

"I could eat," William said. "Can you please order me a Reuben?"

Kian collected everyone's orders and then waited for Toven to come back with the wheelchair. "What would you like?"

"I'm not picky. Whatever you're having is good for me."

Kian arched a brow. "I'm ordering the only vegan sandwich they have on the menu. Are you sure that's what you want?"

"It's fine."

Unlike Annani, Toven was not a prima donna. In fact, he was more accommodating than Kalugal, who must have inherited his penchant for flair and drama from the same source Annani had—his maternal grandfather. Ahn had been the consummate politician, and according to Annani, his leadership had never been challenged, not even by Mortdh. He'd been the most powerful god, but that wasn't the only reason no one could have imagined any other god taking his place. He'd had that innate something extra, a dramatic flair that his daughter had inherited, and so had some of his grandchildren, specifically Amanda and Kalugal.

Toven parked the wheelchair next to Mia. "Do you want to change seats?"

"I'm fine for now. But if I need to visit the bathroom, I'll need the wheelchair."

"About that." Syssi winced. "None of the bathrooms in the office building are wheelchair accessible."

"I'll carry you." Toven sat down next to Mia and turned to Kian. "Let's talk business."

"Indeed." Kian handed him the draft he'd prepared. "As we've discussed over the phone, you are going to purchase most of Hunter and Gabriel's shares and some of Syssi's. The equity and voting shares will be equally split between you and Syssi at fifty percent each, but they will represent only forty percent of the profit-sharing stock. The founders will retain ten percent each."

Toven's main objective was to have control over the company, but he conceded to sharing it with Syssi as long as it was only the two of them, so neither could make a major decision without the other. The problem with that was giving Hunter and Gabriel a stake in the company without giving them the deciding voting rights. It had been solved by creating two classes of stocks.

After reading through the one-page document, Toven passed it over to Mia. "What do you think?"

"It looks fine to me," she said. "I'm just surprised at how short it is. I expected the contract to be at least as hefty as my medical record."

Syssi laughed. "The final draft will probably be much longer, mainly for Hunter and Gabriel's sake. I'm fine with sealing the deal with a handshake."

"So am I." Toven turned to her. "As long as the main items we agreed upon are spelled out, so there is no future disagreement, we don't need the legalese to complicate things." He smiled. "It's not like we can take each other to court over disputes."

Syssi waved a dismissive hand. "Fates forbid we ever get there. We are both reasonable people, and we are in agreement about the major issues. We can negotiate over the minor details."

"I have a few that are not that minor." Toven turned to William. "The first thing I want to do is bring more machines here. From what I heard, there is a long waiting list of village residents for the two you have, and that's unacceptable. I want to have enough machines so Mia and I can go on an adventure whenever we please without feeling guilty about making others wait."

William cleared his throat. "The demand is high, but I think that four additional machines would suffice. The problem will be finding space for them. Up until recently, we only had two curtained-off areas, but we've added walls, and now we have two dedicated private rooms, but we will need four more."

The rooms in the lab were also tiny and spartan, nowhere near as nice as the ones in the Perfect Match studios.

"Then we need to build a studio in the village." Toven shifted his eyes to Kian. "Since Mia and I will be frequent users, I will cover the expense of building it."

Kian didn't like the idea of Toven financing building projects in the village. He was fine with the god owning half of Perfect Match, but he wasn't ready to give him a stake in the village. Then again, he'd let Kalugal pay for developing and building his section, which was a much bigger deal than a studio, so it wasn't rational to deny Toven.

Still, it wasn't the same. Kalugal had pledged his allegiance to the clan, while Toven was a free agent, and the only guarantee they had of him not turning against the clan was that his children and grandchildren were members.

"I was thinking about charging for the service." Kian leaned back and folded his arms over his chest. "In time, the proceeds will cover the expense. The problem is finding space for a new common building. I'm not willing to shrink the lawn area, or sacrifice greenery for more buildings, but we have vacant residences that could be converted into studios. Most of the houses have only two bedrooms, but we can use two adjacent homes to house the four new machines, or three to house all six. I'm sure that Ingrid can convert them to look just as good or better than the Perfect Match studios."

Toven nodded. "That's an acceptable solution. I also need space for a creators' studio. Mia wants to try her hand at designing environments, and I would like to move some of the work that's now done in the Perfect Match headquarters to the village. I understand that William has many programmers working on different projects, including developing new adventures."

"I do," William said. "They all have workstations in the underground lab, but we are at capacity. I have no people to spare for more projects." He scratched his head. "We have many programmers in the clan, but I could always use more." He looked at Kian. "Can you incentivize computer studies?"

Kian doubted that would help, but it never hurt to try.

He nodded. "I can do that."

8

TOVEN

"I don't want Mia to work underground." Toven uncrossed his arms and draped one over the back of Mia's chair. "That's not an environment conducive to creativity."

"I agree," Syssi said. "Maybe some of your programmers would like to work aboveground? Their productivity might increase."

William shrugged. "It's possible. But I'm going to work remotely for the next several months, and the lab won't function as well without me, so I wouldn't suggest making any changes while I'm gone."

"Where are you going?" Toven asked.

"I'm running a new project at Safe Haven."

"I have an idea." Syssi's eyes lit up with excitement. "After you are done there, we can move the Perfect Match headquarters to Safe Haven. Everything will already be set up, and it would be a waste not to utilize the lab there beyond this one project."

William frowned. "I don't see how that can help. First of all, the lab in Safe Haven is too small to serve as headquarters, and secondly, it's also underground, and for a good reason. It's much easier to secure."

A knock on the door put a temporary halt to the conversation, and as it opened and a very tall and very skinny woman entered with a tray of drinks in one hand and a large paper bag in the other, Toven had no doubt that she was the Kra-ell female who Mia had wanted to meet.

Aliya was lovely, beautiful in an alien way that didn't resemble any of the goddesses he remembered. Had her ancestors come from the same place as the gods?

His father hadn't mentioned another humanoid species sharing their corner of the universe, but he'd hinted that humans were not the gods' first genetic experiment. They had created other intelligent life by combining their genetic material with that of local primitive life, speeding up its evolution to leap over hundreds of thousands of years of natural processes.

Had the Kra-ell been one of their creations?

"Thank you, Aliya." Kian took the bag and the tray from her. "I apologize for dragging you up here."

"It's my pleasure." She looked at Toven and then at Mia. "Hi."

"Hello." Mia smiled at her. "You can blame me for that. Ever since I woke up from my transition, I'm constantly hungry."

"Congratulations on turning immortal." Aliya looked down at Mia's missing legs. "I heard about you, and I've met your grandparents. They are very nice. I'm glad that you're getting your legs back. I don't know if my people can regenerate like that."

As a long moment of awkward silence stretched over Kian's office, Aliya's olive-toned skin went a shade darker. "I'm sorry. Did I say something inappropriate? I'm still learning what's okay to say and what's not, and I don't understand many of the English idioms."

"You didn't say anything wrong," Mia reassured her. "I heard about you too, and I was curious to see you. You are very pretty."

Aliya chuckled. "For an alien."

"For anyone," Mia said. "Your beauty is different, but that's what makes you look so exotic. Is it okay if I draw you? I'm an artist."

"Yeah, I know. Your grandparents told me that you illustrate children's books."

"I also draw for my own pleasure, and those pictures have more mature themes." Mia sent Toven a reproachful sidelong glance. "But no nudes or anything suggestive." She turned back to Aliya. "I like to draw interesting faces."

After Orion had shown her the journal he'd stolen, Mia had asked to see Toven's other journals that contained drawings of his lovers and the comments he'd written to help him remember them. It was a very bad idea for her to see the sheer amount of them, but thankfully, the originals were stored in a safe in Switzerland. He'd offered to show her the scans he'd made on his computer, but after seeing a few pages, Mia had decided to wait until he could show her the actual journals.

Aliya shrugged. "I don't mind you drawing me as long as you don't make it public. I don't like being put on display." She pushed a lock of hair behind her ear, which was slightly pointed.

"I totally get it," Mia said. "I'll give you a copy, and you can do whatever you want with it."

That got a smile out of Aliya. "Awesome. I'll give the picture to Vrog. When do you want to do it?"

"We are moving into the village this Wednesday. So maybe this weekend?"

Aliya nodded. "Let me know when and where." She turned toward the door. "Enjoy your lunch."

"What about your grandparents?" Syssi asked when the door closed behind her.

"They are moving with us," Toven said.

Kian turned to him. "What about their home in Arcadia?"

"They are excited to move into the village," Mia said. "But we've decided to do it in stages. At first, we will spend the weekdays in the village and the weekends back in Arcadia. That way, I can keep seeing my friends until the new headquarters are set up in the village, and we can bring them here."

Kian frowned. "I wasn't aware of any such plans."

"We suspect that they are Dormants," Toven said. "I felt an immediate affinity toward them, and Lisa confirmed my suspicions. I know that's not enough to prove that they are indeed Dormants, but once they start dating immortal males, we will find out sooner or later whether they can be induced or not."

Kian groaned. "I'm not okay with that. We have Safe Haven for trying out potential Dormants. If you want your friends with you, you should consider moving there. You don't have to work in the underground lab. You can work in one of the lovely bungalows we've built there."

Mia turned a pair of worried eyes to Toven. "My grandparents like the village, and the machines are here. The idea was to make Frankie and Margo testers of adventures. What are they going to do in Safe Haven?"

Toven took her hand. "Don't worry. We are not moving to Safe Haven." He turned to Kian. "I will compel the girls to keep the village and its occupants a secret, and since they are both young and attractive, we won't have to wait long for them to find inducers. They'll turn immortal in no time."

Looking like he'd swallowed a bitter pill, Kian nodded. "You will be responsible for them."

"I am perfectly aware of that." Toven shifted his gaze to William. "How soon can we bring four additional machines to the village, and how long will it take to set them up in the homes Kian will dedicate to them?"

"I need to talk to Hunter. If he has the parts and sends them to me, I can have my people assemble them in a week. The setup will take a few more days."

"After you talk to him, let me know."

"I will."

Leaning over, Toven picked up the printed piece of paper Kian had prepared. "Do you want me to sign it?"

"No need. I'll have Edna draft a proper contract, and I will forward it to you for review. If there are no changes, we will sign on that. I'll have the accounting department calculate how much money you will need to transfer to Gabriel and Hunter and how much to Syssi."

Toven smiled. "I'm glad that it's only half of what I originally planned to pay. If you don't mind, and Hunter and Gabriel agree, I would prefer to make it an installment deal. Too much money changing hands at once will attract attention that neither of us needs."

"I agree." Kian looked at Syssi. "Is that okay with you?"

"Sure." She extended her hand to Toven. "Let's shake on it, partner."

9

WILLIAM

"How do I look?" William buttoned up his new shirt.

Pursing his lips, Max nodded. "Not bad. For a nerd, you clean up nicely."

He had to agree. The shopping trip the Guardian had taken him on had been a success. He'd gotten a new pair of dress shoes, three shirts, one pair of slacks, and two pairs of jeans. Everything was either two or three sizes smaller than what he usually ordered online, and he couldn't remember looking that good since he was a teenager.

William had always been more interested in books and learning than running around hunting or playing sports like the other boys, and he loved to eat, so he'd always been a little padded, but ever since he'd dived into coding, the weight had piled on until he'd gone from plump to fat. Hannah had started him on the journey of eating better and moving more, but the biggest change was the result of him joining Ronja and Darlene on their quest for improved health.

He was still a little overweight and had another twenty or thirty pounds to lose, but on his six-foot-two-inch frame, that wasn't a lot.

"Glasses on or off?" he asked the Guardian.

"You don't need them unless you are in front of a computer screen, so why wear them?"

William had been asked that question many times, and the simple answer was that they had become part of his persona, and he felt naked without them. But he'd been told that his blue eyes were pretty, so maybe he should not wear them when he wanted to impress Doctor Kaia Locke?

On the other hand, the interview with her was already making him nervous enough, and he would be even more nervous without his glasses on.

"I look smart with them on." He put the glasses back on top of his nose. "It's a job interview, not a date."

Max snorted. "A date? We don't go on dates. We hunt for hookups." He draped

28

his arm over William's shoulders. "What say you we go clubbing after the interview? You've got new clothes, and you look hot. The ladies are going to be all over you."

William hadn't gone hunting in months, and even though he wasn't as obsessed with sex as other immortal males, the dry spell was too long even for him. That being said, he hated what the others called hunting, but he hated paying for pros even more, so that didn't leave him with many options.

Maybe now that he'd actually put a little effort into how he dressed, the ladies would come to him.

Yeah, right.

He was getting a few appreciative looks here and there, but usually that was the extent of it. On the rare occasions when his lab mates managed to drag him out to a club, no one hit on him, despite his new and improved appearance, and it wasn't because he was too intimidating. He simply didn't exude masculinity like the other immortal males. Or maybe he had a tattoo on his forehead that spelled Mega Nerd and was visible only to women.

William was a teddy bear, or rather that was the impression he gave.

On the inside, he wasn't as soft and cuddly.

Well, that wasn't true. He was a romantic, and he enjoyed being polite and chivalrous, and that made him seem soft.

No female had ever called him a tiger.

With a sigh, he turned away from the mirror and collected his wallet from the entry table. "That depends on how well the interview goes. If she accepts the offer, I will be in a mood to celebrate. If she doesn't, I'll be bummed. I need her."

Max clapped him on the back. "Lay on the charm, buddy."

"I'll do my best."

Max had escorted him before on other out-of-town trips, and he was glad that Onegus had assigned him to accompany him on this one as well. He was fun to be around, wasn't as buff as the other Guardians, and he didn't look like a bodyguard.

Perhaps he could pass for a chauffeur, but that didn't solve the problem either. William didn't want to look like the kind of guy who had one. It was okay for Kian to be driven around, but even he would have gladly given that up if he didn't have to take two bodyguards with him every time he left the safety of the village.

"Do me a favor, Max. When we get to the house, drop me off and park a block away. If they ask, I'll say that a friend gave me a lift and is coming back to pick me up later."

"No problem, but you'll have to leave the earpiece open and broadcasting. I need to be able to hear what's going on."

"I'm not going to wear it. It's going to stay in my pocket."

Max shrugged. "Good enough for me. But if anything smells fishy, put it in. You can claim to be hard of hearing."

"I don't expect any trouble in the suburban family home of Doctor Locke, but if I get ambushed by her or her younger siblings, I'll put the earpiece in."

"Yeah, yeah." Max grabbed the keys and opened the door to their hotel room. "You can never know where danger lurks, and as the boss likes to say, better safe than sorry."

10

KAIA

"When is Gilbert coming home?" Scooping up one of Idina's dolls off the floor, Kaia dumped it into the laundry basket that she was using as a collection bin for the toys her little sister and brothers had left strewn all over the living room. The poor Barbie had fallen victim to one of Idina's foul moods and was missing all of her clothes and half her hair.

"He'll be here." Her mother wiped Evan's hands with a wet towel.

"I know that he will, but the question is when. William is going to get here at seven, and Gilbert told me to wait for him. What am I going to do? Take the guy out for a walk?"

"You know Gilbert. Intimidating strangers and keeping them off balance is something that he actually enjoys doing."

Ryan was still eating, and the nanny was trying and failing to keep the area around him clean.

Kaia snorted. "Yeah, I don't envy the guy. Gilbert is going to give him a military-style interrogation. If he shows up on time, that is."

Her mother, the responsible adult in the house, had come home from work early to get everything ready for the meeting, but Gilbert was still a no-show, and Kaia had no intention of waiting for him. Still, she would have preferred him to be there. The guy had a nose for crooks and lowlifes, and if William was either, Gilbert would sniff him out and wipe the floor with him.

Her honorary stepdad took no prisoners when he was in his family-protector mode.

Kaia wished she had his skills, but despite memories of her prior life, she was still too naive and trusting for her own good.

"Leave the toys," her mother said. "Berta and I will finish cleaning here. You need to change and do something with your hair. It's a mess."

Smoothing a hand over her long wavy hair, Kaia looked down at her stylishly torn jeans. "Why? This is my best pair. They are comfortable, and I look great in them."

"You are a PhD, and you are being interviewed for an important job. You need to dress appropriately even if you have no intention of taking it. The academic world is not that big, and the competition is stiff. If William McLean forms a negative impression of you and talks about it in his academic circles, it could hurt your chances of getting the job you actually want."

"All because of an outfit? That's a bit of a stretch, don't you think?"

Her mother rolled her eyes. "Do you have to argue about everything? Just go upstairs and change into something nice and conservative. The white button-down blouse I've gotten for you is perfect for an interview."

"I look like a nun in it," Kaia grumbled. "But fine. It's worth wearing a nun outfit if it gets me off cleaning duty." She looked at the messy living room and groaned. "Why did I think that inviting him to my house was a good idea? I should have met him at a coffee shop."

She loved her chaotic home, but William would probably be horrified. Hopefully, the twins would be asleep by the time he arrived, or the interview would turn into a circus. Idina wouldn't be asleep yet, but she was okay unless she didn't like the guy. Her little sister had a bit of a mean streak, and she pinched people who rubbed her the wrong way.

Up in her room, Kaia walked into her closet and looked at her selection of clothes. Very few were job-interview appropriate, and the white blouse her mother had gotten for her was one of her only two choices. The other one was a dark blue blouse with ruffles at the sleeves that made her look like an escapee from an Amish community. Another gift from her mother.

Karen Locke was many things, but fashionista wasn't one of them. She had terrible taste in clothes.

Heaving a sigh, Kaia pulled her T-shirt off and shrugged the blouse on. Buttoning it up to her neck, she chuckled at her reflection. "I look like a librarian." Pulling her jeans off, she reached for the only skirt hanging in her closet.

It was calf-long and had little blue flowers printed on the fabric. It wasn't ugly, but together with the white blouse, it was awful.

Gilbert would love to see her wearing it. The guy was obsessed with protecting her and Cheryl's virtue, and he made all kinds of weird rules about having boys over. If either of them took a guy to her room, the door had to remain open at all times.

He was such a hypocrite.

If he was so concerned with their reputations, he should have married their mother, but despite having three kids together, Gilbert and her mother hadn't made things official. Nevertheless, he was very protective of his adopted daughters. Not that anything had been officially done about that either, but he always referred to her and Cheryl as his daughters, and she liked that he cared deeply about them.

That didn't mean that she should dress like a librarian to please him, though.

Perhaps wearing a pair of jeans that didn't have tears in them would be enough to make her mother and Gilbert happy.

Despite how full her closet was, very little of its content was wearable. She'd outgrown most of it and should either give it to Cheryl or donate it to charity.

Perhaps her mother was right, and she should get a few work-appropriate outfits, but she hated shopping, and she didn't care much about clothes.

Kaia was most comfortable in jeans, T-shirts, and flip-flops.

After finding a pair of jeans that passed inspection, she pushed her feet into a pair of ballet flats, brushed her long wavy hair and pulled it into a high ponytail, and finished up by spraying a little perfume on her neck.

That was as much prep as she was willing to put into meeting the recruiter. After all, she wasn't going out on a date, and it wasn't as if she needed to impress him with her looks. What was inside her head was much more important to him than the outer packaging.

11

WILLIAM

*A*s Max pulled up next to Kaia's house, William regarded the mansion-sized home with a sinking feeling in his heart.

When Roni had done a background check on Kaia and her family, he'd found out that her mother was a sysadmin for a large defense contractor, which meant that everyone in the household had gone through rigorous background checks, and since Roni hadn't had to dig deep in search of red flags, William hadn't bothered to read through the file either.

Roni had mentioned that the unofficial stepdad was a successful builder and that the family was affluent, but owning a house like that in this neighborhood indicated that they were more than that.

They were rich.

Money was not going to be as important to Kaia and her parents as prestige, and she would prefer a job that would earn her recognition rather than a secret project for which she would get no credit.

"Fancy house," Max said. "To have a place this size in this neighborhood, they have to be loaded."

"It would appear so." William opened the passenger door. "Please, park where they can't see you."

"Yes, boss." Max gave him a two-finger salute.

William waited until the Guardian drove away before walking up to the front gate. It opened before he had a chance to press the intercom button, which meant that his arrival had been monitored. There was a camera mounted on one of the pillars holding up the gate, but it was an older model that was popular for home installations. Still, it wasn't the cheap kind, and whoever had installed it had done a good job.

As he walked through the gate, it closed behind him, and the front door opened.

The intimidating human who stepped out gave him an unabashed critical once-over. "William McLean, I presume?"

"That's me." William gave him his best smile and offered him his hand.

The guy took it and squeezed hard. "Gilbert Emerson. Kaia's stepfather."

Karen Locke and Gilbert Emerson weren't married, but they'd been together for twelve years and had three kids in addition to Kaia and her sister, so the guy was solid, and he seemed to be taking his fatherly duties seriously.

"A pleasure to meet you, Mr. Emerson."

"Call me Gilbert." The guy cracked a smile and draped his arm over William's shoulders as if they were best buddies. "I expected someone older. Are you really the chief scientist of the project, or are you just the recruiter?"

"I'm older than I look, and I'm the chief."

"You must have been a prodigy like our Kaia. Where did you go to school?"

They were still standing outside the door, and the guy was already in interrogator mode. His hostility was evident, but it was coming from a good place. Gilbert was looking out for his family.

William took a step away, getting out from under the guy's arm. "Let's get inside, so I won't have to repeat my life story and credentials for your daughter and the rest of the family."

Gilbert smiled, seeming satisfied for some reason.

Perhaps he liked that William wasn't intimidated by him.

Kaia's stepdad was tall, only an inch or so shorter than him, and he was a little padded around the middle but still handsome. He was in his late forties, had most of his hair, and he had a certain charm about him despite the assertiveness that bordered on aggression and the directness that bordered on incivility.

"I'm buying time for my better half and the nanny to wrestle the twins to bed. We won't be able to talk while they're awake."

Just then, an angry wail sounded, and it was immediately joined by another one. Then the wails turned into a loud demand. "Dada!"

Gilbert dropped his head in resignation. "I've been summoned. Just tell me where you went to school, and I'll leave you to talk with Kaia."

"The University of Glasgow." William let some of his Scottish accent bleed through.

"A Scot, eh?" Gilbert clapped him on the back. "I thought I detected a slight accent."

"Gilbert!" an angry female voice called. "Get up here."

"I'm coming!" He stayed exactly where he was. "So, what is a Scot doing in the Bay Area recruiting bioinformaticians for a secret project?"

"I was offered a job in Los Angeles straight out of college, and I stayed."

"Gilbert!" A tall blond walked out the door. "Invite Mr. McLean inside and go to your sons." She cast William an apologetic smile.

This was unmistakably Doctor Kaia Locke, and she was stunning.

Instead of the enormous glasses she'd worn in her graduation photo, she wore fashionable frames that didn't detract from her natural beauty, and a beauty she was.

Doctor Kaia Locke was dressed in slim jeans that accentuated her long, trim legs and a dressy white shirt that was a little too conservative for a young woman her age, implying an innocence that her eyes belied.

CHAPTER 11

She reminded him of Annani. A young body housing an old soul.

"Hello." He smiled and offered her his hand. "Please, call me William."

12

KAIA

William McLean looked nothing like what Kaia had imagined, and seeing him standing on her doorstep triggered two opposing emotions.

First, her heart sank because the guy had the face of a sweetheart, not a conniving manipulator, so he probably had had nothing to do with Tony's disappearance, and a moment later, excited butterflies took flight in her belly because he was way too attractive for a chief scientist.

Why the hell did the guy have to be so handsome?

Then again, maybe his appearance was misleading. With that guileless, nice-guy expression, he could easily ensnare his unsuspecting victims.

"Please, call me William." He offered her his hand.

Did he omit the doctor on purpose, or did he keep forgetting that he was a PhD like she was?

Or maybe he didn't have a doctorate? Come to think of it, he'd never introduced himself as one in all their online communications.

"Kaia." She narrowed her eyes at him before clasping his hand.

As their palms touched, an electric current zinged between them, sending a pulse of longing to all of Kaia's neglected feminine parts.

She tried to pull her hand out of his grasp, but he held on for a split second too long before letting go. "Just Kaia?" He smiled. "Not Doctor Kaia Locke?"

She shrugged. "I keep forgetting that I'm a PhD. It feels weird to be addressed as doctor. What about you? Do you have a PhD that you are not flaunting for some reason?"

"I don't." He pushed his glasses up his nose. "I'm a software engineer, and I didn't pursue a doctorate. I needed to start working."

Kaia tilted her head. "Didn't they offer you a stipend?"

"Money wasn't the reason I needed to start working." He shifted from foot to foot, reminding her that she was just as lousy of a host as Gilbert and was keeping him on her doorstep instead of inviting him in.

She moved aside, clearing the doorway. "Please, come in. We can continue our conversation sitting down."

"Thank you." He turned sideways as if he was concerned about passing through the doorway with her blocking part of it.

William was tall and slightly padded but he wasn't huge. Maybe he used to be and still retained the habits of a big guy?

An old memory of making the same move in her previous life flashed through her mind. She'd been a large man who had always been self-conscious about his height, his big protruding belly, and mostly about his thick, meaty fingers. Inelegant and unfitting for a mathematician, they'd been the source of endless embarrassment.

Kaia still caught herself looking at her hands from time to time and being pleasantly surprised to see the slender fingers she had in this life. Maybe that was why she gave them much more attention than her hair and even her face, filing her nails and applying fresh polish as soon as the old stuff started peeling.

"The dining room is the safest bet." She led him to the only room in the house that didn't get invaded by her younger siblings.

"You have a lovely home," William said as he followed her.

"Thank you. My stepdad built it. There was an old house on the property when he bought it, but he demolished it completely and built a new one for us."

"He did a very nice job." William pulled out a chair for her.

"Thank you." She smiled and lowered herself as gracefully as she could to the seat instead of dropping into it like she usually did.

His gentlemanly gesture deserved a ladylike response.

These days it was so uncommon for guys to do things like opening doors and pulling out chairs, but somehow it didn't seem odd for a young man like William to act so old-fashioned. He seemed older than his years, and the impression she got was that he was a very kind person.

She wasn't sure whether she should hope that he was the man he seemed to be or hope that he wasn't. If William was a good guy, he wouldn't be able to help her, but on the other hand, it made the prospect of joining his team appealing and not for professional reasons.

It had been a year since Kaia broke up with the only boyfriend she'd had, and she hadn't been in a rush to replace him, but meeting William changed things.

He was at least ten years older than her, if not more, so he might try to stay away, but she saw how he looked at her, and he wasn't indifferent.

It would be nice to have a boyfriend who wasn't intimidated by her academic achievements.

"Do you want to hear about the project, or are we waiting for your parents to join us?"

"Let's give them a few more minutes." She smiled apologetically. "Gilbert will chew my head off if I start without him. In the meantime, you can tell me about my competition. Who else have you interviewed so far?"

"You are my first," he admitted. "The others are not as good, and I really hope that you'll consider joining my team because I don't think the others could do the job without you leading them."

Evidently, William wasn't a skilled recruiter. That had been way too honest, giving her the leverage to demand whatever she wanted in exchange for agreeing to work for him.

"Oh, wow." Kaia flipped her long ponytail over her shoulder. "You're putting a lot of confidence in a greenhorn. Who are the others, if I may ask? I probably know all the bioinformaticians in the area."

William pulled a folded piece of paper from his shirt pocket and handed it to her. "These are the people I'm meeting with tomorrow. I don't know who will make the team."

She scanned the list. "These are all good people." She refolded the note and handed it back to him. "The fact that I got my PhD while being ten years younger doesn't mean that I'm better than them. It just means that I have an unnaturally fast learning ability." And previous knowledge that had been the foundation of her academic success, but that was a secret no one besides her mother knew, and even she thought that Kaia was making it up.

"You're being too modest." William put the note back in his shirt pocket. "I've read your thesis and the papers you published. I consider myself a smart guy, but it took me a while to understand them."

"Are you a bioinformatician?"

He shook his head. "I'm a software engineer, and I enjoy coming up with new programs and new inventions that make life better for people."

If anyone else had said that to her, she would have regarded it as a nice sales pitch, but William looked and sounded so sincere that Kaia believed him.

Then again, she wasn't the best at judging character.

Where the hell was Gilbert? She needed his nose for crooks and manipulators.

No more wailing was coming from upstairs, and even Idina hadn't run in to poke her nose into the dining room. Cheryl had her in the den, and they were watching one of Idina's favorite animated movies, but the moment she realized that they had a guest, the little demon would want to see him.

"It's no wonder that you had trouble understanding my papers. You are not a bioinformatician."

He smiled sheepishly. "I usually don't have trouble understanding papers from fields that are unrelated to my particular expertise, but genetics seems to be written in a whole different language."

"That's because it is. It's the language of life."

13

WILLIAM

*A*s the wailing upstairs suddenly resumed, a little girl ran into the dining room and leaped into Kaia's lap.

"I'm Idina," she introduced herself. "Who are you?"

William was about to answer when Kaia's other sister rushed in. "She tricked me. She said that she was going upstairs to get her teddy bear." She trained an apologetic set of eyes on William. "I'm Cheryl, Kaia's sister."

"I'm William. It's nice to meet you."

"You didn't say that to me." The toddler pouted. "Say it's nice to meet me too."

"It's very nice to meet you, Idina." He offered his hand to the little girl and looked into her brown, cunning eyes. "How old are you?"

"I'm three." She put one small hand in his for a handshake and lifted the other with three fingers up. "How old are you?"

"Idina," Kaia said in a reproachful tone. "That's not polite to ask."

"Why? He asked me."

"She's right." William smiled. "I'm thirty-two."

Idina narrowed her eyes at him. "No, you're not."

Stifling a chuckle, he asked, "How old do you think I am?"

"Twenty-seven."

That wasn't a bad guess for a little girl. When he'd been heavier, he'd looked a little older, and thirty-two had seemed reasonable, but after losing weight, he looked younger.

"I'll take twenty-seven if you're selling."

She scrunched her nose. "How can I sell twenty-seven? I don't have it."

"Enough with the questions." Kaia pushed to her feet with Idina in her arms and handed her over to Cheryl. "You can either go back to watching your movie, or you can go upstairs and get ready for bed."

"I don't want to go. I want to stay here!" The child tried to wiggle out of Cheryl's hold, and when that didn't work, she started kicking her sister.

39

"Stop it!" Cheryl tried to catch her legs.

"I'm sorry about that." Kaia shook her head. "This house is just impossible. Do you want to go for a walk?"

"Gilbert is not going to like that," Cheryl grumbled while wrestling Idina to stop kicking her.

"I can't hear myself think in here." Kaia walked up to the front door and opened it. "Tell him that William and I are taking a walk around the block. If he wants, he can catch up to us."

"Fine." Cheryl carried the wiggling child away.

As Kaia closed the door, shutting the chaos behind her, William let out a breath. "I love children, but after today, I'm not in a rush to have any. I'd rather be the uncle who can walk out whenever he wants."

"It takes some getting used to." Kaia tugged on the elastic holding her ponytail, releasing her long hair from its confines. "They are at their worst just before going to bed because they are tired and cranky, but other times they are a joy." She smiled. "They are generators of love."

As the wild mass cascaded down her shoulders, framing her pale face in a golden halo, she looked ethereal, but it was an illusion.

He'd met her less than half an hour ago, but in that short time, he'd learned that Kaia wasn't a delicate flower. Her smart eyes betrayed not only a sharp mind but also a strength of character.

"You don't look like your sisters," he said to break the silence stretching between them.

Cheryl and Idina had dark hair and brown eyes, while Kaia was blond with blue eyes and skin that was nearly translucent.

"Cheryl looks like our mom, and Idina looks like Gilbert. I look like my father." She pulled her phone out of the back pocket of her jeans. "He looked a little like you. I can show you a picture." She scrolled through her photos until she found what she'd been looking for and held the phone up to William.

He had to admit that she was right. The young man's smiling face bore some resemblance to his, and their coloring was similar. There was also something in the guy's expression that made William like him. "He's a handsome fellow, and he seems like a nice guy."

"He was. He died when I was five." Kaia turned the phone off and tucked it back in her pocket. "He was also an engineer like you."

"What happened to him?"

"Heart failure." Kaia sighed. "This makes me too sad. Let's talk about something else. Tell me about your project."

William debated how much he could tell her without lying. "You might think of it as a translation project. We have charts upon charts of instructions that are written in what I believe is a genetic code, and to decipher them, I need skilled bioinformaticians."

She arched a brow. "What happened to the people who made those charts?"

"Regrettably, that person is no longer with us." They had never even set foot on Earth, but that was as close as William dared to get to the truth.

"I see. So, the author passed away, and you need someone to decipher what he or she wrote in code."

"Yeah, that's about it."

CHAPTER 13

"Why is it such a big secret? What do you think is in those charts?"

"If I tell you, it's not going to be a secret. I can't tell you more before you sign the confidentiality agreement."

"Can you at least give me a hint? I can't commit to a project without knowing what I'm going to work on. I don't want to be involved in the creation of biological weapons or anything that could be used to harm people."

Without knowing what she was talking about, Kaia was surprisingly close to the truth.

"We suspect that these journals contain information that might revolutionize medicine and help a lot of people, or it might reveal something dangerous that could do the opposite. Until we know for sure what is in them, we can't let anyone get their hands on that information, and if we discover that it's bad, we will destroy it."

"So, I was right. It could be a biological weapon."

"Or a cure-all for cancer. We won't know until we decipher the code and translate the writings."

In essence, that was true. Mass-producing Odus could be a great boon, freeing humanity from all sorts of manual labor, but it could also be a disaster if there was no way to prevent them from being turned into weapons. And if the journals held the secret to immortality, that could create a whole new set of problems as well.

14

KAIA

"But what if a member of your team sells the information after the project is done?"

A signature on a nondisclosure agreement wasn't a fail-proof way to prevent the information from being leaked or sold, and the only way to guarantee that didn't happen was to silence the scientists who had worked on it for good.

Perhaps that was what had happened to Tony.

Perhaps he'd been recruited to work on a secret project, and once it was completed, they'd offed him to keep him from revealing what he'd learned. William didn't look like a murderer, but what if someone else had done the killing, and he didn't even know about it?

"We are not going to allow anyone to take notes out of the lab. I also designed a protocol that will keep the information encrypted at all times. To access it, the team members will get a fob that generates a new code every two hours, and they will have to input it to keep working."

"That sounds very sophisticated." She cast him a sidelong glance. "Did you have leaks in the past, and is that why you are so careful?"

William shook his head. "This is the first time I've needed help on a project that I can't get from my own people, who I trust implicitly. I'm forced to assemble a team of strangers, and I'm doing my best to mitigate security leaks and other problems before they are created."

Again, William sounded so sincere that Kaia had a hard time holding on to her suspicions.

And he was also so damn likable. He gave off a vibe of a big teddy bear, safe and cuddly, and she had the odd urge to crawl into his arms and put her head on his chest.

Was it because he reminded her of her father?

Hopefully not, because that would just be sick. She was attracted to the guy, for goodness sake, and she didn't have daddy issues.

CHAPTER 14

"What if someone has an eidetic memory?" Kaia looked at William from under lowered lashes. "They could walk out of your lab with all the information stored inside their heads. You can't encrypt a brain."

He smiled sheepishly. "I thought about that loophole as well, and I hired a powerful hypnotist to make the team members forget what they worked on."

"Ingenious, but a little out there. I don't believe in hypnosis. Only weak-minded people can be hypnotized."

He frowned. "Has anyone tried to hypnotize you and failed?"

"No."

"Then how do you know that you can't be hypnotized?"

Kaia shrugged. "I was curious about how hypnosis works, so I read about it. People who are suggestible and eager to please are easily controlled by a skilled person who knows how to manipulate those weaknesses. I'm neither suggestible nor eager to please, so I'm not hypnotizable."

William opened his mouth, closed it, and then opened it again as if he'd changed his mind about what he was going to say. "You need to experience it once before deciding that it doesn't work on you."

"True, and I'm willing to put it to the test, but I'm ninety-nine percent sure that I can't be hypnotized."

A smile lifted his perfectly shaped lips. "As long as you leave that one percent open, you're not a lost cause. So, did I pique your interest in my project?"

"You did, but to be honest, I'm probably going to accept the job offer from Stanford. I've gotten better offers from private research companies and other universities, but I want to keep living at home, and that's an overriding factor."

William stopped walking and turned to her. "Do you really want that, or are you doing it because your family wants you to stay home?"

"Both. It might surprise you, but for me, family comes first. I love my siblings, and I don't want to be away from them." She smiled. "Despite the noise and the mess, I adore them."

"I get it, believe me. I love my family as well, but you need to think about your future and what's best for your career."

Kaia laughed. "A project that I can't talk about and a work experience that some hypnotist is going to make me forget will not help my career."

"That's true, but the camaraderie and connection you'll develop with your teammates are priceless, on a personal level as well as the professional."

She tilted her head. "Are you talking about romantic involvement?"

The guy actually blushed, which was adorable. "Not at all, but that can be another bonus. Working and living with your teammates is a unique experience, especially when the project you are working on is interesting and challenging. That's something you won't be able to do later in life when you are married with two and a half kids and a dog."

He wasn't wrong, and a part of her yearned for the adventure and for the change of pace, but a larger part needed to cling to her family and never let go.

"Life is short, William, and job satisfaction is not as important as the people I love and who love me back. Money doesn't motivate me either. I just want to make enough to cover my expenses."

15

WILLIAM

*T*hat was a very mature statement from someone as young as Kaia, but then it shouldn't have surprised him. Other than her appearance, nothing about Kaia was young. She didn't talk like a nineteen-year-old or behave like other girls her age.

In fact, her approach to life was more mature than his, and he was ancient compared to her.

Before the lab grew to the mega factory it was now, he'd spent most of his time in isolation, working on projects that fascinated him and filled his mind and his heart. He'd felt lonely at times, but not enough to leave his lab and pursue contact with people. The one time that William had been motivated to take a break from his work was when he'd met Hannah, but after that relationship had fizzled out, he'd dived even deeper into his projects.

Still, he was an immortal, and unlike Kaia, he was not going to run out of time to find his true love and strive for more balance in his life.

Casting a sidelong glance at her, he felt an absurd longing for her to be the one for him, and that made even less sense than his former infatuation with Hannah.

He'd been drawn to Hannah and had felt an affinity toward her because she was a scientist and a fellow brainiac, same as Kaia, but she'd been a mature woman in her late twenties, not a kid.

Kaia was beautiful and sexy, but even acknowledging her attractiveness made him feel like a damn pedophile. Legally, she was permissible, but morally, she wasn't.

Regardless of his hormones deciding to act at the least opportune time, he needed her on his team, and he had to convince her to join, hopefully without thralling her, but he might not have a choice.

"What about the excitement of discovery?" He looked into her big blue eyes. "I live for that. Sometimes I can't fall asleep at night because my brain keeps churning up new ideas or new angles to approach what I'm working on. It's like living on high-octane fuel. I'm always hyped up." He chuckled. "People say that I talk too fast, but that's nowhere near the speed at which my mind works. I couldn't slow down even if I wanted to."

Kaia regarded him with a curious expression on her beautiful face. "I envy you. I don't get excited about much, and especially not about work." Her lush lips lifted in a small smile. "I get excited when my baby brothers learn a new word, or when they try to walk. I get excited when Cheryl gets an award at school. She's so smart, and she has her own Instatock channel for which she produces daily content, but people don't make a big deal out of her achievements because of the shadow I cast, and it makes me feel bad." She pushed a strand of hair behind her ear. "Maybe if I went away for a while, they would start noticing her more."

William's heart leaped with hope. "Then come to work for me. A few months away is nothing in the grand scheme of things, and with your bright star shining somewhere else for a little while, Cheryl will get her chance in the spotlight."

"That's something to consider." Kaia let out a breath. "We should head back. The little ones are probably asleep by now, so my mother and Gilbert can join us."

As they reached the gate it opened immediately, and a moment later Gilbert opened the front door. Standing with his arms crossed over his chest, he glared at William. "Took you long enough."

"Are the little ones asleep?" she asked.

"Yes." The guy diverted his glare at Kaia.

"Then we can talk inside." Unperturbed by the glare, she walked past him.

As the guy stepped aside, letting William in, a smile tugged on his lips, suggesting that the glare had been just for show. He wasn't emitting any hostility either.

When William entered the living room, a pretty brunette rose to her feet and offered him her hand. "I'm Karen, Kaia's mother. I'm sorry I wasn't here to greet you when you arrived."

"That's perfectly all right." He shook her warm palm. "You and your mate had your hands full."

She tilted her head. "Mate? I like that. Is it a Scottish expression? Gilbert told me that you are originally from Scotland."

"You are?" Kaia asked. "I didn't detect any accent."

"That's because I usually hide it." He affected an exaggerated Scottish accent. "I pretend to be an American."

"Don't. Your accent is so sexy."

"Kaia," her mother said in a stern tone.

"It's okay, Mom." She patted her shoulder. "William is cool, and he's not a stick in the mud. You can relax."

Well, that was good to hear. He must have made a good impression after all.

"Please, sit down." Karen motioned to one of the oversized armchairs. "Can I offer you something to drink?"

Whiskey would have been great but inappropriate. "A glass of water would be wonderful. Thank you."

"I'll get it." Cheryl got to her feet and walked out of the room.

Gilbert sat in the armchair across from him and assumed a regal pose worthy of the king of the castle. "So, what have you two been talking about during your walk?" He turned to look at Kaia. "I hope you didn't make any decisions without consulting with us first."

"We talked about William's project and the team he's assembling. I know everyone on his list of candidates, so if I decide to take his offer, I will not be working with strangers."

Talk about surprises. Only moments ago, she'd said that she'd prefer to stay home and take the job offer from Stanford.

Had thinking of her sister living in her shadow been what had made all the difference?

Curiosity getting the better of him, he tentatively reached into her mind, got the shock of his life, and retreated as fast as he'd entered.

Kaia's mind wasn't just her own. She shared it with an older man, or rather thought of herself as one. One moment she examined things as Kaia, a nineteen-year-old girl ready to embark on an adventure, and the next, she examined them from the point of view of a lonely, middle-aged man.

1 6

KAIA

*W*illiam looked as if he had seen a ghost. Could the stunned expression on his face be the result of her expressing a tentative interest in joining his team?

To be honest, she'd given him conflicting cues, one minute claiming that she wanted to accept the offer from Stanford and the next giving his offer another thought.

It had been inspiring to hear him talk about the exhilaration he felt when thinking about new ideas or working out a problem with a product or software he was developing. She wanted that too, and then thinking about Cheryl living in her shadow and not getting the recognition she deserved from their mom and from Gilbert and the rest of the family worked in favor of accepting William's offer as well.

Could she live without them for three to four months, though? She would miss the little ones too damn much.

They were growing so fast, and every moment with them was precious. If she went away, would they even remember her when she returned?

"What's wrong?" Gilbert asked William. "You look pale all of a sudden."

He heaved a sigh. "I just thought of a flaw in one of my designs." He forced a smile. "I know it's random and unrelated to what I'm here for, but sometimes my mind just gets away from me and goes galloping in strange directions."

"Kaia is the same way." Cheryl walked in with a tray loaded with soft drinks and an assortment of things to snack on. "Sometimes she just spaces out and doesn't even hear me talking to her. You two will get along great."

William turned hopeful eyes at Kaia. "Are you seriously considering my offer?"

"I am. The position at Stanford will become available only at the end of October, which will give me four months to work on your project if I decide to join. The problem is that I'm not willing to be away from my family for the entire time.

47

I will need to go home at least every other weekend, and I want them to be able to visit me. If you can compromise on the isolation, I'll give it serious consideration."

William's eyes shone as if he had just been informed that he'd won a Nobel Prize. "I might be able to make it work. The project is top secret, but I can make special accommodations for you." He rubbed the back of his neck. "I need to figure out the details, but I will make it work one way or another. I have a feeling that you are the key to deciphering those schematics. The other candidates are capable people, and they might be good, but none of them are as brilliant as you."

His compliments made her feel self-conscious, and Kaia shifted on the couch. "Thank you, but that's an exaggeration, and I'm not being falsely modest. I have a very good command of mathematics, and that gives me an advantage, but it doesn't make me a genius."

Cheryl snorted. "Just take the compliment, Kaia. You have a PhD at nineteen. I think that proves you are a genius."

"I'm not." Kaia folded her arms over her chest. "You think that it's great to be called a prodigy or brilliant, but it's not. It puts pressure on me that I don't want. What if I can't pull off a miracle? What if I disappoint William? I constantly need to prove myself."

"You don't." Her mother took her hand. "You should only do the best you can, and if that's not enough, then it's not your problem."

"True." Kaia let out a breath. "I just want to be normal."

She wanted to go on a date with a guy her age without having to lie about her achievements, but then she also wanted to have something interesting she could talk with him about, and that was much tougher than lying and pretending to be a normal college girl.

She was a freak, and not just because she was smarter than most people or had a PhD in bioinformatics.

"We all want something we can't have," Gilbert said. "And being so-called normal is overrated." He crossed his legs at the ankles and leaned back. "It's damn boring, that's what it is. Right, William?"

"Absolutely." William nodded.

Gilbert grinned. "I'm glad we see eye to eye. So where is this secret project of yours located? Or is that a secret as well?"

"It's on the Oregon Coast, and the location is serene and beautiful."

"That doesn't tell me much," Gilbert said. "If we are to let Kaia join your team, we need to see the place first and make sure that it's well-appointed, that she has her own room which she can lock, and that there are other women working on the project. I don't want her sleeping in army barracks or eating field rations, and most importantly, I need to make sure that she's safe." He looked at her and smiled. "You're not just a brain, Kaia. You are a beautiful young woman, and men are pigs."

She rolled her eyes. "I can take care of myself."

Gilbert had insisted on her attending a Krav Maga self-defense course for women, and surprisingly, she enjoyed it and became very good at kicking ass.

"I know. But let's be realistic. Unless you carry a gun and are willing to use it, you are not safe."

"You have nothing to worry about in that regard," William said. "No harm will come to Kaia on my watch, and I'm going to be there twenty-four-seven from start to finish."

"They think that she's too young to leave home, which is absurd since the girl is an adult and has a PhD. I hope that after they meet me, they will agree to let her join." He waved a hand over his face. "My harmless, nice-guy appearance will finally be good for something."

Kian chuckled. "You *are* a harmless, nice guy. I hope you convince her to join. Is she pretty?"

William shrugged. "I'm not the kind of guy who allows himself to be blinded by physical beauty. Kaia's beautiful brain is of much more interest to me than her physical appearance." Especially since she was nineteen, and William had never been drawn to young women.

He preferred mature females who knew what they wanted and didn't waste time on games.

"Kaia what?" Kian flipped his laptop open.

"Doctor Kaia Locke." William shook his head. The guy was a two-thousand-year-old immortal, but he was acting like a frat boy.

Most men, including the mighty Kian, judged people, and especially females, based on their looks. William wasn't indifferent to beauty, but he deemed exceptional brains and strength of character much more important than a person's appearance.

Kian typed in the name, lifted a brow, and kept reading. "Doctor Locke has a very impressive résumé, and I suspect that under those monster frames, she's a looker."

William had seen Kaia's graduation photo, and even though her dark-framed enormous eyeglasses hid most of her face, he couldn't help but notice her lush, sexy lips, and the secretive smile that hinted at a sense of humor. But since she was only nineteen, Kaia Locke would never become anything more than a colleague.

Taking off his glasses, William rubbed the lenses with a corner of his Hawaiian shirt. "I believe that Doctor Kaia Locke is more concerned with science than she is with trivial things like fashionable frames and makeup."

Kian lifted his hands in the air. "I meant no offense. Are you taking the jet?"

"I don't need the jet to get to the Bay Area. I booked a commercial flight."

Kian shook his head. "I want you to take the jet, and I'm sending a Guardian with you."

That was what William had been afraid of. "Why?"

"Did you forget? We lost Mark in the Bay Area."

William winced as a spear of pain pierced his heart. Given their shared field of expertise, Mark and he had been close, and he still mourned his loss.

He wasn't the only one.

Mark's murder had shaken up their family. It was the reason Kian had decided to pull all of their people from the Bay Area, build a hidden village for the clan, and have everyone living where they were protected and safe.

But that had been four and a half years ago, and a lot had changed since.

"I didn't forget, and I never will, but we haven't heard from the Doomers in months. Lokan says that Navuh is busy breeding the next generation of smart warriors, and until he achieves that, he isn't going to come after us."

Kian leaned forward and pinned William with his intense eyes. "That might be true, but we know that they run drug and prostitution rings in California. You

17

WILLIAM

*K*ian would probably pop a vein when he heard about the compromises William was considering for Kaia, but to get her on his team, he was willing to incur the slightly increased risk along with the boss's wrath.

Safe Haven had been chosen for the research so the team members wouldn't feel like prisoners, but that didn't mean that they would be allowed to leave the compound or receive visitors. The idea was to keep them in a controlled environment, where they could be relatively free and interact with the small group of paranormals, but not with the outside world.

They would still be allowed to make phone calls, but those would be monitored by security, and given the compulsion they would be under, the risk of them blurting out something was minimal.

After the project was done, William would thrall them to forget what they'd been working on, and Emmett and Eleanor would add compulsion on top of that. The same would have to be done to everyone who had interacted with the scientists. Thralling them to forget that they had ever seen or talked to them could be performed by the Guardians assigned to the project, and for safe measure, Eleanor could add compulsion that would prevent them from talking about it.

Besides, the team would work on small sections taken from different journals, and that would not provide them with the entire picture. William only needed them to decipher enough of the scientific language so he could take it from there.

But before he made any promises, he needed to verify that Kaia and everyone in her family, aside from the little ones, were susceptible to thralling. In his experience those who could be thralled could also be compelled, so his thralling tests should be enough. If any of them were immune to thralling, though, they might still be susceptible to compulsion, but he would have to put them on the phone with either Eleanor or Emmett to test it.

Compulsion was a strange ability, and it varied greatly in strength as well as in

49

the susceptibility of the subject to compulsion by others. Kalugal was a powerful compeller, and so was Emmett, but both of them could be compelled by Annani. Eleanor was a weaker compeller, but she was immune even to the goddess's compulsion. Turner wasn't a compeller, but he was immune to both thralling and compulsion.

"William?" Kaia asked. "Are you still thinking about that flaw in your design?"

"I'm sorry." He smiled apologetically. "As I said, my mind tends to run off in different directions at the most inopportune moments. Did someone ask me a question?"

"I did," Gilbert said. "When can we see the place?"

"First, Kaia needs to agree to join my team. We can condition it on your approval of the accommodations, but I'm not going to lower my security standards just to satisfy your curiosity."

Gilbert nodded. "I understand. What else?"

"I will have to run a security check on everyone who wants to visit."

"We've already been vetted," Kaia's mother said. "I work for a defense software and hardware contractor, and I have a very high security clearance. They also checked Gilbert and the girls, and they all passed." She smiled. "We are a strange bunch, but we have no skeletons in our closets."

"Speak for yourself," Gilbert said. "I have a few fossils in mine that I need to get rid of."

"Yeah, your cutoff shorts need to go," Cheryl murmured. "You look ridiculous in them."

He affected an offended expression. "I only wear them in our backyard. No one can see me."

"I can." Cheryl grimaced. "And that's painful."

Kaia lifted her hand to stop the bickering. "We've kept William here long enough. He has eight more candidates to interview." She rose to her feet and turned to him. "I need to sleep on it, and I'll let you know my decision tomorrow. If you need to run background checks on us, go ahead, but I don't want to meet with security personnel and get interrogated, and I don't want to subject my family to that either. Once was more than enough."

William put his glass of water on the coffee table and got up as well. "There is no need for that. My guy will do some internet snooping, and that should suffice."

Andrew could probably pull the dossier that the government had compiled on the family, and if not, Roni could find out if there were any shadows hanging over Gilbert, who was the only one William considered a suspect, but not too seriously. The guy liked to stir things up, but he seemed harmless enough.

"Do you need to call a taxi?" Kaia asked.

"A colleague is picking me up. I should text him." William pulled out his phone and typed up a text to Max even though the guy had heard everything through the open earpiece in his pocket.

When he was done, he put the phone back in his pocket and smiled at Kaia's family. "It was nice meeting you all, and I hope we will have many more opportunities to meet in the future."

The surprising thing was that he meant it. He liked Karen with her no-nonsense attitude, and Gilbert with his penchant for drama, and he loved Cheryl with her sensible murmured comments.

But most of all, he loved Kaia with her brilliant brain and her lush lips and long legs—

Yeah, he needed to stop that train of thought. She was a kid, and if she joined his team, she would be a subordinate. Nothing could happen between them.

"I'll walk you outside," Kaia offered. "We can wait for your friend together."

He had a feeling that she wanted to talk to him in private, and even though he shouldn't, he was thrilled to be alone with her again.

"Thank you. That would be great."

18

KAIA

It was probably futile to ask William if he knew anything about Anthony, but if Kaia didn't do it now, she would regret it later, especially if she decided to decline his offer, and this was her last opportunity. As long as William still hoped she would accept it, he would be more motivated to help her.

Kaia waited to confess until they were standing outside the gate. "When I invited you to come over, I had no intention of accepting your offer." She gave him an apologetic smile. "I don't know what magic you used to make me consider it."

"My only magic is logic. But if you had no intention of accepting, why bother?"

She took a deep breath. "Because I hoped you would help me find my friend. He's also a bioinformatician, and a year ago, he accepted a similar offer to work on a secret project that was supposed to last a few months. No one has heard from him since. His parents and his sister think that he's dead, and they are obviously distraught, but there is nothing they can do. No one knows who recruited him or where he went. I refuse to accept that he's dead, and I want to find out what happened to him."

William frowned, his amiable expression turning hard. "Do you think that I had something to do with your friend's disappearance?"

She shrugged. "Now that I've met you, I don't think so. You are too nice of a guy to be involved in something shady." It never hurt to throw in a compliment to get in someone's good graces. "But maybe you can speculate about who might have taken him. Most of the big players in the bioinformatics field know each other."

William didn't seem appeased by her compliment, and his frown only deepened. "I come from a different field, so I'm not familiar with other players, but I can look into it."

"Thank you." Hope surged in her heart but then evaporated when she considered that he might be throwing empty promises her way to get her to accept his offer.

"I will need more information about your friend. His full name is a good start, and if you have a picture of him, that will save my people the effort of locating it. I also need to know when he left for the new job, and if you have an exact date and time, that would be helpful. Did he have social media accounts?"

William's very specific questions revived her hope that he at least intended to look into Tony's disappearance. "I can provide a picture, and I can find out what day he left, but his social media accounts would not be helpful. Tony is a geek and socially awkward. He might have browsed social media to look at pictures and videos of hot girls, but he never posted anything."

The creases in William's forehead smoothed out. "If you can talk about Anthony's browsing habits with such indifference, you are either very open-minded and don't have a single jealous bone in your body, or he wasn't your boyfriend."

So that was why William had seemed so bothered. It wasn't because she offended him by her suspicions, but because he had thought she'd manipulated him to help find her boyfriend. It was all true except for the boyfriend part, so if that was the only thing bothering him, he must be interested in her for more than her brain.

As excitement swirled in Kaia's chest, she felt guilty for thinking silly romantic thoughts while Tony was missing and might be dead.

She chuckled sadly. "Tony was my best friend, and at some point, he might have harbored hopes for being more, but I never felt that way about him."

When William looked doubtful, she added, "He's twenty-eight, which is way too old for me."

Kaia realized her mistake as soon as the words had left her mouth. William was thirty-two, and telling him that she didn't want to date Tony because of his age would make him think twice before initiating anything. And the worst part was that age had nothing to do with her not wanting Tony that way.

He smiled. "Thanks for making me feel old."

"I didn't mean it that way, and it wasn't only the age difference." Perhaps she could still save the situation. "I just wasn't attracted to him." She leaned closer to William. "Tony has a handsome face, but he is shorter than me. I know that it shouldn't matter, but it does. I want my boyfriend to be at least my height." Five feet and nine inches wasn't that tall, so it wasn't unreasonable of her to want a guy who was at least that.

Tony was also a bit of a condescending ass, not to her, but to others, and although he was fun to hang around with and smart enough to talk about every-thing, he wasn't boyfriend material.

Squaring his shoulders, William straightened to his full height, which was a good five to six inches taller than her, and she liked it a lot, but then he slouched back and let out a breath.

"I'll see what I can do. I know an excellent hacker, but he's extremely busy right now. The more information I can give him, the less work he would have to put into finding your friend's trail."

"You would really do that for me?"

"Of course, but I can't promise you that it will be done right away. It might take my hacker friend weeks to get to it."

Kaia wasn't surprised. She'd anticipated that William would use her request as leverage to sway her decision. Unless she joined his team, he wouldn't ask his friend to dig into Tony's disappearance.

She didn't mind.

As long as she had a shred of hope of finding what happened to Anthony and maybe rescuing him, she was willing to do whatever it took.

"I'll be forever grateful to you if you find Anthony for me." She wound her arms around William's neck and planted a quick kiss on his lips.

He didn't return the kiss, he didn't put his arms around her, he didn't even breathe.

The poor guy was stunned.

"It's okay." She laughed. "Gilbert is not going to kill you for kissing me."

"I didn't kiss you." He found his voice. "You kissed me."

"It was a small token of my appreciation." She lifted on her toes and kissed him again. "Goodnight, William, and thank you again."

19

WILLIAM

*A*s Kaia rushed back into the house, William remained rooted in place, a stupid smile stretching his face.

She'd kissed him. On the lips.

Was it just gratitude?

Or was there more to it?

Was she attracted to him?

Had she felt the connection the way he had?

He hadn't sniffed arousal, but maybe she hadn't felt it until he'd promised to help her find her friend.

"Are you just going to stand there?" Max said through the open window.

William hadn't even noticed the car pull up to the curb. "Sorry." He opened the passenger door and got in.

"Judging by the smile on your face, I assume it was a success." Max pulled out into the street. "Keeping the earpiece in the pocket was a bad idea. I heard only every other word."

He suspected that Max had heard everything just fine. It was no coincidence that he'd pulled up to the curb a moment after Kaia had kissed him and had gone back into the house.

"Sorry about that. I don't know why the fabric of my pocket would cause interference."

"Maybe it was your phone?"

"That's possible. I should have put it in my other pocket." Usually, he wouldn't have overlooked a detail like that, but he'd been distracted by Kaia and his attraction to her.

"I heard that she was going to sleep on it, which is better than an outright no, but what's your sense? Was it just a brush-off, or is she considering it seriously?"

"I think she is serious."

He still wasn't sure how things had turned out the way they had, and what had been the turning point. Was it his promise to help find her friend?

"That's great news." Max cast him a sidelong smile. "I found a nice club where we can celebrate your success."

The last thing William wanted was to go hunting for a hookup. He was still reeling from the meeting, and what he needed was a stiff drink.

"I'd rather go to a bar if you don't mind. I'm not in the mood for female company."

Max frowned. "What's wrong?"

Like most immortal males, the Guardian was always in the mood, so he couldn't understand how and why William wasn't.

"Nothing is wrong. I need a drink to calm down after the meeting, and I need to figure out how to adjust our safety procedures to accommodate Kaia. She wants to go home at least every other weekend, and she wants her family to be able to visit her."

"I heard that part."

"Her mother and stepfather also want to see Safe Haven before giving their approval."

The Guardian shook his head. "That's too risky."

"Not necessarily. I can mitigate most of the risks. Her mother works for a defense contractor and has a high-security clearance. Her partner and older daughters have gone through briefings as well. Kaia is susceptible to thralling, but before allowing her family to visit, I still need to check whether they are susceptible as well."

The truth was that William wasn't sure about Kaia's susceptibility. He'd been able to peek into her mind, which suggested that she was, but he still needed to make sure that he could erase her memories and plant fake ones.

He also needed to find out why she thought of herself as a middle-aged man. He wasn't a psychologist, but it could be a coping mechanism, a way for a very young woman to deal with the world of academia where her peers were much older than her.

Or maybe it had to do with her missing friend?

He shifted to face Max. "Did you hear what Kaia told me about her missing friend?"

"I heard some of it, but first, tell me where you want me to take you. Are we going back to the hotel? Or am I looking for a pub?"

"The hotel has a bar. We can get a drink there, and if you find someone to hook up with, I won't have to call a taxi to take me back."

"True." Max let out a breath. "The hotel bar doesn't offer much of a selection, but it will do."

William chuckled. "I guess you are not referring to their selection of whiskeys."

"That too. So what do you think happened to Kaia's friend?"

"It's a long shot, but he could have been taken to the island. The guy has a PhD, and he's young and good-looking. He fits the profile of Navuh's currently preferred studs."

Max looked doubtful. "The Doomers are not the only bad guys out there, and if bioinformaticians are in such high demand, he could have been taken by the Chinese, the Russians, or one of the smaller players. It's not uncommon for scientists to be abducted and forced to work on secret projects, especially those that have to do with weapon development. It's also not uncommon for the kidnappers to get rid of them once the project is done."

"Then I hope he was taken to the island. Serving as a breeding stud might be humiliating, but it's better than being dead."

20

KAIA

*A*s Kaia returned to the house, she could barely contain the excitement swirling in her belly. Schooling her features required a major effort, but she couldn't let her mother and Gilbert see her smiling like some silly girl with a crush on an older guy.

What had possessed her to kiss William?

Not that she regretted doing it, but usually she wasn't that impulsive. It was the gratitude, and Kaia was going to stick to that version even under torture. She would never admit that she'd been staring at William's lips throughout the interview and imagining how they would feel against hers.

They'd felt amazing, but William hadn't risen to the occasion. Well, one part of him had, but the rest had remained frozen. She'd hoped he would wrap his arms around her and take over the kiss, but he'd been either too stunned or afraid to touch her.

It definitely was the strangest interview she'd ever had. William hadn't asked her any questions about her qualifications, and he hadn't tested her knowledge. He'd just assumed that she was exactly the person he needed for his project. In fact, they had switched roles, with her being the interviewer and him being the interviewee.

Had he passed the examination?

Given Gilbert's frown, William hadn't passed his nose test, but given her mother's knowing smile, he'd passed hers. Cheryl was busy on her phone, no doubt checking her Instatock channel to see how many likes and shares she'd gotten in the past hour.

The girl was obsessed with social approval, and that wasn't healthy.

Kaia sat next to Gilbert and draped her arm over his shoulders. "So, what does your nose tell you? Is William a crook?"

Gilbert shook his head. "He seems like a good guy, but he has too many secrets,

58

and he feels guilty about keeping them from us, which worries me. He might be an awesome fellow, but his business partners might be crooks."

"How does that work? Why would a straight shooter involve himself with bad guys?"

Smiling indulgently, Gilbert patted her knee. "People who find themselves in tight corners, or get pushed into them, sometimes have no choice but to compromise on their moral standing."

"True." She leaned against his side. "So, what should I do?"

"Do you want to go?" her mother asked.

"I do, and I don't. I've never left home, I've never lived in dorms, and I missed the whole college experience because I was the genius freak who started college at fourteen. The project will only take a few months, so it's not like I'll be away for all that long, and it might be fun."

Cheryl lifted her head from her phone and smirked. "Admit it. You want to go because you like William."

There was no point in denying that because it was the truth, just not in its entirety. She didn't want to tell them about William's promise to help find Tony. If they thought that was the reason she was considering going, they would never allow it.

Kaia was an adult, and she didn't need their permission, but that's not how their family worked. Her mother had asked Kaia and Cheryl's permission before she'd started dating Gilbert, even though they'd just been little girls and still missed their father. If they had said no, she wouldn't have gone out with him and would have missed out on the best second chance ever.

"Of course, I like William. He's smart, polite, and handsome. I don't have to dumb myself down to talk to him."

"He's too old for you," Cheryl said.

"A thirteen-year difference is not that bad." Kaia took her arm off Gilbert's shoulders and got up. "Especially for someone like me who has nothing to talk about with people her age."

Her mother winced. "That's why I wanted you to join that high IQ club, but you refused to go after attending the introductory meeting."

Kaia rolled her eyes. "What a bunch of freaks, myself included. One or two freaks in a room make things interesting, but a room full of freaks is just depressing." She sat next to her sister. "Am I right?"

"If you say so." Cheryl went back to scrolling through her Instatock account.

Her sister wasn't much of a talker, and engaging her in a conversation was like pulling teeth.

"A thirteen-year difference is huge," Gilbert said. "He's definitely too old for you."

She had to kill that subject before her family started obsessing about her wanting to date an older man. "I was just teasing. Even if I was interested, William is not because he thinks of me as a kid."

"Right." Cheryl snorted. "That's why he couldn't take his eyes off you."

"As if you would know. You were babysitting Idina." Kaia sighed. "Let's move on and focus on what's relevant. Let's say that we go there and it's just as beautiful and luxurious as William claims, and I accept the offer. I can't stand not seeing the little ones for more than a few days, and I will only be able to fly home every other weekend. We need to figure out how we can make it work. I will need you to come to visit me and bring Cheryl, Idina, and the twins with you."

"Did you hear that?" Gilbert looked at her mom. "She only cares about the babies. You and I are chopped liver."

"You're not chopped liver." Kaia laughed. "I want to see you too, but you are not going to change in two weeks or two months. Unlike you, Idina, Evan, and Ryan change from day to day, and I don't want to miss any of it. Besides, babies have short memories, and they might forget me."

"They are not going to forget you," her mother said. "Not even if you don't come home every other week." She looked at Gilbert. "But I don't think we would be able to visit you more than once or twice throughout the duration of the project. It's difficult to travel with the twins. Just the amount of stuff we need to take with us is staggering."

"What about Eric? He can fly you back and forth with all the things for the twins."

"My brother charters his planes to earn a living," Gilbert said. "He's not our private pilot."

"What if you pay him?" Cheryl asked. "Then we will be just like his other clients."

"He's not going to take money from us."

"Can you at least ask?" Kaia cast him a pleading look that was sure to break through his resistance.

"Don't look at me with those puppy eyes," he grumbled. "Fine. I'll talk to Eric."

"Thank you." She pushed to her feet and walked over to him. "You're the best." She leaned and kissed his cheek.

Gilbert grinned. "I know."

WILLIAM

*I*t was after two o'clock in the afternoon when William was done with his last interview, and he hadn't heard from Kaia yet.

Should he call her?

Text her?

"Are there any more candidates on your list?" Max asked after dropping the silencing shroud he'd maintained throughout the interviews.

It had been the Guardian's idea to hold the interviews in a Starbucks but keep them private without the interviewees realizing that. Meeting in a public place made it feel less cloak-and-dagger and put the candidates at ease. After all, the project couldn't be about developing something nefarious if they were discussing it in a Starbucks.

"Corinne was the last." William leaned back in his chair. "Now, I'm ready for coffee."

"Me too." Max got to his feet and walked over to stand in line.

Sitting in a coffee shop all morning and sipping on water had been its own kind of torture, but William had heeded Darlene's advice to avoid caffeine during the interviews.

Even without stimulants, he talked too fast and had to remind himself to slow down, and Darlene had noticed that after drinking coffee, he got worse. William hadn't had any yesterday before the meeting with Kaia either, and he'd done well keeping his talking speed in check.

As his mind drifted back to her, he realized that he hadn't asked her even the most basic questions. He hadn't tested her knowledge because he wasn't qualified to do that, and after reading her published articles, he knew that she was exceptional. But he hadn't asked her any personal questions either, like whether she preferred coffee or tea, or whether caffeine made her jittery. He'd gotten to know her family, though, and how important they were to her. Her decision would largely depend on their approval and their willingness to come to visit her, and that would also depend on Kian and whether he would approve of the visits.

William hadn't called the boss yet, and if he didn't hear from Kaia, the only thing he would have to report was that he'd assembled a team of mediocre bioinformaticians who had no chance in hell of deciphering the journals.

Max returned with two grande cappuccinos and a stack of sandwiches and pastries. "That should do it for now." He handed William a paper cup.

"We could have gone to a proper restaurant for lunch." William took the lid off his cup.

"I'm too hungry to wait." Max pulled out one of the sandwiches and unwrapped it. "It would have taken at least an hour until we found a place to eat, sat down, ordered, and food was served. I wouldn't have lasted that long." He dug into his sandwich with gusto.

A couple of months ago, William would have attacked the food with the same fervor, but he'd taught himself to slow down and enjoy what he ate instead of gobbling it down.

When Max was done with his first sandwich, he wiped his mouth with a napkin and unwrapped the second one. "Any of them any good?"

"The sandwiches?"

"No, the candidates. Who did you decide to hire?"

William put his sandwich down. "Doctor Corinne Burke is an experienced bioinformatician, and she is eager to take the job. She's recently divorced, needs the money, and even more than that, she needs a break. She's taking a sabbatical, so it's not an issue for her to be gone for a few months. Owen Ferrel has just gotten his Master's, so he's a total greenhorn, but he's decent, and with proper guidance, he could function as an assistant. The same goes for Kylie Baldwin."

"So, you got two PhDs to do the deciphering work, one who is experienced and one who is not, and two donkeys to assist them with the tedious parts."

William chuckled. "More or less. I didn't hear from Kaia yet, and without her, I don't have a team. Corinne can lead the effort and organize the research, but she doesn't have Kaia's innate talent."

Glancing at the people sitting around them, Max leaned forward. "Then thrall her," he whispered. "Too much is at stake to leave it to the whims of a nineteen-year-old."

William smiled. "Shame on you, Max. You're supposed to uphold the law, not conspire to break it."

The Guardian shrugged. "The law is open to interpretation. You might claim that the research is vital to the clan's future, and therefore thralling a human to get it done is justified. Edna is not going to argue with you over that."

"I know." William let out a breath. "I'm just not comfortable with it."

"Do you want me to do it?"

He didn't want the Guardian anywhere near Kaia's brilliant mind, and not just because there was a second personality living inside of it. Her mind was like a fine-tuned instrument, and the slightest interference could be detrimental. In her case, compulsion would have to suffice, and if Kian had a problem with that, William would suggest dual compulsion by Emmett and Eleanor to make it iron clad.

Compulsion might be more intrusive than a thrall, but it caused no damage to the brain.

"I'll convince her to join my team the mundane way." He smiled. "With a bribe. She wants me to find her friend, and I'm going to use that as leverage. It's not honorable either, and I should help her regardless of her joining my team, but it's not as bad as thralling her to sign the contract."

Max shrugged. "Whatever works." He took a big bite of his second sandwich and washed it down with a gulp of cappuccino.

Sipping on his own coffee, William let his thoughts drift back to the strange duality inside Kaia's mind. She didn't behave or speak like an old man. She was mature for her age, but that was because she was smart. Sometimes, however, she acted her age, like when she'd suddenly kissed him on the lips.

Damn, that kiss still played havoc on his mind, not to mention other parts of his body that were not as astute.

He had to find out what the deal with the middle-aged guy was. Was it a memory? A play-pretend? A spirit like the one who used to live in Nathalie's head?

How could he find out more about it without invading Kaia's mind again? The less he messed with that precious brain of hers, the better.

Perhaps he could call Syssi and ask her advice. She would easily come up with a diplomatic way to pose the question to Kaia, but she was so busy these days, and he didn't want to bother her. Besides, everything he told her would go straight to Kian, and William hadn't figured out a strategy for dealing with the boss yet.

22

MIA

"I'm in love." Mia's grandmother kissed Okidu on the cheek. "If I ever leave my husband, it would be for you."

The butler grinned. "I am honored, mistress."

Kian had loaned them the cyborg to help with packing and loading their belongings into the clan's bus. It had made the entire process physically effortless, but it was still difficult emotionally.

Last night, Mia had cried when she said goodbye to Margo and Frankie, and they had shed a few tears as well, and then the three of them had laughed about how ridiculous they were being. They were going to see each other on the weekends and talk on the phone as many times a day as they wished. It was also only a temporary arrangement until Margo and Frankie could join her in the village, but that wasn't a sure thing yet.

Hopefully, the new developmental division of Perfect Match would be set up sooner rather than later, so her friends could quit their jobs, move into the village, and start working for Toven.

Margo and Frankie were ecstatic about dropping their dead-end jobs and becoming testers for Perfect Match adventures, and after she'd explained that the other partners were paranoid about leaks, they were even okay with moving into a secret compound. But she hadn't told them the rest of the fantastic story yet. That would have to wait for when it was time for them to move, and that was also when they would have the option to decline.

Although knowing those two as well as she did, they would be all for it. Neither had health problems, so transitioning would be a breeze for them, but there were downsides. Their families couldn't visit them in the village, and they would have to lie to them, which would be a big problem for Frankie, and to a lesser extent for Margo. It was also possible that they weren't Dormants after all, and if they didn't transition, the entire house of cards would come crashing down. They would have to leave the village after their memories of it were erased, and they would have to go back to their boring jobs. The clan could help them find better employment, but knowing that they were not guaranteed a happy ending might be a deterrent.

"Stop flirting with the cyborg, Rosy," her grandfather grumbled as he helped his wife climb the steep steps of the bus.

"Why? It's not like I mean it, dear. It's just a bit of fun, and unlike a man, Okidu is not going to take it seriously."

"Shh," he admonished. "We are in the middle of the street. Someone might hear you."

She waved a dismissive hand. "There is no one out here, and even if there was, they would just think that the old lady has dementia and is talking nonsense."

"God forbid." Her grandfather huffed out a breath.

Once her grandparents were seated in the bus, Toven lifted Mia off the wheelchair, carried her into the bus, and put her down. "Do you want me to bring the chair?"

"I have a new one waiting for me in the village. We can leave it here and have one less thing to schlep back and forth."

"True." He wheeled the chair back to the house.

"It's not going to be easy switching homes every week," her grandmother said. "But I have to admit that it's exciting. We will get to meet new people and go on virtual adventures."

Her grandfather groaned. "You can go if you want, but I'm not about to let these immortals strap me into a chair and attach electrodes to my head."

"You will." Her grandmother patted his knee. "Stop being such an old man."

After Toven had locked the house up and joined them in the bus, Okidu pulled into the street, and they were on their way.

"When are our cars arriving?" Mia asked.

Toven took her hand. "Last I checked, they were working on the modifications, so it should be done soon, but the shipping will take a couple of weeks."

Mia sighed. "I wish the delivery coincided with our move, but things seldom work out that seamlessly." When he frowned, she lifted her other hand. "I'm not complaining. I'm so full of gratitude that I could burst."

But that didn't mean that everything was perfect.

Orion, Alena, and Annani were not in the village, and it would be several more weeks until they returned from their trip. That meant that the reconciliation between father and son would have to wait, and so would Toven's reminiscing with Annani about the good old days of the gods.

He needed that to process the grief he'd bottled up for five thousand years, and once he finally let it all out, he might get his glow back and shine like the god he was.

"The good news is that your grandparents' cars are ready," Toven said.

"Awesome." She gave him a smile. "They would have hated being chauffeured everywhere."

Toven leaned to whisper in her ear, "I don't think your grandmother would have minded if the chauffeur was Okidu."

"She was just teasing." Mia leaned her head on Toven's arm. "I want that car to be here already."

It was her ticket to freedom. She couldn't bring her own modified car to the village because it didn't have the special windows that turned opaque or the self-driving capabilities. Toven could have gotten a car from Kian, but he wasn't happy with how basic the model was, so he'd ordered two SUVs for them, both with special modifications for her motorized wheelchair. Toven's SUV had a passenger side lift and no seat on that side, and hers had the same arrangement on the driver side, in addition to all the other modifications that made it possible for her to drive using only her hands. Once the vehicles arrived, she would no longer need to be carried around like a sack of potatoes and would get her independence back.

Mia couldn't wait.

Toven shifted in his seat to look at her grandparents. "I hope you remember that we are invited to dinner at Kalugal's tonight."

Her grandfather winced. "Can we be excused? People our age shouldn't eat that late. The heartburn will keep me awake all night, and I will be good for nothing tomorrow."

"You can eat a snack before," Mia suggested. "And not eat much at dinner."

"You know me." He sighed. "I'm on the see food diet. When I see it, I eat it. I have no self-control."

"I can help with that," Toven offered. "Do you want me to compel you not to touch anything during dinner?"

"And miss out on all the great food Kalugal's cook is making? No way. Besides, I don't want you taking over my will. It's enough that I can't say the word immortal in the company of other humans. My mouth just refuses to obey me, and that's disturbing."

Mia cast a sidelong glance at Toven, communicating with him wordlessly. How was he going to give her grandparents his blood without thralling them? To do so after her grandfather had explicitly said that he didn't want Toven in his head was just wrong.

She would have to come up with a story and lie to them about the benefits of Toven's thralls to get them to agree. But then if they told any of the other immortals about it, her lies would be exposed.

It was a conundrum, and at the moment, the solution eluded her.

Could the Fates give her a hint?

They had been so generous with what they'd bestowed on her so far that asking for more seemed like pushing her luck, but she needed help, and unless Toven came up with something clever, she would have to go against her grandfather's explicit wishes.

23

WILLIAM

*I*t was after three o'clock in the afternoon, and Kaia hadn't called yet.

With a sigh, William sat down on his hotel bed and looked at his phone, willing it to ring. He also wanted to speak with Darlene before she went home for the day, but he didn't want to miss a call from Kaia.

It was odd that no one was calling him from the lab. He'd left Marcel in charge, expecting the guy to call him every five minutes with questions, but his phone had remained silent throughout the two days he'd been gone, and wasn't that sad.

He'd even checked to make sure that there was nothing wrong with the device, but everything worked like it was supposed to. He wasn't getting calls because no one missed him, and Marcel was doing just fine without him.

Evidently, he wasn't as irreplaceable as Kian had thought he was.

Maybe he should use Max's phone to call Darlene. That way his line wouldn't be busy when Kaia called.

The Guardian was in the adjacent room, watching a game on the television and cheering on his favorite human team, whatever the sport or the name of the team was.

William couldn't care less. Sports had never interested him, not as a participant and not as a spectator.

After long minutes passed and his phone remained silent, he let out a breath and called Darlene.

She answered right away. "How is it going, boss?"

"Good." He smiled, happy to hear her sounding so cheerful. "I have most of my team members lined up."

"You don't sound enthusiastic. What's the catch?"

She'd gotten to know him pretty well since her arrival at the village. More so since she'd started working at the lab.

"My best candidate, Doctor Kaia Locke, still hasn't given me her final answer, and that's why I'm calling you. I need your advice."

"Get her chocolates. That always works for me."

He chuckled. "I'm not asking her on a date."

"You're not?" She sounded genuinely surprised. "Why?"

"Why would I? She's nineteen, and I'm trying to recruit her. Can you think of a more inappropriate move than to ask her to go out on a date with me?"

"Yeah." She sighed. "You're probably right. Do you like her?"

William nodded. "I do."

"I mean as a woman, not just a brain."

"She's nineteen, Darlene."

"So what?"

He shook his head. "Just drop it. She's too young for me, and I'm about to become her employer."

"I thought that was what you needed advice on."

"It's not. I took a peek into Kaia's mind, and I saw something very strange. When she thinks of herself, she switches between thinking of herself as Kaia, a young woman, and a middle-aged man. I don't want to intrude on her thoughts, I don't want to thrall her unless it's absolutely necessary, and I don't know how to ask her about it without creeping her out."

"Don't ask her anything before she signs the contract, that's for sure. After she spends time with you at Safe Haven and gets to know you, you can tell her that she gives out a vibe of a much older person, and that it's slightly masculine. By then, she might trust you enough to tell you the truth, or she might tell you to mind your own business."

"What do you think it could be?"

"No clue, William. You should ask Vanessa."

"Right." He pushed his glasses up his nose. "As if she has time for that. You are the only one I can talk to about Kaia," he admitted. "I just hoped that as a woman you would have a clue about what's going on in her head. Does she have a split personality? Is it her way to cope with a chaotic world?

"I wish I could help you, but I can't."

It had been worth a try, and he hadn't really expected Darlene to have answers for him. "How are things going at the lab?"

She sighed. "It's boring here without you. Roni never talks while he works, and Marcel is kind of dull. I miss you telling me about this or that idea or how you're going to improve this or that gadget."

"I thought you were bored by my stories."

"Never. I just lost you when you talked at the speed of a machine gun. Are you following my advice and slowing down when you talk to the recruits, and especially Doctor Kaia?"

"I do when I remember."

"I should have come with you, and I should come to Safe Haven with you as well. You need someone to keep you organized. I don't want to even imagine what a mess you're going to make in that brand new office. Besides, you need someone to train with you, or you won't do it and you'll gain back all the weight you lost."

The more Darlene talked, the more he liked the idea of her coming to Safe Haven with him. He'd become so much more productive since she'd started working at the lab. He no longer misplaced things and had to waste time looking for them, because she knew where everything was, and he no longer forgot to order parts and then had to wait for them because she made sure he was on top of that.

"I like your idea."

"Which one?"

"Of you joining me at Safe Haven. I could use an administrator."

"Yay!" Darlene shrieked in his ear. "I can get out of here."

He chuckled. "You weren't a prisoner."

"I know. I like the safety of the clan, but going to Safe Haven is like branching out without actually leaving. I'll get to meet the paranormal talents, and maybe I'll find my one and only among them. But even if I don't, we are going to have fun out there."

"Sure thing. It was nice chatting with you."

"Same here. Good luck with your lady."

"Thanks." William ended the call, glanced at the time, and put the phone down on the bed.

He'd spent twenty minutes talking to Darlene, and no call had come in during that time. If Kaia didn't call soon, he needed to accept that her answer was a no and decide what his next move should be.

When his phone rang, he snatched it off the mattress, and his heart skipped a beat when he saw Kaia's name displayed on the screen.

"Hello," he said in the most nonchalant tone he could muster.

"Hi. I'm sorry for not calling earlier, but I was waiting for my uncle to get back to me and tell me when he could get here. Does eight in the evening work for you? By then the babies are going to be asleep for sure."

"It's perfect. Am I going to get grilled by another member of your family?"

"Yeah, sorry about that. Eric is Gilbert's brother, and he has two private planes that he charters. When Gilbert called him to ask if he'd be willing to fly us to Oregon, and Eric heard about you, he insisted on meeting you in person."

"I see. Are you waiting for him to form his opinion, or did you make up your mind?"

"Oh, I made up my mind yesterday after you promised me to look for Tony. Now I just need to convince my family that this is a good move for me, so do your best to impress Eric."

William let out a silent breath. "You don't know how relieved I am that your answer is a yes. Anything I should know about your uncle?"

"He's a younger, cockier version of Gilbert, but he's a great guy. You're going to like him."

"I don't know if I can handle an enhanced version of Gilbert. The original was tough enough."

Kaia laughed. "You'll do fine. Gilbert says that you're a good guy, and he has an infallible nose for people's characters. And if Gilbert thinks that you are okay, Eric is not going to give you a hard time."

24

DARLENE

*A*fter doing a victory dance in her tiny office in the lab, Darlene dropped into her rolling chair, lifted her legs up, and put them on the desk.

She could finally move out of Geraldine and Shai's house without her mother bursting into tears at the mere mention of her wanting a place of her own.

Maybe if she started calling her Mother, Geraldine would stop trying so hard to make up for all the years she'd missed from her life. After all, it hadn't been her fault, but it just felt weird to address a woman who looked young enough to be her daughter as Mother.

If she did that just to appease Geraldine, it would sound as fake as she imagined it would feel.

It was too early to call it a day, but since everyone in the lab made concessions for the fragile human, no one would bat an eyelid if she went home even earlier than usual. The others worked fourteen- and sixteen-hour days, and in the beginning, she had tried to keep up with their stamina and prove that she was just as strong despite being human, but it had taken only a few days for her to realize that she couldn't keep up.

Maybe if she were in her twenties she could, but at nearly fifty it was too taxing, especially since she also trained at the gym every day.

It was time to find an immortal male to induce her, so she could turn immortal and forget all about feeling dizzy after a run on the treadmill or needing a Motrin after lifting weights. Saying goodbye to wrinkles and saggy skin would be even nicer.

So what if she hadn't found the perfect guy yet? Any male that she could see herself getting naked with would do, and there were plenty of handsome bachelors in the village who didn't mind that she looked old enough to be their mother.

The problem was that she minded.

Maybe it was vanity, but she was a woman, and she wanted to look better than the guy she was having sex with. Or maybe it was just an excuse, and she was still not over her divorce even though it had been finalized.

Ugh. If only there was a store that sold courage. She would have spent her entire salary on that.

Pushing away from her desk, Darlene got up and walked out into the main lab.

"I'm going home." She stopped by Roni's chair and kissed the top of his head.

He frowned. "Are you feeling sick?"

"I'm feeling great." She grinned. "I'm going to celebrate. William invited me to come with him to Safe Haven to help keep everything organized."

Her son smiled. "That's awesome, but I hope that you will come to visit often. You've only just gotten here, and I enjoy having you around."

"Oh, sweetie." She leaned and kissed his cheek. "You don't know how much it means to me to hear you say that." She straightened up. "Maybe I shouldn't do it."

"Go." He waved a hand. "You need a change of pace after the divorce. Treat it as a vacation and take some of the classes they offer in the retreat. Most of it is New-Age nonsense, but it can be relaxing and reaffirming."

"That's not a bad idea. I'll do that, if I have any free time left, that is. Keeping William organized is a full-time job."

"Tell me about it." He reached for her hand. "Have fun, Mom. You deserve it."

"Thank you."

As she made her way back to the house, Darlene reflected on what Roni had told her and how good it had made her feel. She hadn't been the best of mothers, and yet he'd forgiven her, called her Mom, and told her that he loved her and liked spending time with her. Those were the kinds of goodies that all mothers lived for.

She shouldn't withhold that from Geraldine.

So what if it was awkward the first few times she called her Mom? She would get used to it, and it would mean the world to her mother.

Walking into the house, she knew that she would find Geraldine in the kitchen preparing dinner like she did every day.

"Hello, sweetheart. You're home early today. Is everything okay?"

"Hi, Mom." Darlene kissed her on the cheek. "Everything is perfect. What's for dinner?"

The spatula dropped from Geraldine's hand, and she stared at her as if she was an apparition. "You called me Mom."

"Does it bother you?"

"Bother me?" Tears started flowing down Geraldine's cheeks. "No, it doesn't bother me." She threw her arms around Darlene and squeezed hard. "I love you so much, and it means the world to me that you found it in your heart to call me Mother again. I'm so happy."

Great, now she didn't want to spoil Geraldine's mood by telling her that she was going with William to Safe Haven, but it was better to get it over with.

"I have great news, Mom." She unfolded herself from Geraldine's arms. "William invited me to join him at Safe Haven for the duration of the project. Both of us will probably come back for a visit every other weekend, so you are not going to miss me too badly."

Geraldine's chin quivered, but she smiled through the tears. "Does it mean that you two are getting together after all?"

"No, Mom." It was already easier to say that word. "We are just friends, but maybe one of the handsome Guardians Onegus assigned to the project will catch my eye."

25

ELEANOR

*E*leanor leaned back in her chair and looked out the window of her home office at the surf down below. Kian had chosen a great location for the paranormal division. The elevated plot meant that every bungalow had at least a partial ocean view, but hers was near the top of the hill, and had the best view of them all.

Emmett had wanted them to live in his cottage, or rather down in its luxurious underground quarters, but she didn't want the shadows of his past hanging over their relationship. He'd had orgies in those rooms, and even if she got new mattresses and new bedding, she wouldn't be able to get past the sleazy images lingering in those walls.

Poor Mey had no doubt encountered worse when she listened to the echoes embedded in walls. People were far less nice in private, and the stories the walls told her were probably mostly nasty.

What a dubious talent that was.

Eleanor, on the other hand, had been blessed with the best talent an immortal could have. Compulsion was a rare and incredibly useful ability. The only problem with it was the need to exercise restraint and not abuse it, and sometimes the line between necessary and abusive was blurry.

Before getting caught by the clan, Eleanor had used her talent often and not always out of necessity or for the greater good.

Hell, she'd abused her power, and the worst of it had been compelling a man she'd been in love with to act as if he loved her back, when he could barely stand her.

But that was in the past, and she was a different person now.

She had a man who loved her with the same intensity she loved him, and she had been put in charge of an important program, not by compelling her way through the ranks but by earning Kian's trust and respect.

Gazing out the window, Eleanor surveyed her little empire.

She could see all the other bungalows that comprised the paranormal enclave of Safe Haven, which was one more reason to work from her home office rather than the one in the main building, which also housed the program's two classrooms and another tiny office for its instructors. She used it only when she needed to confer with them or the damn doctor, who was a pain in her rear.

Thankfully, his clinic was in a separate bungalow.

She had the guy under such strong compulsion that he couldn't fart without her permission, but he was unpleasant to put it politely, and a sleaze bucket in a more colorful language.

Eleanor couldn't wait to get rid of him, but she still had a long way to go until that objective could be achieved.

First they needed to figure out who, if any, of the paranormals were Dormants, and that was a problem. Aside from Andy, who was still a kid, the rest had formed relationships with others in their group, so introducing them to immortals was not an option unless those relationships fell apart.

Lisa might be able to sniff out the Dormants among them, but Kian didn't trust her ability enough to rely on it exclusively.

When Eleanor had still been the program's recruiter, Mollie and James had already been an item, Jeremy had his eye on Naomi, and Abigail had been regularly hooking up with Dylan, but they hadn't been officially a couple. After she'd left, Spencer and Sofia had gotten together, Jeremy and Naomi had solidified their relationship, and so had Dylan and Abigail.

Compelling them to fall out of love was as impossible as compelling them to fall in love in the first place, but she could compel them to do things that would sabotage their relationships.

Not that she was going to do that if there was any other way. Even if Kian would have approved, Eleanor wasn't callous enough to tear those couples apart.

The males could be tested without breaking up their relationship with their partners, but if they transitioned and their partners didn't, that would also be a problem.

Eleanor could see no easy solution for any of that.

The easier part of her job was dismantling the program. When the doctor continued to report insignificant findings, and the talents kept producing dismal results, the government would eventually lose interest and their contracts wouldn't get renewed. But that meant waiting until the current ones expired, which wasn't anytime soon.

Those who turned out to be Dormants could disappear to the village the same way Jin and her group had done, but those who didn't, would stay, and she would have to stay with them to keep up the charade.

It wasn't a hardship.

Eleanor loved her position of authority in Safe Haven, and not just because of the independence it afforded her and the prestige. Applications for the new paranormal retreats were exceeding expectations, and if even one potential Dormant was found in each group of guests, it would be a tremendous achievement.

Eleanor felt honored and privileged to be in charge of a program that could potentially breathe new life into the clan.

26

KAIA

"*E*ric." Kaia rushed over to her uncle and wound her arms around his neck. "Thanks for coming." She kissed him on both cheeks. "Ugh, you're prickly."

Laughing, he put his hands on her waist. "I came as soon as I could, and I didn't have time to shave for you. I need to check out that guy before I let him lure you to his lair."

"William is harmless." Kaia let go of him. "Even Gilbert says that, and he doesn't trust anyone."

"Yeah, I know all about his infallible nose." Eric bent to whisper in her ears. "His ability to sniff out crooks is just as inflated as the rest of his ego."

Kaia slapped his back playfully. "Look who's talking. You two can compete for the award of who has the bigger one." Her cheeks heated as she realized how that had sounded, but to clarify would make it even worse.

"I'd win." Eric winked. "Where are the little monsters?"

"Asleep, I hope. Mom and Gilbert are upstairs with them, and I don't hear crying. Can I get you something to drink?"

"I'm hungry." Eric beelined for the kitchen. "Are there any leftovers from dinner?"

"Always." Kaia opened the fridge and pulled out a glass container. "Berta doesn't know how to cook small portions."

"Why should she?" Eric took the container from her, grabbed a fork from the drawer, and walked over to the kitchen table. "You are a big family." He opened the container and dug in.

"Don't eat it cold. Let me warm it up for you."

"No need. It's good as it is."

"Bachelors." She pulled out a chair and sat next to him. "When are you going to find a girl and settle down?"

"Never." He collected another forkful. "I learned my lesson the first time around."

"Gilbert went through a nasty divorce as well and look how happy he is now."

"He got lucky. I'm very happy to remain a bachelor, thank you very much."

It was better to drop the subject before he got upset. Anytime anyone mentioned his ex-wife, Eric's good mood evaporated. Kaia didn't know the details of what had gone wrong in their marriage, but from what she'd heard, the woman was nuts. When she'd gotten mad at Eric, she slashed all the tires on his car and threw his big screen television outside. How she'd even managed to lift it was a mystery.

"Tell me about this job," Eric said. "It must be spectacular for you to give up Stanford for it."

"I'm not giving it up. The project should end before I need to start at Stanford. That position will only become available in October when the professor leading the research retires."

"Why didn't he retire at the end of the year?"

Kaia shrugged. "I don't know. I'm very lucky that he will, though. It doesn't happen often. I know the postdoc who's going to replace him, which is why I'm getting the job despite my lack of experience. I will take over the postdoc's position when he's appointed to head of the lab."

Eric dropped the fork inside the empty container, "Are you excited about working at the university?"

"Yeah, I am."

"You don't sound excited."

She shrugged. "I was very excited until William told me about his project. I can't wait to learn more details about it."

"Are you allowed to tell me what it is?"

"I'm not sure myself. It's about deciphering another scientist's work, which he'd written in code. William thinks once we crack it, we will find information that will revolutionize medicine, but that's all he's willing to tell me before I sign the nondisclosure agreement."

"Sounds mysterious." Eric leaned back in his chair and rubbed his flat stomach. "Gilbert tells me that the lab is somewhere on the Oregon Coast. Do you know where on the coast it is?"

Kaia shook her head. "How many private airports are there in that area?"

"Several. I need to know which one is the closest."

"So, you're going to fly us there?"

"Of course. I want to check the place out myself."

Kaia worried her lower lip. "I don't want you losing business because of us. We can fly commercial."

"With the little monsters? I don't think so. Besides, family comes first. Right?"

"Always."

Gilbert and Eric's parents were gone, and neither of them had children with their exes. The only family they had was a sister who lived in Ohio and was also divorced and didn't keep in touch, so when Gilbert had started dating her mother, both brothers had adopted them as their own.

They'd started as family by choice, and after Idina and then the twins had been born, they had also become a family by blood.

27

WILLIAM

*B*y the time Gilbert and his brother had finished grilling William, his shirt was sticking to his back, and he was craving a stiff glass of whiskey. Those two could work for Turner.

Luckily, he'd prepared well for the meeting. Max had thrown questions at him at a rapid rate, and he'd come up with the answers on the spot.

With how fast William's brain worked neither Max nor the brothers had a chance to trip him up, but it had been an intense experience, especially since he'd been distracted by how good Kaia looked today.

Instead of the librarian's blouse she'd worn yesterday, she had a simple T-shirt on, and the light pink fabric and low neckline did little to hide the sumptuous curves underneath.

"I'm sorry for the third degree," Eric said. "But we had to make sure that Kaia was in good hands. I intend to visit frequently to ensure that she's doing okay. I don't need to know what you're working on, but I need to know that she's well."

That would be a problem, but William would cross that bridge when the time came. Right now, he needed to close the deal. "You don't need to apologize. I'm glad that Kaia has such dedicated protectors."

Eric smiled. "No hard feelings then?"

"None."

Kaia let out a breath. "Can I talk now?"

"Of course." Her mother turned a warning look at the brothers. "You guys are done, right?"

"For now." Gilbert crossed his arms over his chest and directed a look at William that was meant to be intimidating.

Kaia turned to him with an apologetic smile. "How did the interviews with the other candidates go? Did you manage to recruit anyone else?"

"I hired Corinne Burke, Owen Ferrel, and Kylie Baldwin. Do you know any of them?"

"I know them mostly by reputation, and they are all good. Owen is not the brightest of the bunch, but he's hard-working. You won't be disappointed. Corinne is average, but she's more experienced, and Kylie is probably the best of the three."

"Will you be comfortable working with them?"

"I haven't heard anything bad about any of them, so I hope they are easy to work with." She flicked her long hair behind her shoulder. "The only difficulty I can foresee is them bristling about a kid leading the team." She trained her big blue eyes at him. "Not everyone can see past that."

Had that comment been directed at him?

William wasn't sure. "I'm putting Corinne in charge of organizing the findings, but I'll make it clear that they all answer to you. Anyone who has a problem with that can leave."

His answer seemed to satisfy Kaia. "Thank you. If they are professionals, they will stay."

"So, do we have a deal?" He looked at her and then her mother, Gilbert, and lastly at Eric.

"We do," Kaia said. "I'll sign the nondisclosure agreement whenever you want, but I will sign the contract only after my family approves of the location." She gave him an apologetic smile. "I feel like a prima donna for making such unreasonable demands."

"That's okay. You have a right to be demanding. I feel privileged to have you on my team."

"When can we see the place?" Gilbert asked.

"The other team members are arriving next Sunday, and we start working on the project on Monday. If you want, you can come on Saturday and stay for the weekend. The research lab is located in a high-end resort that serves as a spiritual retreat."

"Are you talking about Safe Haven?" Eric asked.

"How did you know?"

"A woman I dated participated in one of those. She wanted me to come with her, but I'm not a very spiritual guy. She said that the location was beautiful and that the accommodations were simple but comfortable."

"It's under new ownership, and it's much more luxurious than it used to be when your friend was there." William took off his glasses and looked into Eric's eyes. "Please don't mention where Kaia is working to anyone." He used a shallow thrall that was directed not just at Gilbert's brother. "I also need you all to sign a nondisclosure agreement. To ensure the safety of everyone working on this project, it's very important to keep the location a secret."

A thrall wasn't as strong as a compulsion, especially the kind William had just used on the brothers and on Kaia's mother, but if they were so concerned with Kaia's safety, they wouldn't volunteer the information anyway.

Gilbert frowned. "Who are you afraid of and why?"

"Scientific espionage is rampant, and everyone wants a leg up in the game. I'm protecting my people from every conceivable risk."

The guy didn't look satisfied by the vague answer, but he must have under-stood that William couldn't disclose more than he already had, and he didn't ask him to clarify.

CHAPTER 27

"Let's sign those agreements," Kaia said. "Do you have them prepared?"

"I do." William rose to his feet and took his satchel from the back of the chair. "Since Cheryl is a minor, I will need her legal guardian to sign the agreement for her." He pulled the stack of papers out and handed a copy to each one of them. "It's pretty straightforward but go ahead and take your time reading through it."

Edna had written the agreement in her uncompromising style, so it sounded draconian, but he didn't expect anyone to object. With Karen working on sensitive defense technology, they were all familiar with the need for secrecy.

Once everyone was done reading and the documents were signed, William collected them and put them back in his satchel.

"Thank you."

"We can't stay for the weekend," Karen said. "We will come on Saturday and fly home the same day. If we find the place agreeable, Kaia will sign the contract and stay. If we don't, we will take her back with us."

"I'm sure that you will find the accommodations more than adequate, and the resort is beautiful."

"How come you are doing it there?" Kaia asked. "Is it safe with all the guests of the resort and the people maintaining it?"

"It's safe. The lab and the team's accommodations are located in a separate restricted area that has every security measure conceivable. We will be sharing it with another group that's engaged in unrelated research, but they are bound by the same nondisclosure agreements as the ones you've just signed. I'm confident that the research will remain confidential."

The compulsion they would be under would ensure that.

"Is the other group using the same research facilities we will be using?"

He shook his head. "They have their own, but you'll be sharing the dining hall and the gym with them. I didn't want my team to spend months in isolation. It's not good for morale."

"I bet." She rubbed her hands on her jeans. "I'm nervous. I've never been away from home for more than a few days."

"You'll be fine," her mother said.

"Yeah, I will."

William pushed to his feet. "Thank you all for hearing me out and for supporting Kaia's decision."

"You're welcome," Karen said.

Gilbert got to his feet and walked over to him. "Nothing is finalized yet."

"I'm aware of that, but I have no doubt that you will love the place."

"That remains to be seen."

Kaia patted Gilbert's arm before threading hers through William's. "I'll walk you out."

"Thank you," he said again. "I will see you all next Saturday. Let me know if you change your mind about staying for the weekend, and I'll have rooms prepared for you."

"I would like you to stay." Kaia turned a pair of pleading eyes to her mother. "It will make it a little easier for me."

Karen released a breath and looked at Eric. "Is it okay with you?"

"I need to check my schedule. I might not be able to fly you back, but I'll try to move things around."

28

KAIA

$\mathcal{K}$aia was impressed. William had not only survived Gilbert and Eric's interrogation, but he'd done it while she'd been purposely distracting him.

The T-shirt had been a strategic choice designed to draw his attention to her ample cleavage. After the nun-style blouse she'd worn yesterday, that was a big improvement, but its success had been partial. She'd confirmed that he was attracted to her, which after his stunned reaction to her kiss last night she hadn't been sure about, and she'd also discovered that despite his healthy male appetite, William was a gentleman.

She'd caught him glancing at her cleavage several times and then quickly shifting his gaze back to her eyes with a guilty expression on his handsome face.

Other girls might have been offended, but she found it adorable.

Regrettably, he hadn't been distracted enough to reveal more than he'd intended.

He'd let slip a few details that had helped Eric figure out the location, and later she was going to google Safe Haven and find out more about it, but he hadn't revealed anything about the people who were financing the project. Were they big pharma? The military? A secret government organization?

Judging by his simple clothes and affable attitude, William wasn't wealthy, so he was just an employee of the organization. Heck, he hadn't even rented a car. He had a friend dropping him off and picking him up.

"I should text Max." William pulled out his phone and typed up a message.

"How long before he gets here?" she asked as they walked out the gate.

"About ten minutes."

"Good, so we have time to talk about Anthony. Did you have a chance to check whether your hacker friend could look into his disappearance?"

Looking guilty, William shook his head. "Yesterday it was too late to call him, and today was very busy. I'll call him tomorrow."

Kaia knew he wasn't going to do that. He was using it as a bargaining chip until she signed the contract, and she could understand that, but she would have preferred if he were just honest about it.

"You're not going to do anything until I officially join your team, are you?"

He swallowed. "I really didn't have time, and even if I did, I don't know when Roni will be able to look into it. He's swamped with work."

"If you find out anything before next Saturday, call me or text me. Any little bit of information would be appreciated. I hate not knowing what happened to him, and I feel terrible for his parents who think that he's dead."

"I promise to call Roni tomorrow, and I'll plead with him to make time for this."

"Thank you." She rewarded him with a big smile.

He nodded, and as his eyes shifted to her lips, Kaia wondered if he expected her to kiss him again, but after the strange way he'd reacted last night, she wasn't sure.

"I'm sorry for kissing you yesterday. I was so grateful for your help that I acted on impulse."

"Nothing to be sorry about."

She tilted her head. "You looked shocked."

He swallowed again. "I was taken by surprise, but I would be lying if I said that I didn't like it."

"You were frozen."

He closed his eyes for a brief moment. "What else could I have done? You are beautiful and brilliant, and I can't help my attraction to you, but it would have been inappropriate for me to respond the way I wanted to. Even if you were not about to start working for me, the age difference alone is enough for me to keep my distance."

That was a very good answer that explained his reaction without offending her, but it also nipped in the bud any ideas she might have harbored about stealing another kiss.

"Thirteen years difference is not a lot, and I'm not working for you yet."

He chuckled. "I'm sure your mother and Gilbert have a different opinion, and rightfully so."

Tucking her hands into her back pockets, Kaia shrugged. "My family's opinion is important to me, but they don't get to decide who I can date. Besides, on the inside, I'm even older than you."

It was true, but she didn't expect him to agree with her. Surprisingly, he nodded.

"You are very mature, and you are smarter than most people I know, but it still doesn't make it right." He lifted his hand and waved at the approaching car. "My friend is here."

"It's goodnight then." She offered him her hand. "But regrettably, without a kiss."

Taking her offered hand, William moved faster than a big man like him should have been able to. Wrapping his arm around her waist, he pulled her against his chest and planted a quick kiss on her lips. "Goodnight, Kaia."

Talk about a surprise.

What had made him do that?

"Goodnight," she remembered to say as he ducked into the idling car.

He opened the passenger-side window. "Until next Saturday."

Lifting her fingers to her lips, she smiled. "I can't wait."

29

KALUGAL

"Welcome to my home." Kalugal held the door open for Mia, Toven, and Mia's grandparents. "My name is Kalugal." He offered Mia's grandmother his hand.

He had a bit of a snob reputation that he needed to overcome, especially this evening, which was why he hadn't sent one of his men to open the door and lead his guests to the dining room.

"I'm Rosalyn." She shook his hand with a warm smile on her kind face.

"Curtis." The grandfather offered him his hand. "Your home is much bigger on the inside than it appears to be on the outside."

"It's like Doctor Who's Tardis," Mia said.

Kalugal had heard about the British television show, but he hadn't watched it and had no idea what a Tardis was. Did it have anything to do with being tardy?

Probably not, and he wasn't going to ask. He wasn't in the mood to delve into a discussion about British television.

"The magic was performed by the clan's very talented architect." He motioned for them to follow him into the elevator. "Most of the structure is located underground, but the skylights bring in plenty of natural light and fresh air. At night, the automatic shutters go up, so the artificial lighting is not visible from above."

"That's a shame," Mia said. "You can't see the stars."

"I wondered about that." Curtis waited for Toven to wheel Mia into the elevator before taking his wife's hand and following. "When we stayed in the village during Mia's initial stages of transition, the shutters closed each evening as soon as the sun came down, and when we opened the front door at night, the light in the living room turned off. It was so dark that I was afraid Rosy would stumble on the steps. I thought that it was about saving on electricity or about preventing bugs from getting into the house. Now I know the real reason why it was necessary."

"The lights turning off as soon as you open a door or a window is a new security measure." As the elevator stopped at the lower level, Kalugal held the door open until his guests got out. "As the village grows, it becomes more important to control its visibility at night."

"Why do you have an elevator in the house?" Mia asked. "I'm glad that you do, but immortals don't need it."

"True, but my wife is expecting, and once our son is born, the stairs will become problematic."

He intended to put gates on both ends of the stairs and have everyone in the household use the elevator exclusively. Boys were fragile until they reached puberty and could transition, and he was going to make sure that no harm came to his son.

As they entered the sprawling dining room, Mia's grandmother gasped. "This is like a banquet table in a fairytale. It's huge."

"Who else is coming?" Toven asked. "I thought that you were just inviting the close family."

Kalugal smiled. "That's a lot of people, and I also invited Syssi and Kian, Amanda and Dalhu, and Andrew and Nathalie." He leaned closer to the god. "I had to invite Kian, or he would have suspected me of trying to plot something with you."

Not that he would have been wrong, but at this stage in the game, Kalugal was only sending out feelers to assess how potentially useful his newfound uncle could be to him.

He'd invited the usual gang for the simple reason that Kian and Amanda included him and Jacki in all of their family's gatherings, and he could do no less. Besides, he liked having them over.

The good-natured rivalry he and Kian routinely engaged in was fun, and so was sharing a cigar and a glass of whiskey with his cousin. They were more like brothers than he and Lokan were, perhaps because they had more in common. He and Kian were both leaders of their communities and shouldered many responsibilities, but that was where the similarities ended.

Kalugal was one of a kind and proud of it.

Lokan was too uptight, and Kian wasn't exactly an island of tranquility either. Both his brother and his cousin were overly serious and somber. Perhaps he would find more in common with Toven, although given his initial impression of the god, that wasn't likely.

"Hello, everyone." Jacki walked into the dining room wearing a very fetching outfit of a pair of white maternity trousers and a loose, yellow silk blouse. "Please, sit down. We can have some wine before the others get here."

"Are they bringing the little ones with them?" Mia asked hopefully.

"Not tonight." Jacki smiled. "The moms wanted to enjoy a quiet dinner with adults, so the girls are having their first sleepover at Nathalie and Andrew's home. Ella and Wonder are babysitting."

"That's a shame." Mia pouted. "I hoped to see them."

"You'll have plenty of opportunities." Toven moved a chair away from the table, making room for Mia's wheelchair. "Now that we are living in the village, you can probably see them every day."

"You can catch Phoenix and Ethan at the playground most afternoons," Jacki said. "And sometimes Syssi and Amanda take their little ones for a stroll and stop by to chat with Eva and Nathalie. During the day, Phoenix attends a preschool, while Allegra and Evie are with their mothers at the university. Amanda converted her office to a nursery, and they hired a human nanny to look after the babies while they work."

"Isn't that dangerous?" Toven asked. "Kian told me about the attack at Amanda's lab four and a half years ago. If her location was compromised before, it can happen again."

"That's not likely." Kalugal uncorked a wine bottle. "The one who discovered the lab's location was Dalhu, and he's no longer a threat."

"Oh my." Rosalyn put a hand over her chest. "From enemies to lovers to fated mates. Now, that's a story I would love to hear."

30

TOVEN

*B*y the time Kalugal had finished his abbreviated version of Dalhu's story, starting with his past in Navuh's camp and up to his capture by the clan, the rest of the guests had arrived, and Amanda had added all the spicy details that Kalugal either hadn't known or deemed inappropriate to share in polite company.

Kian glared at his sister, either for what she had done back then or for telling the story shamelessly, and Dalhu looked like he wanted the floor to swallow him whole.

What had surprised Toven the most, though, was not that Amanda had fought tooth and nail for her right to keep the mate the Fates had chosen for her, but that Annani had helped her against her son. She could've ended the feud between the siblings by simply decreeing it, but she'd gone about it in a roundabout way, letting Kian slowly realize that Dalhu was worthy of Amanda, and that he was the right mate for her.

"I wonder," Nathalie said. "How did Annani's probe of Aliya go? No one told Andrew and me anything."

"That's because there was nothing to tell," Kian said. "Aliya's childhood memories were all scrambled, probably because of the trauma she'd suffered. What she remembered were parables that Jade had liked telling the children, and there had been nothing useful we could learn from that. But Annani said that Jade was a talented storyteller, which surprised me given what her tribespeople had said about her."

"That actually makes sense," Syssi said. "Aliya said that she learned English from the movies Jade brought back from her travels abroad. That means that she enjoyed watching fictional stories and that she appreciated what the children could learn from them."

Amanda waved a hand. "Don't spoil it for me. I've gotten used to thinking of her as a monster. I don't want to hear that she did nice things for her people."

"The only one who describes Jade as a monster is Emmett," Kian said. "Vrog waited for her return for over two decades, and he still talks about her with respect. So does Aliya." He grimaced. "I bet some clan members think of me as a monster as well."

"No one thinks that." Syssi slapped his arm playfully. "And they never did, even when you were much grumpier."

Kalugal chuckled. "He was even worse than he is now?"

Shai nodded. "I can attest to that. Married life agrees with him."

"Traitor." Kian cast a mock glare at his assistant.

Onegus, who had been Kian's chief Guardian many years before Kian had met Syssi, kept an impassive expression and didn't comment, which was probably wise.

Next to Toven, Curtis shifted in his chair. "When is dinner going to be served?" he whispered, forgetting that all the immortals could hear him just fine. "It's nearly nine o'clock."

Kalugal lifted his hand, and a moment later several men entered the dining room carrying trays.

"Is everyone hungry?" asked a guy in a white apron who looked more like a drill sergeant than a cook.

"Yes, we are," Amanda grinned at him. "What have you made for us today, Atzil?"

"A feast worthy of a king." His eyes darted around the table until they landed on Toven and widened to the size of saucers. "Or a god." He bowed deeply. "I'm honored to serve you today, Master Toven."

"It's just Toven. I let Okidu address me as master because I know it's futile to argue with him, but we live in an era where no one should be considered another's master. Not that demanding obeisance was ever okay. It took thousands of years for the gods' teachings to finally have an effect, and for humans to embrace the ideas of democracy and equal rights, in no small part thanks to Annani."

From across the table, Kalugal eyed him curiously. "As far as I know, the gods enjoyed their grand status very much. I doubt they considered humans or even immortals as equal."

"They didn't," Toven admitted. "And at the time, they were entitled to that elevated status. But they led by example. The gods governed themselves in a democratic way, with all the advantages and pitfalls that democracy entails, and they wished for humans and immortals to emulate them."

Kalugal didn't look impressed. "They didn't practice democracy on their home planet. They had a king."

Evidently, Mortdh hadn't been as tight-lipped with his son as Ahn had been with Annani, but given that Kalugal hadn't been close to Navuh, or at least that was the impression Toven had gotten, he wondered how his nephew had learned that.

"There was a king, but his rule was similar to Ahn's. He couldn't make any major decisions without his council's approval, and he had to politic the same way Ahn did."

"What else can you tell us about the gods' home planet?" Syssi asked.

"That's more or less it. I know that at some point, there was a war that had started as a rebellion, but my father refused to elaborate on it."

3 1

KIAN

*K*ian had a feeling that Toven knew more than he was willing to reveal, and he wondered why he saw fit to keep it to himself. Then again, he had nothing to base that feeling on. The god had a poker face to rival that of the best professional players, schooling his expression and tone to perfectly align with his words. Given that he was the oldest being on Earth, he'd had plenty of time to perfect it.

He waited until dinner was over to spring the question that had been nagging him ever since Okidu had gifted him with the journals. "You are seven thousand years old." Kian leveled his gaze at Toven. "You must know things about the gods' origins that my mother doesn't. Do you know why the Odus were used in the gods' war?"

Toven's lips lifted in a sad smile. "I wasn't told, if that's what you're suggesting, but the answer to that is simple. They are an incredible weapon. Whoever designed them limited their capacity to learn, and by doing so avoided the danger that artificial intelligence poses to all organic beings. The moment AI becomes self-aware, the first thing it will do is eliminate the competition. And since its capacity to learn is limitless, no biologically limited beings could stand in its way."

Talking in generalities was a great way to avoid answering the question, but Kian wasn't about to give up that easily. "I'm aware of the dangers of AI, but we are not there yet. I'm more interested in the why and how the Odus, who had been created as domestic servants, had been turned into soldiers."

Toven shrugged. "Someone figured out that an indestructible servant who is programmed to obey its master could be used as a weapon. If someone attacked you when you were with Okidu, wouldn't he destroy them?"

"He would shield me, and he would do his best to protect me, but he would not attack unless I commanded him to do so."

"There you go." Toven waved a hand. "Maybe the Odus were used to defend their masters. My father clammed up anytime I asked him about it. The only thing

88

he told me was that the technology had been banned, the instructions for building them destroyed, and the Odus had been decommissioned. He said it was a great tragedy, and he didn't want to talk about it." Toven smiled. "Ekin always championed the underdog."

"You mean humans," Syssi said.

"And Odus." Toven leaned back in his chair. "I have a theory, but it's only speculation."

"Let's hear it." Kalugal uncorked another wine bottle and started refilling everyone's glasses.

"I think that Ahn, Ekin, and their sister Athor were rebels and that they were involved in what happened to the Odus in some way. The king couldn't execute his own children because it would have looked bad for him, given that he needed to maintain the illusion of democracy, so he sent them on an expedition to Earth, probably to mine for gold, and when everyone back home had forgotten about them, he severed contact with them. Our advanced technological devices were falling apart, and there was no way to fix them because the supply chain had winked out, and there were no replacement parts. My father tried to find solutions using materials that were readily available on Earth, but it was akin to being stranded on an island and trying to make do with what was there. He was a brilliant scientist, but no single person can encompass the knowledge of an entire civilization to recreate its technology from scratch."

Kalugal nodded. "I came to a similar conclusion, but it's also possible that something happened on their home planet. Perhaps it was conquered by other space-faring people, or perhaps its sun exploded, or some other disaster brought an end to their planet or just their ability to communicate with their satellites."

"That scenario is too sad to consider." Jacki put her hand on her husband's arm. "Let's talk about a more pleasant subject." She smiled. "Kalugal is finally taking me on a proper archeological dig in Egypt. We are leaving on Sunday." She put her hand on her substantial belly. "I want to do that before Junior gets here."

"You can't be serious," Amanda gaped at her. "You only have two weeks to go. What if your labor starts in Egypt? Do you want to deliver your baby in a Third-World country?"

Jacki shrugged. "I'm immortal. I can deliver Junior in a field, and I'll be fine."

"Yeah, but Junior might not be." Amanda turned to glare at Kalugal. "I can't believe that you agreed to this insanity. I thought that you had more sense than that."

"We are only going for three days, and Bridget says that Jacki's belly hasn't descended yet, so there is still time."

"Don't tell me that Bridget green-lighted your trip. If Jacki gives birth in an Egyptian hospital and immediately heals right in front of their eyes, you will have to thrall everyone in there."

"I can do that easily, so that's not a problem." Kalugal sighed. "But perhaps you are right, and we should wait until after Junior is born. We can go a month later and hire a bunch of nannies to take with us on the trip."

Jacki pouted, but Amanda's impassioned speech seemed to have achieved its intended result.

"Fine. So Egypt is out. But I want to go somewhere fun. We haven't been anywhere since we returned from China."

"How about Catalina Island?" Amanda suggested. "It's not far, and you can charter a luxury yacht to get there. If your labor starts, we can pick you up with the helicopter and bring you straight to the clinic."

"I guess that could be fun as well." Jacki rubbed her belly. "I had my heart set on Egypt, though."

Kalugal took her hand and covered it with his other one. "We will go as soon as you are up to it, and Junior is okay to travel."

"Six weeks," Amanda said. "That's the absolute minimum. I would wait until he is at least one year old before taking him to a place like that, but that's me."

"What about you?" Jacki asked Syssi. "How long are you going to wait before traveling with Allegra?"

"I haven't given it much thought, but I don't think I need to wait until she's one year old to take her with us on a short trip."

They hadn't been anywhere in the longest time, and even though it terrified Kian to take Allegra out of the village, Syssi had already taken the first step by taking her to work with her.

"Allegra is five months old. Where would you like to take her?"

"Not Egypt, but Hawaii could be fun."

"When?"

"In a couple of months."

Kian turned to Shai. "Put it on my schedule."

"Yes, boss."

3 2

KAIA

*I*dina climbed onto Kaia's lap. "Where is Uncle Eric taking us?" She bounced up and down on Kaia's knees.

The advantage of flying on a private jet was that there was no need to shush the little ones, and they could make as much noise as they pleased. Although so far, the twins had been relatively quiet, and Idina was just asking questions and not mutilating Barbies or pinching anyone, so all was good.

"I've told you already. We are going to a nice resort on the beach, and we are going to meet William. Do you remember him?"

"Yeah. The guy with the glasses and the brown shirt with the creases."

Chuckling, Kaia ruffled her sister's curly hair.

Idina remembered the oddest things about people, and she noticed things that a three-year-old shouldn't. Maybe they were raising another prodigy. Although in Idina's case, she would grow up to be an evil dictator. The girl could be the sweetest thing one moment and a mean monkey the next.

Cheryl lifted her head. "He must have bought a new shirt for the interview and didn't wash it before wearing it. That's why it still had creases from when it was folded in the packaging."

"You noticed that too? How come I didn't?" Kaia didn't even remember the color of William's shirt. All she'd seen were his incredible blue eyes.

Well, she'd stared at his lips as well.

Cheryl snorted. "You were too busy looking into his pretty blue eyes and kissable lips."

"Hey." Gilbert shook his finger at her. "You are too young to notice a guy's lips, and especially one who is old enough to be your father."

"I'm fifteen, Gilbert, not five, and William is only thirty-two, so maybe he could have made a baby when he was seventeen, but he didn't. Besides, I was talking about Kaia noticing his lips, not me." She cradled her phone in her hands, looking at it with sad eyes. "I need a satellite plan. I hate being in cyber limbo. Do they even have internet in that place?"

Kaia winced. "I don't think so. It's supposed to be a spiritual retreat, and I read that the guests have to leave their phones in a safe until the retreat is over. If there is an emergency, they can use the phone in the office."

Looking like she was about to pop a vein, Cheryl clutched the phone to her chest. "That's barbaric. I'm not letting anyone touch my phone."

With a sigh, their mother shifted Evan to her other thigh. "You need an intervention. You are addicted to that device, and it's not healthy."

As the two started arguing about Cheryl's obsession with her phone, or rather her Instatock channel, Kaia adjusted Idina on her lap and closed her eyes.

Eleven days had passed since she'd last seen William, and she hadn't stopped thinking about him and the two kisses they'd shared. Not that they qualified as proper kisses. Neither had involved tongues and both had lasted less than a second.

After she'd texted him that Eric couldn't make it on Saturday and they could only arrive on Sunday, William had called to give her the name of the airport Eric should use and to coordinate the time for picking them up. He'd also apologized for his hacker friend's busy schedule and had asked for more information about Tony, but since Kaia hadn't heard back from him, Roni the hacker had probably still been too busy to look into it.

Either that or William was dragging it out on purpose to make sure that she signed the contract.

"Are you sleeping?" Idina asked.

"I'm napping. You should nap too."

"Okay." She cuddled closer, pulling her legs up and tucking them under her.

Kaia leaned down and kissed her sister's curly mop of hair and sniffed the sweet baby smell she somehow still had. She was going to miss her and the twins so much. Heck, she was even going to miss Cheryl and her grumpy comments.

As tears prickled the back of her eyes, she closed them again and visualized William to distract herself.

Would he come to greet her? Or would he just send a driver to pick them up?

She hoped he would come. If he'd been thinking about her even half as much as she'd been thinking about him, he would be there.

"I don't want you to go," Idina said with her eyes still closed. "I'm going to miss you."

"I'm going to miss you too." Kaia kissed her head again. "But we can talk on the phone and do video calls. It's not like you're not going to see me."

"You said they will take away your phone."

"I'm not going to let them do that. I'll tell them that I need to call my little sister every day."

"Good. And if they say no, pinch them really hard." Idina demonstrated while twisting her little face into an evil expression.

Kaia chuckled. "You shouldn't pinch people. It's not nice."

Idina huffed. "It's not nice to take people's phones either."

"This project is going to be good for you," her mother said. "You need to stretch the umbilical cord a little farther, flap your wings, and live a little."

"Children should stay close to their parents," Gilbert grumbled quietly, so as not to wake up Ryan, who was asleep in his arms. "People are meant to live in tribes. All those blue zones where people live to be over a hundred have one thing in common. They live in small villages and are actively social."

"They also eat healthily," Cheryl said.

He stifled a snort. "I bet that's not as important as their emotional health."

"We are going to grow up and get married one day." Cheryl put her phone in her backpack. "What are you going to do? Build a gated community just for your kids and their spouses so they stay close to you?"

"You bet your sweet pickles that's precisely what I will do. I will commission a big billboard with a picture of all of us smiling and waving, and it will say—if it's good enough for my family, it's good enough for yours."

It was so like Gilbert to find a profitable angle in everything.

"You're weird." Cheryl's lips twitched with a suppressed smile. "That's a horrible idea for a billboard. No one will buy your houses."

"They will buy. They always do. I build nice homes."

"That you do," her sister conceded.

"Does it mean that you will come live in my gated community?"

She gave him one of those penetrating looks that made people uncomfortable. "Maybe I will, and maybe I won't."

WILLIAM

*W*illiam sat at the front of the bus, just behind the driver, and checked his emails, forwarding most of them to Darlene to take care of.

It had been such a smart decision to bring her along. She was taking care of everything.

She'd arranged the flights for his three other recruits, made sure that their rooms were ready, and arranged for a car to pick them up at the airport. She'd also met them when they'd arrived at Safe Haven and had shown them to their rooms. The only thing William had done was introduce them to Eleanor and Emmett, and he'd left them with those two to get compelled.

It was so easy to delegate things to someone who was smart and capable and didn't need things explained to her twice.

It was a shame that there was no spark between them.

Darlene was a good woman, precisely the type William usually went for, but even before he'd met Kaia and had gotten infatuated with the sexy nineteen-year-old, he and Darlene just hadn't clicked.

"How many people are we picking up?" The bus driver pulled into the airport's parking lot.

"Four adults, a teenager, a toddler, and twin babies."

"Do I need to get a porter to bring their things?"

"They are not going to have a lot of baggage because they are not staying the night. They are going back later today."

Hopefully, minus Kaia, and he didn't expect her to arrive with loads of suitcases. She wasn't the type who cared about clothing and shoes. Her suitcase would probably be full of books just like his was.

"You can wait here," he told the driver. "I'll get them."

The private airport's small terminal was nearly deserted, and there were plenty of seats to choose from. William selected one next to the glass wall overlooking the runways.

CHAPTER 33

Kaia's uncle was scheduled to land his jet in about ten minutes, so William had plenty of time to mentally prepare for seeing her again. He needed to keep himself in check and stifle the attraction he felt for her. Perhaps if he appeared uninterested, Kaia would stop flirting with him, and he could retain his sanity.

Fates, the girl was a blessing and a curse at the same time.

She was the key to deciphering the journals, he had no doubt of that, but it was difficult enough to stay away from her when she wasn't looking at his lips with hungry eyes or just flat out kissing him.

He needed to keep his distance as much as was possible under the circumstances, which was going to be impossible since they would be working together for the next three to four months.

Out of the three bungalows that were assigned to the lab, he'd chosen the one that was the farthest from Kaia's. Each bungalow had two bedrooms, a small living room, and a kitchenette, and the rooms were more or less the same, but there were small differences, mainly in which direction the windows were facing and whether there was an ocean view or not.

Since the others had arrived earlier, he'd made sure to reserve the nicest room for Kaia ahead of time so no one else would snatch it, and he assigned the other room in that bungalow to Kylie.

Corinne and Owen were sharing the other, and he had one to himself. He'd offered the other room in his bungalow to Darlene, but she'd asked to get a place all to herself, so he'd gotten her one in the paranormals' section.

After spending months in Geraldine and Shai's home, Darlene craved privacy, and he could totally empathize with that. Besides, she needed to find an immortal male to induce her, and if one of the Guardians assigned to the compound caught her eye, she would be more comfortable bringing him to her place if she didn't have a roommate.

William was rooting for Max, but so far, it didn't look like she liked him any more than she liked the others.

When the private jet touched down, William swallowed the ball of stress that had lodged in his throat, pushed to his feet, and walked out to meet Kaia and her family.

3 4

KAIA

"*H*ow long is the drive?" Cheryl asked a few minutes into it.

William turned around. "About an hour and a half."

Kaia pretended to be absorbed in Idina's picture book to avoid his eyes.

Their meeting at the airport had been awkward. William had been polite, courteous, and full of smiles for everyone, but he'd seemed detached.

He'd shaken her hand, but despite the form-fitting T-shirt she had on, his eyes hadn't roamed over her body like they had outside her house while he'd waited for his friend to pick him up.

It looked like from now on, William would be all business. This would be her place of employment, and he would be her boss, so he was probably afraid of breathing the wrong way and getting sued for sexual harassment, which would be catastrophic not only on the personal level but also given the secret nature of the project.

How could she convince him that he had nothing to fear from her?

It didn't matter if she was the one who initiated, that would still expose him to potential trouble, so the only way would be to earn his trust. Once he realized that she would never do anything to harm him unless he really deserved it, he might become less guarded around her.

Besides, even if he ended up hurting her and deserved retribution, she wouldn't go through the court system to get it. If he was right and she was indeed the only one who could decipher those writings, sabotaging that would be the best payback.

Maybe that was what William was afraid of?

Damn. She didn't like that dynamic one bit. Perhaps someone else would have thrived on the rush of power she had over him, but Kaia hated being feared, and she didn't want to spend the next three to four months of her life in an awkward situation with a guy who was attracted to her but was fighting it with all his might.

"That's one hell of a schlep." Gilbert leaned down and picked up the toy Evan had dropped on the floor. "Between the flight and the drive to and from the airport, a whole day is wasted."

"Thanks for stating the obvious." Cheryl went back to her phone. "But if I have cellular reception the entire way, I have no problem with this part of the trip." She snapped her head back up. "William, are you going to take our phones away once we get there?"

He looked at her over his shoulder and smiled reassuringly. "You must have read old information. It used to be that guests were required to give up their phones for the entire duration of their stay, but now only those who participate in the spiritual retreat have to surrender theirs, and only during classes. They get them back at the end of the day."

Cheryl let out a relieved breath. "What about cellular reception? Is it any good there?"

"It's decent, and there is also Wi-Fi. Before we bought the resort, only the offices were connected to the internet. Now there is access everywhere except for the lab." He turned to look at Kaia. "Things are little stricter with the research team members. I'll explain later during the briefing."

Kaia nodded, despite the alarm bells that had gone up in her mind. She still hadn't signed the contract, and if William sprang some draconian restrictions on her, she was going to bail.

Being able to talk with her family every day was a hard line she wasn't willing to cross. If he wouldn't allow her that, she was going back home despite her attraction to him, her curiosity about the project, and the satisfaction she expected from solving a mystery no one else could solve.

There was no guarantee that she would actually be able to do that, but William was confident that she would, and since he'd read all of her published papers, he might have a good reason to be so sure. Perhaps he'd found something in them that led him to believe she had what it took to decipher the writings.

What about Tony, though?

Roni the hacker was her only hope of finding out what had happened to him. If she bailed, he wouldn't bother helping her.

Could she survive weeks at a time without talking to her family?

She had no choice.

No one else was looking for Anthony, and she was his only hope. Even if he was dead, his family deserved to know how and where he died and to bring his body home for burial.

3 5

WILLIAM

$\mathcal{W}$illiam had never been happier to see Darlene than when the bus stopped at Safe Haven's parking lot.

She would take over and engage everyone in conversation, giving him a few minutes to recuperate from the stress of spending the last two hours with Kaia and trying his best not to look at her beautiful face or ogle her young supple body.

He'd purposely sat at the front of the bus while she'd sat a few rows behind him, but he hadn't expected to feel her eyes burning holes in his back throughout the drive.

It had been torture to keep from turning to look at her.

She had one of those tight-fitting low-necked T-shirts on that didn't leave much to the imagination, and her faded jeans hugged her legs and her backside perfectly.

Kaia didn't wear any makeup or jewelry, but her nails and toenails were painted pink, and she had flip-flops on her pretty feet. She looked beautiful and sexy and ready for a day at the beach, but the outfit was totally inappropriate for meeting her co-workers and signing contracts.

Evidently, Doctor Kaia Locke was not one to follow conventions, and that made him like her even more.

As soon as everyone was out of the bus and the twins had been put in their double stroller, William introduced Darlene. "This is my administrative assistant, Darlene." He turned to Kaia. "Doctor Kaia Locke, her mother Karen Locke, her stepfather Gilbert Emerson, her uncle Eric Emerson, her sisters Cheryl and Idina, and in the stroller are her brothers—Evan and Ryan."

Eric was the first one to offer Darlene his hand. "A pleasure to meet you."

The look she gave him was one that William hadn't seen her giving anyone before, and the fact that he'd noticed it despite his own turmoil meant that it was blatant enough for everyone to see.

"The pleasure is all mine," she purred. "Thank you for bringing the entire family to check out Safe Haven."

"I'm glad that I did." He held on to her hand a moment longer than necessary. "My niece is very important to me, and I need to make sure that she's treated as the precious, unique diamond that she is."

Kaia rolled her eyes. "Stop it, Eric. You're embarrassing me." She offered Darlene her hand. "I'm Kaia, and you can drop the doctor part. Each time someone calls me that I have the urge to look over my shoulder and search for the person they are referring to."

Shaking her hand, Darlene laughed. "That's how I felt when I first got married and people addressed me as Mrs." She shifted her eyes to Eric. "But now that I'm single again, I can go back to being Miss."

What had gotten into her?

This wasn't the Darlene William knew, the one who was reserved, rarely smiled, and was all work and no play.

Evidently, it took the right guy to bring that part out of her, but Eric was human, several years younger than her, and he looked like a player.

Maybe that was precisely what she wanted? A short fling with an attractive guy who she was confident wouldn't stick around?

If so, good for her. She deserved some fun after spending decades with that shitty husband of hers.

After all the handshaking was done and Darlene introduced herself to the little ones, they headed into the lodge.

Kaia had brought only one suitcase, and she refused to let anyone take it from her. Rolling it behind her, she fell in step with him. "Have you and Darlene been working together long?"

The others followed Darlene, who led them to the coffee station.

"Not at all. She started working for me less than a couple of months ago, organizing my mess."

"That's surprising." Kaia slung the strap of her little purse over her body, so it rested on her other hip. "You seem very comfortable with each other."

Detecting a slight sarcastic tone, William tilted his head to look at her. "What are you trying to say?"

She shrugged. "Nothing. I just wonder whether you went out with Darlene before she started working for you or during."

Hadn't she noticed the way Darlene had reacted to Eric? Maybe she had and thought that Darlene was doing that in retaliation for something?

"Darlene and I never dated." He smiled. "We were introduced by mutual friends who hoped something would come out of it, but we just never clicked that way. We became friends when we both joined another friend on her mission to get healthier. If not for Darlene, I doubt I would have gotten back in shape and lost thirty-some pounds. She just didn't let me quit, and if I didn't show up for our morning runs or evening workouts, she would come to my lab and drag me out."

"This lab?"

He shook his head. "This one is reserved just for special projects. It's not where I usually work."

"And where is that?"

He winced. "I can't tell you that. It's another secret location."

Kaia tsked. "You are full of secrets, aren't you?"

"I like to be mysterious." He waggled his brows, hoping to make her laugh.

36

DARLENE

$\mathcal{I}$t had been years since Darlene had flirted with a guy, but Eric somehow brought out the naughty side of her that had lain dormant during her marriage.

His irreverent charm combined with his bad-boy good looks made him the perfect specimen for a fling, someone to celebrate her newfound freedom with. He looked to be in his late thirties or early forties, which was a little too young, and he was also a little too handsome for her, but he seemed interested, and that was good enough for her.

Darlene wasn't looking for a long-term relationship. She still had to find an immortal to hook up with, but the hunky immortal Guardians were too intimidating. Thinking of getting in bed with one of those perfect bodies should have been arousing, but it had the opposite effect on her.

Perhaps it was stupid vanity, but she wanted to look at least as good as the guy she was with, and despite the weight loss and the better shape she was in after all the training she'd done, her breasts were still droopy, and the cellulite on her thighs was still there.

Never again would she allow herself to be someone's compromise, and that was precisely what she would be for one of those perfect male specimens.

They wanted her because she was a Dormant, the granddaughter of a god, so they vied for her attention as if she were a Venus.

Perhaps after she lost those last fifteen stubborn pounds and got a boob job, she would be ready to take on one of them as a lover. Until then, though, she could start the journey of rediscovering her sexuality with a human man who looked just a little younger than her and not like he could be her son.

When Kaia's family was done touring the lodge with all of its new entertainment options, she led them outside. "Do you want to see the new gym? It has two heated lap pools, and you can reserve a time slot for swimming." She smiled at

Kaia. "You'd better be there on time or they will give your slots to someone else. They only allow one person at a time in the pools."

"I'm not a fan of swimming." Kaia cast a sidelong glance at William. "Do you like to swim?"

His eyes momentarily roamed over her young body, but then he forced them away from her and grimaced. "I don't like any kind of exercise, but swimming and running are not as bad as weight training because I can think of other things while doing that, so it's not a total waste of time."

The poor guy had it bad for the girl. What a shame that she was too young and was about to start working for him.

"I want to go to the pool." Kaia's little sister tugged on her hand. "Let's go."

"We didn't bring swimming suits, Idina," her mother said.

"I swim in my underwear in our pool at home."

Kaia tugged on her hand. "But we are not home, are we?"

The child pouted. "Can I see it?"

Idina was very articulate for a three-year-old, and she was adorable.

"Yes, you can." Her father lifted her and placed her on his shoulders.

"Do you swim?" Eric fell in step with Darlene.

She nodded. "Every morning since I got here. I reserve the five o'clock time slot."

"Ouch." He grimaced. "That's an ungodly hour. I'm not willing to wake up so early even to see you in a swimming suit. I haven't gotten out of bed before seven since I finished my last tour of duty."

It seemed that he was definitely interested.

"And when was that?"

"A long time ago." He chuckled. "If you are trying to guess how old I am, I'll save you the trouble. I'm forty-two."

That was what she'd guessed, and even though he was a few years younger than her, it wasn't a no-no. "Don't expect me to return the favor. I'm not going to tell you how old I am."

"Then I'll have to guess. Thirty-five?"

Darlene laughed. "You are such a charmer, Eric. You can't possibly think that I'm that young."

"Are you coming in?" Kaia's sister held the doors to the gym open. "Or do you prefer to stay outside and flirt?"

Eric pointed at her with a mock stern look. "Watch it, sprite. Being my favorite niece doesn't mean that you can be disrespectful to me."

She chuckled. "You tell each of us that we are your favorite, and besides, I was just stating the facts."

"You and your sisters are my favorite nieces." He rubbed the top of her head as he and Darlene stepped through the door.

"We are your only nieces, and Kaia and I are not even officially yours because Mom and Gilbert don't want to get married."

"Paperwork doesn't mean anything." Eric put his hand over his heart. "You are my nieces in here, and that's the only thing that counts."

As tears prickled the corner of her eyes, Darlene got angry at herself for being such a sap.

CHAPTER 36

Eric was a player, and he'd known that she would love hearing him say that.

Perhaps she should tell him that he didn't need to work that hard. She was more than ready to say yes, please.

ERIC

*D*arlene obviously wasn't thirty-five, and she hadn't bought the line, but women loved that crap, and it never failed to work.

She was about his age, maybe a year older or younger, and given that his typical hookups were in their early and mid-twenties, that was much older than what he usually went for, but there was something about Darlene that drew him to her.

She was pretty and had nice curves in all the right places, but she wasn't a great beauty. It was something in her expression, or maybe her eyes that were a little sad, a little introspective, but also smart, welcoming, and warm.

Perhaps he was getting too old for girls who were nearly half his age, or maybe seeing Kaia blossom into a young woman forced him to realize that all too soon, she would be in her twenties as well, and it would be gross to have sex with women who were his niece's age.

He still remembered her as a seven-year-old girl, still traumatized by her father's sudden death and putting a brave face on for the sake of her mother and baby sister. Kaia was one of the strongest people he knew, and he was proud to be called her uncle, even if it was only an honorary title.

Fourteen years was long enough for Gilbert to get over the nastiness with which his first marriage had ended, and he should marry the mother of his children and officially adopt Kaia and Cheryl.

But maybe it was Karen who didn't want to make it official?

She'd loved her first husband and had been devastated by his loss, so perhaps this was her way to remain loyal to his memory. It wasn't logical, but affairs of the heart rarely were.

"That's my lane." William pointed to the pool on the left. "And that's Darlene's." He pointed to the one on the right. "She drags me out here at five o'clock every morning. I'm just grateful that the pools are heated, or it would be even less pleasant than it is."

"That's a strange arrangement." Gilbert walked down the aisle separating the two rows of gym equipment and the two lap pools. "It would have been more economical to build one pool with two lanes than two separate ones."

As William went into a long explanation of why it had been more expeditious to use single-lane pre-fabricated lap pools, Darlene gazed at him as if he were the brightest star in the sky. To be tasked with leading the genetic research project, he was probably brilliant, but a woman looked at a guy with such admiration in her eyes and a smile on her lips only if she had the hots for him, and Eric didn't like it one bit.

Why had Darlene flirted with him if she was in love with William?

The guy was way too young for her, but then he couldn't fault her for wanting a handsome, smart dude. She was a free agent and could hook up with whomever she wanted.

"You really like him," he said quietly next to her ear.

She turned to look at him with puzzlement in her eyes. "Who, William?"

"No, Gilbert," he said sarcastically. "Of course, William. You looked at him as if you were in love with the guy."

A smirk lifted one corner of her lips. "What if I were?"

"He's too young for you."

"Oh, I don't think so. A three-year difference isn't that much."

"Three?" He arched a brow.

"Yeah. Do the math." Amusement danced in her eyes. "William is thirty-two, and I'm supposedly thirty-five."

When William finished his explanation, he turned to Darlene. "Are you ready to show Kaia and her family the bungalow she'll be staying in?"

Casting a quick smile at Eric, she waved a dismissive hand at William. "You can do that. After all, you chose the room for her."

As William glared at his assistant, his cheeks turned red. "I just wanted to make sure that Kaia roomed with Kylie, who is closer to her age."

"That's what I meant." Darlene smiled at him sweetly. "If you want me to come, I will," she said with enough reluctance to make it clear that she didn't want to tag along.

Perhaps he'd been wrong, and she wasn't in love with William?

Threading his arm through hers, he said, "I'm parched. So, if you don't need Darlene, she can show me where to get a Coke."

"We don't have Coke at the lodge." William looked at his assistant. "The directors insist on only healthy soft drinks."

"We have great-tasting cucumber-infused water." Darlene tugged on Eric's arm. "When you are done inspecting the bungalow, you can join us at the cafeteria. I'm sure everyone is hungry."

"I am." Idina started wiggling on Gilbert's shoulders. "Can I come with you?"

"Don't you want to see my room?" Kaia asked

For a moment Idina looked unsure, but then she sighed dramatically. "I want to see it, but I also want to go to the cafeteria after that."

"No problem, munchkin. Let's do that quickly because I'm hungry too."

"Phew." Eric wiped pretend sweat off his brow. "That was a close call."

"She's adorable and speaks so well for a three-year-old."

"Idina is three and a half, and she's been talking like a teenager since before she was two."

ERIC

As they walked back to the lodge, he wrapped his arm around Darlene's shoulders, and she didn't even bat an eyelid at it.

"You didn't answer me about William. Is he or was he your boyfriend?"

She laughed. "Nope, never was, and never will be."

"Why? Because he's too young, or because he's your boss?"

"It's not an age issue. I like William a lot, but we are not each other's types. But even if we were, I work for him. It's bad to mix business with pleasure."

"So you're single?"

She lifted her face to him and smiled. "I am. How about you?"

"Very single and have no intention of changing my status." He pulled the lodge's door open for her.

"Is that supposed to scare me off?"

"No, I just don't like to lead anyone on."

She chuckled. "You're painfully blunt, but I like it, and I will be as blunt with you. I've just finalized my divorce, and I haven't been with anyone other than my ex for many years. I'm not looking for Mr. Forever. I'm looking for Mr. Right Now, and you seem like the perfect guy to celebrate my new single status with."

It was music to his ears.

Eric grinned. "You have a good eye, missy. I am the perfect choice to celebrate with."

3 8

KAIA

"It's a beautiful room." Kaia sat on the bed and pulled Idina onto her lap. "The mattress is very comfortable."

So far, the boys had behaved splendidly. Curious about all the new people and sights, they hadn't cried or protested even once about being strapped in their stroller.

"Let me see." Cheryl sat down beside her and smoothed her hands over the coverlet. "Everything is so luxurious. It really is like a high-end resort."

At the doorway, Gilbert grudgingly nodded. "I have to admit that it's much nicer than what I expected. Good job, William." He clapped him on the back. "You really care about your team."

"I want them to feel pampered. It's not easy to leave their friends and family, and I didn't want them to feel as if they were living in a boot camp on top of that. I want it to be a pleasant experience for everyone involved."

"Hi." Kylie Baldwin squeezed by Gilbert's bulk. "Welcome aboard, Kaia." She walked over to her and extended her hand. "I feel privileged to be working with you on this project."

She hadn't given her final okay yet, but after seeing the accommodations Kaia had run out of objections, so she was most likely in.

"The feeling is mutual." She shook Kylie's hand. "Let me introduce you to my family. They came to check out the place."

"It's beautiful, isn't it? I didn't expect to be working in a resort."

"Neither did I." She proceeded to introduce her family, and when all the hand-shaking was done, she asked, "Where are the other team members?"

"Corinne and Owen are in their bungalow. We just came back from lunch."

"I'm hungry." Idina looked up at Kaia. "Are we going to eat now?"

"Yes, sweetie." She lifted her off her lap and set her down on her feet. "Let's go."

"It was nice meeting you all," Kylie smiled before heading to her room.

"I can't believe that I'm actually doing this." Kaia shook her head as she took Idina's hand.

"You brought a suitcase," William said. "You must have expected to stay."

She smiled nervously. "I kept thinking that something would come up and I would decide to go back home." She looked at her baby brothers. "It's going to be tough to be away from them."

"You're going to be okay." Her mother wrapped her arm around her waist. "You will come home every two weeks, and we will try to visit at least once a month." She shifted her gaze to William. "Now that we've seen how lovely it is here, we might stay for the entire weekend the next time we come, provided that Eric will be able to fly us."

"Darlene can book seats for you on commercial flights, and I'll gladly cover the cost."

Gilbert cast him a glare and puffed out his chest. "I can afford to fly my family to Oregon. When is the contract signing going to take place?"

"It can wait for after you leave." William rubbed the back of his neck. "With how difficult it is for Kaia to part from her family, I don't want her to miss any time with you."

"We want to go over the contract with her," her mother said in a tone that brooked no argument.

William shook his head. "I'm sorry, but that won't be possible. The contract contains sensitive information, and it's for Kaia's eyes only."

"I don't like it," Gilbert said. "Kaia is young and inexperienced. She wouldn't know what to look out for and might miss some of the catches and pitfalls."

Kaia wanted to roll her eyes, but she stifled the impulse out of respect for Gilbert. Her ability to process new information outpaced his by a wide margin, and she was trained to pay attention to the small print, but he still saw her as the little girl he'd taken under his wing twelve years ago, and he wanted to take care of her.

She patted his arm. "It's okay, Gilbert. I can read a contract just as well as you can. After lunch, William and I will go to his office, and you'll wait for me in the cafeteria. If I have any questions, I will give you and Mom a call."

That seemed to appease him, but he still cast William a suspicious glance from under hooded eyes. "I hope for your sake that you will deal honestly with Kaia." He turned to her. "Take a pen, and if anything seems vague or can be interpreted in more ways than one, underline it, and when you are done, call us before signing anything."

"Yes, sir." She saluted.

"Can we go now?" Idina tugged on her hand.

"Let's find Uncle Eric." Gilbert lifted her onto his shoulders. "I hope he's still in the cafeteria with William's assistant trying to charm the sweet-smelling petunias off her."

"What's petunias?" Idina asked.

Kaia wanted to ask what the hell he'd meant by that, but not in front of William. Were petunias a code name for panties? And why were they sweet-smelling?

"Petunias are flowers." Her mother glared at Gilbert. "You really need to pay attention to what you say in front of her. She's much smarter than you think."

"Oh, I know." He patted Idina's back. "She's Daddy's brilliant little girl. Right, Idina?"

"Yes." She planted a kiss on the bald spot at the top of his head.

Kaia glanced at William, curious to see if he was bothered by Eric moving in on Darlene, but he seemed no more and no less stressed than he'd been since he'd first greeted them at the airport.

Was he still worried that she would decline his offer? Or was he worried about working with a girl he was attracted to but thought of as forbidden fruit?

39

WILLIAM

$\mathcal{A}$s William entered the code lock of the door leading to the office wing of the lodge, Kaia patted her belly. "I ate too much, and now my brain is foggy from all the food. I won't be able to concentrate on the contract."

"I doubt it." William led her down the corridor to Emmett's office. "Your brain is a fine-tuned machine that keeps churning no matter what. It probably solves problems for you while you sleep."

She laughed nervously. "How did you know?"

"Because mine does the same."

"Is your office located here in the lodge?"

He pushed his glasses up his nose. "My office is at the lab. We are going to use Emmett Haderech's for the contract signing. He's the founder of Safe Haven, and he and his partner are going to be there to witness it."

She frowned. "How are they connected to the project? I thought that you were only sharing the facilities with them."

"I'll explain when we are inside, but I can give you a hint. Emmett's presence is needed to ensure the project's secrecy."

Her eyes widened, and she leaned closer to him. "Is he the hypnotist?"

Putting a finger to his lips, William nodded.

"I didn't expect to meet him today." Kaia looked worried. "What if that doesn't work on me?"

He took her hand and gave it a gentle squeeze. "Without you, the team is worthless, so let's hope that it does."

"It didn't occur to me that I could still be turned down." She let out a breath. "I don't know whether I should hope that it will work or hope that it won't."

He stopped in front of Emmet's office and turned to her. "Do you still have doubts?"

Given how fast her pulse was racing, Kaia was either concerned about meeting Emmett, getting hypnotized, joining the project, or all of the above.

110

"I haven't seen the lab yet, and that's where I will be spending most of my time. Can I see it before I sign the contract?"

"Is it really that important for you to see the lab, or are you just stalling?"

She smiled sheepishly. "You caught me. I want to see the lab, but it's not going to influence my decision unless it's horrible. Though after seeing how much effort has gone into the bungalows we will be staying in, I have no doubt that the lab will be at least adequate. Besides, if I don't like working there, I won't put in as many hours, so you should hope that I'll love it."

"I think you will. It's underground for security reasons, and it has a thick door that can withstand one hell of a blast, but it's spacious, well-lit, and nicely furnished. We have two couches down there, a kitchenette, a bar, and even a ping-pong table for when we need to let off steam."

William had never played ping-pong, but he'd gotten the idea from an article he'd read about keeping employees happy. The couches and the break room had been inspired by the same article, and he even asked Ingrid to figure out a way to incorporate some of those ideas into the village lab.

"I don't know how to play ping-pong," Kaia said. "But the setup sounds lovely. Are there any desks and chairs in there as well? After all, we are supposed to put in some work, not just lounge around and play ping-pong all day."

"Of course, there are. The other stuff is there for when we need to take a break or to brainstorm." He gave her a reassuring smile before knocking on Emmett's office door. "I'm looking forward to brainstorming with you. I'm sure it's going to be delightful."

Her demeanor changing in an instant, she gave him a look full of promise. "I'm looking forward to that as well."

Damn, the girl wasn't subtle, and she'd gotten him to respond precisely as she'd intended.

Stifling a groan, William depressed the handle and opened the door.

"Hello, sweet child." Emmett rose from behind the desk and walked over to Kaia. "How lovely you are." He enfolded her in his arms, the long sleeves of his white robe hanging down the back of her thighs.

Kaia cleared her throat. "It's nice to meet you, Mr. Haderech."

"Call me Emmett." He released her from his embrace and motioned for her to take a seat on one of the chairs in front of his desk.

"Where's Eleanor?" William asked as he sat down on the other chair.

"She had to step out for a few moments, but we don't really need her here." Emmett put his finger on the folder with Kaia's contract and pushed it toward her. "Before you open the folder, I need you to listen carefully to what I'm going to say."

Swallowing, she nodded.

"You will never discuss, write down, mime, or use any form of communication to reveal the details of this contract with anyone other than William. Is that clear?"

His words had been laced with a heavy dose of compulsion, and even though it hadn't been directed at William, he could feel its effect. Hopefully, Kaia had felt it as well.

"What if something is not clear and I need to ask my mother or Gilbert for advice?"

"William will explain everything in detail, and a smart girl like you will have no

trouble understanding it. It's not written in legal jargon, and it's straightforward."
Emmett grinned. "Basically, it says that if you tell anyone outside your team or William any details about the research, we will have to kill you."

She gasped, her eyes darting to William.

Emmett's attempt at humor was a big mistake given what had happened to Kaia's friend, but he didn't know about the missing scientist.

"Bad joke, Emmett." William shook his head. "Really bad."

"My apologies." Emmett reached for Kaia's hand across the table. "I just couldn't help myself. Although to be frank, the monetary consequences of breaching the confidentiality are so bad that you might wish we killed you instead of taking away all of your money."

"I don't have any." She pulled her hand out of his grasp. "I'm nineteen."

"Right. But after this job is done, you will have plenty of it." Emmett leaned back. "Now put your hand over your heart and repeat after me. I, Doctor Kaia Locke, will never reveal any details about the research conducted in this facility to anyone other than those working directly with me on it."

She put her hand over her heart as he'd instructed, but instead of repeating his words, she tilted her head and put her hand down. "What about you and Darlene? Are you involved in the research? I need to know precisely who I'm allowed to talk to about it and who I'm not."

A cold shiver ran down William's spine. Kaia should have repeated Emmett's instructions like a robot. The fact that she'd stopped to ask more questions suggested that she was immune to compulsion, which wasn't possible. He'd tested her susceptibility to thralling, and he'd had no problem entering her mind.

Emmett looked at her with the same concern in his eyes. "Eleanor, Darlene, and I are not directly involved in the project, so you shouldn't discuss it with us collectively or individually. You can only discuss it with William, Doctor Corinne Burke, Kylie Baldwin, and Owen Ferrel. Is that clear enough?"

"You should have said so from the start." Kaia put her hand over her heart. "I, Doctor Kaia Locke, will never reveal any details about the research conducted in this facility to anyone other than those working directly with me on it."

"Very good." Emmett smiled. "I need you to do one more thing for me before you open that folder." He pointed at William. "Tell him what you were thinking about just now."

"I was thinking that you are trying hard to appear indifferent to me, but you are failing." Her eyes widened in alarm, but she continued. "I know that you're attracted to me, and no matter how hard you try, you can't deny it, so just stop fighting it."

William swallowed. "Am I that transparent?"

"Yeah, you are." She turned to Emmett. "Did you hypnotize me to do that? I didn't want to tell him what I was thinking."

Emmett grinned. "I did. I had to test you to make sure that it worked."

She frowned. "I didn't feel anything, and I was sure that it hadn't worked. I would have known if you hypnotized me, and besides, I'm not hypnotizable."

"Evidently, you are. I'm very good at what I do."

Shaking her head, she turned back to William. "Are you okay? You look a little frazzled."

"I thought I was doing a better job of hiding my very inappropriate attraction to a girl who is much too young for me to even notice that way."

"Don't sweat it." She opened the folder and pulled out the contract. "It is what it is, and we can't control how we feel about people. We can only control what we do about it." She sighed. "I just don't want it to be awkward between us."

Kaia sounded so mature, but the fact remained that she was nineteen and probably still a virgin, though given how forward she was, maybe she wasn't. It made no difference.

She was off limits.

40

DARLENE

"*I* need to change the boys' diapers." Karen rose to her feet. "Can you point me in the direction of a changing station?"

"We don't have one." Darlene followed Karen up. "If you haven't noticed, there are no kids here." She leaned closer. "The community members who run this place believe in free love and no children, if you know what I mean, and no kids are allowed in the spiritual retreats."

"That's just sad." Karen slung the strap of her enormous baby bag over the stroller's handle. "I'll just take them outside and find a bench. I have a changing pad."

"I'll come with you." Gilbert rose to his feet. "Come, munchkin." He ruffled Idina's hair. "Help Mommy and Daddy change your brothers' diapers."

"Okay." The girl looked at her uncle. "Do you want to come change poopie diapers?"

"No, thank you. I smelled their poops before, and I'm not getting anywhere near that."

"I'll come too." Cheryl smirked under her breath. "We've been here half a day and didn't get to walk on the beach yet."

"We can take a walk," Karen offered. "But we don't want to be gone for too long. Kaia should be back any minute now, right?" She looked at Darlene. "How long does it take to read the contract?"

"Not that long. The other team members were done in less than half an hour. I don't know what is taking Kaia so long."

"She's reading it with a magnifying glass." Gilbert took Idina's hand. "Let's change those diapers."

As the family headed out, Darlene sat back down next to Eric. "I admire your brother and Karen for having three little kids at their age. I have only one son, and even though I was much younger when I had him, I still remember how difficult it was."

CHAPTER 40

"How old is he?" Eric pulled his chair a little closer to hers.

Darlene smiled. "I'm not going to tell you because that will reveal my age. Do you have kids?"

"Nope, and even though I adore my nephews and nieces, I'm glad that I don't. My ex is a piece of work, and the only smart thing I did when I married her was to refuse to have kids with her."

"Is that why she divorced you?"

He looked at her down his nose. "Who said that she divorced me? Perhaps I divorced her?"

"You wouldn't be as bitter. You would feel guilty. Ask me how I know."

"How?"

"My ex was a piece of work as well, and I was the one who filed for divorce. But despite all the crap he had done to me, I still feel guilty about ending my marriage."

Eric's face darkened. "What did he do?"

"I'd rather not talk about it." She put a hand on his thigh. "Am I going to see you again?"

"Do you want to?"

"I wouldn't have asked if I didn't, and you are leaving soon."

He leaned so close to her that his breath tickled her ear. "I would have loved to stay, but I have to fly my brother and his family home. I'll come back here as soon as I can."

Darlene wasn't sure she believed him. He'd just met her, and she wasn't a great catch worthy of flying over for, but as the saying went—hope springs eternal.

"You didn't ask for my phone number, but I'll give it to you anyway. If you manage to work out a visit, let me know." She pulled out her phone, anxious to see if he would give her his number.

He regarded her with hooded eyes. "I might get back here tomorrow. I had a client scheduled to charter the jet for the next two days, but he didn't put down a deposit, which was due today, and since I haven't heard from him, I assume that he has changed his mind. But until I hear from him, I can't just take him off the schedule. He's been chartering my jets for years."

Eric's explanation had been too long and too detailed for it to be a brush-off, but she still couldn't believe that he was so eager to hook up with her. Had he been going through a dry spell?

That was doubtful.

He was handsome and charming, and he was a pilot who owned two private jets. That made him irresistible to 99.9 percent of the single ladies' population, and probably fifty percent of the not-so-single one as well.

"Call me as soon as you hear from your client, and I'll arrange for a driver to pick you up at the airport."

"Nah." He leaned back. "That would spoil the surprise. I'll get a rental and drive myself over here."

"Sounds romantic, but that's not a good idea." She leaned closer to him. "Because of the research, the security around the resort is insane, and any unrecognized vehicle is stopped and inspected."

Eric didn't look concerned. "I'll risk that. What are they going to do, shoot at me?"

"No, but they are going to stop you and search the car, and it won't be pleasant."

She was probably exaggerating, but Darlene didn't want him to surprise her. If she was going to hook up with a guy for the first time in twenty-three years, she wanted to be mentally and physically prepared.

He leaned closer and brushed his lips over her cheek, sending shivers through her body. "I want you to wait for me with bated breath, but I don't want you to be prepared for my arrival. When I get here, I'll sweep you off your feet and take you straight to bed."

"Oh my," she said breathlessly. "I won't be able to sleep tonight."

"Good." He leaned back. "Then you won't mind if I call you in the middle of the night to talk dirty to you."

She looked around her in alarm, but no one seemed to have heard him. Leaning toward him, she whispered, "Is that your thing? You like dirty talk?"

Eric smirked. "Among other things."

WILLIAM

*D*arlene stood next to William as they both watched Kaia say a tearful goodbye to her family. "Poor girl. She seems so confident, so strong. I didn't expect her to fall apart like that." She chuckled. "Roni couldn't wait to get out of the house. The moment he turned eighteen, he moved out even though he was just exchanging one prison for another."

It broke William's heart to see Kaia cry her eyes out as she hugged her baby brothers and kissed their cheeks.

"She's very attached to her younger siblings. I don't think it would have been as difficult for her if it was just the adults and Cheryl. She must have strong maternal instincts."

"That reminds me." Darlene looked up at him. "Did you ask her about the old guy inside her head?"

"He was middle-aged, not old, and no, I didn't." Grimacing, he whispered, "I had a hard enough time just controlling my libido."

"I don't know why you are fighting it so hard. So she's young, but she's very mature, smart, and she's into you. So, what's the problem?"

"She's practically a kid. I feel like a pedophile for even thinking about her as a woman."

Darlene shook her head. "She is a woman, William, legally and otherwise, and you two are a match made in heaven. Where are you going to find another lady who is smart enough to actually challenge you? Besides, wasn't Wonder only nineteen when she and Anandur first met?"

"That was different. Wonder is ancient. She's older than Annani by a year or two."

Huffing out a breath, Darlene put a hand on his bicep. "Wonder had spent all those thousands of years in stasis, and she'd only accumulated nineteen years of experiences. I bet that Kaia is more mature than Wonder was when she fell in love with Anandur. In fact, Kaia's soul is so old that she might as well be my age."

He cast her a small smile. "How did it go with the uncle? Are you two going to see each other again?"

"I hope so. We've exchanged phone numbers, and he said that he would try to return as early as tomorrow, but I'm not holding my breath. Eric is a player, and frankly, I don't know what he sees in me when he can get women half my age."

"Maybe he likes more mature ladies? I for one prefer older women who know what they want, and who don't play games."

"You just described Kaia. She knows what she wants, and she's not bashful about it."

Perhaps that explained why he was so attracted to her. It wasn't just about her incredible brain and her sexy, young body. It was also about her assertive attitude and her directness.

"She kissed me," he admitted. "It was to thank me for agreeing to help find her friend, but she kissed me on the lips, so it couldn't have been just about gratitude."

"Good for her!" Darlene said a little too loudly. "Sorry," she whispered. "I got excited. Was it a real kiss, or just a peck?"

William felt his face getting warm. "It was more of a peck, but she did it with gusto."

"I see. So no tongue."

"Fates, you sound like a teenager, but then in immortal terms, you are."

"Really?" Darlene tossed her hair back. "That makes me feel so much better about my age."

"You are a beautiful woman." He patted her arm. "I don't know why you are so self-conscious."

She sighed. "Twenty-seven years with a man who loved pointing out all my flaws have done a number on me. I know now that I was beautiful back then, but I'm no longer young, so no matter how hard I work on my body, it's not going to look like it did in my twenties."

"It will when you transition." He didn't want to butt his nose into her private affairs, but they were friends, and he felt like he needed to remind her of what should have been obvious. "I get it that Eric is charming and handsome, and he seems less intimidating than the immortal males available to you, but you will be wasting your time and his if you pursue a relationship with him." He rubbed the back of his neck. "Max is a nice guy, and he's interested. Why won't you give him a chance?"

She shifted her gaze to Eric, who was hugging Kaia and murmuring encouragement to her. "I haven't been with anyone other than Leo in over two decades, and I need to re-enter the dating scene gradually. Eric is not relationship material, and I don't have any expectations from him other than a few tumbles between the sheets. If that goes well, I'll take the next step and look for a suitable immortal male."

"There was no one in the village who appealed to you?"

She shook her head. "Maybe I should visit your clan in Scotland and check out the selection there."

"And leave Roni? And what about your mother and sister?"

She shrugged. "If I find someone there, I'll just drag him to the village with me. I'm a Dormant, which makes me worth any sacrifice, right?"

William didn't know whether she meant it or was just being sarcastic, but it was a good opportunity to show his friend his support. "You are definitely worth it, Darlene. And not just because you are a Dormant. You are smart, beautiful, and capable. Any man, whether human or immortal, would be lucky to have you as his mate."

42

KAIA

*K*aia waved at the bus as it drove away with her family. The torrent of tears refused to abate no matter how much she tried to staunch it, and now, in addition to that, a choking sensation in her throat was adding to her distress.

She kept waving until the bus left the parking lot, and she couldn't see it anymore unless she ran after it, which she was tempted to do.

It was irrational to get so emotional over a short two-week separation, but she couldn't help it, and she hated the feeling of being alone. Her family was her fortress, her source of strength, and without them, she felt like a leaf that had fallen off a tree and drifted away, carried on the wind.

"Let me show you the lab." William put a gentle hand on her shoulder but stayed behind her, giving her a moment to regain her composure. "You can get a sneak peek at the journals."

Wiping the tears off her cheeks with the back of her hands, she heaved a sigh. "Is Darlene coming with us?"

"I can't," Darlene said. "I don't have the security clearance. I don't even know what you will be working on."

"Right. I forgot." Kaia finally turned around.

Given the pitying look in William's eyes, she must look as dreadful as she felt. Her eyes were probably red and puffy, and she needed to blow her nose, but she didn't have tissues in her tiny purse.

"Can we stop by the lodge first? I need to visit the ladies' room."

"Of course." William lowered his hand to the small of her back.

She appreciated that. The cold seeping throughout her body had nothing to do with the weather, and only the warm human contact he offered could remedy it.

Darlene followed them into the lodge. "Do you want me to come with you to the bathroom?"

"I'm okay." Kaia gave her a small smile. "Thanks for everything."

"Anytime." Darlene enfolded her in her arms. "If you need anything, and I mean even if you just feel lonely and want to talk, call me. I left my number on a sticky note stuck to the toaster in your bungalow."

"Thank you." Kaia moved out of the woman's embrace and ducked into the ladies' room.

Thankfully, there was no one there, and she released a shuddering breath before reaching for a paper towel to blow her nose into.

A look in the mirror confirmed her suspicions. Her eyes were red and puffy, and her cheeks looked blotchy. Some girls looked pretty when they cried, but Kaia wasn't one of them.

It was good that she didn't cry often. Cheryl, who was a little sarcastic and liked to make snarky comments about everything and everyone, cried like a baby when watching a sad scene in a movie. But Kaia didn't cry, not even when she was just as moved by the story.

Maybe it was because of the memories she carried with her from a life as a man who hadn't been allowed to show emotions as freely.

After splashing her face with cold water, Kaia felt a little better, but after she'd dried it with a couple of paper towels and looked in the mirror again, she groaned. Her appearance hadn't improved much, but maybe it wasn't all bad. William would be relieved, not because she was sad—he'd seemed genuinely disturbed by her tears—but because it would be easier for him to resist his attraction to her.

He'd offered to show her the manuscripts to cheer her up or to distract her, and it had been a good move. She was curious to see them, and if she started working right away, she wouldn't be thinking about her family and how much she was going to miss them.

When she walked out of the bathroom, William pushed away from the wall he'd been leaning against and walked up to her. "Are you feeling better? Do you want something to drink? Tea, perhaps?"

"I want a Coke, but you don't have any, so I'll settle for tea."

"If you want a Coke, you'll get it." He pulled out his phone and typed up a message so fast that his fingers blurred. "Not immediately, but it will get here in about three hours." He put the phone back in his pocket. "The bus driver will buy a crate of it on the way back."

"That's so nice of you. Thank you."

"Don't hesitate to ask for anything you need or want." He put his hand on the small of her back again, the warmth of it again chasing the cold away. "My job is to make you happy."

She smiled up at him. "What if I want to go to Paris? Will you take me there to make me happy?"

"Of course. Right after the project is done."

"What if I want to go into space? Will you pay a million dollars to get me a spot on the shuttle?"

He laughed. "I'm not that rich. You are a dangerous young lady, and I shouldn't make open-ended promises to you."

"I was just teasing. I don't want to go to space."

What she wanted was a handsome, smart, and adorable nerdy guy with a heart of gold, and getting him wouldn't be nearly as difficult as getting a seat on the space shuttle.

4 3

WILLIAM

$\mathcal{K}$aia sat in front of the computer, leaning so close to the screen that her nose was nearly touching it. "Whoever wrote this had very neat handwriting. It almost looks like print." She rolled the chair back and looked at William. "I need to see the originals or at least a printout of the screenshots you took. I can't decipher anything if I have to look at snippets. I need to go back and forth and compare sections."

William had been afraid of that, but he'd hoped that with her genius, Kaia could start deciphering Okidu's journals page by page.

"I can print out the first journal for you, but it can't leave the lab, and I don't want you sharing it with the others unless there is no other choice. My idea was for you to give them limited tasks that would prevent them from putting the puzzle pieces together."

Frowning, she slid the chair closer to his. "What do you think is in those journals? And where did you find them?"

He'd expected that question, and he had prepared a fictional story that he hated to tell Kaia, but the less she knew, the better.

"The journals were found in an archeological dig, and we don't know who the author was."

She glanced at the screen and adjusted her glasses. "What's your theory?"

He smiled. "I have several, but as a scientist, you will roll your eyes at all of them."

"Try me." Her blue eyes shone with curiosity. "You'll find me very open-minded to the supernatural, the alien, and even to conspiracy theories if they are well thought out."

That was good to hear, but his so-called theories were fabrications loosely based on the truth.

"My first thought was that the journals had been written by alien scientists who had somehow gotten stranded on Earth. Their technology didn't survive the trip, and they wanted to preserve their knowledge because they didn't want to forget it, or maybe they were dying and didn't want it to die with them. They recorded everything using the tools available to them and buried the treasure for future generations of humans to find and make use of."

Kaia leaned even closer to him, her knees almost touching his. "When were they written? Did you have the journals dated? That would give you a good estimate of when those aliens arrived on Earth."

"It wasn't a very long time ago. They were written in journals that were manufactured in this century."

Her eyes widened. "When? In the fifties? Were they found near Area 51?"

The leather-bound journals that Okidu had used had been manufactured in China since the early 2000s, but he needed to preserve the air of mystery around them to keep Kaia misinformed.

"I'm sorry, but I can't tell you that. The information is classified."

She pouted but then shrugged. "I'll probably figure it out when I decipher the writings." She slid the rolling chair back to her station and put her nose to the screen again. "It really looks like an alien language. What are your other theories?"

"It could have been written by humans who used some sort of code that my most advanced software couldn't crack because I didn't have the key. It's possible that it's hidden within the manuscripts, and only a worthy scientist will be able to uncover it."

"Like Excalibur." Kaia pretended to pull a sword out of the rock. "Am I the worthy scientist?"

He smiled. "Evidently, I wasn't, but then I'm not a bioinformatician, and after many hours of poring over the symbols, I had the brilliant realization that the code is genetic and that I would need to assemble a team of people who are experts in that sort of code."

She nodded. "That was a smart move. Any other theories?"

"Yeah. That the crate full of journals contains the ramblings of a lunatic, and I'm wasting incredible resources and valuable time on nonsense that just appears scientific."

"You don't really believe in that one, do you? You wouldn't have gone to all the trouble of building this super-secure lab and equipping it with computing power that could rival Stanford's."

"No, I don't. My favorite is the first one. Aliens." He smiled and waggled his brows.

She laughed as if he'd done the funniest thing. "You look ridiculous when you do that thing with your brows, but it's adorable." She leaned forward and poked his cheek with her finger. "You have such cute dimples when you smile. You should smile more."

William could barely breathe.

Kaia was leaning over him, her ample breasts nearly spilling out of her low-necked T-shirt, and her feminine scent filling his nostrils.

Sensing his distress, she leaned away and looked at him with those eyes that looked too old on such a young face. "I'm sorry for invading your personal space." She chuckled. "I tend to do that when I get excited, and I'm with people who I like and trust."

He didn't want her to feel guilty about something that wasn't her fault.

"I'm glad that you like and trust me, and if I weren't so damn attracted to you, I wouldn't have even noticed that you were in my personal space, because I tend to do the same with people who I like."

Kaia grinned. "We are so much alike, you and me. Maybe too much."

"What do you mean?"

She shook her head. "Never mind."

"Now that you've blurted that out, you can't leave me hanging. Why are we too much alike? In what way?"

44

KAIA

*S*ometimes Kaia's mouth ran away from her, saying things she shouldn't have. What was she going to tell William? That she often switched to thinking from a man's perspective? That she knew precisely what was going through his head when he got a peek at the tops of her breasts because she remembered having those feelings as Edgar?

Men were visual creatures, and they went from zero arousal to a hundred in a millisecond. William was probably sporting one hell of a hard-on right now, and he was desperate to adjust his painful erection in his pants but didn't want her to see that.

"We both have blue eyes and wear glasses." She turned back to the screen, giving him the opportunity to get more comfortable.

"Why is that a problem?"

Because she sometimes looked at her own body in the mirror and got excited, not as Kaia, but as Edgar, and that was not only confusing but also disturbing.

"It's hard to kiss when the two people kissing both have glasses on." She leaned as if to get a better look at the strange symbols while seeing nothing but a blur.

"Do you have a lot of experience kissing someone with glasses?"

"Other than you? Yeah, I do." She didn't turn to look at him.

Let him stew on that for a while.

She squeaked in surprise when he pulled her chair toward him, and when he wheeled it around, so she was facing him, Kaia got an even bigger surprise.

It must have been a trick of the light, but his eyes were glowing, and since he was wearing glasses, it couldn't be light reflecting from contact lenses.

"Was it Anthony?" he growled.

"Not that it's any of your business, but I've already told you that there was nothing romantic between us. I never kissed Tony."

"Did he kiss you?"

She narrowed her eyes at him. "What is it to you?"

125

"I don't like being manipulated, and I don't appreciate you thinking so little of me. I suspect that you told me that Anthony was just a friend because you assumed that I wouldn't help you look for him if I thought that he was your boyfriend."

"Would you have helped me if he was?"

"Yes, I would."

Perhaps, but he wasn't entitled to play the saint when he was dragging his feet about helping her until she signed the contract and came to work for him.

"So why didn't you? Because you were waiting for the contract to be signed before you helped me?"

"That was true in the beginning, but for your information, I forwarded everything you gave me to Roni. He hasn't gotten back to me yet, and that's because he has his hands full at the moment." William pulled out his phone. "I'll text him right now and ask if he's had a chance to look into it."

"It's Sunday."

"Right." William put his phone down on the desk. "Roni's mate doesn't allow him to work on Sundays. I'll text him first thing tomorrow morning."

Looking at the device, Kaia frowned. "How come you can have your phone in here and I can't?"

He smiled. "Because I'm the boss. Besides, yours won't work down here. Mine is special."

"I bet."

"You still didn't answer my question. Who was the guy with glasses you kissed? Was he a fellow student?"

"Why are you so interested in my love life?"

"You didn't mention past boyfriends in the security briefing."

Ah, so that was what bothered him.

Kaia was willing to bet that William had assumed she was still a virgin and had never had a boyfriend. When she'd mentioned kissing a guy, he'd gotten angry because he was jealous, and not because of the potential security breach caused by the omission of a former boyfriend from the list of friends and acquaintances she'd provided.

He was lucky that she knew how a male's brain worked and how influenced it was by testosterone. Otherwise, she would have been offended.

"It was close to two years ago, didn't last long, and we didn't stay in touch. There was no reason to mention him in the briefing."

Kaia had been seventeen at the time and desperate to explore her sexuality, but since she'd gone through puberty surrounded by people twice her age, there hadn't been anyone she could have explored it with. They'd still regarded her as a kid when she'd turned into a woman. Besides, she hadn't wanted an older guy either. The problem was that when boys closer to her age had heard that she was on her way to earning her PhD, they'd thought she was either a liar or a freak and had hoofed it away.

She was a liar, and a very good one at that, but her lies ran in the opposite direction.

Her only option was to lie about her academic achievements and claim that she was a regular girl who was homeschooled.

When she'd met the cutest boy at a Starbucks, that was what she'd told him, and they'd started dating.

CHAPTER 44

It had been fun.

He was eighteen, a little older than her, and he'd already had sex, or so he'd claimed. If he had, he hadn't been very experienced, and it had been a little awkward at first, but after a few times, it had gotten better, and she'd started to enjoy it. But then he'd gotten into a good college in Ohio, and that had been the end of it.

He'd promised to call and come to visit her during vacations, but he'd stopped calling after a couple of weeks, and she'd gotten the message.

It hadn't been a great loss, and Kaia hadn't been heartbroken over it, but she hadn't had time to pursue another relationship while working on her thesis and publishing papers in scientific journals.

4 5

WILLIAM

*W*as Kaia telling the truth?

William wasn't great at detecting lies, but he sensed that she was evading his inquiries with half-truths. Then again, unless whatever she was hiding was connected to the journals or could sabotage the safety of the research, it was Kaia's right to tell him as much or as little as she pleased.

Theoretically, she could have had a boyfriend at seventeen, but practically, it was unlikely. She'd been working on her doctoral thesis at the time and had no contact with people her age, and she'd told him that older guys didn't interest her.

But that had been a lie as well. If she was showing interest in him, a pudgy, dorky guy that was as charming as a physics textbook, then he probably wasn't the first older man she'd pursued.

It was none of his business, especially when he was trying to keep a professional distance from her and shouldn't get too close to her. But he couldn't deny the burning need to unravel the mystery of Doctor Kaia Locke. He had to know what she was about, what was the truth and what was a fabrication, and why she had a male persona hiding behind her delicate, feminine features.

Perhaps he could goad her into revealing the truth.

"I find it hard to believe that you had only one boyfriend at seventeen and no one since. Or was he just the only one with glasses?"

Kaia threw her hands in the air. "What do you want from me, William? First, you don't believe that I've ever had a boyfriend, and then you don't believe that I've had only one? Make up your mind."

He let out a breath. "I'm sorry. It's just that you baffle me. On the one hand, you are a young woman who is still strongly attached to her family, but on the other hand, you have the maturity and insight of a much older person, and to be frank, I sense something masculine in you, and I don't know where it's coming from."

That was probably the worst way to ask Kaia about her other persona, but it was too late to take it back.

She huffed with her big eyes full of indignation. "Figures. When a woman is successful and assertive, she gets accused of being masculine. I didn't peg you for a chauvinist, William McLean."

"I'm not a chauvinist." He took his glasses off and wiped them with the corner of his shirt, but he'd forgotten that it wasn't one of his Hawaiian silk ones, and the fabric of the new shirt he was wearing was the wrong kind for cleaning glasses. "I'm sorry if my ill-phrased comment offended you, but I'm just very intuitive, and that's the vibe I get from you. Perhaps I'm mistaken."

Hopefully, the line Darlene had suggested would work better than his previous fumbling attempt.

"Ugh." Letting out a breath, Kaia closed her eyes and slumped in her chair, looking defeated or pretending to be. "You think that I'm into women."

"I didn't say that, and I didn't think that. It was just an observation, and it was obviously wrong. Can we forget that I even mentioned it?"

"Nope." She opened her eyes and looked at him with a naughty smile lifting one corner of her lush lips. "You challenged my femininity, and now I have to prove to you that I'm all woman." She rose to her feet, took a step toward him, and put her hands on the armrests of his rolling chair. "Can I kiss you? Or are you going to freeze up on me again?"

He wanted to grab her, plunk her on his lap, and do much more than just kiss her, but he wasn't going to do any of that.

"Don't. You're thirteen years younger than me, and you're my subordinate. It would be criminal of me to succumb to the temptation."

She didn't back up. Instead, her smile widened. "For it to be criminal, I would need to be underage, which I'm not, and you would have to be in a position to take advantage of me, which you're not. You need me for this research much more than I need this job, so if either of us could be accused of using their advantageous position to coerce the other, it would be me, not you. So, I'll ask you again. May I kiss you?"

4 6

KAIA

*C*ould William hear her heart pounding?

Kaia heard it loud and clear, but maybe it was the sound of her blood pulsing in her veins?

Would he call her bluff and laugh in her face?

She didn't lack confidence, but she'd never been so daring. Something about William had awakened a naughty side of her that she hadn't been aware she had until he'd shown up in her life. It spurred her to goad him and torment him until he broke down and surrendered to that wild thing pulsing between them.

A pained groan was her only warning before his hands landed on her waist, and she was hoisted up and plunked onto his lap, the evidence of his desire a hard ridge under her bottom.

"You have half a second to say no," he gritted as he whipped his glasses off.

Was he kidding her?

"Yes."

As his palm closed around her nape, he commanded, "Close your eyes."

"So bossy," she teased but found herself wanting to obey.

Bossy William was sexy, and if he thought that his assertiveness would scare her, he couldn't be more wrong. Kaia had absolutely no doubt that if she wanted him to stop, all she had to do was say the word.

As if to prove she was right about that, his lips hovered over hers for a long moment, giving her the opportunity to retreat if she so pleased, but she had no intention of doing that. Instead, she closed the distance between them and fused their mouths.

When his tongue swiped over the seam of her lips, she opened for him with no hesitation, and when it found hers, the deep growl reverberating in his chest made her want to purr in satisfaction.

Winding her arms around his neck, she ground her bottom against his hard length, eliciting another sexy growl from him that went straight to her breasts, stiffening her nipples.

Then his hand tangled in her hair, tugging on it gently, and heat flooded her core. She'd never felt desire so all-consuming. William was a man and compared to the inferno of fire he was igniting in her, her one and only boyfriend had been a tiny candle, no pun intended.

His hand trailed under her T-shirt, finding the bare skin of her stomach and making her heart thunder in her chest, but he never moved it up as she hoped he would.

All she could do to quench her thirst was to grind herself over his straining erection.

When he pulled his hand out from under her T-shirt and released her mouth, she groaned in frustration, but she knew better than to press her luck by pushing him to go further.

Her lips still tingling from his kiss, Kaia was afraid to open her eyes, not because she was waiting for him to tell her that she could, but because she was afraid of what she would see.

Would he look guilty, disappointed, or angry?

Would he tell her that it could never happen again?

She wouldn't be able to bear it if he did. Not today, not when she still felt fragile after saying goodbye to her family.

"Kaia," he said her name as if it was a prayer. "Look at me."

Given his pained tone, she knew what he was about to say.

Resting her forehead against his, she whispered, "Give me one more moment to enjoy this before you tell me it can never happen again."

"That's not what I was going to say."

"It wasn't?" She lifted her head and looked into his intense blue eyes that were still shining with that strange inner glow.

Brushing his fingers over her cheek, he drew a line down to her jaw. "It's been an emotional day for you, and I should have realized that you felt vulnerable and needed to do something, anything, to make you feel better. I hope that you won't hate me tomorrow for taking advantage of that."

Ugh, the man was infuriating. Lifting her hands, she cupped his cheeks and glared right into his glowing eyes. "Don't you dare turn this into something ugly. It was the best kiss I ever had, with the best man I ever met, and it was beautiful."

A small smile bloomed on his handsome face and then turned into a big grin. "This really was your best kiss ever?"

"Hands down, no competition. You are an amazing kisser." Tucking her head under his chin, she smirked. "I hope that you are not going to hate me tomorrow for taking advantage of you."

He chuckled. "If you are stealing my lines, I'm going to steal yours. This was the best kiss I ever had as well."

"But? I can practically hear the but in your tone."

"But this is as far as I'm willing to go while we are working together."

"What about after the project is done?"

"By then, we will know each other better, and if the attraction is still there, we will take it to the next step."

William thought that he was so smart, but she knew what he was trying to do.

By offering her a small carrot, he hoped that she would back off and give him a break.

If there was any merit to why he was resisting, or if he wasn't into her as much as she was into him, she would have respected his wishes, but since his reasons were nonsensical, she would keep pushing until he caved in and gave her what she wanted, and that was all of him.

"I guarantee that it will be there, even stronger than it is now, because we will be fighting it for months. You are just sentencing us to unnecessary torment."

He chuckled. "I'm a big believer in the merits of delayed gratification. All good things come to those who wait."

47

WILLIAM

*W*hat a liar he was, feeding Kaia that line about delayed gratification. Perhaps it had been true in the past when he'd been too busy to even think about female company, but she was bringing out all of his suppressed male immortal urges, including a dominant bent that William had never felt before.

Well, that wasn't true.

He was running a lab that had grown from a solo endeavor to an enterprise with dozens of people working for him, and he couldn't have done a good job of heading it if he didn't have leadership qualities, which required at least some degree of dominant tendencies.

Sexually, however, he'd never been assertive, and he had been more than happy to follow the female's lead.

Then again, he had never been pursued with such determination by a nineteen-year-old who thought that she was the boss.

Not that she was necessarily wrong. Kaia had him by the balls in more ways than one.

"Let's get out of here." He lifted her off his lap and set her down on the floor. "It's almost dinner time, and you should say hello to the rest of your teammates before we go to the dining hall."

"Are we going to dine in the lodge cafeteria?"

"No, we share a separate, smaller dining room with another program."

From now on, they wouldn't be using the lodge. Their bungalows and the lab were in a separate fenced-off area, but they would make use of the gym and the dining hall in the paranormals' section of the resort.

William wasn't happy about sharing the facilities with the paranormal program, but it didn't make sense to build a separate kitchen and dining hall for his team. Each one of the nine paranormals was under Eleanor's control, so in the event that one of his four team members let something slip despite the strong compulsion they were under, it would be easily contained.

The only one he was worried about was the doctor, but Eleanor had him so firmly under her control that the guy was nearly catatonic.

Kaia ran her fingers through her tangled hair. "I need to stop by my room and freshen up, if you know what I mean." She winked at him.

He had no idea what she meant, other than perhaps wanting to brush her hair. Maybe she wanted to wait until her lips were no longer swollen from their kiss, and her cheeks were no longer rosy with excitement, and her eyes were no longer glossy from desire...

Damn. He needed a breather before he could let anyone see him as well. His new jeans were uncomfortably tight, and not because he'd overeaten at lunch, and his eyes were probably still emitting light.

Kaia hadn't commented on that, so maybe she hadn't noticed, but that was doubtful. She watched him like a hawk, deciphering and learning him just as she did with every complicated project she'd ever tackled. If he wasn't super careful around her, she might figure out that he wasn't human.

"We can take a walk on the beach," he suggested. "It's not too windy today, and the ocean is calm."

"I would love that." Kaia lifted her ridiculously small purse off the desk and slung the thin strap across her body. "What's the protocol for locking the lab?" She took his hand.

"It locks itself." William led her out the door. "There are cameras everywhere, and the moment the door closes behind us, the locks and alarms engage. Only I can open the lab, and it requires the scanning of my iris."

As they reached the top of the stairs, he lifted his eyes to the scanner to open the second out of the three doors.

Kaia eyed him from under lowered lashes. "Aren't you worried that the people in security saw us kiss?"

The Guardians would have a field day teasing him about it, especially Max, but he wasn't too worried about that. What bothered him was them seeing Kaia in his arms, looking aroused and flushed. No one other than him was allowed to see her like that.

Hell, he shouldn't have seen her like that either.

Thankfully, they hadn't done anything more than kiss, so no harm was done to Kaia's reputation or his.

"We've done nothing wrong, and given the circumstances, I was the perfect gentleman. If I refused to kiss you, I would have offended you and hurt your feelings, which wouldn't have been very gentlemanly of me. So I kissed you, but I gave you every opportunity to change your mind, and I didn't put my hands anywhere I shouldn't have."

"I see." She looked a little put out. "So that's why you succumbed to my charms. You knew that if I wanted to cause you trouble, you would have proof of your good behavior."

He stopped and turned to her. "It was definitely your irresistible charm. I forgot all about the cameras, and it didn't occur to me that we were performing for an audience until you mentioned locking up the lab. I would have never willingly given the guys in security a show."

That seemed to appease her, but she still looked like a kid who had lost her favorite new toy.

When they went through the third door, she looked up at the camera together with him, watching it scan his iris. "This place is so 007. If someone wanted to infiltrate the lab, they would need to knock you out, haul you down here, and shove your eye under the scanner. Or they could just cut out your eyeball."

"That's so gruesome. Where did you come up with that idea?"

She smiled. "Movies. To mitigate the risk, you should have scanned another person's eyeball. Then there would be two, cutting your risk in half."

"Are you volunteering yours?"

Kaia pursed her lips. "To be entrusted with such a treasure, I'm willing to take the risk."

48

KAIA

*D*inner had gone by with Kaia replaying the kiss in her mind and stealing glances at William while trying to keep up the conversation with her teammates. She'd been so absentminded that the others probably doubted she was as smart as William had claimed. She could barely remember what they'd talked about.

As they all headed back to the bungalows, William stopped in front of hers and Kylie's. "I'll see you all bright and early tomorrow morning."

"Do you want to come in for a cup of coffee?" She looked at Kylie. "Do we even have coffee? I haven't had the chance to check yet."

"We do, and we also have a pod coffee and cappuccino maker, and surprisingly, I found a box full of Coke, which given Safe Haven's healthy nutrition dictum, is akin to finding pot in a church. You are all invited." She waved her hand to include Corinne and Owen.

"Thank you." Kaia cast William a grateful smile. "I forgot that you asked the bus driver to get Coke for us."

He nodded and smiled back. "Thank you for the invitation, but I still have a lot of work to do tonight, and I'd better get on it, or I will be working until morning."

Bummer. Kaia had hoped they wouldn't have to say goodbye yet.

"It's Sunday," Corinne said. "You should allow yourself some time off, or you'll burn out."

"I happen to love what I do, so I doubt I'll burn out anytime soon, but I agree that balancing work and leisure is important." He cast a quick glance at Kaia. "I'm not very good at that."

It was her fault. She'd kept him from doing his work.

William hadn't left her side since she'd arrived in the morning. Well, not all of it had been her fault. He had to eat, so lunch and dinner didn't count, and it was also his job to introduce the team members to each other, so that didn't count either. Her culpability had been limited to three or four hours, and some of it had been work-related, so Kaia didn't feel too guilty for keeping William occupied with other things.

Despite the separation anxiety she'd suffered earlier when her family had left, it had been one of the best days she could remember in a long while.

Nothing could rival the elation she'd felt when her siblings had been born, but time spent with William was a close second, especially when it involved kissing.

"Does anyone have any questions before we part for the evening?" William's eyes darted to Kaia.

"What time are we supposed to get to the lab tomorrow?" she asked.

"Breakfast starts at six in the morning and lasts until seven-thirty. I'll meet you all at the dining hall at quarter to eight, and we will head to the lab together."

"What about our phones?" Owen asked. "You said that we couldn't bring them into the lab. Should we leave them in our rooms?"

"You can do that, or you can bring them with you and hand them over to me before we enter the lab's building. I'll put them in a secure locker."

When they all nodded, William's eyes shifted to Kaia again. "Well, goodnight, everyone." He smiled.

"Goodnight, William." She forced a smile back.

Why was it so difficult to part ways with him? She'd spent most of the day with him, and she was going to see him tomorrow morning. She shouldn't feel anxious because she was going to spend the night without him.

Perhaps she was still experiencing the lingering effects of her earlier anxiety attack?

It didn't make sense for her to feel such a strong pull toward him.

If she combined all the hours she'd spent with William so far, it would be less than one day, and she couldn't even think of him as her boyfriend. He was just a guy who she'd kissed a couple of times.

Nevertheless, as she watched him enter his bungalow and close the door behind him, she fantasized about sneaking inside in the middle of the night and curling up next to him in bed.

She wasn't going to do that, but knowing that the possibility existed eased the anxious feeling pressing on her chest.

"Do you want to hang out in our bungalow?" Kylie offered to Corinne and Owen.

Corinne shook her head. "Thanks, but I'm tired, and I want to veg in front of the television."

Owen looked like he was debating whether to accept Kylie's invitation or keep Corinne company. "I'll call it a night as well." He smiled at Corinne. "We can veg in front of the television together. What do you like to watch?"

As the two continued to their bungalow, Kaia followed Kylie into theirs. "Have you tried that coffee maker already?"

"I did, and it's great. Do you want me to make you a cappuccino?"

"Yes, please." Kaia plopped down on the couch and reached for the remote. "I like Corinne's idea. Do you want to watch a movie?"

"What do you have in mind?"

"William said that they have all the latest movies on their server, even those that are still playing in theaters." She started scrolling through the selection. "How about *One Morning in Barcelona?*"

Cheryl had seen it in the theater with her friends and had said that it was silly but sweet and funny. It was the perfect combination to lift her mood before she called home and talked with her mom.

Kaia had made such a scene when her family said goodbye that her mother was probably worried about her. She'd texted her and Cheryl during dinner to tell them that she was feeling better and would call them after the twins were asleep, and she needed to sound cheerful and upbeat to convince her mother that it was true.

"Isn't that a chick flick?" Kylie finished frothing the milk and poured it into two cups.

"It is." Kaia was in the mood for something light and romantic, but maybe Kylie was a movie snob and liked to watch only foreign drama. "Do you want to watch something else?"

"No, a chick flick sounds awesome. It was a stressful day, and I want to relax with something silly." She handed Kaia a mug. "I didn't put any sugar in because the vanilla soy milk is already sweetened."

Kaia grimaced. "The one thing I really don't like about this place is their so-called healthy nutrition. If we can't get some snacks in here, I'm going to lose weight."

"You shouldn't let that happen." Kylie sat next to her on the couch. "You have a killer figure. What's your secret?"

Good genes and being nineteen, but she wasn't going to say that because it sounded condescending.

Kylie was in her late twenties, which was still young, but she hadn't been taking good care of herself. Most postdocs didn't. They worked too hard and got paid too little.

"I walk a lot while pushing a double stroller with my twin baby brothers in it. Surprisingly, it's a great workout and burns a lot of calories." Kaia kicked her flip-flops off and tucked her legs under her.

Kylie pursed her lips. "Interesting. Perhaps once this project is over, I'll look for a second job babysitting twins and get workouts as a bonus. Does your mom need help?"

"We have a nanny, but I can ask."

Kylie sipped on her cappuccino for a few moments and then put the cup down on the coffee table. "It's probably none of my business, but is there something going on between you and William?"

Was she asking because she was interested in him?

Kaia had the urge to bare her teeth at Kylie and tell her to stay away from him, but instead, she shrugged. "Maybe. I like him a lot, but he thinks that I'm too young for him."

Kylie snorted. "Of course, you are. You're practically a kid."

Shrugging again, Kaia pressed play on the remote. "Let's watch the movie."

The body she was occupying might be young, but her soul wasn't. She was, however, inexperienced, and it wasn't limited to sex. Edgar Rosu had been a bachelor and a loner, and if he had any relationships with women, Kaia didn't remember them. She had vague memories of him looking at women and lusting after them, but no actual sexual or amorous encounters.

What she remembered most vividly was the mathematics that had fascinated Edgar so thoroughly that he'd forgotten there was more to life than academia.

49

JADE

"I need access to the computer." Jade hated to ask Igor for anything, but the internet was the only connection she had to the outside world, and she needed his permission to use it.

He lifted his head and pinned her with his hard eyes. "What for?"

He didn't tell her to sit down, so she remained standing and schooled her facial features to hide her hatred for him. "I ran out of ideas for stories to tell the children. I need inspiration."

It was a Kra-ell tradition to teach the young through stories and parables, but since the old tales about the struggles of Kra-ell heroines, the tribal wars that had decimated the number of males, and the queen who had altered their future held no meaning under Igor's rule, she relied on human fairytales to teach them the basic tenets of what it meant to be honorable and to strive to become the best versions of themselves.

"Go ahead." He waved at the small desk in the corner of his office.

"Thank you."

Jade hated that she had to do it under his watchful eye as well, but what choice did she have?

Igor had told her time and again that she should be thankful that he was so generous with her, and that the privilege of using the internet would remain hers only as long as she was his prime female. Jade would have gladly passed that dubious honor to another, but the privileges that came with it were worth the sacrifices. As the prime, she had some maneuvering room to ease the lives of the other females and their young.

Besides, she still would have been forced into his bed whether she was prime or not, so the only thing she would have accomplished by acting up would have been to lose the little freedoms she'd fought so hard for.

She was too smart to let that happen just to satisfy her need to lash out.

Sitting at the small desk with her back to Igor, she flipped the laptop open and typed the subject of her search into the browser—becoming the best version of yourself. There were many Kra-ell parables that examined the subject and inspired youngsters to push harder for excellence, but they didn't fit the circumstances of the children living in the compound. She needed new stories that would speak to them and inspire them.

Scrolling through a long list of articles and blog posts, she clicked on one that looked promising, read a few paragraphs, and then continued to the next. After about an hour, she had two articles printed out and a list of topics she could develop further. That was more than enough, but she wasn't ready to leave the internet yet.

Hopefully, someone would come into Igor's office and distract him long enough for her to find out what was going on in the world. It would be even better if he left while letting her stay.

Jade had done that so many times before that she no longer feared discovery. Igor had never caught her or called her out on that, so either no one was checking, or he didn't mind her little forays into forbidden websites.

After all, there was nothing she could do with that information aside from satisfying her curiosity. No one knew that she even existed, and even if there was someone searching for her and the other females, she couldn't ask for their help because of Igor's compulsion.

An hour later, she was still scrolling and pretending to read more articles about reaching one's full potential, but no one had come into the office, and Igor hadn't left even once. She was about to give up and end her search when she clicked on the last article on the sixth page, and a picture of a man in a white ceremonial robe came up.

He looked ridiculous, like one of the prophets from human scriptures, but there was something familiar about his dark eyes. Leaning closer to the screen, Jade enlarged the picture, and barely contained her gasp. Those were Kra-ell eyes, a hybrid's eyes to be more precise, and she knew who they belonged to. The one who'd run off years ago, the hybrid compeller who had been able to throw off her hold on him.

Veskar, who according to the virtual brochure was calling himself Emmett Haderech these days, ran a spiritual retreat that taught, among other things, how to achieve one's full potential.

It was such a fundamental Kra-ell concept that it had to be him.

Finally, she had found a member of her tribe who was free. Except, Veskar hadn't been a member of her tribe for many years. He'd always been smart, so she wasn't surprised that he'd used his compulsion ability to make money, and since he'd been doing that for decades, he was also smart enough to avoid discovery.

Good for him.

Should she contact him?

There wasn't much he could do to help her, unless he'd found another Kra-ell tribe after leaving hers. His compulsion ability was no match for Igor's, so on his own, Veskar was useless to her. Besides, even if he could, she doubted that he would be inclined to help her. There had been no love lost between them. But he might be willing to help the other females of their tribe.

Did he even know what had happened to their compound? Did he know that his father was dead?

But even if he could do nothing to help them, just knowing that someone on the outside knew that they were alive and that they were being held against their will would bring Jade more hope than she'd had in twenty-two years.

It wasn't likely that the queen would send new settlers after so many years, but if she did, Veskar could tell them about his tribe's fate.

The problem was figuring out a way to contact him without alerting Igor.

50

DARLENE

"Good morning." Darlene stopped next to Mollie and James's table. "Can I join you?"

Of the nine paranormals, they were the only two in her age group. Mollie was a year or two younger and had post-cognition ability, and James, who was a remote viewer and a weak telepath. He was in his mid-fifties but didn't look it.

Mollie smiled. "Of course."

"Good morning." James leaned over and pulled out a chair for her. "How are things going on the other side of the fence?"

Darlene put her plate down on the table and sat down. "Can't you just read my mind?" she teased.

Eleanor had told her that James's newfound telepathic ability was limited to feelings and impressions. If he could read her actual thoughts, Darlene wouldn't have been sitting with him and his girlfriend at breakfast.

"Let me see." He closed his eyes. "You feel disappointment, and I can tell that it has to do with a man." He opened his eyes. "Am I right?"

"You are. Good guess." She took a sip of her coffee to hide her grimace.

A message from Eric had waited on her phone this morning, letting her know that he couldn't make it after all.

It shouldn't have surprised her.

A guy like him wouldn't put so much effort into hooking up with a woman who was older than him and looked it.

The fact that he'd left the message at three o'clock in the morning probably meant that he'd done it at the end of a date, no doubt with some twenty-something hottie who had still been in his bed when he typed up the text.

Except, the message also said that he was flying Kaia's family for a visit on Saturday, and they would all stay for the weekend, so there was that.

Darlene had no right to feel jealous, and she should be glad that he was coming at all, but she would believe it when she saw him.

"It's not a guess," James said. "I can read your aura, and it seems muted, which indicates either depression or disappointment, but since you don't seem depressed, I assume that it's the latter."

She gave him a tight smile. "I thought that Spencer was the aura reader."

"I am," the guy said from the next table over. "And I agree with James. Your aura is dimmed compared to how it was yesterday, so you must have gotten some bad news today."

His girlfriend just smiled. Sofia's claim to fame was the ability to affect the flip of a coin or dice, but according to Eleanor, her talent was negligible.

Darlene shook her head. "You people are freaky."

Mollie laughed. "We will try to behave when your scientists get here." She glanced at her watch. "Are they joining us for breakfast?"

"It's still early, but they'll be here." Darlene put a tiny bit of jam on her toast. "William is meeting them here."

As the dining hall door opened, she hoped it was William with members of his team, but it was just Eleanor, who walked in with Abigail, Dylan, and Andy.

"You are up early." She regarded her flock. "Did you join Darlene and William in the gym this morning?"

Darlene snorted. "I had the place to myself. William didn't show up, and when I called him, he grumbled something about sleeping only two hours and hung up on me."

"He and Kaia make a cute couple." Dylan pulled out a chair for Abigail at the table next to Spencer and Sofia.

Was he suggesting that William had spent the night with Kaia and that was why he hadn't shown up for their swimming session?

Evidently, the guy wasn't a good judge of character despite his paranormal talent. It was something called claircognizance, which was supposedly the ability to acquire psychic knowledge without knowing how or why he knew it.

"They are not together," Darlene said.

Dylan arched a brow. "Are you sure? I had a strong feeling that they were."

Breakfast with the paranormals was turning into an episode of *The Twilight Zone*, and Darlene was starting to doubt the wisdom of mixing the two groups together. If the scientists had heard that conversation, they would have laughed their butts off.

On the other hand, maybe it wasn't such a bad idea to introduce them to phenomena they couldn't explain. It might get them thinking, and it might teach some humility to those know-it-alls who believed that science had all the answers.

Perhaps they were right, and one day the paranormal would acquire a scientific explanation, but for that to happen, they first needed to acknowledge that the phenomena were real.

WILLIAM

*A*s a loud ringing woke William up, he groaned and reached for his phone, intending to turn the alarm off and go back to sleep, but it wasn't the alarm. It was a phone call, probably Darlene calling him again to get him to the gym.

"I'm not swimming today," he barked without even opening his eyes. "I got in bed less than two hours ago." He ended the call, dropped the phone on the night-stand, and when the ringing started again, he covered his head with a pillow.

If anyone needed him urgently, they could get ahold of one of the Guardians and send them over to knock on his door.

When the ringing stopped, he sighed in relief, but a moment later it started again. He was going to fire Darlene and send her back to the village.

With a groan, he tossed the pillow aside and grabbed the phone, opening his eyes this time to check that it was really her and he wasn't about to bark at Kian.

It was indeed Darlene, but as he glanced at the time, his anger flew out the window. It was quarter to eight, and he was late collecting his team from the dining hall.

"Hi," he answered as he threw the blanket off. "I'm sorry about before. I thought it was still early in the morning."

She chuckled. "As long as you get here in the next fifteen minutes, you're forgiven. I told everyone to grab another cup of coffee, and I asked the kitchen staff to keep it open. Do you want me to prepare a plate for you?"

"Maybe something to go."

"No problem."

"You're the best, Darlene. See you soon."

And to think that a moment ago he wanted to fire her. The woman deserved a raise.

When he was dressed and ready to go out the door, his phone rang again, but this time it was Roni.

That was odd. The guy never started his workday before nine in the morning.

"Good morning," William answered as he closed the door behind him. "You're calling early. What's the emergency?"

"After your text message from last night, I figured it was urgent and came in an hour earlier to check on Kaia's friend."

William had sent it before going to sleep, and he hadn't expected Roni to do anything about it right away.

"Thank you. What did you find?"

"He booked a flight to the Maldives. Coincidence?"

A shiver ran down William's spine. "Perhaps. The Maldives is not just a hub for the Brotherhood. Anything else?"

"That's it. After that, he disappeared from the face of the net. His emails remained unopened, and he didn't send any. Not from his main address, anyway. He might have one of those throwaway emails. His bank account shows a fifty-thousand-dollar deposit right before his trip, but there was no activity beyond automatic payments that kept going. The same is true for his credit cards. There were a couple of charges from airports on the day of the flight, and nothing since."

Fifty thousand dollars wasn't a big enough amount to pay a scientist for participating in a secret project that was supposed to last several months, but it could have been just the deposit. Was that a new mode of operation for the Brotherhood?

According to Lokan, brainiacs were lured to the island by promises of free, unlimited sex and then returned to their homes at the end of their sex vacation. But maybe the Brotherhood had started using an additional tactic and was luring them with a promise of a job?

Traffickers had been employing that method for ages, promising young girls and their families a modeling job, or even something more mundane like a nanny position with a rich family. The Brotherhood might have decided to expand their recruiting net and implemented a method they were all too familiar with from their trafficking operations.

After the men got to the island and realized that there was no project, they could be blackmailed into silence by compromising pictures taken of them with the ladies. Either that or something more nefarious, like offing them once they'd done their job and impregnated a Dormant.

"So, what's our next step?"

"I would suggest asking Lokan for help. You have the guy's picture, so if he's on the island, he shouldn't be too hard to find."

"If he's in the Dormants' enclosure, which is what the brainiacs are brought to the island for, then Lokan can't help us. He doesn't have access to them."

Roni chuckled.

"It's Lokan we are talking about. The compeller who can walk into people's dreams and who plotted to kidnap Ella and Vivian. He will find a way."

"I don't want him to take unnecessary risks to help a human."

"Of course not. But he might be able to help without exposing himself to risk. It doesn't hurt to ask."

"You're right. What time is it in China?"

"It's eleven at night. He should be awake."

CHAPTER 51

"I'll send him a text. Thanks, Roni. I really appreciate you coming into the lab early to do this for me."

"Hey, that's what friends are for. Good luck with Kaia."

How the hell could Roni know that there was something going on between them? William hadn't even talked with him since Kaia's arrival.

"What do you mean?"

"I spoke with my mother. She says that you are smitten and that Kaia is lovely."

William was going to have words with Darlene. She was supposed to keep everything going on in Safe Haven a secret, but apparently, she didn't think that included his private affairs.

"Kaia is nineteen."

"So what? I was eighteen when I met Sylvia. She was twenty-six at the time, and look at us now. We are living our happily ever after. The heart doesn't care about age, and as long as the lady is not a minor, it's not a crime to fall in love with her."

"I'm not in love."

"I wasn't either, but then I was. Keep an open mind. That's all I'm saying."

"I will. Thanks again, Roni." William ended the call and checked the time.

He was beyond late, but Darlene was keeping the team occupied, and they could wait a few minutes longer.

Walking at a brisk pace, he typed up a text to Lokan, asking him to call back.

Lokan's call came in a couple seconds later. "What can I do for you, William?"

After he explained the situation, Lokan heaved a sigh. "I can ask my servant to snoop around. He's human, so he can get in almost everywhere, and my compulsion keeps him from telling anyone what he is doing for me. I'll call him tomorrow."

"Thank you, Lokan. I appreciate your help."

"Is this guy important to the research you're conducting? Or is it just a favor for your lady friend?"

Evidently, the rumor about his infatuation with Kaia had spread so quickly that it managed to reach as far as China.

"It's a favor for my friend, who is crucial to the project. The other people on my team are just good enough to be her helpers. Without her, we don't have a chance."

"I understand. You need to keep her happy to get her to do her best."

"Precisely."

"I'll do what I can."

52

KAIA

*K*aia nibbled on a piece of toast and watched Corinne and Owen exchange smiles when they thought no one was looking. The two had obviously hooked up last night, and she was envious.

Corinne was older than Owen by at least eight years, and it didn't seem to bother either of them. Why did William have to be such a prude?

Yesterday, she'd finally managed to break through his resistance, and for a few glorious moments she'd basked in her success, but he'd put a damper on that with his insistence that other than kissing, there would be nothing more between them until the project was done.

What century was he living in?

Talk about frustrating.

Kaia had no problem with taking it slow, but by slow she meant a couple of weeks, maybe a month, but not more than that. She had waited long enough for the right guy to come along, and now that she'd found him, she was antsy and impatient to explore this thing between them.

She'd never met a guy who'd made her feel like this before, and not all of it was good. She loved how awakened her body felt, how aware, but her brain was functioning in a diminished capacity because most of its bandwidth was taken up by William.

If she wanted to shorten the wait time by breaking the code faster, she needed to get her head back in the game. But she needed to be realistic. She'd seen those alien scribbles, and although she could discern a pattern right away, she had no database to compare them to and no software to run them through. It would be like translating a foreign language with no key. It wasn't impossible, but it wasn't something that could be done quickly either.

On the other side of the dining hall, Kylie laughed, drawing Kaia's attention. She was chatting with the older couple, James and Mollie, if Kaia remembered their names correctly, the only two who lingered after the other paranormals had

148

left along with their boss. Even Darlene had excused herself, saying that she had an urgent matter to attend to and couldn't wait for William.

There were nine paranormals in Eleanor's team, and Kaia had tried to memorize their names when they had been introduced, but she remembered only some of them. Their fascinating talents, though, she remembered vividly.

Perhaps she should talk with Eleanor about her own paranormal thing? Were memories of a past life considered a paranormal talent?

Probably not.

Besides, Kaia had learned early on not to talk about that. People reacted with either dismissal or amusement when she talked about her strange memories, and no one other than Cheryl had ever believed that they were real, not even her own mother.

When Kaia had told her that she remembered being a man in her past life, her mother suggested visiting a therapist. She'd thought that Kaia was making up a male persona as a result of the trauma of losing her father, and that she was coping with grief by clinging to the belief that a person didn't end when their bodies quit.

It made sense, and it was a comforting thought, but her memories were real.

Kaia had found references to Edgar Rosu in a couple of books dealing with the history of mathematics and the different mathematicians who had contributed to the field throughout recorded history. Rosu, a mathematician who'd lived through both World Wars, hadn't been famous enough to be featured in a documentary she might have seen as a kid, so she couldn't have heard about him and somehow assimilated his persona. Besides, she'd had those strange memories even before her father had died, and she even remembered telling him about them.

He'd laughed, ruffled her hair, and said that he would always love her, even if she turned out to be a grumpy old man.

Kaia had been three or four at the time, but the memory of that exchange was so vivid in her mind that it still brought tears to her eyes every time she thought about it.

Her father would have never suggested a shrink.

Not that she'd ever gone to see one. She'd wiggled out of it by lying and saying that she'd made it up. Her mom had figured that it had been a phase, and there had been no more talk of visiting a psychologist.

The only one who she'd confided in was Cheryl, but the secret was safe with her sister. The girl was like a vault, and no secret she'd been entrusted with ever got out.

"Good morning, team." William strode over to their table. "I apologize for being late. I had an important phone call I had to take."

He seemed a little frazzled.

"Did you work all night?" Kaia asked.

"Most of it," he admitted. "Is everyone done and ready for their first day of puzzling out a mystery?"

"I am," Kaia said. "Darlene left a bag for you." She handed it to him. "She asked me to remind you to drink water."

He glanced longingly at the coffee dispenser and then nodded. "I'd better stick to water for now." He opened the dining room's door and held it open until they all stepped out.

"What's wrong with coffee?" Kaia asked. "I saw you drinking it yesterday."

"I need to limit my consumption of caffeine." He chuckled. "People say that I talk at the speed of a machine gun, and Darlene noticed that it gets worse after I drink coffee."

Kaia hadn't noticed that. Had he been trying to slow down for her sake?

He shouldn't have bothered. She had no problem with fast talkers. She had a problem with people who talked too slowly.

Patience was not one of Kaia's virtues.

53

WILLIAM

*W*illiam had been debating all morning whether to tell Kaia about what he had learned from Roni. It was nothing earth-shattering, and suspecting that Anthony was on the Doomers' island was pure speculation on their part, so it wasn't worth mentioning even if he could tell her about it. All he had for her was Anthony's last known location, and that could wait for later. He didn't want to raise her hopes and distract her from her work.

In only a few hours, she was making tremendous progress and pulling the entire team behind her.

Following her advice, he'd printed several pages for her and her three helpers, and he'd let them brainstorm ideas and jot down notes. Naturally, Kaia was the one leading the effort, and to distract her was to slow down their progress.

As a knock sounded on his open door, William lifted his head. "Do you need me?"

Standing in the doorway to his office with a yellow pad clutched in her hand, Kaia gave him a suggestive smile. "Always. May I come in?"

Swallowing, he motioned for the chair in front of his desk. "Please." He was already hard just from that one sultry look and grateful for the desk hiding his reaction.

She closed the door behind her, walked over, and pulled out a chair. "Do you want to see what I have so far?"

"Of course."

"It's not much, but I think that these symbols represent the four bases. I just don't know which one is which yet, and to figure it out, I need to see a larger sample. You said that you would prepare one for me."

"I did, but I don't want you working on it in front of the others. You will have to do it in here."

It would be torturous to have her sitting in front of him all day, but he would leave the door open so that neither of them would succumb to temptation, and so the others wouldn't think they were doing anything inappropriate.

"Okay." She seemed all too happy to comply, and William had a feeling her reasons had nothing to do with the genetic code she was eager to translate.

"I didn't mean now. It's your first day, and I think it should be spent on bonding and learning to work as a team. You can start tomorrow."

Looking disappointed, she nodded but remained seated. "I hate to be a nag, but did you call your hacker friend?"

"Roni called me this morning. He found out that Anthony booked a flight to the Maldives around the time you said he'd accepted the job. But since it's a popular tourist destination, he might have gone there to relax before starting the project. Did he tell you anything about where he was going?"

She shook her head. "Tony couldn't afford a vacation in a place like that unless he got a big advance or a signing bonus, and he didn't mention either. But that could have been confidential as well, so he couldn't tell me about it. When I nagged him to give me some details, he said that it was located on the other side of the world. So maybe he was referring to the Maldives."

"The islands are also a hub, so he could have continued to Indonesia, Australia, New Zealand, and even Japan, but Roni didn't find any connecting flights booked under Anthony's name."

She frowned. "So that's it? That's all Roni, the great hacker, has been able to find?"

"He's not done yet. He just wanted to let us know that he found something." William smiled. "Don't underestimate what he has done. Roni is swamped with work, and he came to the lab an hour earlier than usual to do this for you."

When she still didn't look impressed, William added, "Just so you can fully appreciate what a sacrifice that was, you should know that Roni is not a morning person, and he's never volunteered to come in early for any of the other projects he's working on, some of which are much more important to us than your missing friend."

"I appreciate that, I really do." She let out a breath. "It's just that I was hoping for a clue, and unless Roni can find out where Tony went after arriving at the Maldives, that's a dead end."

There was another possibility that had occurred to William that Kaia wasn't going to like.

Leaning over the desk, he took her hand. "The Maldives are also a popular transshipment destination in the illicit drug trade. Do you know if Anthony dealt in drugs?"

She snorted. "Tony didn't even smoke pot. He was just your average nerdy postdoc, looking for a job that paid more than minimum wage."

"Are you sure? Maybe he didn't use drugs but dealt in them? Did he ever flaunt money he shouldn't have had?"

Kaia shook her head. "He drove an ancient yellow Toyota hatchback that was worth less than a hundred bucks, and his mom bought his clothes at Costco. That's the opposite of flaunting."

William frowned. "He was twenty-eight, and his mother still bought his clothes for him?"

"He lived at home and worked sixteen-hour days. Tony wanted to head a lab someday and to teach, but the competition for professorial positions is brutal, and he isn't the brightest of the bunch. He was struggling to publish a paper in a decent scientific magazine, and I think that was what eventually broke him and the reason he took on the secret project. He was starting to realize that he would never get the publications he needed to move his academic career forward, and that he would have to settle for work in the private sector."

"Is that so bad?"

"It was for Tony. His dream has always been to become a professor."

54

KAIA

*K*aia left William's office disappointed, and not just because the information the hacker had found about Tony wasn't much.

Except for the brief moment when William had taken her hand, he'd been all business, acting as if what they'd shared in the lab yesterday had never happened.

Perhaps she should visit the security office and ask to see the recording to prove to herself that she hadn't dreamt the kiss up.

It wouldn't be the first time Kaia had had dreams so vivid that she confused them with real memories. But she'd told Cheryl about it when she'd called her last night, so unless the call had been part of the dream, the kiss must have been real.

As Kaia sat at the team's round conference table, Corinne eyed her with a smirk on her face. "I thought that you abandoned us in favor of our handsome boss."

Kaia didn't feel like explaining herself, but she had to say something. "I showed him our progress."

"Right," Owen murmured without lifting his head off the page he was scribbling notes on.

Ignoring his comment, Kaia peeked at what he'd written. "What do you have there?"

"Nothing mind-bending. I'm just translating a couple of lines assuming that this one is the G, this one is the A, and so on. Then I'll try a different combination to see which one looks like something I recognize."

It was a good idea, but the problem with that was that there were many more symbols than just the four representing the familiar nitrogenous bases.

"You should ask William to write a software for us to feed the symbols into," Corinne said. "Doing this by hand will take forever. Darlene told me that he's a genius with software development, but he's also a hardware man. He's an inventor."

CHAPTER 54

Pride for William swelled in Kaia's chest. "We have to figure out what we need first."

William had never bragged about his accomplishments, but Kaia had figured that out from his comments about lying awake at night and thinking about new ideas and solutions to problems he was having with what he was working on.

"He's handsome for a brainiac," Kylie said. "If he lost some weight, he would be a hunk."

The comment angered Kaia much more than it should have. "Watch it, Kylie. The people in security hear and see everything that happens here. You don't want to offend the boss. Besides, William is perfect the way he is. A guy like him doesn't have time to spend hours in the gym just so he can look pretty for the ladies. He has much more important things to do."

Owen, who was skinny as a twig, pretended not to be part of the girly conversation, but she saw him smiling under his breath as if he had some advantage over William because of that. He couldn't hold a candle to her guy, not in looks, and certainly not in brains.

Looking up at the cameras that weren't even trying to be hidden, Kylie winced and lifted her hand to hide her lips, dipped her head, and whispered, "I didn't say anything bad. I said that he was handsome for a brainiac. He just needs to get rid of the little padding he carries around the middle."

Kaia shrugged, not bothering to speak quietly or hide her mouth. "I like it that he doesn't have washboard abs. What's more pleasant to hug, a plush teddy bear or a Barbie doll Ken?"

Laughing, Corinne followed Kylie's example and lifted her hand to hide her lips from the camera, whispering "That depends on the purpose of the hug and who you're hugging." She cast Owen a lascivious glance. "I like my boyfriends thin."

"To each her own." Kaia tried to keep the irritation out of her tone and rose to her feet. "Anyone want coffee before we go back to what we are paid to do?"

"I can use a cup," Kylie said.

Corinne and Owen were too busy eye-screwing each other to respond.

Anger still pulsing through her, Kaia filled the coffeemaker's tank with water, and pushed a pod into the slot with too much force, so it dropped into the trash compartment.

Cursing under her breath, she pulled it out and tried again, pushing gently until it snapped into the slot.

She loved everything about William, and she didn't want to change a thing about him. The problem was that he didn't feel the same. He thought that she was too young for him, and technically he was correct, but he didn't have the whole story and wasn't going to get it either.

55

WILLIAM

*K*aia had left the door slightly open, so William couldn't help but hear the entire discussion regarding his hunkiness or lack thereof, including the whispered parts.

He loved that Kaia had gotten offended on his behalf when Kylie had suggested that he needed to lose weight, and he loved even more that she had no issue with his padding. If that was what she liked, he had no problem being her cuddly teddy bear. Hell, it was the perfect excuse to stop swimming every morning.

But what had put a big grin on his face was that she'd defended him.

The girl was a fighter, and she took no prisoners.

He wondered who she'd gotten that from. Karen Locke seemed like a delicate, soft-spoken woman, but he'd seen the steel determination in her dark-brown eyes, not to mention the way Gilbert had silently deferred to her despite the alpha-male show he'd put on.

The guy was an extrovert who loved making waves, but his partner was no less formidable and probably more dangerous. If either of them had an issue with him not treating Kaia right, he would have been much more afraid of her mother's retaliation than Gilbert's.

When his phone rang, William knew it was Max before looking at the screen.

"Did you hear that?" Max asked. "Because if you didn't, you can come up here, and I'll replay it for you. I can even make you a copy for safe keeping."

"Yeah, I did, and thanks for the offer, but don't make a copy. That's not what the surveillance is for. We are not supposed to spy on their private conversations."

"Yeah, yeah. They are also supposed to be working instead of gossiping about their hunky employer. Way to go for your girlfriend, though. The way she defended your honor made me all tingly on the inside and seriously jealous. I want one just like her."

William groaned. He wasn't going to hear the end of it from Max and the other Guardians. As he'd suspected, they'd all seen the recording of his and Kaia's kiss by now, and he regretted not erasing it last night. Although, it probably would have been too late anyway. He had no doubt that the Guardians on duty watching the kiss live had made a copy to show the others. They were bored, and they had nothing better to do than gossip.

"Kaia is not my girlfriend. She's a young human who's infatuated with me for some inexplicable reason. She'll get over it."

Liar. He didn't believe that she would, and neither would he, so why had he said that?

Max chuckled. "I'd say that the epic kiss proves otherwise but I digress. I also called to tell you that lunch is on its way and to open the door for Paul."

"Thanks. The breakfast Darlene packed for me is long gone, and I'm hungry." He rose to his feet. "I'll see you later." He ended the call before the Guardian came up with more comments about Kaia.

That was the problem with living and working with family. Nothing was sacred, and everyone felt as if they had the right to meddle in everyone else's business.

One would think that centuries-old immortals would act more mature than that, but as he'd realized a long time ago, characters didn't change with age, especially when the bodies housing them didn't reflect that and were still working perfectly. Calamities and happy times had a short-term effect, either dampening or raising moods, but after a while, a person's character returned to its base state.

"Lunch is here," he said as he walked through the lab. "I need another set of hands to help me carry the delivery to the break room."

"I'm on it." Kaia got up to her feet and followed him to the door. "Are we getting Safe Haven's standard fare or can we place orders next time?"

"I wish we could, but we get whatever they make in the kitchen on a given day." He lifted his head, so his eyes aligned with the scanner and then took a step back as the door started to swing in.

"It leaves a lot to be desired," Kaia said.

As the door swung all the way, the Guardian delivering the food nodded at William and smiled knowingly at Kaia. "Here you go." He handed William the tray piled high with covered dishes and Kaia the two paper bags that he'd carried hanging from his forearms. "Someone should have thought to build an elevator in here. I could have wheeled a cart instead of carrying all that."

"There were schedule and budget constraints." William gave him a smile. "Thanks for bringing it in."

As Paul saluted and pivoted on his heel, William moved away from the door, and it started closing.

"How did you get away with not installing an elevator in here?" Kaia asked as she followed him to the break room. "Isn't it required to make all new public places accessible?"

"I wasn't in charge of the building project, so I don't know, but this lab is supposed to be the opposite of a public place. The idea was to make it as inaccessible as possible, not the other way around."

KAIA

*K*aia went through the notes her team had collected, including the ones she'd written, and when she was done, she looked up at the cameras and moved the pages so they weren't in direct view of it.

William was so concerned with security, and yet the people in the security office could see everything that was going on in the lab, and what was worse, they were recording it. It would be child's play to zoom in and read not only the notes but also the photocopies of the originals that William had given them.

Her stomach was rumbling, reminding her that it was time to call it a day and go get dinner, but she sensed that she was starting to get a whiff of an idea, and she wanted to stay and run with it before it dissipated.

The others had left more than an hour ago, but William had returned after escorting them out, and he was probably hungry as well. The lunch they'd eaten in the break room was more of Safe Haven's healthy fare, which was more suitable for rabbits than people, and it had left her unsatisfied.

It seemed like that was the story of her life lately.

"Ugh, don't be so dramatic." She lifted the stack of papers and strode to William's office.

He lifted his head and smiled. "Done?"

"For today. I'm hungry, and there are a few things I want to talk with you about." She glanced at the camera. "But not in here."

He blushed, probably assuming that she wanted to play, which she did, but it wasn't about that.

"It has to do with a security concern I have."

"You do?" He took his glasses off, looking at her with his incredibly blue eyes. "I assure you that it's top-notch."

"Yeah, you've told me that." She motioned for him to get up. "Let's talk on the way to the dining hall."

"Okay." He gave her an indulgent smile.

She didn't say a word until they were out of the building. "You must be aware that the people in security can see everything we are working on. On top of that, everything gets recorded. How hard would it be for them to make a copy and sell the info?"

"Very hard." He took her hand. "First of all, I know each one of the guys working there, and I trust them implicitly, and secondly, no one can make a copy of the recording or send it out. It's a closed circuit, and it erases every twenty-four hours."

Kaia shook her head. "Even I know how to circumvent that. I could just whip out my phone and record whatever is on the monitor screen. It might come out blurry, but that's easy to fix with the right equipment."

He chuckled. "That's precisely what those idiots did with the recording of our kiss. But as I said, I trust these people. I've known them and worked with them for many years."

"You are too trusting." She followed him inside the dining hall. "We need to continue this talk later."

Her teammates were already gone, and the paranormals must have eaten early as well. A single red-headed guy whose name she'd forgotten was sitting a couple of tables over. He was the aura reader who was about her age. Spencer? Was that his name?

When he lifted his head and smiled, she waved. "Hi. How was dinner?"

"Terrible," he mouthed. "I say we fire the cook."

She gave him the thumbs up. "I'm adding my name to that petition."

After they loaded their plates with mushy stuff that was barely recognizable, they walked over to one of the tables and William pulled out a chair for her. "Why the sudden concern with security?"

"Thank you." She sat down. "Given that I just started working today, I wouldn't call it sudden." She leaned closer to him. "I was going over what we've done today, and it occurred to me that one of the cameras was pointing directly at the table where I was sitting." She collected some of the mush onto her fork. "The stuff we are working on might be dangerous and worth a lot of money to someone with dastardly plans."

"What makes you think that?"

"I have a hunch." She put the fork in her mouth.

Surprisingly, the mush was not as bad as it looked. She tasted zucchini, eggplant, and peas.

For the next several minutes they ate in silence, until the red-headed guy stopped by their table on his way out.

"You have a very strange aura," he told Kaia. "I've been watching you for a while to make sure I wasn't seeing things."

Kaia tensed. Could he sense her previous self? Wasn't she the same person, the same soul, just in a different body?

Hopefully, he wouldn't say that she had a masculine aura.

"What do you mean by strange?"

"You have two auras, and I've never seen anyone who has two. One is so bright that it's almost blinding, and in comparison, the other one is dimmed, but if it was on its own, it would have been just like any other aura. The other thing that's strange about the secondary one is that it flickers on and off. One moment it's there, and the next it's gone."

"What does that mean?" William asked. "Does Kaia have a split personality?"

"That's what I thought." The guy threaded his fingers through his curls. "Do you?" he asked.

"Not as far as I know." She forced a smile. "One aura probably belongs to my big ego, and the other one to its ugly twin. Sometimes I think that I'm the most advanced human in the world, and other times I think that I'm a big fraud."

Both statements were exaggerations meant to throw the guy off, but there was a kernel of truth in them.

Kaia had a big ego, which she tried to wrestle down so she wouldn't appear condescending, but she also owed her so-called genius to things she'd learned in a previous life, so she was a bit of a fraud.

The guy gave her a tight smile. "I just hope that you don't have a parasitic spirit latching onto your bright aura."

Goosebumps rose over her arms. "Is that a thing? Have you encountered a spirit like that before?"

"No, but when I was thinking about a possible explanation for what I was seeing, that was one of the things that popped into my mind."

Rubbing her arms, she let out a relieved breath. "You scared me."

"Sorry. I didn't mean to." He raked his fingers through his red curls. "Well, goodnight. I'll see you tomorrow at breakfast."

"Goodnight, Spencer," William said.

When the door closed behind the guy, he smiled. "Well, that was odd."

"Tell me about it." Kaia rubbed her arms again. "He shouldn't be going around and creeping people out with his so-called aura readings."

William lifted one shoulder in half a shrug. "I bet he doesn't do that outside of this place. He knows that it's safe to give voice to his unique talents here."

"I guess."

Life must be difficult for those paranormals. They had an extrasensory perception that they hadn't asked for, and when they shared what they knew, they were regarded as freaks or lunatics. Still, Spencer should have exercised more discretion before blurting out things like parasitic spirits.

Kaia pushed her plate away. "Are we done? I feel like taking a shower to scrub that other aura off."

"We are." William rose to his feet and collected their plates. "Is the need to scrub urgent? Or are you up for a walk on the beach? You can share the rest of your concerns with me while we get some fresh air."

"That sounds even better than soap and water. Let's go."

57

WILLIAM

*T*he second aura Spencer had seen was no doubt the middle-aged man living inside Kaia's head, but the way she'd reacted made William think that she didn't know what he was or where he'd come from. Otherwise, she wouldn't have been so freaked out by Spencer's comment.

When she rubbed her arms for the third time, he wrapped his arm around her. "It's windy." It was only a gentle breeze, but it was chilly, and it gave him a great excuse to do that. "Do you want to get a jacket?"

It had been on the tip of his tongue to tell her that her teddy bear could keep her warm, but then he would reveal that he'd overheard what she'd said to Kylie and Corinne.

"I'm fine." Kaia leaned closer to him. "It's so beautiful out here, and it will get dark soon. I don't want to miss any of it."

A dense marine layer hung low over the beach, coloring everything a mono-chromatic gray and making the ocean look ominous as the waves forcefully splashed against the rocks. The sound was so loud that it was making conversation difficult.

Nevertheless, William loved the coast's harsh beauty, the salty smell of the water, and most of all, the feel of Kaia's back under his arm.

She had on one of her flimsy T-shirts, and he could almost feel the texture of her skin under the fabric. It was perfectly smooth, and although she was wearing a bra, she probably didn't need it to hold up her generous breasts.

He had to admit that there were certain advantages to youth, and those fleeting gifts of human beauty shouldn't be squandered. Then again, they were meant to please human males who were also young and in their physical prime, so healthy babies could be born.

The survival of the species was a delicate and beautiful dance, just not always. Sometimes, things got ugly, especially for young females.

At the thought, his fangs started elongating and his venom glands filled up. His aggression was spurred by the need to protect her from anyone who wished her harm, but since there were no potential threats lurking at Safe Haven, it was entirely uncalled for, and so atypical of him that he scared himself.

What was it about Kaia that brought out those primitive male urges?

Did it have anything to do with her double aura?

He moved his hand to rub her arm up and down. "Do you have any idea what Spencer was talking about?"

"No clue," she answered immediately as if she'd been waiting for him to ask. "I think that auras are bullshit. Our bodies emit an electrical charge, and sensitives might be able to sense it, or maybe even see it, but I most definitely do not emit more electricity than the next person."

He widened his eyes in mock surprise. "You don't? I think that you are the brightest star in the sky. Are my eyes playing tricks on me?"

She tilted her head and looked up at him with a smile tugging on her lips. "We both need to get our prescriptions checked, and maybe Spencer needs glasses as well. I thought that I saw your eyes glowing on several occasions, but it must have been a reflection from either your or my lenses."

William swallowed. "It must have."

He knew that his eyes had been emitting light, but he'd thought that she hadn't noticed, and he'd been glad that he hadn't needed to thrall her to forget what she'd seen. With how precious Kaia's mind was, he was afraid to get in there and cause even the slightest damage. Thankfully, she explained the glow away and he hadn't been forced to thrall her.

"You wanted to talk more about security," he changed the subject.

"Right. I got distracted by this magnificent view." She looked at him and not the ocean. "You said that the guys working in security were idiots, which probably meant that they aren't the sharpest tools in the shed, but you also said that you trust them. What if they are as trustworthy as you believe they are, but they blurt out something about the research we are doing in the wrong place, and at the wrong time? Someone who wants to find out what you are working on could overhear, and that someone might get motivated to infiltrate the lab or its computers and steal the information."

"Don't worry about it. I've got all angles covered."

"That's not good enough. That stuff is alien technology, and it's biological in nature. If those are instructions for how to build human bodies, people would kill to get their hands on them. It scares me."

She was so amazingly close to the truth that the short hairs on the back of William's neck prickled.

"How did you figure that after one day of investigating?"

Kaia shrugged. "For now, it's just a hunch, but I'm usually right. You were impressed by the research papers I published, right?"

"Very impressed. The subject matter was well researched, the calculations impeccable, and the findings were very well substantiated. I couldn't find fault with any of your methods or results."

She smirked. "Would it surprise you to know that it didn't take me more than a couple of months to submit for review and that I didn't have to make any revisions before my papers were published?"

"It would. That rarely happens." They reached an outcropping that created a natural enclave protected from the wind. "It often takes years to publish a paper in a respectable journal." He led her to the enclave and sat down with her on a flat rock shaped like a bench.

"The reason the articles took me so little time and didn't need revisions was that I knew what would work and what wouldn't." She scooted closer to him, and he wrapped his arm around her. "Gilbert has a nose for crooks and fakes, and I have a nose for science. The funny thing is that we are not related."

58

KAIA

*W*illiam took her hand. "You're probably the smartest person I've ever met, and I've met my share of very smart people. Did you ever hear of Perfect Match?"

"The virtual fantasy studios?"

He nodded.

"Who hasn't? Their commercials are all over. What about them?"

"I helped the founders work out the kinks in their programming. Those guys are brilliant, and the machine they invented blew my mind." He smiled down at her. "I think it was the first time in my life I was jealous because they came up with an idea that was more revolutionary than any of mine."

"But they needed you to work out the bugs, so you were smarter than them."

He shook his head. "It's much easier to find mistakes in someone else's work than to create something original. They were too close to it to see where the problem was."

William's modesty was one more thing Kaia loved about him. Was she in love with him, though?

She'd never been in love before, so she didn't know the difference between love and sexual attraction or infatuation. Furthermore, he was sending her mixed signals, and she didn't know where she stood with him.

Yesterday, he'd told her that kissing was all he would allow until the project was done, and today he'd been a little distant. But then he had taken her for a walk along the coastline, which could count as a romantic gesture, and he led her to this secluded spot that was perfect for making out.

Did he just want another kiss, or did he want more than that?

Kaia was all for more, their proximity and William's unique masculine scent sending heat down to her center, but she wasn't going to push him. It was bad when guys did that to girls, and it was equally bad when the pressure came from the girl.

That being said, she could hint at wanting more and let William decide whether he was ready or not.

It sounded ridiculous even in her mind. He was thirty-two, most likely not a virgin, and yet he was more skittish than a sixteen-year-old girl.

Talk about role reversal.

Maybe she was a little too masculine for a woman? Spencer had scared the crap out of her with that aura reading of his. Thankfully, he hadn't said anything about it being manly.

Snuggling closer to William, she lifted her face to his and smiled. "Guys usually bring girls to spots like this to make out."

"This wasn't my intention." He smiled, and his eyes zeroed in on her lips. "But now that you brought it up, I won't be able to stop thinking about kissing you." He lifted his finger and rubbed it over her lower lip. "You have the most kissable lips of any woman I've ever been with."

A surge of jealousy turning her vision red, Kaia narrowed her eyes at him. "You make it sound as if you've kissed scores of women. How many are we talking about?"

"Enough to know that none had lips as succulent as yours or had even a fraction of your appeal. You are one of a kind, a precious jewel."

Clever man, showering her with compliments to take her mind off the subject of his previous lovers.

"I would have never pegged you as the Don Juan type. When did you have time to kiss all those other lips?"

He laughed. "And I would have never pegged you as a relentless temptress and a jealous monster." He dipped his head and feathered a kiss over her lips. "Although I enjoy your jealousy more than I should, let's not talk about any lips other than yours."

Oh, so now he was eager for a kiss.

Maybe she should throw more jealous tantrums at him to goad him into making love to her.

"Are you going to talk, or are you going to kiss?"

Just as before, he moved faster than was humanly possible, lifting her off her butt and settling her in his lap, and this time, he didn't wait before fusing their mouths.

Kaia groaned, the tension she'd felt all day long finally finding a release in William's arms.

As his tongue dueled with hers and his hands roamed over her back, she did what she'd been too shy to do the day before and snaked her hands under his shirt to touch his skin.

He was so warm and nearly hairless, and under the slight padding covering his abdomen and chest, she felt hard muscles.

Feeling brazen, she roamed a little higher and thumbed his nipples. They hardened immediately into two little pebbles, and as a growl started low in William's chest, he deepened the kiss, devouring her.

Her own nipples stiffened inside her lightly lined bra, aching to be touched, and as she pressed her chest to his in a futile attempt to relieve the ache, she hoped he could feel them and get the hint. But if he didn't, she was just going to take his hands and put them where she wanted them.

59

WILLIAM

*K*aia was going to be the death of him. Well, not really since he was immortal, but the sweet torment she was causing him combined with his guilt over taking what she was so freely offering was slaying him.

She was temptation and sin personified, and William was salivating to get his mouth on those hard tips she was pressing into his chest.

With a groan, he yanked her T-shirt up over her chest, pulled the flimsy bra cups down, and closed his palm over one generous swell.

The shuddering moan Kaia uttered in response undid him.

It was as if she'd been starving for his touch, and now that he'd finally given in to her silent pleas, she fell apart with relief.

"Kaia," he murmured against her lips as he plucked at her nipple, eliciting another delicious moan from her.

"Yes," she murmured back. "Whatever it is, the answer is yes."

Fates, if only he could live with the guilt of accepting that yes.

He had to put his mouth on those sweet berries, though. Despite the vow he'd made to her and to himself to limit their passion to kissing until the end of the project, he just couldn't say no to that.

It didn't matter that they were outside and that it wasn't even dark yet, and it made no difference that someone might walk in on them. He needed to get a taste and bring her a few moments of bliss as much, if not more than, he needed to take his next breath.

Letting go of her mouth, he dipped his head and kissed one turgid peak, then the other, and then came back for the first and sucked it into his mouth.

It was delicious, and the sounds she made were even more so. Kneading, plucking, and lightly pinching one nipple with his hand, he sucked and licked the other.

Kaia threaded her fingers into his hair, holding him to her, and as she ground her bottom over his hard shaft, he could feel her sweet feminine center through the thick fabrics of their jeans. It was quite evident that she was ready for him if he decided to take her, but he would never forgive himself if he did.

Compared to him, she was a child, and he was a pervert for succumbing to his baser needs.

Kaia didn't act like a child, though. She was all woman. Reaching with her hand between her legs, she rubbed the seam of her jeans in sync with the gyrating motion of her bottom over his erection. Her lack of inhibition was the sexiest thing, and he was so close to erupting in his pants and letting his fangs elongate that he doubted his ability to prevent either. The only thing capable of cooling his fervor was the thought of walking back to his bungalow with a big wet stain on his groin.

When a powerful climax shook Kaia's entire body, and she threw her head back, his restraint nearly snapped, but he gritted his teeth and managed to force himself back from the brink.

Partially.

He hadn't erupted in his pants, but his fangs had elongated, and he was struggling to wrestle them back.

Releasing her nipples, he tugged the bra cups up, the T-shirt down, and wrapped her in his arms. Cocooning her in his embrace, he rocked her gently until her tremors subsided.

"Wow," she whispered into his chest. "I didn't know I could orgasm so hard just from nipple play."

William chuckled. "Glad to be of service." He rested his chin on the top of her head to prevent her from looking at him.

Without reaching release, wrestling his fangs to retreat was a monumental struggle, and even though the sun hadn't set yet, and the glow from his eyes wouldn't be noticeable, he preferred to wait a few moments before letting her look at him.

"What about you?" Kaia murmured.

"What about me?"

She gyrated her hips over his shaft, nullifying his efforts to force his fangs to retreat. "You didn't climax."

"I don't have to." He kept his chin over the top of her head. "But I would appreciate it if you didn't grind your perfect bottom over my erection. I'm trying to regain control."

"I like you better without it."

He snorted. "If you have any mercy in your heart, don't make me walk back to my bungalow with a big wet stain on my pants. I'd rather you bury me out here in the sand."

"I wouldn't do that. But I can think of a very easy way to prevent a stain." She reached for the top button of her jeans.

He put a hand over hers to stop her. "Don't. This was more than enough."

"For today," she added.

"Until the project ends," he corrected.

"We shall see about that."

60

KAIA

Funny how sex worked so differently for women than it worked for men. Guys reached their climax, and that was it for them. They were happy. Kaia had orgasmed like a firecracker during her too-brief interlude with William, but instead of feeling sated and relaxed, she'd gotten recharged with enough energy to power all of Safe Haven and several neighboring towns.

It hadn't happened immediately.

William had walked her to her bungalow, they'd kissed again at the door, and then he'd said goodnight and continued to his own place. The energy had started building back up when she'd gotten into her room and the replay had started.

Standing in the shower, she imagined William doing the same over at his place. He hadn't climaxed when she had, and she had no doubt that he'd gotten right to it as soon as he entered his bathroom.

Closing her eyes, she saw him bracing a hand against the shower wall, the other fisting his erection, his hand going up and down his shaft as he imagined that he was inside of her.

Had he climaxed already? Or was he still at it, his hand movements synchronized with hers?

Kaia closed her eyes, dipped her finger into her heated core, and then gently rubbed the magical spot at the apex of her thighs. With her other hand squeezing her breast, she imagined that William was with her in the shower, touching her, kissing her, filling her…

Kaia exploded with a tormented moan leaving her throat, but she wasn't done. The sexual energy still pulsing through her needed to be released, and it took another round until her body calmed down. Heck, it got so depleted of energy that she lacked the strength to stand and had to sit on the shower bench to finish washing.

After she was done, she got dressed in a pair of loose shorts and a sleep camisole and padded to the kitchenette to make herself a cup of tea to take to bed. The door to Kylie's room was closed, but Kaia could hear music playing.

Hopefully, it had been loud enough to cover for her bathroom activity. She wasn't ashamed or even embarrassed about her self-pleasuring, but it wasn't something she wanted to share with Kylie.

Still, she wanted to talk to someone about her feelings toward William, and the only one she could do it with was Cheryl, who was too young to hear about Kaia's sexual frustrations.

Could she talk with her mom?

Her mother wasn't a prude, and she knew that Kaia wasn't a virgin, but she might worry that William was taking advantage of her because he was older and he was her boss, but mostly because Kaia wasn't home.

Heck, she'd only arrived at Safe Haven yesterday. Her mother would be shocked to learn what she'd been up to. She wouldn't believe that Kaia had been the instigator and would accuse William of coercing her young daughter.

It was better not to tell her.

Putting the tea on her nightstand, Kaia lay on the bed and stared at the ceiling. Imagining how her mother would view the situation helped her understand William's position.

People might point fingers at him even though he had done nothing wrong, and if she truly cared about him, which she definitely did, she would let up and wait until the project was over. Everyone would be much more amenable to them having a relationship when they were no longer working together, and Kaia was back home.

Would she manage to survive on just kisses for that long?

She would have to, for William's sake, but it was so damn frustrating. The age difference was irrelevant, and so was their workplace situation, but people liked to put things in neat little boxes and frown at anything that didn't fit the norm.

Heck, she had been no different until she'd met William. She'd even told him that Anthony couldn't have been her boyfriend because he was too old for her, but that hadn't been the reason at all.

She liked Tony, but she hadn't been attracted to him. There had been no chemistry, at least not on her part. Tony just hadn't had that extra something that she found so appealing in William.

William was a giver. He was caring, selfless, and always looked out for others.

Tony hadn't been any of those things. He'd been selfish, driven, and conceited, but he had a great sense of humor, and he hadn't minded being friends with the freaky kid while the others had pretty much shunned her.

She wondered what Tony would have thought of William. He probably would have sneered at her choice and asked if she was looking for a daddy figure.

Maybe she was?

Nah. That was baloney. She didn't need a father figure because Gilbert had assumed that role, and she'd accepted him wholeheartedly.

But the truth was that Gilbert, William, and her father had more in common than met the eye, so maybe she liked the fatherly types?

They said that girls married men who were similar to their dads and guys married girls who were similar to their moms, so there was that.

KAIA

When her phone rang with the familiar FaceTime ringtone, Kaia smiled and lifted it to her face. "Hi, Mom."

"What are you doing in bed so early? Are they working you to the bone out there?"

"Not at all. We took an hour break for lunch, and we were done at five-thirty and went to get dinner."

"How is the project going?"

"Great, but I can't tell you anything about it."

"I know. How are you getting along with your teammates?"

"We spent today mainly brainstorming ideas, and tomorrow we are going to dive in deeper."

"You look relaxed, and you sound happy, but I'm going to make you even happier. Eric can fly us over early on Saturday and fly us back Sunday night. We can spend the entire weekend with you."

It did make her happy, but not as much as it should have. If she spent the entire weekend with her family, she wouldn't spend it with William, and she was going to miss his company.

"That's awesome. I didn't expect you to come back so soon. You said that you couldn't make it here more than once a month."

"The truth is that I didn't plan on it, but Eric called and said that he has one of his jets available for the entire weekend and that he can fly us, so I jumped on the opportunity." Her mother chuckled. "I think he wants to see William's assistant again. The two of them hit it off."

"I noticed. Darlene is really nice. After I had my meltdown when you left, she gave me a hug and told me to call her whenever I felt lonely and needed to talk to someone."

That was an idea that Kaia hadn't thought of before. She could talk with Darlene about William. The two were friends, and Darlene might know things about him that would help her understand him better.

"Did you take her up on her offer?"

Kaia shook her head. "There was no need. I acclimated faster than I thought I would. I'm getting along well with William and with my teammates. Last night, I watched the chick flick that Cheryl recommended with my roommate."

"Is there a movie theater in the area?" her mother asked.

"We watched in our bungalow. They have all the latest movies on their servers."

Her mother smiled. "I'm so glad that you are finding your place there. You need to spread your wings a little."

"Yeah. I'm glad that I took this job. It's a fascinating project, and I got to meet some very interesting people. Did I tell you about the paranormals we share the dining hall and gym with?"

"You mentioned them yesterday."

"I know a lot more today than I knew yesterday." Kaia pushed up against the pillows. "Do you want me to tell you about them?"

"Sure. If it's not part of the secret."

"I don't think it is."

170

61

WILLIAM

*W*illiam's day had passed in a blur of activity, saving him from dwelling on his crumbling defenses and how fast things were progressing with Kaia.

The girl was a force of nature on all fronts, and he had a feeling that the project would be finished much faster than he'd expected. In the two days she'd been working on decoding the journals, she'd already managed to translate words written in the gods' language, which he had no idea how she could have possibly done, and she cracked the first set of schematics, figuring out exactly what they meant.

So far, she hadn't figured out more than he had already known, but given that he could read at least some of the language, it was nothing short of awe-inspiring.

"Are we done for today?" he heard Corinne ask.

"I need a little more time," Kaia said. "But you can go ahead. I'll join you in the dining hall later."

They couldn't leave without him opening the lab's door for them, and the scanner that they thought scanned only his iris also scanned them to make sure they weren't taking anything out of the lab.

He pushed to his feet and walked out of his office. "I'll escort you upstairs." He turned to Kaia. "Are you sure that you want to stay? I can come back for you, but I suggest that you call it a day and come with us to eat dinner."

Chewing on her lower lip, she looked at the sheets of paper strewn over the table. "I need to organize this mess before I leave."

"I'll help you," Corinne offered.

Kaia nodded. "Thank you. I didn't feel hungry until William said the word dinner, but it hit me full force now."

"That's because the food here is not filling," Owen grumbled. "I would give my left testicle for a juicy hamburger with fries."

William's mouth salivated.

Would it be a huge security risk if he took the team out for a proper dinner?

The nearest town was an hour's drive away from Safe Haven, and he would need to take a couple of Guardians with him, but they would be happy to get a real meal as well.

"All done." Corinne put the neat stack of papers on Kaia's desk.

William scooped it up. "Give me a moment to put them away."

No one could get into the lab and take the papers, but he didn't want to leave them lying around. It took him less than a minute to put them in the safe in his office.

As he and his team went through the second door at the top of the stairs, his phone rang, and when he pulled it out of his pocket and saw the name, he rushed them out through the third door before answering.

"Hold on for one moment," he told Lokan, and looked at Kaia. "I have to take this. I'll meet you later in the dining room."

When she nodded, he went back into the building and waited until the door closed behind him. "I'm with you. What did you find out?"

"My servant snooped around, and what he found out was that someone resembling your guy's description and going by the name of Tony had been brought in about a year ago, but he left shortly after arriving. I sent him to check the departure ledger, and his name wasn't there, so he didn't leave the island. He could be dead, or he could be imprisoned, or it could have been some other Tony. They don't record last names in any of the ledgers that are accessible to servants."

"Do you have access to the ones that contain the full names?"

"I do, but I'm not scheduled to visit for another five weeks."

"Do you think it's significant that Tony is a bioinformatician? Does Navuh have a need for one?"

"I don't think so. The guys he brings in to breed the Dormants are young, in their mid- to late twenties, and smart. Those are the only criteria he cares about. He doesn't care if they are physicists or psychologists as long as their IQs are high, and they have a proven record of academic success."

Leaning against the wall, William let out a breath. "I have a feeling that it might be significant that a bioinformatician was brought to the island. Maybe Navuh decided to crack the immortal code. With all the scientists he lures to the island, he could open a research facility."

Lokan chuckled. "You are giving him too much credit. He's not that sophisticated. That being said, Losham is. I'll give him a call and check what he's up to. The thing about Losham is that he likes to brag, so he might share with me his latest schemes."

"Given that a year has passed since Anthony was taken, those schemes were hatched a while ago."

"True. Anything else I can do for you?"

"Not that I can think of. Thanks for the help."

"No problem. I'm happy to assist in any way I can."

As Lokan ended the call, William put the phone in his pocket. Was it worth mentioning to Kian that Navuh had had a bioinformatician brought to the island? And perhaps Turner as well?

William wasn't sure, but when in doubt, it was always prudent to err on the side of caution.

62

KIAN

"William." Kian held the phone to his ear as he closed his office door. "How is the research going?"

The project had only started the day before, so he wasn't expecting any groundbreaking discoveries, but if William was calling him this late, he might have some news.

"Better than expected. Kaia was worth every moment I invested in recruiting her and all the concessions I made for her."

"Glad to hear that." Kian took the stairs down to the lobby. "Turner wasn't happy when I told him that you allowed Kaia's family to accompany her to Safe Haven, and he even dug deeper into their background. Did you know that Eric Emerson was a fighter pilot in the Air Force?"

"It was in the security brief that Karen Locke's employer had prepared. The entire family passed the security check with flying colors. Did Turner discover anything worrisome?"

"Not really, which is why I didn't call you. What's up? I know that you are not calling me because you miss me."

William chuckled. "The truth is that I expected to be miserable away from my lab and my crew, but I'm enjoying it here. Having Darlene and Max with me is a big plus, and I love being right next to the ocean. It's a nice change of scenery."

Kian waved at Wendy and Wonder, who were heading home as well. "Wait until it gets cold. You are not going to like it as much then."

"I hope the project will be done by mid-fall, and it seems likely that it will. Although, I'm still not sure what we are supposed to do with what we learn from those journals once they are deciphered."

"We'll worry about that then." Kian quickened his strides, eager to get home and sweep Allegra into his arms. "Anything else you want to talk about?"

"Yeah, there is. Can you think of any reason Navuh might need a bioinformatician?"

The short hairs on the back of Kian's neck stood up. "Why do you ask?"

"Kaia's friend was also recruited for a secret project that was supposed to take a few months, but it has been a year since anyone has heard from him, and his family thinks that he's dead. I asked Roni to do some snooping, and he found out that Anthony had booked a flight to the Maldives, but he hadn't booked a connection or a return flight. We know that the Maldives is one of the hubs that the Doomers use, so I asked Lokan to check if the guy was on the island."

"You shouldn't have done that. A missing human is not worth risking Lokan for."

William was silent for a long moment. "It was important to Kaia, and I basically bribed her to join the program with the promise to look into her friend's disappearance. After talking to Roni, I contacted Lokan to see if he could think of any reason Navuh might want to get his hands on a bioinformatician. He couldn't think of any and offered to look into it. He's also going to call Losham to see if he's up to anything."

"That's even more dangerous."

"I assumed that Lokan wouldn't have offered to help if he thought that it was too risky, but he was more than happy to help and promised to send his servant to snoop around the Dormants' enclave."

Kian slowed down his steps. "Did he find the guy there?"

Usually, the brains were kept on the island only until they impregnated a Dormant, and then they were shipped out. They assumed that the women were pros, sent to pleasure them, and they had no idea that their seed was being stolen and they were fathering children.

"Someone there remembered a guy who matched Anthony's description and went by the name of Tony, but since they don't use last names, we can't be certain that it was the same guy."

"So, he's no longer there?"

"He's not, but he didn't leave the island. The servant checked the records, but no one named Anthony or Tony was listed in the departures log. Lokan said that he must be either dead or imprisoned."

"There might be a third option. Is Anthony a good-looking guy?"

"He's young, and I guess some would call him handsome. Why?"

Kian had a suspicion that he wanted to investigate, more to satisfy his curiosity than any useful investigation. The guy wasn't his responsibility, and if Kaia's friend had let himself be lured to the island with promises of free sex with beautiful women, he deserved what he'd gotten.

"Do you have a picture of him you can text to me? I want to see what he looks like."

"I'll do it right away."

A second later, Kian's phone pinged with an incoming message, and as he clicked it open, his suspicion was reinforced.

"Anthony has similar coloring to Navuh, and their facial bone structures bear some resemblance as well. We know that Navuh brings human servants who look like him to the harem for the immortal ladies to enjoy, so he can claim their children as his own. If he's breeding a new generation of warriors by pairing Dormants with smart men, it makes even more sense for him to do the same with breeding the immortal females whose sons he claims."

CHAPTER 62

William let out a long-suffering sigh. "What am I going to tell Kaia?"

"Nothing for now. Kalugal's scheduled call with Areana is tomorrow morning. He could ask her if a smart guy named Tony arrived at the harem about a year ago."

63

KAIA

ylie rose to her feet and picked up her plate. "Are you going to wait for William? He might not show up at all." A hint of a smile tugged at her lips. "He's so scatterbrained that he might have forgotten that he told us he would join us later, and went home."

Kaia bristled at the rude comment, but she wrestled her temper down. "William is not scatterbrained. He's brilliant, and sometimes his mind races ahead of him, so he appears distracted, but I assure you that it works like a well-oiled machine."

Kylie waved a hand in dismissal. "It was a poor choice of words. I meant that he spaces out. Although with how much he likes to eat, it's unlikely that he forgot about dinner, and if he did, his growling stomach would remind him. He's probably still stuck on that phone call."

Kaia nodded. "Maybe it was from his other lab, and he had to solve a problem for them. I'll wait a little longer, and if he doesn't show up, I'll call him."

Kylie looked around the empty dining hall. "The kitchen staff probably want to call it a day and go home."

"I'm sure that they'll keep the place open for William." And if the cook made a fuss, Kaia would fill a plate for him and take it to his place.

Kylie shrugged. "You're probably right. I'll see you later." She put her plate and utensils in the dirty dishes bin and walked out the door.

Leaning back, Kaia cast a sidelong glance at the serve-out window, glad to see that no one was giving her the hairy eyeball for not vacating the premises and letting them close up for the night. Perhaps she should ask them to prepare a plate for William before they put everything away and finished cleaning up. Pushing to her feet, she walked up to the window.

Only the cook was there, her two helpers already gone, and when she noticed Kaia standing at the window, she walked over. "What can I do for you?"

"Not for me, for William. He is running late, and I don't want him to miss

176

dinner. Are you in a hurry to close up? Should I get a plate for him and bring it to his place?"

Maggie wiped her wet hands on her white apron. "You can if you want, but you don't have to. I'll put all the leftovers in the refrigerator, and he can come later and warm himself a plate whenever he wants."

"Are you going to leave the place open for him?"

She should have realized that William probably had the code for the lock.

"The kitchen is never closed," Maggie said. "If anyone is in the mood for a snack in the middle of the night, they can come in and get it."

"I didn't know that. Thanks for telling me."

"You're welcome." Maggie smiled. "The coffee dispenser is also left on all night, and I leave a basket of fruit out."

"That's very nice of you. Thank you."

A plate with cookies would have been even nicer, but Maggie had to follow Safe Haven's health protocol.

At least there was coffee, and it wasn't bad, so it wasn't totally nuts.

Kaia walked over to the dispenser and poured herself a cup. Perhaps she could still take a plate for William, using it as an excuse to go to his bungalow.

Ever since their make-out session yesterday, she'd been fantasizing about seducing him. William had no idea what he had done by giving her that incredible orgasm. He had awakened a ravenous monster who needed more and wouldn't rest until she got it.

Thankfully, deciphering the journals and what she was uncovering was so fascinating and all-consuming that she hadn't been bothered by carnal thoughts throughout the day. But now that her mind was free to wander, the cravings she'd managed to subdue last night had returned with a vengeance.

Glancing at the door, she made up her mind, rose to her feet, and walked up to the counter. "I think I'll take a plate for William after all. Can I come into the kitchen and prepare it myself?"

Maggie shook her head. "I'll prepare it for you. I need to finish cleaning in here."

"Thank you." She waited by the counter as Maggie filled up a plate, covered it with a lid, and brought it out to her.

"Remind him to return the dishes tomorrow morning."

"I will. Thank you, and goodnight."

Maggie smiled. "Enjoy your evening."

"You too."

If Kaia's plan succeeded, she was going to enjoy the evening very much indeed.

64

WILLIAM

*A*s William opened the lab's topmost door, the sun was already setting. How long had he been on the phone? It hadn't felt like an hour had passed, but as he glanced at his watch, he was surprised to see that it was after seven.

Dinner was most likely over by now, but he knew he wouldn't stay hungry. Maggie never threw away the leftovers until the next morning, saving them in the refrigerator for those who missed dinner or got the munchies in the middle of the night.

He'd been guilty of both.

With Ronja and Darlene's help, William had gotten better about his food intake, but he still had a hard time fighting the urge to stuff himself whenever he was stressed. It wouldn't be the first time he'd reheated a plate in the microwave and ate alone in the dining hall, and most times, he didn't mind that. On the contrary, he enjoyed the peace and quiet.

Not this time, though.

He regretted the missed opportunity to spend time with Kaia and talk about things that weren't related to their research and get to know her better. Though given how consumed they both were by the secrets waiting for them to decipher, they probably wouldn't be able to help themselves.

That seemed to be their theme in more ways than one. He still couldn't believe that he'd let himself get carried away last evening.

How could he have been so careless?

He'd bared Kaia's body in full daylight, where any passerby could have seen them, and he feasted on her nipples like a savage.

Except, even though guilt was eating at him, he couldn't bring himself to regret it. Every delicious moment of it was etched in his memory—the way she'd reacted with such unabashed abandon, the sounds she'd made, the way she'd climaxed, the way she'd looked after they'd been done.

Well, she'd been done. He'd been in agony, but it was worth it.

178

He'd enjoyed giving Kaia pleasure more than he'd enjoyed receiving it from any other woman.

Fates, he was a pervert.

He sucked in a breath as he saw the object of his obsession walking toward him with a covered plate in her hands.

"You missed dinner." She smiled shyly. "So, I got you a plate to eat at home." She handed it to him.

"Thank you." He didn't know what to do next.

Should he invite her to join him?

Should he just smile back and say goodnight?

Should he tell her what he suspected had happened to her friend?

"I thought that we could go to your place and talk about the research." She glanced around before leaning closer to him. "I didn't want to say anything in front of the others, but the stuff I'm decoding is blowing my mind. They haven't realized what they are working on yet, and if you want to keep it that way, I need to know. It will seriously limit the help I can expect from them."

Looking around, William was glad that they were alone. It wasn't a topic to discuss in public, but he didn't want to take her back to the lab where they would be closeted together, and he didn't want to take her to his place either. Things might get out of hand again.

"We can talk in the dining hall."

"Maggie is still in the kitchen, and the cleaning staff is probably there already, mopping the dining room. Besides, there are security cameras in there as well, and we need privacy." A mischievous smirk lifted one corner of her mouth. "I didn't find any cameras in my bungalow, so I assume that there are none in yours either."

"There aren't."

Damn, the girl was scrambling his brain. He knew that there were cameras in the kitchen and dining hall and some on the outside of the building as well. He'd just forgotten about it because he couldn't think straight with her standing so close to him.

"Then let's go." She threaded her arm through his and started walking. "Did Roni find out anything new about Anthony?"

What was he supposed to tell her?

Even if he could tell Kaia that her friend might be being held captive on the Doomers' island and used as a breeder of a new generation of smart immortal evildoers, she wouldn't believe him.

"We are still investigating."

"We? Is there anyone else besides Roni looking into it?"

"Yeah, but I can't say more about it. The source has to remain confidential."

Kaia tilted her head. "In what way is that different than Roni? I don't know who he is, where he is, or what he does. You can tell me about the other sources in the same way."

"Roni works with me. The other two sources are part of my organization, but even mentioning them could put them in danger. That's why I can't tell you anything about them."

"I get it. They are informers."

In a way, Lokan and Areana were precisely that. Only they were much more.

"You guessed right."

"Who do you suspect took him? Do you still think that it has something to do with drugs?"

Again, in a way it was because that was what the Brotherhood did these days to finance its operations.

"Drugs and prostitution."

Her eyes widened. "I hope that you don't think that Tony is involved in that. He might be a prick sometimes, but he's not evil."

"I didn't say that he was. I suspect that he's a victim, not a perpetrator."

65

KAIA

*K*aia's throat was suddenly dry, and her words came out in a whisper, "In what way? Why would they use a scientist for prostitution? He isn't even that good-looking."

She'd heard that it wasn't only women who fell victim to trafficking, but for the men, it usually meant slave labor, not slave sex. For the most part, women didn't hire male prostitutes, but given that an estimated ten percent of men preferred other men, it was possible that some of them were willing to pay for it, and a small percentage of them were psychos who didn't care whether the guy they were bonking was offering himself willingly or not.

Heck, some of them might even enjoy forcing themselves on a reluctant victim, the same as some thrived on hurting women.

Regrettably, there was no shortage of evil people who made life miserable for the rest of the human population that was mostly good, or at least neutral.

Kaia couldn't understand how people could be so evil, not from a woman's perspective and not from what she remembered from the male point of view of her previous life. It took someone seriously twisted to rape another person.

God, poor Tony.

How was she going to save him?

William regarded her with sad eyes. "I don't know any of this for a fact. It's all speculation, and you shouldn't get needlessly upset. Your Tony might be somewhere on the beach in the Bahamas, getting a tan while sipping on margaritas with paper umbrellas. Perhaps he met a fascinating, beautiful lady while working on his special project, and they decided to live on the money they'd just made and enjoy life. Maybe he was paid so well that he figured he never needed to work again."

Did the longing she saw in William's eyes hint that he'd been describing his own fantasy and projecting it onto Tony?

Was that what he wanted for the two of them?

William might fantasize about spending a few days in the Bahamas with her, but she doubted that he wanted to quit his job and live on the money he'd made so far.

He was too driven, not by ambition, because he didn't care about status or prestige, but by the burning curiosity to discover new things, create new technology, or come up with ways to improve people's lives.

She knew that because she was the same. Maybe that's why she was so drawn to him.

When they passed by her and Kylie's bungalow, Kaia cast a furtive glance at the windows, glad to see that the shutters were down.

"Do you want to let Kylie know that you are going to my place?" William asked as he opened the door to his bungalow.

He must have caught her glancing at the windows and misinterpreted it. He thought that she was worried about being alone with him, while her concern had been Kylie seeing her walking into his place and gossiping about it tomorrow.

"Maybe later." She followed him inside and pulled out a chair next to the small round table in his living room. "I would rather avoid her questions and speculations."

"As you wish." William took the lid off the plate before putting it in the microwave. "So, what did you want to talk to me about?"

"I think that your first theory was right, and we are dealing with alien technology. I was able to decipher several of the symbols with the help of the schematic drawing. When it occurred to me that they might be molecules, things started falling into place. I deciphered the symbols for oxygen, carbon, hydrogen, nitrogen, calcium, and phosphorus. Do you know how?"

"I can't wait to hear that." He took the plate out of the microwave with his bare hand and carried it to the table.

"Isn't the plate hot?"

"Not really." He put it down and pulled out two more empty plates from the cabinet along with utensils for both of them.

Sitting down, he pushed the loaded plate she'd gotten for him to the center of the table. "Dig in."

"I've already eaten. I'm not hungry." She pushed the plate toward him, and it was scalding.

Was the guy so distracted that he hadn't noticed his fingers getting burned? Or was he playing macho and didn't want to admit that he was hurting?

She glanced at his hands, but they both looked fine. Maybe he wasn't sensitive to heat.

"I'm still waiting to hear how you did that."

"Right." She leaned back in her chair. "First, I should start by saying that I figured out what the symbol for percentage was. We've already deciphered their numerical symbols, so when I got that, it was a game-changer. I copied one of their tables, and when I substituted their numbers for ours and then replaced their symbol for percentage with ours, I immediately knew what I was looking at. It was the chemical composition of an average human body in terms of elements and compounds. Oxygen is the most abundant at sixty-five percent, carbon is next at eighteen percent, then it's hydrogen, followed by nitrogen, calcium, and phosphorus. The rest are small amounts of other trace elements and metals." She looked into William's eyes. "I think that those journals contain information about human biology. The thing was that the next table had symbols that didn't represent anything that should be in a human body, and that table was on the same page as the other one. I'm still trying to figure out what it's about."

66

WILLIAM

$\mathcal{W}$illiam wasn't surprised that Kaia had figured that out. What he was astonished by was that she'd done it in two days.

"First of all, congratulations. You are unbelievable. And secondly, you are right about not revealing your suspicions to the others. It would seem that these aliens left us blueprints to build a human body."

Kaia's eyes widened. "You are brilliant. I didn't think of that. I thought that they investigated humans to learn more about us." She waved a hand. "With all the stories about alien abductions and medical examinations, I thought that maybe there was a kernel of truth in them. When I was a kid, those stories scared the bejesus out of me. I thought, what if they abducted me? But then I figured that advanced aliens wouldn't need to kidnap humans to learn what they were made from. They would have scanners that would tell them everything they wanted to know without them having to even touch a human."

If William wasn't beating himself up for steering Kaia in a direction he should have kept her away from, he would have been amused by her story. He could imagine the young Kaia pondering the probability of alien abduction and realizing that the stories didn't make sense.

He might have to thrall her later and remove that suggestion from her mind, but he hated messing with her brain. Unless it was absolutely necessary, and there was no other way to control what she knew and what she took away with her from the research, he wasn't going into her head.

Maybe he could just redirect her mind to think in other directions.

Getting to his feet, he collected his plate and put it in the tiny sink in the kitchenette. "What other alien theories did you examine as a kid and debunk?"

"Let me see." She pushed away from the table and moved to sit on the couch, patting the spot next to her for him to join her. "I was fascinated with unidentified submerged objects. I imagined an underwater alien base in the deepest ocean trenches, but I haven't been able to debunk that yet. Many of the sightings were

184

reported by very reliable witnesses, like navy officers and pilots, so we can't assume that they were all nuts. There are places so deep in the oceans that even our most advanced equipment can't get down to them and check whether anything or anyone is hiding in those depths."

She scooted closer until her thigh was touching his, and that small contact was enough to cause him great discomfort.

Clearing his throat, William moved his thigh an inch away. "What about unidentified flying objects?"

"Same thing, but with a twist. Many were reported by air force pilots, radar operators, and the like, so they can't be dismissed either, and their velocity and maneuverability defy the laws of physics as we know them. As for where they are hiding, I have two theories. One is that unidentified submerged objects and unidentified flying objects are one and the same, and they hide in the deepest regions of the sea, and my other theory is that they have an underground base on the dark side of the moon. Until both are debunked, I'm willing to go out on a limb and accept that not only are we constantly visited by aliens, but that they also live among us and always have." She gave him a bright smile. "As proven by those journals you found. What I don't know is why they are here and what they want. As far as I know, they are not interfering in human affairs, so maybe they are here only to watch."

If Kaia only knew how close she was to the truth, she would be ecstatic. Maybe one day she would discover it for herself, but she wouldn't learn it from him.

Not unless she was a Dormant.

Could her incredible mind be considered a paranormal ability?

And what about the undeniable pull between them?

Except, he'd been wrong before. Hannah had worked in Amanda's lab, was incredibly smart, both Syssi and Amanda had liked her a lot, and he'd felt a connection with her as well. It hadn't been as powerful as what he felt with Kaia, but then Hannah hadn't been forbidden fruit.

She hadn't been so young, she hadn't been his subordinate, and he hadn't had to work as hard to resist her when he'd needed to. Hannah's brain had been no less precious to him than Kaia's, and he couldn't bite her as often as he would have liked because he'd been reluctant to thrall her too frequently.

Thankfully, he had great self-control, and he'd often pleasured Hannah without biting her or even flashing his fangs, but he wasn't sure he would be able to do the same with Kaia.

In fact, he was certain that he couldn't.

But maybe if he was careful, his thrall wouldn't cause any damage. The only time he'd entered her mind was when they'd first met, and that had been a long time ago. He could probably thrall her again safely, but that was the devil on his left shoulder talking.

The angel sitting on his right shoulder demanded that William stay strong and resist temptation.

67

KAIA

"As fascinating as the subject of alien visitations is, I still have work to do, and it's getting late." William got to his feet. "I'll escort you to your place."

Kaia stifled a groan. She'd expected him to do what he thought was honorable, but she'd hoped his desire for her would overpower his need to follow the rules he'd set for himself.

William didn't have a poker face, and she could read his emotions as clearly as if he was actually expressing them out loud and sharing his inner struggles with her.

He'd been waging war with himself since the moment he'd invited her into his bungalow, wanting her to stay, craving her, but he'd decided to be a damn gentleman and do the right thing.

Or the wrong thing.

Kaia had a very different opinion on what was right and what was wrong, but since she'd promised herself not to push him, she couldn't call him out on his bullshit. Or maybe she should? If she didn't take the initiative, months would pass until she got him to take her to his bed, and she couldn't last that long.

To hell with that.

She might be only nineteen, but she knew that life was fleeting, and every moment wasted was a moment lost forever. She had no intention of wasting the moments of her life on being timid and dancing around someone else's misguided opinions and sensitivities.

And if that meant taking risks and stepping on toes, she was willing to accept the consequences.

"I don't want to go." Kaia crossed her legs and looked up at him. "Do you really have work to do, or is it an excuse to get rid of me?"

He swallowed, his Adam's apple bobbing up and down. "I don't want to get rid of you, and I always have work that can't wait. But whether I do or don't, you shouldn't be here."

"Why not? I've read very carefully over the contract I signed, and there was no clause prohibiting fraternizing between teammates, and that includes you. There was no clause about fraternizing with the boss either. If we both want me to be here, there is no reason for me to leave."

Letting out a resigned breath, William sat back down on the other side of the couch. "I guess work can wait a little longer. Can I offer you a cup of tea?"

"Coffee would be better."

"Coming up." He rose to his feet and walked over to the kitchenette.

Now what?

Resigned was not the emotion Kaia had been going for, and she didn't know how to turn things around and get William in the mood for making love.

Should she take her shirt off? Would that be a big enough clue for him? Or did she need to go to his bedroom and get naked for him to get a hint?

When he returned with two cups of coffee, she gave him her sweetest smile. "You know what I've just realized?"

He lifted a brow. "What's that?"

"I know very little about you, while you know everything there is to know about me." Well, except for one thing, but that had no bearing on their relationship. "You said that in order to take this thing between us a step further, we need to get to know each other, but you never talk about yourself. I don't even know where you live when you are not working on deciphering alien science."

A ghost of a smile lifted one corner of his lips, and when he took his glasses off to wipe them with a corner of his shirt, the sight of his blue eyes took her breath away. They seemed to be glowing with an inner light.

Was he an angel? Or maybe an alien?

Kaia stifled a snort.

It would be just her luck to meet a hot alien who needed help finding his way back home. Was Darlene an alien too? Or did he have her under his thrall because he needed a human prop to perfect his human act?

"I'm originally from Scotland, but I've lived in Los Angeles for many years, and that's where my permanent home is."

That didn't sound too otherworldly.

"What about relationships? Have you ever been married?"

He shook his head.

"What about girlfriends?"

He nodded.

The guy who usually talked up a storm had turned mute when asked personal questions, but that wasn't going to deter her.

"How many, and have you been in love with any of them?"

William smiled. "I feel like I'm being interrogated."

"That's because you are. I'm shortening the entire getting-to-know-each-other period by not beating around the bush."

"I thought that I was in love once, but in retrospect, I wasn't. I liked her a lot, though, and then she moved away, and we lost touch."

Kaia narrowed her eyes at him. "You aren't going to tell me how many girlfriends you've had, are you?"

"Other than Hannah, none are worth mentioning. She was the only one I had feelings for, and I told you about her. What else would you like to know?"

Kaia wasn't done with questions about his ex-girlfriend, but she knew when it was time to retreat and regroup, and when it was time to push forward, and she needed to give it a rest for now.

"What kind of music do you like to listen to?" she asked.

"Instrumental, mostly classical."

"Nothing contemporary?"

"It's not that I don't like it, but lyrics distract me from my thoughts, so I prefer instrumental music. There is always something I need to figure out, and I don't have time to listen to someone singing about their broken heart."

"Makes sense. So, I guess you don't watch movies either."

"I do, but rarely. I've seen all the *Star Wars* movies, *Guardians of the Galaxy*, *Wonder Woman*, *Lord of the Rings*, and the *Harry Potter* movies."

"The boy who lived." She laughed. "Those are some of my favorite movies as well. In the music department, though, my horizons are broader. I like the oldies like the Red Hot Chili Peppers, Night Wish, and even older ones like Queen and Pink Floyd."

68

WILLIAM

"*I*t's almost midnight." Kaia leaned her head on William's arm. "Is your bungalow going to turn into a pumpkin when the clock hits twelve?"

It took him a split second to get the reference. "Aren't you confusing fairytales?"

They'd been talking for hours, and apparently Kaia's mind lost some of its sharpness when she was tired. If she fell asleep on his couch, William would be relieved but also disappointed.

"Yes, I am." She looked up and smiled at him. "I'm about to kiss the prince, and I don't think he's going to turn into a frog."

William had known that this moment was coming, and evidently Kaia wasn't tired enough to forsake her seduction plan.

She'd thought that she was being very clever, but he'd seen right through her so-called let's-get-to-know-each-other excuse and had made all kinds of promises to himself to turn her down gently. Except, on some subconscious level, William must have accepted the inevitability of what was about to happen between them, knowing that he wouldn't be able to resist.

"I'm no prince, but you are definitely a princess." He hooked a finger under her chin. "My princess." Dipping his head, he took her lips in a gentle kiss and wrapped his arm around her.

The moan she released into his mouth was one of longing mixed with relief, the sound making him feel guilty for denying her for so long. Except, it hadn't been long at all.

Kaia had arrived on Sunday, and it was only Tuesday, or rather Wednesday morning. He had succumbed to her charms practically without a fight.

But what choice did he have?

To deny her would hurt her feelings and sabotage the project, and keeping her at arm's length was causing them both pain. He'd hoped she would back off and wait patiently for a more appropriate time, but that wasn't in Kaia's nature, and he was done fighting the insane attraction between them.

"William," she murmured against his lips. "Take me to your bed."

The word bashful was not in Kaia's vocabulary, and he was glad that it wasn't. It made her what she was—a force of nature, a goddess of science, a woman to be reckoned with.

"Your wish is my command, my lady."

As he lifted her into his arms and carried her to the bedroom, Kaia wound her arms around his neck and purred like a satisfied kitten. "You're so strong. I love how easily you can carry me."

"You're light as a feather."

She threw her head back and laughed. "What a sweet liar you are. But I don't mind." She tightened her arms around his neck and tilted her head up to kiss him.

Sitting on the bed with her on his lap, he took over the kiss. She melted into him, and as a needy groan escaped her throat, William's immortal instincts screamed for him to take care of that need, to satisfy his female, and to claim her as his own.

He delved deeper with his tongue, dueling with hers and preventing it from entering his mouth and discovering that his canines had elongated and that their sharp points could draw blood.

With a warning growl, he squeezed her tighter to him, but her need was so great that she didn't heed the warning and reached under his shirt. The feel of her hands roaming over his naked skin obliterated the last of his resistance, and as the dam burst inside of him, he snaked his hand under her T-shirt to cup her breast over her bra.

She trembled, crying out as he pulled the bra cup down and dipped his head to take the succulent berry between his lips.

This time they weren't out in the open where anyone could see them. There was nothing stopping him from baring her completely and taking her as he'd yearned to do since the first time he'd seen her.

When she clutched at the back of his head and held him to her breast, his eyes rolled back in his head, but he couldn't just let himself revel in the pleasure of holding her in his arms, smelling the intoxicating aroma of her arousal, and suckling on her breasts. He had to take care of his princess, and she was aching for him to touch her where her need was the greatest.

Reaching down, he rubbed his fingers over the seam of her jeans, his shaft getting impossibly hard as he felt her heat through the thick fabric. Her moans grew frantic as he pressed his thumb to the apex of her thighs, and with her hips gyrating faster and faster over his erection, he was just as close to climaxing as she was.

Kaia was so ready for him that he could have taken her right there and then, but he wasn't going to. He would pleasure her with his hands and his tongue, bringing her to one climax after the other, but as much as he wanted to make her his, he wasn't going to claim her tonight.

69

KAIA

*K*aia trembled from the intense pleasure, but it wasn't enough. William's mouth sucking on her breast and his fingers rubbing that most sensitive spot through her jeans was a sweet torment, and she could climax just from that, but tonight, she wasn't going to settle for just kissing.

She wanted it all.

When he released her breast and lifted his head to take her lips, she pushed on his chest, and as he tumbled down on the bed, she knew she wouldn't have been able to do that unless he'd allowed it. Despite his soft appearance, William was insanely strong, and if she wasn't already beyond turned on, that would have done it for her.

Kaia followed, lying over him and rubbing her aching sex against his rock-hard erection. Impatiently yanking his shirt apart, she didn't care that buttons were flying everywhere. The growl leaving William's throat was not one of anger over the shirt's destruction, but of hunger that she was eager to satiate.

Rolling her under him, he settled between her thighs, gripped her wrists, and pinned her hands above her head. "Naughty, naughty girl," he tsked.

"Are you going to punish me?" she teased.

"I am." He dipped his head and nipped her ear.

When he released her hands and slid down her body, Kaia smiled. She'd never had anyone pleasure her with his mouth, and if that was how he was going to punish her, she would get naughty as often as she could.

As he kissed her center through her jeans, she reached down, intending to shove her jeans off, but he batted her hands away and yanked them down her hips, pulling them off along with her skimpy panties.

"Ohh," she moaned as he blew air on her heated flesh.

"Beautiful," William murmured before lightly kissing her lower lips. "Did you ever have anyone lick your gorgeous pussy?"

Kaia almost climaxed just from hearing him say that. She'd never have expected prim and proper William could ever talk dirty.

"No," she whispered. "You're going to be my first."

His head whipped up, and he looked at her in alarm. "Are you a virgin?"

She laughed. "Just a cunnilingus virgin and eager for a change of status."

His worried expression evaporating, he smirked. "Not as much as I am eager to change it." He dipped his head and treated her to a long lick that had her hips shooting up.

"Stay still, my naughty princess." He gripped her thighs, pinning them down. "Close your eyes and enjoy."

Kaia wanted to watch, but William's tone brooked no argument, and she had a feeling that if she didn't comply, he would stop what he was doing.

Besides, it was sexy as hell to be ordered around by him, but only in bed.

"Yes, master," she teased when she closed her eyes and let her head fall back on the mattress.

Her reward was a flick of his tongue over that most sensitive spot that had her seeing stars behind her closed lids.

As he went on to feast on her, licking, nipping, and nuzzling, she was helpless to do anything other than moan, not even able to undulate her hips because he was pinning them down, but that just added to her arousal.

Then he let go of one side, and a moment later, he thrust his tongue into her sheath while his thumb pressed over the center of her desire. As the orgasm shot up and exploded out of her, she screamed his name.

He kept licking and thrusting until the tremors subsided.

Her eyes were still tightly closed as he climbed over her and took her lips in a scorching kiss, the zipper digging into her sensitive flesh, making her realize that he still had his pants on.

"William," she murmured against his lips.

"Shhh, it's okay." He pumped his hips over her, rubbing his hard length against her mound. "Keep your eyes closed, princess."

She was too blissed out to object, but she couldn't understand why he wasn't getting rid of his pants and filling her up with that magnificent erection she could feel through his pants.

Reaching down, she yanked on the waistband, but he caught her hands again and pinned them over her head while kissing her hard enough to bruise her lips.

Kaia wanted to tell William that she needed him inside of her, but he was possessing her mouth and holding her hands, and his big body was pinning her under him. There was nothing she could do other than surrender.

70

WILLIAM

The devil on William's left shoulder was riding him hard, whispering in his ear that Kaia wouldn't be satisfied with the orgasm he'd given her, that she needed to be claimed as much as he needed to claim her. But the angel on his right shoulder pleaded with him to exercise restraint, to get off her and run into the bathroom before she saw his fangs and his glowing eyes, and he was forced to thrall her.

Hell, he didn't even have a condom, and if his suspicion was correct and she was a Dormant, he would induce her transition without her consent, and she would never forgive him for that.

As she released a strangled mewl into his mouth, he realized that he was crushing her with his bulk, and as he lifted off her and braced on his forearms, she sucked in a breath.

"I want you in me, William," she hissed. "If you are not inside of me in two seconds, I'm opening my eyes."

How the hell did she know that this was the most effective threat she could use on him? And why did her assertiveness chase the angel off his shoulder, leaving only the devil behind?

"Keep your eyes closed," he commanded as he lifted just enough to push his pants down and kick them off him.

The smile lifting her lips was full of satisfaction, but he wiped that smirk off her face with one brutal thrust, burying himself inside of her.

Her orgasm had prepared her for him, but she was tight, and when she cried out, he had a moment of panic and stilled immediately. But then that satisfied smile returned to her lips, and she lifted her long legs, wrapping them around his waist and gripping his ass with her hands.

"You're mine." She dug her fingers into his flesh and arched her hips, getting him to go even deeper.

"I'm yours," he growled against her ear. "And you're mine."

He was out of control, and if she opened her eyes right now, she would see him in his full immortal glory, his fangs fully elongated, and his eyes blazing blue light.

Keeping his head down, his cheek tucked against hers, he reached between them and circled his thumb over her clit.

"William," Kaia moaned his name.

As his thrusts became faster and stronger, he had to remove his thumb, and as he felt his seed rising in his shaft, he pushed the slightest of thralls into Kaia's mind, preparing her for what he was about to do next.

Licking her neck, he pulled out of her and fisted his erection, and as he sank his fangs into her neck, he came all over her belly and her thighs. She climaxed under him, the venom inducing a chain of orgasms that went on and on for nearly as long as he kept spilling on top of her.

When it was all done, and Kaia was soaring on the clouds of bliss, he withdrew his fangs, licked the puncture wounds closed, and lay on top of her for a moment to catch his breath.

Pulling out and finishing outside had been a feat William doubted any other immortal male could have accomplished, but he wasn't proud of himself for achieving the impossible.

He imagined the angel on his right shoulder shaking his head at him in disapproval, while the devil on his left shoulder was dancing a victory dance and flipping the angel off.

They had both acted recklessly, just for different reasons. Kaia didn't know that he couldn't give her sexually transmitted diseases or get her pregnant, and even if she was on the pill, she should have made sure that he put a condom on. She was young and impulsive, and perhaps she could be forgiven, but he was tempted to treat her to a good spanking for how irresponsibly she'd acted.

Except, knowing her, it would only encourage her to be even naughtier. It hadn't escaped his notice how throaty she'd sounded when she'd asked him if he was going to punish her.

Brazen, assertive Kaia yearned to yield control, and he was more than happy to play along.

But then, he wasn't blameless either. He didn't have the excuse of youth and impulsivity, and he shouldn't have allowed things to progress so quickly between them. Perhaps he should let Kaia spank him, although he doubted she would enjoy it as much.

The image put a smile on his face, but then the reality of what he'd done slapped it off his face.

The thralling Kaia would need at the end of the project was substantial, and the responsible thing would have been to avoid thralling her until then. By giving in to his impulses and her insistence, he was endangering not only her but also the safety of the project.

71

KAIA

*A*n obnoxious beeping noise woke Kaia from the best dream ever, but her annoyance was quickly replaced by a fuzzy warm feeling as she registered the arm draped around her and the warm body pressed against her back.

She was in William's bed, in his arms, and it was much better than any dream. Well, since the dream had been about him, it was nearly as good, but the real thing was always better.

"Good morning." She turned around and kissed him on the lips. "Or is it still night? What time is it?"

He opened his eyes and smiled. "I thought that I was dreaming, but you are really here."

She chuckled. "Funny, I dreamt about you too, and then that annoying beeping started, and I woke up. What was it?"

"My alarm." He sighed. "I'm supposed to be in the gym at five, but I think I'm going to skip it today." He pulled her closer against him. "I might never get out of bed at all."

"I wish we could stay here all day and snuggle, but I need to get to my bungalow before Kylie wakes up and starts the gossip train." She kissed him again and then pushed on his chest. "I need to pee."

He grumbled something under his breath but let go of her.

She found her clothes folded neatly on the nightstand and pulled the T-shirt and panties on before padding to the bathroom.

After she'd passed out, William must have cleaned her up and collected her clothes because she remembered them being carelessly tossed on the floor.

After taking care of her bladder and brushing her teeth with her finger, she padded back to the bedroom and sat on the bed. "Wake up, sleepyhead."

Instead of opening his eyes, he yanked her down to him and wrapped her in his arms. "You are way too cheerful for someone who slept only two hours."

"I'm happy." She couldn't stop smiling. "But I don't want to do the walk of

KAIA

shame. I'd rather sneak into my room and tell Kylie that we were working on the project, and I fell asleep on your couch."

A frown tugged on his brows. "Are you embarrassed about spending the night with me?"

"Never. I'll shout it from the rooftops if you are okay with that, and I'll tell everyone that we are officially together. I'll also move my things in here and sleep with you every night."

He smiled. "I would like that."

That was a surprise. He'd been so concerned about having a relationship with her because she worked for him, and now he didn't mind telling everyone about it?

"Really? That's a big departure from where you were just yesterday."

"Things have changed, and I have no intention of hiding our relationship. I'm going to get mercilessly teased and accused of cradle robbing, but I can live with that. You are not a shameful secret, my princess Kaia. If anything, you are a great prize to be proud of."

"That's music to my ears." She relaxed against his chest. "Are you going to tell Darlene that you're not joining her today for a swim?"

"I'm just not going to show up." His hand traveled down to her bottom, and he gave it a hard squeeze. "You should get a good bare bottom spanking for being so careless."

If not for his serious tone, she would have thought that he was teasing. "What do you mean by careless?"

"You're impulsive. You didn't verify that I had a condom, and that's careless. I happen to be clean, but allowing a guy you've just met to have unprotected sex with you is irresponsible."

Talk about spoiling the mood. From floating on clouds, she'd tumbled down into detention.

"I'm on the pill, so pregnancy prevention was covered, and you are too much of a dork not to be clean. I knew that I had nothing to worry about."

"A dork, eh?" He playfully slapped her bottom. "I'm a nerd, not a dork. Even an old lecher like me knows the difference."

She laughed. "You are both a dork and a nerd, but so am I, so we are in it together. You are also a sexy hunk of a man, not an old lecher or a cradle robber. And you are mine. But I still need to get to my room, shower, and put on fresh clothes before going to breakfast."

"Not yet. Stay for a little longer."

72

WILLIAM

*W*illiam lingered in bed long after Kaia left to shower and change, basking in the afterglow of the best lovemaking he'd ever experienced despite pulling out at the last moment.

Kaia hadn't commented on that, so perhaps her memories of those final moments were fuzzy thanks to his venom and the slight thrall he'd managed right before he'd bitten her.

Waking up with her in his arms had been phenomenal, but if he wanted many more mornings like that, she needed to move in with him, and that would make some waves. He needed to come up with a strategy to deal with the responses to their relationship.

People were going to snicker and make comments, but he could handle it. The question was whether Kaia could. Even those who didn't know how old he really was would frown on their relationship.

A thirteen-year difference was a big deal for humans at any age, especially when the girl was as young as Kaia.

Her stepfather was going to kill him, or at least try, and so would the uncle. Hopefully, that wouldn't ruin things for Darlene, who had high hopes for the guy.

Perhaps he should propose to Kaia?

Would her family still be angry if they were engaged?

And why did the prospect of calling her his fiancée appeal to him so much?

Closing his eyes, William did something so atypical that it could only mean that he was in love. He prayed to the Fates, beseeching them to make Kaia his mate. Well, first she had to be a Dormant, and then his mate. Or was it the other way around?

When his phone rang, he expected it to be Darlene berating him for not showing up for their swimming session again, but as he lifted it, the picture on the screen was Kian's.

His anxiety spiking, William pushed up on the pillows and accepted the call. "Good morning, Kian."

"Good morning. I hate being the bearer of bad news, but I just got off the phone with Kalugal. He asked Areana about Tony, and she confirmed that he's in the harem, which means that he's not getting out. No one ever does."

William swallowed the bile rising in his throat. "So, your hunch was right. Is he at least being treated well?"

"Of course, he is. The harem is Areana's domain, and she takes care of her people." Kian cleared his throat. "Was Anthony Kaia's boyfriend?"

"No, he wasn't. They were just good friends."

"Good. Areana told Kalugal that Tula took Anthony as her lover, and she refuses to share him with the other immortal ladies."

"That's one hell of a coincidence. Is he happy there?"

"Kalugal didn't comment on that. Obviously, he's not suffering, and he's under Navuh's compulsion to donate his seed the natural way, but he's a young man who had a bright future to look forward to, and it's been taken away from him. He can't be too happy."

"Can we rescue him? We can do it the same way we extracted Carol from the island."

"I feel bad for the guy, but I'm not risking our people and a war with Navuh to rescue a human."

"Yeah. You're right. I shouldn't have even suggested it. I just don't know what to tell Kaia."

"Don't tell her anything. As far as she's concerned, you couldn't find any more information about her friend. Case closed."

William didn't want to lie to Kaia. He was already lying to her about too many things.

"I'll think of something. Thank you for calling me right away."

"You're welcome. I'm sorry I didn't have better news for her."

After Kian ended the call, William got out of bed and padded to the bathroom. Turning the water on in the shower, he got under the spray, braced his hands on the tiled wall, and hung his head. While the hot water sluiced down his back, he tried to come up with a way to tell Kaia about Tony without lying to her, but at the same time not telling her about the island and how he knew about it.

If Tony was Tula's lover, then perhaps the story about him finding a girl and enjoying his time with her was not such a big departure from the truth. It would be a lie by omission, and that wasn't as bad as a complete fabrication.

But knowing Kaia, she would ask questions that he couldn't answer, so maybe Kian was right that the best strategy was not to tell her at all.

73

KAIA

"Good morning." Kylie had a knowing smirk on her face as she walked into their small living room. "Where were you last night? I went to sleep after one in the morning, and you weren't here yet."

As a dozen different considerations flashed through Kaia's mind, she took a long moment to answer. She didn't want to hide her relationship with William, and he didn't want that either, but despite what she'd told him about shouting it from the rooftops, she wasn't the type of girl who freely shared details about her sex life with her friends. It was nobody's business.

"I was with William." She lifted her phone and pretended to be absorbed in her sister's Instatock channel.

"I thought so." Kylie walked over to their coffee maker, stuffed a pod into the slot and a mug under the spout, and then leaned against the counter with her arms crossed over her chest and that annoying smirk still playing over her lips. "Working late on the decoding, I presume?"

The sarcastic tone aggravated Kaia, and the answer dancing on the tip of her tongue was that she'd had mind-blowing sex with a spectacular man and had woken up in his arms this morning, which had also been an amazing experience, but it was none of Kylie's business.

"Among other things." Kaia put her empty coffee cup in the sink. "I'm heading out to get breakfast. Are you coming?"

"Yeah." Kylie took the freshly brewed cup of coffee and brought it to her lips. "I just need a few sips."

Tapping her foot on the floor, Kaia waited for her to finish drinking even though she would have liked nothing better than to walk out the door and leave her nosy roommate behind.

She'd hoped to have a better relationship with Kylie, perhaps even form a real friendship that they could maintain after the project was over and they returned to the Bay Area, but there was something about her roommate that just rubbed her the wrong way. Kylie wasn't horrible, but she wasn't bestie material either.

Not that Kaia had ever had a bestie. Tony had been her closest friend, but he was a guy and much older than her, so he didn't really count. Besides, he was gone, so the only one left was Cheryl. Her sister was four years younger than her and had no prior life memories, but she was a very old soul. Cheryl was level-headed and direct, and Kaia could always count on her to tell her the truth and watch her back.

Perhaps she could call her later and share the wonderful news about her and William. Not about the sex, of course. She would only hint at that, but about them officially becoming a couple.

"I'm ready to go." Kylie put her cup in the sink.

As they walked out the door, she threaded her arm through Kaia's and leaned closer to whisper in her ear. "So, what were the other things you and William did last night?"

"We talked." Kaia smiled sweetly at her.

Thankfully, Kylie wasn't stupid and got the hint. "Fine. If you don't want to talk about it, it's your choice." She tilted her head to look up at Kaia. "Did you know that the Safe Haven community practices free love?"

"I've read about it. Good for them, but it's not for me. I'm too possessive to share."

"Yeah, I don't like to share either. I can't imagine falling in love with someone and watching him with another woman, but I wouldn't mind just having fun for a while and choosing a different guy each night. And what's even better, it's ladies' choice with them. The men have to wait to be invited. They can't initiate, but they can try to impress the ladies to get an invitation. How cool is that?"

Kaia opened the door to the dining room. "I can see the merit of that, and kudos to them for empowering women, but it's not for me. I'm a one-guy girl, and I want my guy to be a one-girl man." She waved at Darlene, who was sitting with Eleanor and three of the paranormals.

William wasn't there yet, and she wondered whether he was still sleeping. Had she exhausted him so thoroughly last night?

The thing was that she couldn't remember what happened from the moment right before she'd blacked out from bliss, and it bothered her. It had been literally mind-blowing sex because her mind had shorted out, and stuff like that just didn't happen to her.

74

WILLIAM

*W*illiam was struggling to keep the information Kian had shared with him from Kaia. He'd even skipped breakfast so he wouldn't have to face her in a social environment, but once their workday ended, he would have no more excuses. He had to come up with something that he could tell her that wouldn't be a complete lie but would also give her hope and not devastate her.

He was a smart guy, and he should be able to think of something before Kaia lost her patience and demanded answers.

Sitting across the desk from her and keeping it bottled inside of him was pure hell.

As Kaia lifted her head and looked at him, William forced a tight smile. Seeing his pinched expression, she lowered her head and went back to the stack of photocopies he'd printed for her to work on, but not before he'd caught the pained look in her eyes.

After what they'd shared yesterday, she'd probably expected smiles and covert kisses, not a nervous wreck who was giving her the silent treatment. He'd even left the door to his office wide open so they were in plain view of the other team members.

William hoped that she would take it as his attempt to act professionally during work hours, and not as his reaction to their intimacy of last night and this morning.

If it hadn't been such a reality-altering experience, and he wasn't falling in love with her, it would have been much easier for him to lie to her or to pretend that he didn't know what happened to her friend. It would have been just one more thing he couldn't talk about because the clan's security demanded it.

But Kaia was his mate, he could feel it in every fiber of his being, and he would be very surprised if he was wrong. And if he was right, he had to tell her the truth about everything anyway, so why wait and live with the torment?

"I need to make a phone call." He got to his feet.

Kaia lifted her head and looked at him with those big sad eyes of hers, cementing his decision. "I can leave if you need privacy. I can use a coffee break." She was out the door before he had a chance to object.

As she closed it behind her, he dropped back into his chair and let out a breath before picking up his phone and calling Kian.

"William," the boss answered in his usual gruff voice that people took to mean that he didn't have time for them. "Anything new with the decoding?"

"Plenty, but that's not what I'm calling about. I think that Kaia is a Dormant and that she's my mate. I'm going to tell her everything tonight, including what I know about her friend."

There was a long moment of stunned silence. "What makes you think that she's a Dormant? Does she have any paranormal abilities?"

"Not as far as I know, unless her uncanny ability to translate the gods' language and genetic coding counts. It's like she was born with the knowledge, but that could be attributed to her brilliance. The others don't have a clue about what they are working on. Well, I'm exaggerating. They have a vague idea, but since only Kaia has access to larger portions of the manuscript, she's the only one who has the big picture."

"What about affinity?" Kian asked.

"That's actually a good indicator. Eleanor and Darlene like her a lot, and that's not because Kaia is such an easily likable girl. She's assertive and direct, and she's quick to anger, which doesn't endear her to her teammates. But that could also be because of envy. She's a kid, and she's smarter and more accomplished than the three of them combined."

"You sound like you are in awe, not just in love."

"I am, and I feel like an old lecher lusting after a nineteen-year-old who works for me, but as Kaia pointed out, I need her much more than she needs me, so she's in the position to coerce me, and not the other way around."

Kian chuckled. "I like her already. But that doesn't mean that you should tell her everything. You can give her the general overview about immortals and Dormants and get her consent to induction, but you can't tell her about obtaining the information about her friend. That would endanger Lokan and Areana, and especially Areana. Navuh wouldn't kill his mate over this, but he would confiscate her means of communications with us, and we can't let that happen. He could even retaliate by hurting those she loves, and one of those is Tula, Wonder's sister."

"How is Kaia going to jeopardize their safety? For the next two weeks, she's not going to leave Safe Haven, and in that time, we will know whether she's a Dormant or not. And with the security systems we've put in place, no one can get to her either."

"What about her family? They are coming to visit her this weekend."

Onegus must have updated Kian about that, but it wasn't an issue either.

"She's already under compulsion not to reveal anything about the research. I can ask Eleanor and Emmett to include this as well."

"You can't tell Eleanor and Emmett about Areana. They don't know that we can communicate with her, and if they don't know that, how are they going to compel Kaia not to reveal it?"

"I don't have to give them any details. I'll find a way for them to form an umbrella compulsion. Besides, I won't mention Areana by name. I will just tell Kaia that we have a source in Navuh's harem."

"I don't like it," Kian grumbled.

"I have no choice. I've bitten her once already and had to thrall her. I don't want to do that again. Her brain is too precious to mess with, not just to me but all of us. She holds the key to the translation."

"Fine. Just be careful."

As relief washed over William, he closed his eyes for a brief moment. "Thank you."

"Don't mention it, and by that, I mean, don't mention it to anyone ever. I can't believe the concession I'm making for you. If it was anyone else…"

"I know. I'm special, and I'm truly grateful."

75

KAIA

*W*illiam was acting strange, and the only explanation Kaia could think of was that he regretted last night.

But he'd been so loving this morning. And what about all that talk about her being his great prize and him being proud to win her?

What, or who had changed his mind?

She glanced around the table at her teammates. Kylie was scribbling on her yellow pad, Corinne was trying to figure out the chemical composition of one of the materials that William had partially translated, and Owen was working on a spreadsheet. None of them looked guilty or were giving her weird looks, so they weren't the culprits.

Perhaps Darlene had told William to back off?

The woman seemed to like her, and Kaia liked her back, so the only reason for Darlene to do that was if she thought that William was taking advantage of her. But if the two were old friends, she should know that William would never coerce anyone into doing what they didn't want to do. He was a good man.

The door to his office opened, and as he stepped out, William immediately zeroed in on her as if none of the others were there. "I need to talk to you." He walked over to the table and offered her a hand up.

That was it. He was going to tell her that they couldn't continue whatever they'd started and would have to limit their interactions to the lab. Or something like that.

Swallowing the lump that had formed in her throat, she took his hand and tried to suck in a breath, but all she got was a trickle of air.

"It's okay," William murmured quietly as he led her to the lab's door. "There is no reason for alarm."

Her panicked expression probably made him think that she was expecting bad news from home, not from him. But what if that was what he'd come to tell her?

"What happened? Is my family okay?"

"I didn't hear anything to indicate otherwise. The thing I need to talk to you about has to do with what we are working on."

Kaia didn't believe him.

When they were outside the lab, she turned toward the bungalows, but William took her hand and guided her in the opposite direction. "We are going to the lodge."

"Why?" After the first day, they had been told not to go there because a new retreat had started, and they were not supposed to mingle with the guests.

"We need to talk with Eleanor and Emmett."

That was even stranger. "They are not supposed to know what we are working on. What do we need to talk to them about?"

Maybe they had been the ones to turn William against having a relationship with her?

"It's related to your contract." He sounded exasperated.

She hoped he wouldn't try to pull that one on her. Kaia had an excellent memory, and she'd read the entire contract carefully.

Tugging on his hand, she forced him to slow down. "There was nothing in there about prohibiting relationships between team members. I would have remembered if there was."

William stopped, turned to her, and before she knew what was happening, his hand cupped her nape, and his lips smashed over hers in a scorching hot kiss.

He kissed her like a starving man, like he couldn't get enough of her, and as she put her hands on his chest and melted into the kiss, he wrapped an arm around her and pulled her into his body.

When she had to come up for air, he let go of her and looked into her eyes. "I'm not trying to get rid of you. The opposite is true. I want to keep you with me for as long as I can."

As his meaning sank in, Kaia's eyes widened. So that's what he needed Emmett and Eleanor for—witnesses for their marriage contract.

"I like you a lot, William. I might be even falling in love with you. But I'm not ready to get married after knowing you for three days."

He laughed. "We are not going to the chapel or the courthouse. We are just going to the lodge. Can you wait patiently for a few more minutes instead of jumping to conclusions?"

"I can't help it." She let him lead her at an even faster pace. "That's what I do. I gather clues and put them together. I do it even in my sleep. How do you think I can decipher that alien language?"

76

WILLIAM

*A*s William knocked on Emmett's office door, Eleanor opened it and smiled. "Good afternoon. Please, come in."

"Welcome." Emmett spread his arms in his prophet pose, the long sleeves of his robe fluttering in the breeze blowing through the open window. "Please take a seat."

When William had called ahead and explained what he needed them to do and why, both Emmett and Eleanor had congratulated him and wished him and Kaia the best of luck, and there had been true warmth in their voices.

Eleanor rolled her eyes at her mate. "You can drop the theatrics, Emmett. Your flock is not here to witness it."

William didn't mind. As long as the compulsion worked, Emmett could pretend to be an angel and flap a pair of fake wings. It would probably be an improvement over his Moses act.

The guy pouted. "How did I end up with a grouch like you who doesn't appreciate a good act? I'm a performer. I need an audience."

"You have it." Eleanor leaned and kissed his bearded cheek. "Every day, almost all day long. I want to see the real Emmett from time to time."

"My love." The guy beamed at his mate.

The two were an odd couple, and right now they seemed to have forgotten that William needed their services.

Looking confused, Kaia leaned closer to him. "What's going on?"

"Emmett and Eleanor are a loving couple, but they are two very different people. Emmett likes to live on a stage, while Eleanor is more down to earth."

Kaia still looked confused, but she nodded.

Eleanor patted her mate's arm. "We have a job to do."

"Right. Do you want to go first?"

"Sure." Leaning against Emmett's desk, Eleanor crossed her arms over her chest and her feet at the ankles. "The reason you are here is that William is ready to reveal more secrets to you, and he needs our help to ensure that you don't breathe a word of what he's about to tell you to anyone, and that includes Emmett and me."

Kaia turned to him with an offended expression on her beautiful face. "You could've just asked. I would have never broken your trust. Besides, I've already signed a confidentiality agreement."

He took her hand and leaned toward her. "It's not entirely up to me, and the lives of many people depend on that information remaining a secret."

"Then why tell me at all? I don't want to know something that means life or death to people. I don't want that kind of responsibility."

"You're smart," Eleanor said.

William had a plan, and he knew precisely how he was going to play it. "It's about Tony."

Kaia's head whipped around to Eleanor. "Where do I sign?"

The woman chuckled. "It's not a written agreement. It's a verbal one. You will not repeat anything William tells you is a secret to anyone but him, and only when you are sure that no one else can hear you. You will not write it, mime it, or communicate it in any other fashion either. Now, repeat what I said and swear an oath."

Kaia looked as if she wanted to say something else, but she did exactly as Eleanor had commanded her instead. When she was done, she looked at the woman with narrowed eyes. "Are you also a hypnotist like Emmett?"

"I am. And just to cement it, Emmett is going to repeat what I just did."

William was surprised. Emmett's compulsion hadn't worked as immediately and as strongly on Kaia as Eleanor's. Perhaps she was the stronger compeller?

Turning to him, Kaia rubbed a hand over her temple. "How do they do that? I wanted to ask that question before repeating what Eleanor said, but I couldn't. It was like a compulsion."

"Because that's precisely what it was," Emmett said. "Eleanor is a strong compeller, but I'm even stronger, and the doubling of our powers will ensure your silence."

William was no longer sure that Emmett was right about being the stronger compeller, but this wasn't the time to comment on it.

Kaia looked like she was about to bolt, but Emmett stopped her with a simple command. "Sit down."

Her bottom hit the chair with a thwack.

Later, William would have a word with Emmett about his Doctor Evil performance. There was no need to scare Kaia, and he could have just done the compulsion the way Eleanor had done it.

"Ignore his theatrics." William squeezed her hand. "He will do exactly what Eleanor did, no more, and no less."

7 7

KAIA

*A*s they left Emmett's office, Kaia stopped right outside the door and turned to William. "That was the weirdest hour of my life, and I've had a few that I didn't think could be topped." Like standing naked in front of the mirror, looking at herself through the eyes of a man, and touching her own breasts. "But I have a feeling that things are going to get much weirder than that."

"You have no idea." He took her hand and brought it to his lips for a soft kiss. "But don't worry. The rest of it is going to be much more pleasant. I apologize for Emmett's unnecessary theatrics. I don't know what has gotten into him." He lowered her hand and led her down the corridor toward one of the lodge's side doors.

"You said that the secret had to do with Tony."

"It does, but I can't tell you about it without explaining a few things first, and those are not the type of things I can tell you out here." He opened the door and held it open for her. "Let's go to my bungalow."

Kaia smirked. "I have no objection to that, but aren't you forgetting something?"

He frowned. "What?"

"The other team members. They are stuck in the lab, and they can't get out without you opening the door for them. Thankfully, lunch was delivered before we left, so they are not starving."

"Right." William rubbed the back of his neck, with a sheepish smile lifting the corners of his lips. "We need to stop by the lab and let them out. Everyone gets the rest of the day off. I bet they are going to love that."

"No doubt." Kaia leaned into him as they kept walking. "You really should scan another person's eyeball so someone else can open those doors." She narrowed her eyes at him with a mock stern look. "Talk about irresponsible. If something happens to you, how are we supposed to get out?"

"You are right. I'll get Max to lend me his eye." He winked at her.

"You seem so different from the way you were this morning. I was sure that you were regretting what happened between us."

Remembering the private phone call he'd needed to make, the puzzle pieces fell into place. "You called someone and asked permission to tell me the truth, didn't you?"

"Yes. And the reason I was in such a dreary mood all morning was that I couldn't tell you all the things I wanted to, and it was eating away at me. There should be no secrets between people who love each other."

Love? Was he telling her that he loved her?

In a way, he'd already said that in so many words this morning.

Did she love him back?

How could anyone be in love with someone after knowing them for three days?

William stopped in front of the lab door. "Do you want to come in with me? Or do you want to wait out here?"

"I'll come with you. I need to organize my papers."

She'd left them on William's desk in a neat stack, and since he'd locked the door behind him, it wasn't necessary, but she didn't want her teammates to start asking him questions about her without her being there.

When he opened the third door, Corinne gave him a glare worthy of a stern matriarch. "I was starting to worry that you'd abandoned us here."

"I would never do that." He sent an overt smile Kaia's way. "I came to get you out. Everyone gets the rest of the day off."

"What's the occasion?" Owen asked.

"I have a headache." William didn't even bother to sound convincing. "I need to lie down and have my girlfriend rub my temples." He wrapped his arm around Kaia's shoulders.

Corinne shrugged. "If you want to dig your own grave," she murmured under her breath, "it's no skin off my nose."

William pretended that he hadn't heard her, but Kaia's skin wasn't as thick as his, and Corinne's jab hurt. It implied that William was manipulating her to get her in his bed, or that she was manipulating him to later extort him with threats to sue him for sexual harassment. It cast a sleazy light on both of them.

She was tempted to say something biting back, but William squeezed her shoulder reassuringly, and she decided to let it go.

Her teammates would get used to them being a couple, and in a day or two it would be old news, and everything would return to normal.

Or so she hoped.

WILLIAM

$\mathcal{O}$n the way to his bungalow, William had thought long and hard about the way he was going to present things to Kaia. She had an open mind, and after dealing with the journals and what they contained, she wouldn't dismiss his story as the ramblings of a madman.

He didn't expect to encounter too much disbelief from her.

Nevertheless, he was nervous as he put down two glasses of water on the coffee table and sat down next to her on the couch.

"Everything I'm going to tell you from now on is a well-guarded secret." He took her hand and clasped it.

She nodded. "I wouldn't tell a soul even without the hypnotic compulsion. It wasn't necessary."

He believed her, but he hadn't had the luxury of trusting his instincts on that.

"I got the boss's approval to let you in on the biggest secret in the world under the condition that you undergo compulsion to never reveal it."

"The biggest?"

He smiled. "After I tell you what it is, you can tell me if you think it is the biggest or not."

Kaia let out a breath. "Just get on with it, then. I can't stand the suspense."

He nodded. "I'll start with a brief overview, and after I'm done, you can ask me to elaborate on the parts you want more information on." He sucked in a breath. "The mythological gods were real people, and they had children with humans who were born immortal. The immortals had the gods' powers to manipulate human minds, but to a lesser extent. When those immortals took human mates, though, their children were born mortal. It was later discovered that the children of female immortals carried the immortal genes in a dormant state and that there was a way to activate them. Most of the gods perished in an attack launched by one of their own, but a few survived, and some of the immortals and humans who carried the godly genes survived as well."

CHAPTER 78

Kaia regarded him with interest, and so far, she didn't look as if she was about to declare him insane and walk out the door, which was encouraging, but he hadn't gotten to the part of him being one of those immortals.

"The survivors split into two opposing camps. The one I belong to is headed by a benevolent goddess whose mission is to continue her people's work and help humanity progress and evolve. The other camp is headed by the immortal son of the god who murdered the other gods, and his mission is to rule supreme over an enslaved humanity. Lately, he decided to improve the quality of the immortal warriors he breeds on his island, so he started attracting smart young men to breed the dormant females he keeps enslaved there."

William lifted his glass and took a sip of water before continuing to the part she would find most relevant. "Your friend is one of those smart young men, but unlike the others who have no idea that their seed is being stolen and go home after their sex vacation is over, he's been sent to Navuh's personal harem because of his slight resemblance to the despot. That way, Navuh can claim that all the children born to the immortal females he keeps there are his. Anthony is alive, and he's treated well, but he's never going to leave that island."

For a long moment Kaia just gaped at him, then she leaned down, took her glass, and drank half of it in one go. "If anyone other than you would have told me this story, I wouldn't have believed it. But I know that you are not crazy, and you are not prone to making up fantasies either. So, my question is, how do we get Tony out?"

William's heart swelled with pride and a big smile spread over his face. "I knew you wouldn't freak out and run away screaming that your boyfriend is a madman."

She narrowed her eyes at him. "I have many more questions for my so-called boyfriend, starting with how old you really are, but for now, I want to know what can be done for Tony."

William's smile wilted. "Nothing, I'm afraid. The island is home to about twenty thousand immortal warriors, and my clan is tiny in comparison. Even if Tony was one of us, we wouldn't have dared to start a war with Navuh to get him out."

That wasn't entirely true, but to tell her more meant exposing Areana and her role in Carol's extraction, and he'd promised Kian not to do that. Besides, it had no bearing on his relationship with Kaia, and Anthony was an unlucky human, not a clan member.

Kaia let out a breath. "At least he's alive. Do you know that for sure?"

"They don't use last names on the island, so I can't be a hundred percent sure, but I doubt that they have another scientist named Tony who also matches your friend's description."

"I assume that you have an informant on the island."

He nodded.

"Can he pass a message to Tony? Just so he knows that he hasn't been forgotten?"

"I'm not sure. I'm not the one who's dealing with the informant, and I doubt my boss would authorize it."

That part was close enough to the truth. William was no longer in charge of communications between Areana and Annani or Kalugal at the pre-agreed times. That job had been assigned to one of the guardians back at the village.

211

"Is your boss the goddess?"

"The goddess is the head of our clan, but she leaves the day-to-day management to two of her children. Her son is my boss."

"How many kids does she have? Were their fathers human? Where does she live?" Kaia chuckled. "Don't tell me that it's on Mount Olympus."

KAIA

"It's not on Mount Olympus." William's eyes shone with that inner light Kaia now knew she hadn't imagined. "She lives in a place called the sanctuary, and no one knows how to get there except for her Odus, who fly her people in and out of there."

"The Odus?"

William took his glasses off and reached for a corner of his shirt to wipe them with, but then stopped and put them on the coffee table. "Immortals don't need glasses. I wear them to protect my eyes from the computer glare, and since I spend most of the time in front of the screen, I usually don't bother taking them off." He smiled. "I feel naked without them." He took in a long breath. "The Odus are what you would call cyborgs, but the technology to build them was banned on the gods' home planet. Seven of them were either sent or brought to Earth, and they belonged to our Clan Mother, the goddess. She assigned one to each of her five children, whose fathers were indeed human, but one of her sons was killed, so his Odu returned to her. Not too long ago, the one taking care of her surviving son gifted him with a surprising birthday present. A trunk of handwritten journals containing the blueprints of how to build an Odu. That's what you've been working on. We are trying to decipher the gods' scientific language."

So that was where the journals came from. Now everything clicked into place, painting a fantastic picture that she had no doubt was true. If she wasn't embarrassed to show her excitement, Kaia would have danced in a circle singing, 'I knew it.' She'd always suspected the mythological gods had been aliens, but she couldn't come up with a reasonable explanation for why they had disappeared. William had provided her with the missing piece of the puzzle that had finally unlocked the mystery and confirmed her suspicions.

"Did you try to take one apart to see how it worked?" she asked.

William's eyes widened with an expression of horror. "The goddess wouldn't allow it, and even if she did, I wouldn't have dared. The Odus are like members of our family, and to open up one of their brains would have been like operating on one of my cousins without knowing if I could put them back together again."

"I get it." She leaned back. "Are they sentient?"

"I believe so. They are constantly learning, but their creator limited their ability to learn. They were supposed to be domestic servants, and I assume that was done so they wouldn't become dangerous, but they were used as weapons nonetheless, and that's why the technology to make them was destroyed, and they were decommissioned."

"Can I meet one? I mean an Odu?"

"Perhaps. It depends on a few things."

"Like what?"

William chuckled. "You never cease to astonish me. The questions you ask are not the ones I prepared answers for. Aren't you wondering why I told you all of this?"

She was, but then other questions intruded, and she'd lost her train of thought. "At first, I thought that you told me all this because of Tony, but since there is nothing that can be done for him, it didn't serve any purpose other than to let me know that he's alive, but you could have told me that without revealing all the background story. Was it because of what I was decoding? Was I getting too close to figuring out what those schematics were for?"

He shook his head. "That's not it at all, but it will certainly help you now that you know the big picture. I told you the brief history of gods, immortals, and Dormants because I suspect that you carry the godly genes, and if you do, being intimate with me might activate them. I didn't want to do that without your consent."

So far, everything William had told her had sounded logical, but now he'd managed to stun her.

Kaia lifted her hand. "Wait a minute. Are you telling me that I can turn immortal?"

"Yes."

"How?"

"Look at my teeth."

He smiled wide, and for the first time ever, she noticed that his canines were longer than usual, and as she looked closer, they elongated in front of her eyes.

"What the heck, William? Why do you have fangs? Are immortals vampires?" Her hand flew to her neck. "Did you drink my blood?"

He laughed nervously. "We don't drink blood. Immortal males inject venom, which delivers incredible orgasms and has healing properties, so you have nothing to worry about on that account. But when that happens during sex with a Dormant, it can induce her transition, and that's something to worry about. Not for you because you are so young, but for older Dormants, it might be dangerous."

"What if I'm not a Dormant? What would it do to me?"

"The venom has euphoric, aphrodisiac, and healing properties. It gives you orgasms, trips to fantasy land, and a wonderful sense of well-being when you wake up."

She'd experienced all of that with him, which meant that he'd bitten her, which meant that he could have already induced her.

Panic seizing her, she touched her neck again. "You've bitten me."

CHAPTER 79

"I did."

"We had sex. You could have induced my transition already."

His cheeks reddening, William shook his head. "To induce a Dormant, two things have to happen at once. One is unprotected sex, meaning insemination, and the other is the venom bite. You don't remember it, but I pulled out before climaxing. If you don't want to be induced, using a condom would prevent it."

Kaia barked out a laugh. "So that's why you were so angry about me not insisting on you using a condom." She wagged her finger at him. "You were the one who acted irresponsibly. If you didn't have a rubber, you shouldn't have had sex with me at all." Another laugh escaped her throat. "Talk about sexually transmitted diseases. I could have caught immortality from you."

WILLIAM

*A*s Kaia collapsed in a fit of giggles, William realized that she must have reached the limit of what she was able to absorb and pulled her into his arms. "It's all too much at once, and you didn't get enough sleep last night. Maybe you should take an afternoon nap, and we can continue talking about it when you are rested."

Hiccuping, Kaia wiped the tears from her eyes and let out a sigh. "Maybe I'm still inside the trip your venom sent me on. But wait, that doesn't make sense. I can't be inside the trip if this is not real because I wouldn't know about it. But maybe you slipped something into my water?" She leaned over, lifted the glass off the table, and sniffed it. "Smells fine, but that doesn't mean anything." She extended her tongue and lapped at it like a dog. "It tastes fine too."

She was losing it.

"I really think you should take a nap." He got to his feet with her in his arms, walked over to the bedroom, and put her down on the bed. "Do you want me to undress you?"

"Please do." She eyed him with amusement dancing in her eyes. "But you have to get naked too. I didn't get to see you fully nude last night."

He was relieved to hear her sounding bossy as usual and in control of her emotions.

"I'm shy." He took off her flip-flops and dropped them on the floor.

"No, you're not." Kaia stretched her arms over her head. "You are a scion of gods, an immortal. How can you be shy?"

"I was just joking." Not really, but he would go with that.

"But if you are immortal, and so were the gods, how did they die?"

"Gods and immortals can be killed. It's just a little harder to do. Immortality means that we don't age and we don't get sick."

"Fascinating. How old are you?"

CHAPTER 80

"Too old for you." He pulled her jeans down her hips. "I've told you that already."

"I'm an old soul."

"Not as old as me." Leaving Kaia's T-shirt and underwear on, William pulled the blanket over her, kicked his shoes off, and lay next to her over it.

This wasn't about sex, and despite her bravado, Kaia was exhausted, overwhelmed, and she needed warmth, comfort, and sleep.

"Give me years," she insisted. "I want to know."

"I'm over three hundred years old, which is considered young for an immortal but ancient compared to you."

She lifted the blanket. "Get in here but take off your pants first."

"Yes, ma'am."

He did as she commanded and pulled her into his arms. "You don't need to decide anything right away. You are young, and there is no rush. We can use condoms until you tell me that you want to give immortality a go."

She lifted her eyes to him. "If there is no rush, why did you tell me now?"

"Because I can't make love to you without biting you, and to make you forget that I need to thrall you. One thrall is harmless, but more than that can cause damage, and you are too precious to me to risk it."

"Am I precious to you? Or is it my brain?"

"Both. But given how uniquely gifted you are, I'd rather err on the side of caution and not thrall you at all."

"What about what Emmett and Eleanor did to me? Isn't that dangerous to my precious brain?"

"It's not. Compulsion works differently, and not all immortals can do it. In fact, very few can, and I'm not one of them. That's why I needed their help."

"Good." Kaia yawned and closed her eyes. "I don't mind playing kinky games with you and letting you boss me around in bed, but only when I want it. I would hate it if you compelled me to do things I didn't want to do."

"I would never do that." He kissed the top of her nose.

For a moment, he thought that she'd fallen asleep, but then she asked, "The kinky games or the compulsion?"

He laughed. "I'll play any game you fancy, but I will never compel you unless the security of my clan demands it."

"I get it. I would do anything to protect my family as well." She cupped his cheek and leaned up to kiss his lips. "And I would do anything to protect you too."

His heart surged with emotion. "Why?"

"Because I'm falling for you, my handsome, immortal prince."

DARK WHISPERS
from afar

THE CHILDREN OF
THE GODS 63

I. T. LUCAS

INTERNATIONALLY BESTSELLING AUTHOR

1

WILLIAM

"*B*ecause I'm falling for you, my handsome, immortal prince."

Those were the last words Kaia had said to William before closing her eyes and letting out a sigh.

Reeling from the impact of her proclamation, he took a brief moment to bask in those words and to come up with some of his own, but by the time he was ready to tell her that he'd fallen in love with her the first moment he'd seen her, she was fast asleep.

With her glasses perched crookedly on her nose, her long blond hair tangled, and her lush lips parted, Kaia looked so adorable that William just wanted to keep watching her so he could memorize everything about her. But even though she was sleeping peacefully, she couldn't be comfortable.

As he took her glasses off and put them on the nightstand, it occurred to him that he hadn't told her that she would no longer need them after transitioning.

There were still so many things he needed to tell Kaia, and now that he knew how receptive she was to his version of history, he was looking forward to it instead of dreading it.

There had been no disbelief, no shock, not even awe. Kaia had listened to his fantastic story as if she hadn't been surprised to hear that the mythological gods had been real, and she hadn't batted an eyelash when he'd told her that they'd taken human lovers and produced immortal offspring.

But he'd only given her a brief overview of the history of gods and immortals, and he hadn't gone into detail.

In preparation for the grand reveal, William had collected several articles discussing the Biblical narrative and how it echoed more ancient tales describing real events. He'd even stored them on an app on his phone to show Kaia, but she hadn't needed convincing.

He'd just been confirming what she'd suspected all along.

When his phone buzzed with an incoming message, William was tempted to ignore it, but he had a feeling it was from Kian, and the boss probably wanted an update.

Reluctantly pulling his arm off Kaia, William turned around and picked up the device. As he'd suspected, the text was from Kian, and it was one word long. *Update.*

When the boss was down to single-word commands, it was better not to keep him waiting.

Gently pulling his other arm from under Kaia, William managed to get out of bed without waking her. Last night, the girl hadn't slept more than two hours, and she'd still worked all morning as if she were already a supercharged immortal.

That was the power of youth. Even humans felt invincible at her age.

After pulling his pants on, William padded out of the bedroom and closed the door behind him as soundlessly as he could.

When he placed the call, Kian answered right away. "How did it go?"

William knew what the boss was worried about, so he opened with that. "I didn't mention knowing anyone on the island. Kaia assumed we had an informant, and I just confirmed without saying who the informant was. We didn't go into any details about the Doomers either. I just told her that the original immortals had split into two opposing camps, good and evil, and that I'm on the good team."

"Did you tell her about Annani?"

"I told her that our clan is led by a goddess."

William had made the mistake of telling Kaia that there had been more than one survivor, but since he didn't fear that any of the information would leak from her, he wasn't worried about it.

"How did she take it?" Kian asked.

William chuckled. "As if I was confirming what she already knew. Kaia thinks that there is a very high probability that sightings of unidentified flying objects are real, and that aliens could be hiding in the depths of our oceans or on the dark side of the moon. Compared to that, my story of gods and immortals was tame. She didn't even ask me to show her proof and just accepted everything I told her at face value."

"Lucky you." Kian let out a breath. "Most Dormants have a real hard time suspending their disbelief. Did she ask you if we can get her friend out?"

"She did. I told her that we couldn't. Then she asked if we could relay a message to Anthony. I said that I'm not sure because I'm not the one dealing with the informant, and that I doubt my boss would authorize it."

"The boss wouldn't," Kian said. "If Anthony gets a message from Kaia, he will wonder how she knew where he was, and how she managed to relay the message. He's under Navuh's compulsion, so even if he swears to keep it a secret, he won't be able to hold on to it."

"You're absolutely right." William was embarrassed about his failure to think it all the way through, but he wasn't going to admit to Kian that his acuity suffered when he was near Kaia. "I preferred the nameless, faceless boss to take the blame for refusing to send the message to her friend."

Evidently he wasn't immune to the effect a testosterone spike had on males.

Kian snorted. "If Kaia is a Dormant, I won't remain nameless and faceless for long. She'll come to live with you in the village."

William winced. "She hasn't given me an answer yet, and since she's so young, there is no rush."

"No one says no to immortality unless they are afraid of dying during the transition, and at nineteen, Kaia has nothing to fear."

"It's more complicated in her case." William sat on the couch and propped his feet on the coffee table. "She's very attached to her family. They are so important to her that she might give up immortality to avoid separation from them."

"How old is her mother?"

"Karen is young enough to transition, provided that she has no health issues, but she's in a loving, committed relationship, and she has five kids, two of them being one-year-old twins. She might not want to risk it either."

"Obviously. But let's worry about that when the time comes. Step one is to confirm that Kaia is a Dormant, and that means inducing her. When she transitions, we will move to step two and see what can be done about her mother and her siblings."

2

KAIA

*A*s Kaia's brain started waking up, she turned on her side and reached for William, but he wasn't there. Had she fallen asleep in his arms, or had it been a dream?

And what about all the things he'd told her?

Was all that part of the dream as well?

She remembered William telling her that he was an immortal and that she was a carrier of godly genes, but Kaia had had strange dreams before, so that wasn't out of the ordinary for her.

Chuckling, she turned on her back and looked at the ceiling. She had lucid dreams of her prior life as a man, so nothing William could have told her in a dream or otherwise would surprise her.

She remembered him carrying her to bed and helping her undress, but she didn't remember them making love, and since she had her T-shirt and underwear on, it was proof that they hadn't done anything more than cuddle. She could've fallen asleep in his arms and then dreamt up that conversation.

It was one hell of a vivid dream, though.

Kaia sighed and turned her head to look out the window.

It was still day outside, but it was getting dark, and given how empty her stomach felt, that seemed about right. She'd missed dinner, and William must have gone without her.

Hopefully, he would bring her a plate. If he didn't, she would demand to be taken out on a proper date and fed a proper meal, and by that she meant a juicy hamburger with a double order of fries.

As Kaia's mouth watered, her stomach made an angry, demanding sound that got her out of bed in an instant.

Grabbing her neatly folded jeans off the dresser, she smiled. They'd been tossed on the floor when she and William had gotten in bed, and he must have picked them up and folded them for her. It was a very sweet gesture from a guy who needed help remembering where he'd put his glasses.

When Kaia was done freshening up and walked into the living room, William was there, and as he turned to her with a big grin spreading over his face, a mirroring grin spread over hers. She hadn't expected to find him there, and she'd expected even less to realize how happy it would make her to see him there waiting for her.

"Good morning, Princess." He walked up to her and pulled her into his arms. "I hope you're hungry."

As Kaia glanced at the small dining table William had set up for two, noting all the little details he'd added to make it fancy and romantic, her heart swelled with love for him. The table was covered in a white cloth, and a slim vase with two red flowers peeked from between the pile of covered plates he'd brought from the kitchen.

"This is lovely. Where did you get the flowers?"

William chuckled. "The flowers were easy. Emmett has them growing in his little private garden next to the cottage that he no longer uses." He pulled out a chair for her. "The tough part was finding a round tablecloth. Darlene cut it out from a large bedsheet."

Instead of sitting down, she lifted her arms and wound them around his neck. "If you keep doing such sweet things for me, I'm going to fall in love with you."

"I'm counting on it." He put his hands on her waist and pulled her against his body. "Are you okay? I mean, given all you learned before your nap?"

Kaia tilted her head up and pressed a soft kiss to his lips. "When I woke up, I wasn't sure I hadn't dreamt it. You are a three-hundred-year-old immortal, right?"

"A little older than that. I'm three hundred and thirty-two years old, but who's counting?"

She laughed. "So that's where the thirty-two came from."

"It's coincidental. I've been using thirty-two since I originally turned that age." He steered her toward the chair. "Let's sit down and eat dinner before it gets cold."

"Thank you." She sat down. "What time is it? I left my phone in my bungalow."

"It's ten minutes to eight." He sat across from her.

"Wow. I slept for over six hours. You shouldn't have waited for me. You must be starving."

"I have enough reserves." He patted his stomach. "I can afford to lose some weight."

Kaia grimaced. She hated when William referred to himself as overweight. So what if he had a little padding? The small layer of fat cushioning the hard muscles underneath felt wonderful when his body was pressed against hers.

"You're perfect the way you are." Removing the lid off her plate, she lifted her fork but paused before spearing a piece of potato. "I find you very handsome." She stabbed the fork into the chunk and lifted it to her mouth.

William shook his head. "I used to be much heavier than this, and if I don't watch it, the weight will pile back on in no time. I like to eat, and I hate any form of physical activity. If left to my own devices, I would sit in front of the computer screen for sixteen hours a day while shoving sandwiches and snacks into my mouth."

Kaia reached for the can of Coke William had put in front of her plate. He must have gone to her place to get it, and wasn't that sweet?

The guy was a keeper for too many reasons to list.

"Don't worry. I'll keep you active and won't let that happen." She popped the lid.

William arched a brow. "Oh, yeah? How?"

"I have a physical activity in mind that you'll enjoy taking part in very much." She took a sip. "And I'll make sure that you engage in it at least once a day."

3

JADE

"Come." Jade tugged on Kagra's sleeve. "I need to burn off some steam. Let's hunt."

Jade hadn't had a private moment with her second-in-command since discovering Safe Haven and its leader's true identity, and she burned with the need to share the news with the only person she could talk to.

Kagra's brow furrowed. "Just the two of us?"

"Yeah. We won't go far. I'm not very hungry. I'm just restless and need an outlet for my energy." Jade shrugged her jacket on and walked out the door.

Kagra followed. "We should take some of the young ones with us."

"Not today." Jade looked down her nose at the guard blocking her way. "Move. We are going hunting."

The guy didn't budge. "Your leave is not on the schedule, and therefore not authorized. I can't let you go without a badge from security, and you know that."

Jade bared her fangs at him. "I'm the prime, and Kagra is my second. We can go hunting whenever we please. If you need badges from us, go to the office and get them."

Her claim wasn't entirely true. As Igor's prime, Jade had more leeway than the others, but Kagra didn't. Nevertheless, the guard responded to her natural dominance as she'd expected, dipping his head and doing as she'd commanded.

Getting authorization to leave the compound wasn't a big deal, and all she needed to do was stop by the security office on the way and get badges from the officer in charge. There was nowhere to run, and even if there was, the compulsion and the collars around their necks made it impossible.

Igor just wanted to keep tabs on everyone in his compound and know where they were at all times.

In that, he and she were alike, and if he wasn't murderous, immoral, and irreverent scum, she would have agreed with his security measures.

When Jade had been in charge of her tribe, when she still had a tribe, she had similar procedures in place, but the difference was that she'd never murdered or enslaved her people, and the procedures had been put in place to keep everyone safe.

Nevertheless, she'd failed spectacularly to ensure her tribe's safety despite how careful she'd been, and she was still paying the price for that failure with her own flesh.

Staying on as Igor's prime and making sure that no other female took her place wasn't about pride, and it wasn't only about gaining information and helping the other females he'd abducted and enslaved either. It was also a self-inflicted punishment.

Not that she'd managed to learn much from him throughout her twenty-two years serving him. She still couldn't figure out how Igor had found her tribe or the others. She'd tried to get him to tell her, but regrettably, he wasn't one of those villains who liked to brag.

The guard returned with their badges. "Next time, go to the security office first."

As she took the badge and affixed it to her jacket, Jade cast him a glare. "Open the gate."

He opened his mouth but then quickly closed it and opened the gate without saying a thing.

Jade stifled a satisfied smile. She could still get most of the males to respond to her demands as long as they weren't in direct opposition to Igor's.

Over the years, she'd tried to use that small advantage, but Igor was too smart, and his commands to his men ensured that none of them would aid in her escape or respond to her attempts at stirring up resentment and making them rebel.

When they were on the other side, Kagra chuckled. "You haven't lost it yet. You are still the alpha."

"It's not something that can be lost. You're either born with it, or you are not." Jade let out a breath. "What you call my alpha power only works on the rank and file, and you have it too. But since Igor is immune, and so are his lieutenants, it does us no good."

"Still, Igor chose you as his prime even though you make it no secret that you despise him and want him dead."

"The only reason he tolerates me is that he wants strong offspring."

"You also offer him a good fight." Kagra grimaced. "He gets off on subduing an alpha female."

"That he does." Jade swallowed the bile rising in her throat and shook her head. "Let's run."

There was a very thin line between the Kra-ell sexual dominance dance and rape, and Igor and his cronies had crossed it by a wide margin. But the only way she could deal with her situation was to not dwell on it.

The day she allowed it to consume her, she would lose her mind.

Running and hunting helped, but today she had a lot to talk about with Kagra, and hunting had just been an excuse. Slowing down, Jade sniffed for water and charged toward the river. The Karelian's woods were so dense that even though she'd hunted in them for years, she still needed the scent of water to orient herself.

At the riverbank, she found a fallen log to sit on and motioned for Kagra to join her. "Do you remember Veskar?"

"Of course. You hated him and made his life so miserable that he broke his vow of loyalty to you and escaped."

Jade kicked a rock into the river. "You were still so young back then, so it might have looked that way to you. Veskar was immune to my power, and I was hard on him to get him to fall in line, but he was untamable. He was a disruptive influence on the other hybrids, and I was glad to see him go."

Kagra nodded. "I'm glad that he left. I hope he and Vrog survived. If they were in the compound, they would have been slaughtered along with the other males of our tribe."

Jade swallowed the lump that had formed in her throat. "Veskar is alive, and he's done well for himself."

Kagra narrowed her eyes at Jade. "How do you know that? Have you always known where he was and didn't tell me?"

"I had no idea where he was or even that he was still alive. I just found out where he was this Monday. I was searching the internet for inspirational stories for the children, and I stumbled upon a commune called Safe Haven. They run spiritual retreats that teach humans how to become the best versions of themselves. The commune leader calls himself Emmett Haderech, and he's none other than our Veskar."

"Are you sure?"

Jade shrugged. "I'm fairly certain that it's him. He's grown an enormous beard and long hair, probably to hide the fact that he looks too young for the age he's supposed to be, but even though he's a hybrid, I recognize Kra-ell eyes even when they are half-human. The question I've been debating is whether I should contact him."

"What for? He can't do anything to help us, and you'll just put him in danger."

"You're right. He can't help us on his own. But he might be affiliated with other Kra-ell. We thought that we were the only pod that had survived, but we know now that many more made it. There might be more Kra-ell out there."

Kagra's eyes widened. "What if the royal twins survived? Either one of them could take on Igor."

Jade put her arm around Kagra's shoulders. "I wish they were still alive, but I know that they perished. Who do you think sabotaged the mother ship and why?"

"Igor," Kagra whispered.

Jade nodded. "That's what I suspect. He either planned a coup even before we left the motherland, killed the royals en route and sabotaged the ship to cover up the murders, or he just took advantage of the disaster to rise to power."

4

WILLIAM

*E*ver since Kaia's comment about the physical activity she intended to engage him in, William had been sporting an uncomfortable hard-on, but he refused to let it dictate his plans for the evening.

They still had a lot to talk about.

Pushing her plate away, Kaia leaned back. "I can't take another bite." She rubbed her stomach. "It's amazing how even goop tastes good when I'm hungry."

"Goop?" William got to his feet and started collecting the dishes. "Maggie is a gourmet chef. Don't let her hear you call her cooking goop."

Kaia shrugged. "So it's healthy and gourmet, but it's still mostly goop. When I woke up, I planned to make you take me on a proper date and feed me a proper meal." She followed him up. "But then I saw the table you set up for us and forgot all about it."

Damn. Kaia was right. He should take her to a nice restaurant and show her a good time. She deserved proper courting from him, and to be wooed and charmed.

"I should take you out. Where would you like to go?"

"It's nothing fancy. I'm dreaming of juicy hamburgers and fries." She glanced at the sink that was okay to rinse a coffee cup in, but no more than that. "Do we need to carry everything back to the kitchen?"

"We can do it after we have coffee." He put the plates into the paper bags he'd brought them in. "I'm sure you have many questions for me." He loaded the coffeemaker.

"I haven't given it much thought yet." She walked over to the couch and sat down. "I fell asleep before I had time to process what you told me, and I was too hungry to think about it while I ate."

His Kaia was a fast thinker, and she didn't need long to process what he'd told her, which hadn't been all that much to start with.

William eyed her with a frown. "That's not like you. What's going on?"

"I'm not the genius everyone thinks I am. It's just that some things come more easily to me than others. Everything that has to do with math and computations is intuitive to me. The rest is just as hard or as easy as it is for the average person."

"I doubt it." William leaned against the counter and folded his arms over his chest. "There is nothing average about you. What I have you working on requires much more than computational skills. It requires intuition and multi-faceted thinking, and what you've managed to do so far is nothing short of miraculous. I had the advantage of understanding at least some of the gods' language, and I still couldn't figure out the instructions. You had no prior knowledge, and you've done better than I have."

"You are not a bioinformatician." She closed her eyes briefly. "I knew what to look for. You didn't. Besides, I have a knack for solving puzzles." She pulled one leg under her and shifted sideways to look at him. "Now that I know that those journals contain instructions on how to build a cyborg, I'll probably decipher the rest in no time, but I need to know more about the Odus. You told me that those writings could contain information that would be greatly beneficial to humanity or just as greatly detrimental. I want to know what you meant by that."

He should have expected Kaia to focus on the science. Just like him, this was her comfort zone and what she was confident about.

"What do you want to know about the Odus?" He brought the two coffee mugs to the table.

"To start with, just some general information. How strong are they? How much do they weigh? What can they do? How do you control them?"

"They are incredibly strong, and they are nearly indestructible. I have no idea what they are made from. I assume that their outer layer is biological but that their inner organs are mechanical in nature, or maybe some of them are biological and some are mechanical." He rubbed the back of his neck. "I think that their creator based them on himself and used his genetics to create the outer biological layer. They can regenerate from injuries even faster than immortals, and if that's included in the instructions, we might be able to use that knowledge to give the same regenerating ability to regular human bodies, basically turning them immortal."

Kaia narrowed her eyes at him. "Do you have any doctors or scientists in your clan? Don't they know why your bodies can repair themselves so fast and why they don't deteriorate like all other living things?"

"Our chief physician has been trying to find the secret to our longevity for decades, but she's an MD, and what she knows about genetics is apparently not enough. We don't have any geneticists or bioinformaticians in our clan."

"Interesting." Kaia lifted her coffee mug and took a sip. "People thought that once the human genome was deciphered, we would have all the answers, but biological systems don't work like computer circuits. They adapt, systems take over for each other when needed because an area is damaged, and external factors determine gene expression. It's much more fluid than anyone had suspected. I'm not really surprised that your doctor couldn't figure it out. But a manual for building cyborgs might have the answers we are seeking."

"My thoughts exactly. But discovering how to make humans immortal without altering their fertility could be disastrous. Talk about overpopulation."

Kaia tilted her head. "What about your kind? Is your fertility altered?"

"It is. Otherwise, immortals would have overrun the Earth. That's why our enemy doesn't let the Dormants transition. As long as they are in their dormant state, they can produce children at a normal human rate. Once they become immortal, their ability to conceive drops to nearly nothing. Centuries can pass before an immortal female has a child."

5

KAIA

"Centuries?" Kaia's gut clenched. "So, if I turn immortal, I might not have children for centuries to come?"

It made sense that the procreation rate of immortals would be much lower to compensate for their incredibly long lifespans, but it hadn't occurred to her until William had brought it up.

"That's the downside." He gave her a tight smile. "The upside is that it's never too late. You can have children when you've lived for thousands of years. Annani, our Clan Mother, had her first daughter when she was over three thousand years old, and she continued to have four more children, but that's uncommon for an immortal female, let alone a goddess."

"That's terrible." Kaia's hand shook as she put down her coffee mug. "I always thought that I would have a big family. When it was just Cheryl and me, the house felt empty, and then Idina was born, and we came alive as a family, and two years later the twins arrived, and it became chaotic, but I love it." She wrapped her arms around herself. "There is so much love to spread around. I can't imagine living for thousands of years and having no children."

For a long moment, William seemed lost for words. "The clan is a family," he said after a while. "I know that it's not a substitute for having your own children, but once you become one of us, you'll never feel alone. I never felt the need to have kids of my own, and although I yearned for a mate, I wasn't lonely, not since my lab became a large enterprise teeming with people. When it was just me, I couldn't wait for someone to stop by for a chat."

His words had registered somewhere in the back of her head, and Kaia promised herself to talk to him about it some other time, but she was still stuck on the issue of waiting to have children for centuries or a millennium.

"If turning immortal means that I might not have children for hundreds or thousands of years, then I don't want to transition before I have at least two, and preferably four." She frowned. "My mother is a Dormant too, right?"

"Correct. And so are your sisters and brothers."

"What about Gilbert?"

"Probably not."

"Then how is my mother going to transition? She's not going to leave Gilbert. Can she transition and still keep him?"

William winced. "That would be problematic on several levels. First of all, transitioning at her age is risky, but it's probably still okay if she hurries up. Secondly, she will need an immortal male to induce her, which is a problem since she's with Gilbert. And thirdly, long-lasting relationships between immortals and humans are not possible for obvious reasons. Kian might make an exception and allow Gilbert into the village with his mate and his children, but his mortality would be heart-wrenching for your mother."

It would be terrible, and Kaia didn't want to think of how it would affect them. Hopefully, the journals would supply the answer for turning regular humans immortal, so she could keep her stepdad with them forever.

If only she could go back in time to save her father, turning him immortal before his heart gave out. But not even William or his Clan Mother, the goddess, could perform a miracle like that.

Reminded that the lives of her loved ones could be snuffed at any moment, Kaia resolved to ensure that everyone else in her family turned immortal as soon as possible.

"What about my sisters and brothers? How are they going to be induced? Cheryl could have sex in a few years, but what about the little ones?"

"Idina is probably still young enough to transition just from being around the goddess, and the boys will be induced when they reach puberty. For males, it's less problematic. All they have to do is fight an immortal male and spur him into biting them and injecting them with his venom."

She lifted her hand. "Hold on. How is Idina going to transition just from being around the goddess? And how is she going to spend time with her?"

"I don't know how it works, but it does. The little girls go with their mothers to the sanctuary, and they turn immortal in no time. I assume it's easier for the girls because they don't only possess the immortal genes but also transfer it to the next generation."

Kaia shook her head. "That doesn't make any sense. Adult women need both venom and semen, pubescent boys need just venom, and little girls can be induced just by the goddess's presence? You're a scientist, William. Does that make sense to you?"

William shrugged. "Not everything can be explained by science. We don't know how thralling and compulsion work, and immortals and Dormants have other paranormal talents that can't be scientifically explained either."

As the puzzle pieces rearranged themselves in Kaia's mind, her eyes widened. "Is that why you have paranormals here? Do you think that they might be Dormants? Is that how you go about finding them?"

William snorted. "That would be at least semi-scientific, but that's not how it usually works. We hope to find Dormants among people with paranormal abilities, but so far, that's not how most of them were found."

"How does it usually happen?"

"The Fates bring Dormants and immortals together like they did for us."

CHAPTER 5

"The Fates." She grimaced. "Are you serious? The Fates?"

"I am, and trust me, it wasn't easy for me to accept, but we had so many pairings that were the result of seemingly random encounters that I could no longer deny the facts."

The truth was that she should know better than most people that paranormal phenomena were real. She not only remembered a past life, but she'd also found proof of it. So why should she find the idea of fate so outrageous?

Kaia lifted a hand. "I'm willing to suspend disbelief for a moment and accept that fate is a thing. But you are talking about The Fates. Do you mean the three Fates from Greek mythology?"

"Yeah." He rubbed a hand over his jaw. "I know how crazy that sounds. The Fates weren't invented by the Greeks. Like most everything else in their mythology, including their pantheon, they inherited them from prior civilizations, and the originals were the gods themselves and their belief system. I too thought that the Fates were just a fantasy, but I have been proven wrong."

Kaia groaned. "So, what am I going to tell my family? That the Fates want my mother to leave the father of three of her five children so she can turn immortal?"

"You shouldn't tell them anything yet."

6

WILLIAM

*K*aia glared at him. "What do you mean? They are coming here this Saturday. What am I supposed to tell them?"

William took her hand. "It's not certain yet that you are a Dormant, and we won't know if you are until you transition. Why worry them needlessly? And what's more, why dangle immortality in front of your mother and sister and then take that hope away?"

Letting out a breath, she pulled her hand out of his and slumped against the couch pillows. "So much for no rush and having children before transitioning. I might have time, but my mother doesn't."

William hadn't asked her who she planned to have those children with, and he didn't want to. His fertility wasn't any better than that of an immortal female, so him giving her a child in time before she needed to attempt transition was unlikely. Could he tolerate her having one with a human male?

If Kaia was a Dormant, her children would turn immortal no matter who the father was, so denying her that option because he was jealous would be criminally selfish.

He couldn't think of her with another male, but artificial insemination was an option he would be willing to consider.

Could he, though?

He wanted Kaia to have his children, not some random human sperm donor's.

She put a hand on his thigh. "What's going on in your head? You look as if you are chewing on a mouthful of lemons."

"I'm just trying to figure out how it can all work out, and I don't like any of the solutions."

"Care to share your musings with me?"

Not really, but now that Kaia was privy to his biggest secret, William had lost his excuse to keep things from her.

"You said that you wanted to wait until you had children, but you didn't specify who you wanted to have them with."

Kaia smiled suggestively. "Are you volunteering?"

As anxiety over baring his soul to Kaia dried out his throat, William swallowed. "I know that we've just met and that talking about mating and having a family is premature, but nothing would make me happier than having children with you."

"You are right. It is premature." She patted his thigh. "I don't want to rush into getting pregnant right away, but since I've already completed my studies and my financial future is secure, I don't intend to wait too long." She took a sip from her coffee that was probably already cold, grimaced, and put the mug down. "I might be old-fashioned in that regard, but unlike my mother and Gilbert, who have three children together and yet are happy with their nonbinding arrangement, I want a wedding ring first."

Fates, the girl was decisive, and she went for what she wanted, like a bulldozer.

"Are you proposing?" He must have gotten infected by her bravado to chance such a loaded question, and now that it was out of his mouth, he waited anxiously for her answer.

Kaia tilted her head and eyed him from under lowered lashes. "Are you saying yes?"

Sneaky girl. "It's unfair to turn the question around, but if you are proposing, then I'm saying yes."

She laughed. "Talk about being irresponsible. We've known each other for less than a week."

He clasped the hand she'd put on his thigh. "What does your heart tell you?"

The smirk slid off her face. "My heart tells me that you are the one and that I will never find anyone as perfect for me as you are. But if I'm not a Dormant, and I can't turn immortal, we don't have a future together. I might be terribly old-fashioned, even compared to my own mother, but I want to be married to the father of my children." She swallowed. "Even if he's not my perfect prince."

"Then your choice is clear. You need to allow me to induce you before having children, and if you turn immortal, you'll just have to wait patiently to have them."

Kaia closed her eyes. "You can't expect me to give you an answer now." She opened them and leveled her gaze at him. "I need to give it a lot more thought. It's not a decision that can be taken lightly."

"That's perfectly understandable." He lifted her hand to his lips and kissed her knuckles. "I just need to give you one more piece of information to consider." It was one of the hardest things he'd ever had to confess, but there was no way around it. Kaia had to have all the facts before making her decision.

"Don't tell me that there are even more caveats."

"Unfortunately, there are. Immortal male fertility is just as low as the fertility of immortal females. I most likely can't get you pregnant even in your dormant state. It kills me to tell you that, but if you want to have children before becoming immortal, you need to consider having them with a human male. If you are indeed a Dormant, your children could become immortal no matter who their father is. I wanted to suggest artificial insemination, but you made it clear that you want to be married to the father of your children, so I guess that's not an option, and neither am I."

As tears pooled in the corners of Kaia's eyes, William expected her to tell him that it was over between them. Instead, she cupped his cheeks and kissed him lightly on the lips before pulling back. "I can't fathom a future without you in it, and I will not be the one to walk away. My choices, whatever they are, will always include you. Regrettably, that's not true on your side. If I can't turn immortal, it will be over between us."

"It won't. I will not let it happen. If you can't turn, I'll take whatever time you have to give me."

Kaia shook her head. "I will not do that to you. Watching the people you love die while you live on is a hell I don't wish on anyone."

7

KALUGAL

"You're home early." Jacki looked up at Kalugal with anxious eyes. "Did something happen at work?"

She was sprawled on the chaise in their bedroom with a pillow propping her enormous belly.

"Nothing happened." He knelt in front of her and pressed a soft kiss to her lips. "I couldn't concentrate at work and decided my time would be better spent with my beautiful wife. How are you doing?"

Jacki was a week late, and he was going out of his mind with worry. Bridget had said that it was uncommon for immortal females to go more than a day or two over their due date, and she'd given Jacki a device to wear twenty-four-seven to monitor the baby's heartbeat. On top of that, their son was a big boy, which amplified Kalugal's anxiety. Bridget had prepared them for the possibility that Jacki would need a C-section, another rarity for immortal females.

The monitor was the only thing keeping him from losing his freaking mind.

"As well as can be expected." Jacki cupped his cheek. "I'm so glad that Amanda talked us out of going to Egypt. I didn't know the last two weeks would be so miserable. I spent the morning floating in the tub."

He frowned. "Is the heartbeat monitor waterproof?"

"It has a water-resistant probe that I used."

He let out a breath. "Our son loves his mommy so much that he doesn't want to leave her womb." Kalugal feathered a kiss on Jacki's stomach. "But Mommy is uncomfortable, and Daddy is anxious to meet you, so you need to hurry up and be born."

"He'll come when he's ready." Jacki put a hand on her belly. "I love you."

"I love you more than words can express." He took her hand and started kissing one finger at a time.

When she winced, he thought that he'd accidentally nicked her with his fang, although it was highly unlikely that it could happen when they were not elongated.

"I'm sorry," he murmured against her fingers, searching for the one he'd nicked to lick the hurt away.

"About what? Making me pregnant?" She winced again. "Or telling Junior that it was time for him to be born?"

Understanding dawning, he felt his heart sink down to his gut. "Are you feeling contractions?"

He'd been waiting for this moment for months, but now that it was here, he was terrified.

"I'm not sure." Jacki frowned. "Real ones wouldn't be coming so soon one after the other, so it's probably nothing. But I've had false contractions before, and Bridget said to call her anytime I felt them."

"I'm calling her right now."

Kalugal pulled out his phone and called the doctor.

She answered on the second ring. "Is it time?"

"We are not sure. Jacki had two small contractions, one after the other, so she thinks it's the false ones again."

"At this stage of her pregnancy, I prefer for her to come to the clinic. And just in case it's the real thing, bring an overnight bag with you."

"Yes, doctor. We have it ready, and we are on our way." He looked at Jacki's face, searching for signs of distress. When she seemed fine, he relaxed a little. "I'll carry you to the golf cart."

She shook her head. "I should walk. If this is the start of labor, walking will speed things up."

Kalugal wasn't sure that he wanted things to go faster than they should, but it was Jacki's decision. He was just glad that he'd bought a golf cart for his household's exclusive use, so he wouldn't have to send someone to search for one of the clan's that was available.

Pushing to his feet, he offered her both hands and gently heaved her up. When she tried to find her flip-flops and couldn't see where they were because her belly was in the way, he knelt on the floor again and put them on her feet.

Jacki threaded her fingers through his hair. "Thank you. That's very sweet of you."

He pushed up and leaned over the belly to kiss her cheek. "I don't kneel for anyone except for you, my queen."

She rolled her eyes. "I'm a girl who grew up in the foster system. If I'm the queen of anyone, it would be the queen of underdogs."

Folding his arm behind her back, Kalugal smiled. "Even if that were true, I would still be your perfect loyal subject. I'm the guy who had to run for his life from his father, so I might be viewed as an underdog." He led Jacki into the elevator and pressed the button for the ground floor.

"Your father wouldn't have harmed you. In his own twisted way, he loves you."

Kalugal had often wondered about that. It had been arrogant of him to think that his father hadn't known that he was alive and that he couldn't find him. With enough resources and dedication, Navuh could have discovered his whereabouts when Kalugal had lived in New York and then in the Bay Area. That he hadn't could mean one of two things. One, that his father didn't care enough, and as long as Kalugal didn't try to overthrow Navuh, he was content to leave him be. The second was that his father loved him and wanted what was best for him.

The latter was unlikely, but Kalugal could fantasize that it might be true and that his father wasn't a monster.

There was also a third possibility.

Life in the Brotherhood and the constant rivalry between the so-called brothers was dangerous, so perhaps Navuh wanted one of his two true heirs to be away and in hiding in case something happened to Lokan.

That his father hadn't found the clan yet was also puzzling.

Navuh probably could have done away with Annani and her people a long time ago, but then he wouldn't have a nemesis to dangle in front of his people and unite them in hatred of it. The Brotherhood needed a mighty enemy to keep from falling apart, and since no human army or regime fit the bill, that left only Annani and her clan of immortals.

8

JACKI

Six hours later, Jacki held their son in her arms. "He looks like you." She smiled up at Kalugal.

Even though she'd done all the work, the poor guy seemed more worn out than her.

Men.

Hiding her smile, she kissed the top of their son's head. It was covered in the softest dark fuzz, and he had quite a lot of it for a newborn. That extra week in the womb hadn't been for nothing.

Thank God that she hadn't needed a C-section as Bridget had feared, but she couldn't have done it without the epidural. Junior's birth weight was nine and a half pounds, and birthing a child this size naturally would have been a nightmare.

"I think he looks like you." Kalugal put his hand on the baby's bottom.

Jacki caressed their son's downy head. "He has your coloring."

"This hair can still fall out, and he could turn blond."

Unlike most men, her husband seemed disappointed that his son looked like him.

"Let's ask Gertrude what she thinks," she suggested.

The nurse had been a wonderful midwife. Her calm demeanor and cheerful attitude had made the process almost fun. She'd kept making jokes at Kalugal's expense, which he'd taken without complaint, and the many words of encouragement and compliments she'd paid Jacki had compensated for not having a mother to hold her hand during the birth of her first child.

As usual, thoughts of her mother and what had prompted her to give up her child saddened Jacki, and this was not the time to get melancholy.

"I already have." Kalugal grimaced. "She said that Junior looks like me."

"You sound so disappointed."

His eyes widened. "The love I feel for him and for you could fill up the

242

universe. It's just that I kept imagining a boy with soft blond curls and blue eyes. A little angel like his mother."

Jacki chuckled, her hand caressing the baby's incredibly soft back. "First of all, I'm not an angel, and secondly, I kept imagining a little dark-haired daredevil with a charming smile and smart eyes like his father."

"You think that my smile is charming?"

She laughed. "Despite your enormous ego, you're such a glutton for compliments."

"Only from you. I need to know that I please you, my love." He put a hand over his heart. "It's ingrained in my immortal male makeup."

"You are the best husband any woman could wish for and the wisest," she said, only semi-mockingly. "And that's why you need to name our son." She batted her eyelashes at him.

Jacki had come up with more than a dozen names that Kalugal hadn't liked, but he hadn't offered any suggestions of his own.

"We will name him together."

She sighed. "You didn't like any of the names I came up with."

"I don't want to call our son Jonah after David's brother. It's bad luck to call a baby after someone who died prematurely."

Jacki groaned. "We can call him Guntar after your professor persona." At this point, she was willing to work with that. Their baby boy needed a name other than Junior.

Kalugal shook his head. "It has to be an original name and none that I've used in my disguises."

"Then how about something simple like a good old-fashioned biblical name. Benjamin, or Abraham, or Jacob?"

"Knock, knock." Syssi stood at the open door with Kian behind her. "Can we come in and see the little prince?"

"Of course." Kalugal rose to his feet. "I wondered what was keeping you."

"Allegra woke up and got fussy." Syssi walked up to the bed and leaned down to kiss Jacki's forehead. "How is Mommy doing?"

"Awesome. I had an epidural, and Bridget and Gertrude were wonderful." She cast a smile at her mate. "Not so much to Kalugal, but it was all in good humor."

He shook his head. "They ganged up on me, but I didn't let them bully me. I wouldn't leave the room through all the checkups they did."

"Good for you." Kian clapped him on the back and then pulled a cigar out of his pocket. "Do you want to step outside and smoke a celebratory Cuban?"

"Thank you, but I'm not leaving my wife and son's side. I'll take a raincheck."

"As you wish." Kian put the cigar back in his pocket. "So, does Junior have a name yet?"

Jacki grimaced. "He doesn't. We are open to suggestions."

"How about Darius?" Syssi said. "It means the upholder of good."

"In what language?" Jacki asked.

"Old Persian. There were several Persian kings and princes with that name, and most people associate it with rich and kingly because of Emperor Darius the Great. It sounds very regal."

"I like it." Kalugal looked at Jacki. "How about you?"

"I like it too." Jacki caressed her son's back. "But it's such a big name for such a small boy."

Kian peered at the baby from the other side of the bed. "This little boy will one day be a big man."

"Amen to that." Kalugal grinned. "My son was born for greatness. He's going to be the next Darius the Great."

Jacki rolled her eyes. "Is there a nickname for Darius?"

"Rius, or Dar," Syssi said. "But they don't sound cute. How about just Ri? Or Riri?"

"We can come up with a nickname later." Kalugal leaned down to look at his son's little face. "What do you say, buddy? Do you want to be named after Persian kings?"

"Darius," Jacki said to taste the name on her lips. "Dary. That's what I'm going to call him." She chuckled. "I wonder how long he's going to let me call him that. If he's anything like his daddy, he'll demand to be called Darius the Great as soon as he understands what it means."

9

KAIA

*A*s morning arrived and Kaia's alarm blared, she was already awake despite spending most of the night thinking over her options.

She hadn't stayed at William's, not because she'd been worried about Kylie making nasty comments in the morning, but because she needed to distance herself from him to think things through without him distracting her.

Regrettably, though, she hadn't come up with any perfect solutions, and each permutation required compromises that were too painful.

Family came first, but in this case, she would be sacrificing her future family for the one she had now. Her mother was forty-seven, which according to William, was already too old to transition smoothly, so she couldn't wait for her grandchildren to arrive first.

Even if she got pregnant today, nine months was a long time.

But what if her mother was willing to get induced without waiting for Kaia to transition?

Right. As if she would have sex with some random immortal for a hypothetical chance of immortality. If Kaia transitioned, though, it would be proof that her mother carried the immortal gene, and then she might consider doing that. But she wouldn't do it on a maybe.

Still, even if her mother agreed, which she most likely wouldn't, Kaia didn't want the father of her child to be some random sperm donor. She wanted him to be the man she would spend the rest of her life with. But since that man was William, they needed to figure out how to have sex without him biting her and inducing her transition instead of getting her pregnant.

Was it even possible?

Perhaps she could put a muzzle on him, but she wasn't sure he could ejaculate without biting her. Even if he could, though, his fertility was so low that he might not be able to impregnate her for years to come if ever, and in the meantime, she might get too old for induction.

The easiest course of action was to give up on her wish to have children. She could let William induce her right away, and if she transitioned, her mother would be a confirmed Dormant and could decide what she wanted to do.

But even that wasn't simple. Kaia didn't want to decide on a monumental thing like that without consulting with her mother and Gilbert, and she definitely didn't want to go through the transition without having them and Cheryl by her side.

With a sigh, she threw the blanket off and slid out of bed. Perhaps a cup of coffee or two would clear her mind enough so she could come up with a new angle.

When Kaia emerged from her bedroom, Kylie greeted her with a knowing smile. "Good morning. Coffee?" She put a pod into the machine.

"Yes, please." Kaia handed her a mug to put under the spout.

"I'm surprised that you came back last night." Kylie leaned against the counter. "I was sure you were going to spend the night at William's."

Kaia shrugged.

She didn't owe her roommate an explanation. Even if the two of them were besties, she couldn't share with Kylie any of her dilemmas and ask for her advice.

"Are you two going to move in together?"

"Maybe." Kaia pulled out the mug from the machine, added cream and sugar, and stirred. "Let me ask you something." She leaned against the counter next to Kylie. "Do you think I'm too young to have a kid?"

Kylie gasped. "Are you pregnant? Oh my gosh. William will be in so much trouble."

She sounded disgustedly gleeful.

"Relax. I'm not pregnant. I was just thinking that people wait to have children later in life because they want to finish their studies, get a job, and get settled. But I've already done most of it, so why wait?"

Kylie eyed her suspiciously. "Getting pregnant to trap a guy is idiotic. You must know that. You're young and pretty, and you should spend the next ten years partying and sampling the selection. Don't settle for the first guy who shows interest in you."

Why were people so quick to judge, and why did they tend to gravitate toward the worst conclusions?

"William is not my first, I have no intention of trapping him, and he's certainly not someone to settle for. He's a rare find." Kaia pushed away from the counter. "I'm going to the dining hall."

She should have known better than to ask Kylie for advice. Darlene was a much better choice.

"Don't get all pissy at me." Kylie caught up to her. "Hearing the truth is not always pleasant, but I would be a shitty friend if I lied to you. William is smart and handsome, but he's too old for you, and I find it disturbing that he's taking advantage of an employee. Is it even legal for him to have sex with you?"

"I'm an adult. I can have sex with whomever I choose. And just so you know, he didn't initiate anything. It was all me, and he tried to resist me."

"And he has conveniently failed. You are so naive, Kaia."

1 0

WILLIAM

*T*he door to William's office banged open and Kaia walked in, slamming the door behind her.

"I've had it with them." She dropped into one of the chairs in front of his desk. "They are behaving like middle schoolers and giving me shit about us being together. Can you fire them? I don't need them to complete the project. You and I can do it by ourselves."

It was tempting, especially since he could just take Kaia to the village and close down the lab in Safe Haven, but it wasn't fair to the others. Besides, Kian would be upset about spending all that money on the new lab for nothing.

"I've gotten a few smirks and nasty looks as well." William swiveled his chair to the side. "Come here." He patted his knees.

Pouting, Kaia got to her feet, walked around the desk, and sat in his lap. "Are you going to fire them?" She wrapped her arms around his neck.

"No, but I'll have a talk with them." He kissed her lightly while rubbing soothing circles on her back.

William wasn't looking forward to having a talk with the team.

He didn't like confrontations, and if not for Kaia, he would have just pretended not to notice the looks and whispers. But for her, he would go to war and battle nasty attitudes with the ferocity of a dragon.

Her forehead furrowed. "Why not just get rid of them?"

"Because the contract obligates me to provide them employment as much as it obligates them to work for me."

"If you pay them what's in the contract, they wouldn't mind not having to work for the money."

"Come on, Kaia. They can't be that bad, and they are helpful. You give them all the tedious tasks that would be a waste of your time. Isn't that punishment enough?"

When she shrugged, he added, "I can also ask Maggie to make their lunches so nasty that they will beg to be released from their contract."

He didn't get the laugh he'd expected.

Resting her head on his chest, Kaia let out a breath. "Their help is marginal, and now that I know what I'm dealing with, I'm even more careful about what I let them work on. I don't want them to figure out the big picture. It would be so much less stressful if it were only the two of us."

"Let's give it another week. I'll take the team out for dinner in one of the neighboring towns, buy everyone drinks, and hopefully, that will do the trick. If not, I'll ask Eleanor to compel them to smile at you throughout the workday and say nothing about our relationship."

This time, he got the laugh he'd expected before. "They will figure out that they are under compulsion, but thanks for offering me the option." She straightened in his arms. "What do you think about me moving in with you?"

His heart skipped a beat. "That would be wonderful." He never would have dared to suggest it, but to have Kaia in his bed all night, every night, would make him tremendously happy. "When?"

"Today after work. I don't want to see Kylie's smirking face first thing in the morning."

"What about your family? They are coming to spend the weekend with you, and I'm sure Gilbert will not be happy about your new living arrangement."

Mirth dancing in her eyes, Kaia scrunched her nose. "He's probably going to punch you. Please, don't kill him."

That was an odd comment. He'd told her that immortals were stronger than humans, but he was no warrior.

"I'm not much of a fighter, so you should worry about me more than you should worry about your stepfather."

"You are very strong, though, right?"

He nodded. "Compared to a human."

"So, if you punch him back, it could be dangerous. Gilbert is not the young stud he thinks he is."

"I will not punch him back. I can seize his mind and make him believe that he's okay with us being together."

"Don't do that." Kaia cupped his cheeks. "I want my family to accept you and our relationship because they like you and see how happy you make me. I don't want them to be coerced, thralled, or compelled to give their approval."

"Are you sure? What if your mother and Gilbert throw a major tantrum?"

"They won't. I'll be subjected to some talking to, and probably you'll get the same treatment, but they will not make a scene. After all, I'm an adult, and I get to choose my own boyfriends."

William wasn't sure at all that there would be no scene. Gilbert liked stirring things up, and he enjoyed being the center of attention. He might do it just for kicks-and-giggles.

Perhaps he should have Max with him when he confronted the overprotective patriarch of Kaia's family. The Guardian could restrain the guy.

"Have you told your mother about us?"

Kaia shook her head. "Only Cheryl knows that there is something going on between us, and the secret is safe with her. She won't tell anyone."

CHAPTER 10

"Good. So we have time to prepare a strategy. Any suggestions?"

Kaia chuckled. "We could throw an engagement party. If they know that you are serious about me and not just using me for your sexual needs, they would be more accepting."

He arched a brow. "I thought you were a very close-knit family. Don't they know you better? You would never let anyone take advantage of you, and so far, it's been more about your sexual needs than mine."

He regretted the words as soon as they left his mouth. It was true that she'd been the one to push for them to get together, but he wanted her just as much and probably more than she wanted him. And as for his needs not being fully fulfilled yet, it had been his choice to withdraw and not finish inside of her. He had done it to protect her, but he didn't want her to feel guilty about it.

Luckily for him, the comment didn't upset Kaia, probably because her mind was still focused on her family.

"That's all true," she agreed. "But Gilbert likes to pretend that I'm still a little girl. And speaking of needs, did you get condoms?"

Evidently, his comment hadn't flown over her head, but his Kaia was a pragmatic lady, and instead of playing games she thought of solutions, which he should have done instead of waiting for her to remind him.

William felt his cheeks warm up. "Not yet."

"I can get them at the nurse's office at the lodge," she offered.

He didn't even know that the nurse had them. "How do you know that you can get them there?"

"It makes sense. They preach free love in those retreats, and the community members practice that philosophy, so they must provide protection."

"I think that they demand proof of contraception from the females, and if they also screen everyone for sexually transmitted diseases, they might not have condoms. Perhaps I can get them when we take the team out for dinner."

"I don't want to wait that long." She clasped his cheeks and pulled his head down for a kiss.

11

MIA

*A*t five o'clock on the dot, Mia put away her journal and stored her coloring pencils in their box.

For the past week, she'd been writing down her ideas for Perfect Match adventures and sketching the environments she envisioned for them. Before meeting Toven, she'd done most of her storyboarding on the tablet, but he'd converted her to paper journals. The beauty of using them was that she could flip back and forth between the pages, and she would always have a physical copy of her journey. The downside was that making changes wasn't as easy, and her journals were messy.

How did he manage to keep his so neat and tidy?

Practice? Or did he have everything perfectly organized in his mind before putting it down on paper?

Mia sighed. He was a god with endless time to master every skill, and he was also brilliant. Why the heck had the Fates chosen her for him?

He deserved someone so much better, and she wasn't even thinking about her disability. Her heart was now perfectly healthy, and her legs were growing, and in a year, she would be physically whole. But she hadn't become any smarter or more talented, and he was still light-years out of her league.

Perhaps she would get an answer for that disparity today.

Amanda and Syssi were coming over to test her enhancing ability, and if they confirmed it, then perhaps what the Fates had in mind for her was to boost Toven's performance. Mia had no problem with being his supercharger and having no special talents of her own. It would at least make more sense to her as to why she'd been chosen for him.

Turning around, she drove her chair to the living room.

The motorized wheelchair was wonderful, allowing her to drive around the village and visit her neighbors, who happened to be part of her family. Well, Toven's family, but even though they weren't married yet, they regarded each other's relatives as their own.

Mia's life was so perfect that she was afraid of hoping for more things, like her legs to be done growing already and her friends to be able to move into the village, find mates of their own, and turn immortal.

If Frankie and Margo proved to be Dormants, plenty more members of their extended families could be Dormants too, join the ranks, and make more clan people happy. There were so many immortal bachelors and bachelorettes yearning for a meaningful, life-long partnership. If she could, Mia would find each and every one of them a mate so they could all be as happy as she was.

For now, though, her contribution could be enhancing some of their powers, provided that Syssi was right about her being a booster. She and Amanda were bringing along several immortals to test the hypothesis.

The original plan was for her to test her ability at the university, enhancing the performance of the people volunteering there, but Amanda had pointed out that her boosting ability would be most beneficial to the clan if she could enhance the skills of other immortals.

When the doorbell rang, her grandmother rushed out of the kitchen.

"I've got it." Mia zoomed over to the door and opened it. "Good afternoon, everyone."

Out of the four additional immortals accompanying Amanda and Syssi, Mia knew only two.

"You know Vivian and Ella." Syssi said.

"I do. Hello, ladies."

"Hi." Ella leaned down to give her a brief hug. "How are you doing?"

"Excellent, thank you." Mia moved her chair back to let everyone come in.

The tall, broad-shouldered female offered Mia her hand. "I'm Kri."

"And I'm Michael, Kri's mate." The only guy in the bunch offered her his hand.

"I've heard that you are both Guardians."

Michael smiled. "Kri is a Guardian. I'm still in training."

His mate patted his shoulder. "Michael is what we call a Guardian in training, but he's already gone on several missions with me."

When Mia's grandmother walked into the room, a few more minutes were spent on introductions, and then Amanda motioned for everyone to sit around the dining table. "Let's get to it, people. I've left Evie with Dalhu, and I want to be done as quickly as possible."

Syssi chuckled. "And I left Allegra with Kian. Both our daughters are perfectly fine with their daddies."

"Let's begin with Michael." Amanda motioned for him to get closer to Mia. "I also want to test if proximity has an effect."

"Michael is a telepath, but he can only read emotions and intentions." Amanda waited for him to switch places with Vivian. "He can't read thoughts. I'm going to think something very specific, and he will try to read my mind."

"What do I need to do?" Mia asked.

"Nothing. You didn't do anything special when you were with Syssi, so we must assume that you do it involuntarily."

Amanda turned her gaze toward Michael, and for a long moment, no one said a word. When she was done thinking, she smiled at him. "What did you sense?"

He had a curious look on his face. "It was definitely stronger than usual, but I still couldn't hear your thoughts. You were thinking about a fashion show, with models going up and down the runway on impossibly high heels and sashaying their hips in an exaggerated way. I felt your yearning to be there in person, and a little sadness about not being able to attend."

"Excellent." Amanda clapped her hands. "It wasn't a verbal mind communication, but your visuals were much better than usual." She regarded Mia with appreciation in her incredibly blue eyes. "Let's see what you can do for Vivian. She can communicate mind-to-mind verbally, but only with her daughter. Ella and her mother can have a mind-to-mind conversation as if they were talking on the phone, and it's not affected by distance. They can be on different sides of the world and still be able to talk to each other."

"I'd rather Ella went first." Vivian motioned for her daughter to take the seat next to Mia. "You're the more powerful telepath."

"Can you hear the thoughts of people other than your mother?" Mia asked.

Ella shook her head as she took the seat Michael had vacated. "I have a little more control over the communication with my mother, but I still can't read the thoughts of others. Let's see if sitting next to you will enable me to hear Syssi's thoughts."

"Here it goes," Syssi said.

A long moment passed with the two staring into each other's eyes, and then Ella grinned.

"You were singing 'Itsy Bitsy Spider' in your head."

"Yes." Syssi clapped her hands. "Were you ever able to do that before?"

"Not with anyone other than my mother."

"I want to try." Vivian got to her feet and traded places with her daughter. "But this time, I want Kri to think something at me. She doesn't have a paranormal talent, and maybe that affects the results as well."

"I have a talent." Kri pouted. "How come no one knows about it?"

Michael chuckled. "Because no one expects you to be a calming influence. You are so intense."

"I'm not." She crossed her arms over her chest, her biceps bulging like a bodybuilder's. "I'm calm and collected."

"Can we go back to the experiment?" Amanda asked.

When everyone nodded, she waved her hand at Kri. "Think of something."

After a long moment, Vivian shook her head. "Nothing. I couldn't hear or sense anything."

Kri turned to her mate. "Michael. You give it a try."

It took only a couple of seconds for a grin to spread over Vivian's face. "Yellow, green, red, purple, and white. You were thinking about those colors. I could see them as if they were flashcards in my mind."

"That's exactly what I imagined." Michael lifted off the chair and high-fived Mia. "Congrats on the most awesome talent."

"Wow," Mia whispered. "I didn't believe it until now."

"You've got it, girl." Ella high-fived her as well. "I'm curious to see what you can do for Cassandra's talent. With you at her side, she might be able to blow up an entire building."

"I don't think so," Amanda said. "I think that Mia can enhance only certain talents. We need to do further testing to dial it in, but that should be done at the university lab."

12

KAIA

$\mathcal{W}$ith a frustrated sigh, Kaia glanced at the time displayed on her computer screen and willed it to be five-thirty already.

The underground lab felt stifling, her colleagues were annoying, and despite the fascinating research subject and the progress she was making, the day had been dragging on.

She couldn't wait to get topside.

But the truth was that it wasn't about her teammates or the tension in the lab. Halfway through the day, Corrine and Kylie had gotten tired of making comments about her and William, and Owen hadn't said anything to begin with. The cause of the antsy feeling was that she still didn't have clarity on what she was going to tell her family when she called home tonight.

When the clock finally announced that it was dinner time, Kaia let out a breath, collected her papers, and got to her feet.

"I can put everything in the safe," she offered to take her teammates' notes as well.

When they handed her their work without comment, and Corrine even smiled at her, Kaia wondered whether William had told them to back off. If he had, he'd done it by using a thrall, because she hadn't heard him talking with anyone about anything that didn't have to do with the project.

As she walked into his office, he took the papers from her and dropped them into the safe. "Ready for dinner?"

"Can we take it to go and eat at your place?"

He eyed her with a frown. "Are they still bugging you?"

She shook her head. "They either got tired of picking on me or you thralled them to stop."

"I didn't do anything." He wrapped his arm around her shoulders. "They must have realized that acting like idiots was unbecoming of scientists. Let's eat a quick dinner in the dining hall and then have coffee at my place."

253

"Yeah. You're right. I will not hide, and I will not cower."

"That's my girl." He kissed the top of her head. "On the way, you can update me on the progress you've made today."

She nodded.

When they were outside, she waited for the others to get ahead of them to tell William her findings. "We don't have the technology to grow skin, muscles, and the internal organs for the cyborgs. If we manage to build them, they are not going to look human."

He slowed down his steps. "Didn't they include instructions on how to make that happen?"

She shook her head. "The information I've deciphered provides molecular structure for some of the tissues, but so far, I found no reference to the equipment they used to actually produce them in mass quantities. We have the ability to make small quantities of skin by taking skin cells from patients and growing them into personalized artificial skin grafts. They are used to help burn victims. We can even genetically reprogram skin cells into their more primitive state, in which they have the potential to become almost any other type of cell in the body, including brain cells. But it's difficult to turn those cells into self-renewing stem cells for a particular organ. At this time, scientists are working on producing muscle stem cells as a treatment for muscle-wasting disorders like muscular dystrophy, but the research is still in its infancy. It will be decades before the research and the biotechnology reach the state where tissue and organs can be produced in quantity."

"Unless we discover how to make it happen faster with the help of Okidu's journals. So far, you've just seen part of one journal."

Kaia had known there were more than the one she'd been working on, but she underestimated the quantity of the remaining journals. No wonder William was reluctant to dismiss the rest of the team.

"I hope you don't intend to keep the team here until all the journals are deciphered. It will take years."

"I don't." He opened the door to the dining hall. "Once I have a grasp of what I'm looking at, I'll continue with my own team."

He meant the immortals working in his other laboratory.

With her family occupying whatever brain bandwidth was left over from her work, Kaia had neglected to ask more questions about William's people.

How many were there?

He'd said that the enemy had tens of thousands of immortal warriors and that his clan was tiny in comparison.

Had he meant a few thousand?

A few hundred?

Were there other immortals in Safe Haven apart from William, Eleanor, and Emmett?

The answer to that was probably yes. William had told her that he trusted the guys in security implicitly and that he'd worked with them for years, so they were probably immortal as well.

What about Darlene, though?

She looked to be in her forties, and that meant that she was human. Otherwise, she would look as young as the other immortals.

Well, Emmett's age was impossible to determine, but under his beard and long hair, and his flowing robes, he probably looked just as young as William and Eleanor.

As they collected their trays from the kitchen window and carried them to the table, Kaia looked around the dining room to check if anyone was paying them any attention. Her teammates were busy chatting with the paranormals, and only Darlene waved at them from where she was sitting with James and Mollie.

"Is Darlene like the others in your family?" Kaia asked in a whisper.

"Not yet, but we hope that she will soon join us."

So, Darlene was a potential Dormant. "Do you know that for sure?"

William nodded. "Her mother, sister, and son are all part of the family."

Interesting. So, they were all immortal except for her.

"How come she hasn't joined already?"

William sighed. "Up until very recently, she was married to a verbally abusive jerk. She wasn't ready to enter a new relationship."

Kaia snorted. "She seemed very ready to me. She and Eric hit it off right away."

"They did, but he's not what she needs."

Kaia's smile died on her lips. "Right. She needs one of yours to become a family member."

"Yeah. But she fancies your uncle. She knows he's not looking for a relationship, so he seems like a good choice for her first foray into the dating scene."

"That's a shame." Kaia lifted the lid off her plate. "They seemed to fit so well together, and I hoped that Eric had finally found a woman he could connect with. The guy needs to stop dating girls half his age."

William arched a brow. "Said the kettle about the pot?"

She laughed. "I'm not dating girls or guys half my age. That would be illegal."

13

WILLIAM

*A*fter dinner, William escorted Kaia to her bungalow. "Are you sure you don't need my help?"

He was thrilled about her moving in with him, and he didn't want to chance her changing her mind. If he helped pack her things and moved them into his place, she wouldn't have time to second-guess her decision.

"I have only one suitcase, and it has wheels." She smiled at him with understanding in her too-old eyes. "I'm perfectly capable of rolling it a hundred feet or so to your place." She put her hand on the door handle but hesitated before going in. "It might be a while before I come over, though, so I don't want you to worry if I don't show up in the next ten minutes. I didn't call my mom yesterday, and I'm sure she left least ten messages on my phone demanding that I call her as soon as I can."

"Why didn't you call her last night?"

"I was overwhelmed, and I didn't know what to tell her. She always knows when I'm trying to hide things from her. She can hear it in my voice."

He took her hand. "What are you going to tell her?"

"I don't know yet, and that's why it might take a while. I need to figure out how to tell her about us without actually telling her that we are together. I don't want her freaking out and boarding a plane tonight, but I want to give her a hint, so she won't be totally shocked when she gets here and finds out that I moved in with you."

He didn't want her to get in trouble with her family, and as much as it pained him to admit it, the smart thing to do would be to wait until after they left. "Maybe we should wait. If you move in with me Sunday night, it will give you a whole month to drop hints and prepare them."

Kaia smiled. "That would be the prudent thing to do, but it would also be dishonest and cowardly, and that's not how I roll. I'd rather fess up and face the music than hide and lie. You are not a shameful secret, William." She rose on her toes and kissed his lips. "You are my Prince Charming."

Ducking into her bungalow, Kaia left him standing with a stupid smile stretching across his face.

He liked being her Prince Charming even though he hadn't earned the title yet. Kaia deserved to be courted properly, with flowers and chocolates and romantic candlelight dinners at fancy restaurants.

William hadn't done any of that, but he was going to.

First, though, he needed to stop by the nurse's office and get condoms, provided that she had them. It wouldn't be very Prince Charming of him to let Kaia pick them up.

Snorting a laugh, he turned on his heel and strode in the lodge's direction.

The girl was something else. She didn't have one shy bone in her body, and he loved that about her, but he had to man up and be just as fearless as she was, or she would lose respect for him.

Was it old-fashioned of him to think that? Did women still want their men to be brave and fearless?

"Hey." Darlene walked up to him. "Where are you going?"

Great. Now she would want to know why he was going to the lodge, and since he'd just made that speech in his head, he would have to tell her.

"To the lodge."

"I'm heading there too." She tilted her head. "Are you coming to watch the movie?"

It would have been so easy to lie and tell her that was the reason, but to be worthy of Kaia, he had to be brave.

Or not.

He could also be evasive.

"What movie are they playing tonight?"

"*The Runaway Bride.* I'm a sucker for silly romantic comedies. You should have brought your team with you." She smiled conspiratorially. "Or just one team member. Is Kaia joining you later?"

"She's not." He swallowed. "She's packing her things and moving into my bungalow."

"Yes!" Darlene pumped her fist in the air and then jumped to hug him. "I'm so happy for you."

"Thanks." He awkwardly patted her back. "Regrettably, the other teammates are not as happy about us getting together. They think of me as a cradle robber and of Kaia as an opportunistic girl who's sleeping with her boss to gain favor."

"Screw them." Darlene waved a dismissive hand. "They don't know what they are talking about, and their opinions are irrelevant."

He shook his head. "I need them to work with Kaia and not make her life miserable. I plan to take them all out to dinner and have a talk with them. Can you find a nice place in the area and make reservations?"

"I would gladly do that, but there is nothing in the area. The nearest town is an hour's drive away, and I doubt it has any decent restaurants."

"I know, and I don't mind the drive. I think the team is starting to develop cabin fever, and that's why they are being nasty to Kaia and me. A road trip would be good for them."

"Aye, aye, captain." Darlene gave him a two-fingered salute. "I'll take care of everything, and if you need me to talk some sense into them, I will gladly do that as well." She squared her shoulders. "Am I invited to the dinner as well?"

"Of course. And you should also allow for at least two Guardians. Kian will not approve an outing without a proper escort."

14

KAIA

*K*aia was done packing in minutes. She hadn't folded anything and had just emptied the dresser drawers into her suitcase, collected her toiletries, her laptop, her phone, and all the chargers, and dropped them in the suitcase as well.

If she hurried, she could be out of the bungalow before Kylie got back from dinner, but that would be a coward's move, and Kaia was no coward.

As she'd expected, her mother had left her several messages, and she needed to call her, but she could do that from William's place. Then again, if she was waiting for her roommate to return, she could do that now.

As Kaia sat down on the bed with the phone in her hand, she wondered whether she should launder the bedding. Supposedly, someone from the community had been hired to clean the place once a week, but she didn't know if that included changing the bedding and towels.

Probably.

The community ran the resort, and they did that for the guests of the lodge, so they probably did the same in the bungalows.

"Stop stalling." She bit down on her lower lip and called her mother.

She picked up before the first ringtone. "Kaia, I was worried about you. Why didn't you call me last night?"

It was on the tip of her tongue to say that she'd fallen asleep in front of the television, but her mother would sense the lie right away.

Was it her paranormal talent? Or just something every mother could do?

"I had a lot on my mind that I needed to sort through."

There was a long moment of silence, and then her mother sighed. "Are you still troubled by Anthony's disappearance?"

Kaia hadn't thought about Tony at all last night, but in a strange way, he was connected to everything she'd learned.

Coincidence?

259

Fate?

"Of course. It's not like he's been found."

"I don't want to sadden you, but you need to face the possibility that you're never going to see him again."

If her mother only knew how right she was.

"I know. I still hope he will get free somehow."

"Free from what?"

Kaia squeezed her eyes shut. "From whoever is keeping him. I refuse to believe that he's dead."

"I hope you are right. Let's move to a less depressing subject. How is the research going? Any breakthroughs since Tuesday?"

Kaia could only talk in generalities, but her mother knew that and was satisfied with what she could tell her.

"Nothing major. We are just chipping away at it one paragraph at a time."

"Do you still think that you will be done ahead of schedule?"

"I don't know. It's a massive project, but I don't think William intends to decipher everything at one go. We might be done with the initial stage sooner than he expected."

"Good. I want you back home. The house feels empty without you."

Kaia chuckled. "I doubt it. How is Idina doing?"

"She's excited about visiting you. She packed her swimming suit in her backpack along with her teddy bear, and she was ready to go. She asks if you went swimming in the pool."

"I didn't but tell her that I will go swimming with her when she gets here."

"That will make her day. I have to go, sweetie. Ryan is screaming his head off. Evan probably took his favorite tiger away from him."

"Bye, Mom. Give everyone kisses from me."

"Will do."

As her mother ended the call, Kaia let out a breath. That had been easier than she'd expected. She had lied only by omission, which wasn't a big deal. Her relationship with William was the only thing she could have told her mother, and that could wait until Saturday. All the rest was locked down inside of her by compulsion, and she couldn't tell her about it even if she wanted to.

Given the sounds coming from the living room, Kylie was back, and she wasn't alone. Corrine and Owen were there as well, which was going to make moving out doubly awkward, but whatever.

Once it was done, it would be behind her.

Stalling for a few more minutes, Kaia opened every drawer, checked the bathroom, and even peeked under the bed to make sure she hadn't missed anything.

When there was nowhere else to look, she took a deep breath, extended the handle of her suitcase, and opened the bedroom door.

Kylie's eyes zeroed in on the suitcase. "Where are you going?"

"I'm moving in with William."

"Are you sure that's smart?" Corrine asked. "If you have a fight, it will be very awkward to work together."

Kaia looked pointedly at Owen and then back at Corrine. "We are not going to fight. William and I see eye to eye on most things." She pasted a sugary smile on her face. "We are a match made in heaven."

"Congratulations." Kylie rose to her feet and pulled Kaia into her arms. "It was fun rooming with you for a few days. I hope it works out between you and William, but if it doesn't, I'll happily share this bungalow with you again."

Surprisingly, she sounded sincere.

Maybe Kaia had been too quick to judge them all. "Thank you. It means a lot to me." She briefly hugged Kylie back. "I'll see you all tomorrow at breakfast."

As she opened the door and walked out, the crisp air dried off the sweat from her brow and cooled down her overheated skin.

It had gone much better than she'd expected, and she was glad to have that one hurdle behind her. But that had been the easy part. Her family would not be as accepting, and going by her teammates' initial response, Kaia would have one hell of a fight on her hands. It would have been so much easier if she could just tell them the entire story.

Or maybe not.

Perhaps it was better to pace the shocking revelations.

In a way, it was similar to her baby brothers' immunization shots. Instead of throwing everything at them at once, it was better to give them smaller shocks over an extended period of time.

15

WILLIAM

*W*illiam paced around the bungalow's living room. It was only fourteen feet across, and the pacing made him dizzy, but he couldn't stop. He was restless for reasons that had little to do with his daring expedition to get condoms.

Getting them from the nurse's office had been much easier than he'd expected. She hadn't been there, the door had been open, and he'd found a basket full of them on her desk with a note instructing guests to help themselves.

No one had seen him going in or leaving.

He'd filled up his pockets with an assortment without checking sizes or quality, so hopefully, at least some would work. His experience with using condoms was limited, and he hadn't bothered with them since Hannah had left. Even while they'd been dating, he'd been reluctant to thrall her, and had held off as long as he could. Eventually, though, she'd become impatient, and his resistance had crumbled. Still, they'd been intimate only a few times before she'd left.

Hannah must have thought that he had a low libido, and compared to other immortals, that might be true, but not compared to human males. He'd done it to protect her, but as the saying went, no good deed went unpunished, and she'd left him.

Well, she'd left because she'd gotten a position in another lab that had been closer to her family, so it wasn't only about him, and if he'd cared about her enough, he would have followed, but he hadn't.

If a similar thing happened with Kaia, he would go after her to the ends of the earth and find a way to keep working for the clan remotely.

William didn't regret his time with Hannah. She'd gotten him started on a healthier lifestyle, and she'd given him a crash course in having a meaningful relationship with a woman. In a way, she'd prepared him for his truelove mate.

When the knock he'd been awaiting sounded at the door, he rushed to open it for Kaia and pulled her into his arms. "What took you so long?"

She chuckled. "It wasn't long at all. I thought that talking with my mother would take me much longer, but I was saved by Ryan demanding her attention."

He took the handle of her suitcase and rolled it toward his bedroom. "I made room in the closet for your things."

"I don't need much space." She followed him into the room. "One drawer for underwear and a second one for T-shirts and jeans, and I'm good."

"You didn't bring any dresses?"

"I don't even own any." She looked at the bed that he'd made while waiting for her. "Why are you asking?"

"I want to take you out on a proper date to a nice restaurant. I thought that you would want to wear something nice."

She sat on the bed and dropped her flip-flops on the floor. "I'm not the fancy restaurants kind of girl, and I don't need a nice dress to get a hamburger. Gilbert likes taking us to fancy places, and the truth is that I rarely enjoy the food." She smiled. "We are spoiled by Berta, who is an excellent cook."

"Who's Berta?"

"Our nanny and cook."

He sat next to her and draped an arm over her shoulders. "You said that you didn't know anything about me, but I don't know much about you either. What's your idea of a perfect date? What do you like to do for fun? What are your expectations from your guy?"

She leaned into him. "I love it that you want to please me, but I'm very easy to please. My idea of a perfect date is a walk on the beach with a smart guy who I can talk to about things that interest me. An ice cream cone for a snack, a hamburger with fries and an ice-cold Coke for lunch or dinner, great sex for dessert, and I'm as happy as can be." She put her head on his shoulder. "As for fun, I like all of the above, and as for expectations from my guy, all of the above plus honesty and kindness." She took his hand and brought it to her lips for a kiss. "So, as you can see, you meet all of my requirements, and the only thing you haven't done yet is treat me to an ice cream cone, a burger, and fries."

"I want to do so much more for you."

She lifted a finger. "I forgot one thing. Did you get condoms?"

William chuckled. "You are the least romantic female I've ever met, and I love that about you just as much as I love everything else. You're perfect."

Reaching into his pocket, he pulled out one of the packets he'd gotten earlier and handed it to her. "I grabbed a bunch. So, if this one is no good, I have plenty more."

She turned over the packet in her hand and then handed it back to him. "If you are counting on me to know what to do with one of these, don't. I've never put one on a guy."

"There is a first time for everything." He hooked a finger under her chin and pressed a soft kiss to her lips. "Just thinking about you putting it on me got my fangs going."

Her eyes widened. "Let me see."

Smiling broadly, he gave her a full view of his elongating fangs. "Do they scare you?" The question came out slurred.

"Yeah, they do. They are huge." She lifted a finger. "Can I touch one?"

He nodded. "Just be careful. They are very sharp."

16

KAIA

*T*he other time Kaia had seen William's fangs, they must have been only partially elongated, and looking at them now, they were monstrously long.

But even with the glowing eyes and the sharp fangs, William somehow still looked harmless. As her mother used to say, it wasn't about what gifts people were blessed with or disabilities they were burdened with, but what they chose to do with them. A good example of that was the guy with the highest IQ in the world who was bartending in a small town.

William might have the fangs of a saber-toothed tiger and the strength of a gorilla, but he would never harm anyone unless he was protecting those he loved.

As carefully as she could, Kaia touched one fang with her finger, not near the sharp point but higher up, and then gently smoothed it down.

When William closed his eyes and a groan escaped his throat, she realized that his fangs were sensitive and that having them touched turned him on.

"Can I touch the other one?"

His answer was another throaty groan, and as Kaia got emboldened and smoothed her finger down the other fang, she wasn't as careful and nicked it on the sharp tip.

"Ouch." She tried to pull it out, but William caught her hand and sucked the finger into his mouth.

As his tongue swiped over the small injury, the pain stopped, and when he released her finger, there was no trace of the nick.

"How did you do that?"

"My saliva has healing properties." He looked at her from under hooded eyes. "It can also do all kinds of other interesting things."

She remembered those things, and the memory had her core tighten in anticipation. "You have a very talented tongue, but today, I want to experience you coming inside of me."

"One does not negate the other." He slid down and kneeled at her feet. "Let me worship you, my princess."

"Well, if you ask so nicely." She whipped her T-shirt over her head. "Can you turn off the light?"

He looked at her with a smile tugging on his lips. "Are you being shy?"

She smirked. "I'm being romantic. Some things are better done in the dark."

"Indeed." William pushed to his feet, walked over to the light switch and flicked it off, plunging the room into nearly complete darkness.

Some moonlight filtrated through the semi-opaque window treatments, and William's glowing eyes provided additional illumination, but she could still barely make out his features.

"How come you can't turn the lights off with your mind?"

"I can't control inanimate objects." He kneeled before her again and tugged on her jeans. "I can only control the minds of sentient beings."

"No animals?" She lifted her bottom to help him take her pants off.

"Animals are sentient, but some have such limited brain capacity that they can only respond to the simplest suggestions." Chuckling, he shook his head. "Does this qualify as dirty talk?"

Kaia laughed. "For me, it's the dirtiest. And if you start talking about aliens hiding in the depths of the oceans, I might orgasm."

He arched a brow. "What about an alien underground base on the dark side of the moon?"

Kaia affected a moan. "Stop. You'll give me multiple orgasms before we even start."

He laughed. "You're funny."

"If you don't believe me, take off my panties and see for yourself."

Her offer turned the amusement in his eyes into raging desire. "Oh, I intend to." He nuzzled her over her panties, hooked his fingers in the elastic, and slowly tugged them down. "You smell delicious." He pressed a kiss to her folds. "And you taste delicious as well."

As it dawned on her that he had his fangs next to the most sensitive part of her, Kaia fought the urge to close her legs. "You're not going to nick me, are you?"

"Not by accident."

As he scraped his fangs over her inner thigh, she shivered in part from excitement and in part from fear.

"But don't worry." He lifted his glowing eyes to her. "I promise you that you'll know only pleasure from me."

Kaia wasn't averse to a little erotic pain, but she was still learning William's peculiarities, and if she was honest, those fangs still scared her.

Slow and gentle was the name of the game for now.

Letting out a breath, she lay back and braced on her forearms. "I trust you."

"Thank you." He kissed her folds again. "Your trust means a lot to me." He lifted her legs over his shoulders and pushed his hands under her bottom. "Gorgeous." He murmured for a moment before licking into her.

17

WILLIAM

hen Kaia exploded all over William's tongue, throwing her head back and calling out his name, he fought the urge to bite into her inner thigh and release his venom right there and then. One day he would do exactly that, but since this would be her first time experiencing his bite, fully aware and also remembering it later, he wasn't willing to squander the delight of her offering him her neck.

He had never experienced a female's willing surrender, never had even thought of it as something that he desired, but now that he could have it, he craved it more than his next breath.

As Kaia's tremors subsided, he pressed one last kiss to her drenched folds, lowered her trembling legs to the bed, and with immortal speed, took off his clothes.

Pushing back to fully lie on the bed, Kaia chuckled softly. "I wondered if you could move so fast, or was it just my perception that was warped, but you really do have a vampire's speed."

Smiling to reveal his fangs, he grabbed the condom packet off the nightstand and tore it in half. "Let's see how fast I can do this."

She lifted her hand, the movement lethargic from her post-orgasmic bliss. "Take your time. I want to watch."

William didn't like anyone watching him undress, let alone put a condom on, and this was highly uncomfortable for him. But he was no longer a fat guy who never had sex with the lights on and always thralled the female's memory of him afterward. Even now, after the weight loss and the training, he was still far from a sexy Adonis, but he was okay to look at, and Kaia accepted him the way he was and didn't want him to change.

"I hope I remember how to do it." He tried to roll the condom on his shaft, but the thing was either too small, or he was doing it wrong, and it tore. "Damn."

"Let me do it." Kaia shifted on the bed and rose to her knees. "I've never done it before, but it's not rocket science." She snorted. "Or maybe it is." She looked at his shaft and licked her lips.

As his manhood swelled even more in response, William doubted Kaia would have better luck putting the condom on him than he'd had.

For a long moment, he just stared at her gorgeous body, transfixed by the sight of her breasts.

She was so unabashed, so free with her body that it was enviable. But then she was perfect, and he wasn't.

Kaia smirked. "Not so fast now, big boy, are you?"

Was she referring to his overall size or to the size of his manhood?

Hoping it was the latter, William leaned down, picked his pants off the floor, and pulled out a new packet.

"I hope this one is the right size." He handed it to her.

Kaia looked at it for a moment before tearing it with her blunt front teeth. "This one is an extra large. It should fit." She beckoned him to get closer.

As her palm wrapped over his shaft, the grin her comment had put on his face was replaced with a hiss, and when she leaned down and kissed the tip, he nearly climaxed.

"If you don't want me to come all over your face, don't play with me."

"Who said I don't want that?" She rolled the condom on his staff with deft fingers. "But we should save that for later." She let go, lay back down, and cupped her breasts. "Come to me."

He was on top of her before the last word had left her mouth, and as she spread her legs to cradle him between them, his shaft found her entrance like a heat-guided missile.

Kaia moaned as he gently pushed just the tip into her, arching to take more of him inside her. She was slick from orgasming only moments earlier, but she was tight, and he wanted this to be the best sexual experience she'd ever had, even before the venom made it so.

Wrapping her arms around him, Kaia lifted her head and licked at the seam of his lips, demanding that he let her in, and although his first instinct was to deny her entry and take over the kiss, he wrestled it down and opened for her.

Her tongue darted in, and as she swirled it around his right fang, his restraint was shot, and he surged the rest of the way inside of her.

She gasped into his mouth, but he detected no distress in the sound, and as he pulled nearly all the way out and surged back in, the throaty moan she emitted was all about pleasure and need and not about pain.

"William," she whispered against his lips. "You fill me up so perfectly."

He couldn't agree more.

The need to go fast and hard was so strong that it threatened to overwhelm his resolve to go slow, but he was still mindful of Kaia's human fragility and wrestled the animal threatening to take over.

It had never risen so close to the surface before. When William had heard other immortal males talking about it, he assumed that they didn't have enough control over themselves, but now he understood how difficult it was to keep the beast subdued when the sexual encounter was as explosive as this one.

Letting go of Kaia's mouth, he continued controlling the force of his thrusts until he felt her nearing another climax. With only seconds to go, she turned her head, offering her neck, and he had no choice but to let the beast take over. Somehow, he still retained enough reason to lick the spot before biting down and ejecting his venom along with his seed into her.

Kaia exploded again, her climax nearly as violent as his, and as another one hit her a moment later, her eyes rolled back in her head, and she blacked out.

Panting, William remained suspended over her for long minutes, the blissed-out expression on her beautiful face soothing his worry and assuring him that she was perfectly fine.

Even if he'd been a tad too rough, no trace of it would remain by the time she floated back to earth, and there would be no ache in her body to indicate otherwise.

1 8

JADE

*T*wo months had passed since the last time Jade had been summoned to Igor's bedchamber. Two blessed months to mentally recuperate from the humiliation.

But she was in her fertile cycle again, and the bastard either kept a calendar to keep track of his breeders' cycles or he had sniffed out her fertile state despite the strong soap she cleaned herself with and the fragrant oils she used to rub all over her skin to throw him off.

The worst part, the most humiliating, was that her body responded to that murderer. She had no control over it. Kra-ell females were programmed to challenge their males and allow only the strongest the chance to impregnate them, and Igor was no doubt the strongest and most ruthless she'd ever been with.

Except, nothing about coupling with Igor was according to Kra-ell traditions. The females were the ones who were supposed to summon the males and not the other way around. On top of that, the females in Igor's compound couldn't refuse a summons, while according to Kra-ell customs, the males were not obligated to accept the invitation and could refuse it. It rarely happened, and only when the male's station was far above the female's or if her leader objected. To receive a summons was considered a great honor for a male, and to refuse it was considered a great offense to the female.

The system was perfect for their society and given to them by the Mother of all Life. To turn it on its head the way Igor had done was a great affront to the Mother and to their customs, and since he and his men didn't allow the females the right of refusal, the correct term for sex in the compound was rampant rape.

It didn't matter that once Igor overpowered her, Jade's traitorous body welcomed him inside of her. She hadn't invited him, and she didn't want to be with him. They weren't animals, and nonconsensual sex couldn't be defined as anything other than a violation.

Jade's one ray of hope was her discovery of Veskar's whereabouts, or Emmett as he called himself these days.

For the past two days, she'd been trying to come up with a plan for contacting him without getting caught or alerting Igor and his cronies to his existence, but so far, she had only a seed of an idea. She needed to phrase her email to Veskar in a way that would let him know it was from her, but to anyone else, it would seem like an innocent inquiry about some random crap she needed for her teaching.

She was known for her parables and her twisting of human fairytales, so if she were to write the email in such a way, Igor might not catch on to the secret message hidden within it.

Veskar might not be able to help her or want to get involved, but hopefully, he didn't harbor that much resentment against her that he would betray her trust or ignore her plea for help. At the very least, he would know that she and the other females were still alive and their general whereabouts. She couldn't give him an exact location, but she could give him broad coordinates. It was a tall order to hide all that between the words of a parable or a fairytale, but she'd figure it out.

When Jade reached Igor's chambers, the guards posted at his door opened it for her, and she gave them a haughty look as she walked in. She wouldn't give them the satisfaction of looking distraught or reluctant. If they thought she was willing, she could retain at least some scraps of her dignity.

Igor knew how much she hated him and that she would kill him on the spot if she could, but the sick bastard enjoyed her hatred and used it against her.

As usual, she found him sitting in his favorite throne-like chair in front of the fire.

"You summoned me." She remained standing at the doorway.

He demanded of her and all the other females to call him master, but she didn't unless he forced the issue.

"I did." Igor turned in his chair and regarded her with a frown. "Why are you dressed in your work clothes?"

"I didn't have time to change. Your summons was to come right now, and as you know, I have no choice but to obey your commands."

"One of those commands is for you to change into traditional formal robes, and yet you find ways to defy me time and again."

Jade stifled a smirk. It was a tiny and insignificant rebellion, but to defy him in any way felt like a victory, and she needed those small wins.

Dipping her head in mock respect, she hid the twitch of her mouth. "When you command me to show up right away, it overrules your previous command to change for the occasion."

For a long moment he regarded her with his cruel eyes, and despite her bravado, Jade could barely control the trembling of her limbs. He'd whipped her several times during her years of imprisonment, and he'd reveled in her pain. She was careful not to cross the line and give him an excuse to punish her so severely, but the truth was that he could do whatever he wanted to her whenever he felt like it.

"Get in the shower," he commanded.

Jade released a covert breath and dipped her head. "Yes, master."

19

KAIA

"'m going to work in the main room." Kaia rose to her feet, walked over to the other side of the desk, and kissed William's cheek.

He pulled her down on his lap. "Why? Don't you like being all alone with me in here?"

"I like it too much, which makes it hard to concentrate."

Sitting in front of William was distracting. Her mind kept wandering to last night, and she'd caught herself daydreaming about the bite, the explosive orgasms it had triggered, the euphoria, and the incredible trip through alien worlds.

Kaia had never experimented with drugs, not even weed, but she doubted any hallucinogen could rival that experience. She could easily get addicted to that and turn into a nymphomaniac.

William nuzzled her neck. "I have a solution for that. I can lock the door and do naughty things to you on my desk."

She laughed. "How is that going to solve the problem of my inability to concentrate for more than five minutes? Every time I look at you, I'm reminded of last night, and I start daydreaming."

His smile was all smug male satisfaction. "If we do as I offered, you will no longer have to daydream." His hand snaked under her T-shirt, rubbing gentle circles on her belly.

Yeah, as if blacking out for several hours would help with her workflow. After William had bitten her, Kaia had been out for at least three hours, and when she'd floated back down from the clouds, she'd felt so refreshed that she'd woken William up and had her way with him again.

He hadn't bitten her the second time, though. Evidently, immortal males had no limit to the number of times they could make love, but their venom glands weren't as randy.

As his hand inched up to her rib cage, she put her hand over his to stop him.

"I'm trying to downplay our relationship for the sake of teamwork. This is not helping."

Grimacing, he pulled his hand out from under her T-shirt. "Yeah, you're right. Which reminds me that I need to check with Darlene about our outing this evening."

"What outing?"

"Did I forget to tell you? I asked her to find a nice restaurant in one of the nearby towns and make a reservation for eight."

Kaia frowned. "Eight in the evening? Isn't that late for dinner?"

"The reservation is for five-thirty in the evening for eight people."

Her frown deepened. "Did you hire more people and didn't tell me?"

Talk about absentminded. Most times it was adorable, but sometimes it got annoying.

"Of course not. I wouldn't forget a thing like that. There are five of us on the research team, Darlene is coming with us as well, and I need to take at least two Guardians along."

"Oh." She pushed out of his arms and got to her feet. "Since the nearest town is an hour's drive away, you will need to cut the day short. We have to leave Safe Haven around four o'clock to get there on time."

"Right." He rubbed a hand over the back of his neck. "I didn't think of that."

Kaia put a hand on her hip. "In fact, you should let everyone go at two, so they can get ready. Especially if it's a nice restaurant. If it's a burger joint or a pub, we can go straight from here."

William chuckled. "A pub is not an option. You can't order alcohol."

That was so ridiculous. She was a damn PhD, could vote, get married, and have kids, but she couldn't order beer in a pub.

"Can't you get me a fake ID? I'm sure you and your people make them in-house."

Being immortal and living in hiding probably required them to have multiple serial fake IDs. Their faces didn't age, so every ten years or so they needed to get a new ID with a different name.

That must be so confusing.

Was William using his first name in all of them and just changing his last name?

Someone someday might notice that there were several Williams who looked identical and had different last names.

"We have a guy," William said. "He does an excellent job of producing fake documents for us, but he won't be able to make it and ship it here before we go out this evening. If I order it now, I can get it in a few days." He pulled out his phone and typed something on the screen faster than humanly possible.

"Seriously?" She gaped at him. "You are getting me one? I was just joking."

He stopped typing. "Do you want one or not?"

"Of course I do." She sat back in her chair and leaned her elbows on William's desk.

Her mother and Gilbert wouldn't be happy about it, but she didn't have to tell them everything. It wasn't as if they didn't approve of her having the occasional beer or a glass of wine at home. And she didn't plan to get drunk or do something outrageous with the help of her fake ID. She just wanted to order one measly beer with her meal.

"All done," William said as he finished typing the text.

WILLIAM

"Thank you." Kaia smiled.

She was so beautiful, but when she smiled, she was breathtaking. "You're most welcome."

William couldn't take his eyes off her. In fact, he hadn't been able to wipe the smile off his face since waking up this morning with her in his arms. It had been almost as good as the two bouts of lovemaking last night, and if they hadn't overslept, he would have treated her to another round before work.

Thankfully, Darlene had given up on him showing up for their morning swim and hadn't called him at four-thirty in the morning to wake him up.

Kaia crossed her arms over her chest. "When you're done staring at me, call Darlene and ask her how fancy the restaurant is where she made the reservation. I don't have anything to wear other than jeans and leggings."

He stared at her for a moment longer. "You are so stunningly beautiful that it doesn't matter what you wear."

Her smile was brilliant. "Thank you, but some of the fancier places frown upon customers showing up in flip-flops and T-shirts."

"I can always thrall them to think that you are wearing an evening gown and stilettos."

Kaia laughed. "I thought that it was against clan law to thrall humans for frivolous reasons."

"It is, and it's also against the law to thrall people to gain an unfair advantage. But it's not strictly enforced, and I'm not a lawman, but I am a council member, so I guess I need to hold myself to higher law-abiding standards."

Kaia lifted a brow. "You didn't tell me that you are a council member."

William shrugged. "Sometimes I forget. I'm first and foremost an engineer and an inventor, and my domain is the tech lab. I leave the politics to others."

Kaia nodded. "I get it. I hate politics too. Most people are in it for the money and not because they want to serve the public. The whole system is built on companies financing candidates who will look after their interests when elected." She chuckled. "The United States is probably the only country in the world where corruption is part of the system and perfectly legal."

"It's not like that in the clan. The goddess's children who manage the clan affairs as regents, dedicate their lives to protecting our people and providing for them. Their share in the clan's profits is significantly larger than that of members who don't contribute their work to the clan, but it is in no way proportional to what they've had to sacrifice over the years nor to the amount of work they still put in to this day."

Kaia unfolded her arms. "I want to know more about the clan and how it's run, but you'll have to tell me about it later. Right now, you need to call Darlene and find out about the reservation."

"Right." He picked up his phone and dialed Darlene's number.

She answered right away. "Hello, boss. Did you sleep well this morning?"

"Kaia and I slept splendidly." Switching to the speaker so Kaia could hear, he smiled. "Thank you for not calling to wake us up."

"Yeah, thanks for that," Kaia said.

Darlene laughed. "I value my life. Despite how sweet you usually are, I didn't want to push my luck."

"Thank you. Did you find a restaurant in the area?"

"I found a seafood restaurant with decent reviews, but it's nearly a two-hour drive from here. All the ones that are closer are simple eateries. Do you still want me to make a reservation?"

He looked at Kaia, who was shaking her head. "Simple is good. I won't need to change into anything fancy, which I don't have."

"I can lend you something," Darlene said. "You're taller than me, but I'm wider, so the difference should even out."

William wasn't sure how that could work, but what did he know about women's clothing?

"Are you sure you have stuff to spare?" Kaia asked.

Darlene chuckled. "I brought two full suitcases with me, and they are filled with new stuff. After being kept on a strict budget most of my life, I went a little wild with mail order. You'll have a lot of never-before-worn items to choose from."

Kaia pouted. "Is that seafood restaurant really so highly rated?"

"It looks promising," Darlene said. "After what we've had to eat here all week, I can't wait to order a plate of succulent shrimp."

Kaia's eyes lit up. "Okay, I'm sold. When can I come over to borrow something?"

"Right now, if you want. It's not like I have to drive from the office. It's a five-minute walk."

William didn't want to point out that she was supposed to stay in the office, but the truth was that she didn't have much to do now that the team was settled and Kaia and Corrine were keeping the lab organized. But Darlene was still remotely taking care of his stuff in the main lab back home.

Kaia looked at him. "When are you letting everyone out of here today?"

"If we make reservations for six in the evening, I think two o'clock dismissal should do it."

"Can I come over then?" Kaia asked Darlene.

"I'm looking forward to it. I always wanted to have a daughter I could go clothes shopping with. I had a couple of shopping trips with my mother and sister, and those were fun, but it's not the same."

Kaia leaned over the phone. "I hate to spoil your fun, but I'm going to be the only one shopping, and it's going to be from your closet."

"It's as close as I'm going to get unless my son gives me a granddaughter."

21

KAIA

*K*aia stared at her computer screen, the symbols blurring into a shadowy, incoherent mass. Focusing on her work hadn't been any easier in the main room than it had been in William's office, but for a different reason.

No longer being exposed to his male magnetism didn't mean that her imagination couldn't provide the missing stimuli or that she could push the memories of last night's passion aside. Besides, her mind had found more issues to obsess about.

How could she reconcile being with William and having children in the foreseeable future?

Could she have both?

Should she try to have children before attempting to transition?

Or should she transition first and let fate decide when to gift her with a child?

Could she have a child from a sperm donor for William to raise as his own?

That was the best compromise she could think of. William would be a wonderful father even if the child or children weren't biologically his, and one day, in a few centuries, they might be blessed with a child who would be.

Her family was doing wonderfully despite her and Cheryl not belonging to Gilbert biologically and not referring to him as their father. That wasn't because they didn't love him or didn't accept him as a father figure, but because calling him Dad would have felt like a betrayal of their biological father's memory.

Nevertheless, their family worked great, and it was proof that her idea of using a sperm donor could work.

But then there was the issue of her mother's age. She didn't have the luxury of time to wait for Kaia to have a couple of kids if she were to successfully attempt transition.

Why did it have to be so complicated?

Kaia really needed to talk to someone, but she couldn't because all of this was a secret, and she'd been compelled not to share it with anyone but William.

Once two o'clock finally arrived and William's office door opened, she turned her computer off, pulled out her fob, and collected her papers.

After everyone's work was locked in the safe and William opened the lab's door, Corrine put her hand on Kaia's arm. "Do we have you to thank for this outing?"

"It was William's idea, but my complaining about the food might have inspired him."

"Good job." Corrine patted her arm. "Keep complaining."

"Yeah," Owen said. "I've already started developing cabin fever. Isn't that odd?"

"It's too soon." William climbed the stairs. "It's the idea of being isolated rather than the isolation itself that gets to you."

"I know." Owen was right behind him. "It's not like I get out a lot when I'm back in the Bay Area. I'm either working or in my apartment."

"We only see each other and the paranormals," Kylie said. "That's not enough. I want to see new faces. Let's make an outing to a restaurant a once-a-week treat."

William looked at her over his shoulder. "I'll see what I can do."

When they were out of the building and the others headed to their bungalows, William took Kaia's hand. "They seem to be getting used to the idea of us being together."

She nodded. "It was a good decision to just flaunt it instead of trying to hide it."

He wrapped his other arm around her. "I'll escort you to Darlene's place."

It was only a few minutes' walk away, but she wasn't complaining.

"Can I talk with her about the stuff you told me?"

"I don't see why not. She knows most of it. The only thing she doesn't know is what we are working on, and I would like to keep it that way."

"Why? Don't you trust her?"

"I do, and I also trust many others who have no idea what I'm working on out here. But the fewer people who know about it, the better. Not everyone is good at keeping secrets, and this is important." He sighed. "There is still so much I need to tell you, but whenever we are alone, we get distracted by other things."

Kaia lifted a brow. "Is that bad?"

"No, it's good." He stopped in front of one of the bungalows in the paranormals' section. "Have fun with Darlene." He leaned and kissed her cheek.

"Wait." She held on to his hand. "How are you going to release me from Eleanor and Emmett's compulsions so I can talk to Darlene?"

"Easy. You need to keep everything I told you a secret from everyone except Darlene. Just don't tell her about the project or about the informant we have on the Doomer's island. That's classified information as well."

Kaia frowned. "I don't think this will work. You can't pick and choose which part of the secret I can reveal and which I cannot."

"I can't. But I trust you not to reveal things I asked you not to."

"I'm glad." She leaned up and kissed him on the lips. "I'll see you in a bit."

"Take your time." He squeezed her hand. "I'm jealous about every moment you spend with someone else, but you need someone who is not me to talk to, and Darlene is a great listener."

22

DARLENE

"Welcome to my humble abode." Darlene pulled Kaia into a quick hug. "We are going to have so much fun."

Kaia seemed a little taken aback by the exuberant display of affection, but Darlene didn't care. She was in a great mood today and dressing up a doll-like Kaia was going to be super fun.

"Thank you for inviting me." Kaia looked around the messy living room. "Who are you rooming with?"

"No one." Darlene led her to the bedroom. "I asked for a bungalow all to myself, and William graciously provided one for me. Don't mind the mess. It's part of my therapy." She opened the closet door. "Pick whatever you want."

Kaia thumbed through the selection of outfits hanging in the closet. Most were brand new with the tags still attached, and some Darlene hadn't even tried on yet. She was waiting until she lost a few more pounds before she dared to get into the size eight dresses she'd ordered.

"Forgive me for asking, but how is mess therapeutic?" Kaia pulled out a black dress and looked it over. "My mother drilled it into my head that a well-organized room is a reflection of a well-organized mind." She hung the dress back in the closet.

"She isn't wrong." Darlene pulled out a pink one that she knew would look lovely on Kaia. "It's just that I lived with a neat freak who terrorized me for over two decades to the point that I got an anxiety attack if something was out of place. I'm curing myself of that by ignoring the mess."

"Good for you." Kaia eyed the dress as if it was indecent. "You want me to try this on?"

"It's going to look lovely on you. I don't know what possessed me to order it for myself. It doesn't go with my coloring, and it's too tight in the hips." She gave Kaia a once-over. "You have slim hips and large breasts, which is the perfect shape for this dress."

"If you say so." Kaia took the hanger from her. "Well, it doesn't hurt to try, right?" She put it on the bed. "It's what I tell Idina when she doesn't want to eat something." She whipped her T-shirt over her head and dropped it on the bed as well. "I tell her to take one small bite, and if she doesn't like it to spit it out." She kicked her flip-flops off and pushed her jeans down.

The girl had a killer body, which was so unfair given that she also had a beautiful face and a brilliant mind. Darlene was a god's granddaughter, but her gifts were much more modest than Kaia's.

"I hate you," she said jokingly. "How can you be so perfect?"

Snorting a laugh, Kaia took the dress off the hanger and pulled it over her head. "Thank you for the compliment, but I'm far from perfect." She shimmied into the tight dress, trying to pull it down to cover more of her thighs. "Isn't that too short for me?"

"A little," Darlene admitted. "And the pink color is too light for you. You look like an albino." She reached into the closet and pulled out another black dress that was slightly longer than the one Kaia had looked at before. "Try this one on."

"Thank you." Kaia looked relieved to take off the pink one. "Maybe you should return it. It still has the tags on."

"I might do that when I get back to the village." Darlene took the dress from her, put it on the hanger, and returned it to the closet.

"Do you like it there?" Kaia unzipped the black dress and pulled it on.

"I love it." Darlene zipped it up for her. "I've never been happier. But then, I'm finally free, and I get to spend time with my son, so that might be the reason. I also found out that my mother wasn't dead, that I have a sister, and that my grandfather is a god."

"Wow." Kaia's eyes widened. "William didn't tell me any of that. Heck, he didn't tell me much at all." She smirked. "We often get distracted."

Darlene laughed. "I bet." She looked Kaia over. "There is a mirror in the bathroom. Go take a look."

"I want to hear all about your grandfather and the mother that you thought was dead but wasn't."

"First, choose what you want to wear tonight, and then I'll make us coffee and tell you my story." She narrowed her eyes at the girl. "You know that you can't reveal any of the things I'm about to tell you?"

Kaia put her hand over her heart. "Your secrets are safe with me. Can I tell William?"

"He already knows everything there is to know about me." She gave Kaia a slight push into the bathroom and followed her inside.

"I love it." Kaia smoothed her hand over the side of the dress. "It's not too tight or too revealing, but it's still sexy." She turned to look at herself in profile. "Do you think I can wear it with flip-flops? I have a black pair."

Darlene grimaced. "You need nice pumps with a dress like that."

"I don't have any with me. I only have one pair of sneakers and three pairs of flip-flops."

"What's your shoe size?"

"Nine and a half." Kaia wiggled her toes. "I have big feet. My sister calls me Frodo."

"That's mean. You have very nicely shaped feet." Darlene sighed. "Regrettably, my shoes won't fit you, so you are stuck with the flip-flops."

Kaia grinned. "I'll rock that look." She pulled off her glasses, put them on the vanity, and then tugged on the elastic holding her long hair and shook it out.

When Kaia let her hair down, she looked like a supermodel. It was long, wavy, and full, and it framed her face in a gold halo.

"Wow." Darlene took a step back. "Why the hell do you keep that hair in a pony-tail? It's gorgeous."

"It gets in the way." Kaia flipped it over her shoulder. "So, what do you think? Can I get away with wearing flip-flops?"

"You can, but can you see without your glasses?"

"I'm farsighted, so yeah, I can see, but it's not going to be comfortable." She lifted the glasses off the vanity and put them back on. "That's much better."

"You know that you won't need them after your transition."

Kaia nodded. "I'm not going to miss them, that's for sure. I tried contact lenses, but they irritated my eyes, and I figured looking good wasn't worth the pain."

Darlene laughed. "You're a rare breed, Kaia. Most women are willing to suffer a lot to look good. Take stilettos for example. In my opinion, they are torture devices that some sadist designer invented to torment women with, and yet, they are not only willing to wear them but also to pay a lot of money for the privilege."

"Or corsets." Kaia stepped out of the bathroom. "Why would anyone subject herself willingly to that?"

23

KAIA

"*L*eave it on," Darlene said as Kaia reached behind herself to unzip the dress. "Is there a chance you will let me do your makeup?"

Normally, Kaia would have said no, but Darlene seemed so happy to play dress-up with her that she didn't have the heart to refuse.

"You can if you want to, but I don't look good with a lot on. A little mascara and some lip gloss are the most I can get away with. Anything more, and I look like a clown."

With her fair skin, even the lightest blush and a smidgen of color on her lips looked fake.

"I will just line your beautiful eyes with some shadow and add mascara. You don't need any more than that." Darlene pulled out a chair and motioned for Kaia to sit down. "So, how are you taking the whole thing? William said that you weren't overly surprised when he told you about the shadow world of immortals no one knows about."

"I was surprised, just not shocked. I have always believed that humans are not the only intelligent species in the universe, and I also believe that we have had many alien visitors throughout our history. The one thing I never imagined was that I might be part of that as well." She wanted to say immortal but couldn't.

Evidently, the compulsion still prevented her from repeating what William had told her, but she could work around it. None of what she'd said was sharing what he'd told her. Those had been her thoughts and beliefs long before she'd met him.

"I assume that you already started working on it?" Darlene opened a makeup bag and pulled out a brush and a shadow palette.

"Not yet. I need time to think things through."

"What is there to think about?" She opened the palette and swirled the brush in the powder.

"You didn't do it right away either. Is it because of your age? Are you afraid of attempting it?"

"That's not it." Darlene hooked a finger under Kaia's chin and tilted her head up. "I'm a god's granddaughter, which means that I am close to the source, therefore I have better odds of transitioning successfully, so I'm not worried about being too old, and I'm taking my time. It's just that I'm recently divorced, and I'm still healing from the scars caused by my marriage. I need to re-enter the dating scene gradually, and jumping into bed with a hunky immortal who looks my son's age is intimidating." She swiped the brush over Kaia's eyelid.

So that was why Darlene had been flirting with Eric. He was her chosen training-wheels lover, not someone she wanted long-term. That would be her immortal inducer.

"I guess Eric is not as intimidating."

Darlene nodded. "I know that he's a player and that he's not looking for a relationship, and that makes him perfect for my re-entry."

"I understand, but I'm disappointed that nothing can come out of it. It's time for him to stop chasing women who are too young for him and settle down with someone closer to his age, but you need one of your own people to do that thing for you."

Darlene took a step back and regarded her with a frown. "Are you still under compulsion not to talk about what William told you?"

"He tried to remove it, but it didn't work." Kaia smiled. "But I'm managing to work around it."

"Clever girl." Darlene dropped the shadow palette into her makeup bag and pulled out mascara. "Now that you know why I'm still human tell me why you are not jumping on the immortal bandwagon with both feet."

"It's the fertility thing. I've always wanted a big family, and I didn't want to wait long before having it. If I accept William's proposal, I will have to give up that dream, so I'm trying to figure out a way around it."

"There is no way around it." Darlene brushed mascara over Kaia's lower lashes. "That's the way it is with immortals. But you might get lucky and not have to wait for centuries to have a child. Kian and his wife have a little girl, and they met only four or five years ago."

"Is Kian's wife like me?"

Darlene nodded. "She was the first Dormant the clan discovered, and that's also a great story, but I will tell you about it some other time. We need to talk about you and what's keeping you from immortality."

"It's good to hear that Kian and his wife got lucky, but I can't count on it. I even considered having a kid or two before changing, but William said that he probably couldn't get me pregnant so quickly, so I thought about getting artificially inseminated, but that doesn't solve all of my problems either. If I'm a carrier, my mother is a carrier as well, and since the only way to prove it is to go for it, I have to do it quickly because she's not getting any younger."

Darlene finished applying the mascara, dropped it in the makeup bag, and sat on the bed facing Kaia. "When you dreamt of a big family, you didn't know that you were a Dormant and that you had all the time in the world to have a child. Now that your circumstances have changed, you need to adapt your dreams to your new reality. Besides, what if you are not a Dormant? Do you want to have some random stranger's children and then discover that you did that for nothing?"

She hadn't thought of that, but while it was a chilling thought, it wasn't a deal-breaker. "I come from a blended family, and it's great. I would prefer to raise my children with their father, but it's not as important as having them in the first place."

Darlene shook her head. "I had Roni with a guy I met at work while I was separated from my ex, and he had no idea that Roni was his. I went back to my ex-husband and convinced him that he was the father. My ex must have suspected that it wasn't true, and even though he never demanded a paternity test, he was a shitty father. But at least I knew who the real father was and that he was a good guy with a great brain that Roni has been lucky enough to inherit. When you get pregnant from a sperm donation, you don't know anything about the other half of your child's genetics. They can tell you all kinds of stories at the clinic, but you will never know for sure. And let's face it, genetics determine at least half of a person's character. Don't you want to know that your child is not going to have murderous tendencies?"

Kaia rolled her eyes. That's a bit far fetched, don't you think?" Nevertheless, her conviction was starting to falter."Artificial insemination is just one of the ideas floating around in my head. Given my mother's situation, it's not likely that I'll go that route, but it makes the decision to attempt this thing right now even harder. Perhaps my mother should attempt it first, and in the meantime, William might get me pregnant." She shook her head. "I can't believe I'm considering any of this. I'm nineteen. I'm not ready to become a mother."

Darlene leaned forward. "Do you love William?"

Kaia swallowed.

They'd known each other for a week, and it was stupid to think that she was in love with a man she barely knew, but the thing was that she did know him, and he was the best man she'd ever met. Even if he wasn't immortal, and she wasn't a Dormant, she would have wanted a future with him.

"I do."

Darlene smiled. "Then that's your answer. You need to rearrange your priorities accordingly. I would never tell you to abandon your dreams for a man, but in this situation, it's a no-brainer. Regardless of your mother, you need to find out whether you are a Dormant before you make any other decisions about your future, and that means going for the transition now with the knowledge that you might have to wait much longer to fulfill your dream of having a large family."

24

WILLIAM

$\mathcal{A}$s Kaia opened the door, William's breath caught in his throat.

She had been beautiful before, with her hair gathered in a ponytail and in loose-fitting jeans, but she was absolutely stunning in a black mini dress with her wild hair cascading down her back and shoulders.

"We are not going anywhere." He pulled her into his arms. "I don't want any men to see you looking like that and ogle you."

She laughed. "Those who ogle would do that no matter what I wear. Besides, I'm yours." She kissed his lips. "So all they can do is be jealous."

Kaia's words made William's heart soar with emotion. She'd told him that she was falling for him, and she'd even told him that she couldn't fathom a future without him in it, which was as good as saying that she loved him, but she hadn't said those words to him, and she'd never said that she was his before.

He hadn't told her that either, not because he didn't feel it but because he didn't want to spook her. For the same reason, he also hadn't told her about the powerful bond immortal couples formed or about the addiction that, in time, would prevent her from desiring anyone but him.

How could they talk about spending eternity together and having a family without going through those important steps? Those affirming words needed to be said, and he also needed to tell her what she should expect.

Kaia wasn't a coward, and she wasn't rash either. She could handle him telling her that he loved her, and she might be okay with the bond, but the addiction might scare her.

"I like to hear you say that you're mine." He took her hand and led her to the couch. "You know that I'm yours, right?"

She smiled nervously. "It's still nice to hear."

"Does that scare you? Are we going too fast?"

Kaia barked out a laugh. "I should be the one asking you that question. I was the one pushing for us to get together."

"So why are you nervous?" He clasped her hand.

She closed her eyes and let out a slow breath through her nose. "I need to tell you something, but I don't know how to do it right." She opened her eyes. "So, I'll just say it. I love you."

When William opened his mouth to tell Kaia that he loved her too, she lifted a hand to stop him. "I know that you're going to say it's not possible to fall in love after knowing a person for only one week, but we are perfect for each other. I will never find another man like you, and I'm not talking about the immortality part. I would have felt the same if you were human. In fact, I would have been less conflicted about our future together if you were not an immortal with sucky fertility because I want kids."

Even her comment about his fertility couldn't wipe the smile off his face. "Are you done?"

She nodded.

"What I wanted to say was that I love you too. I fell in love with you on the doorstep of your house back in California. And you are right about us being perfect for each other. You might be young and haven't met a lot of people to compare me with, but I have been around for a long time, and I've never felt for anyone anything even remotely close to what I feel for you. I'm looking forward to spending eternity with you, and that's a very long time."

"I feel the same." She gave his hand a light squeeze. "Do immortals adopt children?"

"We can't adopt human children for obvious reasons, but if an immortal couple gets married and the lady has children, her partner can adopt them." He lifted her hand to his lips. "If you decide to have kids before your transition, I'm fine with that." He narrowed his eyes at her. "I can't get you pregnant in time, so your only alternative is artificial insemination because I can't think of you with another man. Once you transition, I will adopt your children and raise them as my own."

"Thank you for being so considerate." She slumped back against the couch pillows. "But I'm not going to do that. Even if I was willing to get pregnant right away, which after giving it a little more thought, I've decided that I am not ready for that, my mother doesn't have the time to wait nine months or eighteen months until I have the minimum two kids that I want. Besides, it will really suck if, after having those kids and attempting transition, I find out that I'm not a Dormant and that we don't have a future together. I would have rushed for nothing while giving up on raising my children together with their father."

It pained William that he couldn't give Kaia everything she wanted, but there was always a chance that the Fates would bless them with children sooner rather than later.

25

KAIA

*W*illiam didn't look as relieved as Kaia had hoped he would be. In fact, he looked pained.

"What's the matter? I thought you would be happy that I'd given up on the idea of having kids before transitioning."

Wrapping his arms around her, he lifted her into his lap. "I'm sorry that I can't give you everything you want."

She cupped his cheek. "You've given me more than I ever expected from a guy, and you might also give me immortality. All I'm giving up on is my impatience. I will just have to wait until we are blessed with a child, no matter how long it takes. Darlene helped me realize that I need to change my perspective on things and adjust to my new reality."

"I'm glad that you have someone to talk to about all this. Most Dormants don't have that luxury."

"I know, and it helped a lot. But just so you know, the compulsion still holds. I had to talk around it, but luckily, Darlene had no problem figuring out what I was talking about."

"I'm sorry about that. I was concerned that the only ones who could change it were Emmett and Eleanor."

"Yeah, I suspected the same, but it was worth a try. It was also good practice before my family arrives tomorrow." She winked at him. "I can tell them everything despite the compulsion."

The panicked expression on his handsome face made her laugh.

"Don't worry. I won't tell them anything." She sighed. "It will be difficult enough to tell them about us being together. Gilbert is going to flip."

"How about your mother? Will she be more accepting of us?"

Kaia chuckled. "She's going to flip on the inside and try to appear reasonable on the outside. She will try to convince me very calmly and logically why I should not be with a man thirteen years my senior, especially after knowing him for just one week. Even Cheryl tried to talk me out of it."

He arched a brow. "You told your sister?"

"I told her that I've managed to break through your defenses and that you've given in to my advances. She said that you were the smart one and that I probably pursued you so incessantly only because you were resisting, and I always have to win. Then she added that my stubbornness would one day bite me in the ass."

"Was she right about any of it?"

"Totally wrong." Kaia lifted her face to him and kissed the corner of his lips. "I pursued you because you were awesome, and I wanted you, and you wanted me back. Your reasons for resisting me were nonsensical."

"Not really." He let out a breath. "If you are not a Dormant, we are both in for a lot of pain. I convinced myself and you that you must be a carrier of the immortal genes because of the insane attraction between us, but it would have been a lot smarter if I had kept my heart protected until I knew for sure."

"The heart wants what the heart wants." Kaia shifted so she could put her head on his chest. "That's what I'm going to tell my family, and I hope that they accept it."

He rubbed small circles on her back. "Would it help them accept us if we got engaged?"

She chuckled. "Are you proposing?"

"I've already told you that I want to spend eternity with you. Our clan doesn't require a legal document to accept a couple's union, and marriage is optional. Some have a party to celebrate their joining, and the goddess is more than happy to preside over the ceremony, but it's not legally binding."

She lifted her head to look at him. "Can we have a human wedding with a marriage certificate and all?"

"Sure. But it, too, won't be legally binding because I don't really exist in the human records. I have a fake last name and fake documents."

That should have occurred to her. "Will those fake documents pass inspection for the purpose of obtaining a marriage certificate?"

He nodded. "We are very good at altering official records."

"Then it's good enough for me." She lifted her hands. "We can't be officially engaged without a ring."

"Then I'll get one when we go out tonight."

She laughed. "I was just joking."

"But I'm serious. I want to get you a ring."

"Good luck with that. By the time we get there, all the stores will be closed."

"Let me worry about that." He kissed the top of her head. "I'll find something. But it's only going to be a placeholder until I can buy you a proper ring."

"I don't need anything fancy."

"You might not need it, but I want to give you a ring that reflects my adoration of you. The problem with that might be that it would be too heavy a ring to wear."

Kaia laughed. "What's the largest diamond in the world?"

"I have no clue."

"I remember reading somewhere that it weighs over a pound. I need to start exercising my finger muscles." She wiggled her ring finger. "I wonder how much it's worth."

CHAPTER 25

He kissed the top of her head again. "Not nearly as much as you."

"And to think that I'm worth that much despite being a diamond in the rough. Once I get refined, I'll be worth much more."

William's chest shook with suppressed laughter. "You can't be worth more. There is no larger number than infinity."

"Not true. In cardinal and ordinal numbers, there are other bigger infinities which are surreal numbers."

He laughed. "You are such a gorgeous geek."

26

WILLIAM

*I*t was a shame to ruin Kaia's good mood with the things William still needed to tell her, but she needed to know.

"There are a couple of things I failed to mention."

She lifted one blond brow. "More caveats? I thought we were done with those."

William rubbed the back of his head. "I should have made a list. I keep forgetting about aspects of my people's physiology that you have no way of knowing, but that's not an excuse."

Kaia waved a hand. "Just tell me and get it over with. The preamble is scaring me."

He swallowed. "The first thing is the bond. Immortal couples who are truelove mates form an unbreakable bond. That's why marriage is optional. Once that bond snaps into place, it's good for life and beyond."

Smiling, Kaia cupped his cheek. "That's very romantic, but I doubt it's true in this life or the one beyond. It's most likely a myth."

"It's as much of a myth as gods and immortals are. Trust me, it's real. If we are each other's truelove mates, neither of us will ever even look at anyone else with desire."

"Fine." She shrugged. "I hope that's true because once I commit, it's forever."

"Even if I annoy you and you can't stand to be around me?"

"Not going to happen, and I don't like to indulge in what-ifs." She narrowed her eyes at him. "Just to be on the safe side, though. Do you have any annoying habits that I should be aware of?"

"I talk too fast, I'm obsessed with my work, I don't like going out much, and I love to eat."

"That's it?"

"Isn't it enough?"

She laughed. "You don't talk too fast for me. I'm also obsessed with my work, but I like going out, especially if it's to get something good to eat, so I think we can compromise on that."

"You've got yourself a deal." He took her hand and shook it.

"Don't you want to hear about my annoying habits?"

"Nope. Nothing you can do would ever annoy me."

Her eyes were full of mirth. "Remember you said that when I blast music in our house and dance in my underwear."

"Is that supposed to be a deterrent?" He moved his hips to let her feel the erection that had sprung up beneath her bottom. "I'm looking forward to seeing you dancing in your underwear."

"Don't forget the blasting music. Gilbert hates it when I do that."

The guy fulfilled the role of her father, but he wasn't, and it bothered William to think that she had done that.

"Do you dance in your underwear in front of him?"

"Not anymore. I did that when I was little, but now I do it in my room."

"Good to know." He let out a breath. "The next thing I'm going to tell you is connected to the first, but it's a little more difficult to accept."

She rolled her eyes. "Just spit it out already."

"My venom is addictive. Well, not just mine. All immortal males' venom is. If a female is repeatedly bitten by just one male, she becomes addicted to his venom. She craves only him and is sexually repulsed by others. Also, her scent changes, so the other immortal males know that she's taken, and they can't feel attraction toward her either."

Kaia pursed her lips. "That's one hell of a nifty trick to ensure fidelity. What about the males? Do they get addicted to the females?"

"They do, but it takes a little longer."

"Why is that?"

"I don't know. It's just the way it works. In the days of the gods, they used to frequently switch partners to avoid getting addicted."

She frowned. "Do any of your people still do that?"

He shook his head. "So far, all the clan matings have been truelove matches, and the couples welcomed the bond along with the addiction."

"Then I welcome it too." She tilted her head. "What happens when one of the mates dies? I know that it almost never happens, but you said that immortals can be killed, so I assume some have fallen in battle. What happened to their mates?"

"Withdrawal is long and difficult, but eventually, the effects of the addiction diminish, and the living partner can find love with someone new, but they won't be truelove mates. You get only one."

27

KIAN

$\mathcal{K}$ ian had sensed Syssi approaching a moment before a soft knock sounded at his office door, and as he rose to his feet to open it for her, she walked in with Allegra strapped to her chest in a baby carrier.

"Is everything all right?" He kissed his wife and daughter.

It was only ten minutes after three o'clock, and Syssi usually wasn't back from the lab until five.

"Everything is fine." She kissed his cheek. "Allegra kept going Baba all day long, so I figured she missed you and cut my day short."

"Baba," Allegra agreed while flailing her legs and arms.

"Say Dada, sweetheart." He unstrapped her from the carrier and lifted her into his arms.

Bridget said that Allegra was just babbling and that it was too early for her to mean Daddy by that, but he and Syssi disagreed. Her Baba and Dada babbles were very obviously directed at him.

"Dada." She smiled at him with a challenge in her big blue eyes.

"That's right." He kissed both her cheeks. "I'm your Dada." He turned to Syssi. "She knows exactly what she's trying to say, and she understands when we are talking about her."

"I know." Syssi sat on one of the chairs in front of his desk. "I had an idea on the way home. What do you think about spending this weekend at Safe Haven? I met Gavin this morning at the café, and he kept boasting about the bungalows and how perfectly they'd turned out. It made me curious to see the completed project."

Syssi wasn't the spontaneous type, and informing him on a Friday afternoon that she wanted to go to Safe Haven the next day was atypical of her.

"Are you sure you want to do it this weekend? If we go next week, we will have more time to plan."

"Dada." Allegra's little hand closed over a strand of his hair, and she gave it a mighty pull.

Kian winced. "Don't pull on Daddy's hair, sweetie. It hurts." He tried to gently dislodge her tiny fingers, but she got a stubborn expression on her little face and refused to cooperate.

"What's to plan?" Syssi leaned over and tapped on their daughter's fist. "Let go, Allegra."

She released his hair immediately but kept staring defiantly into his eyes.

"Sometimes this girl scares me." He stared back. "It's like she's trying to communicate things with her eyes and daring me to understand her meaning."

"She wants to go on a trip." Syssi smiled at Allegra. "Right, sweetie?"

"Baba." Allegra smiled sweetly back as if to say, "You finally got it."

"I guess that's a yes." Kian let out a breath. "I'll tell Shai to make the arrangements."

"We can stay at Emmett's bunker," Syssi said. "I talked with Anastasia, and she said that Emmett and Eleanor are staying in one of the bungalows in the paranormal enclosure. Eleanor wanted a fresh start in a structure that wasn't contaminated by Emmett's past shenanigans."

"You mean orgies."

"Shhh." Syssi looked at Allegra. "Watch what you say in front of her."

"Right." He leaned and kissed her soft cheek. "Sugar and spice and everything nice. That's what little girls are made of."

Syssi laughed. "Boys are made from the same things until they reach puberty and can think of nothing but sex. Anyway, don't dismiss Eleanor's preference as superstition. If Mey can hear echoes left in the walls then Eleanor is right to not want to live there."

"And you don't mind staying there with our daughter despite that?"

"Not really. What's the difference between that and any hotel room?"

Kian grimaced. "Thanks for planting that thought in my head. From now on, we are only staying in rooms that were never occupied before."

She laughed. "Thankfully, neither of us is sensitive to echoes. I want to bring Okidu along, though, and have him change all the bedding with the stuff we will bring with us, including mattress toppers. Anastasia promised to send a cleaning crew to the cottage to make it ready for us, but the mattresses there were not as comfortable as what we have at home, and the bedding was not as soft."

Kian smiled. His wife wasn't picky in most things, but she was choosy about her coffee and her bed, and he loved indulging both.

"I see that you have everything planned already. Is there anything else you want me to take care of?"

She nodded. "If you don't mind, I would like you to allow Brundar and Anandur to bring their mates along. I feel bad about taking the guys away for the weekend, and I know you can't travel without them."

Kian pursed his lips. "Technically, I can. There are guardians posted in Safe Haven, and if they pick us up from the airport, I don't need to drag the brothers with me."

"Baba," Allegra said in a demanding tone. "Baba."

Syssi smiled. "I think I know what she's trying to say. She wants Anandur, Brundar, Wonder, and Callie to come with us."

"Baba," Allegra said in an affirmative tone and followed it with a smile.

Kian shook his head. "I'm officially stunned."

"Why? Just because your six-month-old daughter can communicate her desires so expressively? We know that she's special."

"That she is." He hoisted Allegra higher on his chest so he could kiss her sweet cheeks. "She's Daddy's brilliant little girl."

28

KAIA

"Is that the place?" Darlene asked as the bus driver stopped in front of the restaurant.

"That's the one." He opened the door.

"It doesn't look as fancy as it purports to be." Darlene rose to her feet. "I hope the food is good."

Max followed her up. "Don't judge a book by its cover."

She turned to look at him over her shoulder. "That's what I usually do, and more often than not, I'm right."

"Whatever works for you, darling." He put his hand on her shoulder.

Kaia smiled.

The two had been engaged in flirtatious banter throughout the nearly two hours it had taken to get to the restaurant.

During the ride, William had kept his arm wrapped around Kaia's shoulders, held her hand, and kissed her cheek or her temple every five minutes or so, and at first, there had been some quiet snickers, but as time had gone by, her teammates had found Max and Darlene's shameless flirting more interesting.

If not for the fact that Eric was arriving the next day, she would have been all for Darlene and Max getting it on tonight, but Eric would be disappointed.

After spending the weekend with Darlene, he would probably lose interest like he was known to have done with all of his other conquests, and after he was gone, Darlene could move on to Max with renewed confidence in her sexuality.

Should she have a talk with Eric and warn him to show Darlene a good time? He was used to women half her age that weren't interested in long-term relationships any more than he was, so he might not know what to do with a woman who had a wounded soul that needed mending.

As the bus stopped next to the restaurant's front door, her teammates and the two Guardians accompanying them disembarked and followed William and Kaia inside.

Only a few tables were occupied, which wasn't a very promising sign. If the food was good, the place should be packed.

"Hello." The hostess smiled at William. "McLean party of eight?"

"That's us."

"Follow me." She collected a bunch of menus and led them to a long table on the far side of the restaurant.

"What about the bus driver?" Kaia asked. "We should invite him to eat with us."

"I did." William pulled out a chair for her. "He doesn't want to hang out with us. He wants to go to a local pub." He leaned closer. "Look over the menu and order for me whatever you want. I have a quick errand to run."

He probably meant the ring, but she didn't want to ask him in front of everyone. "Is there anything you don't like to eat?"

He chuckled. "Do I look like a picky eater? I'll eat anything that's put in front of me."

"Lucky you." Corrine nudged her. "When the two of you get married, you won't have to work hard to prepare meals for him. Picky husbands are a drag."

Kaia was ready to answer that she loved to cook and that it wouldn't be a problem even if William was picky, but he stopped her with a hand on her shoulder. "When we move in together, I'll cook for Kaia. My princess will not have to do anything other than use her brilliant mind to solve genetic puzzles." He winked at her. "I'll be back as soon as I can."

When he left, Corrine put a hand on her heart. "I take back every negative word I've ever said about William. He's a treasure. My ex expected me to do all the cleaning and cooking as if we were in the fifties. Finally, I got sick of waiting on him hand and foot, and I left his sorry ass."

"Good for you," Darlene said. "My ex was like that as well. Did yours come from a rich family?"

Corrine nodded. "Yours too?"

"Yeah. Guys like that grow up with a maid doing all the housework, and when they get married, they expect their wife to do everything for them as if she's the new maid."

Kaia wondered how William had grown up. Shame on her that she hadn't asked him about his mother, who was probably still around and looking like she was his sister.

Did he even have siblings?

With how low the immortals' fertility was, that was probably a no.

Was his family rich?

He'd said something about a share in the clan's profits. As a council member and his clan's tech authority, he was probably paid well. Did he have a maid cooking for him back home?

Kaia lifted the menu. "I don't know how good of a cook William is, but even if he's great, I'm not going to let him hog the kitchen. My family has a nanny who also cooks for us, but from time to time, I like to unwind by preparing something special for dinner. I'm not just a brain."

Owen gave her a meaningful look. "You definitely are not just a brain."

As Corrine cast him a glare, the restaurant's front door opened, and a family with four kids entered. The three boys looked like they were about two years apart, with the oldest being about eight and the youngest four, and their sister was about a year old.

Compared to her younger siblings, they were very well-behaved, and as the father doted on his daughter, Kaia's heart squeezed with envy.

She wanted that.

She wanted to have a little girl with William and watch him go crazy about her. And she wanted to have a bunch of sons who would be as handsome and as sweet as their father and who would adore their mother.

For a human, it was such a simple thing to wish for, but she was something more and at the same time, something less.

Evidently the saying about balance was right, and when fate bestowed a gift, it usually took away something in return.

WILLIAM

"I'll take this one." William pointed to a diamond ring with a simple platinum band.

"Excellent choice, sir." The jeweler pulled it out of the display case and placed it on the counter. "If the lady needs it adjusted, come back with her, and we can have it done in a week."

"It will fit her just fine." William handed the guy his credit card.

"Nice ring," Max said. "Kaia is going to love it."

"It's just a placeholder until I can get her something nicer."

The store owner looked aghast. "This is a very fine ring, and the diamond is top quality."

"I don't doubt it for a moment." He gave the guy a tight smile. "And knowing my fiancée, she will not want it replaced by a bigger diamond, but half a carat is just not enough for her."

It was the largest the store had.

The guy looked as if he'd taken a bite out of a lemon. "I'll wrap it up for you."

"Thank you."

Max chuckled. "Are you trying to compete with Kian? The ring he gave Syssi requires a security guard to accompany her whenever she leaves the house with it on."

"Didn't she have a fake made?"

Max shrugged. "What's the point of owning a ring like that if she has to exchange it for a lookalike?"

"True. But I'm not going to buy Kaia an extravagant ring like that. Not because I can't afford it but because it will look strange on a nineteen-year-old girl who's most comfortable in jeans and flip-flops."

Come to think of it, Kaia might not like diamonds at all. Maybe he should get her a sapphire?

Moving to the next display over, he looked at the non-diamond rings, but none of them caught his eye. The diamond ring he'd chosen was simple and modern looking, and Kaia was going to like it. If not, he would know what she preferred when he replaced it.

"Here you go, Mr. McLean." The jeweler handed him a small bag with the ring box inside of it. "Here is the receipt and your credit card back."

"Thank you. I appreciate you staying open late for me."

The guy smiled. "I'm glad to help a young man in love. Congratulations on your engagement, and the best of luck to you and your bride."

"Thank you."

When they were outside the store, Max clapped William on the back. "I don't know whether I should congratulate you or not. You said that you were doing it to appease Kaia's family, but since you think she's your one and only, perhaps congratulations are in order?"

Max's words sent a spear of fear through William's heart.

He was taking it for granted that Kaia was a Dormant when all he had to base it on was their intense attraction to each other. She was incredibly smart, and her ability to decipher the journals bordered on paranormal, but it was far from proof.

The Fates supposedly rewarded those who had suffered greatly or had sacrificed a lot for others with a truelove mate, but he hadn't suffered, and he doubted his work for the clan qualified as a sacrifice. William loved what he did, and his work fulfilled him and satisfied him.

Kaia had suffered, though. She'd lost her father at a young age, but then the Fates had provided her family with a good man who cared for them. He was no substitute for the father they'd lost, but he made their lives better.

William let out a breath. "Let's hope that she transitions. You can congratulate me then."

When his phone rang, William reached into his pocket to pull it out, expecting it to be Kaia calling to tell him that the food had arrived, but the number on the screen was Kian's.

"Hello, boss."

"I hope I'm not interrupting your dinner."

"You're not. I left the team at the restaurant to run a quick errand. What can I do for you?"

"I wanted to give you a heads up that Syssi and I are coming to Safe Haven for the weekend. Naturally, Anandur and Brundar are coming with us, and they are bringing their mates along. We will stay in Emmett's old bunker, and Anastasia is taking care of the arrangements, so there is nothing you need to do, but I thought you would want to know."

William shook his head. "That's really bad timing. Can you come next weekend?"

"Why?"

"Kaia's family is arriving tomorrow as well, and I will have my hands full with them. Kaia thinks that they will not be happy about her dating a man thirteen years her senior."

Kian chuckled. "Imagine what they would do if they knew you were three hundred and thirteen years older than her."

William grimaced. "Frankly, I don't think it would make a difference. Can I persuade you to postpone your visit?"

"Syssi and I are not going to bother you. She wants to see the completed development, but we don't need you to show us around. Eleanor and Emmett can do that. Naturally, we would like to meet Kaia, but if that doesn't work out because you have a war on your hands, so be it. We will meet her when you bring her to the village."

William let out a breath. "We don't know for sure that will ever happen, but I hope it will. When are you arriving?"

"We are leaving here at around eleven, so we should land at around two o'clock and arrive at Safe Haven at around four in the afternoon. Does that work for you?"

"Kaia's family will get here a little earlier. The lodge's dining hall closes at two and opens again at five for dinner, but I spoke with the kitchen's manager about keeping the dining hall open for them. I hope they'll be done by the time you get there."

"If not, we will stop by to say hello and continue to the other side of the dining hall. Don't worry about it. I don't expect you to drop everything to spend time with us."

"I want you to meet Kaia, and I'll try to work it out. If her family is not as incensed about our relationship as we expect them to be, would you be averse to having dinner with them?"

Kian groaned. "You know how much I dislike spending time with humans, but Syssi would want to meet them, so I guess I will have to suffer through it."

"Thank you. I appreciate your sacrifice."

"Yeah, yeah. I'm not doing it for you. I'm doing it for my wife."

William chuckled. "The things we do for love."

30

KAIA

$\mathcal{T}$he food arrived a couple of minutes before William and Max walked back into the restaurant, but given William's expression, his mission to get her a ring hadn't been successful.

"What happened?" Kaia whispered as he sat down next to her. "Was the store closed?"

"It was open." He lifted his fork and stabbed it into one of the prawns.

For a guy that usually talked a mile a minute, he was strangely tight-lipped.

"They didn't have what you were looking for?"

He put the fork down and turned to her. "I got what I wanted." He leaned closer to whisper in her ear. "I got a phone call from the big boss. He and his wife are coming to Safe Haven tomorrow. I asked him if they could move their visit to next week, but he said no."

Kaia's gut clenched. "Is he coming because of me?"

William shook his head. "Let's talk about it on the way back."

After that intro, Kaia couldn't wait for the meal to be over. What could the clan's leader possibly want with her?

Maybe he was worried that she was taking advantage of William? Their whirlwind romance probably seemed as suspicious to him as it would no doubt seem to her family, and maybe he assumed that she had an ulterior motive the same way her family would assume William had. Well, in William's case, the suspected ulterior motive would be simple lechery, but in her case, it would be something more nefarious.

Romeo and Juliet, anyone?

Except, her Romeo wasn't a teenage boy, and he didn't answer to his family.

Or did he?

What if his boss told him to leave her? Would William do as he was told?

When they were finally done with the meal and got on the bus, she took William's hand and led him all the way to the back, hoping that the others would stay up front, but Corrine and Owen followed them and took the seat in front of them.

Whatever. Kaia could wait no longer to find out what William's boss wanted with her.

"Why is Kian coming to Safe Haven?" she whispered.

"His wife wants to see the completed project. They were here in the planning stages, and she's curious to see how it turned out."

She narrowed her eyes at him. "Are you sure it has nothing to do with me?"

He took her hand. "They want to meet you, but after I told him that your family is coming and that we expect them to raise hell over our relationship, he said that they could wait to meet you when you come to the village."

Relief washing over her, Kaia slumped in the seat. "I was afraid that they wanted to check out the temptress who snagged their genius tech guy."

He chuckled. "I'm sure that they do, but that's not the reason for their visit." He wrapped his arm around her shoulders. "On the upside, you might get your wish to meet an Odu sooner than later. Kian is bringing his butler along."

Her mood instantly brightened and Kaia straightened up. "That's fantastic. I'm so excited."

Smiling, William leaned over and kissed her cheek. "You are a strange girl, Kaia. You're about to meet a demigod, but you're more excited about meeting his butler."

"Okidu is much more interesting to me than your boss."

"Okidu?" Corrine turned around. "Do you mean Enkidu?"

Damn, Kaia hadn't bothered to whisper her last sentence, so maybe that was all Corrine had heard, but what if she had overheard more of their conversation?

When in doubt, it was always better to get the other party talking. "What about Enkidu?"

Corrine looked confused, which was precisely what Kaia had intended. "I heard you say Okidu, and I thought that you confused it with Enkidu. Enkidu was King Gilgamesh's companion in a famous story from Assyrian mythology."

Kaia remembered something about a legendary Mesopotamian figure called Gilgamesh who had sought immortality, but she didn't remember the details.

"Yeah, I was trying to remember that legend. Wasn't Gilgamesh the guy who claimed to be three-quarters god and searched for the secret to immortality?"

If Corrine had heard William talk about a demigod, that would cover it.

"That's the one." Corrine grinned. "But his friend's name was Enkidu, not Okidu."

"Gilgamesh was the king of Uruk," William said. "Enkidu was created to be his servant, and he was described as a wild man, someone who was strong enough to stand up to Gilgamesh. Later, he became the king's friend and companion. When Enkidu died, Gilgamesh was heartbroken and grieved his loss."

"What do you mean by created?" Kaia asked. "By whom?"

"The gods, I guess."

"Interesting." Kaia leaned back.

What if Enkidu was an Odu? The similarities were too much to be a coincidence. A created servant whose name was almost identical to Okidu and who was very strong. The main difference was that Enkidu had died, while the Odus were supposed to be indestructible.

"I want to refresh my memory." Kaia pulled out her phone and typed the inquiry, but the cellular signal was too weak, and Wikipedia refused to load. "It's no use. The reception is just too bad. I'll have to wait until we get back home."

"Home?" William asked softly.

She smiled. "Yeah. Our temporary little home."

DARLENE

*T*here was plenty of available seating on the bus, but Max chose to crowd Darlene with his bulk.

His legs were so long that he had to sit sideways for his knees to clear the seat in front of them, and his shoulders were so broad that Darlene had to squeeze herself against the window to avoid touching them.

It would have been semi-tolerable if the guy wasn't so damn attractive.

She found it impossible not to react to his proximity, but since she was waiting for Eric to arrive the next day, she didn't want to encourage Max.

Was it William's doing?

Up until now, the Guardian had been giving her charming smiles whenever their paths crossed, but their interactions had been limited to brief greetings and a few polite words. Why was he suddenly laying on the charm so thick?

Her hunch was that William had told him about her interest in Eric, and Max had taken it upon himself to seduce her before the guy's arrival.

Wasn't going to happen.

Darlene had a plan, and she was going to stick to it. She would have a short fling with Eric as a test run, and once she regained her confidence, she would give Max or one of his fellow Guardians a chance.

Maybe that was what he was after? To secure his spot at the top of her list once she was ready?

"Am I making you uncomfortable?" He smiled as if he knew the answer to that.

"The seats on this bus are ridiculously narrow. I have to scoot all the way to the window to avoid touching you."

"You can touch me." His smile turned lascivious. "You can even put your head on my shoulder and take a nap if you want." He patted his bulging bicep. "Right here."

"Thank you for the offer, but I'm not sleepy."

CHAPTER 31

"Good, then we can talk."

He'd asked her a thousand questions on the way to the restaurant, and she had nothing more to tell him. "It's your turn to tell me about yourself. I've already told you everything there is to know about me."

"Not true. What is your favorite ice cream flavor?"

"Pistachio. What's yours?"

"Cookies and cream. What's your favorite drink?"

She rolled her eyes. "Please, can we stop with the endless questions? Tell me about your life in Scotland and what you did after retiring from the Guardian force."

He tilted his head to look at her. "How do you know that I retired?" A smile bloomed on his handsome face. "Did you ask about me?"

"It was just a guess. Roni told me that most of the Guardians were recruited from retirement by Bridget's impassioned speech about all the good they could do."

He looked disappointed. "Yeah, I was one of those Guardians." He dipped his head to whisper in her ear. "I joined the force a little over five hundred years ago, and I retired after serving for seventy-two years."

"How old are you?"

"I'm five hundred and twenty-three years old."

"That's ancient," she whispered back. "What did you do after retiring?"

"Many things. I was even a stage actor for a few years." He cast her one of his charming smiles. "I have a good singing voice, and I also joined the opera, but I wasn't getting any leading roles, so I quit."

That piqued her interest. "How come I've never heard you sing?"

He waggled his brows. "Would you like me to give you a private performance?"

She was willing to bet that his idea was to perform for her in the nude, and the truth was that she wasn't averse to that.

"I would love to hear you sing," she skirted around the trap he'd set up for her. "What did you do other than that? Four hundred centuries is a long time to dabble in acting and opera singing."

"For most of my life, I was a stonemason. I love building things, but eventually I got tired of doing that as well. Rescuing victims of trafficking and getting their handlers arrested is a much more fulfilling job." He sighed. "But it's stressful and emotionally charged. Sometimes I miss the quiet of masonry. It's relaxing."

"I get it." Tired of fighting for space, Darlene relaxed and let her thigh press against his. "In my opinion, creating something is much more fulfilling than dealing with mystery and corruption. On the other hand, I'm sure that helping others who have no one else to fight for them is fulfilling as well."

Max nodded. "It would be easier if I had a mate to come home to at the end of the day or the night as it may be. Most of the missions are at night."

Great. Now he was pulling out the guilt card to persuade her to give him a chance.

"It's up to the Fates." She patted his bicep. "Your one and only is waiting for you somewhere out there."

That was not a subtle way to communicate that this was not what she was looking for at present, but it was effective and clear.

"I hope so." He looked into her eyes. "It would be so nice to have someone welcome me when I get back from a mission, ask me how it went, and tell me how proud she is of me for rescuing innocents."

3 2

WILLIAM

When the bus entered the outer security ring surrounding Safe Haven, everyone's phones started buzzing with incoming messages.

"After that long drive through the countryside with no reception anywhere, I feel like we are back in civilization." Kaia read over her texts.

Kaia and her teammates didn't know that their lines were tapped, and William felt bad about that, but it was either that or not allowing them to have phones at all.

"Cheryl is asking what she should pack and if it's cold here at night." Kaia typed up a quick answer. "I told her that a hoodie should do it."

Corrine turned around. "Now that you have reception, you can read up on the epic of Gilgamesh."

"Right." Kaia typed the search term into the box and started scrolling through the endless selection of articles. "This is going to take a while." She leaned against William's side.

He'd read the poems in their original Sumerian, or rather the parts that had survived, but it had been a long time ago, and he didn't remember much.

Kaia kept reading until the driver eased the bus into its parking spot by the main lodge.

"Did you find anything interesting?" William asked as they stepped out.

"Plenty. But I'll tell you about it at home."

That was enough to put a grin on his face. "I have a little something to give you when we get there."

"I almost forgot." She reached into his pocket and palmed the small box. "I can't wait to see it."

Kaia didn't sound as excited as he'd hoped she would be, but perhaps that was because she was treating their engagement as a ruse, or maybe she just wasn't the type of girl who got excited about things like that. She seemed more interested in the Gilgamesh legend than she was in the ring.

When they said goodbye to the others, William asked, "So, what did you find out that's so fascinating?"

She glanced over her shoulder at Kylie and waited until her former roommate entered her bungalow and closed the door behind her. "Did it ever occur to you that Enkidu could have been an Odu?"

"The name is similar, but Enkidu was created as a wild man, not a cyborg."

"That's true, but the whole story is about gods and immortals and legendary monsters. Gilgamesh was a harsh king who abused his power and behaved amorally, so the goddess of creation made Enkidu in order to teach Gilgamesh a lesson." Kaia followed him inside. "At first, Enkidu was a mighty wild man who lived like an animal, which could be a metaphor for him having to learn even the most basic things about acting like a human." She put her wallet-size purse on the coffee table and sat down on the couch. "You said that the Odus learned by mimicking human behaviors, so that could be what the legend was trying to show."

"That's an interesting hypothesis." William walked over to the kitchenette. "But they sent him a temple prostitute to teach him about being human, which an Odu wouldn't have known what to do with. They don't have sexual urges or even the appropriate organs."

He loaded the coffeemaker, wishing that he'd thought ahead and gotten wine for the occasion, but all he had was a bottle of whiskey, and he doubted Kaia would want that.

"That could be an allegory as well. I don't know for what, but I'm sure that if I give it some thought, I'll figure it out. Maybe it was meant to show that women were morally superior to men. After all, they chose a sacred prostitute to teach him about morality and not some old sage. When she brings Enkidu to the city, he's nice and helpful to the shepherds and trappers he'd terrorized before, and when he sees Gilgamesh on his way to take a bride on her wedding day, as was the king's nasty custom, he stops him. Meaning that Enkidu internalized what he had learned from the prostitute and became morally superior to the king."

"Coffee?" William asked.

"Yeah, sure. It helps me think. After engaging in an epic fight, Gilgamesh and Enkidu become good friends. In the next chapter of his life, Gilgamesh is bored and decides to journey to the gods' forest and kill the guardian who keeps mortals from entering the gods' realm. Enkidu is the voice of reason, advising against such a foolish quest, and he ends up being punished by the gods for killing their guardian, and dies."

William handed Kaia the coffee mug and sat down next to her. "The Odus are practically indestructible. They can't die."

She took a sip of coffee. "I might be wrong, but I think it's an allegory for what happened to the Odus in their home world. They were created to be servants and companions and to mimic all the good behaviors of the gods. But an ambitious ruler with crazy ideas decided to use them in warfare. The ruler won, but the Odus paid the ultimate price for the victory. In the legend, Enkidu's death is portrayed as a descent to the underworld. I think Enkidu was an eighth Odu who got separated from his brothers and sent to Earth."

"Where is he now?" William put his mug on the coffee table and pulled the small ring box out of his pocket.

Kaia pouted. "That's the one part I don't have a theory for."

CHAPTER 32

He laughed. "Just that one?"

"Yeah." She eyed the box in the palm of his hand. "It's just a fun mental experiment with what-ifs, but you must agree that there might be something to it."

"It's possible."

She seemed satisfied with his answer. "Can I see the ring now?"

33

KAIA

$\mathcal{K}$aia stifled a chuckle when William slid off the couch and went down on one knee before her.

"Will you marry me, Kaia Locke?" He opened the box.

She gave the ring a cursory glance and was about to act out a scene, pretending that the proposal was real and making some comic remarks about it, but William's hopeful expression gave her pause.

He wasn't a good actor, and he seemed serious.

Was she ready to commit to him?

Before seeing the family in the restaurant, her answer might have been yes, but with her heart yearning for what they had, her resolve was shaken.

Looking into his eyes, she chewed on her lower lip. "I thought that this would only be a placeholder until you get me a real engagement ring."

"It is a placeholder, but I hope that our commitment to each other is not dependent on the size of the diamond."

That was such an offensive thing to say. Did he really think that she'd hesitated because she didn't like the ring?

"It's not about the diamond, and you know it. The ring is lovely, and I would be more than happy with it being my permanent engagement symbol. I just need a few more days before I can say 'yes'." She folded her arms over her chest. "Keep the ring until then."

William frowned. "I thought that you already gave me your answer. You said that Darlene helped you rethink your priorities."

It was true. She had said that, but she'd just shared with him her deliberations. She hadn't made a steadfast commitment to him yet.

Besides, she still hadn't told William her secret, and accepting his marriage proposal before fessing up to that wouldn't be right.

With a sigh, she unfolded her arms and leaned over to close the box. "There is something you need to know before you propose to me for real. I thought that I had more time to tell you my secret, but if you are serious about this proposal, then you should know who the girl you plan to spend the rest of your very long life with really is."

William remained on the floor, his hand extended with the box resting on his palm. "There is nothing you can tell me that will alter the way I feel about you."

She lifted a brow. "What if I'm a murderer?"

He smiled. "You're not, and if you were, you would have had a good reason for committing murder."

It was good to know that he had such faith in her. But then, who would suspect a nineteen-year-old professor of murder?

"Let's hit a pause button on the proposal." She patted the spot next to her. "Come sit with me."

William turned to put the box on the coffee table and then pushed up and sat next to her. "So, what's your big, scary secret?" He reached for her hand.

Kaia swallowed. "Do you remember what the aura guy said he saw?"

His eyes widened. "About the parasitic spirit?"

She nodded. "Only it's not a parasite. It's all me. I remember pieces of my previous life as a man who was a gifted mathematician. The mathematics is what I remember best from that life. That's what made me a prodigy. But I also remember other things." She lifted her hand and wiggled her fingers. "I was a big guy, and I hated my sausage-like fingers. I lusted after women, but I was too shy to pursue them, and I lived a lonely life."

William looked perturbed but not repulsed, so that was a relief.

"How do you know that those memories are yours from a past life and not those of an invading spirit?"

Kaia pursed her lips. "I think I would have known if those weren't my own memories but someone else's. Are you asking because of what the aura guy said?"

He nodded. "If those are just memories of your past life, you shouldn't have two auras."

She waved a dismissive hand. "How reliable is that guy anyway? Did he ever make an observation about a strange aura that was proven correct?"

"I don't know. I will have to ask Eleanor. You should also talk with Nathalie. She had a parasitic spirit living in her head for many years, but she's always known that he was a separate entity. Then that spirit passed on and made room for a much nicer spirit." He smiled sadly. "The spirit of someone very dear to me. Mark was a gifted programmer who was murdered by our enemies."

Kaia felt the blood drain from her face. William had told her about the immortals splitting into two opposing camps, but he hadn't told her that the others were murdering his people.

"Is that why you have such formidable security around Safe Haven? Are you afraid they will find out about the research and attack us?"

As her mind processed the information and its implications, her fear ratcheted up several notches.

William's enemies were also immortal, which meant that they were as strong and as fast as the Guardians in his security detail. But there were many more of the others, and they could easily overpower the small unit assigned to their lab.

What if an attack happened when her family was visiting? Should she call them and tell them to cancel their visit? But what would she tell them? If she told them about the danger to the lab, they would demand that she return home right away, and if she refused, Gilbert and Eric would come right over and make a scene.

34

WILLIAM

*K*aia looked apprehensive, and William couldn't blame her. He hadn't told her anything about the clan's war with the followers of Mortdh, or rather Navuh, and he could see that mentioning Mark's murder had her imagination filling in the blanks.

"You have nothing to worry about." He gave her hand a reassuring squeeze. "At this time, our enemies are not planning any attacks on us. They are busy breeding their new smart army, so we have a couple of decades of reprieve. Besides, their mode of operation is not to attack us directly but to ally themselves with countries that don't aspire to the ideals that our clan promotes, like democracy and equal opportunity for all. The Doomers do their best to undermine our work."

Kaia chuckled. "Doomers? Is it a nickname?"

"Doom is their acronym. They are the Brotherhood of the Devout Order of Mortdh. It just works out nicely in English."

"So, if they are not a clear and present danger, why the insane security around Safe Haven?"

He sighed. "First of all, we can never know when or why the Doomers will change tactics. They haven't attacked us directly because they can't find us, but if they ever do, they will strike against us. The likelihood of that is marginal, but on the remote chance that it will happen, we prefer to err on the side of caution."

The truth was that he was no longer sure that Navuh sought the clan's destruction. The clan did a great job of hiding, but it wasn't impossible to find, and Navuh wasn't dumb. It had occurred to William that the despot was content with using Annani and her clan as a means to unify his people, and annihilating that unifying factor didn't serve his best interest.

Finding an enemy to vilify was a common tactic that was successfully employed by despots and tyrants throughout history as a means aimed at rallying their troops behind a cause. But once that enemy was no more, a new enemy had to be found, or the entire underpinning of the rotten structure collapsed.

"And what's the second reason?" Kaia asked.

"Humans are no less of a threat, especially when something as valuable as the secret to eternal life could be attained."

She let out a breath. "Since the only two people who know what we are working on are you and me, I'm not worried about humans."

"We are not the only ones," William admitted. "I suspected that we might find answers in Okidu's journals from the moment Kian had told me about them, and I shared my suspicions with him and the clan council."

"But no humans other than me know about it, right?"

He nodded.

She waved her hand at the box on the table. "Then you'd better give me that ring and marry me as soon as possible."

William tilted his head. "Why the sudden change of heart?"

"I just realized that once the project is completed and you no longer need me, your best option to keep it a secret is to eliminate the only human who knows about it. I'd better turn immortal as soon as I can."

Was Kaia joking? Or was she serious?

It was hard to tell with her, not because she didn't emit emotional scents, like Turner, but because she emitted such a smorgasbord of them that it was impossible to isolate just one.

"I would never harm even one hair on your head. If by the end of the project you haven't transitioned, I will thrall you to forget what you've learned."

She narrowed her eyes at him. "So once my job is done, my mind will no longer be precious to you?"

"Of course, it will. But a one-time thrall is not dangerous, not even when it involves eliminating many memories."

That wasn't entirely true, but William was positive that Kaia was a Dormant and that she would transition successfully.

She shook her head. "I don't know why we are arguing about hypotheticals."

"I'm not arguing." William took the box and opened it again. "I love you, Kaia. And even a hundred spirits living in your head won't change that. If you feel the same about me, say yes. But if you don't, or you're not sure that you do, there is no rush. You can wear the ring with no obligation attached."

Looking at the ring, Kaia chewed on her lower lip. "I'm sorry for ruining your romantic proposal."

His heart sank. "I understand." He handed her the box.

She lifted her hand to stop him. "No, you don't. I want to say yes, but I can't. What if I don't transition? If I'm just a regular human, you can't marry me. You will need to erase my memories not just of the project but of everything that you told me and probably of our relationship as well."

"I know in my gut that you are my one and only, and I'm willing to put my heart on the line and commit to you as if you have already transitioned. Are you willing to do the same?"

She hesitated for a moment longer and then nodded. "But I want a do-over. I don't want our engagement to come on the heels of an argument."

William's heart floated up from his gut back into his rib cage and flapped its wings in excitement.

Hooking his finger under her chin, he dipped his head and sucked on that luscious lower lip that she'd been nibbling on. When she was breathless and panting from the kiss, he let go of her lips and leaned back.

"I love you, Kaia. Will you be mine? Will you marry me?"

She smiled. "Yes, William. I love you, and I will marry you provided that I transition." She wound her arms around his neck. "Now take me to bed."

35

JADE

"Do you know what day it is today?" Jade asked the eight little ones gazing at her with adoring eyes.

"It's Saturday," Gaycha said.

She was an intelligent three-year-old, and she wasn't afraid to speak up. She showed potential as a future prime.

"And what happens on Saturdays?" Jade asked.

"Story time." Rikon clapped his hands.

"That's right." Sitting on a large pillow, with the little ones sitting on smaller ones in a semi-circle facing her, Jade put her hands on her knees. "Which story would you like to hear today?"

"Can you please tell the one about the prince and the princess?" Gaycha asked.

It was the kids' favorite story, and Jade had told it hundreds of times before, at least fifteen times to this group alone. She'd changed the story over the years, creating many variations but maintaining the core principles she wanted to convey.

She was treading on dangerous ground.

Through her stories, Jade tried to teach the young ones the true way of the Kra-ell, but that's not how Igor's compound operated, and she had to be careful how she worded it. If Igor didn't like her teaching methods, he would not allow her anywhere near the kids.

"Aren't you tired of hearing that story over and over again?" she asked.

All eight kids shook their heads as one.

"Please," Rikon pleaded.

"Okay." Jade folded her legs into the lotus position, which was a signal for the kids to do the same. Not all had mastered the pose yet, but they were doing their best, and one day soon, they would all sit with their backs straight and their legs folded in the proper position.

"Since you've heard the story so many times, you can help me tell it. Who wants

316

to go first?"

As always, Gaycha lifted her hand. "I do."

"Go ahead."

"A very long time ago, in a land far, far away, lived a strong and just queen."

"Excellent opening." Jade motioned for Radina to continue.

The girl swallowed, her big eyes growing even larger. She was a timid little thing, and if she didn't grow some backbone soon, the others would eat her alive.

"The queen set her eyes on a king from a strange faraway land," Radina said so quietly that it was almost a whisper.

"Speak up, Radina. You are a strong Kra-ell female. We do not speak in whispers."

"I'm sorry."

Jade lifted a brow. "Don't be sorry. Just continue the story in a louder voice."

The girl squared her shoulders and thrust her chin out. "The king saw the queen, and he thought that she was beautiful and strong, and he desired her."

"Very good." Jade looked at Moshun. "Continue."

"The king didn't know the Kra-ell way, and he offended the queen, but he didn't mean to. It was an accident."

"What did the queen do?" Mondy asked.

Jade smiled. That was as far as the kids could recite the story. From that point on, they would start messing it up. "The queen told the foreign king that he could not be hers because he was not of her people, and the law prohibited her from mating him."

"But she liked him," Mondy said.

"Yes, she did. And then what happened?"

"War." Moshun pumped his fist in the air.

"Not yet." Jade lifted her hand. "The queen and king started to meet in secret, hiding their relationship from both their peoples. But when their secret was discovered, and their people got angry, demanding that they never meet again, the king left his people and went to live with the queen."

Jade paused when Kagra entered the room and leaned against the wall.

Kagra waved a hand. "Please, don't let me interrupt the story."

She'd heard it many times before, in at least ten different versions.

"The king's people thought that the queen had bewitched him," Jade continued. "So, they declared war on her lands, demanding that she release the king from her snare. The queen refused because she was proud and selfish and wanted to keep the handsome king. The war was long and bloody, and many good people died needlessly, all because the queen and king cared more about each other than about their duty to their people."

"Your story is depressing." Kagra walked over to the semi-circle of kids and sat between Moshun and Radina. "We want a story with a happy ending. Right, kids?"

They were raising Kra-ell, not humans, and Kra-ell didn't believe in happy endings and love and all that other nonsense that humans drugged themselves with.

The best ending a Kra-ell could hope for was to die honorably in battle.

"If you want a happy story, you will need to ask Kagra to tell it." Jade unfolded her legs and got up. "My stories don't have happy endings. We are Kra-ell, and we live for the glory of battle and the honor of serving the Mother of All Life."

36

KAIA

*A*s the bus neared the airport, Kaia took the ring off and put it in her purse. Next to her, William tensed. "Why did you do that? The engagement was meant to placate your family. Did you change your mind about it?"

"No, I still think that it will help, but if I show up with the ring on my finger, it will be immediately obvious, and things will get ugly fast. It will be better if I ease them into it."

He let out a breath. "You know your family. I trust your instincts on that."

"I wish I was as confident in myself as you are in me. I don't know if the engagement will make our relationship more palatable to them or the other way around. Without a ring, they can dismiss it as a fleeting infatuation. The ring might act as a call to battle."

"By them, I assume you mean Gilbert."

Kaia shook her head. "Gilbert makes a lot of waves, but he's harmless. My mother is the one I'm worried about. She is extremely protective of Cheryl and me, and she's always suspicious of boys." Calling William a boy was just wrong. "I mean men. My mother is not the trusting kind."

William chuckled. "Your mother is a smart woman. Men have one thing on their minds when it comes to desirable women, and it usually isn't platonic love."

She shrugged. "Nature ensures the propagation of the species. Imagine a world in which men were content to sit around and wait for women to come to them." She lifted a pair of mock innocent eyes to him. "Oh, wait. That's what you did."

"I guess I'm lucky my lady didn't forget her past life as a man and took the initiative."

"Gah." She elbowed his side. "It's not cool to bring that up in that context. My past memories had nothing to do with it." She scrunched her nose. "Well, that's not entirely true. My assertiveness has nothing to do with it, but my understanding of how men think does. I don't get offended by comments that I know were not meant to offend, and I also understand the male sexual drive on the one hand and the inhibitions on the other. It's not easy to be a guy."

That was especially true of big guys who took up too much space. She remembered Edgar trying to make himself look smaller so as not to intimidate people. He'd hunched his shoulders, tried to get out of people's way, and smiled a lot even when he hadn't felt like it.

"Does your family know about those memories?" William asked.

"I told my mother about it when I was younger, but she thought that I'd invented an imaginary male friend as a result of the trauma of losing my father. She wanted to take me to a shrink, so I told her that I had just imagined it and that was it. I told my sister, and she said that she believed me, but it was a long time ago, and we haven't talked about it recently. Other than that, I didn't tell anyone else."

He leaned toward her and kissed her lips. "Thank you for trusting me with your big secret."

"You trusted me with yours, so I trusted you with mine."

"I ensured mine would remain a secret with compulsion, and I feel bad about it."

She patted his knee. "Don't. You had no choice because your boss demanded it. Besides, if my secret gets out, I might get threatened with visits to a shrink, while if your secrets get out, your life and the lives of all your clan members would be in danger."

William glanced at the Guardian sitting at the front of the bus, then shifted his eyes back to her. "I forgot about him." He motioned with his head to the guy and then dipped his head to whisper in her ear, "Immortals have exceptionally good hearing."

Damn. So now three people knew about her past life.

Kaia whispered back. "Can you ask him to keep it to himself?"

"I'm not sure that he heard anything, and even if he did, it wouldn't make him think any less of you. Paranormal phenomena are common among immortals and Dormants."

"Yeah, you told me that. I wonder how Eleanor's group would feel about my past life. They would probably be more open than others to accept it as real." She chuckled. "What do the paranormals call regular people, mundanes?"

"I don't know. I don't think they have a special term for non-paranormals. You should talk to Eleanor first, though."

It could be an interesting experience to talk openly about remembering her past life, and maybe even get some feedback. The aura guy would be the first one she would approach.

The problem was that Kaia usually met the paranormals during meals in the dining hall, and most of the time, her teammates were there as well. The last thing she needed was to give them more ammunition against her.

As the driver parked the bus and opened the door, the three of them got out, and Kaia cast a quick look at the Guardian, checking to see if he regarded her differently than before, but the guy just smiled politely and said nothing.

Taking a fortifying breath, Kaia released it slowly through her nose and took William's hand. "Let's get this show on the road, shall we?"

37

WILLIAM

*W*illiam stood with the Guardian who'd accompanied him and Kaia to the airport, and watched her hugging and kissing her mother, her sisters, Gilbert, and Eric.

"Lots of love in that family." Conrad crossed his arms over his chest. "Should I offer to help with their luggage?"

"Thank you for the offer, but I would wait until they are done."

"Roger that."

The Guardian's words tugged on William's heart strings. Once Kaia's family learned of their engagement, that happy reunion would be over, and he hated being the cause of strife between them.

Kaia scooped one of her baby brothers into her arms and peppered his smiling face with kisses. "I missed you so much." She hugged him tightly to her, which he didn't seem to mind at all.

Winding his little arms around her neck, he gave her a sloppy kiss.

Kaia laughed. "I even missed your slobbery kisses."

The other twin didn't like being left out, wiggling in his mother's grip and flailing his arms toward his sister.

"Wait your turn, you little monster." She walked over to William and handed him the baby. "Hold him while I get Ryan."

The boy didn't protest as William held him suspended in front of him, debating whether he should hug him like Kaia had done, or put him over his shoulders the way Idina demanded to be carried around.

The boy looked at him with curiosity in his eyes, lifted his little fist and stuck it in his mouth.

"Hold him against your chest," Cheryl advised. "But don't squash him. Do it gently."

"Have you never held a baby in your arms?" Gilbert asked.

"I haven't," William admitted. "They are so small and fragile." He offered the boy to his father. "I'm afraid I'll hurt him."

Gilbert didn't make a move to take his son from William. "You can carry Evan for a little bit. He seems to like you."

William frowned. "He does?"

"Yeah. He didn't kick you in the nuts yet, so he must like you."

William looked down at the boy's feet, which were dangling right in front of his crotch, and lifted him higher, putting him against his chest.

Gilbert grinned. "You see? It's not that difficult."

The baby wiggled, wanting to turn around and look at his father.

"What do I do now?"

Gilbert sighed and reached for his son, but the boy refused to leave William, clinging to his shirt and making an angry face at his father.

"I guess you're stuck with him. Just turn him sideways and make sure that you don't drop him."

"I won't drop him." William did as the guy had instructed, and Evan calmed down. Settling in his arms, he chewed on his fist, covering it in slobber.

Idina tugged on her father's sleeve. "I want William to carry me."

Gilbert made a pouty face at her. "You don't want your daddy to give you a ride?"

She sighed dramatically. "Okay, you can carry me," she said like she was doing him a favor.

William would have preferred to carry the girl, who looked sturdy enough, but her brother had claimed the spot and wasn't willing to give it up.

"Can I help you with the luggage?" Conrad asked Kaia's mother.

"Thank you." Karen pointed him to the pile that Eric had taken out of the small executive jet. "Eric can't handle all of that, and the rest of us have our hands full."

"No problem." Conrad squared his impressive shoulders. "That's what I'm here for."

He was there to provide Guardian escort, but that answer was better.

As William led the procession toward the bus with the baby in his arms, he felt everyone's eyes on him, and it was unnerving. Well not everyone's. Cheryl was typing on her phone while walking.

Kaia and her mother looked at him with amusement in their eyes, Gilbert cast him suspicious glances and exchanged silent looks with his brother, and Conrad was stifling laughter while carrying most of the family's luggage.

When they were all seated in the bus, Evan finally agreed to let go of William and sit in his father's lap, and Idina immediately jumped on the opportunity to take his place.

"My children seem to like you," Gilbert said. "Do you get that a lot from kids?"

There weren't that many children in the village for him to be exposed to, and William hadn't had many opportunities to be around them.

"I don't get to interact with kids much," he admitted. "I spend most of my day in the lab, and sometimes I even sleep there. I don't have much of a life outside of it."

"That's no way to live," Eric said. "When I was still in the Air Force, I had no life either. I retired as soon as I could and never looked back."

"And now you live the merry life of a bachelor." Gilbert bounced his son on his knee.

"Perhaps those days are coming to an end." Eric looked at William. "I hoped Darlene would come along to pick us up."

"I'm sure that she wanted to come, but she had to stay behind and take care of a few things for me." William adjusted Idina in an attempt to make her stop swinging her leg and banging it against the seat in front of them. "I wanted her to keep an eye on the kitchen staff in the lodge so they wouldn't close the dining room like they normally do. I asked them to have a late lunch waiting for you when you arrive." He looked at Eric. "We will have the entire dining hall to ourselves, and Darlene is going to join us there."

Karen gave him a grateful smile. "I didn't know that they closed the kitchen between lunch and dinner; if I did, I would have timed our arrival better."

"That's okay. My boss is arriving at Safe Haven an hour later, so I need the place to stay open for him and his party as well."

"Where is he coming from?" Eric asked.

"He's flying in from Los Angeles."

It was a big city, so telling them that was pretty meaningless.

Gilbert arched a brow. "I'm surprised that you came with Kaia to collect us from the airport when your boss is arriving today as well. Won't you get in trouble for not picking him up?"

William shouldn't have mentioned Kian, and it was no wonder that Gilbert was suspicious.

Groaning internally, he assumed an impassive expression.

"I offered, but he preferred to rent a van. He's not one of those bosses who enjoys his people groveling."

Gilbert still looked suspicious. "Tell me about him. Is he a scientist like you?"

"He's a businessman. My lab and the things we work on are just a small fraction of the holdings he manages."

"Like what?" Gilbert pressed.

"Developing and building, among other things. Mostly office buildings and hotels." Again, it was just a small part of the clan's investments, but he didn't need to list them all.

That got a smile out of the guy. "A fellow builder. I would like to have a chat with him."

"I don't know if he will have time." William swallowed another groan. "He's also a bit of a recluse."

Kian had said that he would agree to have dinner with Kaia's family because Syssi would want to meet them, but if they became hostile after learning about the engagement, dinner with them would not be a good idea.

38

DARLENE

*N*ervous butterflies fluttered in Darlene's belly as she waited for Kaia's family to arrive at the dining hall.

She'd spent the morning getting ready, shaving what needed to be shaved, exfoliating, putting a moisturizing mask on, doing her hair, and obsessing over which outfit to wear. Darlene had wanted to accompany Kaia and William to the airport and greet Eric, maybe even have him show her his jet, but William had been right to put her in charge of making sure they had a proper meal waiting for them upon their arrival.

If she hadn't been there to intervene with the kitchen staff, they would be eating lunch leftovers that they had to reheat themselves.

She had to remind the chef that the new owners of the resorts were arriving soon after Kaia's family, and if the big boss didn't like the service, he might hire a new chef and new kitchen staff.

That had worked like a charm, and the kitchen had gone into a frenzy of preparing vegan dishes for Kian. When she'd pointed out that he was the only vegan of the bunch, the chef shrugged her shoulders.

The others would have to make do with the vegan fare as well, but Darlene had a feeling that it would be an improvement over the parboiled fish and dry chicken breasts that they usually served for lunch and dinner.

Blah.

Safe Haven was a beautiful place, and Kian's renovation had turned it into a luxurious resort, but she needed to have a talk with him about the food, especially if he wanted the guests to return.

Or maybe he didn't want repeat customers, and the bland food was intentional?

After all, the idea was to attract people with paranormal abilities, so if they didn't have what the clan was looking for, the only reason to tempt them to return would be financial.

Nah. Kian probably didn't know that the fancy chef he'd hired was not all that she'd claimed to be. Though given the smells coming out of the kitchen now, she'd made a special effort to impress him.

When the doors to the dining hall finally opened, and William ushered Kaia and her family in, Darlene's eyes met Eric's, and when he smiled at her, her heart did a happy little flip.

Max might be more handsome and pack double the muscle, but there was a certain cocky charm to Eric that Max didn't have and that Darlene found irresistible.

He also was more age appropriate for her, but that was an illusion. Max only looked like he'd just turned thirty. The Guardian was ancient.

She should remember that when the thing with Eric ended and she moved to the next stage of her plan. Not that she wanted to, but she had no choice.

Eric wasn't long-term material. He was human, and he was a player who was not interested in settling down.

"Hello, Darlene." He walked over and took her hand. "You look even lovelier than I remembered."

"It's funny, but I wanted to say the same thing to you."

"Oh, thank you." He put his other hand over his heart. "Do I look lovely today?" He batted his eyelashes.

"You look even more handsome than I remembered and cockier as well."

"Cocky is my middle name." He wrapped his arm around her shoulders. "How have you been?"

"Great. And you?"

"Wonderful." She leaned closer and whispered in his ear, "I couldn't stop thinking about you."

His hand squeezed her shoulder. "Same here," he whispered back.

"Can we sit down anywhere?" Karen asked.

"Yes." Darlene ducked out from under Eric's arm. "The entire dining hall is ours for the next hour and a half."

"Did you hear anything from the boss?" William asked.

"Not since they boarded the plane. But I estimate that they will get here around four in the afternoon."

"We should hurry." William walked over to one of the tables and pulled out a chair for Karen.

"I would like to meet your boss." Gilbert sat next to Karen.

"William already told you that he doesn't like to interact with the plebs." Eric pulled a chair out for Darlene.

"It's not that," William said. "It's just that he's a very private person, and he doesn't like attention."

It was precisely that.

Hiding a smile, Darlene unfurled a napkin and draped it over her knees. Perhaps it was just her impression, but Kian was a snob. He might tout democracy and champion humanity, but he regarded most humans as plebs, and so did Kalugal. Her grandfather wasn't any better, and Annani was on a whole different level of haughty.

Toven and Annani were gods, so they were entitled to their feelings of superiority, and maybe as demigods, Kian and Kalugal were entitled to that as well. But Orion and Geraldine were also demigods, and yet they didn't flaunt it, weren't stuck up, and were comfortable pretending to be human.

It was probably a matter of personality.

Eric wasn't a god or a demigod, but he certainly acted like one.

39

KAIA

$\mathcal{T}$he ride to Safe Haven had gone well, with Gilbert and William talking about his boss's building projects and the rest of them listening to the conversation. When Gilbert found out that Kian had used 3D printing technology to have the bungalows built in record time, he had a thousand questions for William that, thankfully, her guy knew how to answer.

Evidently, William was involved in the clan's projects and was well-informed about the tech that went into all of them. Kaia's area of expertise was much narrower, and she made a promise to herself to expand her horizons once she transitioned and joined the clan. There was so much she could learn from William, and she would have limitless time to learn as much as she wanted.

Provided that she transitioned.

But first, she had to deal with her family and get them to accept William as her fiancé.

To hide her frayed nerves, Kaia held Ryan on her knees, bouncing him up and down and eliciting happy giggles from him even after the food had been served.

There were no highchairs in the lodge's dining hall, but her mother had come prepared with boosters for the little ones that attached to regular chairs.

"Put him in his seat, Kaia," her mother said. "He needs to eat."

Reluctant to let go of her shield, Kaia lifted her baby brother and strapped him into the booster.

"This is not bad," Eric said to Darlene. "After your preamble about the vegan meal, I was afraid we would be served the same slosh as last time, but this is actually better."

"It's like what the grumpy food critic ate in *Ratatouille*," Cheryl said.

"I think it is actually ratatouille," Karen said.

There was also creamy mushroom pasta, which Kaia assumed was made with coconut cream, and two bowls of family-sized salads for them to share.

"Do you like it?" William asked Idina.

CHAPTER 39

She nodded. "I like vegetables."

For the next few moments, everyone got busy eating and commenting about how tasty everything was, but Kaia could barely taste anything.

She'd spent half the night trying to come up with a clever way to ease into announcing her and William's engagement, but dancing around a subject had never been her forte. She was the direct type who liked to shoot first and deal with the consequences later.

Maybe she should do just that and stop agonizing over it. The problem was that she knew her shot would backfire, and she wasn't sure she could deal with a combined attack from Gilbert and her mother.

Maybe talking with Eric first and getting him on her side was a better plan?

It could have been if not for Darlene.

Kaia suspected that the two would disappear right after dinner and not emerge until Sunday afternoon, when it was time for Eric to take everyone back home.

"So, Kaia." Gilbert pushed his empty plate aside and gave her a penetrating look. "Is there something that you want to tell us?" He shifted his eyes to William, then back to her.

Damn. He'd guessed it.

The challenge in his tone was a call to battle, evaporating Kaia's resolve to ease her family into the news. Gilbert had fired the first shot, giving her the ammunition she needed to fire hers.

"Your nose is infallible, Gilbert." She gave him a bright smile while opening her purse and pulling out the ring. "William and I are engaged." She slipped the ring over her finger.

A stunned moment of silence followed, but it didn't last long.

"Are you out of your effing mind?" Gilbert threw his napkin over his plate as if he was throwing down a gauntlet. "You've known the guy for a week."

She shrugged. "When you meet your one and only, you know it. William and I are perfect for each other."

"You're nineteen, Kaia," her mother said. "You shouldn't be engaged to anyone." She looked at William. "No offense, William. You are a nice guy, and if Kaia were twenty-five and you had dated for a couple of years prior to getting engaged, I would have congratulated you and started working on the wedding plans. But Kaia is nineteen, you are thirty-two, and you've known each other for a week. That's a hard no."

"Did you knock her up?" Gilbert spat.

"I'm on the pill," Kaia spat back.

Gilbert didn't even shift his gaze to her and was still glaring at William. "Accidents happen. Otherwise, I can see no reason for two intelligent people to rush into getting married."

Evidently, the engagement had been a mistake. It was making things worse, not better.

"We are not rushing," Kaia said. "And we are not planning a wedding yet. The only reason we got engaged so quickly was to show you that we are serious about each other, and this is not a fling. William and I are in love, and we want to be together. That's all."

Her mother let out a relieved breath but then shook her head. "I'm glad that you are not running off to Vegas to get married, but you need to think of your future and whether what you feel now can endure." She cast an apologetic glance at William. "Right now, the thirteen years difference might not seem like much to you, but when you are forty and William is fifty-three, the difference will become more problematic."

Gilbert was still engaged in a glaring battle with William, who was glaring back but saying nothing.

It was a good tactic to let them vent out all of their objections before responding to them and escalating things into a shouting match, but it required patience that Kaia didn't have.

"What I want to know is how you coerced Kaia into sleeping with you," Gilbert snarled at William. "What power do you wield over her?"

"He didn't coerce me into anything." Kaia folded her arms over her chest. "I was the one who initiated everything, and William tried to resist me."

"You didn't resist hard enough." Gilbert was starting to get red in the face. "You should have realized that Kaia is a young girl, who's away from home for the first time in her life, alone, vulnerable, and latching on to the only person available to her. But you took advantage of her infatuation, and that's deplorable." He turned to look at Kaia. "We are taking you home."

WILLIAM

*G*ilbert's words hit William in the chest like a volley of daggers. He was right, and William was deplorable for not realizing why Kaia had pursued him with such determination.

He'd seen how she'd fallen apart saying goodbye to her family and how she couldn't stop crying. How could he have overlooked all that?

The answer was simple. He wanted her, and it had been easy to just accept that she'd wanted him back for the same reasons and not because she needed to fill the hole in her heart that her family's absence had created.

"I'm sorry," he murmured. "I've acted despicably."

"What?" Kaia's head whipped around, and she looked at him as if he had lost his mind. "You haven't done anything wrong, and neither have I. We fell in love because we found in each other our other half." She turned to Gilbert. "Do you really have so little faith in me? Am I the kind of girl who is so desperate for love that she clings to the first guy who shows interest in her?"

Gilbert's eyes softened as he gazed at her, but his expression remained determined. "At home, you are surrounded by love. Out here, you find yourself alone and away from the protective cocoon of your family, so it's not surprising that you sought someone to fill that void. If you were older and more aware of your feelings, you would have understood that and would have proceeded with more caution. But you are young and impulsive, and you think that you are smarter than everyone. That might be true in regard to science, but it's not true for relationships. Nothing can replace life experience when it comes to feelings, and I'm telling you that what you feel for William is not the mature love that makes a marriage work."

She snorted. "Look who's talking. You and Mom have three kids together, and you are still not married. Maybe you are the one who's not mature enough."

"Kaia," her mother admonished in a stern tone. "We are talking about you, not us. Gilbert and I are in a committed, mature relationship, and we don't need a document to bind us."

"You can't seriously compare us to you," Gilbert said. "Your mother and I met as mature adults, we are only two years apart in age, and neither of us took advantage of the other's vulnerability."

"Oh yeah? Mom was a young widow with two little girls. Maybe you took advantage of her?"

"Pfft." Gilbert waved a dismissive hand. "You're just proving my point about you being immature and impulsive by hurtling accusations at me that you know perfectly well are untrue."

"You're too quick to judge," Eric told Gilbert. "Kaia is very mature for her age, and she's not impulsive. Besides, you would not have been so opposed to their relationship if William was a few years younger. Would you have been foaming at the mouth if he were twenty-three?"

"I'm not foaming at the mouth, and a twenty-three-year-old boyfriend would have been borderline acceptable, provided that they were just starting to date and taking it slowly."

Eric glared at his brother. "Age is not important, and thirteen years is not that much. Why can't you just accept that they are in love?"

Gilbert snorted. "You are guilty of the same thing, so of course, you would come to his defense. Dating twenty-something-year-olds is only slightly better than dating teenagers. Frankly, you are an embarrassment to the family."

"Is that so?" Eric pushed to his feet. "Then maybe I'll remove my embarrassing presence from here, and you can find yourself another way to get back home?" He turned to Darlene. "How about you and I fly to Miami for the weekend? I have good friends out there."

"Please, Eric." She tugged on his hand. "Sit down. Both you and Gilbert need to calm down. You are scaring the kids."

No one had paid any attention to the little ones, but now that Darlene had brought it up, William looked at Kaia's four siblings.

Idina seemed fascinated by the argument and didn't look scared at all. Cheryl seemed worried and was holding Kaia's hand under the table, but the twins were on the verge of tears, their eyes wide and the corners of their mouths turned down in identical mournful expressions.

"I'm perfectly calm," Eric said with a fake smile on his face and sat back down. "Gilbert just needs to stop being an asshole."

Idina gasped. "Uncle Eric said a bad word."

"I meant asshat." Eric patted her head.

"You said asshole. I heard it."

Gilbert smiled at her. "Your Uncle Eric made a mistake, sweetie. One of many."

"That's it." Eric threw his chair back. "I'm out of here." He offered Darlene a hand up. "Are you coming?"

She cast William an apologetic glance before taking Eric's hand. "I think everyone needs some space to cool down. Let's take a walk on the beach."

41

SYSSI

*E*mmett's underground bunker had undergone an interior design transformation since the last time Syssi had stayed there with Kian and Allegra. Eleanor must have used Ingrid's services to get rid of everything that reminded her of what Emmett had been up to in those rooms. The interior designer's signature look was evident not only in the transformed guest suites but also in the common rooms, making Syssi feel at home. The only things that remained almost unchanged were the kitchen and the bathrooms. Those rooms had gotten a fresh coat of paint, but none of the fixtures or the cabinetry had been replaced.

Okidu bowed. "I shall put everything in the closets, mistress."

"Thank you." Syssi handed Allegra to Wonder, folded the stroller, and gave it to Kian. "I can't wait to see the bungalows."

"We can go there now," Eleanor offered.

"I'm starving," Anandur said. "Let's eat first."

"That's a good idea." Syssi followed Kian up the stairs. "If we go now, we will have the place to ourselves. At five, the dining hall opens to the lodge's guests."

"Then we definitely need to go now," Kian said. "I'd rather avoid having to smile at random humans. I just hope that Kaia's family is out of there already. I promised William that we would stay out of their way."

"Why?" Anandur asked.

"Kaia expects opposition to her and William's relationship, and he expects a fight." Kian opened the cottage's front door. "I'd rather not be there and get dragged into the argument. If they say anything offensive about William, I might overreact."

"I'm curious to see the girl who has stolen our William's heart." Anandur closed the door behind them. "But right now, all I can think about is food. What do they serve in the lodge?"

"We hired a new chef," Kian said. "She came highly recommended, but I haven't sampled her cuisine yet. I hope she's good."

"Where did you find her?" Callie asked. "Is she a famous chef?"

Kian shrugged. "She's not famous, but she's a graduate of the Culinary Institute, and I stole her from a competitor hotel chain. I can't remember her name, though. I think it's Jasmine something, but I will have to check with Shai."

Syssi laughed. "You never take notes because you have him next to you. But what about the times you don't?"

"I remember what's important."

Callie threaded her arm through Brundar's. "I can't wait to sample her cooking. It's probably excellent."

"How is your restaurant coming along?" Syssi asked. "You have a village of anxious customers awaiting the opening night."

"I know." Callie grimaced. "That's what is keeping me from opening right away. I don't have enough staff to serve all the tables, and I know the demand will be high." She looked at Wonder. "Any chance that I can steal you away from the café? Now that Aliya is working there, you can leave."

"Not really. Wendy is starting college this fall. She said she would work as many hours as possible, but it would depend on her class schedule."

As they were about to enter the lodge, the door opened, and Darlene stepped out with a handsome guy by her side.

"Good afternoon." She looked perturbed. "How was your flight?"

"Excellent." Syssi looked at the man standing next to Darlene. "I'm Syssi." She offered him her hand.

"Eric, Gilbert's brother." He shook hers and then turned to Kian. "I guess you're the reclusive boss William told us about?"

Gilbert was Kaia's stepfather, and Eric was her uncle. Syssi connected the dots. What was he doing with Darlene?

"That's me." Kian shook Eric's offered hand. "This is Brundar, his lovely partner Callie, and that's Anandur and his much better half, Wonder."

Eric shook everyone's hand and then knelt next to Allegra's stroller. "And who is this beautiful girl?"

"Ba." She reached with her hand and patted his cheek.

"Is your name Ba?"

"Her name is Allegra," Syssi said.

"A beautiful name for a beautiful little girl." Eric pushed up to his feet. "It was nice to meet you all. Darlene and I are going for a walk on the beach. Would you like to join us?"

"Thank you," Anandur said. "But we are hungry."

Darlene winced. "I can ask the kitchen staff to deliver your meal to the cottage. It is World War III in there."

Eric nodded. "My brother is unhappy about Kaia dating a guy thirteen years older than her, and he's not bashful about expressing his opinion."

"Yeah," Darlene concurred. "He's threatening to take Kaia back home with them."

"He can't do that," Kian said. "She has a contractual obligation to stay until the end of the project."

Eric nodded his agreement. "Not to mention that Kaia is an adult, and he can't force her to leave. He's just making her and William miserable for no good reason. William seems like a very nice guy, but he's too mellow and polite to stand up to Gilbert."

"We should go in and help William," Syssi said. "We will introduce ourselves and sit at the next table over. Your brother will not be nasty in front of strangers, and he will have to back off William."

Eric snorted. "You don't know how pig-headed my brother can be."

42

KAIA

A long moment of awkward silence stretched over the table after Eric and Darlene's departure.

Kaia had never heard Gilbert talk like that about Eric, not to his face and not behind his back. He'd joked about his brother's dating habits, but it had always sounded good-natured. He must be really riled up to lash out at him like that.

"You shouldn't have said that." Her mother glared at Gilbert. "What has gotten into you?"

"I don't know." He let out a sigh. "I lost it for a moment there. The only thing that bothers me about Eric's penchant for women who are too young for him is that he's not looking for someone suitable to settle down with. I don't want him to be one of those guys who are still alone and childless in their late fifties, wearing a damn toupee and baking their skin in tanning salons to look younger. That's the image I had in my mind when I said that he's an embarrassment to the family. I was thinking of him in the not-so-distant future."

Kaia had to admit that the picture Gilbert had painted of future Eric was depressing. It was good that Darlene viewed him only as a step in her journey of self-discovery and not as a possible partner. She was too old to have children, and Eric deserved to be a father.

He'd had a shitty experience, getting married young to a person who turned out to be a control freak with rage issues. It had soured him for future relationships, but his marriage had ended four years ago, and it was about time for him to get over it.

As the dining hall's door opened, everyone shifted toward it, expecting to see Eric and Darlene returning, but it wasn't them.

Kaia knew immediately that the guy pushing a stroller with a baby girl in it was William's boss. Kian was the most stunning male Kaia had ever seen. A god, or rather a demigod. No human was that perfect, and neither were the immortals she'd met so far.

How did he manage to go unnoticed? Did he thrall everyone he encountered to forget him? Or did he just live the life of a recluse as William had told them, and avoid being seen in public?

The two men walking right behind him were unnaturally gorgeous as well, and given how their eyes scoped the dining hall and her family, it was pretty obvious that they were Guardians. They were both wearing light jackets even though it wasn't cold, and Kaia was willing to bet that they were hiding weapons under them.

The three women and the baby in the stroller were all beautiful, but they could at least pass for humans. The blond with the kind face was no doubt Kian's wife, the tall brunette who looked like an Amazonian warrior woman was with the redhead, and the one with the penetrating green eyes was with the blond Guardian with the stoic expression.

Out of the three males, he seemed the most dangerous despite his angelic features. With his stick-straight blond hair that was even a lighter shade than Kaia's and longer as well, his beauty bordered on feminine, but she knew it for the illusion it was. The guy was deadly, and she would never want to get on the wrong side of him.

"Hello, everyone," Kian's wife smiled brightly. "I hope you don't mind us joining you." She walked over to Kaia's mother and offered her hand. "I'm Syssi."

"I'm Karen." Her mother rose to her feet and shook Syssi's hand.

Gilbert followed her example, pushing to his feet and offering the newcomers one of his charming smiles.

"This is my husband, Kian," Syssi continued the introduction. "And those are his cousins, Anandur and Brundar, and their partners, Wonder and Callie."

As her mother and Gilbert shook hands with everyone, Kaia stood next to Cheryl, anxiously awaiting her turn.

William's boss was intimidating as hell, and so was one of his so-called cousins, but the tall redhead and the ladies seemed friendly.

Kian and the Guardians joined William in the back, and a nearly silent conversation started that Kaia would have loved to be privy to.

"Wonder?" Gilbert shook the statuesque brunette's hand. "Is it a nickname, or is it your given name?"

She smiled brightly. "It started as a nickname, and I decided to adopt it as my legal name."

"I get it." Gilbert nodded. "You look like Wonder Woman." He turned to look at the baby. "And who's the beauty in the stroller?"

"This is Allegra," Syssi said. "Our daughter."

"Enchanted." He leaned down, took the girl's little hand, and kissed the back of it.

"Ba." She smiled, her big blue eyes assessing him with a smart, penetrating gaze.

"I'm Idina." Her sister crouched next to the stroller. "I have two baby brothers. I wanted a baby sister, but I got two boys instead."

"Da." Allegra reached for a lock of Idina's hair and gave it a tug.

"Ouch. Don't do that." Idina glared at the baby.

Kaia tensed, but for once, Idina didn't retaliate.

Syssi laughed. "She'll let go. It's her way to say hello."

The baby did that a moment later and offered Idina the plush toy she'd been clutching in her other hand.

"Thank you." Idina accepted the plush tiger graciously. "What's his name?"

"Da."

Standing behind her mother and Syssi, Kaia cleared her throat, reminding them that she hadn't been introduced yet.

Her mother whirled around and smiled apologetically. "These are my older daughters, Kaia and Cheryl."

Instead of taking Kaia's extended hand, Syssi pulled her into a quick hug and whispered into her ear, "Thank you for making William happy."

43

WILLIAM

*W*illiam thanked the Fates for Kian and Syssi's timely arrival. Gilbert had worked himself into a frenzy of anger, and there had been no chance of reasoning with him without using a thrall, but Syssi had managed to press the reset button with just the calming effect of her presence.

The guy was back to his usual charming self, working on getting on Kian and Syssi's good side. Perhaps now that they were there, Gilbert would be willing to listen to someone other than himself.

When all the introductions were done, and another table had been added to make room for everyone, the twelve of them took their seats.

Unlike before, when the kitchen staff had served everything buffet style, they tripped over themselves to serve Kian and his retinue in person.

"You have a lovely family," Syssi said.

Karen beamed proudly. "Thank you."

"If I may ask, how old were you when you had Idina?"

"I was forty-three. After my husband died, I never imagined I would have three more kids, but then I met Gilbert, and he worked diligently to convince me to have another one." Karen looked at her partner and smiled. "I finally agreed, and Idina brought so much joy to our family that I decided to have one more and ended up with twins." She turned to look lovingly at the boys. "My two cherries on top."

"They are adorable," Syssi agreed. "How did you and Gilbert meet?"

"A mutual friend introduced us. I wasn't ready to date, and when my friend told me about Gilbert, I told her that I wasn't interested. But she tricked us both, inviting us for dinner at her house without telling either of us that the other one would be there."

"It was love at first sight," Gilbert said.

Karen shook her head. "We were both still hurting from the loss of our spouses, and we found comfort in each other's company."

Syssi shifted her gaze to Gilbert. "Were you a widower as well?"

"I was the victim of a nasty divorce, and I'd lost my faith in humanity, not just the female half of it. Karen was incredible, patient, and kind, and she restored my faith in people."

Karen chuckled. "He was so cocky, trying to play the part of a newly released bachelor who was ready to plow his way through scores of women, but I saw the pain in his eyes. He evoked my motherly instincts to comfort and heal, and we became inseparable from that day on."

Gilbert cleared his throat. "There was nothing motherly about what you felt for me." He cast a quick glance at Kaia and Cheryl. "Karen told you the PG version." He leaned closer to Kian and whispered, "The truth was that we couldn't keep our hands off each other."

His stepdaughters couldn't have heard him from the other side of the table, but Kaia must have guessed what he'd told Kian.

"How long after you met Gilbert did it take you to tell Cheryl and me about him?" she asked.

"A week later."

Kaia snorted. "So, you two fell in love in one week, and you have the nerve to doubt my relationship with William because we've known each other for the same length of time?"

"It's not the same," Gilbert said. "Your mother and I were both mature adults, and we were close in age. I'm only two years older than Karen."

Kaia rolled her eyes. "Can you even hear what you're saying? The differences in circumstances are so small that they are negligible. The biggest difference is that William put a ring on my finger as a symbol of his intent to spend the rest of his life with me, while you haven't given my mother one yet."

"I don't want one," Karen said. "I was married once, and I loved your father very much. I love Gilbert no less, but it's important to me to make this relationship different. I'm perfectly happy with our partnership the way it is, and I don't like you and Cheryl pushing us to get married. It has nothing to do with you."

"Huh." Kaia folded her arms over her chest. "William and I have nothing to do with you either, and yet you feel entitled to try to push us apart."

Gilbert's face twisted in a grimace. "I should have known he was trouble the moment he let his Scottish accent come out. The age of consent in Scotland is sixteen. No wonder he sees nothing wrong with seducing a nineteen-year-old. To him, she's a mature woman."

"It is?" Cheryl asked. "So, if I go to Scotland, I can have sex?"

"You can have sex whenever you want," Kaia said. "It's a legal offense for whoever has sex with you, not for you."

Gilbert pointed a finger at Cheryl. "You're not having sex until you are twenty-one."

"Or married," Cheryl chuckled. "I know. You've said it many times before."

She hadn't added that it was hypocritical of him, but William could practically read it in her expression.

How could Gilbert preach abstinence until marriage when he hadn't practiced it himself? Even a bachelor like William knew that do-as-I-say-and-not-as-I-do never worked with kids.

The only way to lead was by personal example.

44

SYSSI

*T*hings were about to get out of hand again, and since the subject was ancestry, Syssi decided to follow the thread and divert the conversation away from William and back to Gilbert and Karen.

"I'm curious. What about your origins, Gilbert?" She asked. "Do you know where your ancestors came from? Perhaps you are part Scot as well."

The guy straightened in his chair and grinned. "I know a lot about my ancestry because I've done quite a bit of research on it, and I'm proud to be a mutt. I'm part Norwegian, part Pole, part Austrian, and part Portuguese."

"The age of consent in Norway is also sixteen," Anandur said. "So, it's not just us randy Scots."

If he had been sitting next to her, she would have kicked him under the table. She was trying to steer the conversation away from William and Kaia.

"What prompted you to research your ancestry?" she asked Gilbert, to keep him talking about himself.

He sighed. "All that's left of our family is Eric, our sister Gabi, and me. Our grandparents and parents passed away, and we didn't have any uncles or aunts. I wanted to find out whether we had any extended family in the countries our grandparents came from."

"Did you find any?"

He was about to answer when one of his sons let out a wail and was soon joined by his brother.

"I'm afraid it's way past their nap time." Karen unstrapped one boy and handed him to Gilbert, and then freed the other one. "We will have to continue this conversation at another time."

The boys stopped crying as soon as they were in their parents' arms, but given the way Evan put his head on Gilbert's shoulder and Ryan rubbed his eyes, it was obvious that the little ones were exhausted.

"We can meet for dinner." Syssi rose to her feet. "I'll have the kitchen deliver it to where we are staying." She smiled at Karen. "You'll have an opportunity to visit the leader's underground facility and hear about all the naughty things that happened in there."

That got Gilbert excited. "What time?"

"Since it's already after four, no one will be hungry until eight."

"That's late for the little ones." Karen turned to Cheryl. "Can you babysit?"

"I don't want to be left out. I want to come and hear about those naughty things."

"You're too young for that," Gilbert said.

She rolled her eyes. "We live in the era of the internet. Do you really think there is anything that can still shock me?"

He shook his head. "I guess not, and it's a shame. Your generation was robbed of the precious few years of innocence our generation had. The world seemed like a kinder place back then."

"It was an illusion," Kian said. "The world was never kind."

He didn't look happy about having Kaia's family over for dinner, but thankfully, he didn't object. Syssi needed time to come up with a strategy to bring Gilbert and Karen around to supporting their daughter's relationship with William, and she hoped to come up with something by dinnertime.

"We can bring their travel crib," Karen said. "Is there a bedroom down there we can use?"

Syssi nodded. "There is one spare bedroom where you can put the boys and Idina to sleep."

"Good luck with that." Kaia took Idina's hand. "She will not want to miss out on the fun." She leaned closer to Syssi and whispered in her ear, "When you tell us about the bunker's history, I'll have her watch a movie on her tablet with the earphones on."

"That's a good idea."

Overhearing her sister, Cheryl grinned. "Count on me not being on my phone for a change."

Gilbert frowned at the two of them. "You two are incorrigible."

Stifling a chuckle, Syssi turned to Karen. "I can tell Darlene that she and Eric are invited, but just in case I can't get hold of her, you should tell Eric about our plans for tonight as well."

Karen nodded. "I will."

"You should invite Emmett and Eleanor," Anandur suggested. "I want to see Eleanor's face when Emmett tells us about the things he did in that place."

"That's not a good idea." Kian lifted Allegra onto his lap. "I need them both alive and well to run this place. It would be difficult to find a replacement for Emmett if Eleanor murdered him."

"That sounds like an interesting story," Karen said. "But we really need to go before the boys get overtired. When they get like that, they cry for hours and can't fall asleep." She looked down at Idina. "She was such an easy baby. I've never had problems like that with her."

Kaia chuckled. "She compensates for it now. Right, Idina?"

The little girl looked up at her sister. "I don't understand what you're talking about."

As all the adults either chuckled or laughed, Idina stomped her foot on the floor. "Stop laughing at me!"

"We are not laughing at you, sweetie." Kaia lifted her into her arms. "You just sounded so grown up when you said that."

"I'm a big girl."

"Yes, you are."

KIAN

*A*fter William left with Kaia's family, Kian signaled for the server. "Can we please get coffee?"

"Of course, sir."

When the guy rushed into the kitchen, Kian turned to Syssi. "You were uncharacteristically engaged today."

Usually, she was shy around strangers, and he'd enjoyed seeing her leading the conversation and striking up such a quick friendship with Kaia's mother.

"William needed help, so I overcame my natural tendency to sit back and listen while others talk. Besides, I like Karen. She seems like such a sensible person, and she's a great mother."

"It's the affinity at work," Anandur said. "Regrettably, her mate is a buffoon."

Wonder nodded in agreement. "I don't know why William didn't say anything in his defense."

Kian shook his head. "William was wise to stay silent. Anything he said would have been held against him. And as for Gilbert, the guy is protective of his stepdaughter, and that's admirable. If Allegra got engaged to someone much older than her, who she had known for only one week and who Syssi and I had never met, I would be just as angry as Gilbert if not more."

Syssi chuckled. "Did you forget how quickly we fell in love? I imagine my dad reacted the same when I told him I was getting married to a guy I met just a few weeks ago, but he trusted my judgment."

"He had Andrew to vouch for me, and both your father and brother warned me that if I ever did anything to upset you, they would cut off my balls and then chop me into little pieces."

Her eyes widened. "They didn't. I can imagine Andrew saying something like that, but not my father."

"Your dad was a little less graphic, but his intent was the same."

"That's kind of sweet," Anandur said. "In a gruesome way." He wrapped his arm around Wonder's shoulders. "If your father was still around, he would have nothing to fear. If I ever deserve my balls to be chopped off, you are perfectly capable of doing that yourself."

Despite how proud Anandur sounded saying that, Wonder winced. "Thanks for reminding me that I'm a freak."

"You're not a freak." He leaned toward her and kissed her cheek. "You are the original Amazonian warrior."

That seemed to placate her, and she leaned her head on his shoulder. "Somehow, you always know what to say."

He clapped his hand over his chest. "That's because it comes from the heart."

After the server brought them coffee and a vegan dessert, Syssi took a few sips and put her cup down. "The fact remains that all of us here fell hard and fast for each other. It's the special connection between truelove mates. The problem is that Gilbert doesn't know about it, and we can't tell him, so he can't understand that a powerful bond already exists between Kaia and William."

Callie nodded. "It was so evident that I could actually feel it. I'm happy that William finally found the right woman to complete him."

"Kaia is perfect for him," Wonder said. "She's brilliant, beautiful, and assertive."

"Dada." Allegra lifted her face to him.

"What, sweetie?"

She stuck her thumb in her mouth and put her head on his chest.

"She's telling you that she's tired." Syssi finished the last of her coffee and pushed to her feet. "We should get back and put her down for a nap."

As the brothers and their mates followed them out, Wonder took in a deep breath. "I can smell the ocean. The breeze here is so much stronger than what we get in Malibu."

"Let's take a walk on the beach," Callie suggested.

"We can't." Brundar wrapped his arm around her waist. "We need to stay with Kian and Syssi."

"No, you don't." Syssi turned to Kian. "Do we need them with us twenty-four-seven?"

"That's my mother's protocol for whenever I'm out of the village, but I can ask for two of the Guardians stationed here to trade places with Anandur and Brundar."

"That's a good solution." Syssi stroked Allegra's head. "Who's in charge of the Guardians here?"

"Leon." Kian pulled out his phone and called the guy.

"Good afternoon," Leon answered. "What can I do for you, boss?"

"Can you send two Guardians to Emmett's cottage? Anandur and Brundar want to take their mates for a walk on the beach."

"I'll do better than that. Anastasia and I will come over to say hello, and we'll bring Emmett and Eleanor with us along with two Guardians who will remain outside."

"Sounds like a plan. We are heading back to the cottage right now."

"We will meet you there."

"Very well." Kian ended the call and put the phone back in his pocket.

"We will walk with you to the cottage," Anandur said.

Kian was disappointed to have his plans for an afternoon delight with Syssi ruined. With the brothers and their mates gone and Allegra napping, it could have been a perfect opportunity, but he couldn't have said no to the visit without sounding rude.

"What's the matter?" Syssi asked. "Don't you want to see them?"

"I do." He put his arm around her while holding Allegra with the other. "I just hoped for some time alone with my wife while our daughter takes a nap."

46

WILLIAM

Outside the lodge, William parted ways with Kaia. "Enjoy your time with your family. I will come to escort you to the cottage at quarter to eight." He gave her a quick peck on the cheek.

Gilbert pretended like he wasn't there, Karen gave him a tight smile, and only Cheryl smiled at him with fondness. "See you later."

Kaia mouthed, "Wish me luck."

William nodded, pivoted on his heel, and headed toward the lab.

It wasn't unusual for him to work on Saturdays, but that wasn't why he was going there. He needed a few moments of solitude to collect his thoughts and decompress.

He'd gotten no more than fifteen minutes of sitting in his chair and staring at the wall before his phone buzzed with an incoming text.

Hoping it was from Kaia, he pulled it out and looked at the screen but was disappointed to see that it was from Kian.

Leon and Anastasia are coming over with Eleanor and Emmett. If you're not busy, come over.

William hesitated before answering.

He needed some time alone, but being among friends would also be therapeutic. After being under attack from Kaia's mother and stepfather, it would be a welcome change to be with people who had his back.

He typed, *on my way.*

When he got to the cottage, he found Max and Conrad sitting on a couple of rocks near the front door.

"What are you doing here?"

"Anandur and Brundar went on a walk with their mates," Max said. "We are just waiting for them to come back, and then we are out of here. Leon and Anastasia are already down there."

"What about Emmett and Eleanor?"

"On their way," Conrad said.

Max eyed William with a frown. "You look like you've been through the wringer. Was it that bad?"

William nodded. "Worse than I expected. Syssi smoothed things over, but I have a feeling that it was just a temporary reprieve and that the battle will resume when we meet again for dinner."

Max nodded. "I'm here for you, buddy. If you need to get drunk with someone, I'm your man."

"Thanks." William gave him and Conrad a thankful smile before heading inside.

Max was a good guy, and he appreciated the words of encouragement even if he had no intention of taking him up on the offer. He'd never gotten drunk, and he didn't intend to start today.

Once he was inside, he pressed the intercom button, and when the door opened, he took the stairs down.

"Hi, William." Anastasia rose to her feet when he entered. "I heard that you had a difficult time with Kaia's family."

Kian handed him a glass of whiskey. "I'm sure you need this."

Leon lifted his glass in a salute. "To truelove mates." He threw the whiskey down his throat. "They are worth every difficulty."

"Amen to that." Kian grabbed the bottle, walked over to Leon, and refilled his glass.

William sat down and put the glass on the coffee table. "We are not sure that Kaia is a Dormant, let alone my truelove mate."

"She is." Syssi walked into the living room. "I'd be very much surprised if she isn't."

"I hope you are right."

"Did you see Darlene on your way here?" Anastasia asked. "Syssi told me that she and Eric went on a walk."

"Eric got angry at Gilbert." William lifted the glass and took a sip. "Darlene offered to take him out on a walk to calm him down. I guess they are still on the beach. She can't take him to her bungalow, so there aren't many places they can go."

"Eric has a room in the lodge," Leon said. "They can be there."

"Right." He finished the rest of the whiskey. "I hope they are not too affected by the family drama."

"What are you going to do?" Anastasia asked.

"You could thrall the guy," Kian offered. "Since Kaia is a potential Dormant, and so are her mother and siblings, his opposition to your relationship is harmful to the clan, and therefore thralling him is justified."

"It won't be necessary," Syssi said. "Gilbert just needs to get over the initial shock. Besides, William can't thrall him into liking him. He will have to do it the old-fashioned way."

"I'm open to suggestions." William rose to his feet, walked to the bar where Kian had left the whiskey bottle, and refilled his glass.

"Just be yourself." Syssi smiled at him. "You are one of the nicest people I know, and Gilbert will realize that sooner or later. The rest is up to us." She looked at Kian. "When they come over for dinner, we will talk about William's position in the clan and his contribution to our safety and prosperity, and also mention that he's a council member."

Kian shook his head. "That will reveal too much about the clan."

Syssi smiled at him indulgently. "We will talk in terms of an organization or a family run business, not a clan, and instead of calling it a council, we can call it the board of directors."

47

KAIA

"Come see my room." Idina pulled on Kaia's hand.

Kaia looked at her mother. "Will you join us after you put Evan and Ryan down for their nap?"

"Of course." Her mother kissed her cheek and followed Gilbert into their room.

Cheryl opened the door. "It's not large, but it's nice."

Two single beds were tucked against the walls with a small chest of drawers between them. The one that was Idina's had a lineup of Barbie dolls propped against the pillow, and Cheryl's tablet was on the chest.

It was such a familiar sight that it tugged at her heartstrings.

Kaia missed home, and her dual nature pulled her in two opposite directions. On the one hand, she was an old soul who'd lived for a long time and was primed and ready to live on her own. But on the other hand, she was a nineteen-year-old girl who wasn't prepared to fly the nest to William's village and only see her family on holidays.

Kaia had thought she had years until she would find a guy she wanted to settle down with. But fate had other ideas. Her guy was a member of a clan of immortals, he believed that she could turn immortal too, and if he was correct, then her mother and her siblings could also turn immortal. But that left Gilbert out, and that along with the risk involved would most likely be a deal-breaker for her mother. She had three little kids that needed their parents, and Kaia wouldn't be surprised if her mother gave up on the chance of immortality to keep what she had now.

If Kaia were in her mother's shoes, she would probably say no to immortality, but she had the advantage of having proof that the soul was immortal, so perhaps gaining physical immortality was not the be-all and end-all that others might view it as.

The problem was that the vast majority of people didn't retain their memories of past lives, so in a way, their previous personas died along with their bodies, and they were reborn to start anew.

On the one hand a fresh start was preferable, but on the other hand, knowing that their essence lived on would alleviate people's fear of death.

But was that a good thing?

Not necessarily.

To appreciate life, people needed to treat it as the precious gift it was.

Idina took off her shoes, climbed on the bed, and took a Barbie doll in each hand.

"You are an embarrassment to the family, Emily," she said in a deep voice. Lifting the other doll, she shook her from side to side. "You are a mean sister, Rebekah."

Smiling at Kaia, Cheryl patted her bed. "You can sit here."

For a few moments, they watched their little sister re-enacting the earlier argument with her dolls.

"Are you really in love with William?" Cheryl asked quietly.

"I am. He's wonderful." Kaia dropped her flip-flops, lifted her feet on the bed, and leaned against the wall. "I suspected that Mom and Gilbert would think that I didn't know what I was doing, but I didn't expect them to put up such a fight. Poor William. I will need to make it up to him."

"William is so nice," Idina mimicked Kaia's voice. She picked up two different dolls, one male and one female. "You are so mean to him. You should be ashamed of yourselves."

Cheryl chuckled. "With Idina on your side, you have nothing to fear. She'll fight for you and William. Right, Idina?"

Their sister treated them to one of her dark looks. "I don't want Kaia to marry William."

"Why not?" Cheryl asked. "They love each other."

"Because she will not come home."

"What if I bring him home with me? Would you be okay with me marrying him then?"

Idina shrugged. "Daddy doesn't like William."

"He will change his mind once he gets to know him. He's the nicest guy I've ever met."

"Really?" Cheryl asked. "Or are you just saying that?"

"No, I mean it. William is smart and sweet."

"What about sexy?"

"He's that too."

A knock sounded at the door, and her mother ducked into the room a moment later. "They were out in two minutes flat. I left Gilbert to watch over them." She sat on Idina's bed. "What did I miss so far?"

"Kaia told me how William is smart, sweet, and sexy, and that she loves him."

"Are you sure?" Her mother leveled her intense gaze at her. "I hope it's not some kind of delayed rebellion against the parents."

Kaia snorted. "You know me better than that. I love my family, and I love our home."

"So maybe Gilbert was right about you feeling sad and lonely and needing someone to fill the void of being away from home?"

"It's not that either." Kaia grabbed a pillow and pushed it behind her back. "If you two weren't so focused on the age difference and on how little time we've known each other, you would have seen how perfect William and I are for each other. I will never find anyone like him again. So, if you force us apart, I will become a cat lady because I could never fall in love with anyone who is less perfect for me than him."

She wasn't hyperbolizing, and she wasn't being overly dramatic. Every word was true, and it filled her with anxiety. If she wasn't a Dormant, William would have to let her go, and becoming a cat lady wouldn't be a joke.

If he erased himself from her memories, it would be a mercy. Otherwise, she would compare every guy she met with the one who'd been perfect for her, and would choose cats instead.

"Oh, sweetie." Her mother shifted to Cheryl's bed and pulled Kaia into her arms. "I want what's best for you, and so does Gilbert. We just don't want you to make a mistake." She kissed Kaia's temple. "I was lucky. I've never had a relationship go bad. Your father loved me very much, and I loved him just as much back. Then I found love again with Gilbert. But Gilbert and Eric weren't that lucky. They didn't choose the right woman the first time around, and they suffered dearly for it. Gilbert doesn't want you to suffer a similar fate."

Kaia hadn't thought of it from that angle. Hearing her mother explain it, she understood where Gilbert was coming from and why he was so strongly opposed to what he thought was her whirlwind romance with an older man.

"What you said helps me understand Gilbert better and makes me less mad at him for making William and me feel bad, but my love for William is not a mistake. I want your approval, but I will not leave William if I can't convince you to approve of my choice. He's not only the man I love and the one I want to spend the rest of my life with. He's important to my future and to the future of our entire family."

Her mother frowned. "In what way is he important to our family?"

"I can't say. Not yet."

"Do you sense it?" Cheryl asked.

Her family was used to her making cryptic comments about the future based on hunches she couldn't explain, and they had learned not to dismiss them. Maybe her subconscious mind collected bits and pieces of random data, and her ability to solve complicated puzzles helped her see patterns that others couldn't. Although, this time, it wasn't a hunch but information she wasn't allowed to share with them yet.

"I don't sense it. I know it."

48

DARLENE

$\mathscr{E}$ric held Darlene's hand as they walked on the beach, the contact sending delicious shivers through her body, and as she imagined that rough, callused hand caressing her skin, she nearly moaned from how turned on she got.

The molten looks he was sending her way weren't helping either. His brown eyes were full of lust, the long black lashes framing them evoking thoughts of a boudoir's curtains.

Heck, with Eric so near, every thought she had was carnal. Mostly, she felt aroused and excited, but some insidious doubt still managed to infiltrate all those sexy feelings.

Years of being told she wasn't exciting in bed had left their mark on her. She'd been too timid, hadn't initiated enough, and her blowjobs had been mediocre at best.

Was it true? Was she a lousy lover? Or was it just part of Leo's campaign to keep her from raising her head?

"What are you thinking about?" Eric asked.

She averted her gaze. "Something I shouldn't."

"Talk to me." He gave her hand an encouraging squeeze. "I'm a good listener."

It was humiliating enough to tell those things to a therapist, which was why Darlene hadn't availed herself of Vanessa's services, let alone a hunky guy that was probably a god in bed.

She smiled up at him. "Sharing those thoughts with a man I plan to seduce tonight would be counterproductive."

A lascivious grin spread over his handsome face. "Why wait for tonight?" He stopped and looked around. "See that outcropping?" He pointed at a rock formation a hundred feet or so in front of them. "I bet I can find us a cave in there."

Darlene laughed. "Even if there was one, which I know there isn't, I'm not keen on the sand getting in my privates."

"Then let's go to your place." He started turning around.

"I'm afraid that's not possible either. I'm not allowed to bring visitors into the secure inner zone."

He frowned. "So, how did Kaia show Karen and Gilbert her bungalow?"

"William made an exception for her and notified the guys in security. If they didn't have cameras all over the place, I would sneak you in, but they would stop us as soon as we crossed the gate."

"We can go to my room at the lodge," Eric offered.

"That would be awkward. Your family is staying next door and might be going between rooms or leaving their doors open."

He shrugged. "I don't care. They should be happy that I'm finally hooking up with a woman my age."

She winced, the reminder of who he usually hooked up with sending a spear of apprehension through her.

"I didn't mean it that way." Eric stopped walking and turned to face her. "You're more than just a hookup to me."

He must have noticed her wince and misinterpreted it.

"I don't need you to pretend that I'm more than a casual fling, and I don't mind being just that. We are both adults, and we are after the same thing." She lifted on her toes to plant a kiss on his lips.

Eric didn't take over like she'd expected. Instead, he waited for her to drop down to her heels, and his expression remained serious.

"If you were just another hookup, I wouldn't have reorganized my entire schedule so I could fly the family over here this weekend. Since the moment we met a week ago, I haven't been able to stop thinking about you. Do you know how many times I've jacked off imagining all the things I'm going to do to you?"

Did that mean he hadn't been with anyone else during that week? And why was he so fascinated with her? She was no great beauty, and her flirting skills were rusty.

Heat creeping up her cheeks, Darlene shook her head. "Why? What's special about me?"

"Everything." He cupped her cheek. "I feel a connection to you that I haven't felt for any other woman. Not even for my ex, whom I was madly in love with, or so I thought." He raked his fingers through his hair, pushing back the wavy bangs. "I can't explain it, but when I look into your eyes, I see a real person. I see a woman who thinks and feels and who has a great sense of humor."

She narrowed her eyes at him. "Everyone thinks and feels, Eric. What makes me more real to you than others?"

"It's something in your eyes. I wish I could explain myself better. But the bottom line is that I'm not planning for this to be a weekend thing and then to never see you again. I'll be back without the family, and I will take you out on a proper date. I can fly you anywhere you want to go."

He sounded serious, and that was a problem. If he were an immortal, she would be elated to find someone she liked so much and who was interested in a long-term relationship with her. But he was human, and she couldn't lead him on with promises of a potential future.

Lowering her eyes, Darlene forced a smile. "Let's take it one day at a time and see where that leads us."

ERIC

*E*ric didn't know what had possessed him to say those things to Darlene. First of all, he didn't plan on settling down anytime soon. Secondly, telling a woman that he was interested in a long-term relationship right from the start was a rookie mistake he hadn't made since junior year in high school.

Women were less predatory than men, but they needed to feel that they had to work for it too. A fish easily caught was just as quickly thrown back into the sea.

Was there something in the sea breeze that had addled his brain? Or was it really something about Darlene?

Given the guilty expression on her beautiful face, she didn't feel the same. If he wanted to salvage the situation and get her naked today, he had to think fast.

"Gilbert's lecture about settling down must have affected me more than I realized. I'm not ready for anything serious." He wrapped his arm around Darlene's waist and pulled her against his body. "So, beautiful, where can I do to you all those dastardly things I've been dreaming about?"

A conspiratorial smile bloomed on her face. "We have two options. We can try to sneak into your room in the lodge without your family seeing us and then make very quiet love, or we can sneak into the bus and go as wild as we want."

He arched a brow. "The bus?"

"Yeah. No one is coming or going today, and the driver parked it in the shade. If you wait for me in the lodge, I can go to my bungalow and pack a couple of blankets to make it more comfortable."

He hadn't made love on a bus before, and he doubted the novelty could compensate for the discomfort, but given the blush coloring Darlene's cheeks, she was excited about it, so why not?

Eric was an adventurous sort, and he was willing to try everything once.

"Sounds like a plan to me." He pulled her against his body, letting her feel how hard he was for her.

She kissed him on the lips. "I can take a shortcut through there." She pointed. "You just need to walk back the way we came to find the lodge."

"Don't worry about me." He turned her around and smacked her bottom to send her on her way. "Don't make me wait too long."

"I won't." Darlene cast him a smile before rushing off.

He loved that her cheeks had pinked when she'd suggested the bus, and when he smacked her ass, they turned flaming red.

There was a level of innocence and expectancy in Darlene that made his heart beat faster with anticipation and desire. Today's young women were more brazen than those of his generation, and it had been a long time since he'd made a girl blush. It excited him more than if she'd stripped naked in front of him and offered to suck him off.

What did it say about him that offers like that no longer excited him?

Was he so damn jaded, or had he gotten too many offers of that lately? Not that he didn't appreciate being treated to an enthusiastic blowjob, but it was somewhat of a turnoff when the offer came after the first date. It became as common as a kiss goodnight on the cheek and just as meaningless.

The last time Eric had been so excited about the prospect of having sex with a new partner had been when he'd met his ex. She'd played the game expertly, pretending she wasn't interested and making him work hard for her, then pretending finally to succumb to his charms.

She'd told him she'd only had two boyfriends before him, and since she'd been only twenty, he'd believed her. Not that it would have deterred him if he'd known that she'd had five or ten or fifteen. All he'd asked for was honesty, and he'd expected loyalty while they were together. When he'd told her that, she'd pretended offense that he could even think she would ever cheat on her man.

He'd eaten up all the crap she'd fed him, discovering years later that she'd kept her bed warm with multiple partners while he'd been gone on missions.

When rumors of her infidelity had reached him, and he'd confronted her, she'd reacted with such a tantrum that he'd once again been fooled into believing that the rumors had been false—a malicious attempt that had been born of envy and meant to besmirch the reputation of a beautiful woman.

God, what a fool he'd been.

How could he have let her play him so well?

Once he'd retired from the Air Force, she'd had a more difficult time playing around, and eventually he could no longer ignore the rumors and the discrepancies in her stories.

Eric had often wondered why she'd done it. Had he been neglectful? Had it been his long absences? Or perhaps she couldn't handle the stress of not knowing where he was and whether he would return in one piece? But those excuses had become invalid once he retired, and yet she hadn't stopped. Maybe it had become a habit, or maybe she had gotten addicted to sex.

Sometimes he wondered whether it was the age difference.

He'd been thirty when he'd met Emma, and she'd been only twenty, but he'd always taken good care of himself and was in excellent shape.

Maybe Gilbert believed that was the reason their marriage had fallen apart, and that was why he was so opposed to Kaia's engagement to William.

Eric was so embarrassed about being played that he'd never told his brother about Emma's infidelity. He'd blamed it on his ex's insane tantrums and her combative personality, which had been true, but those hadn't been the deal-breakers. They'd always made up after her explosions, and the sex had been phenomenal.

Perhaps that was why he'd ignored what had been right in front of his eyes.

50

DARLENE

*D*arlene stifled a nervous giggle as she slunk around the lodge with a laundry bag slung over her shoulder. She wasn't doing anything wrong, and everything in that bag was hers, but she still felt like a thief with a load of stolen loot.

It was kind of exciting, especially given what it was for.

The Guardians in the control room might have seen her leaving her bungalow with her laundry bag, but hopefully no one had guessed what she had in it, and what she was planning to do with the stuff.

If anyone asked, she could say that the washing machine in her bungalow had malfunctioned, and she needed to do her laundry in the lodge.

The trickier part was to sneak into the parking lot behind the resort with no one seeing her.

It was late Saturday afternoon, so there was no way she could avoid bumping into guests roaming around or heading down to the beach, but they didn't know her, and they couldn't possibly guess what she was carrying or why.

Most of what she'd collected had come from her bed, so she would need to launder everything later, but making a comfortable nest for her and Eric was worth the effort.

Her plan was to arrange everything first and then come back for him, but when she finally made it to the parking lot, her heart sank. The damn bus wasn't there.

"What now?" She looked around, searching for an alternative, but the only vehicle there was the resort's delivery van, and when she tried the handle, it was locked.

Maybe the bus was parked in the underground garage?

She'd never been there, but she'd heard that there was a small one that was connected to Emmett's underground cottage. Could the bus even fit in there?

Pulling out her phone, she texted William. *Do you know if the bus is parked in the garage? And if it is, how do I get in there?*

CHAPTER 50

Hopefully, there was another way to get in because she couldn't go through the cottage. Kian and Syssi were staying there, including Kian's guards and their mates. Sneaking through unnoticed would be impossible.

William answered a moment later. *Did you lose something on the way back from the restaurant last night?*

Taking a deep breath, she decided to fess up. It was easier than coming up with an excuse on the spot and inviting even more questions. Eric was waiting for her at the lodge, and he might think she was standing him up.

Well, she intended to, but in a good way.

I didn't lose anything yet, but I plan to lose my inhibitions if you get my drift. I can't entertain anyone in my bungalow and the lodge is too busy, so I thought of the bus.

His return text had a smiley face and a thumbs up. *The bus is parked in the garage next to Kian's rented van. You need to go out of the lodge and turn right. When you get to the hedge, look at it closely, and you'll find the door. I know that it's unlocked, but I don't know about the bus. Text me if you can't get in, and I'll get you the keys.*

She typed back. *You are the best. Thanks.*

Another text came in before she had a chance to return the phone to her purse. *I don't know if anyone notified you about the dinner at the bunker with Syssi and Kian. If not, it's at eight. Tell Eric.*

Darlene glanced at the time on her phone. It was seventeen minutes after five o'clock. That should be enough time for a nice romp in the bus.

Chuckling to herself, she typed a message back. *We will try to be there. If we are not, tell them that we have eloped.*

A message with a laughing face came in a second later.

Her amusement didn't last long, though. When she got to the hedge, the door to the garage was so well hidden that it took her several frustrating moments of looking through the thick greenery and sweeping aside branches before she found it. Thankfully, it was unlocked just as William had promised.

It was cool and dark inside the garage, which suited her plans much better than if the bus was parked outside, and most importantly, it was more private. The chances of anyone walking in on them were tiny, but it was enough to add spice to the adventure.

When she found the bus door open, Darlene let out a relieved breath and climbed inside.

It took her several minutes to set everything up the way she wanted in the back of the bus, and when she was done, she took a step back and regarded her nest. Two blankets covered the floor, several pillows were casually tossed on top for added cushioning, and she'd also brought a thin blanket for covering up. Originally, it had been meant as a means to provide her with a small measure of modesty, but with how cool it was in the underground parking, it would also serve to keep the chill away.

Darlene had also brought a bottle of wine, two glasses, a box of tissues, and a pack of wipes. The only thing she didn't have was a condom, but hopefully, Eric had thought ahead and brought a bunch with him.

One would certainly not do it.

Pregnancy wasn't an issue, but he led an active sex life, and she didn't want to catch anything from him.

The setup was far from ideal, but it was naughty and fun, and it was highly unlikely that Eric had tried anything like this before. She might not have robust sexual experience to wow him with, but she could delight him with a novel environment.

WILLIAM

*A*fter Emmett and Eleanor's arrival, the conversation turned to paranormal recruitment and the Echelon system, and William started to relax.

This was familiar. This was where he was comfortable. He was with people who knew him, respected him, and knew what to expect from him.

Being with Kaia was exhilarating, but it was also exhausting.

William wasn't an old immortal, but he was old enough to be set in his ways, and change made him anxious. He might have thrived on new technologies and scientific discoveries, but the upheaval Kaia's arrival had brought to his personal life was draining.

He was sweaty even though it wasn't hot, and he felt lethargic although he hadn't done anything physically demanding.

"Is Echelon spitting out any relevant information?" Kian asked.

"I sifted through the lists our contact at Echelon provided me, and I have several prospects." Eleanor put her teacup on the table. "The problem is that I will need to recruit them like I did while working for the government." She looked at Kian. "First of all, I will need to travel to meet them, and I need your authorization for that, and I will probably also need to use compulsion to lure them here. How much of it am I allowed to use?"

The boss grimaced. "I don't like the idea of compelling people. Can't we lure them the old-fashioned way? A good salary should do it."

Eleanor gave Kian a one-shouldered shrug. "I can start by offering them a free spot in the paranormal retreat, but they will wonder how I found them. The head-hunter cover worked very well for me before." She smiled. "No one ever asked me how I found out about them. They assumed I had access to their school and college records."

"You were a government agent," Syssi said. "It was natural for them to assume that. You can use that cover now as well. We can make you all the fake documents you need."

"What about my reason for contacting them? I need to come up with something that would sound reasonable. No one gives free retreats to random people without expecting something in return."

If Kian forbade Eleanor from using compulsion, he would be tying her hands and limiting her options. As a newly transitioned immortal, she couldn't thrall, so an ironclad contract was the only way she could ensure that the prospects didn't tell anyone about the lady recruiting paranormal talents for a secret project.

"Who are the potential prospects?" Syssi asked. "And what flagged them?"

"The best one has an interesting story." Eleanor lifted her teacup from the coffee table, took a sip, and put it down. "He was caught cheating on the roulette tables in Vegas, but they couldn't prove anything. He was just cleaning out the house with perfect hunches. They forbade him from ever gambling at any of the casinos there. His picture with the explanation of his uncanny lucky streak was sent to all the security offices of the large hotels, and that brief was what Echelon had flagged. He will be easy to deal with because he's either a master of deception or has a real precognition talent. After the fiasco in the casino, he won't be surprised when he's approached by people interested in his talent."

Syssi's eyes shone with excitement. "Does he live in Vegas?"

"No, he's actually a mathematics student at Caltech. Easy." Eleanor looked at Kian. "If you prefer to send one of the Guardians to get him, that's fine with me."

Leon got to his feet and walked over to the bar. "I wonder if he gambles in the small tribal casinos in the Los Angeles area. Did you check?"

Eleanor shook her head. "It's of no interest to me what he does with his talent. I only want to find out whether it's real. A Guardian could pose as one of Amanda's students and casually mention her lab to the guy. He might be able to lure him in for testing without even having to thrall him."

"Send me the information," Kian said. "I like your idea of getting him into Amanda's lab. Precognition is an easy talent to test."

"Who else?" Syssi asked.

"A woman in Nashville who claims to have precognition. I don't have anything official to support it, but Echelon flagged dozens of phone conversations with people who called her, asking for her help. What lends credibility to her claim is that she doesn't take money for foretelling the future, and she's not famous. People come to her by word of mouth. The others are weaker cases, but I don't mind traveling to see them if my expenses are covered."

Reading Kian's expression, William knew that the boss worried more about Eleanor leaving Safe Haven than covering her expenses.

"Emmett will need to stay here," Kian said.

Eleanor cast her mate a sidelong glance. "That's okay. I will go and come back the same day. I don't plan to make a national tour out of that the way I used to."

"What if you need to bring a prospect in?" Anastasia asked. "They won't be ready to go right away."

"After I ascertain they are worth investigating further, Kian can send someone else to finalize the deal." She smiled at the boss. "It will complicate things, but since you don't want Emmett to join me on my travels, that's the best I can do."

5 2

ERIC

$\mathcal{A}$ s Eric saw Darlene walking toward him, he let out a relieved breath and pushed to his feet. "I thought you weren't coming back."

Her eyes darted around the lodge's common room. "Let's go. We don't have much time." She took his hand and led him toward one of the side doors.

"Why the rush?"

"Syssi and Kian are hosting your family for dinner at eight. Our presence is requested."

"Who told you that?"

She smiled sheepishly. "William. I couldn't find the bus, so I texted him."

He lifted a brow. "So, we are not going to the bus after all?"

"Yes, we are." She walked up to the hedge, reached behind a branch, and pushed open a hidden door. "It's parked in the garage."

It was cool and dark inside, which was perfect for their plans. "Is the bus open?"

"It is." She led him to the door and then up the steps. "And I've already prepared our nest."

When Eric saw the blankets and pillows on the floor, a grin stretched over his face. "Let's close the door."

It took him a couple of seconds to find the lever, and as he pushed on it, the door closed with a hiss.

"I hope it opens just as easily." The tremor in Darlene's voice had nothing to do with fear of being stuck on the bus.

It was all about the anticipation of what was coming next, and Eric vowed to make it so good for her that it would erase any other sexual experience she'd ever had, whether good or bad.

"It does." Turning around, he put his hands on her waist and smashed her soft body against his. When their mouths met, she melted into the kiss, and as he pushed his tongue past her lips, a throaty moan escaped her throat.

The need he heard in that moan made Eric wish that he could tear Darlene's clothes off, throw her down on the nest she'd made, and take her in every conceivable way, but it had been a while for her, and he was her first lover since she'd left her husband.

Darlene needed a slow and tender seduction, and he would give it to her. There would be many more times for them, and he would get his fill of her when she was ready.

Holding her tightly against him, he moved his hands up her back, pushed his fingers into her hair, and kissed her slowly. When they had to let go of each other's mouths to come up for air, he leaned away to study her face.

Her lips were swollen from their kiss, and her eyes were glazed with desire, and at that moment, she was the most beautiful woman he'd ever been with.

Dipping his head, he captured her lips again, and this time his kiss wasn't soft. It was hard and demanding, and as Darlene sagged in his arms, he gripped her waist and walked her backward toward the nest.

Gently lowering her to the pile of pillows, he kneeled beside her and slid his hands under her loose blouse. "May I?"

When she nodded, he dragged it up and off of her and then tossed it behind him.

The bra covering her ample breasts was lacy, soft, and almost sheer, and through the pink lace, he could see her slightly darker pink nipples puckered and awaiting his mouth.

"Darlene," he murmured as he sat back and pulled the bra cups down and under her breasts.

"Yes." Her chest heaving, she arched her back and offered him her bounty.

It was all the encouragement he needed, and as he descended on one of those plump berries and closed his lips around it, another needy moan left Darlene's throat.

"Eric." Her fingers threaded through his hair as she held him to her.

He feasted on her breasts for a long moment before hooking his fingers in the elastic of her pants and tugging them down her hips. He'd left them pulled around her knees and pushed his hands under her panties, cupping her generous ass.

When she trembled in his hold, he didn't know whether it was in anticipation of what he was about to do next or if she was cold. Trailing his fingers down the crack of her ass, he reached her moist petals from behind and got his answer.

"You are so ready for me," he murmured against her nipple.

"I am, and you have too many clothes on."

A dark laugh left his lips as he let go of her nipple and ripped his T-shirt over his head.

"Better?"

Her eyes ate the sight of his bare chest. "Much, but I want to see more." She leaned forward and grasped his belt.

"May I?" she asked mockingly, parroting what he'd asked her before baring her.

"Please." He puffed out his chest, making his pectorals bulge for her to ogle.

Her smile was wicked as she slipped the length of the belt from the buckle and unbuttoned his fly.

5 3

DARLENE

$\mathcal{A}$s Darlene pushed Eric's jeans down to his knees, she paused before reaching for his boxers. Did she have the nerve to pull them down as well?

Instead, she looked into his eyes and put a hand on his chest. He must have spent many hours at the gym to be so chiseled, and seeing how toned and perfect his body was, she had the urge to cover her less than perky breasts and rounded belly.

Not that Eric seemed to notice any of it. As she ran her hands up his defined pecs, his eyes roamed over her body hungrily.

He let her explore for a few moments before folding his arms around her and drawing her to him, and when he kissed her, the passion in his kiss melted away her insecurities. He claimed her with such wild ferocity that she was left breathless and mindless, so much so that at some point, she found herself on her back with him pulling her pants and panties off her.

Evidently, Eric didn't need an immortal's ability to thrall his partners into oblivion. His expert kissing was just as effective.

His eyes never left her as he kicked off his own jeans the rest of the way. When he hooked his thumbs in the elastic band of his boxers, Darlene held her breath in anticipation of the reveal, but he pulled them down so fast that she only got a brief glimpse of his proud mast, and then he was on top of her, that hard length pressing against her center.

Was the guy an immortal pretending to be human? Who else could move with such speed? Or was it just an illusion that her mind had created?

Gripping the back of his neck, she arched into him, making him understand what she wanted him to do. Perhaps another time they could spend long moments on foreplay, but today, her patience had run out, and she was desperate for him to get inside of her.

"Eric," she moaned as he ground his shaft against that most sensitive spot,

ratcheting her need to the stratosphere. "Don't tease me. I need you inside of me."
She hooked her legs around his waist to get more of that delicious friction.

Cupping her cheek with one hand, he gripped himself with the other, but he
didn't push inside her as she'd hoped.

Instead, he paused at her entrance. "I'm clean. I haven't been with anyone for
over a month, and I got checked a week ago."

For some reason, knowing that he hadn't had sex since meeting her eased a
knot of anxiety inside of her that she hadn't been aware of, and a relieved chuckle
left her mouth. "I haven't been with anyone for months. I'm safe too."

A predatory gleam turning his brown eyes amber, he found her entrance a split
second later, and as he slid his length inside of her, she gasped.

He stilled for a moment, his ragged breaths misting the air between them, but
as she smiled up at him and arched up, he pushed all the way in, filling her so deliciously that a tear slid down the corner of her eye.

He kissed the tear away, and for a long moment, he just stared at her as if he
wanted to tell her that he loved her, but that was a silly wish that had no hold in
their reality.

They had this weekend, maybe one or two more, but love had no place in their
summer fling.

And then Eric began to move, burning off her sad musings with the hard
thrusts of his hips that demanded all of her attention.

With him claiming her core and her mouth, it didn't take more than a couple of
minutes for her to climb beyond the point of no return, and as the climax
exploded out of her, his thrusts became savage in their intensity.

As he swelled inside of her and shot his essence into her, Darlene climaxed
again, shouting his name.

When he finally stilled, he let out a groan and shifted onto his side, taking her
with him, so she was half sprawled over him. Her head resting on his chest,
Darlene listened to the wild beat of Eric's heart until it slowed down and
evened out.

Had she ever felt so satisfied after sex?

Not that she could remember. She came twice, only minutes apart. That had
never happened before, and given that there had been barely any foreplay and the
whole thing couldn't have lasted more than ten minutes, it was astounding.

Either Eric had some sex superpowers, or she'd been deprived for so long that
she'd accumulated enough explosives to detonate from any spark.

"I'm sorry," he murmured, his hand caressing her back. "I really wanted it to last
longer than that."

She lifted her head and smiled at him. "I don't think I could handle more.
Already it was the best sex I ever had and the only time I climaxed twice in a row."

54

ERIC

*A*s Eric caressed Darlene's back after making good on his promise, he was satisfied that he'd adequately compensated for his embarrassing first performance.

He wasn't a young buck, but it had been surprisingly easy to get hard again for Darlene. She was soft and feminine, sexy and responsive, and being with her was as easy as water.

"Do you think I can find something to do around here?"

Her hand, which had been lovingly caressing his chest, stilled. "What do you mean? Do you want to participate in one of the retreats?"

He laughed. "That New Age stuff is not for me. Do you think your boss needs a pilot? That's pretty much all I know how to do."

She lifted her eyes to him. "I can ask. We are pretty isolated out here, and the nearest airport is the one you landed at. But I don't know if they can build a landing strip here. The area is rocky and hilly."

"Maybe I can do something else." He kept running his hand over the lush curve of her ass. "Do they need help in the kitchen?"

She narrowed her eyes at him. "Can you even cook?"

"Of course, I can cook. I know how to make scrambled eggs and defrost pre-made dinners. I'm also handy. I worked for my brother's construction firm for a while. But Gilbert and I can get along only when we don't spend too much time together. We are both too headstrong to cooperate."

Darlene let out a breath and put her head on his chest. "I don't think they are going to build anything more on this property. This project is done."

"That's a shame." He threaded his fingers through her hair and tugged her head back to nuzzle her neck. "Do they need a hairdresser?"

She chuckled. "Now I know that you're not serious."

"I'm serious. I want to find a way to be near you."

She lifted her head again. "I'm not going to stay here forever. This is a temporary assignment just until William's project is done."

"I didn't know that." His hand stilled on her back. "Do you know what they are working on?"

"No clue. It's top secret, and I'm just the administrative assistant."

He had a feeling that Darlene knew more than she was letting on, but she probably couldn't talk about it, and it was easier to pretend that she didn't know.

He knew all about keeping secrets. Most of his missions had been classified, and he couldn't tell anyone about the many times he almost hadn't made it but somehow had survived despite all odds.

"What does your boss do?"

"William? He runs the lab here and the one back home."

"I meant the big boss. Kian."

Darlene was in Safe Haven just for the project, and once it was done, she would go back home to Los Angeles. If he wanted long-term with her, he should look for work over there. He could always move his jet operations to one of the many private airports in her area, but he was curious to see whether she was interested in him following her.

The sex had been incredibly good, but for Eric, it was more than that. Just holding Darlene in his arms and talking with her was more pleasant than any interaction he'd had with a woman in ages. The question was whether she felt it too.

"Kian does many things. I know that he develops office buildings and hotels. Why?"

Eric shrugged. "Maybe I'll move to Los Angeles and get a job at his company."

As he felt Darlene tense in his arms, he got his answer. She wasn't interested in him following her to Los Angeles.

"As I said, I'm here for a few months, so if you want to see more of me, you can join a retreat. Not all of them are about New Age stuff. Safe Haven also runs retreats for people with paranormal talents. Do you have any extrasensory perception? Telepathy? Precognition? Remote viewing?"

He chuckled. "I have one paranormal talent, and that's staying alive. The guys in my unit called me the lucky charm. I somehow got out alive from situations that should have killed me, and so did everyone who flew with me. If it had happened once or twice, it could have been just dumb luck, but it happened so many times that it became spooky. After the last time it happened, I decided not to renew my contract for another term. I didn't want to push my luck."

She shivered. "I'm glad. Being a fighter pilot is dangerous."

"Not really. It's less dangerous than almost any other combat position. But I guess I was both lucky and unlucky. I was unlucky to get into more trouble than I should have, but I was lucky to walk away alive."

DARLENE

*W*as it too much to hope for that Eric was a Dormant?
Probably.

He made her feel alive, and being with him was surprisingly easy. Darlene had expected it to be awkward, and she hadn't even had much hope that the sex would be great, but he'd surpassed her expectations on every front.

Maybe that's how all players were, though.

Was that the secret of their success?

They made women feel so good about themselves that they became a coveted prize even when none of the beneficiaries of their attentions expected them to stay?

When Eric's phone rang, he reached for his discarded pants and pulled it out. "It's Gilbert."

"He's probably calling to tell you about the dinner at Syssi and Kian's."

Eric smiled at her before accepting the call. "Are you calling me to apologize?"

The phone was so close to her ear that she could hear Gilbert breathing on the other side.

"I didn't mean it the way it came out. Where are you?"

Eric trailed his hand down to her ass. "Darlene is showing me the sights."

She stifled a giggle by burying her face in his chest.

"Right. Anyway, I'm calling to tell you that we are all invited to dinner at Kian and Syssi's, and they are staying at what they call the bunker. Darlene probably knows where it is."

"I know about the dinner. William told Darlene about it. I guess that if you're going, you've gotten over your anger tantrum and reconciled yourself to accepting Kaia's choice."

"Not even close, but I have orders from Karen to behave. Kaia is in love with the guy, and Karen told me to back off and let it play out. If it's not meant to be, it will fizzle out on its own."

"Darlene says that William is a sweetheart, and that Kaia is lucky to snag him."
Darlene nodded her agreement and whispered. "The best guy I know."
When Eric squeezed her butt, she patted his chest. "After you, of course."
"That's better." He smiled.
"What's better?" Gilbert asked.
"Your attitude. I'm glad that Karen talked some sense into your stubborn head."
"Yeah, yeah. All is hunky dory now when William is thirty-two and looks younger than that. But in twenty years, he's going to be over fifty while Kaia will be only thirty-nine. That's a big difference. At that age, people's health starts to decline along with their looks. She's too young to see it now, and maybe he is too, but it's going to be a problem."
Eric winked at Darlene. "You're only as old as you feel. Besides, they are in love. What are you going to do? If you fight it, you're going to alienate her and make your entire family miserable."
Gilbert let out a long-suffering sigh. "Don't you think I know that? I need to apply pressure to force Kaia to re-evaluate her feelings and make sure that she really wants him. She had known the guy for seven days, and she accepted his marriage proposal. That's crazy, and it's very much unlike Kaia. He might have some unhealthy influence on her, and if she's unsure how to end it, she can use me as an excuse to get out of the relationship without souring things between her and her boss. That way, they can at least finish the damn project."
Darlene was impressed. Gilbert had pretended an anger tantrum not to stand in Kaia's way to love and happiness but to give her a way out if she needed it. The guy was either an excellent actor, or he was putting a spin on it because he felt embarrassed about the way he'd acted.
"Maybe they are really in love," Eric said. "Sometimes the simplest explanation is the correct one, and there is no need to search for hidden motives and undue influence."
"Maybe," Gilbert said. "That's what I want to find out."
Eric chuckled. "So, your posturing was all for show?"
"Not all of it, but some. I don't think that William is right for Kaia, mainly because of the age difference, but I won't stand in the way of her happiness if that's what she really wants."
Eric sighed. "Don't assume that all marriages where there is a big age difference between the partners end badly just because mine did. Emma was a psycho, and I was too blind to see that."
"You also dated her for only two months before proposing to her."
Eric closed his eyes. "We thought that she was pregnant."
"She tricked you," Gilbert said. "The woman was a master manipulator even though she was still a kid."
That explained so much. Eric had married a woman who had been much younger than him, and he'd done it after knowing her for a very short time. No wonder Gilbert was freaking out over Kaia doing the same. Well, the situation was reversed in that in his mind William was the cradle-robber, but it was similar enough.
"Yeah, she probably did, but at the time, I was in love and naive enough to believe her."

When Eric ended the call, Darlene lifted her head and braced it on her forearm. "How old were you when you got married?"

"I was thirty, and I don't want to talk about it." He pulled her on top of him. "So far, this has been one of the best days of my life, and I don't want to spoil it by talking about her."

5 6

WILLIAM

*A*fter leaving Kian and Syssi to prepare for dinner, William stopped by his bungalow to shower and change.

When he was done combing his hair, he removed his glasses, cleaned them with a wipe, and put them back on. But as he stood in front of the vanity mirror, he took them off again and put them on the counter.

He wasn't going to sit in front of a computer screen, and the sun wasn't glaring on the Oregon coast even at midday, let alone at seven-thirty in the evening. He had no valid excuse to hide behind the frames.

Not that he owed an explanation to anyone, but he felt that it was time to stop using the glasses as a crutch.

Given that he expected the battle with Kaia's stepfather to continue, it wasn't the best time to give up his imaginary shield, but since he was already facing so many changes, one more shouldn't make a difference.

Taking a calming breath, he glanced one last time at the folded glasses and then turned on his heel and headed out.

The lodge was less than ten minutes of an easy stroll away, but William strode with purpose in his steps and made it in half the time. Walking down the corridor to the rooms the family occupied, he didn't know which of the three doors to knock on. The larger room housed the parents with the two boys, but the other two were the same size.

Which one was Kaia in?

Pulling out his phone, he started to text her, but as he heard a chorus of female laughter, he knocked on the door it was coming from.

Kaia opened up with a big smile and pulled him into a hug. "I missed you." She kissed his cheek.

Inside, Cheryl and Karen were seated on one bed while Idina was bouncing on the other with a doll clutched in each hand.

"William!" She jumped off the bed and lifted her arms to him. "I want to ride on your shoulders."

"We were just talking about you," Karen said.

"I hope only good things." He bent down and put his hands on the little girl's tiny waist.

As he picked Idina up, Cheryl gave him a discreet thumbs up from behind her mother's back.

Did she mean that what they'd talked about had been all good?

"Gilbert should be ready in a few minutes," Karen said without acknowledging his comment.

She'd changed into a pretty navy-colored dress, and with her dark hair curled and cascading down her shoulders, she looked effortlessly beautiful, but he didn't know whether it was okay for him to compliment Kaia's mother.

Cheryl had also changed into a new outfit, pairing black jeans with a short-sleeved white shirt. The fabric had tiny holes in it that were embroidered, but it wasn't lace. It had some other name that eluded him at the moment. Was it eyelet?

Kaia was still in the same outfit she'd worn that morning, probably because she hadn't wanted to miss a moment with her family to get changed.

As the five of them stepped out into the corridor, the next door over opened, and Gilbert walked out, pushing the double stroller with one hand and holding a portable crib in the other.

"Let me help you." William reached for the crib.

"That's okay." Gilbert moved it out of William's reach. "Cheryl or Kaia can push the stroller, and I can carry the crib." He added a tight smile. "You are already carrying precious cargo. Make sure she doesn't fall."

The way Idina was gripping his head, there was no way she would fall, but little kids were impulsive, especially the hellion he was carrying on his shoulders.

"Hold on tight," he told her as he gently gripped her tiny ankles.

Idina's big personality was housed in a small, fragile body, and holding her, William wondered how parents dealt with the anxiety of knowing how vulnerable their children were. The girls in his clan transitioned early, and by Idina's age, they were already immortal, but boys remained vulnerable until puberty, and he wished there was a way to induce their transition earlier.

Maybe Okidu's journals held the answer to that, and perhaps they also had instructions for transforming the children born to immortal males with human partners.

The Fates had been kind to his clan lately, and many Dormants had been found, but there were still so many males without a mate and without immortal offspring.

"What are you thinking about?" Kaia fell in step with him.

"I was thinking about children and how vulnerable they are. Until they reach adulthood, their parents must live with constant anxiety."

"That never changes," Karen said. "You don't stop worrying about your child just because she's all grown up." She smiled at Kaia. "On the contrary. The worst feeling for a parent is helplessness. When our children are small, most of the time, it's easy to fix whatever is troubling them. The older they get, the harder it is to do, and at some point, they no longer listen to you, and you are forced to watch them making mistakes that they are going to regret later. As the saying goes, small kids, small troubles, big kids, big troubles."

Had she been referring to him? Did they still think that he was Kaia's mistake?

"Kaia says that you are sweet." Idina patted his head and then leaned down and kissed his forehead. "I like you."

Surprised, William lifted his eyes and looked into her smiling face. It was framed in soft curls that were now cascading down and blocking his view. "Thank you. I like you too."

Gilbert snorted. "It seems like you've won over all the ladies in my family." He looked up at Idina. "This one doesn't offer her affection easily. I wonder what magic you wield over the fairer sex."

William shrugged. "You should trust their female intuition. I'm a nice guy."

57

KAIA

"Is this where your boss is staying?" Gilbert looked with dismay at the small, one-room cottage.

Kaia had heard about the underground, but she'd never been there. Supposedly, Emmett had orgies down there before he met Eleanor and fell in love with her. William had said that there was more to the story and promised to tell her about it, but they'd been busy with other stuff, and they'd forgotten about it.

They were both guilty of getting completely immersed in whatever they were doing, whether it was work or sex, and they both tended to let other things fall by the wayside. They needed an Odu of their own to remind them of all the things they were forgetting.

"This is just for show." William opened the door and ducked low so Idina's head cleared the header. "There is a sizable bunker built under it, and the entrance is through the cottage."

Gilbert handed the travel crib to Kaia and took the stroller from Cheryl. "I thought that this was a free love commune, not a survivalist camp. What do they need a bunker for, and why is your boss staying underground when he could stay at the lodge?"

William glanced at Cheryl and then cast Gilbert an apologetic smile. "The bunker's history is a long story and not meant for young ears. And the reason my boss is staying there is that it's much more luxurious than the lodge and can house his entire entourage."

Cheryl snorted. "If you were referring to my ears as young, you are mistaken. I've heard and seen much more than you can ever imagine."

As Cheryl and Gilbert started arguing about what kind of content she was exposing herself to, and Karen got busy taking the twins out of the stroller, Kaia sidled up to William.

"Is Kian's butler here?" she asked quietly.

Nodding, William punched in the code to open the door.

"Yay." Kaia clapped her hands. "I'm so excited to meet him."

Cheryl walked over with Ryan in her arms. "Why are you so excited about meeting the butler?"

Thinking fast, Kaia said the first thing that popped into her head. "I've never met a proper British butler."

William had told her about the British television series and the characters that Okidu imitated, specifically the snooty butler. Hopefully, he was doing a good job of it and didn't look too robotic. Her sister was a smart girl, and she would notice if something was off.

As her family made its way down the narrow stairs carrying the twins, the folded stroller, the travel crib, and the big baby bag, Kaia hoped there was room enough down there for all of that.

When William opened the door at the bottom of the stairs, she had just a brief moment to look around as the greetings commenced.

"Good evening!" Syssi welcomed them with a big smile on her face.

The living room was sizable, but most of it was taken up by a long dining table. The couches and armchairs had been pushed against the walls, probably by the super-strong butler.

Where was he?

Kaia waited patiently for all the hellos to be over before turning to Syssi and whispering in her ear. "Where is the butler I've heard so much about?"

"Okidu is getting ready to serve dinner." Syssi threaded her arm through Kaia's. "Come. I'll introduce you." She led her through a swinging door into the kitchen.

The butler was dressed in a charcoal-colored suit, a white dress shirt, and a tie, with a white apron over his outfit.

"This is Kaia," Syssi said. "She wants to say hello."

He smiled broadly. "Hello, Mistress Kaia. How are you this lovely evening?"

He looked and sounded so human that she would have never guessed he was a cyborg.

"I'm great. What about you?"

"I am very well, thank you for asking. How is the work on my journals progressing?"

"We are making slow progress." She looked into his eyes, expecting to see camera apparatus behind the irises, but they looked perfectly organic. "Perhaps you can help us understand what you have written?"

He shook his head. "I just wrote down information that was stored in my memory banks. I know that they are instructions on how to build more of me, but I do not understand any of them." He smiled a little too broadly, and it looked fake but still human. "I am like a printer. The printer does not know what it prints. It just does its job."

She smiled. "I understand. Thank you for explaining."

He bowed. "I am always happy to help in any way I can."

Kaia turned to Syssi. "Is the printer analogy something Okidu was told?"

"I don't think so. Why?"

"Humor is a sign of intelligence."

"I agree." Syssi put her hand on Okidu's shoulder. "Please remember not to say anything like that near the others. They don't know about you."

He dipped his head. "Of course, mistress."

58

SYSSI

"Shall I start serving dinner, mistress?" Okidu asked.

Before answering, Syssi listened to the voices coming from the living room, but it didn't seem as if Eric and Darlene had arrived yet. "You can take out the soft drinks and the wine, but wait until the last two guests arrive to serve the food."

"Yes, mistress." He dipped his head and walked out of the kitchen with a tray of wine glasses.

When she made to follow, Kaia put a hand on her arm. "May I ask you something?"

"Go ahead."

Kaia struggled with what she wanted to say, opening and closing her mouth a few times. "How long have you and Kian been together?"

"About four and a half years. Why?"

"You have a daughter. I was told that's unusual."

Understanding dawning, Syssi nodded. "I wanted a child very much, and I didn't want to wait centuries to have one. Kian and I drank fertility potions that one of the clan's doctors had prepared for us, and we got pregnant within months." She smiled. "Kian thinks that it was a coincidence and that the potions were nothing more than snake oil, but I believe that they helped."

Kaia let out a breath. "I always dreamt of having a large family. Four kids was the minimum I considered, and I entertained the thought of having six. When I learned that it might not be possible after you know what, I started thinking of getting pregnant before doing the thing. But since my mother needs to do the same thing and her clock is ticking, I can't take the time to have a couple of kids before doing it. It's a relief that there is a treatment that might help me conceive sooner rather than later."

Syssi frowned. "Are you under compulsion not to talk about any of it?"

Kaia nodded. "The way it was worded, I can only talk about it with William. He tried to circumvent it so I could at least talk to Darlene, but it didn't work."

"Of course not. You need Eleanor and Emmett to remove the compulsion and reword it, so you can talk freely with those in the know."

"Yeah. I'll ask William to arrange that as soon as possible." She laughed. "I'm usually a direct person, and talking in circles is not my style."

"You're doing very well, given the limitations. It only illustrates how limited compulsion can be at enforcing the keeping of secrets. An intelligent person can find ways around it."

Kaia shifted from foot to foot. "Is the other method available to members of your family better?"

"I think so, but William is adamant about not thralling you. I think he's being overly cautious, but he keeps referring to your brain as a fine-tuned machine that shouldn't be messed with."

"I know." Kaia rolled her eyes. "I sometimes wonder if he's in love with me or my brain."

"Is there a difference between the two?" Syssi asked.

"Yeah, there is. I have a soul." Kaia put her hand over her heart. "And its feelings are no less influential on my character than my logical mind." She smiled. "Don't mind me. I know William loves everything about me. It just annoys me that he talks about my brain so much. I'm not as smart as everyone thinks."

Kaia's modesty was sweet, but it was unfounded. "I beg to differ. William is the smartest person I know, and he needs your help to decipher Okidu's journals. That means that you are at least as smart as he is, if not more."

The girl shrugged. "I'm a bioinformatician, and he's a computer engineer. There are things I know that he doesn't and vice versa. That's why we need to collaborate to find out what's in those journals." She frowned. "William is afraid that the knowledge gained from them might be dangerous, and I agree. I don't know what we should do if that's the case. The knowledge is valuable regardless of what it is used for."

"Precisely." Syssi threaded her arm through Kaia's. "Nearly every new invention or discovery has the potential to be either beneficial or harmful depending on the intent of those who use it." She led Kaia out of the kitchen. "And what's worse, it's impossible to bury it for long. Eventually, the technology or the idea always resurfaces, even if it's on a planet millions of light years away." She winked.

59

KIAN

"Where can I set up the crib?" Karen asked as soon as Syssi and Kaia had gone into the kitchen.

"I'll show you." Wonder rose to her feet with one of the twins in her arms. "Follow me."

"I'll come too." Callie cuddled the other baby boy to her chest.

With all the babies surrounding them, the ladies had their motherly hormones in overdrive, and Kian wouldn't be surprised if the two couples paid Merlin a visit upon their return to the village.

"Do you want to come?" Karen asked Kaia's baby sister.

Sitting in William's lap, she shook her head adamantly, her curly hair bouncing around her small face.

Idina was a fierce one, and Kian had taken a liking to her immediately. He liked feisty girls, and yet his perfect truelove mate was a gentle soul who never raised her voice or made any demands.

But then, that was Syssi's power. She only had to mention something in passing, and he jumped to fulfill her wishes.

Allegra was more like him than her mother, though. She was demanding and uncompromising, but at least she knew how to get it all with a charming smile. He had no doubt that she had inherited that skill from her mother.

When he kissed the top of his daughter's head, she turned to look up at him. "Dada."

"Yes, sweetie. I'm your daddy."

"How old is your daughter?" Gilbert asked.

"She's six months old."

The guy pursed his lips. "She's talking early. My Idina was the same." He smiled at his little girl. "Right, baby?"

"I'm smart." She swung her leg up and down, missing William's shin by a hair. "Like Mommy."

He chuckled. "I get no respect. What about me? Are you smart like Daddy?"

She smiled, but her expression was a little evil. "I'm strong like Daddy." She lifted her arm and fisted her hands. "I'll build houses when I'm big. Like Daddy."

Kian's interest got piqued. "You're a builder?"

Gilbert's lips lifted on one side with a mocking smile. "I'm sure you know everything there is to know about me. The brief your people prepared on my family was quite extensive."

"That might be so, but I didn't read it. William is the one who heads the tech department, and I trust him implicitly. The only thing he needs to run by me is the budget, and I usually approve it without looking at it, either. His contribution to our organization is so massive that he can ask for the moon, and I'll tell my people to get it for him."

It was a shame that Syssi wasn't there to hear his speech. He'd followed her instructions to the letter, and Gilbert seemed duly impressed.

Looking at William, he gave him a once-over as if he was seeing him for the first time. "So, you're a big shot in the organization, are you?"

William gave him a shy smile. "I'm the authority on everything that has to do with technology."

"Nice. You're so unassuming that I would have never suspected that you were such an asset to your boss."

"I'm not really his boss," Kian said. "I answer to the board of directors, and William has one of the seven seats. Since I have to run every major decision through the board, it's more like they are my bosses than I'm theirs."

William was regarding him with a puzzled expression, probably confused by the bullshit he was spewing, and the moment Gilbert looked away, Kian winked and gave William the thumbs up.

"Our William is a genius," Anandur said. "He designed our entire defense system, and he's responsible for most of the patents we hold."

As Kian glared at Anandur for saying too much, William's cheeks got red, and he bounced Gilbert's little girl on his knees to hide his embarrassment.

"Kaia is a genius too," Gilbert said proudly. "I can't take credit for her smarts, but I'm proud to be her stepfather."

Evidently, he'd been too focused on the compliments to notice Anandur's slip up about the defense systems and therefore hadn't asked what they were defending themselves from and why.

Cheryl cleared her throat. "You and Mom are not married, so you are Kaia's and my honorary stepfather."

Pinning her with a hard stare, Gilbert put his hand over his heart. "It's what's in here that matters, not what's on a piece of paper."

"Amen to that." Anandur rose to his feet and walked over to the bar. "A shot of whiskey, anyone?"

"Don't mind if I do." Gilbert followed him up. "What do you have?"

As the two discussed the various whiskey brands on hand, William closed his eyes briefly and let out a breath. "I should give Darlene a call. Maybe she can't find the place. They should've gotten here already."

"I'm on it." Brundar pulled out his phone.

"Who are you going to call?" William sounded anxious.

"The security office. They can find her and bring her and Gilbert's brother here."

William's expression turned panicked. "Don't send anyone looking for them. They'll get here when they get here."

The Guardian lifted one blond brow and kept typing a message on his phone.

A moment later, the device buzzed with an incoming message. "They are on their way. Max found them outside the lodge, and he's escorting them to the cottage."

"Thank the merciful Fates," William murmured under his breath.

Kian regarded him with amusement. "Is there something that you would like to share with us about Darlene and Eric?"

William shook his head. "I have absolutely nothing to share."

6 0

SYSSI

*T*hankfully, Allegra had fallen asleep in Kian's arms before dinner had started, and the twin boys had been sleeping peacefully in the spare bedroom.

Syssi had gone to check on them together with Karen, and they both had melted seeing the boys holding hands in the crib they shared.

Idina, on the other hand, didn't seem to be getting tired at all and continued listening intently to the conversations going on around the table and offering her opinion whenever she had one, whether it was on politics or economics, or the current bear market.

The adults had done their best to stifle their amused smiles at her astute observations, the best being about the bears and how they shouldn't be allowed in the market because they would just eat everything and scare the customers away.

When dinner was done, and Okidu had served hot beverages and dessert, Gilbert leaned back in his chair and patted his stomach. "Thank you for a lovely meal and the even lovelier company. I don't remember the last time I enjoyed an evening with friends so much."

"Thank you." Syssi smiled at him. "The feeling is mutual."

She wondered whether he had many friends, and for some reason she had a feeling that he did not, which reminded her of his comment about having a very small family and researching his ancestry to find more relatives.

She put her coffee cup down and turned to him. "You promised to tell me about your ancestry research and what you've found."

"Yes, I did." Gilbert put his hands on the table. "I was able to find out who my great-grandparents were, but that was as far as I got. I couldn't find anything about their parents."

She nodded. "You were fortunate to find even that. About three years ago, I tried to find out more about my ancestry, but I couldn't find anyone that predated my grandparents. They were no longer alive at the time, so there was no one to ask, and my parents didn't know much either. All I know is that my maternal great-grandparents came from Poland, and my paternal great-grandparents came from Ukraine, although back then, Ukraine was part of Russia."

Gilbert tapped his hands on the table with glee. "What a coincidence. You and I have common roots. No wonder I like you so much."

When Kian released a growl, Gilbert lifted his hands in the peace sign. "As a friend. I have eyes for only one woman." He draped his arm over Karen's back. "From the moment I first laid eyes on her, I never even thought of another." He leaned over and kissed her temple. "I found the love of my life, and she came with two wonderful girls." He looked lovingly at Cheryl and Kaia. "I got two amazing daughters in the bargain."

Looking placated, Kian gave him a tight smile. "Which one of your ancestors was Syssi's great-grandparents' countryman?"

"My maternal great-grandmother. My paternal grandfather was of British descent, and my paternal grandmother was Portuguese. On my mother's side, my grandfather was of Austrian descent, and my grandmother was the daughter of Polish emigrants. They came to the United States shortly after World War I ended."

"Do you know where in Poland they were from?" Syssi asked.

He nodded. "They were from a small town named Gdynia. Today, it's a mid-sized seaport city, but back then, it was just a small tourist town that was part of the German Empire and was called Gdingen. After World War I, Gdynia was reintegrated within the Polish state."

"Interesting." Syssi took a cookie from the communal plate. "Your great-grandparents must have spoken fluent German."

"I assume that they did."

Syssi rubbed a hand over her chin. "I don't know which part of Poland my great-grandparents were from, but I remember my grandmother telling me that her mother could speak five languages, with German being one of them."

"She must have come from a wealthy family," Karen said. "Only the nobility could afford tutors for their children, and it was a status symbol to teach the kids several foreign languages. I bet she also knew French, English, and Russian. In addition to German, those were the main languages of the time."

"They still are," Eric said. "French is the language of love, English is the language of industry and commerce, German is the language of military precision, and Russian is the language of literature."

"Says who?" Kaia snorted. "I only know of French as being the language of love. I've never heard the other ones being described that way."

Eric shrugged. "That's how I think of them. I don't know whether I heard it somewhere or made it up."

Syssi thought of Sumerian and wondered whether it could be called the language of origins. Maybe it was the language that had launched the first human civilization, but it wasn't the original language from which all others had sprung.

That honor belonged to the gods' language. But then, even theirs might not be the original. Another advanced civilization could have started the gods' and another one before that started that one and so on.

It was probably a never-ending cycle, and the original fountainhead most likely no longer existed.

61

WILLIAM

illiam was fascinated by Gilbert's showmanship. The guy enjoyed being the center of attention, drinking it in as if it was his favorite drug. He should have chosen a career in entertainment or in politics. But then, he probably owed his success to his people skills and to his politicking.

Getting permits to build in desirable locations required a lot of both.

"My great-grandmother's family owned a windmill near Gdynia," Gilbert said. "They might have been a little wealthier than their neighbors, but they weren't nobility, and they weren't rich. My great-grandmother's name was Perl or Perla, and she had a sister, Rosa. Perla married a man called Yanek Dorjinsky, and Rosa married his cousin Boris with the same last name. Both couples emigrated to the United States in 1923."

Syssi gasped. "My great-grandmother's name was Rosa, and she also came to the United States at about the same time."

Kian waved a dismissive hand. "Rosa was a popular name back then. It doesn't prove that you are related."

Ignoring her husband's dismissal, Syssi asked, "Do you know what happened to Rosa?"

Gilbert took a sip of coffee, put the cup down, and continued. "Boris died shortly after he and Rosa came to America, and Rosa remarried, but I lost track of her after that."

"What was the name of her second husband?" Anandur asked.

Gilbert lifted his hands in the air. "If I knew that, I could have found her, but my mother didn't remember what her mother had told her about her aunt, and my grandmother was no longer with us when I did my research. I even hired a private detective to try and find Rosa's descendants, provided that there were any, but since he couldn't locate her marriage certificate, he had nothing to go by. The town hall where she'd used to live with Boris burned down in 1927, and that was where the certificate had probably been kept."

CHAPTER 61

"What happened to Perla after she came to the United States?" Wonder asked.

"She and my great-grandfather had only one daughter, my grandmother Sheila, who married an Austrian immigrant named Franz Wagner. They had a son who died as a baby and a daughter, my mother, Stephanie. She married Darren Emerson and had three kids. My brother Eric, my sister Gabi, and me. We don't have any family on our mother's side, and we have only two cousins on my father's side."

"That's why I want to have at least four kids," Kaia said. "I want to have a big family."

When William clasped her hand under the table, she gave him an encouraging squeeze.

"What about you, William?" Gilbert turned to him. "You want to marry my stepdaughter, and you haven't told us anything about your family."

Kaia pretended to frown. "You were raised by wolves, right?"

"I wasn't. My mother had me on her own, so I don't know anything about my father's side. But my mother has a big family with many cousins." He smiled at Gilbert. "Everyone here who is not part of your family is part of mine. Kian, Anandur, and Brundar are my second cousins, and Syssi, Wonder, and Callie are their mates."

"Mates?" Karen asked. "Is that a Scottish term for a significant other?"

"It's a family thing," Syssi said. "They have a tradition of calling their partners mates, and once you're exposed to it, you realize how much easier it is to use a gender and level of commitment neutral term. You can use it for a wife or a fiancée, you can use it for male or female, and you don't need to worry about offending anyone by using the wrong term."

"Pfft." Gilbert waved a hand. "People get offended too easily these days. Instead of worrying about serious things, they focus on minutiae."

"It's not minutiae to them," Cheryl grumbled under her breath. "But I'm all for simplifying things. I'm going to make an InstaTock post about using the term mate for every form of amorous partnership. I bet it will go viral."

"What's an InstaTock?" Kian asked.

She gaped at him as if he didn't know what a cell phone was. "Do you know what YouTube is?"

"Of course."

"And you know what a blog is, right?"

"Naturally."

"Instaock is a short video that is like an opinion blog. You record yourself either making a statement or commenting on someone else's, and then you add filters and background music to dramatize it, so it looks like a movie clip."

"That's an interesting concept," Kian said. "Maybe later you can show me an example."

"No problem. I have my own channel, and you are all welcome to subscribe. The more subscribers I get, the more popular my channel will be. Instatock's algorithm will show my Instatocks to more people."

62

KAIA

*K*aia had seen several of Cheryl's vlogs and had done her sisterly duty of liking and sharing, but she wasn't a fan of social media in general and Instatock in particular. It was even more addictive than the others, and older teens Cheryl's age were obsessed with it.

Her mother leaned over Gilbert and picked his phone off the table. "Is the app you used to construct your family tree available on mobile?"

"It sure is." Gilbert took the phone from her. "I stored everything in the application, and I have some pictures I can show you. I went to Poland to try to claim the windmill for our family." He scrolled on his phone. "I didn't have proof enough to get ownership of it, but I took pictures." He passed the phone to Syssi.

She smiled. "It looks nice." She handed him the phone back. "They must preserve it as a historical monument, surely. It's not operational, right?"

Gilbert puffed out his chest. "I paid for the restoration in exchange for having a plaque with my great-grandmother's maiden name on it. I thought it would help my case in the future."

Kaia rolled her eyes. "That's so like you. You don't miss any opportunity to put your hands on real estate."

"That's what I do for a living, and I do it very well." He kept scrolling. "I also scanned old family photographs into the family tree application. This is my grandmother Sheila as a little girl with her mother, Perla." He passed the phone to Syssi again.

Her eyes widened. "Oh, my God. She looks exactly like my grandmother."

"Who?" Kaia leaned to get a look. "Perla or Sheila?"

"Perla." Syssi pushed to her feet. "I need to get my phone. I will be right back." She rushed down the hallway and returned a moment later. "I need to find her picture." She sat back down and kept scrolling until she found what she'd been looking for. "That's my grandmother as a young woman with my mother as a little girl." She passed the phone to Kaia.

"Syssi's grandmother looks a lot like your great-grandmother, Gilbert." Kaia enlarged the picture with her fingers.

Could Gilbert and Syssi be related?

It would be wonderful if they were.

If their great-grandmothers were sisters, then Gilbert, Eric, and Gabi were Dormants.

Hope surging in her heart, she passed Syssi's phone to Eric, who shook his head in disbelief. "That's one hell of a coincidence." He passed the phone to his brother.

Gilbert took one look at the screen, grinned like he'd just won the lottery, and passed the phone to Karen. "It seems that my ancestry research wasn't futile after all. I've found a relative, and she comes with a big, beautiful family." He offered Syssi his hand. "Hello, cousin."

Shaking it, she turned to Kian. "You know what that means, right?"

"I haven't seen the evidence yet." He waited until his wife's phone was passed over to him and turned to Gilbert. "Let me see the picture of your great-grandmother again."

"Here you go." Gilbert handed him his phone.

Kian put both on the table side by side and examined the old pictures for a long moment.

"It's not conclusive. They both have Slavic features, but these old photos are grainy and yellow. Besides, a physical resemblance is not enough to go by." Kian returned the phones to Syssi and Gilbert.

"The evidence might not be conclusive," Syssi said. "But if you take into account the other factors, the case in favor of this assumption is strong."

"What factors? Kaia is not a blood relative of his, and even if she was, her case is not conclusive either."

Gilbert regarded the two with a frown. "What are you talking about? I thought that William was Kian's cousin, not Syssi's. Or did you marry your second cousin, and you are both related to William?"

Gilbert's conclusion was logical given what he knew, but the suggestion was funny, and Kaia stifled a chuckle.

Syssi lifted her hand. "Give us one more moment, Gilbert." She turned to her husband. "I'm talking about the affinity. Gilbert and Karen fell for each other right away." She glanced at Darlene, who looked as stunned as Kaia felt. "I know that none of this is conclusive, and we need Bridget to run blood tests to confirm that I'm related to Gilbert and Eric, but given my strong urge to come here this weekend, I think that all the signs are pointing in that direction."

A blood test couldn't do that. They needed a mtDNA genetic test to confirm that Gilbert, Eric, and Syssi were third cousins, but given the tension in the room, Kaia felt that it wasn't the right time to mention it.

Kian nodded. "Let's get Emmett and Eleanor in here and share what we know with our guests." He waved at Anandur, instructing him to do that. "Kaia's family will need time to process what they learn, so my regular mode of operation in instances like that is not an option."

"What the hell are you people talking about?" Eric asked.

Kian smiled at him. "Everything will become clear in a few moments." He turned to Gilbert. "While we wait for Eleanor and her mate, you can tell us about your father's side of the family."

Kaia could barely contain the tears of relief gathering at the corners of her eyes.

If Gilbert was a Dormant, her mother wouldn't need to leave him or have sex with someone else to transition. He could transition first and then induce her.

The whole family would become immortal.

But what if she wasn't a Dormant after all?

It would be just damn cruel if, at the end of the day, Gilbert, Eric, and their sister Gabi turned immortal while Kaia, her mother, and her siblings didn't.

63

WILLIAM

"*H*old on," Eric said. "Before my brother gets into our family's history, I want to know what Emmett Haderech and his girlfriend have to do with Syssi being our distant relative and why do we have to wait for them before you can talk to us? Do we have to sign some confidentiality agreement or something?"

"Or something." Kian chuckled. "It's crucial to our safety that what we are about to tell you remains a secret. It's a matter of life and death for us. Emmett and Eleanor are powerful hypnotists, and they can ensure that you don't breathe a word of what you hear to anyone outside your immediate family and us. You can't even tell your sister until she goes through the same process."

"It's not a big deal," Kaia said. "They did it to me, and I could barely feel it." She chuckled. "I thought that it was nonsense until I tried to say something that I wasn't supposed to, and the words wouldn't leave my mouth."

Eric leveled his dark brown eyes on her. "So, you know what this is all about?"

She nodded. "But I can't talk about it because of the hypnotic coercion. It is not airtight, and I found a way to use different words and kind of talk around it, but I can only give hints, and without reference, you might have a hard time following." She glanced at William. "Do I have permission to tell them what I can?"

"Permission?" Gilbert spat. "You're asking his permission to speak? I knew that there was something shady under that innocent good-guy façade." He glared at William. "What kind of power do you hold over our Kaia that she needs to ask your permission to speak?"

Syssi put a hand on his arm. "Relax, Gilbert. It's about secrets that are connected to the research, and William is Kaia's boss. You shouldn't be surprised that she can't reveal anything about her work without his permission."

Gilbert didn't look appeased. "Why are you answering for him? Doesn't he have a mouth?"

William had had enough.

He wanted to build a good relationship with Kaia's family, but Gilbert was the type of guy that would just keep on pushing and attacking until he got pushback.

"I have a mouth," William said. "I prefer not to engage in futile arguments, and I don't want to do anything to upset Kaia, but I can't keep quiet when you keep attacking me. Kian has already told you that the information I shared with her is a matter of life and death for us, and I told her about it only after Emmett and Eleanor used hypnosis to ensure her silence. Furthermore, I'm not a hypnotist, so I can't grant her permission to talk around their hypnotic coercion or deny it. They are the only ones who can."

Surprising the heck out of him, Gilbert laughed. "I was wondering whether you had a backbone. I don't want my Kaia to marry a spineless guy who can't stand up to her or anyone else."

Asshole.

Perhaps he should have just thralled the guy. It would have saved him and Kaia a lot of aggravation.

Though if Gilbert turned out to be a Dormant and transitioned, William wouldn't be able to keep thralling him, and once the guy moved into the village, he would become a constant thorn in William's side. If Gilbert kept acting like an asshole, he would have to put him in his place the conventional way, but he had to do that without ruining their future relationship.

Easier said than done.

Kaia groaned. "You're so bad, Gilbert. You made us both miserable just to see how far you could push William?"

The smile slid off Gilbert's face. "I kept pushing to see how hard the two of you were willing to fight for your relationship, and I'm not done pushing yet. I'm still not happy about you deciding to marry your first boyfriend."

Kaia folded her arms over her chest. "William is not my first boyfriend, and you know it."

"*Pfft.* The fling you had at seventeen doesn't count. You weren't in love, and you didn't even claim to be. And if you bring up Anthony, your mother assured me that he was just a friend."

"He was." Kaia let out a breath. "Still is, I hope." She glanced at William. "I know that he's not dead. But I don't know whether I'll ever see him again."

64

KIAN

*T*he pain in Kaia's voice touched Kian. He wished he could help get her friend off the island, but he wasn't willing to risk Guardians' lives to free a human. In fact, he wouldn't have authorized a rescue even if Kaia's friend was a confirmed Dormant.

"There is always hope," William said quietly.

Idina had fallen asleep in his lap, and he looked as if he was afraid to move a muscle and wake her up.

"I'll take her." Karen rose to her feet. "Can I put her to sleep on the bed next to the boys' crib?"

"Of course." Syssi followed her up. "I'll turn down the blanket for you."

"Thanks." Karen took her daughter from William's arms and carried her to the bedroom.

When they returned, Eleanor walked in with Emmett, who was in his full prophet regalia.

"Hi." She glanced around the living room. "You had a party, and we were not invited?"

"Who's that?" Gilbert stared at Emmett.

"I'm Emmett Haderech, the spiritual leader of this community. And who are you?"

He knew perfectly well who Gilbert was, but Emmett enjoyed playing the part.

"I'm Kaia's stepfather." He turned to Kian. "That's your hypnotist? I wouldn't trust him to hypnotize a chicken."

Kian stifled a chuckle.

The comment was rude, but he understood Gilbert's reaction. He would have thought the same thing if he'd seen Emmett in his white robe and long beard.

"Get up, Gilbert," Emmett commanded.

Gilbert shot to his feet.

"Sit down, Gilbert."

He dropped like a rock back on his chair.

Emmett smiled evilly. "Do you still think I can't hypnotize a chicken?"

"What the hell? How did you do that?" Gilbert looked at Karen. "He didn't even dangle a watch in front of my face or snap his fingers."

"He doesn't need to do any of that." Kaia walked over to Gilbert, stood behind his chair, and put one hand on his shoulder and the other on her mother's. "You all need to suspend disbelief for the rest of this evening."

Gilbert looked up at her. "Did you?"

"I did." She moved to stand between his chair and her mother's. "But you know me. I'm the girl who believes that aliens have been visiting Earth since time immemorial and that they have secret bases in the deepest regions of our oceans and on the dark side of the moon."

His eyes widened. "Is that what it's about? They are aliens?"

"Patience, Gilbert." She patted his shoulder. "Let Emmett and Eleanor do their thing first, and then you'll find out what this is all about."

Emmett pulled out a chair and sat down facing Gilbert. "So, who do I need to compel to keep their mouths shut?"

Kaia rose to her feet. "Let me introduce you to my family. This is Karen, my mother, and the guy you just compelled is my stepfather, Gilbert. On the other side of the table is my uncle, Eric, and that's my sister, Cheryl." She looked at Kian. "I can't tell him anything more unless I'm released from my compulsion."

"We will do that later." Kian motioned for Eric to move closer to his brother and for Cheryl to move closer to her mother. "All of Kaia's family members are potential Dormants. We need to tell them what their options are, and then they will need to go home and think things through. Your job is to make it so they can't tell anyone about it but can still discuss it among themselves. After you are done with them, you will have to change Kaia's compulsion so she can talk with her family and with everyone who knows about it already."

Emmett nodded. "Understood."

Eleanor sat down on the other side of the table next to Syssi. "Do you need me to reinforce Emmett's compulsion?"

Kian nodded. "I don't like sending them home with knowledge of us, but it's a complicated situation, and I can't expect the entire family to leave their lives behind, come to the village, and go for it. So, a double compulsion will allow me to sleep a little better at night."

"Got it." Eleanor nodded at her mate. "Do your thing."

"I need Eric and Cheryl to sit next to Gilbert and Karen."

When they did what he'd asked, Emmett lifted his arms, the wide sleeves of his white gown blocking the family from Kian's view. "Gilbert, Karen, Eric, and Cheryl, look into my eyes and listen to my voice."

390

65

DARLENE

*D*arlene's heart was pounding against her rib cage. It was really happening. Eric was a Dormant, and he was Syssi's distant relative.

They had a future together.

Provided that he wanted it.

Provided that he was a confirmed Dormant.

Provided that he transitioned successfully.

Darlene was terrified for him. Eric was younger than her, but he wasn't the grandson of a god, and transitioning would be risky for him.

Once Emmett and Eleanor were done compelling Kaia's family into keeping what they were about to learn a secret and changing Kaia's compulsion so she could talk with them about it, they left together with the Guardians and their mates to give the family privacy. Anandur and Brundar had probably stayed up in the cottage or right outside its door to guard Kian, but their mates had most likely retired for the night, and so had Eleanor and Emmett.

"I think drinks are in order." Kian rose to his feet and walked over to the bar. "Whiskey, anyone?"

As expected, all the men lifted their hands but none of the women.

"I'll get wine for the ladies." Syssi joined him at the bar and opened a new bottle of wine. "Can I give some to Kaia and Cheryl?" she asked Karen.

"Kaia can have as much as she wants, but Cheryl can have only a tiny bit."

"I don't like wine," Cheryl said. "And before you ask, I don't like whiskey either."

Syssi laughed. "I wasn't going to offer that. Do you prefer a soft drink?"

"Yes, please."

Once everyone had a glass in hand, and they'd all gotten comfortable on the couches and armchairs, Kaia lifted her hand. "Can I be the one who tells my family? I don't know everything yet, but now that I can finally talk about it, I can share with them what I know."

Kian waved a hand. "Go ahead."

Kaia leaned against the table and crossed her arms over her chest. "So here is the scoop. The gods from mythology were not invented by people. They were aliens." She glanced at Kian. "Am I right?"

"It depends on how you define aliens. The gods might have been the first intelligent creatures on Earth, and they created humanity by combining their genetic material with that of an earthly creature, so technically they weren't any more alien than humans, but we know that they came from somewhere else in the universe."

"Good enough." Kaia unfolded her arms and gripped the table. "The gods took human lovers and produced offspring who were immortal but not as powerful as the gods. However, when those immortals took human lovers, the children born to them were human, but the children of the immortal females carried the godly genes in a dormant state and could be turned immortal through a special activation process that I will explain later. But whether a dormant female was activated and turned immortal or not, her children carried the immortal gene, and her daughters passed it on through the maternal line down the generations. What it means is that there could be many humans who carry the immortal gene, and in our specific case, we all do. Bottom line, we can all turn immortal, but the process is not without risk, and it gets riskier the older the Dormant." She turned to Kian. "How did I do so far?"

"Excellent. From now on, it's your job to tell prospective Dormants about our history."

Karen shook his head. "It all sounds fantastical, but you asked us to suspend our disbelief, and I'm trying very hard to do that. I assume that Kian and Syssi and everyone else here that is not part of our family is immortal, correct?"

Kaia nodded.

Darlene wanted to raise her hand and remind him that she was still human, but it wasn't important at the moment, and it would only confuse things.

"Then my question is, how did they find us?"

"Dumb luck." Kaia smiled at William. "Or Fate, as William and his people believe."

"I can take it from here," Syssi said. "Immortals and Dormants feel a special affinity toward each other. So, when William and Kaia fell in love within days, William suspected that Kaia might be a Dormant, and he asked Kian's permission to share his suspicions with her." She smiled at Karen. "Your whirlwind romance with Gilbert is a good example of that. You said that he wasn't your type and that you couldn't understand why you were so drawn to each other, but now you have an explanation. Since you are both Dormants, you felt that special affinity."

Darlene glanced at Eric, and as she caught him looking at her, a silent communication passed between them. Was that special affinity responsible for how strongly they were drawn to each other?

Gilbert shook his head. "Forgive me for bursting the crazy bubble, but it all sounds like a script for a weird science fiction movie, and the affinity explanation sounds like total bullshit. What proof can you show me that you are really immortal?"

"I can take care of that." Kian leaned forward. "I'm glad that the little ones are asleep, or this would have scared them." He shifted his eyes to Cheryl. "I'm going to demonstrate the power immortals have over human minds by creating an illusion.

What you are about to see is not real, but it will appear very real to you. I'm not going to tell you ahead of time what kind of illusion it will be so your stepdad won't say that I hypnotized you all and planted the suggestion in your minds."

"Okay." Cheryl eyed him with skepticism painted over her face. "But if we are all going to see it, why are you telling me about it?"

"I just don't want you to get scared."

She snorted. "I'm not a child." She cast a sidelong glance at Gilbert. "If anyone is going to scream like a little girl, it's this big guy."

He pouted. "I did that to amuse you. The remake of *It* was funnier than it was scary."

"Right." She rolled her eyes before turning to Kian. "Anyway, don't choose Pennywise the clown as your illusion."

"Noted."

66

KAIA

$\mathcal{E}$xcitement thrummed in Kaia's chest as she waited for Kian to do his illusion.

William hadn't shown her any immortal tricks other than his elongating fangs, which in her opinion were a much better proof than an illusion, but perhaps not as entertaining.

The air shimmered, and a moment later, a blue, ten-foot-tall, half-naked Na'vi male appeared in Kian's chair, sitting in the same pose Kian had assumed, with one leg folded over the other and his chin resting on his fist.

Cheryl laughed. "That's what you call scary?"

"I decided to go for something less terrifying," the Na'vi said in Kian's voice.

Karen gaped. "Are you one of those natives from *Avatar*?"

"You see that too?" Eric asked.

She nodded and turned to Gilbert. "Just to make sure that we see the same thing. What is he wearing?"

"A damn loincloth."

"Yup. That's what I see as well."

Kian dropped the illusion. "Do you need more proof that I'm not human?"

"Do you bleed?" Eric asked.

"We do," Kian said. "And to answer your next question, we can be killed. Our bodies are very good at repairing themselves, but no one can regrow a heart or a head."

"What about limbs?" Eric asked.

"We can regrow missing limbs. We have a newly transitioned immortal in our village who had both legs amputated four years ago, and she is regrowing them. But it's a long and difficult process."

"That's amazing," Karen said. "I wish it was possible for humans."

"It might be," Kaia started, but as William shook his head, she remembered that their research was a secret even from most of his clan members.

394

Leaning back in his chair, Gilbert crossed his arms over his chest and grinned at her mother. "I kept telling you that I'm a god. You shouldn't have laughed at me."

Her mother chuckled. "You're not a god. You might be a descendant of aliens, but it's not a sure thing." She looked at Syssi. "Is there a conclusive test for that?"

"Normally, there isn't, but if our doctor can determine that Gilbert and Eric are my relatives, then they are Dormants for sure. For you, though, the only test is attempting transition and hoping it will happen."

Kaia was about to mention the need for a genetic test, but then Gilbert asked, "What's involved in attempting transition?"

Syssi glanced at Cheryl, sighed, and shifted her eyes back to Gilbert. "It's done differently for males than for females, but I need to explain a little more about immortals' physiology. The male immortals have fangs and venom. Their venom glands produce different compositions of venom depending on the trigger. If the trigger is aggression, the venom produced is more potent and can be used to incapacitate an opponent. If the trigger is sexual arousal, the venom produced is less potent, and it is used to provide intense pleasure to their partners. The venom is the catalyst for transition in both male and female Dormants, but since the one triggered by arousal is not as potent as the one triggered by aggression, female Dormants need more than just the venom to induce their transition. They also need to have unprotected sex with an immortal male so his seed is absorbed into their bodies along with the venom from his bite."

"Kinky." Cheryl lifted a brow at Kaia. "Did William induce you already?"

"There is no rush." Kaia wanted to strangle her sister for asking her that in front of everyone. "I'm young and healthy, so I can take my time deciding when and if I want to do it."

"So age is a factor?" her mother asked.

"It is." Syssi took the half-empty wine bottle, got up, and refilled Karen's glass. "The older the Dormant, the more dangerous the transition gets. Kaia has nothing to worry about, and Cheryl has plenty of time until it will become relevant for her, but the three of you don't have that luxury." She sat back down. "I was twenty-five when I went through my transition, and I almost didn't make it. My brother was forty, and he had a difficult transition as well."

"We haven't lost a Dormant yet," Kian said. "So, you shouldn't worry too much about that."

"How old was the oldest Dormant to transition?" Eric asked.

"I think Ronja was fifty-seven." Kian looked at Syssi. "Am I right?"

"I think so."

"Then we should be fine," Gilbert said. "I'm the oldest here, and I'm only forty-eight."

Kaia found it odd that Kian seemed much less concerned with the risks than Syssi. Maybe the reason was that he wasn't as caring as his wife, and he thought nothing of one of them dying.

Or he might know something that Syssi didn't.

"So let me get it straight," Eric said. "To transition, a male Dormant has to be bitten by an immortal male?"

Kian nodded. "Correct. A male Dormant needs to challenge an immortal male to a fight and spur his aggression."

"Does it matter if he wins the fight or not?" Eric asked.

Kian unfolded his arms and leaned forward. "It doesn't, but he needs to offer enough of a challenge to spur the immortal's aggression. If the Dormant is weak or scared, that might be a problem."

Gilbert puffed out his chest. "That won't be a problem for my brother and me."

Eric cast him a smile before returning his gaze to Syssi. "A female Dormant just needs to seduce an immortal male and not use birth control, right?"

"She can be on the pill, but no physical barriers." Syssi pushed a strand of hair behind her ear. "It also helps if a bond forms between her and the male, but it wasn't necessary for some of the female Dormants who were closer to the source than me, meaning that there were fewer degrees of separation between them and their godly ancestor."

67

WILLIAM

*K*aren looked at Kaia. "What's stopping you from attempting it?"

William's jaw dropped. Was Karen encouraging her daughter to go for the transition?

He hadn't expected that.

Kaia laughed. "A few hours ago, you both wanted to take me back home because you thought I was crazy for getting engaged to William after knowing him for such a short time, and now you are asking why I haven't let him induce me yet?"

"We now know much more than we knew a few hours ago." Karen reached for Gilbert's hand. "We could be with each other forever."

He shook his head. "Didn't you listen to Syssi's warnings? Risky means that we might not make it through. We have three little kids. We can't take risks with our lives."

The excited gleam in Karen's eyes dimmed. "You are right." She turned to Syssi. "Since I'd rather not have sex with a stranger, Gilbert will have to transition first, correct?"

Syssi nodded. "The thing is that it will take about six months for him to grow fangs and functional venom glands, and that will mean you will be six months older by then. The sooner you do it, the better, but unless you two have an open relationship, that's the only way it can work for you."

"We do not have an open relationship." Gilbert pulled Karen's hand into his lap. "And I want to go first. If anything happens to me, our children would at least have their mother."

"Don't talk like that." Tears formed in Karen's eyes. "I can't bear the thought of losing you. If I could, I would go first."

"And leave me alone? No way."

"It can still happen even if you go first. I might die when I attempt it six months later."

Kaia lifted her hands. "Both of you stop. We all might not be Dormants at all. I will go first, and if I don't transition then you don't need to attempt it at all. But Gilbert and Eric can go for it regardless of whether I transition or not."

"I'll do it," Eric said. "I'm the only one here with nothing to lose."

"What about me?" Cheryl asked.

"You can't do it." Kaia gave her sister an amused look. "You need to wait until you're eighteen."

"No, I don't. I can have sex now if I want to. I'm the youngest, so it's the safest for me to transition."

Gilbert groaned. "Do you want to kill me before I get the chance to become immortal? You are not having sex until you're twenty-one."

"Right." Cheryl rolled her eyes. "Are there any cute boys my age in your clan?"

Syssi smiled at her. "We have one boy who is a little younger than you, but he's taken."

"Oh, well." Cheryl shrugged. "Then I guess I'm not transitioning anytime soon."

"By the way," Karen turned to William. "How old are you? I assume that you are not thirty-two."

He swallowed. "I'm much older than that."

For now, Gilbert and Karen were still stunned by all that they'd been told, so the number might not evoke an immediate shock, but once they'd processed everything, they would restart their campaign against his and Kaia's relationship. Perhaps he should start with a preamble? Like the age difference between Syssi and Kian?

"By how much?" Gilbert asked.

"Three centuries. But you need to understand that age is meaningless to immortals. Kian is two thousand years old, and Syssi is only twenty-nine, and they are truelove mates."

Eric whistled, and Karen gaped at Kian. "That's incredible. You've seen and experienced so much. What could you possibly have in common with such a young woman?"

"Love," Kian said simply. "I'd never experienced bonding my soul to another. Syssi is what was missing from a very long life that was all about duty to my clan. I'd never been truly happy until she came into my life, and then Allegra was born and made us both even happier."

Karen shifted her gaze to Syssi. "What about you? Did it bother you that your husband was ancient?"

Grinning, Syssi waved a hand at Kian. "Just look at him. I'm married to a demigod who worships me as if I were a goddess."

Kian confirmed with a nod. "And who enjoys every moment of his worshipful devotion."

Karen didn't look convinced, and apparently she'd thought that Syssi had called Kian a demigod because of his looks and not because he was the son of a goddess. If she'd made the connection, William was sure her response wouldn't have been a frown.

"What about chauvinistic attitudes?" Karen asked Syssi without even looking at Kian. "He's lived most of his life in times when women were devalued and oppressed."

A soft growl left Kian's throat. "Not in our clan. My mother is the head of our people, and the females of our clan have always been held in the highest regard. In fact, we value females more than we value males because they are the key to the clan's continuation."

"It's true," Syssi confirmed. "But that also translates into overprotectiveness, which could be perceived as discrimination. There is only one female Guardian, and Kian doesn't allow her to go on missions he deems too dangerous for her."

He crossed his arms over his chest. "I won't let Kri fall into the hands of Doomers, and if that makes me a chauvinist, I can live with it."

"Who or what are Doomers?" Gilbert asked.

"That's a story for another time," Kian said. "We need to focus on the topics at hand, which are your family's potential transition into immortality and William's relationship with Kaia. You need to stop making an issue out of the age difference between them. If you think about it for a moment, you will realize that on the inside, you are the same as you were at twenty. If you still looked twenty, you would feel that age as well."

"I have more life experience now than I had at twenty," Gilbert said. "And I see the world through the prism of my experiences. I can only imagine what that prism would look like in three hundred years, but I'm convinced that it would be very different from the prism of someone born into that future."

William shook his head. "I'm the same now as I was at twenty-five. Since we can't form long-lasting relationships with humans, and Dormants are rare, I've spent all of my adulthood alone and unchanging. Having Kaia in my life has opened a new chapter for me, and being in a loving relationship is as new for me as it is for her. In some ways, Kaia is more mature than I am because she has witnessed your loving relationship. I grew up without a father figure in my life, and I didn't have the privilege of watching my mother interact with a loving partner either."

"I love you," Kaia whispered. "Now and forever more."

"I love you too. Forever and beyond."

Karen sighed. "That's sweet, but I can't wrap my head around you being over three centuries old." She pushed to her feet and pulled Gilbert up. "I'm tired and overwhelmed, and I need to go to sleep. Maybe things will become clearer by morning."

"You shouldn't take too long deciding." Kian got up and offered Karen his hand. "The clock is ticking."

"I know." Kaia's mother shook his offered hand. "Is there a specific deadline by which we need to decide?"

"No, but the longer you wait, the riskier transitioning will be for you."

68

KAIA

*K*aia got to her feet and wrapped her arm around her mother's shoulders. "We will discuss it tomorrow." She smiled at Kian. "We are still human, and unlike you, we need our eight hours of sleep to think clearly."

Needing less sleep was one of the things Kaia was looking forward to. So much more could be achieved with only four-hour nights.

"Words of wisdom." Her mother kissed her cheek.

"Do you need my help to get the boys back to the lodge?"

"Just help us get up the stairs, and we will be fine from there. Once we are outside the cottage, I'll put them in the stroller."

"We can help you." Eric got to his feet and walked over to them. "I'll carry Idina."

"I have a question." Darlene looked at Kian. "Can Eric sleep in my bungalow tonight? We need to talk things through as well."

"I don't see why not. I'll call the security office and ask them to make a key for him. You can pick it up on the way."

"Thank you."

"Thank you for everything," Eric said. "Even if we turn out not to be Dormants, it will be fun to entertain the idea of living forever, at least for a little while."

Kian grimaced. "Don't thank me yet. If you are not Dormants, we will have to erase from your memories everything you've learned about us and gods and immortals."

Eric shrugged. "Well, it's up to fate, right?"

"Absolutely." Syssi threaded her arm through Kian's. "The Fates wouldn't have orchestrated this encounter for nothing. I'm positive that you are all Dormants, and you will come to live with us in our village."

"Which is not on Mount Olympus," Kaia added.

"That's also something to talk about tomorrow." Eric offered Kian his hand. "I need to help Karen and Gilbert with the kids."

CHAPTER 68

When her family and Darlene had said their goodbyes and walked out the door, Kaia returned to thank Syssi and Kian once again.

"I truly appreciate the warm welcome you have given my family." She offered Syssi her hand and got pulled into her arms.

"We are always happy to discover new Dormants who can join our clan, but in this case, I'm overjoyed to have found more relatives. Maybe having you in the village will convince my parents to finally retire and come live with us as well."

"Where are they now?" Kaia asked.

"In Africa. My mother is a pediatrician, and she volunteers in a clinic, while my father enjoys his hobby of photography in his retirement."

"Are they immortal?"

Syssi shook her head. "Regrettably, it was too late for my mother to transition, and my father is not a Dormant."

"How do you know? We would have never known about Gilbert and Eric if not for the story about your great-grandmothers. If Dormants feel a special affinity for each other, then your father might be a Dormant as well."

A pained look crossed Syssi's eyes. "It's irrelevant. He's too old to transition anyway."

She looked so sad that Kaia's heart ached for her. "Perhaps William and I will find the secret to immortality in Okidu's journals. William believes that the gods used genetic engineering to prevent their bodies from aging, and since the biological parts of the Odus' bodies can do the same, it makes sense that the journals contain that information."

The smile returned to Syssi's pretty face. "That would be wonderful." She sighed. "I hope. I wish we knew more about the world of the gods. We could learn from them how to manage a planet of immortals and avoid the pitfalls that a transformation like that will no doubt create." She chuckled. "I'm a seer, and I can't foresee a future like that."

"William told me that most of your visions are about catastrophes, so I'm glad that you can't see a future in which all of humanity is immortal. It means that it's a good possible future."

Syssi cast William a mock glare. "My visions are not all about catastrophic events. I also helped find a couple who were stranded in the desert."

Kian wrapped a protective arm around Syssi's waist. "We don't need to solve the puzzle of an immortal society to take care of your parents. If we find the secret to immortality, your parents will be the first we will offer it to, and knowing your mother, she will not shy away from being the first volunteer."

Syssi winced. "I don't know how it would help her. She already has the immortal genes. The problem is that her body is too old to survive the transition."

"Then I hope the journals contain a solution for that as well." He kissed the top of Syssi's head.

Once again, Kaia noticed that Kian looked less concerned about the safety of transitioning Dormants than his wife.

She was convinced that he knew something Syssi didn't.

If he were emotionally numb or uncaring, he wouldn't be as loving toward Syssi and Allegra.

Then again, he'd said that before meeting his wife, his life had been all about duty, so he might care only about her and his daughter.

Still, Kaia was willing to bet that Kian had information he wasn't sharing, but the question was why? According to what William had told her about him, the guy wasn't selfish, and he'd always placed the good of his clan ahead of his own. Therefore, if he was hiding something, even from his wife, it was to protect something or someone.

69

ERIC

*E*ric followed Darlene to the security office without paying much attention to where they were going and then stood outside while she got the key for him.

His head was spinning with all he'd learned earlier and all the questions he still needed to be answered. Other than not aging or getting sick, casting illusions, and manipulating minds, what else was different about immortals?

He'd spent many hours with Darlene, had sex with her, and she'd felt completely human to him. She also didn't look as young as the others. Even the two-thousand-year-old leader looked to be in his mid-thirties at most.

The only one who looked older was the butler.

Was there an underclass of immortals who aged faster than the others, like in the vampire stories?

Was Darlene one of them?

The butler had acted very subserviently, constantly bowing and calling everyone master and mistress, but Darlene hadn't. Maybe as a female, she enjoyed a higher status?

Kian had said that they valued females more than males, so maybe it was true for the underclass of immortals as well. The males were servants, and the females were treated as equals.

"Are you okay?" Darlene asked. "You were fine back at the bunker, but now you seem to be walking in a daze. What's up?"

"What kind of an immortal are you?"

"I'm not an immortal yet. I'm a Dormant like you."

He let out a relieved breath but then wondered why she hadn't transitioned yet, and the possible answers his imagination supplied were all bad. "What's keeping you from doing it? Are you afraid to attempt it because of your age?"

She shook her head. "I'm quite new to all of this as well, and I decided to take my time. I wanted to finalize my divorce before hooking up with an immortal, and after that, I couldn't find anyone I really wanted to be with." She averted her gaze. "I wasn't willing to compromise or be someone else's compromise either. Never again."

He put his arm around her shoulders and drew her to him. "You are a prize, not a compromise. And that's not empty flattery. I'm drawn to you more than I've ever been drawn to anyone, and that includes my ex, who I thought was the love of my life when I married her."

"Thank you." She smiled up at him. "When you showed up with Karen and Gilbert, so full of charm and confidence, I wanted you like I've never wanted a man before. Now I know that it wasn't just your easygoing flirting and boyish charms. It was the affinity between Dormants."

"It's more than that."

"Yeah." She leaned her head on his arm. "It is."

They were walking at a snail's pace, but Eric wasn't in a rush to get to Darlene's bungalow. "I know that you are only thirty-five, but didn't Kian give you his speech about the ticking clock?"

She laughed. "I'm forty-nine, but my case is different."

So, his suspicions had been right, and there were different kinds of immortals.

"In what way?"

"I'm very close to the source, which means that my transition will probably be pretty effortless despite my age." She cast him an amused glance. "The force is strong with me."

If he wasn't still reeling from all he'd learned, Eric would have found another Star Wars quote to answer with, but his mind was still spinning too fast for him to respond to the reference. "What do you mean by closer to the source? Are the gods from mythology still living among us, and are you a recent descendant of one of them?"

Darlene smiled. "Most of the gods are gone, but you are right about me being a recent descendant of theirs. My grandfather is a god."

Eric stopped walking and turned to her. "For real? My girlfriend is a demigoddess?"

He'd thought she belonged to an underclass of immortals when the opposite was true.

He got himself a royal princess.

Or was it a divine princess?

Darlene didn't laugh. "Am I your girlfriend, Eric?"

"Of course." Stifling a chuckle, he took her hand and put it over his chest. "I didn't ask you officially, but I thought that we were going steady."

A smile bloomed on her face. "We are." She lifted on her toes and kissed his lips, but when he wanted to deepen the kiss, she pushed on his chest. "I want to make one thing clear, though. I'm not a demigoddess. That title belongs to my mother."

"There should be a special title for a granddaughter too—a demi-demigoddess, and I want to be known as a demi-demigoddess's boyfriend. It makes me feel important."

That finally got a laugh out of her.

"Fine. I'll petition the board of titles to add a demi-demigod."

He bowed his head. "Thank you. This oversight needs to be addressed."

"Seriously, though." Her smile turned into a frown. "Since I'm the granddaughter of a god, I'm less fearful about my transition, and I have the luxury of taking my time to some extent. You are younger than me by a good number of years, but given that you are Syssi's relative and her transition was difficult at twenty-five, you should do it as soon as possible. It's not a big deal for males. There is an initiation ceremony. You get into a wrestling ring with an immortal and try to offer him a challenge for a minute or two. Once he gets aggressive enough for his fangs to elongate and his venom glands to fill up, he will take you down and bite you."

Did she think so little of him?

He might not be a professional wrestler, but he could hold his own in the ring.

"Unless the immortal gets into my head and overpowers me that way, it will take him much longer to subdue me. If the fight is fair, I might be the one who will overpower him." Still holding on to Darlene's hand, Eric resumed walking.

70

DARLENE

*D*arlene loved how cocky Eric was, but she knew he was wrong. "Immortal males are much stronger than humans. Even William could overpower you with ease, and the guy is the typical computer nerd who hates exercising."

Eric's expression turned worried. "Could he hurt Kaia? If he's so strong, he might do so without meaning to."

"I don't think that's a problem. These immortal males have been hooking up with human females for centuries. They know that they need to be careful."

"How would you know? You said that you've never been with one."

"I haven't, but my half-sister was still human when she fell in love with an immortal, and she said that he was the best lover she'd ever had, and she's had quite a few."

"Oh, yeah?" He lifted a brow. "Your sister was a player?"

"Define player." Darlene pressed her keycard to the lock on the gate and waved at the camera.

"Someone who never stays long with one partner and is always chasing the next one."

The gate opened without Eric needing to press his card to the reader as well.

She smirked. "Like you?"

"Yeah. Like me," he admitted. "But those days are behind me."

"Because of me?"

He nodded.

Darlene's heart did a happy flip, but she reminded herself that Eric was still stunned by all he'd learned and that it was much too early for him to make promises he might later regret. The truth was that she was excited about a possible future with him, but she'd been hurt before and needed to proceed with caution.

"Cassandra is not a player," she said. "And she never was. She works too hard to have time to chase anyone, and she's so beautiful that I doubt she ever had to lift a finger to attract a guy."

CHAPTER 70

"What does she do?"

"She's the creative director of Fifty Shades of Beauty. It's a cosmetics company that caters to a wide range of skin tones." Darlene opened the door to her bungalow.

Eric grinned. "I know who your sister is. I've seen her picture in one of the gossip magazines, and she is one hell of a looker." He followed her inside. "She looks a little bitchy, though." He waved a hand over his face. "She has resting bitch face."

Darlene laughed. "Cassandra has a temper, and she's assertive, but she's a good person. When a woman looks like that, she needs to fend off a lot of unwanted attention, and the resting bitch face comes with the territory."

"You are a beautiful woman as well, but you are not haughty, and you don't look down your nose at people. You have a kind expression with a little flirtatious-ness mixed in." He cupped her cheek. "You have smiling eyes."

Darlene swallowed. Eric had sex on his mind, and she did too, but they needed to talk. She hadn't allowed herself to fall for him before, but now that her armor had been penetrated by the sword of hope, the flood of emotions pouring in and out was overwhelming, and she saw a future with Eric that she hadn't before.

Would he still talk about long-term when she did so as well? Or would he back away and laugh off his previous declarations of intent?

She pushed on his chest. "Do you want coffee?"

"You know what I want."

She rolled her eyes. "We need to talk. We can do that over wine or coffee. Those are your options."

He shook his head in mock dismay. "You are a tough negotiator. I'll take coffee, black." He smiled. "Because manly men don't put sugar or cream in their coffee."

She chuckled. "You are manly enough for me regardless of your choice of beverage. Do you want sugar and cream or not?"

"Yes, please." He sat on her couch, picked up one of her fashion magazines, and then put it down.

"I don't think you should wait any longer to transition, even if you are the granddaughter of a god. The longer you wait, the riskier it will get regardless of how close you are to the source."

Was that his way of backing out? The classic I'm-not-good-for-you excuse?

Darlene put the pod into the coffeemaker and pressed the button. "You should go first, and when your fangs and venom glands are functional, you can induce my transition."

"That will take too long." He sighed. "I don't think Karen should wait for Gilbert to transition either, but there is no way either of them would even consider her having sex with another male, even if it's for health reasons."

Darlene put the mugs on a tray, added the creamer and a container of sugar, and brought it to the table.

"Would you consider that for me?" she asked.

"I wouldn't be happy about it, but I wouldn't stand in your way or give you grief about it. I don't want to be responsible for holding you back, especially since it could make the difference between surviving it or not."

Darlene's heart sank.

His answer sounded so reasonable, but this was not how a Dormant or an immortal male would have reacted. They were extremely possessive, and they couldn't fathom their mate being with anyone else even if her life depended on it, which meant that Eric wasn't her truelove mate, and she wasn't his.

But perhaps she was wrong?

What would Kian have done if he were in Eric's shoes?

Would he have gambled with Syssi's life and had her wait for him to transition first?

Darlene didn't think so.

Kian adored Syssi, and if sex with another male had been the only thing that could save her life, he wouldn't have stopped her from doing it. He might have asked one of his friends to put him in stasis so he wouldn't be awake for it, but he would never have done anything to risk her life.

Sitting down on the couch next to Eric, Darlene fixed her coffee the way she liked it. "So, are you going to do it?" She lifted the mug to her lips and took a sip.

He nodded. "I have to. I'm the younger, single brother, and I'm expendable. Gilbert has a family."

"Don't talk like that. You are precious to me and to your brother and his children. They need you."

"What about you? Do you need me?"

"I just said that you are precious to me."

"It's not the same as needing me."

"I need you." She closed her eyes briefly and then leveled them at his. "I want to be honest with you. Before I knew you might be a Dormant, I planned on having a short fling with you and using you as a stepping stone in my journey of sexual experimentation." She smiled. "The immortal men everyone kept introducing me to were all too handsome and looked too young. I couldn't see myself getting naked with men who looked my son's age and were perfectly put together."

He frowned. "So, I was the imperfect specimen that was less intimidating?"

"Yes," she admitted. "But it was much more than that. I was immediately drawn to you. Heck, I haven't flirted with anyone with such enthusiasm since I was a college girl. I kept thinking that it was a shame that you were not an immortal, but then I told myself that you were a player and that you were not long-term material anyway."

Eric reached for her hand. "I hope I made you realize how beautiful and desirable you are."

"You did, and I want to see where this thing between us goes. I don't want to take some random immortal into my bed. I prefer you."

A mischievous smirk lifting one corner of his mouth, he leaned toward her. "What if I'm in bed with you and the immortal?"

As the image he painted with his words appeared in her mind, Darlene's cheeks caught fire. "You can't be serious. Are you suggesting a threesome?"

"What if I am? Are you feeling adventurous, Darlene?"

71

KAIA

$\mathcal{T}$he decision to attempt transition as soon as possible solidified in Kaia's mind as she stood under the hot spray in the shower.

She needed to get induced first, and she needed to do it fast. If she failed to transition, her mother wouldn't need to rush into anything, and Gilbert could take his time as well. And if she transitioned, her siblings would have someone to take care of them if the unthinkable happened and her mother or Gilbert didn't make it.

The stress of it was making her heart race and her hands shake as she lathered up the soap. She'd already lost one parent, and she wouldn't survive losing another.

Immortality would be a curse if she needed to live with the pain for eternity.

Would it have been better if William had never found her, and they'd all lived out their lives as humans?

It would surely have been less stressful. In a way, it was easier when no choice needed to be made. Perhaps she should talk it over with her family tomorrow and suggest that they all forget about it. William or some other immortal could thrall the memories away, and they could keep on living in blissful ignorance.

But that was a coward's way out, and as much as she feared for the lives of the people she loved, she couldn't ask them to choose a route she wouldn't choose for herself.

If she were twenty years older, would she have still decided to go through with it?

Probably.

What about thirty years older, when it became really dangerous like it was for Gilbert and her mother? Most likely, she would have decided to chance it then as well.

Kaia had much less trouble with risking her own life than watching the people she loved risk theirs.

Then again, she had proof that the soul continued on and that death wasn't the final step in the journey, so dying wasn't as terrifying to her. Most people didn't have the luxury of remembering their past lives, though, so even though their souls would live on, the person they were before would no longer exist, and that was scary.

Besides, what did it matter if the soul continued in a different body when all the people she loved would be lost to her anyway?

Bottom line, dying was frightening even for people like her who knew it wasn't the end.

Gah, her mind was running in circles.

She'd made her decision to go ahead and attempt transition, and she had to stick with it.

When she got out of the bathroom, William was waiting for her in bed with a fresh cup of tea and a worried expression on his face. "You were in there for nearly an hour. Are you okay?"

"Yeah, I am." She climbed into bed, picked up the cup, and took a long sip. "Thank you for the tea. It's perfect."

"It's lukewarm by now."

"That's precisely how I like it." She leaned against the stack of pillows William had arranged for her. "I made up my mind. I'm going for the transition right away. We can start working on it tonight."

William's eyes widened. "We can't."

"Why not?"

"We need to finish the research first."

"Why? You said that it'll be easy for me. I'll take a break for a few days and then go back to work as an immortal."

"It's not that simple." He put his teacup on the nightstand and turned to her. "You need to be under medical supervision when you transition, and we don't have the clinic set up here yet. If the equipment were here, I would ask one of our doctors to fly over, but without it, they wouldn't be able to do much for you."

"Why do I need medical supervision? You said that it would be as easy as having a cold or flu."

"It will most likely be like that, but on the remote chance that it isn't, and things go south, I want you to have the best medical help possible, and that's Doctor Bridget back in the village. I suggest that we finish the research first, then move into the village, and only then start your induction."

Kaia let out a long breath. "You are not thinking it all the way through, William. Even if the clock wasn't ticking for my mother and Gilbert, there is still the issue of my future after the research is done. If it turns out that I'm not a Dormant, and you erase my memories of you and everything I've learned about immortals, I can go back to my old life and take the job at Stanford, but if I wait too long, that job will be gone. I don't want to miss the deadline for that. Opportunities like that don't come often."

"You are right." He sighed. "It's just that I don't even consider it a possibility that you are not a Dormant."

As William wrapped his arm around her shoulders, Kaia put her head on his chest. "I know, but even though I love your optimism, I need to plan my moves while taking both options into consideration, and I need to find out as soon as possible whether my life is taking a serious detour or staying on course. I also need to know what is expected of me once I transition. What am I going to do? Can I still work in research? Do I have to move in with you into the village? What if I don't like it there?"

"Whoa." William chuckled. "One question at a time, please. I'm sure that you are going to love it in the village because everyone does. None of the transitioned Dormants have complained about living there. And as for what you are going to do, that's obvious. We will continue deciphering the rest of the journals, and then you and I will build an Odu prototype together."

WILLIAM

*G*iven how brightly Kaia smiled, that had been the right thing to say.

Kaia's eyes shone with excitement. "I would absolutely freaking love to build an Odu with you. Now I really want to transition."

William laughed. "Immortality is not exciting enough?"

"You know what I mean." She slapped his forearm playfully. "I want to be immortal, and I want us to be truelove mates forever, but I'm a little scared of transitioning, and I'm very scared of my mom or stepdad not making it through. Changing my career trajectory is not an easy pill to swallow either, and I need a spoonful of honey to make the medicine go down. The prospect of building an Odu with you after we decipher the blueprints is just that spoonful."

"I'm glad that I came up with that."

Kaia narrowed her eyes at him. "So, it was just something you said to make me feel excited about the future? You didn't plan on building an Odu before?"

"I did, and I hope we will not only decipher the instructions but also figure out how to avoid the pitfalls. We need the Odus to be intelligent enough to communicate and learn simple tasks, but we don't want them to be able to learn too fast or too much, or they will become dangerous. I also don't want to make them indestructible. I'm sure that their indestructibility played a big part in the banning of the technology to make them. You and I will have to think long and hard about all those issues and how to solve them."

"We should form a committee of experts. Do you have anyone on staff who is versed in ethics?"

"I don't, but you are right about us needing an ethicist on the team." He leaned over and kissed her temple. "To be frank, I don't think I would have had the guts to tackle such an undertaking without you. Having you working on it with me makes me feel more confident about achieving those objectives. You just came up with an idea to form a committee that wouldn't have occurred to me, and you will probably come up with more things that I failed to address. Combining our brain power and checking each other will be greatly beneficial to the future of this and other research."

Kaia let out a breath. "Your confidence in me is flattering, but I would have never dared to work on a monumental invention like that without you either. Any mistake we make could have dire consequences, which is why we need more capable people on our team who are from different disciplines." She pushed up on the pillows and tugged the blanket up to her chin. "I don't think that we should make the new Odus look as human as the old ones. In fact, we can't. We don't have the ability to make organs and skin yet. Besides, the more robotic they look, the less intimidating they will seem."

"So no sexy mannequins?"

She eyed him from under lowered lashes. "Male or female?"

William worked hard to stifle a smile. "Both. We could make a sexy French maid female model and a hunky Australian male. We will make a fortune."

"Why Australian?"

He shrugged. "I overheard Darlene talk with some of the other clan ladies about hunky Australian actors. I thought it was a thing."

"Thunder from Down Under," Kaia said. "It's a male stripper show in Vegas, and the guys are supposedly from Australia. I thought that you got the idea from there."

Imagining Kaia drooling over some half-naked muscular guys, William felt a wave of jealousy rise up in his chest.

"I haven't been to Vegas in decades, and I've never heard of a male stripper show. Have you seen it?"

"I've seen ads for it," Kaia said. "But I wouldn't go to a show like that even if I could."

"Why not?"

Smiling, she snaked a hand under his T-shirt and caressed his chest. "Watching can be fun, but I prefer touching."

William lifted a finger. "Hold that thought." He picked up his phone from the nightstand. "I need to text Kian and let him know that you want to transition as soon as possible."

Kaia groaned. "Now? He's probably asleep already."

"He's not. It's not even midnight yet."

"Still, can't it wait for tomorrow?" She circled her finger around his nipple, eliciting a pained groan from his throat.

He wanted nothing more than to let Kaia keep playing, but this couldn't wait.

"Your family is leaving in the afternoon, and so is Kian." He pulled her hand from under his shirt and kissed her knuckles. "If you want to transition right away, I need to stop the project, send the rest of the team on vacation, and take you to the village. Your family needs to know where you're going and why, and Kian needs to approve it."

"Gah." She flopped onto her back. "Why does everything have to be so complicated?"

He chuckled. "You and I are the definition of complicated, but that's what makes us special."

"True." She waved a hand. "Call your boss."

"I'll text him and ask him to call me back. I don't want to wake Allegra up or interrupt Kian and Syssi's fun time." William typed while he talked. "We need him to approve your plan, and aggravating him right before asking him to do it wouldn't be wise. The guy is grumpy on a good day."

73

KAIA

*W*illiam's phone rang a moment after he'd sent the text.

"What's the emergency?" Kian barked into the phone.

Kaia doubted that he'd even read the text. There hadn't been enough time.

"Everything is okay. Kaia is here with me, and I'm activating the speaker so she can hear you."

"Hello, Kaia. How are you doing?"

"I'm great. I want to transition as soon as possible."

"I'm glad. Why the urgent message to call you back, though?"

Kian didn't think it was a problem, so why did William?

William shook his head. "It's not that simple. The clinic is not ready, and I don't want Kaia to start transitioning without medical supervision. I would have to stop the project and take her to the village, and I need your approval to do that."

"That's indeed a problem," Kian said. "What's the rush? Why can't you wait until the project is done?"

"I can't," Kaia said. "My mother will want to wait for Gilbert to transition first and induce her when his fangs and venom glands are operational. But if she's not a Dormant and can't turn immortal, he might not want to risk transitioning at his age. But if I transition, he might hurry up, or maybe they would consider using the services of an immortal male. I don't think they would, but they might. My sisters and brothers pose another issue. If my mother and Gilbert know that I will be there for my siblings in case they don't make it, it will make their decision to try it easier."

"I see." Kian sighed. "What are you going to do about the other team members? You can't leave them to work alone."

"I will have to send them on vacation," William said. "Kaia is so young that she probably won't need more than a week or two to recuperate from the transition."

"It can also take up to two weeks for the transition to start," Kian said. "So, the break could stretch into a month, and I don't like that."

William looked at Kaia. "Can we finish it on our own? Or do you need them?"

"We can do it by ourselves, but it will take a little longer, though not by much. Their help is marginal."

"You heard the lady," William said. "I can dismiss the team, and we can continue working on the project in the village."

Kian groaned. "That was one hell of an expensive setup for one week's worth of work."

"I know." William didn't look apologetic at all. "But the setup is not just for this one project. You wanted a scaled-down duplicate of the lab in the village, so we will have an emergency location in case the village is compromised. I would have never invested so much effort and resources into building it for one project that I knew wouldn't take more than a few months. Besides, we didn't know how good Kaia really was. I expected her to be the shining star of the team, but she exceeded all of my expectations."

Kian chuckled. "In more ways than one. Syssi says that we should all meet tomorrow morning and decide on a course of action together with Kaia's family."

"That's a very good idea," William said. "When and where?"

"Here, at ten in the morning. Syssi will arrange for brunch to be delivered."

"I'll let my mother know." Kaia looked at her watch. "I'll text her."

"Goodnight," Kian said. "Don't start anything yet."

William's cheeks reddened. "We won't."

When Kian ended the call, Kaia smirked. "Are you sure about that? We can throw away the condoms and have fun tonight."

"Not yet." He put his phone down on the nightstand. "I'd rather play it safe. We'll wait until we are in the village."

He was such a nerd, but he was her nerd, and she loved him just the way he was.

"Fine. Have it your way." She threw the blanket off and got out of bed.

"Where are you going?"

"I left the purse with my phone in the living room. It's probably dead because I forgot to hook it up to the charger."

"I'll get you a clan phone when we get to the village. They keep a charge twice as long."

"Oh, yeah? How did you manage that?"

He smirked. "I can tell you after you text your mother, but I'd rather do other things."

She lifted a finger. "Hold that thought. I'll be right back."

WILLIAM

"*W*ish me luck." Kaia stopped in front of the lodge.

William squeezed her hand in encouragement. "Good luck. Just remember to speak quietly and remind your family to do the same. The lodge is filling up with guests for the next retreat, and someone might overhear you."

"I'm going to talk to them in my mother and Gilbert's room. It's sandwiched between my sisters' and Eric's room, so there will be no ears on the walls."

"Good, but people passing through the corridor could hear you through the door if you don't keep your voices down, and that's especially true for Gilbert."

She smiled. "Yeah. He likes to dominate the conversation, but I'll remind him to keep it down."

He leaned and kissed her cheek. "I'll see you at the bunker in half an hour."

She gave him a smile. "I love you."

"I love you too." He stole a quick kiss before opening the door for her.

When he got to the cottage, he found Anandur sitting outside on a bench that hadn't been there the day before.

"Good morning." He offered the Guardian his hand. "Is this your new post?"

"I'm waiting for Wonder to get ready. We are going to have breakfast at the lodge and then go for a walk on the beach." He stretched his long legs in front of him and patted the bench. "How do you like my new addition?"

"It's a great idea. It gets stuffy down there."

"I know, right? The air-conditioned air is drying out my skin. I need fresh air and some sun on my face."

William could never tell when Anandur was joking and when he was serious, so he chose to smile noncommittally. "Is Brundar staying to guard Kian?"

"He and Callie are coming with us. Your buddy Max is sending two guys to replace us."

Poor Max. William had encouraged him to pursue Darlene, and the guy had done so with notable enthusiasm, but now that Eric had the potential of turning immortal, Darlene was probably going to stay with him.

"Enjoy your day." William opened the door and walked inside.

When he pressed the intercom button, the door opened right away, and he took the stairs down to the bunker.

"Good morning, boss." Darlene rose to her feet, walked over to him, and gave him a hug.

She was the only one in the living room, so the others must be still getting ready.

"You look happy." He leaned to hug her back.

"I am happy. Eric decided to go for the transition as soon as possible, and Kian told me that Kaia decided to do the same."

"She did. I guess Eric's reasoning is the same as Kaia's. They are both doing it for Karen and Gilbert."

"Good morning, William." Syssi walked into the room with Allegra in her arms. "Kian is on the phone with Shai. He will be here in a moment."

William hoped so. They didn't have much time before Kaia arrived, and he needed to run by Kian the plan he'd come up with during the night.

As Syssi put Allegra on a baby mat on the floor, the girl smiled at the toys hanging from the baby gym and started babbling at them.

"Would you like some coffee while we wait?" Syssi asked.

"Thank you. I would love some."

"Did you hear that, Okidu?" she asked before sitting down on the couch next to Darlene.

"I did, mistress," Okidu answered from the kitchen. "I shall serve freshly brewed coffee momentarily."

"Thank you," Syssi called back.

Darlene sighed. "I wish I had an Odu. Heck, I wish every household in the village had one."

"Your wish might come true one day," William said. "With the speed science is progressing, today's science fiction may very well be tomorrow's reality."

She grinned. "If everything goes well and I transition, I will still be around when that happens."

He couldn't tell her that it might happen much sooner than that.

Darlene had a general idea of what they were working on, but she didn't know it was connected to the Odus. All he'd told her and the others at the lab was that he needed to decipher some of the gods' writings that had genetic components to them he didn't understand. They assumed that it was information contained in Ekin's tablet, which was the source of all their advanced knowledge.

The truth was that there were still sections of the information contained on the tablet that he hadn't decoded, but he understood enough of it to know that they had to do with alien technology and not biology.

Some of the difficulty was the language barrier, and some of it was Ekin's style of writing things down in a code that had been known only to him. William suspected that he hadn't done it to obscure his writings but as a form of shorthand.

He'd been working on that tablet for many decades, and he hadn't decoded even half of it. If he could dedicate all of his time to the tablet, he would probably progress at a much faster pace. But the reality was that he barely had time to keep up with the demands placed on him at the lab, let alone dedicate hours to decoding the rest of the information contained on that ancient device.

Perhaps once they were done with Okidu's journals, Kaia could help him with that as well. It wasn't her exact field of expertise, but as a bioinformatician she was trained in managing data, developing algorithms, and classifying components of biological systems, like DNA sequences and documenting protein expression. She was well-versed in programming statistical models and interpreting data sets, which made her even more qualified for the job than he was.

KIAN

The smell of freshly brewed coffee lured Kian out of the bedroom he used as his temporary office.

"Do you need me for anything else?" he asked his assistant as he walked toward the living room with the phone pressed to his ear.

"No, that's it."

"Thanks for coming in on a Sunday, Shai. I appreciate your dedication."

"No problem, boss. I'm glad I checked your emails. Otherwise, we wouldn't have found out about it until Monday, and a whole day of production would have been lost."

"Well done. Have a great rest of your weekend." Kian ended the call.

"Good morning," William said. "Trouble?"

"Nothing serious." Kian pulled out a chair next to Syssi. "Supply chain issues."

William nodded. "It's affecting every sector."

"Indeed." Kian accepted a mug full of coffee from Okidu. "Thank you." He took a grateful sip. "So, what did you want to talk to me about before Kaia's family gets here?"

"I need your input on what to do with the other bioinformaticians. Kaia says she and I can finish the project on our own. She expects that it will take a little longer, but not by much. I would rather send them on vacation and get them back to work once she's done with her transition."

"Can't you give them something else to do?" Darlene asked. "If you send them on vacation, you will need to erase their memories of what they've worked on so far, and when they return, they will have to start from scratch and wonder what happened to their memories. It would be a mess."

Kian couldn't agree more. "She has a point."

After the enormous investment in building the lab and the smaller investment of hiring the bioinformaticians, it would be incredibly wasteful to close up shop after one week.

"What can I get them to work on?" William asked. "I don't want them to continue the current project without Kaia and me being there to supervise them."

"You could send Marcel to take over," Kian said. "He knows what we are doing here, and you can supervise his work remotely from the village."

As William rubbed his jaw, Kian noticed that he didn't have his glasses on. Had he forgotten to put them on this morning?

Come to think of it, he hadn't seen him wearing them last night either.

Good for him. The guy was starting to care about his appearance. His hair was cut in a fashionable new style, and his new clothes fit him well instead of being a couple of sizes too large.

"I'm not a hundred percent comfortable with that," William said. "But I guess it could work as a temporary solution. Even if they don't make progress in our absence, they will still be here and working."

"Then it's settled." Kian took another sip of his coffee. "The damn supply chain issues are also to blame for the clinic not being ready. We have a paranormal retreat starting in three weeks, and if we are lucky enough to find a Dormant among the participants and we don't have a functioning clinic, we will have to bring them to the village, which defies the whole purpose of doing it here."

The medical equipment needed was pretty standard, and it had been ordered over two months ago. Normally, he would have expected delivery in a couple of weeks, not months, but things were crazy all over the globe, and the shortages were difficult to explain.

"Don't you have a clinic in your old location?" Darlene asked.

"We do, but we don't want to bring Dormants there. It's located in the keep's underground, and they would have to be locked down there for the duration of the trial to see whether they could be induced or not. We've done that before, but that was when the entire Guardian force was living in the keep and manning the security office."

"That's not what I had in mind." Darlene put her cup down. "My idea was to transport the equipment from that clinic to this one, and once what was ordered arrived, to put the new stuff in the old clinic."

"That's a great idea," Syssi said. "It's an immediate solution."

Kian grimaced. "I don't like putting old equipment in a new clinic. I'll have Shai check with the supplier again tomorrow, and if it's not going to get here in time for the retreat, I'll do as Darlene suggests and transfer the equipment from the keep."

"Which one of our doctors will be working here?" Darlene asked.

"Julian and Bridget will be on call and get here as soon as we have a transitioning Dormant," William said. "Gertrude agreed to move out here and run the clinic. She's an excellent nurse who has a lot of experience with Dormants. She should be fine for a few hours until we get one of the doctors here."

76

KAIA

*K*aia had expected her mother and Gilbert to argue against her decision, to tell her that she needed to wait to make sure, but she should have known better. When push came to shove, her family united to provide support for its members.

"We are coming with you," Gilbert said in a tone that brooked no argument. "Your mother and Cheryl can call in sick, and we will stay with you until you transition safely. Did you really think we could go back home when we knew that you were doing something so dangerous?"

"It's not dangerous for me. I'm nineteen."

"I would like to meet the rest of William's family," her mother said. "And I want to be there for you, but I can't take a month-long vacation."

Cheryl smirked as she turned to their mother. "It's not a vacation when you are sick. Tell them that I got the chicken pox, and you caught it from me and that you are highly contagious."

Their mother shook her head. "We are both vaccinated, and even if we get sick, chicken pox only lasts a few days, not a month."

Cheryl didn't back off. "Fifteen to twenty percent of people who got the Varicella vaccine still get it, but in a milder form, and some get complications like pneumonia, that last a long time."

Karen narrowed her eyes at Cheryl. "It seems that you've researched the topic. Were you planning on using chicken pox as an excuse to ditch school?"

Cheryl lifted her hands. "Not for me. It was for Claudia, and her parents approved. Do you remember when she went on a month-long trip to Japan with her family last November?"

"Yeah, I asked you how she could miss so much school, and you said that you would take notes for her."

Cheryl smiled sheepishly. "I answered the question you asked. You didn't ask me what she told the school."

422

CHAPTER 76

Grinning, Gilbert clapped her back. "That's my smart girl."

"Don't encourage her." Their mother wagged her finger at him. "She's too sneaky for her own good."

Idina, who'd been ignoring the entire conversation so far, lifted her head and gave Gilbert a sweet smile. "Am I your smart girl, Daddy?"

"Of course, you are." He lifted her off the bed and threw her in the air.

Idina squealed happily while their mother glared at Gilbert. "I hate it when you do that."

"People." Kaia lifted her hand. "We need to go. We have ten minutes to get to the cottage, and we still need to put the twins in the stroller. We can keep talking on the way."

"We will just carry them," Karen said. "We will leave the stroller here."

Gilbert planted Idina on his shoulders. "We are ready." He opened the door. "Duck!" They both did to clear the doorway.

"I'll take Evan." Cheryl took him out of his playpen.

"And I'll get Ryan." Kaia lifted their brother and hugged him to her. "I'm so glad that you are all coming with me. I don't have to say goodbye." She kissed his soft cheek.

Her mother slung the strap of her enormous baby bag across her body and followed them out. "I don't know if that's actually going to happen. What if Kian doesn't allow us to come unless we all want to attempt the thing right away?"

"I don't think he would do that," Kaia smirked. "I'm too valuable to his clan for him to do anything to alienate me, and I will make it very clear that I want you all with me."

"What if there is no room for us all?" Cheryl asked.

"That could be a problem," Kaia admitted. "We can all stay at William's place, but I don't know how large it is and how many beds he has."

"We will ask all those questions when we get there," Gilbert said. "Maybe some of William's relatives can take us in."

"Where is Eric?" Cheryl asked. "He said that he was going to get something from his room and never came back."

Kaia stopped. "I forgot about him. Should I go back and get him?"

"I'll call him," their mother said.

Eric had been a little strange this morning. He'd spent the night at Darlene's, so he should have been in a great mood, but he seemed subdued, contemplative, with none of his usual banter.

Maybe he was scared of the transition?

"Where are you?" her mother asked.

"You could've told us that you were leaving," she said into the phone. "We thought that you ran away." There was a pause, and then her mother said, "We will be there in a few minutes." She ended the call. "He's already there."

"He's acting strange," Kaia said. "Did he say anything about being scared of transitioning?"

"Not to me," Gilbert said. "He seemed eager to go first."

Eric was doing it for the same reason Kaia was, but unlike her, his transition wouldn't be without risk, and she was worried for him.

77

ERIC

*W*hen Eric arrived at the cottage, he found a new guard sitting on a bench that hadn't been there before.

"Good morning." The guy gave him a once-over as if he was checking him out.

"Good morning. Did the rest of my family get here already?"

"Not yet, but you can go ahead, Eric. Darlene and William are there."

"I'm at a disadvantage." He offered the guy his hand. "You know my name, but I don't know yours."

"Max." The guard shook his hand firmly. "So, you are a Dormant, eh?"

That answered the question of whether the guy was one of the immortals or just a human security guard.

Perhaps he could answer some of the questions Eric had, which he wasn't sure Kian or William would answer honestly.

"Can I join you? I'd rather wait for my family out here, so we can all go in together."

"Be my guest." The guy scooted to make room for him. "Why aren't you with them? I was told that you were having a family meeting about who attempts transition first."

"We did, but we were all crammed into one small room, and I needed air. I went for a walk and lost track of time. When I realized what time it was, I came straight here." He frowned. "Who told you about us? We just found out last night that Gilbert and I might be related to—damn, I can't say her name."

Max grinned. "I know who you mean. And as for how I found out, you will soon discover that the clan is like a hive, and rumors spread faster than wildfire. When you live as long as we do, juicy gossip that breaks up the routine is eagerly shared."

"How old are you, if I may ask?"

Max chuckled. "You didn't take me out, you didn't buy me dinner, and you want to know how old I am? How rude of you!"

424

CHAPTER 77

Eric didn't know whether the guy was joking or coming on to him.

"My apologies. I'm new to all this. Is it rude to ask someone like you how old they are?"

Kaia was right. It was possible to talk around the compulsion, but it was a drag.

"It's not rude," Max said. "But it's not something we do. We don't celebrate birthdays either. Perhaps it's because the passage of time is not as meaningful to us as it is to humans." The guard crossed his arms over his chest. "Patience is one of the first things you will learn as an immortal. There is very little reason to rush."

Eric had a hundred more questions he could ask the guy, but his phone rang.

He pulled it out and accepted the call from Karen.

"Where are you?" She sounded irritated, and rightly so.

He'd told them that he needed to get something from his room, which was code for him needing to use the bathroom, but when he was done, he should have gone back and told them that he couldn't stand how stuffy the room was with all of them crammed in together.

"I went on a walk and lost track of time, so I came straight to the cottage. I'm sitting outside on a bench and having a great conversation with a guard named Max."

"You could've told us that you were leaving. We thought that you ran away."

"I would never leave you stranded. Are you on your way?"

"We will be there in a few minutes." She ended the call.

Eric put the phone away.

"The correct term is Guardian," Max said. "We are much more than guards."

Eric tilted his head. "What do you do aside from guarding the research facility and Kian?"

"Many things." Max gave him an assessing look. "You were a pilot in the Air Force, right?"

"Did you read our family dossier?"

"I was just told the highlights. The clan could use another experienced fighter jet pilot. We only have one with military experience, but the last time he flew a fighter plane was over eighty years ago."

Eric's hackles rose. "What do you need fighter jet pilots for?"

Max shrugged. "A contingency in case of an attack from above."

"Who do you expect to attack you?"

Max snorted. "Everyone. If humans found out about us, they would hunt us down to find out the secret to immortality. And if our enemies found us, they would just annihilate us. That's why it is so important to guard the secret of our existence and our location."

Eric put his hand over his heart. "I can't tell anyone even if I wanted to. I'm under a strong compulsion to keep my mouth shut. But I wouldn't reveal your secret even if I could, and even if my family wasn't about to join your ranks. I will never endanger your people."

"Good to know." The guy clapped him on the back. "I wish you and your family the best of luck."

KIAN

*K*ian nearly spat out the sip of coffee he'd just drunk. "You all want to join Kaia in the village?"

"Of course." Karen wrung her hands. "If my baby is going through a difficult ordeal, I want to be there for her and hold her hand. I know that she has William, and maybe she doesn't need me, but I need to be there for her." She turned to Syssi. "You can understand, right?"

"I do." Syssi turned a pair of pleading eyes at Kian. "They are all potential Dormants. They will arrive at the village sooner or later, so why not sooner?"

"Because they are not all getting induced at the same time."

"I also want to transition as soon as possible," Eric said. "I'm the younger brother, and I'm a bachelor." He looked at Darlene. "For now." He winked at her.

"What about the test your doctor can perform?" Gilbert asked. "If we can verify that Eric and I are Syssi's relatives, then I'm going for the transition as well. I won't even wait for Eric to do it first." He smiled at his brother. "We can do it together." He shifted his gaze to Kian. "Once that's done, Eric can induce Darlene, and I can induce Karen."

Kaia cleared her throat. "Can your doctor perform a genetic test? Because that's the only way to confirm that Gilbert, Eric, and Syssi are related. A blood test is not enough."

"On a limited scale," Kian said. "We talked about getting some new equipment for her, but I don't know if she ordered it. I can give her a call." He crossed his arms over his chest. "But that's not the important issue here." He turned to Gilbert. "Even if you and Eric are confirmed Dormants because of your relationship to Syssi, it's not as simple as you think. Darlene is also a confirmed Dormant because her mother is immortal, but Karen is not." He wanted to add that they were both not so young and shouldn't wait, but he didn't want to state the obvious and offend them.

"Do you have a better plan?" Gilbert asked.

"Kaia needs to transition first. If she does, then Karen is a confirmed Dormant, and you will need to consider letting someone else induce her. The six months she will have to wait for your fangs to become functional might be the difference between her making it or not, and the same goes for Darlene."

Karen sighed. "I'm glad that Cheryl took the boys and Idina to watch a show in the bedroom. It would have been very awkward to talk about having sex with a stranger in front of her." She looked at Kaia. "It's still awkward with you here, but at least you are an adult." She glanced at her mate. "I don't think I can do that. Even if Gilbert is okay with that, I'm not."

Gilbert's lips were pressed together in a tight line, but he didn't say a word.

Kian could understand how the guy felt. If he were in his shoes, what would he have done?

The answer was simple. He wouldn't have risked Syssi's life because of jealousy.

He would have asked Bridget to knock him out while someone else induced Syssi, and then he would have tried not to dwell on it when he woke up. Syssi's life was more important than any other consideration.

Darlene was less of a problem because her grandfather would obviously help her with donations of his blood. But his and Annani's help would also be needed with the older members of Kaia's family transitions.

Toven might also be willing to help Eric because it seemed that Darlene had chosen him as her mate, and Annani might be inclined to help Gilbert because he was Syssi's relative and Karen because she was his mate.

But even with the gods' assistance, Karen shouldn't wait another six months to go for it.

"You don't have to decide anything right now." Syssi reached for Karen's hand. "A week or two won't make a difference, and in that time, you should consider your options. I know it's a difficult option to consider, but given that your life is on the line, I think it's a small price to pay."

"Would you have done that?" Karen asked. "If you were married to Kian, and that was the dilemma you were facing, would you have waited for him to transition first and assume a higher risk for your own transition, or would you have agreed to be serviced by another male?"

"I would have waited." Syssi smiled at Kian. "I would have trusted the Fates to see me through."

WILLIAM

*F*or a long moment, no one said a thing, and William suspected that everyone was thinking about what they would do in a similar situation.

He glanced at Kaia, but she was so young and full of vitality that it was difficult to imagine her in her mother's situation.

But what if she contracted some exotic disease, and the only cure was having sex with another man? What if only the Kra-ell had the antigens for it, and the only way for her to get it was to have sex with one of them?

He would encourage her to do it, but then he would cut out his own heart and give it to her if that was what she needed to survive.

"I wouldn't have let you wait," Kian growled. "I would have done everything to keep you alive."

"I know," Syssi said softly. "I'm glad that we didn't have to do that."

"It's settled then." Kian clapped his hands on his thighs. "We are all leaving today and going straight to the village. Kaia and William will start working on Kaia's transition. Gilbert, Eric, and Syssi will give Bridget samples of their blood, and if they are related, I will choose initiators for them, and we will have a double induction ceremony. Darlene and Karen will have to decide whether they want to wait for their mates to have active fangs and venom or use a surrogate, but they can take a few days to think it through."

"How are we going to get there?" Karen asked. "Can Eric fly us to Los Angeles, and someone will pick us up from the airport?"

"That's one possibility," Kian said. "The other option is for your plane to stay where it is, and you will all fly with us on our private jet."

"We don't have enough room," Syssi said.

"We are not going to use the same jet." Kian rose to his feet and walked over to the bar. "I'll ask Morris to pick us up with the large jet." He poured himself a drink. "Does anyone else want one?"

"It's too early for alcohol." Karen gave Gilbert a warning look. "You are not immortal yet."

He lifted his hands. "I wasn't going to ask."

"I can't just leave my plane at the airport," Eric said. "I rented the space for the weekend, and I need to vacate it this evening. I also have a client who needs it this Tuesday."

Kian nodded. "You have to understand that if you transition, your old life will end. You will have to move into the village and find a new occupation, preferably the kind you can do online. Your appearance will change dramatically, and only so much can be explained away by plastic surgery."

"I don't want to move," Cheryl said from the other room. "I have great friends that I'm going to miss."

Groaning, Karen closed her eyes. "I should have known that she was listening. It was too quiet in there."

"Don't you want to be immortal?" Kaia asked. "Are your friends worth giving up eternal life?"

Cheryl stood at the mouth of the hallway leading to the bedrooms. "I guess not. Can I still keep in touch with them on Instatock?"

"You mentioned that social media platform before," Kian said. "When we get to the village, I want you to show me your channel."

Cheryl grinned. "Gladly." She turned around and went back into the bedroom where her siblings were watching some noisy kids' show.

Kian turned to William. "Have you heard of it before?"

He shook his head. "I don't pay attention to all those social media channels that keep popping out. It's all about nonsense like dance challenges and making silly faces. It's not for adults."

"Speaking of the village," Karen said. "Where exactly are we going to stay? Do you have accommodations for guests?"

"We have plenty of fully furnished vacant houses." Syssi pulled out her phone. "I'll text the person in charge of housing to have two prepared for you."

"I still didn't get an answer about my plane," Eric said.

"I'll fly back home with you," Darlene offered. "We can book a commercial flight to Los Angeles, and someone will pick us up from the airport."

William looked at Kian. "Is that acceptable to you?"

"It has to be. I'll take Kaia's family with me today, and I'll send the jet back with Marcel tomorrow. You and Kaia need to finalize things with the team, and you need to pass the baton to Marcel."

William looked at Kaia. "Are you okay with that?"

She nodded. "Kian's plan is solid." She turned to her mother. "Are you going to be okay in the village without me?"

"Of course, sweetie." Karen sighed. "I hope these homes come equipped with washers and dryers. I brought just enough clothes for three days."

"Don't worry." Syssi smiled. "You will lack for nothing. We shop online and get things delivered just like everyone else."

"Well, our deliveries go through one extra stop, but we still get them the same day."

"I'm excited." Karen looked at her mate. "Are you?"

He snorted. "I thought that having three little kids at our age was as adventurous as we would get, but I was wrong. We are about to embark on the most thrilling adventure yet."

KAIA

This time around, there were no tears when Kaia had parted with her family.

The big red-headed Guardian and his Amazonian beauty of a mate stayed behind to leave enough room in Kian's jet for all of her family members, and they would accompany William and her to the village tomorrow afternoon.

When the bus disappeared behind the curve, William wrapped his arm around her. "Are you okay?"

Smiling, Kaia leaned her head on his shoulder. "I'm going to see them tomorrow, and I have you by my side. It doesn't get any better than that."

He hooked a finger under her chin and turned her face up to steal a kiss. "I have every intention of making things even better."

The mischievous spark in his eyes gave her a good clue as to what those intentions were.

Kaia yawned. "It's been a long day. I'm ready for bed."

He chuckled. "It's only seven in the evening."

"I didn't say that I wanted to go to sleep, only that I wanted to go to bed."

His grin widened. "Great minds think alike." He leaned closer and whispered in her ear. "Are you ready to throw away the rubbers?"

"Am I ever! But you said that you wanted to wait for us to get to the village."

He shrugged. "We are leaving for the village tomorrow, and transition doesn't start overnight. I'm willing to chance it if you are."

She wanted to say that yes, she was ready, but a sudden sense of foreboding changed her mind. "You know what? Let's play it safe. I have an idea that you're going to love, and that doesn't involve condoms." She stretched her neck and whispered it in his ear.

"Sweet, merciful Fates." William's eyes blazed with an inner light. "Would you be really mad if I swung you into my arms and ran back to our bungalow?"

"Mad? I'll be thrilled."

She didn't get to finish the sentence before William did exactly as he'd promised.

Winding her arms around his neck, she threw her head back and laughed, the sense of foreboding washed away by a wave of happiness.

Kaia had always known that her future was bright, but now it seemed brighter than ever.

She was looking forward to spending eternity with the man she loved, building Odus and countless other innovations, and somewhere along the way, perhaps with a little help from the clan's physician, children would come as well.

DARK WHISPERS

from beyond

THE CHILDREN OF
THE GODS 64

I. T. LUCAS

INTERNATIONALLY BESTSELLING AUTHOR

1

WILLIAM

*W*orry about Kaia, her family, and the future of the project had kept William awake throughout the night.

Kaia and her family were being forced to rush into life-altering decisions that might either kill its older members or grant them immortality. And if that wasn't enough, Gilbert and Karen's relationship could suffer irreparable damage.

Karen was running out of time, and even though it was easy to understand her preference to wait for Gilbert to transition first so he could induce her, she might not have the six months it would take for his fangs and venom glands to become fully functional. Karen needed to choose an immortal male to activate her dormant immortal genes, but even though her survival depended on it, she and Gilbert might not be able to get past that and continue as a loving couple.

The continuation of the project was less troublesome, but it had many moving parts, and assembling them into a workable solution had also kept William from getting any sleep.

They had only scratched the surface of Okidu's journals, and there was still a lot to be deciphered before William could dismiss the rest of the team and continue just with Kaia. In fact, she would have to do the heavy lifting because he needed to go back to work on the other projects he'd put on hold.

Last night, after they'd made love and Kaia had sailed off on the wings of euphoria, William had called Marcel, and they'd discussed the progress that had been made so far and what Marcel would do with the team in William and Kaia's absence.

The project would continue with them working remotely from the village and Marcel supervising the team of bioinformaticians, but before William introduced his replacement to the team, he needed to discuss with Marcel a few things about managing humans.

Marcel was a sharp guy, but his people skills were even worse than William's, and the guy hadn't dealt with humans since his days as a student at Caltech.

That was why William was picking him and the pilot from the airport instead of just sending a driver for them. He and Marcel needed the time to go over the rules of conduct and what was okay to tell the team of humans and what was not.

It was time to leave, but that was easier said than done.

Standing at the foot of the bed, he gazed at the sleeping beauty sprawled over the covers, his eyes fixed on her gorgeous face and his feet refusing to move.

William would have liked to believe that Kaia's blissed-out expression was his doing, and that she could sleep so peacefully despite yesterday's shocking revelations because he was such an incredible lover, but he knew it was the venom's lingering effect.

Would she be as relaxed when she woke up?

Probably not. As soon as memories of yesterday's events rushed in, she would without a doubt be stressing over her impending transition and the decisions her family was facing.

With a sigh, William forced his eyes away from Kaia and walked toward the door.

"Where are you going?" she asked sleepily.

William turned around and smiled. "I'm going to pick up Marcel from the airport," he reminded her.

Kaia spread her arms. "You can't leave without giving me a kiss."

He couldn't refuse an invitation like that.

Walking back, he sat on the bed and leaned to lightly kiss her on the lips. "You don't need to get up for another two hours. You should go back to sleep."

She yawned. "I want to call my mother and hear her impressions of your village. Do you know if Marcel gave my family new clan phones? If he did, I need their numbers."

"I'm sure he or someone else from the lab took care of that." William cupped her warm cheek. "I'll get the numbers and text them to you, but it's five in the morning, so your mother is probably still asleep, and you should be as well."

Kaia covered her mouth with her hand and yawned again. "No wonder I'm so sleepy. I hope that Cheryl can download Instatock on her new phone. If she can't check her stats every five minutes, she'll get panicky, and she'll demand to leave right away."

That was an unhealthy obsession, but if her mother didn't object, it was none of his business.

"Cheryl can download any application she wants."

"What about your security? All those apps follow people around and record everything they do on their devices."

"Don't worry about that." He leaned and kissed her forehead. "I designed them in a way that makes it impossible for apps to track anything other than what's necessary for their operation."

Kaia grinned. "My genius boyfriend. But out of an abundance of caution, I suggest that you check this particular app."

"Why?"

She shrugged. "Instatock is only six or seven months old, and it's sweeping an entire generation of teenagers without monetizing a thing. There are no advertisements, nothing to buy, and the application is free. I'm suspicious of its motives."

CHAPTER 1

As his chest swelled with love and pride, William grinned. Even when her body was still mostly asleep, Kaia's mind was fully awake.

"I'll check, but I doubt any application can break through my defenses." He kissed her cheeks one at a time and then added one more to her forehead. "I need to go. Max is waiting for me on the bus."

The Guardian had informed him yesterday that he would be tagging along on the trip to the airport to pick up Marcel and Morris. Unsurprisingly, Kian or Onegus had left instructions that William shouldn't be allowed to leave the safe zone without a Guardian escort.

Kaia pulled the blanket up to her chin. "Text me when you get there." She turned on her side and closed her eyes.

"I will." He forced himself to get off the bed and walk out.

He found Max waiting for him outside his bungalow.

"Good morning." He gave the Guardian a tight smile. "Were you afraid I'd give you the slip?"

Max shrugged. "I could have waited here or on the bus, but I knew the driver would already be there, and he would have expected me to chat with him. I don't have the patience for idle chit-chat, and besides, I prefer not to spend too much time with humans if I don't have to."

William arched a brow. "You didn't mind spending time with Darlene."

The Guardian shrugged again, but William caught the wince he'd immediately replaced with an impassive expression. "She's a confirmed Dormant and a god's granddaughter. She was definitely worth my time."

William wondered whether Darlene's lineage had been Max's main motivation to pursue her. If so, he was glad that nothing had come of it. Darlene deserved to be desired for who she was and not for who her grandfather was. But if Max's feelings had run deeper, he felt for the guy.

"I'm sorry it didn't work out between the two of you." William fell in step with Max. "I hoped that Darlene would dump Eric after the weekend and fall straight into your arms, but now it seems that he's a Dormant as well, and they seem serious about each other."

Max's brows dipped so low that they formed a V. "Even if Eric transitions tomorrow, he can't induce her for another six months. She shouldn't wait so long."

William put his hand on the Guardian's shoulder. "She's a big girl, and she makes her own choices. Being Toven's granddaughter helps her chances, so she's not overly concerned."

"Still, it's not wise for her to wait for Eric to transition."

Detecting real concern in the guy's voice, William was inclined to believe that Max cared about Darlene. "Eric might not transition at all, and then she'll have no choice but to turn to you or another Guardian."

A hopeful smile bloomed on Max's face. "That would be unfortunate for Eric, but I can't say that I would be sorry if he turns out to be just a human. I plan to stay very close to Darlene, so if she needs to choose someone else, I'll be the obvious choice."

"How are you planning to do that from here?"

"I'm not." Max grinned conspiratorially. "I'm way ahead of you. I asked Onegus to reassign me to the village, and he approved my request. I'm coming back with you and Kaia."

2

KAIA

$\mathcal{K}$aia stretched like a lazy cat after an afternoon nap and took a deep breath. She'd fallen asleep right after William left for the airport and had dreamt wonderful dreams about life in the immortals' village.

Could it be as beautiful in real life? Would the immortals be as friendly and smiley as they had been in her dreams?

It was time to find out.

Hoping that William had sent a text with her family's new phone numbers, Kaia reached for her phone.

She hadn't spoken with her mother since her family had departed Safe Haven yesterday afternoon, leaving their phones behind as Kian had demanded, and she couldn't wait to hear everyone's impressions of the village.

After finding the text with the numbers, Kaia rushed through her morning routine, made herself a cup of coffee, and sat on the couch to make the call.

"Good morning." Her mother sounded cheerful.

"I hope I didn't wake you up." Kaia picked up her coffee mug and took a sip.

"I wish. Your brothers wake up bright and early no matter when they go to sleep. I've been up since six in the morning, but I don't mind. I like to start my day early."

Kaia didn't. She loved lazing in bed. "How is the village?" she asked.

"Beautiful, but we didn't get to see much of it yet. When we got here, we were shown the café so we would know where we could get food, and then we were escorted straight to the house that we'd be staying in. Ingrid, the lady in charge of housing here, was kind enough to take a grocery list from me, and this morning, I found everything I asked for on our doorstep."

"Did she get it for you?"

"I don't think so. I think it was one of the Guardians, or maybe Kian's butler. In any case, it was very nice of whoever did that."

"How is the house?"

"It's cute. Much smaller than ours, but Gilbert is happy. He says that everything is built to the highest standards, and he's especially impressed with the sound-proofing. It's incredible. Once you close a door, it's like you are in a recording studio. Complete silence. I'm glad that we brought the baby monitor with us so I can hear the boys."

"Did they get their own room, or are they sharing with Idina?"

"There are only three bedrooms in the house, and from what Syssi said, that's the largest model available at the moment, so it's not like we can get something bigger. Idina and Cheryl are sharing a room, which Cheryl isn't happy about, but Idina refused to sleep in the same room as her brothers. When Eric arrives, he will have to share a room with the twins or sleep on the couch in the living room. I hope he can stay with Darlene at her place, but I overheard her say something to William about there being complications. She might have a roommate that is not comfortable with Eric being there."

"I can't imagine Eric separating from her. If Darlene has a problematic room-mate, she should ask for a house of her own. William says that they have plenty available."

Kaia had never seen Eric so taken with a woman, but then he'd never brought any of his post-divorce girlfriends home for the family to meet. Perhaps that was how he'd acted with all of them, but she doubted that he'd regarded any of the women with the same adoration as he did Darlene.

"I'm sure they will find a solution. He's really into her."

"I know." Her mother sounded excited. "I'm so happy for him. I'm crossing my fingers that all of this comes to pass. It would be very disappointing to find out that we went through all this hoopla for nothing."

Kaia's gut squeezed painfully. "I'm crossing my fingers as well." She swallowed the lump that had formed in her throat. Forcing a cheerful tone by faking a smile even though her mother couldn't see her, she asked, "What else? Did you get to meet anyone other than Ingrid?"

"Not yet. Syssi promised to introduce us to Nathalie, who has a daughter Idina's age and a brother who's a year younger, so they can play together." Her mother chuckled. "Just to clarify, the two-year-old boy is Nathalie's brother, not her son. These people are something else." She paused and then asked in a worried voice, "Is your phone secure?"

"I didn't get a new one if that's what you're asking, but William said that they reroute all communication from here through their servers and encrypt it. Just to err on the side of caution, though, we should talk around the topic of you-know-what."

"Right. So, it's a little strange how they all look so good. Anyway, later today, we are meeting with Doctor Bridget. I hope she can test whether Gilbert and Eric are related to Syssi."

"Kian said that she can perform basic tests, and William told me that she checked the maternal lineage of other newcomers, so I assume that she can determine whether they are related or not. She probably has the equipment needed for checking mitochondrial DNA. It's a much simpler test than the more robust DNA mapping test, and what's needed to conduct it is not expensive."

"It would have been interesting to get more detailed information on their genetics, and I suggested for the three of them to send swabs with their saliva to one of those genetic testing labs, but it would take too long to get the results back. They quote six to eight weeks, and none of us wants to wait that long. Anyway, Kian said that he was not comfortable with sending Syssi's biological information to an outside lab. I get it, but on the other hand, I can't understand why they don't invest in a proper lab of their own. Having access to that kind of information could be crucial for their survival, and it's not only about finding relatives."

Kaia picked up her coffee mug and leaned back. "The equipment needed for mapping an entire DNA sequence is not cheap, and it requires training that an internist doesn't have. But if they are interested and don't mind spending the money on the equipment, I can help them build a lab. I'm not a geneticist, but I'm sure I can find instructions on the internet for what's needed."

These days, one could build a nuclear reactor from instructions available on the internet. The tricky part was getting enriched uranium, and even that wasn't impossible to procure for the right price.

"It doesn't seem like they lack resources," her mother said. "I'm sure they have the money to purchase the equipment, and I have no doubt that they have the know-how as well. Kian told us about some of the cutting-edge technologies they are working on, so I'm sure they have what it takes to build a proper genetics lab."

Kaia sighed. "The problem is motivation to make the investment. Syssi was the first carrier they discovered, and that was only four and a half years ago. After her, additional carriers were found, but they were few and far between. William told me that Bridget suspects that they are not going to discover anything anyway, and it will be a waste of time and resources. When you meet her, ask her why she thinks that."

Her mother chuckled. "I wouldn't understand her explanation. I'm a system administrator, and I know my way around hardware, but all that genetics stuff sounds like a foreign language to me. When you get here, you can make an appointment with Bridget, and the two of you can talk it out to your heart's content."

"I have a better idea. Can you postpone the meeting with her until William and I get to the village? We can all talk with her together."

"I'll ask Syssi if that's possible and if Bridget won't get upset with us for changing the appointment time. As far as our family goes, right now she's the most important person in the village, and I don't want to alienate her from the get-go."

"We wouldn't want to do that." Kaia did some quick thinking. "William is a council member, which I'm sure gives him considerable clout. If he asks to be present at the meeting, Bridget won't object."

3

KIAN

*A*s a knock sounded on Kian's office door, he got to his feet and opened it for Toven. "Good morning. Thank you for agreeing to see me this early." He offered the god his hand.

"This is not early." Toven shook it. "I've been up since six o'clock. Mia and I went for a walk around the village." He smiled. "Well, she rode her wheelchair. I walked."

"Still, I appreciate you coming to see me on such short notice." Kian led him to the conference table.

Somehow, it didn't seem right to have a god sit on one of the guest chairs in front of his desk. Toven was aloof and not really friendly, and their relationship was more formal than any of the others Kian had with people living in his village.

Then again, Toven was a god, and they weren't related, so the distance was natural. Nevertheless, he needed Toven's help, and he didn't expect it to be difficult to convince the god to grant it.

"You said that it was important." Toven pulled out a chair and sat down.

"It is. I'll give you a quick recap to get you up to speed on what's going on. William recruited several bioinformaticians for a project he's working on, and he fell in love with one of them. Naturally, he suspects that she's a Dormant."

"Congratulations. What does it have to do with me?"

Usually, Kian was the last person to beat around the bush, but he was about to ask the god for donations of his blood, and that required some finesse, which wasn't his strong suit. Syssi had suggested that he should tell Toven about the family first and present them in a positive light, and also mention Darlene and her possible bond with Eric. The god would be more inclined to help his granddaughter's chosen mate and by extension, Eric's family. It wouldn't hurt if he also liked what he heard about them.

"I'm getting there. Despite finishing her PhD, Kaia is a very young woman of nineteen who has a loving family she's very attached to. They came to see where she would be working, and when Darlene met Kaia's uncle, sparks flew."

Toven lifted a brow. "I hope the uncle is the mother's brother. Darlene is supposed to find an immortal male to induce her, but if the uncle is a Dormant, he can be induced first and then induce her. Naturally, it is preferable if her initiator is someone she actually likes and can form a bond with."

Kian sighed. "I would like that for her too, but the problem is that it will take Eric six months until his venom glands are fully operational. We are also not sure that he's a Dormant, and even if he is, he might not make it through the transition. He's forty-two."

Understanding dawning, Toven nodded. "You want me to help him along with transfusions of my blood."

"Are you willing to do that?"

"Of course. Darlene is my granddaughter, and I want her to be happy. I'll help her chosen mate, and when the time comes, I will naturally help her as well."

Kian let out a breath. "Thank you. But there is more to the story. Eric is not Kaia's mother's brother. He's her stepfather's brother. But it turns out that there is a strong possibility of Eric and Gilbert being Syssi's third cousins, and the shared ancestress is their great-great-grandmother. She had two daughters. One was the grandmother of Syssi's mother, and the other was the grandmother of Eric and Gilbert's mother. We are meeting with Bridget later today to see if she can verify that they are actually related."

Toven crossed his arms over his chest. "What evidence do you have to support that relationship so far?"

"It's a long story, but the gist of it is that when we met them for dinner, Gilbert started talking about his quest to discover more relatives and the fruits of his research. He showed us a picture of his great-grandmother, and Syssi said that she looked exactly like her grandmother and showed us a picture of her as well. The resemblance is undeniable, and they are all originally from the same geographic area in Eastern Europe, but it still might be a coincidence."

Toven looked Kian in the eyes. "Where do I fit into the narrative?"

"Syssi's transition was difficult, and so was Andrew's, and they were both much younger than Gilbert and Eric. I expect both men will need a lot of help. Kaia's mother is also not young, and since Annani is not here at the moment, you are the only one who can help all of them. I need to know if you are willing to do that. If not, I will have to convince my mother to cut her trip short and come back to the village as soon as she can."

Toven chuckled. "I'm already giving transfusions to Mia's grandparents. If I need to help so many people to transition, I might become anemic. Perhaps you should ask Annani to come back to save me."

Kian wasn't sure whether the god was joking or serious. "I know how much blood is required, and it's not a lot. Even if you give each of them daily transfusions, it shouldn't have an adverse effect on you."

"I know." Toven laughed. "I was just joking. I don't like the idea of becoming a pin cushion, but since I don't expect scenarios like this to occur often, I can deal with it."

"Thank you. I appreciate your willingness to help."

Toven smiled. "I'm glad for the opportunity to pay back at least some of the debt of gratitude I owe you. You've been very generous with Mia and me. You took us in and even allowed her grandparents to live in your village."

"You are family, Toven. Your son is mated to my sister, your daughter is mated to my assistant, your granddaughter is mated to my chief of Guardians, and your great-grandson and your grandnephews are part of our clan as well. Besides, my mother wouldn't have it any other way."

A smile brightened Toven's face. "I am truly blessed to have such a wonderful family. I thank the merciful Fates every day for the joy they've bestowed on me." His smile waned. "But I worry that I might lose it all because I don't deserve it. I didn't earn it. I failed in all my attempts to improve the lives of humans."

Kian leaned toward the god. "You did your best, and you sacrificed centuries to do so. It doesn't matter whether you succeeded or failed. Your failures are just as much a badge of honor as if they were successes—they attest to your tireless effort."

"Not tireless." Toven chuckled sadly. "I grew very tired of trying to do the impossible and allowed myself to sink into a state of ennui."

"You are immortal. You can embark on new adventures. You are already doing it with Perfect Match. Making it accessible to more people will enrich many lives."

"It's a small project, and all I'm offering humans is an escape from reality." Toven sighed. "Still, I hope it's successful. I can't stomach any more failures."

"There are no guarantees, and you might fail again, but you might also succeed. Those who do nothing, though, fail by default."

4

WILLIAM

*A*s William finished telling Morris and Marcel an abbreviated version of the discovery of Kaia's stepfather and his brother's connection to Syssi, Morris rubbed his hands. "I'm looking forward to comparing notes with a young pilot who's flown the latest fighter jet models."

William shot him an apologetic look. "Eric is no longer in Safe Haven. He and Darlene flew to the Bay Area on his executive jet, and from there, they will take a commercial flight to Los Angeles."

Morris didn't seem perturbed. "Then I'll catch him in the village when we return." He looked at Max. "You're coming back with us, aren't you?"

The Guardian nodded. "I am."

"Did Onegus assign you to William permanently?"

Max shrugged. "It depends." He turned to William. "You don't need me in the village, and you don't leave it often, but if you and Kaia plan to return to Safe Haven after her transition, I'll probably accompany you."

"Of course, we are coming back." William cast a silencing shroud around them to keep the bus driver from overhearing their conversation. "It might take time until Kaia transitions, though, and then it might take a week or two until she feels well enough to go back to work."

"Are you sure that Kaia is a Dormant?" Marcel asked. "Does she have a paranormal talent?"

She had memories of past life, but William wasn't sure that counted as paranormal ability. He also wasn't sure that she was right about where those memories were coming from. Spencer had seen two auras around her, and that shouldn't be the case if the memories of a past life belonged to her. She was probably housing a spirit who was pretending to be her incarnation.

In either case, though, Kaia didn't like people to know about her male aspect, and he wasn't going to betray her trust and share it with Marcel.

444

"Kaia has an uncanny ability to solve complicated puzzles that even I can't," he said instead. "So perhaps that ability could be perceived as paranormal."

Marcel looked at their two companions. "I assume that it's okay for me to talk about the specifics of the special project you and Kaia have been working on in front of Max and Morris?"

William nodded. "They know."

Max had been with him in the Bay Area when he'd been recruiting bioinformaticians for the project, and Morris was a veteran on the force whose status was on par with that of the Guardians even though he hadn't gone through Guardian training. The pilot's time in the Air Force and military experience earned him a honorary spot.

"Who else knows?" Marcel asked.

Max spread his arms. "The head Guardians, the Guardians stationed here, the council members, Syssi and Andrew, and whoever else Kian decided to share this with, which probably includes Turner. Bottom line, too many people know about the journals and what's in them."

"There was no avoiding it." William reached with his hand intending to push his glasses up his nose, remembering at the last moment that he no longer wore them outside the lab. "The council had to be notified, the head Guardians are part of the council, and the Guardians stationed in Safe Haven had to know what information leaks to pay attention to."

"That's all true," Max conceded. "And I would trust everyone on that list with my life, but a secret is no longer a secret when so many people know about it." He leaned back and crossed his arms over his chest. "I'm glad to be out of Safe Haven, though. It's like living on a tiny island. It's too quiet, and the selection of ladies is too limited."

Morris eyed him with a raised brow. "I'm sure you didn't lack offers."

"I didn't." Max's lips lifted in a conceited smirk. "The community ladies are very generous with their affections, and most are willing to experiment, but I need more variety, and I need to hunt for my pleasure. It's not as much fun when it's offered to me on a silver platter."

William stifled an eyeroll.

Max never had to hunt for female affection.

Whenever the Guardian had managed to drag him to a nightclub, William had seen the ladies fight over him. All the guy had to do was strike an indifferent pose and hold a beer in his hand and a smirk on his face.

"The village is also like a tiny island." Morris waved a hand in dismissal. "And if you are tired of the selection, you can travel to one of the towns in the area." He turned to William. "You didn't use to have a Guardian assigned to you. Do you have one now because of the project and your knowledge of what's in the journals?"

"I don't think so." William sighed. "I think that Kian is just getting more and more paranoid. I don't leave the lab often, so assigning a Guardian to me would be a waste of a valuable resource. We don't have enough Guardians for all the rescue missions we could be running."

"You're a council member, and your knowledge is invaluable." Marcel cast him a rare smile. "We would be lost without you. Most of what I know I learned from you, not Caltech."

"Thank you." William turned sideways to stretch his legs into the aisle. "Still, when I dated a lady from Amanda's lab, I didn't have a Guardian following me around."

Max snorted. "That's what you think. Ever since the Doomer attack, there is always a team of Guardians sitting in a car outside the university when Amanda and Syssi are there. If something comes up on the security camera feed, they can be there in seconds."

"I know that. I installed the new security system after the attack. But those Guardians are there to protect Amanda and Syssi. When Hannah and I met outside the lab, no one was guarding me."

Max shrugged. "I wasn't on the force back then, but I bet Onegus sent someone to keep an eye on you as well. You are too valuable to the clan. We can't afford to lose you."

William sighed. "Enough about me and my security detail. We need to talk about the team." He turned to Marcel. "You need to remember that they are human and that they can't work eighteen-hour days. You need to adjust your expectations accordingly."

"I'm aware of that." Marcel popped the lid on his water bottle and took a sip. "Did you talk with them about the reason for your and Kaia's departure?"

"We didn't even tell them that we are leaving. I tasked Kaia with coming up with a convincing story, and I hope she'll have it ready by the time we get there."

5

KAIA

*K*aia straightened the throw blanket on the back of the couch, took a step back, and examined what she'd managed to do with William's bungalow.

It hadn't been overly messy before, just a few books lying around, a pair of shoes that had been left by the door, and several coffee mugs that had needed washing. But even when it was nice and tidy, the place lacked personality, and the pretty decor only made it look more like a hotel room.

She hadn't had much to work with, but the throw blanket added a splash of color to the gray couch, the books stacked artfully on the coffee table added interest, and the fluffed-up pillows added softness.

William was due to arrive at any moment with Marcel, Morris, and Max, and she wanted the living room to look inviting.

Kaia chuckled. She could call them the 3Ms for short or the MMM.

She'd come up with two possible explanations for why they were leaving in such a rush, and they needed to choose one and coordinate their stories before William introduced Marcel to the team. He also needed to scan Marcel's iris into the security system so the guy could open up the lab in the mornings and let the team out at the end of the day.

They didn't have enough time to do both before opening the lab this morning, so the eye scanning would have to wait for later. Work at the lab usually started at nine, but perhaps it would be a good idea for William to text the team members that there was a delay and that today they would start an hour later.

When the front door opened, she turned around and put a welcoming smile on her face.

"Good morning, gentlemen." She offered her hand to the one who wasn't smiling. "I'm Kaia."

From what William had told her about Marcel, the guy was a dry stick and rarely smiled, but what William had failed to mention was how handsome he was.

The guy was tall and slim, had great posture for a computer nerd, and he was meticulously groomed and dressed, also uncommon for people in his field.

That being said, his choice of clothing was strange. The black turtleneck was way too warm for summer, even in Oregon, and Kaia suspected that he'd adopted a uniform of sorts, like Steve Jobs had done, and wore the same thing no matter the weather or the occasion. Perhaps the black turtleneck and the tailored gray slacks was a combination he'd gotten complimented on, so he'd decided to stick with it.

"It's a pleasure to meet you." He took her hand. "I'm Marcel."

"I'm Morris." The pilot offered his hand. "I'm the guy who will be flying you home."

"Hi." Kaia returned his smile. "William tells me that you flew fighter planes in WWI."

"I did." He held on to her hand and patted it with his other one. "I can't wait to meet your uncle and talk about fighter jets with him."

"I'm sure he would love to hear the perspective of an old timer like you."

It felt strange to call Morris an old timer. The immortal looked to be in his mid-thirties and had reddish blond hair like Marcel, just not as neatly styled.

"Are you and Marcel related?" She led them to the sitting area.

"Nearly all of us are." Max clapped Morris on the back. "Right, cousin?"

Morris chose an armchair to sit in. "Thank the merciful Fates for the influx of Dormants."

"Kalugal's men were supposed to infuse new blood into our clan." Marcel remained standing. "But things are not progressing as swiftly in that department as we hoped for."

"I'm sorry," Kaia said. "But I'm still sketchy on who is who, so I can't comment on that." She waved a hand at the couch. "Please, take a seat. Can I offer you coffee? We have a pod coffeemaker, so you can choose the type of coffee you like. I can make it strong, medium, or weak."

She doubted any of the immortals would want a decaf.

"The strongest you have, please." Morris steepled his fingers in a worshipful gesture. "I desperately need some java in my system."

Kaia chuckled. "Should I be worried about my pilot being sleepy?" She put a mug under the spout and popped the pod into the slot.

"Never. I can fly Betsy with my eyes closed."

"Betsy?" Marcel lifted one reddish-blond brow. "Since when do you call your plane Betsy?"

"It used to be Matilda, but I got tired of that name, so I changed it a couple of years ago."

When everyone had gotten their coffees, Kaia sat on the couch next to William. "I thought of two possible stories we can tell the team."

"Let's hear them," Marcel said.

"They all know that my family visited me over the weekend, but they don't know where they went from here. I can tell them that my mother has a medical emergency that requires an operation, and I need to be with her and also help my stepdad with my younger siblings. They also know that William is my boyfriend, so we can tell them that he's coming along to provide support for my family and me. The other alternative is to tell them that William is needed in the lab back home because of a problem only he can solve, and I'm accompanying him because we are so in love that we can't tolerate being apart. What do you think?" She looked at the men's expressions.

"I like the second one," Morris said. "It's more romantic."

"The first one makes more sense," Max said.

Marcel shook his head. "I vote for the second one as well. Humans believe that it's bad luck to lie about someone being sick because it might come true. It might be just a superstition, but just to be on the safe side, I wouldn't lie about my mother's well-being." He looked at Kaia. "Especially when said mother is about to attempt transition."

"You're right." Kaia gripped the end of her ponytail and wound it around her finger. "I didn't think of that." She looked at William. "Which version do you prefer?"

"I like the emergency problem that needs solving, but I suggest we modify it to include you. We are both needed to address the issue, and since it's top secret, we are not allowed to share any details with the team."

"Why just me, though? Everyone on the team is a bioinformatician."

William smiled. "Because you are the best, and they all know it."

6

JADE

"What are you searching for today?" Igor asked in his annoyingly calm voice.

The sound felt oily, and it slithered from Jade's ears to coat her organs on the inside and out.

She sat at the tiny desk at the far corner of his office with her back to him and, whenever she could, she searched the internet for news she could share with the others. It was her only window to the outside world, and if he took that away from her, it would be devastating. Especially now that she had a glimmer of hope of reaching out to someone.

Shaking the feeling off, Jade grunted. "I told you what I'm doing. I'm looking for human parables to convert into meaningful stories that I can tell the children. I'm tired of repeating the same fables over and over again."

"Wasn't that what you did a week ago?"

Letting out a breath, she turned around to face him. "I'm constantly searching for new material. Sometimes it's inspirational stories, other times it's motivational stories, and today I'm searching for transformative stories. That's my method of teaching. There are some paid sites that offer material to teachers. I could really use one of those if you'd allow it. They don't cost much."

She didn't really need any of those sites, but she was preparing the groundwork for contacting Veskar.

Igor bared his fangs. "Use whatever you can find for free."

"Yes, sir." She dipped her head in mock deference. "Some sites offer free subscriptions. Can you provide me with an email address I can use for that?" Her heart lodging in her throat, Jade waited for Igor's response.

He waved a dismissive hand. "You can create an email address for free."

"Isn't it dangerous, though?" She pretended not to know that all incoming and outgoing email was rerouted and checked by his men.

"It's not." He scribbled something on a piece of paper. "If they require a mobile phone number to create your email account, you can use this one."

She rose to her feet and walked over to his desk. "Thank you."

As she reached for the note, he held it back. "I heard you are telling the children tales of the just queen and her lover, the foreign king, the father of her twin children."

She could try to deny it or cower before him, but that wasn't what he expected from her, and it might make him suspicious.

Assuming her regular defiant expression, Jade put a hand on her hip. "You have a problem with that?"

"It doesn't matter what you tell them as long as you are not twisting their minds to turn them against me."

"I can't do that even if I wanted to."

Well, of course, she wanted to, but she couldn't say anything negative about him or even imply it.

Before allowing her to teach, Igor had compelled her to sing his praises, but she'd found a way around it. She simply never mentioned him, and since her lessons were always about the distant past, there was no reason to bring him up. What she attempted to do instead was to teach the children the Kra-ell way and let them make up their own minds about what was right and what was wrong.

"You are too smart for your own good, Jade. But if I catch you plotting against me, I'll make you pay."

She swallowed the lump of terror that formed in her throat.

Whipping and torture she could withstand, and even death didn't scare her, but Igor would never kill her. She was too valuable as a breeder, and he enjoyed tormenting her too much to give up his toy.

He would hurt people she cared about to teach her a lesson, and he wasn't above using his own daughter to punish her mother. Most likely, though, he would use Kagra.

"I'm not plotting anything. As you said, I'm smart, and I know what's good for me." She walked back to her desk and the laptop that he allowed her to use only in his office and only when he was there.

"But you should know all about plotting," she murmured under her breath.

"Look at me when you speak to me," he growled.

Goading him wasn't smart, but how else was she going to make him reveal anything?

Jade turned her chair around. "Did you have spies among the scouts? Did they report to you what they found, and that was why you sabotaged the ship?"

She'd tried so many times to get him to tell her something, anything, but so far, she'd failed every time.

"You have a vivid imagination, my dear Jade. How could the scouts report to me? I was born many cycles after they were deployed. They couldn't have known that I existed." He waved a dismissive hand at her. "Go back to the nonsense that you collect to teach the children. Your imagination will serve you better there."

Jade did as she was told.

He was right of course. Igor was more or less five hundred Earth years old, and the scouts had arrived thousands of years before. But he might have gained access to whoever the scouts had been reporting to, if they'd reported anything at all.

They must have known that the children fathered by Kra-ell males with human females could not bear long-lived Kra-ell offspring, and the promises the queen had made to the settlers had been lies.

If they had reported it to the queen and she'd still sent the ship with her children on it to establish a colony, the real agenda must have been different than what the rank and file had been told.

Maybe the queen had just needed to get the twins out of their home world. They hadn't been popular, to say the least, and she might have feared for their lives. She might have destroyed the reports she'd received from the scouting team and had lied by omission.

The queen had lured the male Kra-ell into joining the expedition by tales of the abundance of Earth females they would enjoy, but she hadn't mentioned their lack of compatibility. Jade and the other females had been recruited by promises of leadership positions over the new large tribes that would include many human slaves, both male and female.

Jade didn't regret her decision to join. The Mother had guided her to take part in this adventure, and despite the disaster and having no support, she'd managed to establish a thriving tribe and had enjoyed many good years until Igor had smashed her dreams and murdered most of her family.

At least he'd spared the humans, or so he claimed. She wasn't sure she believed him. There had been hybrid children among them who hadn't manifested Kra-ell features yet, so they might have been released along with their human mothers.

Jade prayed for that to be true.

7

ERIC

"*O*kidu is not a man," Darlene whispered in Eric's ear.

They were in the back of the limousine with the partition up, so there was no need to whisper.

"What do you mean? Is he some other kind of immortal?"

She shook her head.

"Is he trans?"

Eric had wondered why Kian's butler looked older than the other immortals, thinking that he was a subspecies that aged faster, but he hadn't noticed anything feminine about the guy. He was small in stature, but there was nothing delicate about his facial features.

Darlene chuckled. "Funny that you should say that, because he can choose to look like either a female or a male but is neither," she said it in a barely audible whisper. "Okidu is a cyborg."

"No way." Eric looked through the clear glass partition at the butler's reflection in the rearview mirror. "Is he some kind of alien technology?"

During their flight to the Bay Area, Darlene had told him a lot about the clan, but there were many things she couldn't tell him because she was also new to the immortal world and still had a lot to learn.

They flew business class from the Bay Area to Los Angeles so they could have continued talking in relative privacy, but Darlene had fallen asleep, and Eric had followed her example and had napped as well.

"Shhh." She put a finger on his lips. "He has exceptionally good hearing. All the immortals do. They can hear even whispers, but with the partition up, I think we are safe."

"But he's not an immortal."

"He's not, but he's a product of the gods' technology, so he has the same abilities as the immortals and more." She scrunched her nose. "Well, also less in some areas.

453

He's not very smart, and I think the gods did that on purpose. Artificial intelligence might be dangerous to organics."

He smiled. "Are you a science fiction fan?"

"No, but my son is." Her eyes widened. "I didn't tell Roni about you yet." She pulled out her phone. "I should text him."

Eric put a hand on hers to stop her. "Let's make it a surprise. Does he have a good relationship with his father?"

Darlene shook her head. "He doesn't. But it's a long story that I don't want to get into yet."

Every time Eric mentioned Darlene's ex, she clammed up and changed the subject. She'd given him some crumbs of information, so he knew that her ex was a piece of work, but whatever she chose to tell him was always on her terms, and he knew better than to ask.

Eric could understand that.

Her divorce was still like a fresh wound, and picking at it was painful. He'd been the same after his marriage had ended, and it had taken two years before he could talk about it without being consumed with rage.

In that regard, Kian's cyborg butler was a much safer topic.

"Is Okidu the only one the clan has?" Eric asked in a whisper.

Kian had sent his own butler to pick them up from the airport, which meant that the clan didn't have an abundance of cyborg servants.

Darlene shook her head.

"How many do they have?"

"Seven, and they weren't made by the clan. They were a present to the Clan Mother from her betrothed, and she doesn't allow William to tinker with them. She treats them like members of the family."

"Are they sentient?"

Darlene pursed her lips. "I don't know. To me, they look like they are, but I'm not an expert."

"What does William say?"

"He says that it's not a question for an engineer but for an ethicist. What does it mean to be sentient? How can we differentiate between real feelings and mimicry of them? William explained that the Odus learned human behavior by mimicking it."

"That's how children learn as well."

"Precisely." Darlene let out a breath. "The goddess is infinitely wise. She treats them as people, with kindness and respect as if they are sentient."

"What about your grandfather?"

Eric was looking forward to meeting the god, but he was also apprehensive. What if Toven didn't approve of him as a suitable partner for Darlene?

"Toven does the same." Darlene smiled. "In fact, he's quite fond of Okidu. Mia told me that when Okidu came to pick them up from their house, Toven greeted him like a long-lost relative and even hugged him, and he's not a hugger."

"Is he cold?"

She shook her head. "I wouldn't say that."

"So, how would you describe him?"

"Toven is aloof, and he seems condescending, but he doesn't do it on purpose. He's a god, so naturally he feels superior to everyone, including the immortals."

She smiled. "That being said, he's changed a lot since he met Mia, and he worships the ground she rolls over."

Eric wasn't familiar with that expression, but maybe it was a new thing, and he didn't want Darlene to think that he wasn't keeping up with current trends and jargon.

"Is Mia your grandfather's mate?"

Darlene nodded. "She's very sweet. You're going to like her."

"What about your grandfather? Am I going to like him too? Or, more importantly, is he going to like me?"

Darlene leaned closer and kissed his cheek. "He's going to love you."

8

DARLENE

$\mathcal{A}$s the windows of the limousine started to turn opaque, Eric watched the process with fascination. "They have this on Dreamliners, but I've never seen it done on car windows. Are the front ones also opaque?"

"I think so." Darlene leaned against his shoulder. "The Odus know where everything is, including Annani's sanctuary, so it's not necessary, but I never checked. We will enter the tunnel soon, and it will become a little darker and cooler in the car, but that's the only indication we will get. I'm dying to see how the entrance to the tunnels is hidden, but unless I somehow manage to become a head Guardian, that's not in the cards."

Eric regarded her with surprise in his eyes. "Do you want to become a Guardian?"

"No, but only the head Guardians are privy to that information. That's why I said it."

Darlene was babbling nonsense because she was nervous. She still hadn't told Eric that she didn't have a place of her own, and it annoyed her that she didn't have the guts to just say what needed to be said and be done with it.

Years with Leo had conditioned her to always choose safe topics for conversation and never mention anything that might be even a little bit upsetting or uncomfortable to him, which resulted in her often sounding like an airhead.

But Eric wasn't Leo, and she shouldn't repeat the mistakes of the past.

"I need to tell you something." She sighed. "I don't have a place of my own. Before coming to Safe Haven, I stayed with my mother and her partner. I would have asked William to help secure a house for us, but he had his hands full, and I didn't want to bother him."

Eric's hand squeezed her shoulder. "I don't mind staying with your mother and her mate if they don't mind hosting me. I assume that you have your own room?"

"I do, but it's time for me to assert myself and tell my mother that I'm too old to

456

be babied by her. I stayed with her not because I had to or wanted to, but because it would have upset her if I said I didn't want to live with her."

It was a relief to finally tell Eric the truth and an even bigger relief that he hadn't made a big deal out of it.

As the limousine entered the tunnel, the temperature in the vehicle dropped by a few degrees, and it became dark.

"Why did she want you to move in with her in the first place?"

Darlene hadn't told Eric that story yet, and she wasn't in the mood to do it now. In fact, she didn't want to talk about the past at all.

This was a new start for her, and she didn't want to taint it with a history that was better forgotten.

"It's a long story. We haven't seen each other since I was a young girl, and when we found each other again, my mother became clingy and wanted to recapture all those lost years."

"Why were you separated?"

The limousine came to a stop and, a moment later, lurched up as the elevator platform started rising.

"Did you feel that? We are going up in an elevator for cars. Isn't that cool?"

Eric grimaced. "Every time I ask you something personal, you change the subject. I can understand you not wanting to talk about your ex so soon after the divorce, but why can't you talk about your mother?"

He was right, and there was no harm in telling him about her history with her mother. Especially not now when she no longer needed to come up with ways to tell the story without revealing that her mother was a demigoddess.

Darlene sighed. "That story is messed up as well. I thought she had died, and then nearly four decades later, she popped into my life together with my half-sister, and the two pretended to be my cousins, the daughters of my mother's nonexistent twin sister. I know that they meant well, and I know my mother didn't mean to disappear on me when I was twelve, but it still hurt no matter what the explanation was. I forgave her up here." She tapped her temple. "But the heart is not logical."

"Did she fake her own death because she wasn't aging?"

"She was in a nearly fatal boating accident and survived only because she was a god's daughter. Any other immortal would have died from an injury like that. She survived, but her memories didn't, and she didn't know that she had a daughter and a husband who were mourning her death."

As the limousine exited the elevator, the windows cleared, and Okidu lowered the partition. "Welcome to the village, Master Eric." He eased the limo into the designated parking spot and turned toward them. "Shall I bring the luggage to Mistress Geraldine and Master Shai's home?"

Darlene shook her head. "Can we leave it in the limo for now? I'm not sure where we will be staying yet."

Okidu affected a regretful expression. "I am afraid that it is not possible. I have another trip scheduled for later today to collect Masters William, Morris, Max, and Mistress Kaia from the clan airstrip. I need the trunk to be available for their luggage."

"Let's just take it to your mother's house." Eric opened the door. "We can leave our suitcases by the door and leave the unpacking for when we know where we will be staying."

9

ERIC

*I*t seemed like Darlene was carrying even more emotional baggage than Eric had realized. It wasn't just her marriage that had left scars on her psyche, but also unresolved issues with her mother.

Evidently, even a demi-demigoddess's life wasn't charmed, and she had things to deal with like any other mortal.

Normally, he would have stayed away from a woman who needed to work through so much crap, but it was different with Darlene.

He wanted to be there for her, to help her heal from those soul wounds, and if he could, also to facilitate her transition.

He didn't want her to wait six months, though. If he could minimize the risk to her life even marginally by inviting an immortal male into their bed, he would do that with no hesitation.

Since his divorce, Eric had done some kinky shit and had thought nothing of it, so it shouldn't have been a problem, but the possessive way he felt about Darlene made it difficult. He didn't want to share her with another male or a female, but he would if he had to.

"So, what do you think?" Darlene asked.

She'd been showing him the village central square, but he'd been paying only cursory attention to what she'd been saying.

"It's very nice."

She tilted her head. "You don't seem impressed."

"I am. It's a nice little gem hidden from the world. I was just wondering whether you told your mother that you were coming back."

It was one thing for the daughter to come back unannounced, and another thing altogether for said daughter to show up on her mother's doorstep with a guy.

"Of course, I did. If I didn't call her every day while I was away and tell her in detail everything that was happening with me, she would have gone into a crying fit. Naturally, you were the star of my recent reports."

"Oh, yeah? What did you tell her about me?"

She smirked. "That you were a cad."

"Seriously?"

"I told her that you were a charming, good-looking player but that I found you irresistible nonetheless. She wasn't happy about that, but then I told her that you are a potential Dormant, and she said that once you become immortal, you would change your ways and leave your wild days behind."

As Darlene cast him a smile and resumed walking, he fell in step with her, pulling their suitcases behind him. "I wasn't always a player. I was loyal to my cheating wife. After the divorce, I didn't want to get attached to anyone, and I went a little wild."

Darlene gave him a pitying glance. "I'm sorry you had to go through that. Leo was a verbally abusive jerk, but as far as I know, he didn't cheat on me."

So that was the key to unlocking Darlene's tight lips. If he shared his pain with her, she would share hers with him.

"Well, my wife was both. She was disloyal and verbally abusive, sometimes physically as well."

Men didn't like to admit that they had been physically abused by their significant others, but Eric knew he wasn't the only one who had been subjected to that.

He didn't feel shamed by it, though.

The fact that he'd never raised his hand to a woman, not even in self-defense, didn't make him weak. It made him strong.

"What did she do?" Darlene asked softly.

"She threw things at me, slapped me, kicked me, but I never responded physically. I just walked out the door and came back hours later after she calmed down. My mistake was that I came back. After the first time it happened, I should have walked out and never come back. But she always apologized with tears in her eyes and real remorse in her voice, and then we made love, and it was great, so I forgave her time and again."

"You're a good man, Eric." Darlene put her hand on his arm.

"Am I? Or am I just a pushover?"

"You're not a pushover." She sighed. "It's not easy. I believed that people gave up on their marriages too easily, and I didn't want to be part of the depressing statistics. That was the lie I told myself to not feel like a failure. But the truth was that I was afraid of being alone, and I thought that if I left Leo, I would become a cat lady." She chuckled sadly. "And I don't even like cats."

"What gave you the push to leave?"

Darlene smiled. "Discovering that I was a demi-demigoddess. I realized that I should be worshiped, and Leo wasn't the worshiping type."

10

DARLENE

$\mathcal{E}$ric laughed. "You are absolutely right, and I'm honored and delighted to worship you."

"Thank you. I expect some worshiping tonight."

He stopped and turned to her with eyes that were molten with desire. "Come here." He let go of the suitcases and pulled her into his arms. "Let me give you a little aperitif to whet your appetite."

Darlene didn't care that they were less than fifty feet away from her mother's doorstep, and knowing Geraldine, she was standing at the living room window and watching them from behind the curtain.

Eric needed this after his confession, and so did she.

Melting into him, she kissed him with the same fervor he kissed her.

Poor guy.

She couldn't imagine this proud, charming, handsome man being treated so badly by his ex-wife. Hell, he'd been abused to the point of being traumatized.

Compared to Eric's ex, Leo hadn't been so bad. He'd been a cold bastard who'd thrived on putting her down, but at least he'd never hit her or thrown things at her.

Clearly, the woman had mental problems, and Darlene wondered why they had never been addressed. Perhaps she'd refused? Eric was an intelligent guy. She was sure he'd suggested therapy at some point.

When they came up for air, she chuckled. "My mother is probably watching us from behind the curtain, and we've just given her one hell of a show."

"Is she conservative? Will it upset her?"

Darlene laughed. "She's the opposite of that. My mother is unconventional in every way." She should warn him about Geraldine's flights of fancy. "Be prepared to hear some crazy stories." She resumed walking. "My mother still has memory issues, and she fills the gaps with fantastic tales, mostly about the fabulous lovers

461

she had. Talk about being a player. Although in my mother's case, it wasn't really her fault."

Thankfully, Geraldine had enough sense not to talk about her former lovers in front of Shai.

"What do you mean? Were her memory issues so bad that she didn't remember her lovers? Then how could she tell stories about them? Besides, what's wrong with her being a player?"

"Nothing. It's perfectly okay for a single woman to enjoy herself with as many men as she pleases, but she was still married to my father. She just didn't know that she was."

The curious thing, though, was that Orion had tried to bring back the memories of her past boyfriends that he'd confused and muddled, but it hadn't worked. Her mother's head was either too messed up for him to make sense of what was going on inside of it, or maybe Geraldine just enjoyed telling those stories too much to let go of them.

"Was it because of the accident?" Eric asked.

"Yeah." Darlene smiled apologetically. "There is more to the story, but I'll save it for another time."

As they climbed the steps to Geraldine's front porch, the door opened, and her mother flew out, looking like a butterfly in her yellow voluminous skirt and white, form-fitting blouse.

"Darlene!" She pulled her into her arms. "I missed you so much." She squeezed her tight.

"I missed you too," Darlene lied as she untangled herself from her mother's arms. "Let me introduce you to Eric."

The truth was that she hadn't had the chance to miss Geraldine since they'd talked every day.

"Hello." Geraldine wiped the tears from under her eyes.

"It's a pleasure to meet you." Eric offered her his hand.

Her mother took it and then pulled him in for a quick hug. "You are even more handsome than my daughter let on."

"Thank you." He smiled, and one adorable dimple appeared on his left cheek.

"Please, come in." Geraldine ushered them inside. "You must be hungry after so many hours of travel."

"We flew business class," Darlene said. "The food wasn't bad."

"Good. I made dinner early today, but if you're not hungry, we can wait for Shai to get here." Geraldine waved them toward the couch. "Please, sit down and tell me everything."

Eric left the suitcases by the door, took Darlene's hand, and walked with her to the couch.

Geraldine sat in the armchair facing both of them. "Shai wants to meet the man who finally convinced Darlene to end her self-imposed celibacy."

Darlene rolled her eyes. "Really? That's the first thing you say to my new boyfriend?"

Geraldine laughed. "Isn't that funny how mothers and daughters interact the same way no matter what age they are?"

Eric chuckled. "I can't think of you as mother and daughter. Sisters, maybe."

Geraldine's eyes widened. "Speaking of sisters, I almost forgot. Cassandra and

Onegus are joining us for coffee and dessert. Cassy is cutting her day short and coming home early so she can see you."

Eric looked at Darlene. "I don't think we can stay that long. My brother and Karen are scheduled to meet the doctor later today, and we are supposed to take part in that meeting."

"I see." Geraldine's happy smile wilted. "That takes precedence, of course. We will work around your schedule." She rose to her feet. "Can I offer you something to drink while we wait for Shai?"

"I'll get it." Darlene followed her up. "I'm in the mood for beer." She turned to Eric. "Do you want one too?"

"Yes, please."

In the kitchen, she pulled her mother aside. "I didn't want the waterworks to start in front of Eric, but I hope you don't expect us to stay with you and Shai. I want us to get a place of our own."

Surprisingly, Geraldine didn't start crying. Instead, she smiled. "Of course. I only want what's best for you, and right now, that's playing house with Eric." She leaned closer to whisper in her ear. "He's adorable. I felt the affinity as soon as I saw him. He's a Dormant for sure."

"I certainly hope so."

11

WILLIAM

"*I*t's amazing here." Kaia turned in a circle. "I love it." She waved her hand at the café. "Is that the only place to eat in the village?"

"For now," William said. "Callie's restaurant is about to be opened. Everyone is looking forward to the day it does."

"Callie is mated to the blond Guardian, right?"

"She is." Max stopped at a fork in the pathway. "I'm heading home. If you need me, give me a call."

Kaia lifted on her toes and kissed the Guardian's cheek. "Don't be a stranger. As soon as I get settled in William's place, you're invited for dinner."

He lifted a brow. "You cook?"

"I do, and I do it well."

He shook his head. "That's not fair. You're smart and beautiful, and you can cook. Couldn't you have an older sister instead of a younger one?"

Kaia laughed. "Cheryl might be the one for you. You'll just have to wait a few years."

He grimaced. "She's a kid. I can't even think of her that way."

William echoed his expression. "I thought the same about Kaia, and here we are."

"Kaia is at least of legal age." The Guardian clapped him on the back. "Good luck to both of you."

"Thanks," Kaia said.

When they were alone on the path, she looked over her shoulder. "Where is Okidu? He was supposed to bring our luggage to your house."

"He's probably taken a shortcut and is already there, but we are not going to our house. We are going to see your family first."

"Why? I want to see your place and then go to theirs."

He smiled sheepishly. "I asked Okidu to clean up before we got there. I left the

464

place a little messy." That was an understatement, but he didn't want Kaia to think that he was a slob.

"Don't you have a roommate?"

He shook his head. "I used to have one, but once the latest phase of the village was completed, Kian moved the council members, the head Guardians, and most of the Guardian force to the new houses. My roommate decided to stay in the old one."

She threaded her arm through his. "Did you get lonely?"

William chuckled. "I work such long hours that when I come home, it's to shower and sleep. My life is in the lab."

"Not anymore." Kaia leaned her head on his arm. "Things are going to change now that I'm here. I'm going to cook dinners and invite people over. I want us to have a life outside of work."

William swallowed. "I would love that, but I don't know if I can. I have so much work to do, and I'm always behind. I wish I could find a solution for that, but there isn't one. I've already hired everyone that I could hire, and we are maxed out. It stresses me just to think about all the projects that I put on hold so I can work on the journals."

"I have a solution." Kaia smiled conspiratorially. "We will build a team of Odus to help in the lab."

He narrowed his eyes at her. "That's the least suitable work for cyborgs. I want to build gardeners, house cleaners, and maybe construction workers. That's what we need most in the village."

"I was just joking." She tilted her head. "I know that the village needs to remain a secret and all that, but you can bring Emmett and Eleanor here to compel the humans you hire to keep quiet about it. There are many talented people out there who can ease your workload in the lab. We will also need a geneticist and an ethicist, and I don't want to wait for your immortals to get their PhDs in those fields."

"When we get to that stage, we will be back at Safe Haven, and I can hire whoever you want out there."

"Good point. You could also build a proper DNA testing facility out there. You need one."

He stopped and turned to her. "That's a brilliant idea. After we are done with our research, we can convert the lab in Safe Haven into a genetics lab."

"I don't think it's big enough. Some of the equipment is bulky, and you need a whole crew of people to operate it."

"That's solvable." William resumed walking. "What's not feasible is moving Bridget to Safe Haven, and she's the only one who has any knowledge in the field. She's not a geneticist, but she's been doing research on the side for years."

"Why can't she move to Safe Haven? You said that there are three doctors in the village, which doesn't really make sense because no one gets sick."

"We still need to take care of transitioning Dormants, births, injuries, and so on. Bridget is our most experienced doctor, but medicine is not the only thing she does. She's also in charge of running the rescue missions."

"Can't you assign that task to someone else? It's not like a doctor needs to be in charge of raids. One of the head Guardians can do that."

"She's also a council member, and she's mated to a guy who has an office in Los Angeles. She wouldn't want to move, and even if she did, Kian would not allow it."

12

KAIA

*A*fter Kaia was done hugging everyone as if they hadn't seen each other for at least a month, her mother offered to take her on a tour of the house.

It started with the kitchen, continued in the two kids' bedrooms, and culminated in the primary bedroom, which had an awesome bathroom with a jacuzzi tub big enough for two.

"The bathroom is almost as nice as the one in our house."

Her mother nodded. "As I said, this house is very nice but small."

"It's small only when compared to ours." Kaia followed her mother back to the living room. "It's more than sufficient for most families."

"It's smaller than the homes I build," Gilbert said. "And my gated communities are meant for ordinary people, not rich folks."

Kaia shrugged. "I can see myself raising a family in a house like this. It's big enough for a couple with three kids."

"I guess so." Her mother sat on the couch and glanced at her watch. "They should be here already."

"They'll be here soon," William said.

Her mother turned to Cheryl. "Do you mind taking the little ones to our bedroom? You can put on one of the shows they like to watch."

Since the conversation would no doubt include adult themes, Kaia could understand her mother's wish to have just the adults in the living room. But in her opinion, Cheryl was old enough to hear whatever the doctor had to say, and since it involved her future as well, she should. Then again, they needed someone to watch the little ones, and Cheryl had plenty of time until the information became relevant to her.

"Fine," Cheryl agreed grudgingly. "Come on, Idina. Let's go." She picked up the boys and carried them to the bedroom.

For a long moment, a tense silence stretched over the living room as they waited for Syssi and Kian to arrive with the famed physician.

466

"What are your plans for dinner?" Kaia asked her mother to break the silence. "Do you want me to quickly whip something up?"

Her mother smiled. "I have a fridge full of casseroles, stews, and pasta that were left on our doorstep. I assume that when people heard about a family of humans with four kids staying in the village, they assumed that we would need food, but they didn't want to come in and say hello in case we don't transition."

Kaia cast William a sidelong glance. "Is that so?"

He nodded. "Makes sense."

"One of the casseroles is from my mother," Darlene said. "She didn't knock on your door to say hello because she knows how overwhelmed you must feel." She turned to Karen. "She asked me to get your phone number so she could invite you for dinner at her house once you get settled in."

"Darlene's mother is very nice," Eric said. "She's a beautiful woman like her daughter, and she's a great cook as well."

"When did you have time to eat?" Kaia asked.

"Geraldine planned for us to stay for dinner, and when she found out that we couldn't, she insisted we eat earlier. We had to leave before Darlene's sister and her mate arrived, but we got to meet Shai, who is Kian's assistant. A very pleasant fellow as well."

Was Eric putting Shai and Kian in the same category of pleasant fellows? Or had he meant that Geraldine and her mate were both pleasant people?

Kian was many things, but pleasant wasn't one of them. He was intense, intimidating, and too handsome. It wasn't that she was attracted to him, but her eyes were drawn to him like to a beautiful work of art.

Perfect and unapproachable.

The only times the guy seemed remotely human was when he interacted with his daughter.

When the doorbell chimed, Gilbert jumped to his feet and rushed to open the door.

"Good afternoon." Kian strode into the room with Syssi on one side and a petite redhead on the other. "Let me introduce our prestigious physician, Doctor Bridget."

The woman wasn't wearing a white coat or the sensible shoes most doctors wore. She wore loose slacks, a fitted blouse, and a pair of high heels. And yet, it wasn't difficult to guess who she was, and it wasn't just the old-fashioned black doctor's bag that gave her away. It was the air of authority and confidence.

Kaia was willing to bet that even Kian couldn't intimidate her.

"Hello." The doctor smiled brightly.

A round of introductions ensued, and when it was done, and everyone was seated around the dining table with a cup of tea or coffee in hand, Kian turned to Bridget. "The stage is yours, doctor."

She nodded. "I'm sure you have many questions, and I'm here to answer them to the best of my ability. I also brought swabs, syringes, and test tubes with me, so once we are done, I'll take samples from Gilbert and Eric. I already have Syssi's results, so I don't need to take hers."

"Well, that answers half of my first question," Kaia said. "It was whether you could perform the tests and evaluate the results in-house."

"I'll have the results ready by tomorrow. I understand that you are not related to Gilbert and Eric, but I still need a sample from you as well. I like to take a sample before the transition starts. It helps me evaluate your progress during the process and then post-transition. I will also keep your mitochondrial DNA results on file for future reference."

"Do you test the mitochondrial DNA of every newcomer?" Karen asked.

"I do. We have a strong taboo against matings between people of the same matrilineal descent, no matter how far back it goes. Our clan used to be comprised solely of Annani's descendants, so we always treated each other as if we were first cousins, but since the influx of new members in the last several years, it's become important to keep track of who was the descendant of which line. That's why I collect that information from new arrivals. We will need it when the next generation comes of age." She smiled. "As I said, I like to take samples before and after the transition, but many times I don't have access to the before and have to make do with just the after. I'm glad that this time I get to take them from all of you."

No one was getting near her baby brothers and Idina with needles for no good reason.

"You don't need samples from the little ones." Kaia cast Bridget a hard look. "You can take samples from my mother and me. The others are not about to attempt transition anytime soon, so there is no rush."

The doctor returned a hard look of her own, but she softened it with a smile. "I didn't intend to. I'm only interested in samples from those who are about to get induced in the very near future."

KIAN

*K*ian hadn't talked with Bridget about her research in a long time, and he was curious about whether she'd found connections between the Dormants. Jacki and Turner had similar coloring and were both immune to thralling and compulsion, which made him suspect that they had a shared ancestor. Although it could be that they were the descendants of the same male god and not the same goddess or an immortal female.

Kalugal and Lokan had inherited their compulsion ability from Navuh, not Areana, and Orion inherited his ability from Toven. The source was no doubt Ekin, Mortdh and Toven's father, but curiously, Annani had never mentioned that about her uncle. Perhaps he hadn't used it, or maybe he'd inherited it from his father or mother but hadn't manifested the ability and only gave it to his sons.

"What kind of equipment do you have in your lab?" Kaia asked.

Bridget lifted a red brow. "I can give you a tour if you like. What are you interested in?"

"You can obviously perform mitochondrial DNA analysis, but can you do a full gene sequencing?"

Bridget shook her head. "I can't. Now that the prices of the equipment have dropped and the machines themselves have shrunk in size, I've been contemplating equipping my lab with everything needed for full sequencing and playing around with it, but the truth is that I don't have time. I would love for one of our clan members to study genetics and take over the research." She smiled at Kaia. "Are you interested?"

"I'm a bioinformatician. I analyze the data geneticists collect."

"And I am a physician who also heads the clan's rescue operations. I can't wear one more hat."

Kian lifted his hand to stop their oddly combative conversation. He liked both of them, but maybe they just rubbed each other the wrong way.

He turned to Bridget. "Can you please explain to me in layperson's terms what you can find out about people's genetics with what you have, and what more can be learned with better equipment?"

"Yeah," Gilbert said. "I didn't even know that there were different types of DNA. What is mitochondria, and does it have anything to do with hypochondria?"

Kaia chuckled. "Don't take him seriously. He just likes to make silly comments like that to get a rise out of people."

Bridget smiled one of her indulgent smiles. "The mitochondrial DNA is a small portion of the total DNA, containing only 37 of the many thousands of protein-coding genes in our bodies. The chromosomal DNA is encoded in the nucleus of the cells and is contributed by both parents. The mitochondrial DNA is encoded in the mitochondria of the cell and is contributed only by the mother."

"Forgive my ignorance," Eric said. "But what is mitochondria? I'm afraid I wasn't a good biology student." He smirked. "Probably because the teacher was a hottie, and I kept fantasizing about her seducing me instead of paying attention to what she was trying to teach us."

Laughing, Darlene slapped his arm. "I was right to tell my mother that you were a cad. You were bad even as a boy."

Gilbert snorted. "There are no worse pervs than teenage boys. I remember those days, and not fondly."

Bridget waited patiently until everyone quieted again. "Mitochondria are organelles inside the cell that are membrane-bound. They generate most of the chemical energy needed to power the cell's biochemical reactions. But the mitochondrial function is helped by about fifteen hundred genes, so it's not like we can learn the secret to immortality just from looking at the mitochondria." She sighed. "I hoped that would be the case, but it wasn't."

"Why would the secret be limited to the mitochondria?" Karen asked. "If it's made from just 37 genes, it would have been easy to identify an extra one or find one that was different from the others."

Bridget nodded. "That's what I checked for and regrettably didn't find. What led me to research the mitochondria was that the immortal genes are passed through the maternal line and follow the same rules as a mitochondrial inheritance in humans."

"What do you mean?" Eric asked. "How does it work in humans?"

"Females inherit mitochondrial DNA from their mothers and pass it on to both their sons and daughters. Males inherit the mitochondrial DNA from their mothers but do not pass it on to their children. They inherit the Y-DNA from their fathers and pass it on to their sons but not their daughters."

That could explain why Orion had inherited Toven's compulsion ability, but Geraldine hadn't. But it didn't explain how male gods could produce immortal children with human females. According to Bridget's explanation, they shouldn't be able to. Also, unless his maternal grandmother was also a compeller, Annani had inherited her compulsion ability from Ahn, and supposedly, he couldn't have passed it to his daughters.

Perhaps the gods were built differently, and when they mated with humans, they passed their complete DNA to their children, but the offspring's DNA followed the split human structure.

"Now I get it." Eric leaned back in his chair. "That's why only the children of immortal females carry the immortal genes. The immortal males can't pass them to their children."

"Precisely." Bridget gave him a bright smile. "The nuclear DNA is worth investigating, but the secret of immortality is obviously hiding in the mitochondria, which is why I focused my research just on that. When we get a geneticist in the clan, we might consider building a proper lab. But until then, it would be a waste. The equipment is getting better and better, and if we buy it now, it will become obsolete by the time someone from the clan becomes a geneticist."

"We can build a genetic testing lab in Safe Haven," William said. "Over there, we can have humans operate it and just compel them to take the secrets they discover to their graves."

Kian shook his head. "It's too dangerous. Compulsion is not foolproof. But that's a discussion for a different time. Let's focus on Gilbert and Eric's relationship to Syssi."

Bridget nodded. "Are there any more questions?"

"How far back can the mitochondrial DNA be traced?" Karen asked.

"That's an excellent question," the doctor said. "Mitochondrial DNA tests are effective for tracing your maternal lineage up to 52 generations, but they are not accurate. That far back, the test can only tell us the direct-line maternal haplogroup, which can tell us which region of the world the mother's maternal line came from. But since we need only three generations, we are good."

Gilbert let out a breath. "Perfect. We only need to confirm that we share a great-great-grandmother with Syssi."

"What about finding other maternal lineage relatives?" Kaia asked. "You might find many more Dormants that way."

Bridget shook her head. "I don't have access to a large database like 23andMe and others like it to find people who might be related to the Dormants we've found so far."

"I tried it." Gilbert waved a dismissive hand. "It confirmed what I already knew about my heritage, but it didn't find any new relatives that I didn't know about before. If there are any, they didn't submit their samples for testing."

"We can hack into the database." William looked at Kian. "If that's okay with you. Maybe Bridget can find maternal relatives of the other Dormants."

"Do it. If we can find even one more Dormant through the information those labs keep on file, it's worth the effort."

Next to him, Syssi shook her head. "It won't work. Every scientific method we have tried so far has failed. All the Dormants were found seemingly by chance, but when it happened time and again, we had to concede that it must be orchestrated by the Fates."

"The Fates?" Eric asked.

Darlene put a hand on his arm. "Syssi is right. I'll tell you later how Cassandra met Onegus and how Orion was found, and you'll see what she meant by that."

He nodded.

"I have a question," Kian said. "How far back can the Y-DNA test go?"

"Y-DNA testing can tell us some information about our ancient direct-line paternal ancestors going back a hundred thousand years." Bridget reached for her doctor's bag and lifted it onto her lap. "All men living today inherited their Y-chromosome from a single direct-line male ancestor. But like mitochondrial testing, it covers only about one percent of our ancestors. We can learn much more about recent direct-line paternal ancestors going back no more than a thousand years."

"So we can't trace lineage to the original male gods." Kian crossed his arms over his chest.

"That's correct."

That was interesting.

The Sumerian myths talked about the essence of one male god being used to impregnate local creatures and create humanity. Perhaps that god had been the singular male ancestor all Y-DNA could be traced to.

14

ERIC

$\mathcal{A}$fter the swabs had been taken and the doctor had left with Syssi and Kian, Eric and Darlene got ready to leave as well.

Shai had arranged a meeting for them with the interior designer who was in charge of housing in the village, so she could show them what was available.

"Stay for dinner," Karen urged. "You can call Ingrid and ask to meet her later."

Eric gave her a one-armed hug. "It's getting late, and I'm sure she wants to end her workday. When Darlene chooses the house she wants, we will come back for a cup of coffee." He kissed her cheek. "Save us some leftovers."

"I will."

"There is no shortage of vacant houses in the village," William said. "You can have your pick."

"I know." Darlene took Eric's hand. "I want to find out what's available, which is why we are meeting Ingrid at the café to go over the options. It's a big day for me." She sighed. "It will be the first house that I'm not sharing with Leo."

"Good luck." Kaia waved at them before ducking into the kitchen.

Opening the door, Eric leaned down to whisper in Darlene's ear, "I hope you'll be sharing it with me."

"Of course." She beamed at him. "That's why we are meeting Ingrid together."

"Good save." He gave her hand a light squeeze.

Their relationship was progressing at warp speed, which usually wasn't a good thing, but from what he'd heard from the immortals, that wasn't uncommon for them. Dormants and immortals felt an affinity for each other, and those who found their truelove mate fell in love fast and hard.

Was Darlene his one and only, though?

He wasn't a great believer in mystical connections, but he wasn't a disbeliever either. He was a maybe kind of guy, and he was willing to suspend disbelief and embrace the immortals' explanation. It made life easier, and it reduced self-doubt to manageable proportions.

"My head is spinning from all we've learned today." Darlene put a hand on her temple. "The field of genetics is fascinating, but it's so complicated. There are so many terms I'm unfamiliar with that even though Bridget tried to dumb it down for us, I had a hard time following her."

"Same here." He looked at the path forking ahead of them. "To get to the café, we need to take the left turn, right?"

Darlene chuckled. "Left or right?" She pointed to the left. "It's that way. Do you know that the immortals can smell it even from here? Their senses are incredible."

"We are about to become them, so you should start thinking in terms of we, not them."

Darlene looked at him with fearful eyes. "I don't think I'll be able to get any sleep tonight. I'm so anxious to hear back from Bridget."

He stopped and wrapped his arms around her. "I'm going to attempt transition regardless of Bridget's findings. I'm sure that I'm a Dormant even if I'm not related to Syssi. How else would you explain us? We are going to choose a house together, and it feels as natural as if we had been dating for months."

"You are right." She lifted on her toes and kissed him lightly on the lips. "Being with you is so easy. I don't have to work hard to please you. I can be myself, and you seem happy with me the way I am."

He pressed a soft kiss to her forehead. "I don't want to change a single thing about you other than your longevity. I want you to live forever." He leaned away and looked into her eyes. "I want you to go for it right away and not wait until I can induce you."

Darlene shook her head. "How can you say that given what's required for that to happen? Can you tolerate knowing that I'm having sex with another man? Especially after what you've been through with your ex?"

"As long as it's not behind my back, and I'm there with you, I think I can." He sighed. "After the divorce, I experimented a lot. I've done threesomes, some with two women, others with a woman and a man. It was exciting, and I enjoyed myself, but those were people I didn't have an emotional connection with. I know it's going to be difficult to share you with another man, but my difficulty is immaterial. If we find someone who we both like and who is open-minded about sex, I think we can pull it off without it destroying what we have."

15

DARLENE

$\mathcal{T}$he image that Eric's words evoked was Max's smiling face. Darlene remembered vividly how he had looked when he'd flirted with her on the bus, and it wasn't a bad memory. Max had been a little pushy but never obnoxious, and she'd enjoyed flirting with him, but she couldn't see herself with him and Eric in bed.

It was just too scandalous.

After it had become known that Eric was a potential Dormant, Max had backed off, and she'd thought that was the end of it. But when Kaia had told her that Max had requested to be transferred back to the village and had returned with them, Darlene suspected that it had something to do with her.

"We can worry about me later." She took Eric's hand and led him toward the café. "First, we need to find you an inducer, and you need to transition."

"I thought that William would induce me."

She chuckled. "He's not the best candidate for that. William abhors anything that has to do with sports, and he doesn't know the first thing about wrestling. You need to choose someone who is a capable fighter, like a Guardian, and he should be someone you like."

"Why? All I need to do is provoke his aggression. I don't need to be friends with him."

"Wrong. The inducer and the inductee promise eternal friendship to each other."

Eric shrugged. "I can be friends with William. I don't know any other immortal males."

"What about Anandur or Brundar? They are both head Guardians, and they are among the best, if not the best. After all, Kian wouldn't choose inferior warriors as his bodyguards."

Eric frowned. "Brundar is a killer, and he scares the hell out of me. Anandur is just too big. I need someone who I stand a chance against for at least a few minutes. If I'm flat on my back in seconds, it would be devastating to my ego."

Darlene wasn't sure whether he was being serious or not, and she didn't want to make a choice for him. "Choose whomever you like." She waved a hand at the café. "I can introduce you to some of the males. That's Richard." She pointed. "He's a newly transitioned immortal, but it has been more than six months since his transition. He would be honored to be chosen." She scrunched her nose. "But maybe he's not your best candidate. I heard that he had a really hard time entering his transition and required multiple attempts by different immortals. That means that his genes are highly diluted."

"Who ended up inducing him?"

"I think it was Kian, or maybe it was Kalugal? I'm not sure. Anyway, Kian induced Roni after several others failed to initiate him." She snorted. "My Roni is no fighter either. He spurred Kian's aggression by reciting particularly vile slam poetry."

She still had to introduce Eric and Roni, but she wanted a word with her son first. Roni could be very rude without meaning to be, and she didn't want him and Eric to start their relationship on the wrong foot.

After they'd ordered coffees and pastries, they took their order to a table next to Richard's.

He got to his feet and offered his hand to Eric. "I heard that an entire family of potential Dormants is staying in the village. You must be the younger brother who snagged our Darlene."

"That's me." Eric grinned. "Eric Emerson."

"Richard." The men shook hands.

"Can I join?" a familiar voice said from behind her.

Darlene turned around. "Max. What a nice surprise." She felt her cheeks heating up. "I didn't expect to see you here. Of course, you can join us."

She hadn't seen the Guardian standing in line, and given the paper cup he was holding, she knew why. He'd used the vending machines.

"I'm heading home," Richard said. "Good luck to you and your family." He turned to Darlene. "If you need anything, let me know."

"Thank you." She sat down.

Max watched the guy walk away and snorted. "What can he do for you? Are you remodeling a house?"

Was that what Richard did for a living?

As far as she knew, he worked as a supervisor on Kian's building projects. He wasn't a handyman. But who knew? Maybe it was his side gig.

"I might. We are meeting Ingrid to go over housing options."

Max pulled out a chair and sat down. "Together? Isn't that too early?" He turned to look at Eric. "You didn't transition yet, and there is no guarantee that you will. Or did Bridget already confirm that you and Gilbert are related to Syssi?"

"She took swabs from us and said that she would have the results by tomorrow, but I'm sure that I'm a Dormant."

Max lifted a brow. "Based on what?"

Eric cast Darlene a charming smile. "The affinity I feel for all of you and how fast Darlene and I fell for each other."

She swallowed.

He hadn't told her that he loved her, and she hadn't told him that either. It was too early even for Dormants and immortals. They barely knew each other, and the crazy attraction could be all about sex.

Max nodded. "I felt it too." He leaned over and put his hand on Eric's shoulder. "If you didn't select your inducer yet, I'll be honored if you choose me. But you will have to buy me dinner first." He batted his eyelashes. "I'm not going to put my mouth on your neck unless we go out on a date first."

Eric laughed, but Darlene didn't.

What were Max's motives?

Why did he offer himself?

Wasn't he jealous of Eric?

What if he planned to sabotage Eric's induction?

If Max was still interested in her, it would benefit him if Eric didn't transition, but on the other hand, it would be a blow to his ego, which was substantial.

Then again, Max wasn't responsible for the blood pumping in his veins, so if his venom didn't do the job, he would have nothing to be embarrassed about.

16

ERIC

*E*ric followed Ingrid and Darlene around the third house on their tour, focusing on the sound of the interior designer's high heels clicking on the hardwood floor and trying to match a tune to the staccato. The houses differed slightly in their decor scheme, but otherwise they were nearly identical, and he was bored.

Hopefully three times was the charm, and Darlene would settle on the one they were touring now, and they could go back to Gilbert and Karen's place for coffee.

"What do you think?" Ingrid asked.

"It's perfect." Darlene sat on the couch and patted the spot next to her for Eric to join her. "We are not too close to Geraldine or Orion, but not too far away either. If my mother decides to visit me, it will take her five minutes to get here, which will give me enough time to get dressed if I need to or to straighten up things." She turned to Eric. "What about you? Which one do you like best?"

"Frankly? All these little houses look the same to me." He smiled apologetically at Ingrid. "No offense to the decor. I think you've done an amazing job. They are cozy and yet stylish, which is not an easy combination to pull off."

"Thank you." Ingrid sat on one of the armchairs. "That's exactly what I was going for, but with Kian wanting everything done yesterday, I had very little time to plan. That's why there is not much variation in the decor. If I had more time, I would have made each house unique."

"Is Kian always rushing things?" Eric asked.

She nodded. "I'm also designing the decor for the boutique hotels the clan is building, and his instructions are always the same." She squared her shoulders and assumed a hard expression. "Don't reinvent the wheel, Ingrid. Do what you've done before, that worked," she said in a gruff voice. "Time is money."

Darlene laughed. "That was good. I can imagine Kian saying that."

Ingrid rose to her feet. "I'm no longer giving out keys because there is no need

478

to lock the door, but if you want, you can add a deadbolt. I'll mark the house as yours on the village map, so everyone will know where to find you."

"Thank you." Darlene got up. "I appreciate the time you took to show us the homes."

"No problem. I always enjoy showing houses to new members." She turned to Eric. "Good luck with your transition. When should I expect the induction ceremony?"

While touring the homes, Darlene had told the designer about Gilbert and Eric's possible relation to Syssi, and Eric's wish to be induced as soon as possible.

"Tomorrow." He offered her his hand. "Max volunteered to be my inducer, and he's taking care of the preparations."

"Wonderful." Ingrid shook his hand. "I'll be there to cheer you on."

"Thanks." He winced. "Although I'm not sure I want witnesses to my humiliation. Max is a Guardian, and he's immortal. I was told that I have no chance against him."

"No one expects you to last long." Ingrid patted his arm. "It's considered an achievement if you manage to stay on your feet for a whole minute. I'm sure that you could last that long against Max." She gave him an appreciative once-over. "You look like you work out."

Eric could practically feel the glare Darlene was aiming at the designer, and he tried hard not to show his satisfaction.

"Thank you for the compliment." He smiled.

"You're welcome. I'll see you both tomorrow." Ingrid turned on her high heel and walked out.

As soon as the door closed behind her, Darlene turned to him. "I didn't have a chance to say anything before, but I don't think that Max should be your inducer."

"Why not? I like him."

"Because he might botch it on purpose. Max hoped that I would choose him, and when he found out that you are a potential Dormant, he backed off. But he still sees you as a rival. Those immortal males are predators, and they don't give up easily."

"Did you encourage him? I mean before I showed up."

Darlene shook her head. "I was friendly." She blushed. "When I still thought of you as just a weekend fling, I considered Max as my next step. He is attractive, and he has a rough kind of charm, but he's not you." She wrapped her arms around his neck. "The Fates sent you to me, and I knew right away that we would be great together. But I thought that I couldn't have you because I was supposed to find an immortal male to induce me."

Darlene had sounded apologetic, probably attributing his frown to jealousy, and she was right. She just didn't know what was really going through his head.

Max was the perfect solution Eric had been searching for, the ideal third partner in the threesome he had envisioned, but he couldn't get the words out and actually suggest it.

"What's the matter?" She cupped his cheek. "Are you jealous?"

He nodded but then shook his head.

"Then what?"

Eric swallowed the lump in his throat. "Perhaps Max can induce us both."

Darlene's eyes widened. "You want us to have a threesome with him?"

"I don't, but he's the perfect choice. We both like him, he's into you, and I have a feeling he is a little into me as well. He might be bisexual."

"He's not. He was just teasing. Max is as heterosexual as they come."

"How do you know?"

She shrugged. "The way he was devouring me with his eyes when he was flirting with me. He didn't look at you like that."

As a growl rose from somewhere deep in his throat, Eric slapped a hand over his mouth. "Forgive me. I don't know where that came from."

Darlene grinned. "That's just more proof that you are a Dormant. Your possessive nature is rearing its head."

"It's never happened to me before, and I had plenty of reasons to be jealous about my ex."

"She wasn't your fated mate." Darlene smirked. "Somehow, I don't foresee a threesome in our future. You won't be able to handle it, and neither will I. I'm just a simple girl at heart, and I can't see myself doing something so scandalous."

She'd hoped that would make Eric smile, but his expression remained serious.

"We have to." He cupped her cheek. "You are precious to me, and I won't put your life in danger just because the thought of sharing you with another male makes me feel physically ill."

17

KAIA

*W*illiam's house was in the new section of the village that was separated from the rest of the homes by a bridge.

There was another section a little farther away that was also accessible only by a bridge, and William had promised Kaia to take her on a tour the next day and tell her the story of its inhabitants.

As they stepped onto the bridge, Kaia looked up and around, searching for security cameras, but she couldn't see any. It was dark though, so she might have missed them with her human eyes.

"What are you looking for?" William asked.

"I expected a gate and at least some surveillance. You said that this was the secure section where Kian lived."

"They are there," William said. "But they are very well hidden."

"Security cameras?"

"That's what you were looking for, right?"

"Yeah. All the important people live here, so I expected the security to be more robust. Where are they?"

"Some are embedded in the railing. They look like decorative elements."

"Show me."

"I'd better not. I'm not supposed to tell you where they are, and if you are seen staring at them, the guys in security will know that I showed them to you."

"What about sound?" she whispered. "Can they hear us talk?"

"It's turned down. They only turn it up when they suspect something is going on, but thankfully, nothing ever is."

"What do you expect to happen?"

He shrugged. "Nothing, really. Kian needed a bigger place, and he wanted a super secure location for his mother if she ever decided to move into the village, so we amped up the security around this section."

The village was extremely well hidden and inaccessible to anyone who wasn't supposed to be there. The whole place was like a fortress, and making a secure inner zone only made sense if Kian and his mother suspected that they had enemies from within, which was possible even though most of them were related to each other. Not all families were supportive, and some were damn deadly. Brothers killing brothers for power and money.

As a shiver ran down Kaia's spine, she clung closer to William.

There were no streetlights to illuminate the way, and she could barely see a few feet ahead of her, but from what she could glean the homes were bigger than the one her family was staying in.

"I'm glad that the houses are small. My mother couldn't insist on me staying with them because there was no room."

"I think Karen and Gilbert have made peace with us being together. They have more pressing things on their minds now."

"I know." Kaia let out a breath. "We all feel as if we are sitting on a ticking bomb. I'm waiting for my transition to start, my mother and Gilbert are waiting for Bridget to give them the results of the genetic testing, and Eric and Darlene are getting ready for his initiation ceremony. He's so convinced that he's a Dormant that he doesn't even want to wait for the results."

"He might be right." William turned into the walkway of the fifth house from the bridge. "This is us." He led her up the two stairs to the front door. "There are no front porches in this section, and I miss the one I had in my old house, which is funny since I never used it." He pushed the door open and switched the light on.

"Oh, wow. That's much fancier than the one my family is staying in." She walked up to the marble fireplace. "Did you have a chance to use it?"

"Not yet. I only moved here a week before leaving for Safe Haven. Do you want to see the bedrooms?"

Kaia smiled. "Someone is impatient."

A slight blush colored William's pale cheeks. "I've been thinking about getting you in bed all day long, and it has been a long day."

"It's not over yet." She cupped his cheek and pressed a kiss to his soft lips. "Show me your bedroom."

She wanted to take a peek at the kitchen, but that could wait for tomorrow.

William took her hand and led her down the hallway. "There are three bedrooms." He opened the door to what looked like a home office and a library combined. "Ingrid thought that I would like to work from home, so she organized this space for me, but I do all my work in the lab."

Kaia eyed the executive chair and the large desk. "I can use this space if you don't." She walked up to one of the bookcases. "Are those yours? Or did Ingrid fill the shelves with nice-looking books to make your office look good?"

He chuckled. "Those are mine, but they were sitting in cardboard boxes in my lab until now. Ingrid brought them here, cleaned them up, and organized them on the shelves."

"She must be a superwoman to find time for all the things she does."

"Ingrid has help. She doesn't do everything by herself." He tugged on her hand. "Let's continue the tour."

William was obviously eager to get her to the bedroom, and Kaia was eager for that as well, but his office was just too cool for a casual inspection.

"I'll give it a more thorough look tomorrow." She let him pull her out of the room.

"This is the guest room." He opened the door. "Nothing special to see here." He tugged her hand toward the last door. "This is my bedroom." He opened the door to a large room with a massive four-poster bed.

"Did you pick out that monstrosity?"

William was so low-key that she knew he would never have chosen an ostentatious bed like that. What had Ingrid been thinking?

He frowned. "I didn't pick anything in the house. Ingrid chose everything. If you don't like it, we can get a different bed."

Kaia turned toward William and wrapped her arms around his neck. "It can stay. Those carved posts give me ideas."

"Oh yeah? What kind of ideas?" Given the blush coloring his cheeks, he knew precisely what she was thinking about.

Kaia laughed. "The kinky kind, my prince."

18

WILLIAM

*E*ven though William didn't know what those kinky things were and whether Kaia wanted to tie him up or to be tied by him, both options equally excited him, and he got so hard that the integrity of his zipper was threatened.

Lifting her up, he intended to carry her to the bed, but she tapped on his shoulders, demanding to be put back down.

"We need to shower. I'm not getting into this lovely bed with the clothes I've been wearing all day, and neither are you."

That was not a problem. He could think of a few interesting things that they could do in the shower, or the bathtub, or on top of the counter, or inside the closet. Now that Kaia had opened that Pandora's box, all kinds of things floated to the surface that William had never given much thought to before.

He was a simple guy with simple needs, but he was ready and able to fulfill any fantasy Kaia might have, and it excited him to no end to imagine what her brilliant mind could come up with.

"May I carry you to the bathroom?"

She laughed. "Yes, you may."

Shifting her in his arms so he could carry her like a princess, he walked into the bathroom and flicked the lights on with his elbow. "Take your pick. The shower, the tub, or the counter."

"Tsk, tsk. Bossy, bossy." She glanced around the bathroom. "The tub looks super inviting, and it's big enough for two."

"As you wish, your highness." He set her down on the counter and walked over to the tub. "How do you like your water? Hot, warm, or something in between?" He turned the faucet on.

"The third option." Kaia hopped down from the counter. "I need to pee."

"The toilet is over there." He pointed. "And there is also a bidet if you fancy those."

A smile bloomed on her face. "I do. Gilbert put bidets in all of our bedrooms, and I got so used to having one that I can't live without it."

She'd never mentioned that or complained about not having one.

"There were no bidets in the bungalows."

"Tell me about it." She walked into the powder room but didn't close the door behind her. "It was a drag to shower after every poop. And given the goop they fed us in the dining hall, there were a lot of those."

William stifled a snort.

Kaia was so unabashed about everything, and it was just one more thing among many that he adored about her. Even now, she was using the toilet with the door open as if they were a couple who'd been together for years and didn't feel shy about anything...

Or like a couple of guys sharing a dorm room.

That was a sobering thought.

Did she even realize that most women wouldn't talk about pooping with their boyfriends or use the toilet without closing the door?

Did it bother him, though?

As long as it didn't bother her, he couldn't care less. Kaia was Kaia no matter what parts made the whole, and he loved her just the way she was.

After washing her hands, she sauntered over, sat on the lip of the tub, and put her fingers in the water. "It's a little too hot for me. Can you add some cold water?"

"Of course."

He wondered what she would do next. Would she start undressing or wait for him to do it for her?

Her flip-flops were the first to go. She just flung them off and stretched her toes. "Do you know what I miss?"

"What?"

"Cheryl and I used to paint our toenails for each other."

"You can do that tomorrow. You are officially on a semi-vacation."

"I want to see your lab, and I want to meet Roni and everyone else you told me about. Does Roni know about his mom hooking up with Eric?"

The last thing William wanted to do was talk about Darlene or Roni, or Eric. But that was just one more thing about Kaia that was so different from any woman he'd ever met. She didn't need a long buildup. She was on or off in an instant, one moment being all business and talking about their research, or her family, or anything else under the sun, and the next, she could be all over him.

That was also a male trait.

William shook his head. He should stop analyzing everything Kaia did and said through that prism. Every person had feminine and masculine traits combined, and Kaia's were just tilted in favor of the masculine a little more than the average female's.

"I guess we will find out tomorrow." He turned the faucet off and knelt in front of his princess. "Let's not talk about it now." He reached for her jeans button and popped it open. "Tonight is all about us."

Kaia leaned to plant a kiss on the top of his head. "I have a strange feeling in the pit of my stomach," she said quietly. "It's excitement mixed with anticipation and anxiety. Maybe my transition will start tonight."

19

KAIA

*K*aia had been looking forward to tonight. It would be their first time with no barriers between them, but it could also be the start of her transition, and it scared her more than she was willing to admit.

William claimed that it was unlikely it would start right away, but Kaia had a feeling that it would.

She should be excited, but the truth was that she envied all the Dormants who hadn't known what was coming and just enjoyed fabulous sex with an immortal male, ignorant of the consequences.

For some, fear might enhance excitement, but for her it was a mood dampener.

Maybe she was just tired?

William paused with his fingers on her zipper. "What's going on?"

"Nothing." She forced a smile.

Lifting up, he sat on the lip of the tub beside her. "You forget that I can sense changes in your mood. You're anxious."

Kaia let out a breath. "I'm scared," she admitted. "It's hard to feel sexy when I have this sinking feeling in my stomach." She put a hand over her tummy.

He took her hand and lifted it to his lips. "We don't have to do anything tonight, or we can just fool around, or we can use a condom. You've had enough excitement for one day."

William was so sweet, so patient and understanding, but Kaia didn't want to wait.

"We are in the village because of my impending transition, and we have a team idling in Safe Haven awaiting our return. We don't have the luxury of waiting for me to get over my irrational fears."

"They are not irrational, and I don't want you to feel rushed." He wrapped his arm around her and pulled her onto his lap. "Tonight, just let me pamper you. I'll wash your hair, massage your scalp, and soap you all over, and if you manage to

486

relax and get in the mood, we will take it from there. If not, I'll carry you to bed and tuck you in."

"I love you so much," she whispered. "You are so perfect for me that I can't imagine anything tearing us apart. But life is often unfair, and I'm afraid that this fairytale is going to end badly."

"It won't." He tightened his arms around her. "I won't let it happen. We will wait until Annani returns to the village before we attempt your transition. I'll call Kian tomorrow morning and plead with him to ask her to come back earlier than planned."

Kaia lifted her eyes to him. "What can she do to help?"

"She gives her blessing to Dormants who have trouble transitioning. I used to dismiss it as her way to give hope to their mates, but then I realized that being a goddess is not just about being more powerful than her immortal descendants. Annani must exude some kind of energy that we can't detect yet. That's why the little girl Dormants transition just from being around her, and that's how she helps adult Dormants transition when they are having difficulties."

That made sense, and it gave Kaia a boost of confidence. "When is she supposed to come back?"

"She didn't give us exact dates, but I guess two or three weeks. If she's not willing to cut her trip short, we can just wait. We will go back to Safe Haven, continue working on Okidu's journals, and come back here when she returns."

Kaia shook her head. "I can't do that, not after I dragged my family here. What am I going to tell them?"

"The truth. Besides, you didn't drag them. They informed you that they were coming."

"Still, they are here. What about Darlene's grandfather? He's a god. Can't he give me his blessing?"

William grimaced. "I don't know. Toven is supposed to be a powerful god, but something happened to him along the way, and he lost his glow. The popular theory is that he suffered from depression and that it depleted his energy reserves. I don't know if Annani's energy manifests in part in her luminescence, and the fact that Toven doesn't have it makes me doubt his ability to help you. I'd rather wait for Annani, who has a proven record of helping transitioning Dormants, than risk your life because we felt rushed."

Kaia was still stuck on the luminescence. "You didn't tell me that the goddess glows."

"She does, but she can suppress the glow when she wants to appear human, although with her otherworldly beauty, that's not enough. She usually uses a shroud to make herself look plainer."

For some reason, hearing William talk about the goddess helped ease Kaia's anxiety.

"Tell me more about Annani. You said that she's tiny. How tall is she?"

He chuckled. "She's about five feet tall, maybe half an inch over that, has a mane of flaming red hair that cascades all the way down to her hips, and she emits power like a mini nuclear reactor. When you meet her, you'll get what I mean. If she doesn't suppress her power and shroud her beauty, no one could mistake her for a human, but when she does, she can pass for a seventeen-year-old high school girl. The one thing that gives her away, though, is her eyes. The wisdom of the ages is reflected in them."

20

WILLIAM

$\mathcal{A}$t some point during William's pampering, Kaia's expression had turned from stressed to relaxed. She lay sprawled in the tub, her limbs floating loose, her eyes closed, and a small smile lifting the corners of her lips.

He'd put a lot of effort into achieving that change in mood, treating her to a long scalp massage and then giving her feet the same attention, one little toe at a time.

William's clothes were wet, he was so hard that it was painful to bend over, his fangs were demanding their due, and his venom glands were full to bursting, but if that was what it took to get that angelic expression on her face, he would keep tending to her beautiful, nude body until she fell asleep.

Kaia's well-being came before his needs, and her survival came before any other consideration.

He should have thought about waiting for Annani's return before attempting her transition, but he'd been so sure that her youth would make it easy for her that it hadn't even occurred to him. But what if Kaia was the exception? What if she lost consciousness and Bridget couldn't keep her alive?

Kian wouldn't like the change of plans, especially if Kaia's family decided to wait with their transitions as well, but William could handle the grumpy regent.

In his heart, Kian was a romantic, and he would understand William's fear.

The same was true for Annani.

If he asked her to come back to bless Kaia, she would.

Letting out a contented sigh, Kaia turned her head to look at him with hooded eyes. "Take off your clothes, William, and get in here with me. This tub is big enough for both of us."

He hesitated. "It's incredibly difficult to keep it platonic while I'm dressed. It will be excruciating to be naked with you and not take it any further than caresses."

She smiled. "I want much more than caresses from you."

William shook his head. "We didn't bring condoms with us."

"That's okay." Kaia reached for his cheek with a soapy hand. "While you were doing all those wonderful things to me, I was thinking about my transition and decided that we shouldn't wait."

When he opened his mouth to protest, she put a finger on his lips. "The transition is not going to start right away, and when it does, it might go smoothly. Tomorrow, you should talk with Kian and ask him if his mother is willing to be on standby in case of an emergency. If it looks like I'm having a hard time, Toven can give me his blessing, and if that doesn't work, the goddess could get on the clan jet and be here in a matter of hours."

"Annani is in Scotland. It will take her more than a few hours to get here."

"I'm willing to take the risk. I don't want to wait any longer."

William shook his head. "But I'm not."

Kaia frowned. "You were all for it until I opened my mouth. Did I scare you?"

"You did," he admitted. "You told me that sometimes you get premonitions, and you've been hesitant to start working on your transition for a couple of days now. I don't take premonitions lightly."

"It wasn't a premonition." Kaia rose to her feet, the soap bubbles clinging to her gorgeous body and her long, wet hair flirting with her bottom. "Can you hand me the small towel for my hair, please?"

When he handed it to her, Kaia flipped her hair forward, covered it with the towel, twisted both together, and tucked the corners under the sides, making a turban out of it.

He was so mesmerized watching her that he hadn't thought to ready a bath sheet for her.

"Can you reach the big towel?"

"Of course." He turned around, reached for the bath sheet, and unfurled it. "Can I pat you dry?"

She smirked. "Given how long your fangs are, are you sure that it's a good idea? Not that I mind, but you seem to be against making love to me tonight."

He wrapped the towel around her and lifted her into his arms. "There are ways to make love that will keep you safe."

Shifting to circle her arms around his neck, Kaia let the towel slide down and expose her breasts. "I don't want those other ways tonight. It's either all or nothing."

He arched a brow. "Is that blackmail?" He put her down on the bed.

Letting the rest of the towel drop away from her, Kaia batted her eyelashes in mock innocence. "I'm just not in the mood for oral tonight." She cupped her breasts. "I want that magnificent length of yours thrusting in and out of me, and I want your fangs at my neck."

She was killing him.

William groaned. "You're playing dirty, you shameless flirt."

Kaia pouted and turned to lie on her stomach. "Do you want to spank me for being so naughty?" She lifted her gorgeous ass and wiggled it.

William's defenses were crumbling.

Maybe Kaia was right?

He could call Kian tomorrow and ask him to convince Annani to come back right away. Hell, he could call her himself and beg her to return. The goddess liked him, and he was a valuable member of the clan. She wouldn't deny him.

Besides, Annani was the ultimate romantic.

She would do that for love.

21

KAIA

"Ouch!" The hard smack landing on her ass took Kaia by surprise. She hadn't thought that William had it in him.

Her taunting had been meant to get him so aroused that he would forget about her mini-panic attack and succumb to her seduction. Kaia had never expected him to actually accept her invitation and spank her.

"That was for driving me crazy." He massaged the small hurt away.

Would he spank her again?

Did she want him to?

It had hurt a little, but it was also oddly arousing.

Looking at him over her shoulder, she wiggled her bottom again. "I don't think one spank counts as spanking."

His eyes widened. "You want more?"

"How crazy did I get you?"

The next smack was followed by three more in quick succession. "That crazy." William caressed her heated bottom.

Turning around, she made it clear that the game was over. "Take off your clothes."

"Yes, ma'am." William popped a couple of buttons open, pulled the shirt over his head, and tossed it on the armchair that stood in a corner.

Apparently, he had no problem switching roles on a dime.

Kaia loved him when he was bossy, and she loved him when he was obedient, but bossy was just a tad sexier. Nevertheless, she wasn't going to say anything until he stripped for her and she got her fill of ogling him.

When he dropped his pants along with his boxers, freeing his impressive shaft, Kaia licked her lips.

"Do you like what you see?" He stroked the hard length lazily.

"You know that I do." She beckoned him to her. "I can't wait to feel it inside me with no barriers."

CHAPTER 21

Before her eyes, his erection lost some of its volume. "Are you sure about that? I'll be very happy with oral."

"But I won't be." She spread her legs a little, letting him see the moisture that had pooled there just from their little game.

His nostrils flaring, William sucked in a breath. "You're playing dirty again."

She kept forgetting about his immortal sense of smell. He could not only see her arousal, but scent it too, so the effect was doubled.

"Are you going to spank me some more?" she taunted.

"Maybe later." He smiled evilly. "You wanted us both to take a shower, and I haven't yet. I'll do it now." He walked away from her.

Who was playing dirty now? He couldn't get her all hot and bothered and then leave her hanging.

"No, you won't. Come back here."

Looking at her over his shoulder, William smirked. "You'll have to wait patiently, my princess." He walked into the bathroom and closed the door behind him.

"Ugh. Frustrating man."

But if he thought that she would cool off while he was gone, he was mistaken.

Five minutes later, when William emerged from the bathroom with a towel draped over his hips, she was even readier for him than before.

"Did you have a nice shower?" She spread her legs, and the full impact of what she'd been doing hit him hard.

His nostrils flared. "You've been a naughty girl again."

She reached with her hand between her legs and stroked herself. "What are you going to do about it?"

Dropping the towel, he prowled over her and settled between her spread legs. "I need to feast." He looked into her eyes. "You're not going to deny me a taste, are you?"

She'd said that she wasn't interested in oral, but that was when he'd offered it as a substitute for intercourse. She had no problem with oral as foreplay.

It was on the tip of her tongue to tell him to turn around so they could pleasure each other simultaneously, but then she realized that once William's immediate need was fulfilled, he might decide not to penetrate her tonight and wait for the goddess to return.

She smiled up at him. "As long as it's just foreplay, I'm more than happy to be on the receiving end. But I'm not going to reciprocate tonight. You are coming inside of me or not at all."

Chuckling, he shook his head. "You just added to the spanking I'm going to give you later."

Kaia's bottom tingled, and not unpleasantly. "Promises, promises." She lifted her head and smashed her mouth over his.

22

WILLIAM

*K*aia never ceased to amaze William. She was so assertive that discovering she had a playfully submissive side to her was a complete surprise.

He had a feeling that there were many more surprises in store for him, and he was looking forward to a lifetime of them.

When Kaia let go of his mouth, his lips were tingling, and his fangs were pulsing with the need to bite her, but he needed a taste first.

Sliding down her supple body, he paid a short homage to her breasts, just a few swipes of his tongue on each nipple and a couple of kisses, and then he kept going until his face was buried between her legs.

He closed his eyes to enjoy the full impact of her sweet feminine scent, and as he swiped his tongue over her slit, the taste of her had him groan like a beast.

They were both close to the edge, so he couldn't spend as much time feasting on her as he normally would, but he needed to bring her to a quick climax before penetrating her.

He couldn't tolerate the thought of giving her anything but pleasure, but it seemed like she included a little spanking play in that definition, and he had no problem with that.

Whatever Kaia wanted, Kaia got.

In moments, he had her writhing around his tongue, and as he added two fingers to the play, she detonated with a scream that nearly had him spill on the bedsheet.

Only fear of Kaia's retaliation stopped William from biting her inner thigh and releasing onto the bed. She wanted him to come inside her while he bit her neck, and if he disobeyed, he would incur her wrath.

Lifting over her, he gripped his aching shaft and positioned it at her entrance, coating it in her copious juices before pushing in.

She was so slick that he didn't stop and pushed all the way inside her with one thrust.

"William," she gasped his name, and for a moment, he feared that he'd hurt her, but then she added, "It feels so good, so right." Her fingers dug into his buttocks, and she arched up, signaling that she wanted him to move.

He wanted to stay connected like that for a moment longer and savor it a little. The moment he started moving, he would be overtaken by the frenzy of coupling, and their joining would be over too soon. Kaia would black out, and he would lie beside her in agony, waiting for her to wake up so they could go for another round.

When she turned immortal, he could keep making love to her throughout the night, but for now, he had to live with her human limitations.

"William." Kaia bucked up again.

"Give me a few more seconds." He cupped her cheeks and pressed a loving kiss to her lips. "Where are you rushing to?"

She smirked. "Another orgasm or two or three from my beautiful monster."

It was silly of him to love her calling him that whenever his fangs were out, but he did. Kaia was his beauty, and he was her beast, and yet she thought that he was as beautiful in his beast form as he was as a man, when in reality he wasn't a great looker in either.

He didn't doubt her sincerity, though. She saw him through lenses tinted by love.

When he started moving, Kaia's fingers dug even deeper into his butt muscles, and when he swelled inside her and hissed through his fangs, she turned her head and offered him her neck.

He still had enough presence of mind to swipe his tongue over the spot before sinking his fangs into her.

Kaia climaxed, her sheath fluttering around his shaft, and as he erupted inside of her, it kept squeezing until there was nothing left.

Nevertheless, he kept pumping his hips until Kaia's string of orgasms ended, and her body went lax under his.

She was out, a satisfied smirk painted on her gorgeous face, and as William braced on his forearms and looked at her, he hoped they hadn't made a grave mistake.

Premonitions were nothing to sneer at, and the rock sitting in his gut hadn't gone anywhere just because he and Kaia had found a way to rationalize their haste.

The problem with logic was that it wasn't objective, and it was based on what was known. But since the unknown was far greater than the known, trusting in one's logic wasn't logical.

23

KIAN

"Good morning." William walked into Kian's office and sat on one of the chairs in front of his desk. "Thank you for agreeing to see me on such short notice."

"My door is always open to you. You don't even have to make an appointment." Kian leaned back in his executive chair and crossed his arms over his chest. "Now that the pleasantries are out of the way, you can tell me what's bothering you."

William pushed his glasses up his nose. "Is it that obvious?"

"Yesterday, you didn't wear your glasses, and you spoke at a nearly normal speed. Today, you're hiding behind your spectacles again, and you are talking at machine-gun speed, so I assume something happened."

Kian was proud of himself for noticing, and Syssi would be even prouder of him when he told her about it.

William closed his eyes for a brief moment and let out a slow breath. "Kaia and I started the initiation process."

That was what they were in the village for, so it wasn't a great revelation. "Congratulations."

"Well, I'm not sure. Kaia was all gung ho to start up until two days ago, and then she started to feel fearful. To be frank, it scared me. I wanted to stop everything and wait for Annani to return to the village so she could bless Kaia in case she needed it, but then Kaia had a change of heart and seduced me last night."

Except for the first sentence and the slight pause after it, the entire speech was delivered in William's regular manner of a thousand words per minute.

"Good for her. I knew I liked the girl. She has spunk."

"Yeah." William's cheeks reddened. "That she does in spades. But I'm terrified that she might start transitioning before the Clan Mother returns, and there would be no one to bless her. Is there any way you can get Annani to come back earlier?"

496

So that was the reason for William's urgent request to see him first thing in the morning.

Uncrossing his arms, Kian leaned forward. "I know that the prospect of your mate facing any kind of danger is terrifying, but Kaia is very young and seems to be in perfect health. Her odds of transitioning easily are great."

"That's what I thought as well until she started having those foreboding feelings, and I can't dismiss them as irrational fears. I have to take them seriously. Too much is at stake. I can't lose her."

"You won't." Kian put his hands on the table. "I'm just surprised that you, of all people, put so much faith in Annani's blessings. You are an engineer and a scientist, not a spiritualist."

Perhaps he shouldn't have said that.

Kian was surprised that William hadn't figured out the truth behind the so-called blessings yet, and it was good that he hadn't. Reminding him that he was a scientist and should look for a logical explanation was a mistake.

The guy was very good at solving puzzles, and now that he was working with Kaia, who was just as bright as he was, if not more so, and seemed to be an extremely talented puzzle solver in her own right, they could easily figure it out.

"It helped others." William took his glasses off, folded them carefully, and put them on the table. "Our little girls transition just from being around Annani, so I assume that her glow and the palpable energy she emits facilitates transition. I'm the last person to tell you that science has everything figured out. What we know covers an infinitesimally tiny portion of what there is to know."

Kian stifled a relieved breath. William had looked for a scientific explanation for why the blessing worked, but he'd looked in the wrong direction.

"We are in agreement on that." Kian cast him an encouraging smile. "We have another god amongst us, though, and Toven can do everything Annani can. If Kaia encounters trouble transitioning, I will ask him to give her his blessing."

Kian had already secured the god's promise to donate his blood to the older members of Kaia's family, and he didn't anticipate Toven refusing to add her to the list of recipients.

William grimaced. "Toven doesn't glow, and being next to him doesn't feel the same as being next to Annani. She radiates power. He doesn't."

"That's because he's gotten so used to suppressing his glow and his power that his body does it on autopilot. It doesn't mean that he's less powerful or that his blessing is less effective."

William didn't look convinced. "We don't know that. When Mia was transitioning, it was Annani who gave her the blessing, not Toven."

Damn. How was he going to explain that one?

"Mia was in very poor health, and she needed double blessings. Toven had been blessing her ahead of her transition to strengthen her so she could even enter it, and once she got strong enough and the process started, he asked Annani to reinforce his blessings."

Thankfully, William wasn't particularly talented at detecting lies, or he would have sensed the half-truths Kian had been spouting. He was also distraught, so that might have affected his bullshit radar as well.

"Annani has more experience." William cast him a pleading look. "I trust her. Can you please ask her to come back? She's been gone a long time already."

"Fine," Kian relented. "I'll call my mother. She's probably heard already about the family of Dormants visiting the village and is curious to meet them. It might incentivize her to shorten her stay in Scotland. But if Sari calls to yell at me for luring our mother and sister away from her, I'm telling her to direct her complaints to you."

"No problem." William took a deep breath. "For Kaia, I'd fight dragons and angry sisters."

Kian laughed. "I don't know which one is more terrifying."

24

JADE

*J*ade spun her staff in her hands, giving Drova a short reprieve before leaping into the air and swiping it at her daughter.

Drova offered a clumsy defense, catching the stick with her own but then losing her balance and falling on her ass.

It was pathetic that Drova was the best fighter in her age group, but she was still inferior to the weakest female of Jade's former tribe.

Perhaps that would be the downfall of Igor's legacy.

The generation of pure-bloods he was raising in his compound was so inferior that they were nearly as ineffective as humans. When Igor and Jade's generation died out, humans would find these weaklings and eliminate them because there would be no one capable of leading them.

But that wasn't what Jade wanted. If she had her way, Igor would die, preferably a horribly painful death, and she would take over, turning these weaklings into tough warriors worthy of the Kra-ell name.

She could only dream, though. With Igor's compulsion rendering her helpless to affect any meaningful changes, all she could do was pray for his premature death and hope that it happened before he got old and one of his many sons took over.

Drova would never become the next leader of the compound because her father believed in and practiced patriarchy, which was an abomination to the Mother of All Life. She would be given to one of his trusted lieutenants and become a breeder like all the other females.

As long as her father lived, she would be treated well, but once he was gone, all bets were off.

Jade's only satisfaction would be watching Igor's empire deteriorate and crumble.

"You are lucky that no other female here will challenge you." Jade threw down her staff with disgust. "If you were in my tribe, you would have been at the lowest position."

"Then I'm lucky that I'm not in your tribe." Drova jumped back to her feet, picked up Jade's stick, and tossed it at her. "Let's go another round."

Leaning against the fence, Kagra chuckled. "Are you up for more humiliation, girl?"

Drova bared her fangs at Kagra. "One of these days, I'll wipe that smirk off your face. You might have been a beta to my mother's alpha back in your glory days, but you are no one here. I suggest that you either shut up or leave."

"Or what? Are you going to tattle on me to Daddy?"

Uttering a battle cry, Drova launched an attack on Kagra, who hadn't been armed with a staff to defend herself, but she still danced out of the way with ease.

"Here." Jade tossed Kagra hers.

"Thank you, my alpha." She sneered at Drova.

Alpha and beta were human terms, but even though the Kra-ell didn't use those designations, they were fitting.

Except, Kagra had served as a beta only because she was younger and less experienced, not because she lacked leadership.

The three of them were all natural alphas, but being born with an innate ability was worthless without putting in the effort to hone it, master it, and own it.

As her daughter and her second charged at each other, Jade dusted off her pants and walked over to stand by the fence and watch.

"You are telegraphing your intentions, Drova."

Her daughter growled in response.

The girl was physically strong, and she wasn't stupid, but she was lazy and thought that everything would always be handed to her on a silver platter because she was Igor's only daughter and everyone in the compound treated her like a princess.

How wrong she was.

Her father cared about one thing and one thing only, and that was power. He wouldn't hesitate to sacrifice his only daughter and his fifteen sons for more of it.

"Let's go for one last round," Kagra said after disarming Drova for the second time.

"I'm done." Drova picked up her staff and started toward the main building.

"The girl has no respect." Kagra walked over to Jade. "I don't know why you bother training her."

"She has potential, and I haven't given up on her yet."

Kagra cast a quick glance around before leaning closer to Jade. "How is it going with the parable?"

Jade winced. "It was ready, but then it occurred to me that I needed to add a warning about the children," she whispered. "I don't expect anything to come out of it, but on the remote chance that Veskar assembles a force and comes to our rescue, I need to let him know that there are children here."

Kagra let out a breath. "I thought a lot about it last night, and maybe you shouldn't send it at all. If Veskar has allies, they might not come here to rescue us. They might come to eliminate the threat of Igor, and they will kill everyone here, including the females and the children. And if they want more females the way

Igor does, they will kill all the males, including the young ones and those who are not evil."

Her second had two sons, and she'd raised them as best she could so they weren't as bad as the others, but that didn't make them good either. They treated the captive females only slightly better than the rest of their brethren.

"It's a risk that I'm willing to take. If we do nothing, we will die in captivity. I'd rather die fighting."

25

DARLENE

*D*arlene crumbled her coffee cake, picking at it with her fork and making a mess on her plate. "Don't be offended if Roni says something rude." She lifted her gaze to Eric. "It's his style, and he usually doesn't mean anything by it."

They were meeting for breakfast, and Roni was predictably late. Her son wasn't a morning person, and since he didn't have a timecard to punch in, he showed up at the lab whenever he wanted. That didn't mean he was slacking, though.

Fates knew that he worked his skinny bottom off in that place.

Eric put his hand over hers, stopping the cake's destruction. "Why are you so nervous? You said that Roni hated his father. He should have no problem with me."

"It's important to me that the two of you get along, but you are very different people. I don't want your relationship to start off on the wrong foot."

"Don't worry about it." Eric leaned and kissed her cheek. "I'll be my charming self no matter how crusty your son gets."

"Thank you." She lifted her coffee cup and took a sip.

Last night she'd called Roni and had a long talk with him about Eric, the possibility that he was a Dormant, and whether she should wait for him to transition first and induce her or find another solution.

Thankfully, Roni had assumed that she'd meant finding a substitute, not a threesome with an immortal as Eric was pushing for.

Gosh, that was such a scandalous proposition that it made her blush just thinking about it. Well, blushing wasn't her only physical response to the idea, but she wasn't going to admit that the prospect aroused her.

Darlene wasn't a prude, and she'd read her fair share of ménage romances back in the day, but there was a big difference between reading about other people doing it and actually participating in a threesome herself.

How would it even work?

She shook her head.

Now was not the time to be thinking naughty thoughts. Eric might still be a human with a human's limited sense of smell, but Roni was joining them shortly, and she would die from embarrassment if her son smelled her arousal.

"Tell me a sad story," she blurted. "Something really bad."

Eric arched a brow. "Why?"

"Just do it. I need something to distract me."

He looked puzzled. "Wouldn't it be better if I tell you a happy story?"

"No."

A happy tale wouldn't kill her arousal.

"I was Kaia's age when I lost my mother. Our father died less than a year earlier, and she never recovered from his death. She lost her will to live."

Darlene frowned. "Did she die from a broken heart?"

She'd read that it was an actual thing and not just a phrase. It was called broken heart syndrome, and it was life-threatening. It could develop after a stressful event like a breakup or a loss of a loved one, and women in their fifties were the most affected group.

Eric nodded. "Her heart gave up. Gilbert, Gabi, and I had barely recovered from our father's death, and then she was taken from us as well. It was tough, and Gilbert took it upon himself to take care of Gabi and me."

"How old is your sister?"

"She's thirty-eight. I'm the middle child."

"Does she have kids?"

He shook his head. "She got divorced after five years of marriage and hasn't remarried. She's a dietitian and has a successful practice."

"You should bring her here. She might be younger than you, but she shouldn't wait too long either."

"I know." Eric sighed. "Let's see how my induction goes tonight."

"Are you nervous?"

He laughed. "Yeah. Max is a big guy, and he has his eye on you. He won't go easy on me."

That was what she was afraid of.

Thankfully, the ceremony would have many witnesses, so Max couldn't cause Eric excessive damage without someone stepping in to stop him.

"Don't provoke him too much. Just enough to make his fangs elongate."

"I'll be fine." He gave her one of his charming smiles. "I'm not afraid of getting knocked around a bit. Besides, Max is a good guy. He barely knew me, and he volunteered to induce me and to make all the arrangements for the ceremony. We are going to be best buddies forever." He winked.

Was he naive? Or was he just joking?

It was sometimes hard to tell with Eric. He smiled a lot, which she loved, and he didn't take himself or anyone else too seriously, which was great as well.

"Just be careful. Don't trust Max blindly."

ERIC

"Sorry I'm late." A gangly young man leaned over Darlene and kissed her cheek.

He didn't look anything like his mother. Did he look like his father?

"Hello, Roni." Eric offered the guy his hand. "I'm Eric."

"Hi." Darlene's son shook his hand. "My mother told me that you are having an induction ceremony tonight." He pulled out a chair and sat down. "Who is your inducer?"

"Max. Do you know him?"

"Yeah. He's cool. He usually accompanies William when he has to leave the village." Roni gave Eric a once-over. "You seem to be in good shape, but I hope you know that wrestling an immortal is like wrestling a gorilla. They are freakishly strong and aggressive as hell."

"A gorilla, eh? Is that an exaggeration, or are they really that strong?"

"They are that strong." Roni let out a breath. "I had to go through that crap four times, and each time I nearly shat my pants from fear. It wasn't fun."

It hadn't occurred to Eric that he might need to repeat the ceremony. "Why so many times?"

"I wasn't well." Roni took Darlene's plate, picked up several of the larger crumbs of the demolished cake, and stuffed them in his mouth. "I had pneumonia, which we mistook for transition at first. Then I recovered, but I was still weak. I couldn't enter transition until my body was back to normal. We didn't know that back then. Anyway, the last one to try was Kian, and I knew that if he couldn't induce me, no one could. Luckily, it worked."

Eric pieced together the bits of information he'd collected so far, trying to figure out how Roni had gotten to the clan before Darlene, but he just didn't have enough information.

"How did you find the clan? Or how did they find you?"

"It's a long story." Roni collected a few more crumbs and licked them off his fingers.

Eric rolled his eyes. "That's the answer everyone gives me. I need more information."

Roni leaned forward and looked him in the eyes. "It's not relevant to you, so it would be a waste of time telling you a story that someone might have to erase from your memories later. If you transition, you can come over to my house on the weekend, I'll grill some steaks for us, and I'll tell you my story over a couple of beers."

That was direct and only borderline rude, not nearly as bad as Darlene had warned him. Was Roni making an effort to be cordial?

"Thanks for the invitation. I would love to eat your steaks and drink your beer."

Roni grinned. "Have you been treated to Snake's Venom yet?"

Eric's mouth twisted in distaste. "That's one of the worst beers I ever had the displeasure of tasting. Is that what you drink?"

Roni laughed. "You are correct about it being horrible, but immortals metabolize alcohol so fast that any beer that is less potent than that tastes like piss water to us."

That was another factoid to add to Eric's small cache of knowledge about immortals. He knew now not to challenge any of them to a drinking competition.

"So, Eric." Roni leaned back in his chair. "What are you planning to do when you turn immortal? Are you going to sell off your planes?"

Eric shook his head. "I can lease them to a buddy of mine who runs a similar business, or I can offer my services to the clan. I was told that there is plenty of work for an experienced pilot."

That wasn't exactly what Max had told him, but it would do for now.

The answer seemed to satisfy Roni. "So you plan to stay in the village?"

"Of course." Eric wrapped his arm around Darlene's shoulders. "I can't leave my fated mate."

Roni's smile was the first genuine one Eric had seen so far. "That's the right answer. My mother deserves a man who adores her. I hope you erase the memory of damn Leo from her psyche forever."

The vehemence in Roni's voice surprised Eric.

According to Darlene, her ex hadn't been physically abusive, and verbal abuse usually didn't trigger such an angry response. It seemed that Roni had unresolved issues with his father.

"It's not good to hold on to such anger. Maybe you should meet up with your father and talk it out of your system."

The therapy sessions Eric had been through with his ex were good for something, after all. He could spout things and sound like he knew what he was talking about.

"Leo is not my father."

"I understand that you feel resentful toward him, but it might benefit to share with him what you feel. The fact that your parents are divorced does not mean that you can't have a relationship with your father."

Frowning, Roni turned to his mother. "You didn't tell him."

"I did not."

"Then maybe you should."

27

DARLENE

*D*arlene's throat suddenly dried out, and a hundred excuses rushed into her mind.

There hadn't been enough time.

They hadn't known each other long enough.

It wasn't relevant to their relationship.

But the truth was that subconsciously she didn't want to tell Eric that her son hadn't been fathered by her ex-husband and that the affair he was the product of had taken place while she had still been married to Leo.

With what Eric had gone through with his ex-wife, he might not believe her that she and Leo had been separated at the time, and that she was not the kind of woman who cheated on her husband even though she hadn't been happy in her marriage.

"What didn't you tell me?" Eric asked.

She let out a breath. "Roni is not my ex's son, but Leo is listed on Roni's birth certificate as his father, and he raised him as his."

Eric lifted a brow. "So?" He turned to Roni. "What's the big deal? You should be glad that the abusive jerk didn't contribute his genetic material to you."

"Oh, I am." Roni smiled. "But since you are serious about my mother, you should know stuff like that. I don't want you looking at me with suspicious eyes and waiting for my asshole qualities to surface."

Eric chuckled. "From what your mother told me about you, you are far from cherubic. Apparently, nurture is as influential as nature, and you absorbed your adoptive father's behaviors."

Roni tilted his head and eyed Eric from under his thick, dark lashes. "First of all, my style of jerkiness is very different than Leo's, and it's uniquely mine. I'm not like him in any way. And secondly, he's not my adoptive father, or my stepfather, or my anything. He was just the dude who was married to my mother when she got pregnant with me."

Darlene wanted to kick her son under the table, but since there was nothing covering it, Eric would see.

The mirth gone from his face, he turned to her. "You had an affair while you were married?"

"We were separated at the time."

"Why did you go back to him?"

Darlene closed her eyes. "It was a mistake I regretted for years." She opened them and leveled her gaze at him. "I should have filed for divorce and stayed with Roni's father. I met him at work, and he was the sweetest computer nerd ever. He worshiped the ground I walked on but was too shy to initiate anything, and I had to do the seducing. He thought that he'd died and gone to heaven."

"Did you tell him that you got pregnant?"

She shook her head. "I told no one. I went back to Leo and pretended that Roni was his. Leo suspected the truth for years, but he never had the guts to have it tested. Roni and Leo have the same coloring and are about the same height, so it wasn't obvious that they weren't related."

The question in Eric's eyes was so obvious that she didn't need to wait for him to ask it. "That wasn't what ruined our marriage. Leo was a controlling jerk from the start, and I enabled his behavior by giving in to his demands. He treated me badly when he still believed that Roni was his, and he treated me badly when he started suspecting that Roni was too smart to be his son."

"I'm sorry that you had to live through that." Eric reached for her hand. "But if not for those difficulties, you wouldn't be with me here today. You would be happily married to Roni's father. So, I'm not sorry for that."

"True." She lifted their joined hands and kissed his knuckles. "I'm also sorry that you were married to a cheating shrew, but I'm glad that she was horrible and that you divorced her, so you could be with me here today."

"Bravo." Roni clapped his hands. "You two are so sweet that it's nauseating." He pushed to his feet. "I need to get to the lab, but I'll see you tonight at the ceremony." He leaned to kiss Darlene's cheek. "I'll bring Sylvia along if that's okay with you."

"Of course, it is." She beamed up at him. "Maybe after the ceremony, the four of us could get coffee and talk about your initiation trials and how you met Sylvia." She chuckled. "That's one heck of a story." She turned to Eric. "The way Roni and Sylvia met is like a script from *Mission Impossible* combined with *American Pie*."

"I can't wait to hear it." Eric rose to his feet and clapped Roni on his back. "Wish me luck."

"Good luck, Eric," Roni sounded sincere. "May the Fates grant your wishes tonight." He clapped Eric on his back.

"Thank you."

28

KAIA

$\mathcal{A}$ s yet another clan member stopped Kaia and William on the way to the lab, she already knew what he was going to say. She'd heard it from five other people in the last fifteen minutes, and if the pattern continued, it would take them another hour to get to a destination that was ten minutes away.

"Congratulations on finding each other," the guy said. "I wish you and your family the best of luck with your transitions."

"Thank you. I appreciate the support," she repeated the same answer she'd given all the other well-wishers.

"You must be very popular." She took William's hand. "I don't get how everyone already knows about my family and me being here. I just got here yesterday, and my family arrived the night before."

"Rumors spread fast in the village." William forced a tight smile.

For some reason he was a ball of stress, and she didn't know how to calm him down. Well, she knew the reason for his anxiety. He was afraid of her encountering problems while transitioning, but he shouldn't take so seriously the few moments of panic she'd experienced. It was natural for her to fear the unknown, and it hadn't been a premonition because she'd gotten over it. When a premonition was real, it held her in its grip until it came to pass.

William had met with Kian early this morning, and when he'd returned, he'd said that he would tell her about it later. Her suspicion was that the boss had refused to ask the goddess to shorten her trip to Scotland, and that was why William was so anxious.

When they finally made it to the elevator, and no one got inside with them, Kaia leaned against the wall and let out a breath. "Is everyone usually this friendly and welcoming toward potential Dormants?"

"People here are friendly, and since living here is like living on an island, new faces are welcome, but I've never seen them react like that to a newcomer." He smiled shyly. "I didn't know so many people were rooting for me to find my truelove mate."

"You are their lovable tech guy who makes their lives easier."

As she was about to pull him into her arms, the elevator door opened, and William took her hand. "Some would argue that I make their lives more complicated." He led her out of the elevator. "I designed the security measures in the village, and they are not easy to live with."

Things looked pretty utilitarian on the lab level, but there were no well-wishers lurking down the hall, and Kaia let out a relieved breath.

"They should be thankful for that." She lifted on her toes and kissed his cheek. "If not for your ingenious system, Kian wouldn't let them out of the village. Your security measures allow them the freedom to come and go as they please."

"Not everyone thinks things through like you do." He put his hands on her waist. "People, even immortals, only see what's in front of them, and they rarely bother to get to the bottom of things."

Kaia lifted her hand and stroked his cheek with the tips of her fingers. "They love you and appreciate you, so I don't think you are right about your fellow clan members. They are well aware of what you do for them." She pressed a soft kiss to his lips. "Are you ready to show me your domain?"

He nodded, but his brows remained drawn together.

"I thought you would be more excited about showing me your lab."

"I am excited, but my worry over your imminent transition puts a dark shadow over everything."

She sighed. "I assume that Kian said no to asking his mother to come back?"

"He didn't say no, but he didn't say yes either. He's going to tell her about you and your family, and hopefully, she'll be curious enough to shorten her trip to come to see you."

"That's good news, right?"

"It's not as good as if he called her right then and there, and she promised to return immediately. That was what I hoped for."

"It's just a silly blessing, and there is another god in the village who can give it to me. We can ask Darlene to ask her grandfather on my behalf."

"Kian assured me that Toven is just as capable as Annani in the blessing department and that he helped strengthen his mate even before her transition. She had a heart problem."

Kaia shook her head. "Toven's mate was a human?"

"She was a Dormant."

"Are you saying that Toven mystically healed her heart condition even before she attempted transition?"

"Correct."

All that talk about blessings made Kaia nervous.

Did the gods put their hands on those they blessed? Was that how they transferred their healing energy?

Suspending disbelief wasn't difficult for her on a theoretical level. The universe was full of mysteries yet to be discovered, and she didn't like to dismiss anything unless it was completely ridiculous. But it wasn't as easy to do when her life was on the line.

KAIA

"Then we have nothing to worry about, right?" Kaia affected a bright smile and took William's hand. "Toven is obviously powerful enough to help me."

He gave her hand a light squeeze. "I can hear the uncertainty in your voice, Kaia. Don't try to be brave for my sake, and don't dismiss your premonitions. What are you feeling? Are you still apprehensive?"

She put her hand on her belly. "It's not as bad as it was yesterday, but it is still here."

SYSSI

"*I* wonder if Bridget has the results already," Syssi said as Amanda's car drove itself into the tunnel.

"She would have called you if she did."

Syssi sighed. "Yeah, I know. I'm just anxious to find out whether Eric and Gilbert are Dormants. I prayed to the Fates to make it so."

She'd been checking her phone throughout the day and had even considered calling the doctor, but that would have been counterproductive. Bridget would have called her as soon as she found out whether Eric and Gilbert were related to her.

Unless Bridget had the results and they were negative, and she didn't want to deliver the bad news over the phone.

When her phone rang and Bridget's name appeared on the screen, Syssi's heart did an anxious little flip. "It's Bridget."

"Answer it." Amanda turned to look at their daughters who were sleeping in the backseat. "The ringing will wake up the babies."

With shaking hands, Syssi accepted the call. "Hello, Bridget. What's the verdict?"

"You are related to Gilbert and Eric. They are Dormants. Naturally, the same goes for their sister."

"Yay!" Amanda pumped her fist in the air. "We have twin boys for our girls."

"Thank you for letting me know," Syssi said. "Did you call them?"

"I called you first. I thought you would want to deliver the good news yourself."

Syssi cast a sidelong look at Amanda. "Can you take care of Allegra while I pay Gilbert and Karen a visit?"

"Sure thing. I have Dalhu and Onidu to help me at home."

Syssi was still uncomfortable leaving Allegra alone with Okidu even though Annani had told her the Odus had practically raised her children. Unlike her, Amanda seemed fine with Onidu watching Evie, which was surprising, given how anxious she'd been about having another child when she'd first discovered that she was pregnant.

Both of them couldn't wait for Annani to return and spend time with their daughters so they could transition and become indestructible.

Syssi nodded her thanks to Amanda before returning to Bridget. "We are minutes away from the village parking, and I can stop by their place on my way home."

"What about Eric?" Bridget asked.

"If he's not there, I'll ask Gilbert to call him. I don't want to deliver news like this over the phone."

It just didn't seem right. This would change their lives completely, and not all of it was positive.

Aside from the danger that everyone was aware of, there were other issues that needed to be addressed. Karen would need to quit a job that she loved because she couldn't bring her nanny to the village, Gilbert would need to change the way he managed his business or close it down, Cheryl would have to change schools, and so would Idina.

As Amanda eased her new Mercedes SUV into her parking spot, Onidu rushed over to take the double stroller and other baby paraphernalia out of the trunk.

By the time Syssi and Amanda got out of the car, he was already unbuckling Evie's car seat. A moment later, both baby carriers were on the stroller, and they were ready to go.

"I feel sorry for Karen." Amanda sauntered behind Onidu in her high heels. "Taking care of twins without help is going to be tough, especially since she's not used to it. She and Gilbert hired their nanny when Idina was born, and she has been with them ever since."

"When did you get a chance to talk to her?"

"I met her yesterday at the playground. She brought Idina and the boys to play with Phoenix and Ethan. It was heartwarming to see so many little ones at the playground. I wish Kian could have seen it."

He would have loved it.

When the playground had been incorporated into the village square's design, it had been pure wishful thinking on Kian's part that one day it would be teaming with children. Seeing his optimism pay off would make him happy.

"You should have called us." Syssi followed the butler with the stroller into the elevator. "We would have brought Allegra over."

Amanda was the last to enter and pressed the button for the ground level. "When I got to the playground, it was nearly seven in the evening, and they were getting ready to leave."

"Maybe we can organize another playground meetup later today."

"Count me in." Amanda waited for the door to open and stepped out into the pavilion. "I'll walk with you to their house."

They both lived in the newest part of the village, while Gilbert and Karen were staying in phase two, which wasn't on the way, but Syssi was glad for the company.

"What were you doing in the playground at seven in the evening?" she asked.

Amanda lifted a brow. "You seriously don't know?"

"Know what?"

Was Amanda planning a surprise party? And if she was, for whom?

Amanda shook her head. "The village rumor machine is strange. I was sure someone would spill and tell you about Eric's ceremony tonight."

Syssi stopped in her tracks. "What are you talking about? He doesn't even know that he's a Dormant yet."

"Apparently, Eric's so convinced that he's a Dormant that he didn't want to wait. Max volunteered to be his inducer and also to make all the arrangements for the ceremony. Naturally, he came to me for help, but I told him that I no longer had the energy to organize parties and gave him pointers on how to do it himself."

Shaking her head, Syssi resumed walking. "We rode together to work, we spent all day together, and you didn't think to mention it to me?"

Amanda winced. "I hoped you wouldn't hear about it until you got the results. I knew you would start stressing about it and try to talk Eric out of attempting it before he was confirmed as a Dormant."

"So what? You should have told me."

"I know." Amanda cast her an apologetic look. "Can you forgive me?" She added a quivering lower lip.

"Oh, stop it." Syssi slapped her arm. "I know that you're not sorry at all."

30

ERIC

*E*ric's gut clenched as he read Gilbert's text. "The results are in." He looked up at Darlene.

Her hand flew to her chest. "Don't keep me in suspense. Are you related to Syssi or not?"

"Gilbert didn't say. Syssi is at their place, and she's waiting for me to get there so she can tell us together."

Darlene frowned. "Then it's probably a no. No one makes such a big deal out of good news." She gave him a small smile. "But that doesn't mean that you are not a Dormant. You might have the immortal genes without being related to Syssi."

"True." Eric pushed to his feet and offered her a hand up. "Let's find out."

She took it and let him pull her to her feet. "I need to tell William that I'm leaving."

"He and Kaia probably got the same text." He opened the door of her tiny office.

It was a converted closet, but Darlene didn't mind. She was just glad to have a space of her own to work in that was more than a desk tucked into some dusty corner of the main lab. She'd decorated it with two tiny plants, one large landscape painting that served as a fake window, and several framed photographs of Roni at different ages.

The guy hadn't been cute, even as a small boy.

Roni looked pissed in all his photos, and Eric wondered whether Darlene's ex had been as abusive toward him as he'd been toward her. It wasn't fun being around a person who tried to put you down, especially when you were much smarter than the jerk trying to make you feel bad about yourself.

Darlene's so-called office was inside William's larger one, and as they walked out of hers, they found William and Kaia getting ready to leave as well.

"Did you also get a text from Gilbert?" Eric asked Kaia.

"Yeah." She tucked her phone inside her wallet purse. "I don't know why Bridget told Syssi first. I hate the suspense."

Roni swiveled his Batman-like chair around. "You'll find out the results in five minutes. Text me when you do."

"You can come as well," Darlene said. "In a way, it involves you too."

He waved a dismissive hand. "I don't like family drama." Roni smiled at Eric. "Best of luck."

"Thank you," Eric said. "I appreciate it."

What he appreciated even more than the good-luck wish was the smile Roni gave him. He had a feeling that the guy didn't smile often, and never just to be nice to someone he didn't like.

It was a good sign that Roni was making an effort to be friendly, even if it was just for his mother's sake.

When they got to Karen and Gilbert's place, the door was wide open, and through it he saw his brother pacing while Syssi and Karen sat on the couch and talked quietly.

"Here you are." Gilbert threw his hands in the air. "What took you so long?"

"We came as soon as we received the text." Kaia entered the room and zeroed in on Syssi. "Now that we are all here, you can tell us the verdict."

Syssi grinned. "I'm happy to welcome you all into the family. Gilbert and Eric are my third cousins."

"Thank goodness." Kaia dropped into the chair William pulled out for her. "I had heart palpitations on the way here." She cast Syssi a mock glare. "Did you forget that we are still human? We can't take stress like that."

Syssi laughed. "You're nineteen. You can handle it."

"Yeah, I might be able to. But my mother, Gilbert, and Eric are no spring chickens, and neither is Darlene." Kaia slanted a look at Darlene. "You're still hot, though."

"Thank you." Darlene looked embarrassed. "I hope to look much hotter once I transition."

Eric pulled out a dining chair for her. "I think you're hot too, and I wouldn't mind keeping you just the way you are forever, but since that's not on the table, I'll have to resign myself to a younger version of you."

Looking unsure whether he meant it or not, Darlene narrowed her eyes at him. "Says the guy who dated twenty-year-olds up until two weeks ago. I'm sure you'll like the younger version of me better."

31

KAIA

*E*ric looked like he was about to spout more compliments for Darlene when Syssi lifted her hand to stop him. "Does your family know about the induction ceremony tonight?"

Gilbert chuckled. "I tried to talk him out of it before, but now that we know for sure that he's a confirmed Dormant, I'm glad he rushed to secure himself an inducer."

"I thought you were joking," Kaia said. "Is Max seriously arranging your ceremony and initiating you? Since when are the two of you best buddies?"

Max had his eye on Darlene, and he'd flirted with her even though he knew she was seeing Eric. There was no way he was now supporting Eric so enthusiastically. The Guardian was a nice guy, but no one was that selfless.

"They are not buddies." Darlene grimaced. "And it seems strange to me too that Max is doing all of that for a rival."

Syssi's lips lifted in a surprised smile. "Were you dating Max before you met Eric?"

"I wasn't, but Max was hopeful." Darlene looked at William. "Probably with your encouragement."

William lifted his hands in the universal peace sign. "In my defense, I didn't know that Eric would turn out to be Syssi's distant relative. I wanted you to find a nice immortal to partner with, and I happen to like Max. He's a good guy, and there is no way he's doing this for some nefarious motives. Maybe he feels guilty for trying to steal you away from Eric."

"When is the ceremony?" Kaia asked to stop the argument.

"It will start at eleven at night and end a little after midnight." Eric took Darlene's hand and brought it to his lap. "A nice lady at the café explained that it is done at that hour to symbolize a new beginning."

"Who did you talk to?" Syssi asked. "Was it Amanda?"

"It was the nurse," Darlene said. "I forgot her name."

CHAPTER 31

"Gertrude?" William asked.

"Yeah, that's the one."

"Gertrude is very knowledgeable," Syssi said. "She worked with Doctor Bridget for many years, and now she also works with Doctor Merlin, helping him with his fertility potions. She grows herbs in her garden."

The name sounded familiar. Wasn't she the one William had said would run the clinic in Safe Haven?

If she worked with the other doctor to brew fertility potions, she might be helpful in more ways than one.

Except, Kaia was no longer in a rush to get pregnant.

She had to transition first. Heck, they also needed to get married before they had children, but throwing a wedding into a mix of explosive issues would create a nuclear bomb.

Her mother and Gilbert were finally warming up to William and accepting him as her partner, but if she threw in wedding plans, they would once again suspect that he had some kind of unhealthy influence on her.

In fact, she wondered why no one had brought it up yet. Now that they knew that immortals could thrall and compel humans, it must have occurred to them that William could have done it to her.

Not that he ever would, but they didn't know him as well as she did.

"I'll certainly plan to attend." Syssi flipped her long hair over her shoulder. "Is Max planning a party for you after the ceremony?"

"I don't know," Eric said. "We haven't spoken since yesterday. I should check with him."

"If he didn't, we could have a small party in here," Karen looked at Gilbert. "We should take a nap, or we will fall on our faces staying up so late."

He patted her knee. "If Cheryl agrees to watch the little ones, we might be able to steal an hour or two of shuteye before the ceremony."

As everyone turned to look at Cheryl, she shrugged. "Fine. Provided that you let me sleep as late as I want tomorrow."

"It's a deal," Gilbert said.

Syssi rose to her feet. "Kian will be there as well, and Amanda and her mate." She slung the strap of her purse over her shoulder. "I need to start looking for a babysitter." She smiled at Cheryl. "If Eric wasn't your uncle, and you didn't need to be at the ceremony, I would have paid you to babysit Allegra. We have a shortage of experienced babysitters in the village."

Cheryl's eyes widened with two dollar signs popping up on her irises. "Pencil me in for your future babysitting needs."

"I will." Syssi smiled. "I'll see you all later tonight."

When everyone rose to their feet, and a round of hugs and congratulations ensued, Kaia thought about the implications of her mother, Gilbert, and Eric transitioning. Except for Cheryl, who was eager to start a babysitting business in the village, no one was mentioning the future. What were they going to do about their living and work arrangements?

Perhaps it was time to discuss it.

3 2

WILLIAM

*A*fter Syssi left, Kaia went to the kitchen and a moment later returned with a pack of Coke cans. "Anyone want a Coke?"

"I do," Cheryl said.

"I should check on the little ones." Karen rose to her feet. "It's way too quiet over there."

"I thought they were napping," Darlene said.

"They are watching a kids' show." Gilbert walked over to the fridge and took out a pack of beers. "Let's celebrate."

It was Coors Light, which was like drinking soda for William, but he didn't want to be the odd man out, so he accepted what Gilbert was offering.

"I should check with Max about his plans for the ceremony." Eric pulled out his phone. "I don't think I'll be in any state to celebrate after he beats me up and bites me, and I don't want you to organize a get-together if I'm going to be passed out." He looked at Gilbert. "Unless you want to do that regardless of my state."

"It's going to be way past midnight, and I'd rather go to sleep." Gilbert offered a can of beer to Karen, who'd returned from checking up on the kids. "Let's make a toast now." He clinked his can with hers. "To all of us making it through the transition."

"Hold on." Eric was still typing on his phone. "Okay, I'm ready." He put the device back in his pocket and lifted his beer. "To everyone successfully turning immortal." He clinked his can with Darlene's and then with Kaia's. "Did you and William start working on it?"

William felt his cheeks warm up, but Kaia remained unfazed. "Yeah." She cast him an apologetic smile. "Sometimes my family lacks boundaries."

He chuckled. "Mine is way worse. Wait until you get settled in the village, and people feel comfortable with you. Even your ears will catch fire hearing them talk. Immortals are not shy about their sexuality."

"That's actually refreshing." Kaia gave him a seductive look before turning to her mother. "Did any of you give any thought to what you'll be doing once everyone's transitioned? We can't go back to our old lives."

"I don't see why not." Karen put her beer down on the dining room table. "I talked with Nathalie, Syssi's sister-in-law, and she told me that Syssi's brother still works at the same Homeland Security department he did before his transition. If he can do that, so can I."

"Not really," Kaia said. "You can get away with suddenly looking younger with a story about an excellent plastic surgeon, but for how long?"

Karen chuckled. "At least a couple of decades. Just look at the actresses on the big screen and on television. Some of them are in their mid-fifties and look twenty years younger."

"You're deluding yourself." Kaia took a long sip from her coke. "You are forty-five, and in two decades, you will be sixty-five. Given how everyone here looks, you will look twenty years younger than you are now. Do you really think you could pull it off for that long? You couldn't do that even for one decade."

Karen grimaced. "I'm not the type who can be satisfied with staying home and raising kids. I'll go crazy."

"Perhaps you can work remotely?" Darlene suggested. "What is it that you do?"

"I'm a system administrator. I'm responsible for managing the IT infrastructure of the organization. Some of it can be done remotely, but not all."

"Maybe William could use your skills?" Darlene turned to him. "Do you need a system administrator?"

He shook his head. "We are a small operation. Only large organizations with many users need someone like that. Using Karen's skills for our network would be like getting a surgeon to put bandages on scraped knees. It's not going to be satisfying for her."

"I see." Darlene turned to Karen. "What about a change of careers? How much do you love what you do?"

"Love is not the right word for how I feel about my job. It's fascinating, I have access to revolutionary technologies the public has no idea about, and I'm very good at what I do. To give it up will be a big sacrifice for me."

Kaia groaned. "I know that it will be painful for you to give it up, but no job is worth giving up immortality for."

Karen smiled sadly. "That's absolutely true, but that's not the only reason I might not wish to transition." She tilted her head in the direction of the hallway. "I have three little kids to take care of and two lovely older daughters who have already lost a father and who I don't want to leave without a mother."

Kaia paled. "So, what are you saying? That you are not going to do it?"

"I need more time to think about it, and so does Gilbert." Karen took her mate's hand. "We talked about it, and we decided to go back home as soon as we know that you are no longer in danger."

"What if I transition smoothly?" Eric looked at Gilbert. "Will that convince you to give it a try?"

Gilbert turned to Karen. "Not without the love of my life. If Karen doesn't want to risk it, I won't either."

As William felt a wave of panic coming from Kaia, he gave her hand a squeeze. "I think that the dangers of transition are overstated. We haven't lost a transitioning Dormant yet, and that was when we had only one goddess to give them her blessing. We have two now, and with their combined power, the chance we will lose one now is negligible."

Did he believe what he'd just said?

Not really.

If he did, he wouldn't be so stressed about Kaia's impending transition. It was true that the clan hadn't lost a transitioning Dormant yet, but there was always a first time for everything. That being said, he didn't think that Karen and Gilbert should give up immortality. Gilbert was a confirmed Dormant, and if Kaia transitioned, Karen would be confirmed as well. Their fears were not unjustified, but they were overblown.

3 3

DARLENE

he crowd Eric and Darlene found in the gym surprised them both. The place looked like a wedding venue, just without the nice table-cloths, the fancy dishes, or the decorations.

Large circular tables were arranged around a roped-off wrestling mat, and there were enough bottles of whiskey and beer on each one to get even a bunch of immortal males drunk. A few soft drink bottles and some bar-style snacks had been included as well, but they seemed like an afterthought.

Given the no-frills and plenty of booze theme, it was pretty obvious that the event had been organized by a guy, but given the time Max had to put the event together, it was admirable nonetheless.

"Why are all these people here?" Eric whispered in her ear. "Are they all eager to see the human get his butt kicked?"

"Maybe they are here for the free booze," Darlene offered an alternative. "These immortals like to drink. Roni often invites people over for barbecues on week-ends, and I get drunk just from watching the quantities of alcohol they consume."

From the corner of her eye, Darlene saw Amanda heading their way and turned to greet her.

"Good evening." She extended her hand to Kian's sister. "I'm glad you could make it."

"I couldn't help but overhear." Amanda shook it lightly. "Neither the booze nor the wish to see the human getting his butt kicked is the reason for so many coming to watch the ceremony tonight." She turned to Eric and offered him her hand. "I'm Amanda, Kian's sister."

"Enchanted." He smiled at her way too brightly for Darlene's liking and lifted her hand to his lips for a kiss.

"Come and join Dalhu and me at our table, and I'll explain why half of the village is here tonight even though most of them don't know you."

They might not have known Eric, but it wasn't hard to guess that the new guy wearing track pants and a sleeveless sport shirt was the Dormant who was about to get induced, and they also knew Darlene and that he was her chosen. As they walked toward Amanda's table, people smiled and murmured words of encouragement, to which Eric responded with his usual charm.

Her guy knew how to work a room.

"This is Dalhu," Amanda introduced her hulking mate. "My better half."

He rose to his feet, towering over everyone, and offered Eric his hand. "Good luck."

"Thank you." Eric pulled out a chair for Darlene. "Am I allowed to drink before my initiation?"

"I don't see why not." Dalhu picked one of the whiskey bottles. "Are you familiar with this one?"

Eric nodded. "It's good."

Dalhu filled up a glass, handed it to Eric, and looked at Darlene. "Would you like some?"

"No, thank you. I don't like whiskey."

"Neither do I." Amanda waited for Eric to take a sip. "There are several reasons for the impressive turnout, and none are about seeing the poor human getting bested by an immortal, or the free drinks. We don't celebrate birthdays, and very few of us bother with wedding parties, so these initiation ceremonies are an excellent excuse for us to gather and celebrate."

"Sounds reasonable," Eric said. "But no one knows me."

Amanda smiled. "That brings me to reason number two. By now, everyone has heard about the family of potential Dormants visiting the village, and when the rumor spread about you and your brother being confirmed relatives of Syssi, they wanted to get to know you. Reason number three is Max, who's a Guardian, so naturally all of his Guardian friends are here for him. The ceremony is mostly about the Dormant, but it's also about his inducer. You and Max are about to pledge eternal friendship to each other, and it's a big deal. Most clan members don't have siblings, and the ceremony gives men a wonderful opportunity to form brotherly bonds."

Darlene stifled a wince.

Eric's idea of a threesome with Max was kinky enough. Adding to the mix, a brotherly bond between the two men she was supposed to have sex with was over the top.

"Where is Max?" Eric asked. "Is he hiding in seclusion like a bride, waiting for everyone to arrive so he can make a grand entrance?"

"Probably." Amanda took a bottle of tequila and poured herself a shot. "I'm so glad that I'm no longer breastfeeding. I can indulge in some alcohol now."

Darlene frowned. "If Max is waiting to make his entry, who will lead the ceremony?"

"Kian, of course." Amanda poured another glass for Darlene. "Well, he always leads the first attempt, but if a repeat is needed, the second event is much more casual, and someone else might lead the ceremony."

"I won't need a repeat." Eric crossed his arms over his chest. "It's happening tonight."

Amanda smiled indulgently. "Every Dormant thinks that, and yet some need to make several attempts to activate their immortal genes."

"So I've heard. But I can feel it in my gut that it's happening for me tonight." Eric tapped his washboard abs.

Not wanting to dampen his mood, Darlene chose to keep her mouth shut, but she doubted that tonight's initiation would work.

She didn't know Max's lineage and how far or close he was to the source. In any case, he wouldn't have been her first choice as an inducer for Eric.

Darlene would have preferred Kian or Orion to do that. But Orion was still with Alena and Annani in Scotland, and she couldn't ask Kian. If Max failed to induce Eric, though, she would beg Shai to plead with Kian on her behalf.

Could Toven induce him?

She wasn't sure. A god's venom might be too potent, or its aggressive formulation might not be suitable for inducing a male Dormant. She needed to ask Toven whether any of the male gods bothered with initiating Dormants back in the day, but she was quite sure that the answer was no. The immortals of that time had still been very close to the source, and there had been enough of them to induce all the Dormants.

The gods had most likely considered themselves too lofty to bother with their lowly descendants.

KAIA

"*L*ook at this." Kaia waved a hand at the transformed gym. "It seems like the party started without us."

The exercise equipment had been pushed aside, and about fourteen round tables had been brought in and arranged around the fighting arena. With sixteen chairs surrounding each table, there was room for over two hundred people, and more than half of the seats were already taken.

"We are not late." William led her through the tables toward where Eric and Darlene were sitting with a stunning brunette and a dude with shoulders the size of an entry door.

He was so big that he probably needed to duck and turn sideways to fit through a standard-size doorway. Perhaps that was why no one else was sitting at their table. The guy looked intimidating.

Naturally, Eric was perfectly at ease with that mountain of a man, talking with the guy as if they had known each other from high school.

"Hello." The brunette smiled at Kaia. "I was wondering when I would get to meet the famous bioinformatician who stole our William's heart."

Kaia returned her smile. "So far, the only new clan members I've met have been in William's lab."

"Why am I not surprised?" The brunette cast William a mock angry glare and rose to her stiletto-clad feet.

She was so tall in those shoes that she towered over Kaia, which didn't happen often.

The woman pulled her into a tight embrace. "I'm Amanda. Kian's sister." She let go as quickly as she'd attacked and turned around. "This is Dalhu, my mate and the love of my life."

He let out a breath, looking embarrassed about the flowery introduction his mate had given him. "Nice to meet you. Good luck with your transition."

"Thank you." She sat on the chair William had pulled out for her.

CHAPTER 34

"Did you start working on it already?" Amanda asked.

Kaia wanted to roll her eyes. William had warned her about his people's open attitudes toward sex, but she'd thought he was exaggerating so she wouldn't feel bad about Eric throwing that same question at them.

No wonder Eric felt right at home with these people. They also didn't have personal boundaries.

She gave Amanda a slight nod. "Is there an induction ceremony for girls? It would save everyone the trouble of asking if they'd started working on their transition. I'm not shy, but for some, it might be embarrassing."

Amanda snorted. "You are absolutely right. We should have a ceremony for females as well. The problem is that most of the adult female Dormants who have transitioned so far started working on it before knowing that they were Dormants, so maybe the party should be held after the transition."

"What about the clan girls? Don't they deserve to have a party?"

William had told her that they transitioned at a young age, but that didn't preclude throwing a party to celebrate the start of the process, especially since the clan didn't celebrate birthdays.

If Kaia transitioned and became a member, she would change that. Birthdays should be celebrated even if a person had thousands of them.

Amanda tapped a finger on her lower lip. "That's actually not a bad idea. The girls are too young to understand that their little bodies are going through a change, but that doesn't mean that their transition shouldn't be celebrated by those who love them and care for them. I'll talk it over with Syssi. Once my mother returns to the village, Allegra will start spending time with her, so that could count as the start of her transition. We should throw her a big party."

"What about Evie?" Dalhu asked. "Will she start spending time with your mother as well?"

"Of course, but she's too little to be affected by Annani's proximity. We need to wait a few more months."

"Syssi said that she and Kian would come." Kaia turned around to look at the gym's entrance. "My mother and Gilbert are also supposed to be here."

"Are they bringing your younger siblings along?" Amanda asked. "This may be frightening to them."

"Cheryl, my sister, agreed to babysit in exchange for a large sum of money and Gilbert's promise to record the entire match."

Amanda chuckled. "Tell your sister that she will have many clients willing to pay large sums for an experienced babysitter."

"Syssi told her that already," Kaia said.

William wrapped his arm around her shoulders. "You wanted to see a god." He motioned with his chin. "Toven just walked in with Mia."

Kaia's heart lurched into her throat, and she whipped her head around to get her first glimpse.

"Wow. I thought that Kian looked like a god. But this guy is the real thing."

Toven was so perfect that it was disturbing.

Amanda snorted. "My brother is more handsome than him, and I'm not saying that because of sisterly love. Kian is more manly. Toven is a little too soft."

There was nothing soft about the god's predatory gait or the way he scanned the room for danger. People skittered aside to let him and his mate through, and it wasn't just because of the motorized wheelchair she was driving.

There was an air of danger and power about him that Kaia could feel from more than a hundred feet away, and the lack of glow William had told her about wasn't enough to detract from Toven's otherworldly perfection.

35

ERIC

*E*ric stared at Darlene's grandfather, searching for the familial resemblance, but other than similar coloring, they had very little in common.

Darlene was a beautiful woman, but she was not in the same league as her grandfather. Toven was so damn perfect that Eric found it impossible to take his eyes off him.

Despite his willingness to experiment, Eric had never been attracted to other men, and even when his threesome adventures included another guy, they had always been about the woman. But if both he and Toven were single, and the god was interested, Eric wasn't sure he would have refused an invitation.

What was it like to be a god? To be so perfect that people just wanted to be near you, look at you, touch you? No wonder the mythological gods had been a bunch of entitled divas.

Except, that wasn't the vibe he was getting from Toven.

The guy didn't look stuck up or even aware of his physical superiority. Perhaps he was so used to the stares that he no longer noticed them.

Eric wasn't sure what he'd expected the god to look like, but in addition to physical perfection, he'd imagined his expression to be peaceful, maybe a little bored, and more than somewhat condescending. He didn't expect Toven to look discontented, especially since he had his mate by his side, and he hadn't expected him to look unhappy either.

The god proved what Eric had always suspected.

Happiness had very little to do with external factors. Everyone had their innate happiness setting, and even a god who had everything a human could ever dream of couldn't change it.

"I'm so glad the two of you could make it." Darlene rose to her feet and leaned to kiss Toven's mate on the cheek.

Eric followed Darlene up and stood next to her, waiting for her to introduce him.

"How could we have missed it?" The girl smiled at him. "This will be my first time witnessing an induction ceremony."

Darlene put her arm around him. "Let me introduce the star of tonight's main event. This is Eric Emerson."

Plastering his best smile on his face, Eric offered his hand to Toven's mate. "It's a pleasure to meet you."

"The feeling is mutual." She put her delicate hand in his. "I'm Mia."

"Enchanted." Eric skipped on kissing the back of her hand as he would usually do.

If Toven was the jealous type, he didn't want to anger him, and not just because the dude was a powerful god capable of smiting him. He was Darlene's grandfather, and she valued his opinion.

Straightening, Eric offered his hand to Toven. "I don't know what the protocol for greeting a god is. Should I bow?"

Toven surprised him with a genuine smile. "No bowing, please. Ever." He took Eric's hand and shook it lightly.

Amanda chuckled. "The rules are a little different with my mother. A dip of the head is expected, and you should address her as Clan Mother. When she gets to know you better, she will tell you to call her Annani, but until then you should stick with Clan Mother."

"Annani always liked fanfare." Toven removed one of the chairs to make room for Mia's wheelchair. "But since she actually has a clan of people who look up to her, I guess it's appropriate." He sat down next to Mia.

She put a hand on his arm. "You have people who look up to you too. Geraldine and Orion and their kids and grandkids and so on. Your clan will grow, but since it will be intertwined with Annani's descendants, you two will have to come up with proper titles to reflect that."

He took her hand and lifted it to his lips for a kiss. "Fates willing, you and I are going to have children as well, and since they will be born immortal, we might start a clan of our own."

"Fates willing indeed," Amanda said as she lifted her head. "Kian and Syssi are here." She waved them over.

"Karen and Gilbert are right behind them," William said. "They must have met outside."

Toven turned to look at the newcomers.

"Good evening." Eric rose to his feet to greet Kian and Syssi.

"Good evening, cousin." Syssi grinned. "I'm so glad that I can finally say that. I never had cousins before."

"We are a family of renown." Gilbert walked over to Eric and clapped him on the back. "Right, brother?"

"Now more than ever." Eric winked at Syssi.

"Are you ready to begin the ceremony?" Kian asked.

"Max is not here yet." Eric looked around. "We can't start without him."

"He's here." Kian pointed at the table near the entrance. "He was ambushed by his friends the moment he walked in. That's why you didn't see him."

Eric craned his neck. "I see him now."

Darlene took his hand. "Are you sure you want to go through with this? I don't mean the transition, I mean your initiator. I'm still not comfortable with Max doing it."

"I'm sure." He smiled at her. "Max is a good man, and I'm the guy whose talent is staying alive. I will come out victorious on the other side."

3 6

KIAN

*N*o matter how many times Kian had recited the ceremonial words, he hadn't grown tired of them. They still evoked in him a sense of pride and continuity.

Usually the initiates were teenage boys, but there hadn't been many in recent years. In fact, there had been only one, and Parker wasn't born to the clan.

The last initiation ceremony Kian had presided over for one of the clan's boys had been Jackson's and before him Vlad's, and before that Gordon's. The other initiation ceremonies had been for the adult male Dormants who'd joined the clan, but there hadn't been many of those either.

For some reason, there had been a dearth of children in the last couple of decades.

Before Syssi's arrival, Kian had nearly given up hope, but then the Fates had taken mercy on his clan and compensated for the lack of children with an influx of Dormants and had followed up with several pregnancies.

Kalugal's son was the latest arrival, but maybe Kaia's twin brothers would be next. It was still unclear whether she was a Dormant, but Kian had faith in the Fates.

William had dedicated his life to the clan and to humanity's advancement, working day and night to develop new technologies that made everyone's lives better.

He deserved his happily-ever-after.

Besides, Kaia was so perfect for him that there was no way she hadn't been handpicked for William by the Fates.

When everyone in the audience was holding a glass of the ceremonial wine, Kian lifted his and waited until they quieted down.

"Once again, I've changed a few words to adjust for the circumstances, so please don't correct me when you think that I forgot the correct wording."

There were a few chuckles, and when Eric smiled nervously, Max put a hand on his shoulder.

Kian held his glass up as he addressed the crowd. "We are gathered here tonight to present this fine man to our community. Eric is ready to attempt his transformation, and since he's Syssi's cousin, an accomplished fighter jet pilot, and more importantly, Darlene's chosen, he doesn't need anyone to vouch for him."

Kian waited for the chuckles and cheers to subside.

"Max has already volunteered to assume the burden of initiating Eric into his immortality, but I need to ask again." He turned to the Guardian. "Are you sure that you want to be bound to Eric for eternity?"

Max slanted a glance at Eric. "I'm sure."

Kian nodded. "Eric, do you accept Max as your initiator? As your mentor and protector, to honor him with your friendship, your respect, and your loyalty from now on?"

When Eric looked surprised, Kian realized that no one had told him the extent of the mutual commitment Max and he were assuming.

Max lifted a brow. "Now you're having second thoughts?" He batted his eyelashes and put a hand over his chest. "If you abandon me at the altar, I'm never going to forgive you."

People laughed, but as the seconds ticked off, Max's amused expression tightened.

Darlene looked at Eric as he shook his head as if to clear the stupor and offered his hand to the Guardian. "Buddies forever."

When Max clasped it, Eric pulled him into a bro hug, and the two clapped each other on their backs.

"Forever." Max grinned. "But you have to say, I do, or it doesn't count."

"I do."

Kian continued, "Does anyone object to Eric becoming Max's protégé?" He looked around at the faces of those standing closest to him, and for a moment, it looked like Darlene was going to object, but then she shook her head, and he let out a relieved breath.

Raising his wine glass, Kian turned back to Max and Eric. "As everyone present agrees that this is a good match, let's seal it with a toast. To Eric and Max."

As cheers and hoots erupted from the Guardian section of the room, Kian wondered why this particular pairing was making them so excited.

The only adult Dormant to receive such enthusiastic cheers had been Michael.

Was it because Eric was a former soldier, a fighter like them?

Or was it because of Max?

The cheering went on for several minutes, and then Kian lifted his hand to silence everyone again.

"Let's begin. Gentlemen, please take your positions."

37

DARLENE

$\mathcal{I}$t was done, and there was no going back. Max was going to induce Eric, and Darlene had a lump in her throat the size of a tennis ball.

She wanted to be close to the ring, but the table she was seated at was a little farther away, and people's backs were blocking her view. She thought about getting up and getting closer to the ring, but no one was standing, and she was embarrassed to be the only one.

The most she could do was turn her chair so she was facing it, but since those sitting in front of her were taller, she had to crane her neck to see what was going on.

Seeing her distress, William tapped the shoulder of the guy sitting at the table in front of her and blocking her view. "Can you move your chair a little? Darlene needs to see her mate's initiation."

"Of course." The guy scooted his chair aside.

As others did the same, creating a path for her to see the ring clearly, she mouthed her thanks to them.

Kian waited until the commotion was over before giving the signal for Max and Eric to begin, and as soon as he did, Eric lunged forward, diving for Max.

The Guardian hadn't been prepared for the swift attack, and when Eric collided with him, he went down like a rock.

Max had either been distracted by someone in the crowd, or he'd just pretended for Eric's sake, but Darlene didn't care how it had happened as long as Eric had his victorious moment.

"Go, Eric!" She shot to her feet and clapped.

Gilbert, Karen, and Kaia joined her, and even some of the immortals clapped their hands.

As soon as Max was down, Eric started throwing his fists at him, but the element of surprise didn't last. He managed to deliver only two punches before Max threw him off with a roar and went after him.

CHAPTER 37

Darlene's heart sank into her gut.

What if Eric provoked Max into a killing frenzy?

Would the others stop the Guardian in time to save Eric?

Eric didn't give up easily, and he fought ferociously to keep Max from pinning him down, but he was no match for the Guardian's superior strength and training.

Darlene doubted that even a minute had passed before Max had Eric pinned face down on the mat and immobilized. But instead of the fury she'd expected to see on the Guardian's face, Max was grinning.

It did nothing to assuage her fears, though. With his fangs fully elongated and dripping venom, the grin made Max look even more terrifying.

How could any woman find that arousing?

Was she expected to have sex with a monster like that? To let him bite her with those sharp fangs?

Not going to happen.

"I'm never transitioning," she murmured under her breath.

Still grinning, Max hissed through his fangs, "If you wanted to be on top, all you had to do was ask." He struck Eric's neck.

Eric didn't make a sound, but Darlene's breath caught in her throat.

She wasn't the only one.

Everyone in the audience was holding their breath with her, and as the seconds ticked off, the silence stretching over the gym became so oppressive that Darlene couldn't force air into her lungs.

She was getting lightheaded when Kian lifted his hand.

"That's enough," he broke the silence.

Max immediately retracted his fangs and treated the wounds with a long lick.

"You can go to Eric now," Syssi said. "It will take him a couple of minutes to wake up, and he will be loopy when he does."

As Darlene ran into the ring and ducked under the rope, Max turned Eric on his back with surprising gentleness.

"He did really well." The Guardian smiled at her. "You should be proud of him."

With his fangs already half-retracted, he looked a little less terrifying, but she didn't want him anywhere near Eric. "I got him now. You can go."

"What, no 'thank you'?" He leaned away to make room for her.

"Thank you," she gritted out as she checked that Eric was still breathing.

Max crouched next to her and said quietly. "You can sit on the mat and put his head in your lap. That's what mothers of transitioning boys usually do." He winked before pushing up to his feet.

Kicking her shoes off, she did as he'd suggested and sat cross-legged on the mat with Eric's head resting in her lap.

"Someone should have told me what I was supposed to do," she murmured as she stroked his hair.

Somehow, there wasn't a mark on him, and she wondered how that was possible. Had Max even punched him? Or had he just wrestled Eric down?

Bridget ducked under the rope and crouched next to them. "How are you doing?"

Darlene frowned. "You're asking me? Eric is the one who was just bitten."

"He's fine. I can hear his heartbeat and his breathing. But you're as white as a sheet."

"I'm okay now," she whispered.

Thankfully, now that the initiation was over, it was no longer quiet in the gym, and other than the doctor no one made a move to intrude on her and Eric's space. Was that also part of the custom?

"Max was very careful with Eric," Bridget said. "Which isn't easy for an immortal once they are provoked. He was a good choice."

"We didn't choose him. He volunteered." Darlene looked at Eric's smiling face in puzzlement. "Why does he look so happy after getting beaten?"

"It's the venom. It's the one time Eric gets to experience the euphoric high of a venom bite. Don't be surprised if he wakes up randy. The venom is also an aphrodisiac."

"I thought that it only worked like that on females."

"To a lesser extent, it has a similar effect on males. That's how they are incapacitated in a fight. The venom does not paralyze them. It's like a drug. They know what's going on, but they don't care. It takes away their will to do anything but soar on the euphoric cloud."

"So it's not deadly?"

"Oh, it definitely could be. If Max had kept pumping more venom into Eric's system, he could have stopped his heart. Kian stopped him just in time."

38

KAIA

"Have you talked with Eric today?" William leaned against the dresser as Kaia pulled her clothes out of the drawers and spread them over the bed.

She and William and her entire family were invited to Friday dinner at Kian and Syssi's home, and her mother wanted them all to dress nicely, but Kaia had nothing that would pass her mother's approval.

"I didn't. He was hiding in Darlene's office all day, and I didn't want to annoy him by asking him again if anything was happening. Why? Did Darlene say something to you?"

"No." William sighed. "It looks like Eric will have to choose another initiator and do it again."

Almost three days had passed since Eric's ceremony, and he was getting frustrated and taking it out on anyone who asked him if he was feeling anything.

Nothing was happening with Kaia either, but supposedly it took longer for females to start transitioning, so she wasn't worried yet.

Looking at the selection of clothes on the bed, she groaned. "I still don't have anything nice to wear. I should have ordered something."

William hugged her from behind, draping himself over her and looking at the meager spread. "You could borrow that dress from Darlene again. You looked hot in it." He kissed her neck.

"That's not a bad idea. She wanted me to keep it, so I don't think she would mind loaning it to me again."

"If you want to get it from her, you should hurry up. There isn't much time left."

"I'll call her. Maybe she can drop it off here on her way to Syssi and Kian's. They need to pass by the house anyway, and I don't need a lot of time to get ready. I'll just pull it on, and I'll be ready to go."

"That's my girl." He kissed her neck again. "Effortlessly beautiful."

Kaia pulled out of his arms and turned around. "What are you going to wear?"

He looked down at his slacks. "I thought that I would just shower, shave, and get a clean shirt. Why?"

Kaia walked into the closet and pulled down the tux that was encased in a plastic bag. "I want to see you in this."

William chuckled. "I'll be way overdressed. Besides, it's probably too big on me. I lost weight since the last time I wore it."

She pouted. "I just want to see you wearing it. You can take it off later." She put her hands on his chest. "I have a thing for men in tuxes."

His eyes blazing with an inner light, he banded his arms around her and pulled her against his body. "I'm the only man in a tux you will have a thing for. You're mine."

"Oooh, I love it when you get all bossy." She lifted on her toes and kissed him. "But the effect would be even sexier when you are in a tux."

"Give it to me." He pulled the hanger out of her hand. "I'm putting it on right now."

"Shower first." She kissed the tip of his nose and pulled out of his arms. "Hurry up, though. I want to have my way with you before Darlene and Eric get here."

"Give me three minutes." He moved so fast that he was a blur.

Laughing, Kaia sat on the bed with her phone and made the call.

"Hi," Darlene answered. "Let me guess. You need to borrow a dress."

"How did you know? Is telepathy your talent?"

Darlene chuckled. "I wish. Do you want to come over and check out my closet again?"

"I'll just borrow the same dress I wore to the restaurant, and I was hoping you and Eric could stop by William's house on the way to Syssi and Kian's and bring the dress with you. It will take me thirty seconds to pull it on, and we can continue together."

"No problem. We can come over a few minutes earlier."

"Thanks, Darlene." Kaia hesitated before asking, "Anything?"

Darlene sighed. "Nothing. It didn't work."

"Don't sound so defeated. Eric is a confirmed Dormant, so it's going to happen."

"Yeah, I know. That's why I'm not freaking out yet. I guess you have nothing to report either?"

"Nope. But I'm not worried. William says that it takes longer for female Dormants to enter transition. But I get why Eric is so disappointed, though. I also thought that I would beat the statistics and start transitioning right away."

Kaia had hoped that being young and healthy, she would enter transition a day or two after they had started working on it, but it didn't look like it was happening.

"Yeah, I also heard that it takes a long time for females," Darlene said.

"Who did you ask?"

"Amanda. After Bridget, she's the best source of information on everything that has to do with immortals and Dormants. When I want to know something, I hang around the café about the time she returns from work, and I ambush her when I see her passing through."

Kaia laughed. "The human ambushing the demigoddess. It sounds funny."

"First of all, I am not just a human. I am a demi-demigoddess. And secondly, it works. I pretend to just happen to be there, and while I walk home with her, I ask her all the questions I have."

Kaia crossed her legs and leaned her elbow on her knee. "Why can't you ask Roni? He's been with the clan for a while, and I'm sure he knows everything there is to know by now."

"Roni has no patience with his old mother, while Amanda is a teacher at heart, and she loves explaining things. She never makes me feel stupid for not understanding something."

Did Roni make Darlene feel stupid?

If so, the guy needed a talking-to, and she was just the girl to do it.

"If Amanda is so good at teaching, she should run a class for potential Dormants."

"I'm way ahead of you. I'm writing down everything I'm learning, and once I have it organized and proofread, I'll put it up on the clan's virtual bulletin board for anyone who needs it."

"That's a great initiative. When did you start?"

Darlene sighed. "Yesterday. I need to occupy my mind with something or I'll go crazy. Waiting for Eric's transition is nerve-wracking." She chuckled. "The funny thing is that I want him to be immortal, but at the same time, I don't."

Kaia frowned. "Why wouldn't you want him to transition?"

"Because once he does, he will grow fangs, and I'm not looking forward to getting bitten."

"Why? It's amazing."

"Doesn't it hurt?"

Kaia rolled her eyes. "Didn't Amanda explain it to you?"

"I didn't ask her about it. She's Annani's daughter. I can't ask her a personal question like that."

"What about your mother?"

Darlene snorted. "Do you want to talk with your mother about sex?"

"Not really. Anyway, the bite hurts a little, but because it is usually delivered as you are having a mind-blowing orgasm, the endorphins in your body make it barely noticeable, and then the venom takes care of everything, and all you feel is an intense pleasure. Let me put it this way. None of the sex you have had so far can prepare you for that. I'm trying to think of an analogy, but nothing profound comes to mind."

Darlene laughed. "Doctor Kaia Locke, I haven't known you long, but I've never heard you stumped for words to describe anything. If you say that it's indescribable, I don't need you to come up with an analogy. I get it."

39

WILLIAM

$\mathcal{W}$illiam stood in front of the mirror in his walk-in closet and examined his reflection. The tux jacket was loose on him, and he had to add a belt to the slacks to keep them from sliding down, but he still looked better in it now than the last time he'd worn it.

His closet was full of clothes that needed to go to charity. He'd gotten several new items already, but he needed to get more that were suitable for social outings.

Perhaps he and Kaia could go shopping on Sunday. If they were invited to more social events, they both needed to get some nicer stuff than what they wore to work every day.

William had been invited to Friday dinner at Syssi and Kian's only once before. Usually, those evenings were reserved for close family time, but from time to time Syssi also invited close friends and newcomers, like she'd done today.

He wasn't a big fan of dinner parties, but he was actually looking forward to this one. Perhaps what made it different was that he was going with Kaia. It wasn't fun attending social gatherings where he was often the only bachelor, but now he belonged to the exclusive club of mated couples, and he felt like a new man.

William hadn't expected the boost in confidence that having Kaia at his side would provide. They were a team, and she had his back as much as he had hers. There would be no more awkward moments when he would catch too late that people were looking at him with glazed eyes and polite smiles. If he went off on a tangent about some tech problem he was working on, she would nudge him to make him aware of boring his audience, and if he had nothing else that was interesting to the others, he could sit back and let her do the talking.

Being mated to Kaia was blissful, and he was grateful to the Fates for finding him the perfect companion for his life journey.

Kaia knocked on the door. "Can I come in now?"

"Not yet." He pulled the bowtie out of the tux pocket and tied it around his neck with practiced fingers. "Now you can."

He turned around as she opened the door. "What do you think?" He spread his arms and turned in a circle. "Does the tux do it for you?"

"Oh, yeah." Kaia sauntered over to him and gripped the lapels. "Come here, you sexy man." She smashed her lips over his.

Closing his hands over her lush bottom, William hoisted her up and kissed her back, his tongue pushing into her mouth and caressing hers lovingly.

The doorbell ringing pulled a groan out of his throat. "Couldn't they have come fifteen minutes later?"

Kaia pulled away from him with a sigh. "I thought we had more time. I'll keep them busy while you change."

"Why?" He made another turn. "Don't you want to drool over your sexy man throughout dinner?"

The doorbell rang again.

"Ugh. I have to get the door." She pointed a finger at him. "Get changed, but you are wearing this tux again when we get home tonight. I have plans for it."

The husky command combined with her hooded-eyed promise had his shaft swell and pulse. "Yes, ma'am."

After Kaia ducked out of the closet, William considered spending a few moments to take the edge off. Given that they were going to spend the evening with his boss and Kaia's family, sporting a painful erection throughout dinner would not only be tortuous, but also disastrous.

No more than five minutes later, William got out of the closet wearing one of his new pairs of slacks, the button-down shirt he'd worn to his interview with Kaia, and a much calmer disposition.

When he got to the living room, he found her with Eric and Darlene, already wearing the sexy black dress, and her long blond hair cascading in soft waves down her back and front.

That was all Kaia needed to look exquisite. She didn't need makeup or jewelry or high heels to change from a pretty girl to a goddess. Releasing her hair from its customary ponytail and wearing a nice dress was all it took.

"You're breathtaking." He pulled her into his arms for a quick kiss.

"You clean up nicely too." She leaned away to give him a once-over. "I remember this shirt."

"Do you like it?"

"I love it. It's the perfect blend of dorky and stylish."

He wasn't sure that was a compliment, but she'd said she loved it, and that was all he cared about.

"Shall we?" Eric pushed to his feet and offered Darlene a hand up. "It's five minutes to seven."

William took Kaia's hand and followed the two out the door. "It's a two-minute walk to Syssi and Kian's place."

"Being on time means arriving five minutes early," Darlene said. "So we are already late."

William chuckled. "Even if we are, you have nothing to worry about because we won't be the last to arrive. Amanda is never on time."

"My family also believes in the five minutes early rule," Kaia said. "But since my younger siblings' arrival, my mother never manages to actually pull it off. She has to turn into a drill sergeant to get everyone ready and out the door."

Hearing the smile in her tone, William squeezed her hand. "But it's worth it, right?"

"Absolutely. I wouldn't have it any other way, and I want to have a large family too." The smile slid off her face. "But as Darlene has so astutely pointed out, I need to adjust my dreams and aspirations to my new reality. Given how long I will live, my life can't be centered around having children. Even if a miracle happens and we manage to have as many as I want, raising them would only take a tiny fraction of my life."

They'd already reached Kian and Syssi's house, but William halted before taking the steps to their front door.

"You are a brilliant scientist, Kaia, and just like me, you are driven by curiosity and the need to make new discoveries. I know that you want a large family, but your work must be just as important to you."

"It is." She smiled. "I'm not sad about having to shift my thinking and adjust the way I imagined my future. I'm just acknowledging it out loud." She leaned closer and kissed his lips. "I love you, and I want to spend eternity with you making discoveries, raising children, and having fun with our grandchildren and great-grandchildren and so on. Our journey is going to be awesome."

40

SYSSI

*S*yssi sat at the head of the table with Kian by her side and marveled at the blessing the Fates had bestowed on her.

She considered Kian's family her own, but it was so nice to add several from her side.

Gilbert and Eric were talking with Andrew, and watching them together, she could actually see the family resemblance. It was in the way they held their bodies and even in their speech patterns. It proved how powerful nature was versus nurture.

Despite the generations separating them from their original maternal ancestor, they still exhibited similar traits. As for their paranormal talents, Gilbert claimed to have a good nose for crooks, and Eric claimed that his talent was staying alive, but those weren't necessarily paranormal abilities. Even if they were, they weren't nearly as strong or unusual as her foresight or Andrew's lie detecting.

She'd invited Toven and Mia and Kalugal and Jacki, but Kalugal had politely declined her invitation. He and Jacki were concerned about their baby's exposure to humans who might be carrying viruses on them without showing symptoms.

Given that they'd planned to travel to Egypt two weeks before the baby had been due, it was funny that they were so worried about the humans infecting their newborn son. They had been fine with the possibility of delivering little Darius in a hospital teeming with humans in a Third-World country, but now they feared a family of humans who were all perfectly healthy.

Perspectives and priorities changed once people became parents, and in that regard, immortals were no different than humans.

Gilbert put his wine glass down and turned to Kian and her. "Karen and I want to thank you for your hospitality and for the warm welcome you've extended to us, but we've decided to go home Sunday night." He cast an apologetic glance at Kaia and then at his brother. "You two can stay and keep working on your transitions, and as soon as anything happens, we will rush back here. But since we don't know when or if it's going to happen, we can't just sit around and twiddle our thumbs. I have building projects that need my attention, and Karen's boss is about to tear all her hair out if Karen is not back at work by Monday."

It was understandable but disappointing nonetheless. Syssi had hoped that Eric and Kaia's successful transitions would encourage Karen and Gilbert to start theirs as well, and that they would decide to move permanently into the village.

It might still happen, but not as quickly as Syssi had hoped.

Kian emptied his whiskey glass and put it down on the table. "Either Onegus or I will have to sift through your memories and erase everything that has to do with the village and its location. I will also ask Kalugal to reinforce Emmett and Eleanor's compulsion to keep you from revealing what you know about the existence of immortals."

There was no way Kalugal would meet with the viruses-carrying humans in person, and doing it over the phone would be less effective. Kian should have asked Toven to do that, and Syssi wondered why he hadn't.

The god hadn't volunteered his services either.

"Is it really necessary to sift through our memories?" Karen asked. "The compulsion is very effective at keeping us from revealing anything even accidentally."

"Compulsion can be overridden by a stronger compeller," Kian said. "If you fall into our enemies' hands, their leader can get you to talk. I'm not worried about him finding out what he already knows, but I don't want him to have even a hint of a clue about where he can find us. Furthermore, the only reason I'm allowing you to leave with memories of the existence of gods and immortals is that Kaia and Eric need to remain here, and you need to know what's going on with them."

"I don't want you to leave," Kaia said. "My transition might start any time now."

Karen gave her daughter an apologetic smile. "I know, sweetie. But it could also take a week or two, and we can't wait that long. We will come back as soon as it starts."

Gilbert shook his head. "What I'm concerned about is a stranger getting in my head. It's not that I have secrets to hide, but like everyone else, I sometimes have thoughts that I don't want to share with anyone other than my better half." He winked at Karen.

Syssi put a hand over her mouth to stifle the laugh bubbling out of her.

What Gilbert needed to hide was most likely his visits to internet porn sites.

He was a healthy male in his prime, and since he was still human, she doubted that his sexual fantasies were limited to Karen. Humans could be in loving, committed relationships and still indulge in fantasies about other partners. Immortals who had been fortunate enough to be blessed with a truelove mate couldn't think about touching anyone else, even as a fantasy.

Kian laughed. "Don't worry. If I'm the one doing the sifting, I'll make sure to stay away from those kinds of memories, and if it's Onegus, he'll avoid them like the plague as well."

41

KAIA

*K*aia lifted the teacup to her lips and blew air on it to cool it down before taking a sip.

After Gilbert's announcement that he was taking the family home Sunday night, her mood had plummeted.

She barely listened to the conversations going on around the table and hid her face from her mother's watchful eyes by staring at her plate.

William put a hand on her thigh. "Are you feeling alright? You've been uncharacteristically quiet."

Kaia forced a smile. "Are you calling me a chatterbox?"

"No, that's me. But you usually have an opinion on everything, and you are never shy about sharing it." He leaned closer and whispered in her ear, "I was counting on you dominating the conversation so that I wouldn't have to contribute."

That was surprising. William's problem was that he sometimes talked too much, not too little. But that usually happened when he got excited about subjects that interested him. He didn't like to offer his opinion about subjects he didn't know much about.

Kaia tilted her head. "Since when are you shy about saying whatever?"

"I'm not shy. I just prefer to better utilize my neural synapses than wasting them on things that are irrelevant to me."

Nodding, she patted his arm. "Now that I know when you need me to shield you, I promise not to neglect my duties." She let out a breath. "Starting tomorrow. This meal has exhausted me, and all I can think about is getting into bed."

William frowned. "It's only ten at night. Even Idina is still full of energy."

"Idina had an afternoon nap. I didn't." Kaia leaned sideways, rested her head on William's arm, and closed her eyes. "When can we go?" she whispered as quietly as she could.

"Soon." He lifted his hand and put it on her forehead. "You are a little warm."
Kaia lifted her head and forced her eyes open. "Maybe I'm transitioning?"
His entire body stiffened. "I'm calling Bridget."
"What's going on?" Amanda pushed to her feet.
"William says that my forehead feels warm."
A grin spread over the woman's gorgeous face. "It could be the start of the transition. What do you feel?"

The expectant silence stretching over the room was like a thousand spotlights that were directed at Kaia, and the warm feeling she'd had before intensified tenfold, making her sweaty.

She fanned herself with her hand. "Is it hot in here, or is it me?"
"It's not any warmer than it was three hours ago." Amanda put her hand on Kaia's forehead. "You're definitely running a fever." She turned to William. "Did you call Bridget?"
"I texted her. She says we should go to the clinic. She'll meet us there in an hour."
"Why only in an hour?" her mother asked.
"Bridget is at a restaurant in town with Turner, but she's sending Hildegard to the clinic. The nurse can take Kaia's vitals and hook her up to the monitors if needed."

Kaia didn't feel bad enough to go anywhere. She'd gone to classes with a fever and had plodded through even though all she'd wanted to do was sleep.

"I don't need to go to the clinic," she protested. "And there is no need to rush the nurse over there either. I have a little fever that could be a cold or flu, and I'm tired. That's not serious enough to justify a doctor's visit. I can wait for Bridget to return to the village and check my vitals."

"You make a good point." Amanda put a hand on her hip and struck a pose. "Do you have a sore throat?"
"No."
"Runny nose?"
Kaia shook her head.
"Stomachache?"
"Just from stuffing too much food into it. Okidu is a great cook."
"Thank you, Mistress," he called from the kitchen.
"You're welcome," Kaia called back. "And thank you for a wonderful meal."
Smiling, Amanda walked back to her seat. "You might be transitioning, but I don't think you are about to faint and lose consciousness." She pulled her phone out of her purse. "I'll text Hildegard that you will be there in an hour."

As she typed on the glass, her long, manicured nails made clicking sounds that, for some reason, annoyed Kaia.

As a neuroscience professor, Amanda shouldn't have such long nails. It just didn't fit the image. She shouldn't be so beautiful, and she shouldn't be dressed like a fashion model, either.

Kaia was dimly aware that her annoyance had nothing to do with Amanda, who had been very nice to her and her family. She was antsy because all her senses were suddenly hypersensitive. The dress felt scratchy against her skin, the fabric was too thick and not breathable enough, and her bra was too tight, digging into her skin, and the sounds around her were amplified and irritating.

CHAPTER 41

Perhaps she shouldn't have insisted on staying.

Instead of going to the clinic, though, Kaia wanted to go home to change out of the dress and discard her bra. But she'd made such a fuss about staying that it would be embarrassing to say that she'd changed her mind and now wanted to leave.

42

WILLIAM

*O*nce dinner was over, Kian rose to his feet. "Who wants to join me for a cigar outside?"

William wasn't a smoker, but he wanted to ask Kian whether he'd talked with Annani, and he hadn't had a chance to do it privately yet. Now that Kaia was possibly transitioning, he wanted the Clan Mother to be near.

She seemed fine, so it didn't seem urgent, but things could change in the blink of an eye.

Looking at Kaia across the table, he didn't know what to think. After dinner, she had moved to sit next to her mother, and she seemed a little better, but he had to make sure she would be okay without him for a few minutes.

He waited for a lull in the conversation before walking over and putting his hand on her shoulder. "I'm going outside with Kian. Will you be okay without me?"

She smiled weakly. "I'll manage. The question is, will you? You don't smoke."

Her smart eyes communicated that she knew his desire to join Kian had nothing to do with cigars.

"I'm going to keep Kian company while he smokes. Some of our best ideas have come to us over his cigars."

"Have fun." She blew him a kiss.

Gilbert rose to his feet. "I'll join you."

"Do you smoke?" William asked.

"Only occasionally." He put his hand on William's back. "If Kian is offering cigars, I'm not going to say no."

"Same here," Andrew grinned. "It's conducive to brotherly bonding. Right, Dalhu?"

"Right." William looked over his shoulder to see whether Toven and Eric were joining them as well, but they had chosen to stay behind.

Outside, Kian motioned to the four armchairs facing a fire pit table, where his cigar box lay open. "Help yourselves, gentlemen."

As the others got busy cutting the cigars, lighting them, and remarking on the quality, William leaned closer to Kian and asked quietly, "Did you have a chance to talk with the Clan Mother?"

Kian nodded. "They were supposed to return next Tuesday, but she said she would try to be back by Thursday. If she's needed earlier, though, she said to let her know, and she will come as soon as she can."

If there was an emergency, Kaia would need the goddess's help immediately and not eighteen hours later, which was how long it could take Annani to travel from the castle in Scotland to the village, and Thursday was nearly a week from now. If Kaia was transitioning, she would probably no longer need Annani's help by then.

Hopefully, Kian was right about Toven's ability to provide a blessing just as potent as Annani's.

William forced a smile. "Thank you."

"You're welcome."

Not to be rude, he stayed with the smokers a few more minutes and then excused himself and went back to Kaia, but she still wasn't ready to leave.

She was busy convincing her mother to stay and see her through the transition, but he could see on her face that she was suffering.

The girl was stubborn and too proud to admit that she wasn't feeling well.

It took another hour until Kian and the other cigar smokers returned, and then everyone said their thanks and goodnights to their hosts and headed out.

"Are you going to the clinic now?" Karen asked Kaia when they were outside.

"I want to change into something more comfortable." Kaia rubbed her arms. "My skin feels itchy all over, and this dress is not appropriate for a doctor's visit. William's house is right there." She pointed. "It will take me a minute."

He found it strange that she referred to their bungalow in Safe Haven as ours but not to the house.

"We will wait outside," Gilbert said. "The little ones are sleeping, and I don't want them to wake up until we get to the clinic."

Idina was sprawled over Eric's shoulder while the twins slept comfortably in their double stroller.

"I'll do it quickly." Kaia took William's hand and headed to their house.

43

KAIA

The moment the front door closed behind them, Kaia reached for the hem of her dress, pulled it over her head, and tossed it to William. "I'm sorry for the impromptu striptease, but I've been waiting to do this for hours." She unhooked her bra on the way to the bedroom.

"You should have said something. We could have come home earlier."

"I didn't want to spoil anyone's fun." She let the bra drop down her shoulders and tossed it into the laundry basket in the walk-in closet.

William followed her inside. "What should I do with the dress?"

"Just toss it into the basket as well. I'll check later if it needs dry cleaning."

Given what was awaiting her, it was such a mundane conversation, but that was precisely what both of them needed right now to keep from freaking out.

Kaia pulled on one of her most worn-out T-shirts that she usually wore to bed. It had been washed so many times that it was incredibly soft, and the fabric didn't irritate her over-sensitized skin. It was also loose and black, so she could get away with not wearing a bra.

She added a pair of old black leggings that had seen better days, pushed her feet back into the black flip-flops she'd worn before, and gathered her hair into a ponytail.

"I'm ready."

"What about an overnight bag?" William asked. "Should you pack something in case Bridget wants to keep you in the clinic?"

"I don't want to keep my family waiting. Besides, if I show up with nothing, Bridget will have to let me go back to pack, so I might get away with sleeping here tonight." She grimaced. "I really don't want to sleep in a hospital bed."

Kaia slung the strap of her small wallet purse across her body.

She didn't need the money or the credit cards, but she needed somewhere to put her phone. If she'd worn jeans, she could have put it in her pocket, but just thinking about the stiff fabric made her itch intensify.

CHAPTER 43

On the way out, William stopped her before she opened the front door.

"I want one great kiss before we go." He wrapped his arms around her. "I have a feeling that from now on, we will have very few moments alone."

Kaia let herself melt into him for a moment. She had to stay strong, and leaning on William was a luxury she couldn't rely on.

There was nothing he could do to make her transition easier, and it was all up to her.

"I love you," he murmured against her lips.

"I love you too." She clung to him for a moment longer, absorbing his strength. "We need to go. They are waiting for us on the street."

He didn't let go. "Annani is coming back only on Thursday, but she told Kian that she would come as soon as you need her."

That was disappointing.

Kaia hadn't expected the goddess to cut her trip short for her, but she'd hoped Annani would do it for William.

"That's okay. Toven is here, and he seems like a nice guy who loves his grand-daughter. If Darlene asks him to help me, he will."

WILLIAM

*A*s William opened the door to the clinic, Bridget eyed the crowd spilling into the small waiting room with a frown.

"Good evening. Is there a reason for all of you to be here?"

Karen assumed a battle position. "We are worried about Kaia," she said in a commanding tone.

"You can be worried outside in the café." Bridget shooed them out. "It's practically part of my clinic." She looked at Kaia. "Besides, you look fine to me. Most of the transitioning Dormants get here after they pass out."

Karen opened her mouth to argue, but Gilbert put his hand on her shoulder, and she closed it.

Kaia threw her hands in the air. "That's what I was trying to tell everyone. I'm fine. I just have a little fever, and I'm tired." She rubbed her arms. "The only thing that really bothers me is this itching. It feels as if my skin is too tight for my body. Am I going to get taller?"

Bridget frowned. "Let's get you into the exam room." She cast William a sidelong glance. "You can wait out here or with Kaia's family. It's your choice."

He wanted to come in with Kaia, but she hadn't asked him to accompany her, and he didn't want to be pushy. "I'll wait with the family."

Kaia turned around and gave him a quick peck on the cheek. "I'll call you as soon as I know anything."

He nodded. "I'll be waiting."

As they stepped outside and walked over to the nearest table, Karen huffed. "Bridget is way too bossy. She kicked us out so unceremoniously that it was rude."

Gilbert chuckled. "Takes one to know one."

"I'm not bossy, and I'm not rude." Karen glared at him. "I'm assertive."

"If you say so, dear." He pulled out a chair for her.

It was after eleven at night, and the café was deserted, but the vending machines were always on, providing decent coffee and something to eat for those who got stuck without access to anything better.

"Can I get you something to drink?" William waved his hand in the direction of the vending machines.

Karen groaned. "If I'm about to stay awake all night, I'd better have some coffee." She turned to Cheryl. "Can you take the little ones to the house? Eric can carry Idina and help you put them in their beds."

The boys were asleep in their stroller, and Idina was passed out on Eric's shoulder.

"Sure," Cheryl agreed without arguing or asking for payment. "But you have to promise to call me as soon as you know anything."

"I'll text you," Gilbert said. "I suggest that you go to sleep if you can. We might spend the night out here, and someone needs to wake up tomorrow and take care of the little ones."

"Yeah, someone." Cheryl gripped the handle of the double stroller. "That's my middle name. Cheryl Someone Locke."

"Come, munchkin." Eric hoisted Idina higher on his shoulder. Propping her up with one arm, he put his other one around Cheryl's waist. "I'll help you put them in bed."

"I'm coming with you." Darlene joined them. "You might need a third pair of hands. I didn't forget how to change diapers or rock babies to sleep yet."

When they walked away, William turned to Karen. "How do you like your coffee?"

"Black with a pinch of Splenda," Gilbert said. "I'll come with you. I know the precise measurement of that pinch. If you get it wrong, she won't like it." He winked at Karen.

At the vending machines, William inserted his clan card into the slot. "Long espresso?"

Gilbert nodded. "Tell me the truth, William. Is Kaia in danger?"

He let out a breath. "The truth is that I don't know. She should transition with ease, but there is a big difference between should and would. Shit happens, and I just pray that it doesn't happen to Kaia."

"Or to Eric." Gilbert took the cup and added a sprinkle of Splenda powder to it. "He will probably need to go for another round. Only this time, I suggest someone else does it." He looked pointedly at William.

"I can't." William pressed the button for a cappuccino. "It would take a lot to get me aggressive." He chuckled. "I think the only way it could happen would be if someone I love was in danger."

Gilbert tilted his head. "From what I've seen so far, that's not typical for immortal males. Those I met seemed to have testosterone in spades."

William pulled his cappuccino out and motioned for Gilbert to make his selection. "That's not true. It's just that so far, you've been exposed mostly to Guardians. Many of the civilian clan males are not the aggressor types, but if their loved ones are threatened, all of them will find their inner beast, and that includes even the females." He gave Gilbert a small smile. "It's a mistake to think that they could be easily subdued just because they look and act feminine. If the need arises, they will fight like tigresses to protect their family." He handed Gilbert the coffee. "We also have a Kra-ell female who can hand three trained warriors their asses, and Wonder is nearly as strong, but she doesn't like fighting."

In the back of his mind, William knew that he was saying too much and talking too fast, but he was too anxious to stop.

45

KAIA

*B*ridget had taken blood samples from Kaia on the first day of her arrival in the village. She'd also measured every inch of her body, including the length of her fingers and toes, had measured her weight with no clothes on, and checked her responses to stimuli.

She was repeating the entire process now and notating the measurements on her tablet and comparing them to the previous ones.

"Are there any changes?" Kaia asked.

Bridget nodded. "Aside from the low fever you are running, your blood pressure is elevated, and so is your pulse. Those, along with the fever, are usually the first signs. I had another transitioning Dormant who complained of itching, and that was Cassandra. We know that she descended directly from Geraldine, who was born immortal and had only one other daughter, Darlene. But Roni, who is Darlene's son, didn't complain of itching when he transitioned, so it might be unrelated."

"What can cause the itching?"

Bridget shrugged. "There might be many reasons for it. Your nervous system might be overstimulated because of the changes happening in your body, it could be a reaction to stress, or it could be an allergic reaction to the venom. The good news is that it will stop in a few days. In the meantime, I'll give you something to ease it."

"Thanks. So, you are sure that I'm transitioning?"

Bridget nodded. "I suggest that you stay in the clinic tonight even though you seem fine. Things can change in a heartbeat, and I don't recommend taking chances. I'll hook you up to the monitoring equipment, and it will continually measure your blood pressure and your pulse. You don't need an IV, so no catheter. You can get up and use the bathroom whenever you want."

Kaia was all for taking her chances and spending the night in bed with William instead of a hospital bed, but Bridget didn't seem like the type who could be pressured into agreeing to something she was recommending against. Besides, William and her mother would side with the physician, and Kaia couldn't take them all on.

She didn't have the energy.

"Can I go out and tell my family? If I faint on the way, they will see me and bring me in."

Ignoring her sarcasm, Bridget smiled. "Of course. Did you pack an overnight bag?"

"I didn't, but William can do that for me."

She had so little with her that he could stuff all her belongings into a duffle. He wouldn't even need to figure out what to bring.

"You can go home, pack a bag, and come back here. As long as you have someone with you at all times, that's fine."

It was on the tip of her tongue to point out that William was with her twenty-four-seven and that at the first hint of trouble, he could rush her to the clinic, but she knew it would be futile to argue with Bridget, and she was too tired to even try.

Well, she could give it a tiny try.

"William is with me all the time. Why can't I sleep in a comfortable bed with him by my side?"

"Because he's going to fall asleep at some point, and he might miss the signs of you going into distress."

"Are you going to stay with me all night long?"

Bridget shook her head. "I'll supervise Hildegard while she hooks you up to the equipment, and then I'll go home to sleep. If there is no emergency, I'll check on you tomorrow morning." She patted Kaia's arm. "Count yourself lucky. It seems like you will have an easy transition."

"I hope so." Kaia hopped down from the exam table and pushed her feet into her flip-flops. "I don't want to keep you here longer than necessary, so I'll just go out to tell my family the good news, and I'll come back. William can pack a bag for me and bring it here later. Can he stay with me in the patient room?"

Bridget nodded. "We have a cot that we keep for the partners of transitioning Dormants."

"Awesome." Kaia faked a smile. "I'll be back shortly."

She had no intention of having William sleep on a cot. They were going to cuddle on the damn hospital bed, and if Bridget had a problem with that, Kaia would plead with her to let him stay. There was only so much she was willing to compromise on.

46

WILLIAM

*W*hen Kaia walked out of the clinic, William was seized by two warring emotions. One was relief and the other was disappointment. Relief that she was safe and not transitioning after all and disappointment for the same reason.

"What did the doctor say?" Karen asked.

"I'm transitioning." Kaia sat down on the chair William pulled out for her.

"That's it?" Gilbert gaped at her. "No sirens going off and no loudspeakers announcing the news to the entire village?"

Kaia smiled tiredly. "Disappointing, right?"

William reached for her hand. "So, what now? Are we going home?"

"I wish. Bridget said that I could go home and pack a bag, but since she's waiting to hook me up before she can go home to sleep, I don't want to keep her waiting. I told her that you could pack a bag for me and bring it over." She squeezed his hand. "She said they have a cot for the partners of transitioning Dormants."

"I don't want to leave your side even for a moment."

"I can pack your bag." Karen turned to William. "If that's okay with you. Can I go into your house without Guardians descending on me?"

"I can let them know that you are coming. Do you know where Kaia's things are?"

They'd been to the house, and Kaia had shown them around, so Karen should have no problem finding her way around.

"Everything is in the dresser drawers," Kaia said. "I just need pajamas, underwear, and a change of clothes for when Bridget lets me go."

"The duffle bags are on the top shelf in the back," William added.

"Anyway." Kaia smiled reassuringly at her mother and Gilbert. "Bridget insists on me staying in the clinic out of caution. She expects my transition to be easy."

William didn't know what Bridget was basing her observation on, but he trusted that the doctor had told Kaia the truth.

"How did she determine that you are transitioning?" Gilbert asked. "What are the signs?"

"The fever is the most obvious one. Also, my blood pressure is slightly elevated compared to the reading she did when I arrived, and my pulse is faster." Kaia rubbed her arms. "I'm also itchy, which isn't a common symptom. The only other Dormant who experienced that was Cassandra, but there is no way we are related. Geraldine's line starts with her, and she only has two daughters."

William frowned. "Maybe she forgot about having a third one. She has memory issues."

"That's ridiculous." Karen huffed. "How can a woman forget she has a child?"

Evidently Darlene hadn't shared that part of her story with Eric yet, or maybe she had, but he hadn't told the others. In any case, it wasn't William's story to tell.

"Geraldine suffered from complete amnesia following a nearly fatal accident, but the timeline doesn't work. You can't be related."

"We couldn't be related even if Geraldine had a third daughter she forgot about. I wasn't adopted, and I know who my parents are." Karen sighed. "Were. It's still difficult to talk about them in the past tense."

"When did they pass away?" William asked.

"Two years ago. They were taken from me two months apart."

Gilbert reached for her hand. "That's when we decided to have another child. When the doctor told us that we were having twins, we hoped for a boy and a girl." He smiled sadly. "You know, a girl for Karen's mother and a boy for her father. But they are both boys, and we adore them."

"They healed my heart." Karen put a hand over her chest. "Idina healed the hole left by Kaia and Cheryl's father, and Evan and Ryan healed the one left by my parents."

Lost for words, William nodded.

"I assume that your mother is still around," Karen said.

"She is. She lives in Scotland."

"We would like to meet her," Gilbert said. "Does she know about Kaia?"

"She does, but my mother is a cautious type. She wished us both luck, but she said she would only come to visit after Kaia transitioned."

Kaia was in no rush to meet her future mother-in-law. It wasn't that she feared the woman would resent her for stealing her son, but she just couldn't deal with anything else right now. She had enough on her plate.

Perhaps William's mother had realized that and had decided not to add stress to an already stressful situation.

"I should get back." Kaia pushed to her feet. "Bridget is waiting for me." She hugged her mother. "After you bring me the bag, I want you to go to sleep. Nothing is going to happen tonight, and the boys will need you in the morning."

KAIA

*K*aia drifted in and out of sleep throughout the night. Disturbing dreams of her past life had kept waking her up, but she wasn't sure whether they had been about real memories or her mind had conjured them from bits and pieces of stories she'd accumulated in her synapses.

If they were real, she'd been a misogynistic prick. Edgar had hated women. He'd lusted after them, but after several rejections, he'd developed a deep-seated hatred for women and had tried to avoid them.

It couldn't have been real. How could she be such a feminist if in a prior life she'd thought so little of women and their role in society?

Edgar believed that the only thing women were good for was satisfying male urges and popping out babies.

Ugh. What a jerk.

Had his punishment been to be reborn as a smart, successful woman?

Cuddled next to her, William was sleeping peacefully, his face looking so much younger when he was relaxed.

She loved him so much.

Thank goodness that he was so different from the way she'd been as a man.

"I love you," she murmured into his neck.

He smiled in his sleep, or so she thought, but then his hand traveled under her hospital Johnny to cup her naked butt.

"I love you too." He nuzzled her ear and, a moment later, was fast asleep again with his hand still draped over her bottom under her gown.

Kaia didn't mind the possessiveness it implied. It was born of love, not a need to dominate and subjugate like Edgar's.

Except, her butt was in full view of the door, and if Bridget or Hildegard walked in, it could be a little embarrassing.

After her mother had delivered the overnight bag, the nurse offered to take off the blood pressure cuff as well as the stickers and wires so Kaia could change into her pajamas and then put them back on, but Kaia had been too tired and decided to leave the hospital gown on.

As the pressure cuff inflated again, she waited for it to deflate, and when it did, she drifted off to sleep again.

The next time she opened her eyes, William wasn't in bed with her, the blanket was tucked snugly around her, and she could see daylight through the half-closed shutters.

She also needed to use the bathroom, but it wasn't urgent. It could wait for Hildegard to come and free her from the wiring.

A knock sounded on the door, and a moment later, Bridget walked in. "Good morning, Kaia. How are you feeling?"

"Good." She smiled, giving the doctor a thorough once-over.

Bridget was a beautiful woman, with a mane of red hair that was gathered in a loose bun on the top of her head and gorgeous eyes that shone with intelligence. Curly tendrils cascaded down the sides of her face and neck, framing her delicate features and providing color to her nearly translucent skin.

She was petite but had ample cleavage and the kind of ass that men salivated over—sizable but firm—perfect for holding on to.

"You are very pretty, Doctor Bridget." What was happening to her? Why had she said that? "I mean your hair. I love what you did with it. Have you had highlights added to it?"

"The highlights are natural." The physician frowned. "It's so nice of you to notice, but I wonder, did your vision improve?"

Had it?

There were hundreds of different hues in Bridget's red hair that Kaia hadn't noticed before, and there were tiny golden flakes in her blue-green eyes that she hadn't seen before, either.

Was it a change in vision, or was it a new appreciation for the female form? A remnant from her dreams of being Edgar?

"I didn't notice before that your hair had so many different shades of red, and you have tiny gold flakes floating in your irises."

"Your vision might have improved." Bridget walked over to the wall and flicked a switch on.

An eye exam chart appeared on the wall across from the bed.

"Can you read the bottom line for me?"

"I can't."

It hadn't occurred to Kaia before, but she had forgotten to put her glasses on. Snatching them off the side table, she put them on.

"Can you read it with the glasses?"

Kaia shook her head. "It's still blurry."

"Try to read the line above it without the glasses."

The doctor hadn't checked her vision before, so how could she know if her vision had improved?

Surprisingly, though, she was able to recite the letters without her glasses.

"Your vision has improved by a lot." Bridget looked surprised. "That's unusual so early in the process."

"Awesome." Kaia grinned. "I won't mind losing the glasses. Can I ask you for a favor, though? Can you take off the wires and blood pressure cuff? I need to use the bathroom."

"Of course." Bridget put her tablet on the table and freed Kaia in seconds. "William went to get you breakfast. He should be back any moment now."

"Great. I'm starving." Kaia ducked into the bathroom.

48

ERIC

*I*t was Saturday, the fourth day following Eric's initiation ceremony, and he was not showing any signs of transitioning. It was time to concede failure and seek another initiator, but it could wait for Monday.

He wasn't looking forward to facing the pitying expressions of people as they asked the same stupid questions, inquiring about his transition that was obviously not happening.

Right now, he was spending a blissfully quiet afternoon with Darlene, watching *Top Gun* and eating pizza, the two of them enjoying each other's company without the family drama.

Kaia was doing well, but Karen and Gilbert were going back and forth about whether they should stay or leave, and Eric had gotten tired of that. He wasn't going anywhere, and he could keep an eye on Kaia until his own transition started.

As the doorbell rang, he turned to Darlene. "Did you invite someone?"

He'd been so contented, and he hated their time alone getting interrupted.

"I didn't, but my mother is just the type to come for a visit without calling first." Darlene untangled herself from his embrace and pushed her feet into her clogs. "It's probably her."

But when she opened up, it wasn't Geraldine at the door. It was Max, with a six-pack of Corona in one hand and a bag of nachos in the other.

"You are not watching the game?" The Guardian strode into the living room without waiting to be invited as if they were frat buddies.

"What game?" Eric asked.

"Never mind." Max plunked the beers on the coffee table and sat next to him on the couch. "I love *Top Gun*." He grinned at him. "Are you reminiscing about your days in the Air Force?"

"Yeah." Eric dropped his feet to the floor and leaned to reach for the nacho bag. "What happened? Did none of your Guardian buddies want to watch the game with you?"

Max smiled. "I'm taking my initiator duties seriously and taking care of my protégé." He pointed to the Corona. "Do you think any of my Guardian buddies would drink that? I got it for my still very human initiate because we are supposed to bond." He put his hand on Eric's shoulder and kneaded it.

That was a very familiar gesture from a guy that he barely knew, and Eric wished he had immortal senses already so he could figure out Max's agenda.

Was he coming on to him?

Or was it just his style of showing affection?

In either case, he had no problem playing along, provided that Max's expectations were reasonable. There was a limit to what Eric was willing to do with another man.

"I can bond over beers." He lifted his gaze to Darlene, who stood on the other side of the coffee table and seemed unsure about the scene unfolding before her. "Come back and sit next to me. We can share a beer."

She walked around the table and sat on his other side.

The movie was still playing, but none of them were paying attention. There was tension in the room, and it wasn't sexual. It was like the three of them were trying to form a friendship, but it wasn't a good fit.

Eric was reminded of Kian's ceremonial words, which talked about him and Max being a good match. Could lack of compatibility between the initiator and initiate hinder the success of the process?

It wouldn't be part of the traditional wording if it weren't important.

Could that be the reason he hadn't transitioned?

"Listen, Eric." Max rubbed the back of his neck. "It's Saturday, and nothing is happening. Perhaps you need another round."

"I'll give it another day."

Max nodded. "If it still doesn't happen, I have no problem giving you another dose."

"No offense, Max," Darlene said. "But this time we will try it with someone closer to the source."

"There is another possibility." Max made a face. "What if you have some disease you don't know about?" He looked at Darlene. "Roni is very close to the source, and he was initiated several times unsuccessfully because his body was too weak from pneumonia."

"I'm healthy." Eric took a sip from the beer. "Bridget ran a thorough physical on me yesterday, and she said that my biological markers are of a man ten years my junior."

Max frowned. "Maybe you are transitioning with no symptoms? What if your markers are so good because your body is reversing the clock? I heard that Kaia is transitioning so smoothly that she's barely feeling anything. Maybe you are the same."

"I wish." Eric took a long swig from his beer. "Bridget compared my results to those from the physical she had in my file, and the results were almost identical. I'm not changing."

Max put his hand on Eric's arm. "Well, at least you know that you're healthy. That's good, right?"

"Yeah. It is." He was so sick of talking about it. "So, Max, what's new in your life?"

"Not much. I'm going back on missions starting next Monday. For now, I'm on village security detail."

That piqued Eric's interest. "Tell me about those missions. How do you find the dens? What's your mode of operation? What do you do with the victims?"

"Why do you want to know? Are you interested in joining the Guardian force?"

"Maybe I am. After I transition, I will need something to do with my time." He smiled at Darlene. "Sitting in your office and watching you work is fun, but I'm not ready to retire yet."

"You are a pilot," Max said. "Kian will put you on the payroll as one."

"I don't know if that's all I want to do." Eric leaned back with the beer still clutched in his hand. "If I become immortal, I will want to try many different things, and rescuing trafficking victims sounds like a good place to start. It would be immensely satisfying to beat the shit out of the scum that ruined their lives."

He wouldn't kill them. That was too merciful, and he had no mercy for monsters. He would leave them maimed and castrated to live out the rest of their lives in agony.

"You don't have the training." Max pulled another beer from the pack.

"It has been a while, but I got very good training in the Air Force."

Max chuckled. "After you become immortal, and I mean fully immortal with operational fangs and venom, come to the gym to one of our training sessions, and you'll see what I mean. Your training is useless compared to ours."

"I still managed to take you by surprise and knock you off your feet." Eric took a swig from his beer.

Max grinned. "Maybe I let you do that to make you feel good."

"Yeah, right."

The Guardian shrugged. "Perhaps I got distracted."

49

WILLIAM

*A*s Bridget walked into the room with her tray, William winced.

This would be the third time she made a cut on Kaia's palm, and even though Kaia hadn't complained, he hated to see her in pain.

The other two times hadn't been a failure, but they hadn't been a complete success either.

The cut Bridget had made Saturday evening had taken four minutes and twenty-five seconds to heal, and the cut she'd inflicted on Sunday had taken four minutes and nineteen seconds. The healing was still much faster than it would have been if Kaia was fully human, but not nearly as fast as it would have been for an immortal.

"Ready for another test?" Bridget put her tray on the side table.

Kaia sighed. "It's not going to produce better results than the one you did yesterday. Let's face it. I'm only slightly immortal."

Bridget chuckled. "There is no such thing. It's like saying that you're slightly pregnant. You either are, or you're not. Besides, the second time the wound healed six seconds faster than the first time, so there is progress."

Kaia extended her hand. "Let's hope that it's my lucky Monday."

Bridget turned to look at William. "No other witnesses this time?"

He shook his head. "It's just us."

Karen, Gilbert, Eric, and Cheryl had come to witness the first and second tests, but since the progress was so slow, there was no point in making it a spectacle each and every time.

Bridget nodded. "Get ready with the stopwatch."

William took the device out of his pocket and turned it on. "I'm ready."

The moment Bridget made the cut with her tiny surgical knife, William started the counter.

Kaia winced but didn't even hiss, and as they watched the blood well over the cut, Bridget kept cleaning it with gauze so they could see the healing progress. By the time the bleeding stopped, and the last of the thin white line disappeared, there was a large pile of bloody gauze on her tray.

William stopped the watch. "Four minutes and fifteen seconds."

"Well, it is getting better, so that's good news." Bridget scrunched the pile of gauze and disposed of it. "I've never witnessed a transition like this, but then every Dormant is different." She smiled at Kaia. "At least the itching has stopped."

"Thank goodness for that." Kaia rubbed her arms.

William didn't mind that at all. As long as Kaia was okay and not in danger, he was fine with her transition taking as long as it needed to.

"I think it's time William and I went back to Safe Haven and continued our work." Kaia ran a finger over the cut area on her palm. "It doesn't look like I'm going to worsen, and at this rate, it will take months for me to get through the initial stage of the transition. There is no reason for me to stay in the clinic and waste your valuable time."

William had to agree even though he was anxious about Kaia being released.

Her blood pressure hadn't gone up beyond the initial rise, and Bridget had told Hildegard to take readings only twice a day and none during the night. The only monitor Kaia was still hooked up to was the one measuring her heart rate.

Bridget nodded. "You don't have to stay in the clinic, but I want you to stay in the village for at least another week. I want to keep monitoring your progress."

"I'm glad that you agree with me. My family extended their stay to see me through the transition, but they need to go home, and now that I'm officially out of danger, they can finally go."

After it had been established that Kaia was not going to lose consciousness and that her transition was progressing slowly but smoothly, there had been a lot of back and forth about whether they should leave or stay, and in the end, it had been Karen's decision to wait until Kaia got released from the clinic.

"That's up to you and them." Bridget removed the two wires still attached to Kaia's chest and collected her tray. "You can get dressed." She shook her head. "You don't even need pain medication. This is so strange," she murmured as she walked out the door.

Kaia let out a breath and flung the blanket off her. "Let's get out of here. I've been going stir-crazy staying in bed all day."

William chuckled. "You were watching television and catching up on your favorite shows. You weren't going crazy at all."

"It was fun for one day." Kaia took her pajama shirt off and dropped it on the bed. "I'll shower at home. I need to get out of here." She reached into the duffle bag he'd handed her and pulled out a T-shirt.

It was a struggle to keep his eyes on her face and not stare at her breasts.

Kaia hadn't changed physically, but then there had been nothing to improve, and other than a few stolen kisses and caresses under the blanket, they hadn't done much. He missed having her naked under him and over him, and in every position imaginable.

But more than that, William wanted his old Kaia back—the one who had a spark in her eyes and a zest for life and who had thrived on challenges—the one who had been like a breath of fresh air in his stagnant life.

The new Kaia seemed subdued and unhappy, and he didn't know why or how to fix it.

The transition hadn't taken a physical toll on her like it had taken on other Dormants, but it had taken a psychological one.

He assumed it was disappointment, and it was understandable to some extent. But the bottom line was that Kaia was transitioning, which meant that she was becoming immortal, and they would be able to spend eternity together.

That should be enough, right?

What did it matter how long it took?

And yet, Kaia seemed troubled and somewhat muted, and she avoided looking into his eyes. It was as if her spark had dimmed, and she'd lost some of the self-confidence that had been such a huge part of her personality.

He wished he knew how to help her, but the only thing he could think of was arranging for her to meet with Vanessa. The therapist had much better tools to help Kaia than he did.

"I'm ready to go." Kaia collected her glasses from the side table and dropped them into the duffle bag. "At least I've gotten rid of those. I have perfect eyesight now."

"You got immortality." He took the duffle bag from her. "Is it really so important to you how fast you heal? Your body's self-repairing mechanism might be a little slow, but it works, and it's good enough to keep you alive forever."

"I know." She gave him a tight smile. "It doesn't bother me. It's just that I get restless when I have nothing to do. I want to get back to the research."

50

KAIA

*a*s they walked out of the clinic, Kaia pulled her phone out of her purse. "I should call my mom to tell her the good news."

William wrapped his arm around her waist. "How about you call her over a cappuccino and a sandwich? You haven't had breakfast yet."

As her stomach growled in response, she nodded. "Sounds good to me."

"Excellent. I haven't had breakfast yet, either." He led her to a table, pulled out a chair for her, and put her duffle bag on the ground by her feet.

"I thought that you grabbed something when you went home to shower and change."

"No way. I wanted to eat with you. The roast beef sandwich?"

Kaia shook her head. "I'm in the mood for a pastry or a Danish. Or both."

He tilted his head. "Since when have you been craving sweet things?"

She was more of a savory kind of girl, but ever since the Edgar persona had surfaced in all of its tainted glory, even her taste in food had changed.

Kaia forced a smile. "I'm celebrating going home."

"That's indeed a cause for celebration." William leaned and kissed her forehead. "I can't wait to have you all to myself again."

"I can't wait either."

"I'll get us cappuccinos and an assortment of pastries."

"Yummy." She licked her lips.

When William turned his back to her and walked to the counter, Kaia let the smile slide off her face and leaned back in her chair. If she wasn't hungry, she would have preferred to go home, get in the shower, scrub away the sticky film from her body, and if possible, wash away the slimy feeling clinging to her from the disturbing dreams of living the life of a misogynistic jerk.

Heck, it wouldn't have been so bad if it was limited to memories and dreams, but Edgar clung to her even while she was wide awake. She was seeing the world through the prism of his eyes, and it wasn't a pleasant sight.

566

What the hell was she going to do about that?

How could she tell William that she was suddenly attracted to women when she wasn't supposed to be attracted to anyone but him?

Wasn't that one of the main tenets of being truelove mates?

With a sigh, she took out her phone again and placed a call to her mother.

"Kaia, sweetie. How are you doing this morning?"

"I'm out of the clinic, sitting in the café and waiting for William to bring me coffee and pastries, so I'm feeling great."

Hopefully, her mother's bullshit radar didn't work as well over the phone.

There was a moment of silence, and Kaia tensed for the inevitable 'what's wrong' question.

"Did Bridget test you again today?"

She let out a breath. It seemed that her mother didn't suspect anything. "She did, and there was a slight improvement. The cut healed five seconds faster than it did yesterday. I begged Bridget to let me go back to Safe Haven, but she only agreed to let me out of the clinic if I promised to stay in the village for another week. She wants to keep testing me every day to see if the gradual improvement continues."

"That's good news, right?"

"Yeah." Kaia closed her eyes. "My transition is the oddest one Bridget has witnessed, but as William pointed out, the end result is still immortality, and it doesn't matter if I'm going slower than all the others before me."

Her mother chuckled. "My sweet, competitive Kaia. You can't tolerate not being the best at everything."

So that's why her mother's bullshit detector had failed to penetrate Kaia's cheerful facade. Karen thought that she sounded a little off because her pride had been hurt by her underwhelming transition.

Perhaps she could throw in some more misdirection.

"It's not about that." Kaia moved the phone to her other ear. "Well, it's a little about that, but that's not why I'm not jumping for joy. I'm tired, and bored, and I want to go back to work. I got so sick of being stuck in that clinic with nothing to do, and I felt uncomfortable about Bridget and Hildegard coming to the clinic just to look after me while I didn't need looking after. I'm fine, and hopefully, I will continue to improve, but I can do that while working on the project." She sighed. "I really want to return to Safe Haven. The village is nice, but I miss our bungalow over there. It's small and cozy. William's house is too big and too formal. It doesn't feel homey."

"Oh, sweetie. You didn't have enough time to get used to the house. William's place is much smaller than our home in the city, and you never complained about it not being cozy."

"That's because it's full of people, and kids, and toys, and it's always noisy."

"I miss home," her mother said. "If Bridget believes that you are out of the danger zone, there is no reason for us to stay. We can go back."

Kaia had been expecting that, but her gut clenched nonetheless.

"Here is your coffee." William put a paper cup in front of her.

She smiled at him. "Thanks."

Her mother huffed. "Was that sarcasm?"

Kaia rolled her eyes. "I thanked William for bringing me coffee, not you for abandoning me."

"We are not abandoning you. Whenever you need us, we will come running."

"I know." Kaia removed the lid and took a sip. "I agree that you need to go home, but it doesn't make me happy. I enjoyed having you here with me, and I hoped we were all going to stay for good."

Her mother released a breath. "You know it's not that easy. We have a life back home. I have a job that I love doing, and Gilbert runs a profitable business. We can't just leave everything behind."

"Yeah, I bet Berta can't wait for you to return. She misses the boys."

The nanny had been with them since Idina had been born, and she loved the little ones as if they were her own.

"I'm sure she's enjoying the time off. Naturally, I'm paying her regardless of our absence."

"What about Eric?" Kaia asked. "Is he going home as well? Or is he making another attempt?"

"Eric is a big boy, and he makes his own decisions."

51

WILLIAM

*K*aia was quiet as they walked out of the café, probably thinking about her family going home. She hadn't tried to convince them to stay, which William thought was a mistake, but perhaps she just didn't have the energy.

Maybe he should try to convince Gilbert and Karen not to leave.

Eric hadn't transitioned yet, and he wasn't going to unless he made another attempt. But that didn't preclude Gilbert from going for it. And since Kaia was transitioning, there was no longer a question of whether Karen was a Dormant, so she shouldn't wait either.

"Why isn't Gilbert attempting transition? He doesn't need to wait for Eric to succeed, and if he wants to induce your mother, he shouldn't wait."

Kaia shrugged. "They are aware of their options, and they will decide what they want to do. I don't want to push them."

He opened the front door for her. "Maybe you should. I know that you don't want them to leave."

"Naturally, but since I'm going to leave as soon as Bridget okays it, I can't expect them to stay here without me."

She dropped her purse on the entry table and continued to the bedroom.

He followed behind. "Why are you in such a rush to go back to Safe Haven? We can work from here."

Kaia lifted a brow. "Neither of us has done much work since we got here. There are too many distractions, and I'm not talking just about my transition. In Safe Haven, there is nothing to do other than work on our project and make love."

"Speaking of making love." He reached for her waist and pulled her against his body. "I missed you."

He hadn't expected her to react with a grimace or to push on his chest.

"I'm gross. I need to get in the shower and wash off all the sticky gunk from where the wires were attached to me, and you need to get back to the lab. You've missed so much work because of me that it will take you weeks to catch up."

It was all true, but the old Kaia would have jumped in bed with him nonetheless.

Perhaps she needed some time to rest. Or maybe she was right about needing to go back to Safe Haven. She might feel more at home there. Safer.

He let go of her. "I can work from here while you get cleaned up. Once you feel like yourself again, we can go to the lab together."

Kaia cast a longing look at the bed. "I was hoping to take a nap after the shower. I'm still weak."

Alone.

Kaia didn't want him to get in bed with her.

She hadn't said it, but that's what she meant.

"I'll stay right here until you are done in the shower, tuck you in bed, and work from the armchair." He pointed to the bedroom's sitting area. "I'm not leaving you alone at home while you are still transitioning. You might need my help."

"I can call Cheryl and ask her to stay with me while you are gone."

Kaia might have fooled a human, but he was an immortal, and even though she was transitioning, she was still emitting human scents. Before her transition, the scents were so strong and multifaceted that he couldn't take them apart to decipher singular emotions aside from arousal and love. Those were strong emotions that tended to overpower most others.

Anger and hate were also powerful, but Kaia hadn't manifested them before, or at least not strongly enough to be distinguishable from the others.

Now she was emitting both, and he prayed that they were not directed at him.

Who could be the object of her hatred, though?

Perhaps it was just intense frustration, and Kaia was angry at her situation and hated being in the village.

What could he do to make it better?

Right now, it seemed that what Kaia needed was to be alone, and he doubted she wanted even Cheryl to be with her.

"I'll make a deal with you. I'll stay just until you are done with the shower. You can ask your sister to come over and keep an eye on you, but if you want to be alone, I can work with that. I'll send you texts every thirty minutes, and if you don't answer them within five minutes, I'll rush over to check on you."

The relieved breath Kaia let out confirmed his suspicions. "Thank you for being you." She wound her arms around his neck. "I need some time to process what's going on with me, and I need to be alone. I'm glad that you're so understanding, and your feelings aren't hurt."

He pressed a soft kiss to her forehead. "Take as long as you need, and when you are ready, talk to me. We are a team, and I want to help you in whatever way I can."

"I appreciate it, and I wish you could help, but only I can reorganize the mess in my own head."

52

DARLENE

$\mathcal{D}$arlene shifted her gaze away from her computer screen and glanced at Eric.

He'd dragged a chair into her office and was working on the laptop William had lent him, using a flat cardboard box as his lap desk and a bigger one as a footstool. He didn't look comfortable, but when she'd offered to order a proper lap desk for him, he'd said that he was fine and that he didn't want her to spend money on it.

From being convinced that he would transition right away, he now wasn't sure he would transition at all.

It was probably just a temporary slump, and knowing Eric, he would bounce back to being his cocky, optimistic self in no time.

But even when he was brooding, she loved having him in her office.

In the short time they'd known each other, he'd become such an integral part of her that she hated every moment she was away from him. Fortunately, he seemed to feel the same and followed her wherever she needed to go.

They were inseparable.

"What are you working on?" she asked.

He looked up. "I'm exchanging emails with a couple of other operators who are interested in leasing my planes. I have one of them doing me a favor and managing what I already had booked and couldn't cancel, but I'm not making any new bookings, and I still need a source of income."

"Right. We are not original clan members, and we are not mated to one of them, so we don't get a share in the clan profits. Kian gave me an allowance when I moved into the village, but I didn't like getting paid for doing nothing. As soon as William hired me, I asked for the allowance to be canceled."

"How much is William paying you, if I may ask?"

"You may, and it's $4,500 a month."

He arched a brow. "Is that enough? Or let me rephrase. Is that what someone with your skills would be paid in the human world?"

"My skills are rusty, and I'm not sure anyone outside of here would have hired me. I asked for $4,500 expecting to get less, but I got exactly what I asked for, and it's more than enough. Don't forget that we don't pay for housing or utilities or any kind of insurance. I even got a car for free. I offered to pay for it in installments, but Kian refused to hear of it."

Eric smirked. "Then I can afford to do nothing if I want. My pension from the Air Force and what I'll get in lease payments for the planes is more than enough to live on."

She shook her head. "At some point, you will have to fake your own death, and the pension payments will stop. Besides, you need something to do, or you'll go nuts."

"I was just joking. Once I turn immortal, I'll fly planes for the clan. Max said that they could use another pilot. But until then, you are stuck with me in your shoebox of an office."

"Hey, I like my little office. Don't insult it." She looked at the cardboard boxes he used. "Perhaps I can replace my desk with one of those that don't have a back panel, so we can both work on it."

Eric shook his head. "You need a larger office. It's deplorable that William keeps you in this closet." He looked at the door that they had to leave open because when it was closed, there wasn't enough air circulation for both of them in there. "It's not healthy for you to work in here, and you are not immortal yet."

"Neither are you." She sighed. "Have you given any thought to who you want to induce you next?"

He nodded. "I like Andrew. He's been immortal long enough to have his fangs and venom glands functioning properly, but since we are related on our maternal side, it might be a problem given the clan taboo."

"The taboo is only on mating between members of the same matrilineal descent. Kian induced Alena's sons, so it's obviously not a problem for your purposes. But Andrew is not your best choice because he's just as far from the source as you are. You need a stronger immortal."

"What about Dalhu?" Eric winced. "On second thought, forget that I said that. The dude is the size of a mountain, and he's scary. Anandur falls into the same category of being too big, and Brundar might kill me just because he likes killing things. Aside from them, I don't know any other immortals."

He knew Toven, but Darlene wasn't sure they could ask the god to do that or if Toven could even induce a male Dormant. Her uncle, on the other hand, was the perfect candidate for the job.

"Orion is coming back on Thursday, and he's your best choice. He's a demigod, so his genes are the most potent, and he's a very nice guy who's not intimidating at all. You will like him."

"Then it's settled. I'll wait for your uncle."

As the door to the outer office opened, William walked in and headed straight toward her and Eric.

"Good morning, boss." She smiled at him. "I didn't expect you here today."

"Good morning to you both." He put his hand on Eric's shoulder. "You probably heard already that Kaia was released from the clinic earlier today."

CHAPTER 52

"I didn't." He put his laptop and cardboard on the desk and got to his feet. "Congratulations." He offered William his hand.

53

ERIC

"Congratulations to you too." William pulled him into a quick bro embrace. "After all, Kaia is your step-niece."

"That she is." Eric clapped him on the back, and then the two of them took a step away from each other.

In Eric's heart, Kaia was his niece, but no one had thought to inform him that she'd been released from the clinic, and it hurt more than he was willing to admit. What was the deal with Gilbert? Did he forget that he had a brother? Or maybe he'd thought that Eric would begrudge Kaia her successful transition?

If he did, he was dumber than an ox. He sure was as stubborn as one.

Realizing that William and Darlene were staring at him, Eric planted a smile on his face that he hoped looked at least somewhat genuine. "So, what's the next step? Are you going back to Safe Haven?"

"Not yet." William leaned against the doorframe. "Bridget wants Kaia to stay in the village for another week so she can monitor her progress. Her transition is very unusual." He let out a breath. "I'm just glad that she didn't lose consciousness and that it's going smoothly. I don't care how long it takes."

"You were so worried for nothing," Darlene said.

Eric didn't think that William's worry had been excessive. They had all been anxious for Kaia, and he had been anxious for himself as well.

Still was.

His journey into immortality wasn't over yet.

William pushed away from the doorframe. "Kaia had a bad feeling, and as someone who is surrounded by people with paranormal abilities, I don't take premonitions lightly, and I'm not done worrying yet."

"I'm with you on that," Eric said. "I'm crossing my fingers for Kaia."

"Thank you." William smiled, but there was tension in his expression that he didn't even try to hide. "I need to check on what's going on in the lab. I'll see you later."

CHAPTER 53

When William left, and the door to the outer office closed, Eric sat back and took his borrowed laptop from Darlene's desk. "When William and Kaia return to Safe Haven, are you going with them?"

"If William still needs me." She smiled. "You'll come with me, of course."

"What about my transition? I need to stay in the village to be near the clinic."

"Right. I forgot about that for a moment." Darlene pushed a strand of hair behind her ear. "I'll ask William if I can do my work remotely. He'll understand why I can't go."

"What about the new clinic in Safe Haven? Hildegard said that Gertrude was already there setting things up. Maybe it's ready."

"I can check." Darlene turned to her computer screen. "If they got the shipment, it will be notated."

While he waited for her to find out, his phone rang.

"Finally, someone's thinking to let me know that Kaia is out." He accepted the call. "Good morning, Gilbert. Are you calling to share the good news? If you are, you're too late. I just saw William, and he told me about Kaia."

"Where are you?"

"In Darlene's office."

"What is William doing in the lab? He's supposed to be watching Kaia."

Eric frowned. "Why? Did Bridget tell him to watch her?"

"No, but it's obvious. Kaia is still in the initial stages of her transition, and she needs to be monitored." He groaned. "Karen and I asked Kian to arrange for transportation back home tomorrow, but now I'm starting to think that we've been too hasty."

They'd been talking about going home for days, and their scheduled return had been postponed several times before. But now that they'd arranged for transportation, it seemed to be final.

Still, perhaps he could change their minds.

"Darlene's uncle is returning to the village on Thursday, and we are going to ask him to induce me. Can't you stay for my second ceremony?"

"I wish we could, but Karen is right here beside me, and she's shaking her head. She really needs to go back to work."

"Can you come back on the weekend? We can ask the dude to induce me on Sunday."

They hadn't taken into consideration that Darlene's uncle might refuse, but if he did, there were other candidates Eric could ask. He hadn't thought about Shai before, but as Darlene's stepdad, he should be willing to help her. And her sister's mate was the chief of security and a head Guardian, so he was an excellent candidate as well. He wouldn't refuse his sister-in-law's request.

"Maybe I'll come by myself," Gilbert said. "We can't drag the little ones back and forth like that."

"What about you? When are you going for it? You are a proven Dormant, and you don't have to wait for me to transition. Karen is proven too, and she doesn't have all the time in the world to wait either."

"We know, but we need time to think it through."

"What's to think about? You need to do it."

Gilbert and Karen had been going round in circles, one day deciding that they needed to go for it and the next deciding that they couldn't. In his gut, Eric knew

575

that they would eventually get over their fear and attempt transition, but he was tired of the merry-go-round.

Gilbert sighed. "It's not as simple as that. Karen and I are thinking about passing on the offer. We have three small children that we don't want to orphan."

Eric sighed. "You can't be serious."

"We are very serious."

"Look, you and Karen aren't attempting transition simultaneously. If anything happens to you, they will still have Karen, Kaia, Cheryl, and me. It's not like they would have no one to raise them with love and care. And if you make it and then Karen doesn't, they'll have you and all of the above."

"Karen and I discussed all of those scenarios, and both of us agreed that we don't want to go on without the other. Though if your transition goes smoothly, we might reconsider."

54

DARLENE

$\mathcal{E}$ ric ended the call with a groan. "No pressure. No pressure at all."
Darlene had an idea of what Gilbert had said based on Eric's side of the conversation, but she hadn't heard Gilbert's last words that had Eric feeling pressured.

"What did he say?"

"If my transition goes smoothly, they will reconsider."

"That's not fair of Gilbert to put it all on your shoulders."

It was stressful enough for Eric to deal with his own transition and his odds of survival. He didn't need the added worry of his brother conditioning his own transition on how well Eric's went.

On the other hand, she could understand Karen and Gilbert as well. It wasn't an easy decision for a bachelor like Eric or for the mother of a grown son like her, so it must be tenfold more difficult for the parents of two babies and a toddler.

"Maybe we shouldn't wait for Orion," she said. "Kian and Kalugal are also demigods, and they are both here. Perhaps they will agree to induce you. And as for the equipment, some of it was delivered to the clinic in Safe Haven, and some is still in transit, but it doesn't really matter. Your inducers are here in the village."

He leveled his gaze at her. "You didn't suggest either of them before, and I assumed that there was a good reason for it."

She shrugged. "I didn't feel comfortable asking Kian, and Kalugal has a new baby and is not seeing anyone, especially not humans, because he's afraid of bringing viruses to his son. He might refuse because of that. And Kian, well, he's Kian. Not the most approachable of guys. But we can ask Syssi to ask him on your behalf. After all, you are her cousin."

For a long moment, Eric just looked at her, and then he reached for her hand over the desk. "What about your grandfather? A god's genes are the most powerful of all."

"That's what I'm afraid of. Maybe his venom is too powerful. I doubt that the gods bothered inducing Dormants back in the day."

"It doesn't hurt to ask." Eric pushed away the box he used as his footstool and put the laptop on her desk. "Can we go see him?"

"What, right now?"

Darlene didn't like the idea of asking Toven for anything. He might be her grandfather, but he was a stranger to her. During the dinner at Syssi and Kian's, he'd barely exchanged two words with her.

"Yeah, why not?"

"I don't know if he's home."

"Check. Send him a text."

She swallowed. "I'll send my mother a text and ask her to call him."

Toven and Geraldine weren't close either, but her mother had a way with people. If the god could induce Eric without killing him in the process, Geraldine could get him to agree.

Eric regarded her with an amused expression on his handsome face. "I don't think Toven will appreciate the request coming from your mother, your sister, or your son. It needs to come from you and, better yet, from both of us. We can go to his house and knock on the door, saying that we stopped by to say hello on the way to see your mother. If he's not there, we will stay to chat with Mia and wait for him to come home. I bet he doesn't leave her alone for long."

"That's actually a good plan. It's almost noon, so it won't look strange that I'm visiting my mother on my lunch break." She swiveled her chair around and got to her feet. "He will find it much harder to refuse us with Mia around. He likes showing her how good he is." She took her purse and slung the strap over her shoulder.

"So, he isn't good for real?" Eric circled his arm around her waist.

"I don't know. I think he means well. He bought half of the Perfect Match company from Syssi and the two other partners, not because he wanted the business but because he believed that the service should be made available for people with disabilities who can't afford the sessions. That's a philanthropic endeavor, and it implies that he wants to do what's right for people. But he's a god, and he's aloof, intimidating, and impossible to read."

Eric leaned away to look at her. "Are you talking about the Perfect Match virtual reality studios?"

"Have you heard of them?"

"Who hasn't? Since your grandfather and Syssi own it, do you think we can get a discount?"

"We can go for free. The clan has two machines in the village, and I can put our names on the waiting list. Those machines are very popular."

"I bet." Eric snorted. "It's the best porn anyone could have ever imagined. You get a fantasy built to your specifications and a virtual partner to share it with. Sign me up."

Darlene laughed. "It's not just for hookups. People go on solo adventures, and friends go to have fun in exotic locales and do crazy things. The possibilities are endless."

"Did you try it?"

She shook her head. "I'm not very adventurous, and if I had the guts to try it, I would only do it with someone I know and like. What about you? Why didn't you try it yet?"

"Who said I haven't?"

"I would be very surprised if you had. You're too cocky to use a service like that."

"How well do you know me, my love." He drew her against his body and kissed her temple. "I wanted to try it, but spending so much money on a virtual experience seemed frivolous to me, especially since I had no trouble finding real women to hook up with. I thought that it was only good for rich guys who couldn't get sex in real life because they were unattractive or didn't have time. It sure beats employing the services of professional sex providers."

She arched a brow. "Are you sure about that? Those providers, as you call them, are not just in the business of sex. They are also in the business of fantasy fulfillment, and they are real. I doubt a virtual experience can be as good as the real thing."

Darlene had heard people talking about it and singing its praises, but she assumed the claims were exaggerated.

Eric leaned to whisper in her ear. "There is only one way to find out. Do you think they have a threesome adventure? If they do, we could try it out in the virtual world first and see if you like it."

She shook her head vehemently. "Not here, that's for sure. We don't have the same level of anonymity in the village as they have in the commercial studios, and I don't want to become the next piece of gossip to sweep over the entire clan, including those in Scotland and in the sanctuary."

5 5

ERIC

*W*hen they reached Toven's house, Eric knocked on the door, took Darlene's hand, and plastered a wide smile on his face.

She chuckled quietly. "You look like a Tupperware salesman."

"Then let's hope Toven loves Tupperware," Eric said while maintaining his grin.

Unexpectedly, the god opened the door himself.

His brows rose in a surprised expression. "Hello."

"Good afternoon," Eric said. "We are on our way to Geraldine's for lunch, and we thought to stop by for a visit."

The god was still frowning when an elderly lady stepped out from behind him. "That's so nice of you. Please, come in. We were about to sit down for lunch, but if you are on your way to Geraldine's, we can have tea first. We don't get as many visitors now as we did when we just moved in, and it's a shame. I enjoyed it."

The god's frown turned into an indulgent smile as he put his hand on the woman's shoulder. "You've heard the lady. Come on in. I'll get Mia."

Eric had heard that Mia's grandparents were staying in the village despite being human, but seeing her grandmother in person warmed something in his heart.

His mind must have registered the apparent lack of older people, or rather older-looking individuals, and it had bothered him on a subconscious level.

He'd never liked the idea of senior communities or neighborhoods just for young couples. That wasn't how humans were wired. Humans were tribe animals, and they functioned best in blended communities where several generations coexisted and contributed to each other.

Appearances were misleading, though, and in reality, the clan was a tribe with a staggering number of generations coexisting in the village. They just all looked the same age.

The dearth of children, however, was depressing.

"We don't want to inconvenience you," Darlene didn't budge from the doorstep. "We can stop by after lunch."

"You are not going anywhere," Mia's grandmother said. "I can call Geraldine and tell her to bring whatever she made over here, and we can all have a nice lunch together." She waved her hand to encourage them to come in. "We don't get enough visitors, and it gets boring." She laughed. "Who would have thought that a village full of immortals could be boring."

Darlene raised a pair of panicked eyes to him. They hadn't even told her mother that they were coming over.

He leaned closer to Mia's grandmother's ear and said in a conspiratorial voice, "The truth is that we didn't tell Geraldine that we were coming over for lunch, so we can accept your invitation without hurting her feelings."

"Wonderful." She offered him her hand. "I'm Rosalyn."

"I'm Eric." He lifted her hand and kissed the back of it.

"Oh, I know who you are. Mia told me that you were very handsome and charming, and she didn't exaggerate one bit. You are all that and more."

"Thank you."

"Hi." Mia drove into the living room in her motorized wheelchair. "What a wonderful surprise."

"I apologize for the intrusion," Darlene said. "I should have called ahead." She looked at Eric. "My mate is much more impulsive than I am."

"I like that in a man," Mia's grandfather said from the couch. "Assertiveness and boldness are the markers of a winner."

Eric chuckled. "That's what I keep telling Darlene."

From behind Mia, Toven was still regarding them with a raised brow.

He knew that they hadn't come on a social call, but he was waiting patiently for them to state the reason for their visit.

"I heard that Kaia was released from the clinic this morning," Mia said. "Is she out of the woods, so to speak?"

"Not yet." Eric sat on the couch next to Mia's grandfather. "I'm Eric." He offered his hand to the man.

"Curtis. Welcome to the family." He shook his hand with surprising strength for an older gentleman.

"Kaia's transition is unlike any of the others." Darlene sat on Eric's other side. "She's progressing very slowly, but thankfully, very smoothly as well. That's why she was allowed to go home. But Bridget wants to keep testing her for a few more days."

"That's interesting." Toven pulled out one of the dining chairs and sat next to Mia. "What do you mean by slow?"

Normally, Eric wouldn't have shared medical information about his niece, but this wasn't a normal situation. Toven had information that they didn't, and he might have helpful suggestions.

Besides, they needed to ask him for a big favor.

"I don't know the results of today's tests, but Saturday and Sunday, it took her over four minutes to heal from the cut test. It's much faster than it would have taken a human to heal a cut like that completely, so it indicates that she's transitioning, but slowly. Also, her eyesight corrected itself, and she now sees perfectly, so that's another proof that things are changing in her body. It's just taking longer than it did for other Dormants."

"That's interesting." Toven rubbed his jaw with his thumb and finger. "I wonder why Kaia's transition is so different."

5 6

DARLENE

*I*t was the opening Darlene needed. "I hoped you would know more about it. Back in the days of the gods, so many Dormants were initiated, and someone must have collected that data. Were there any anomalies back then?"

Toven shrugged. "I wasn't involved with Dormants." He draped his arm over Mia's shoulders. "Mia is the first Dormant I ever initiated."

Darlene's heart sank.

"Did any of the other gods induce male Dormants?" Eric asked. "Or was it beneath them?"

"To the best of my knowledge, it was always done by immortals. Don't forget that in those days, Dormants were initiated when they reached puberty, so they were still children. The idea was to make the process as fun and as exciting as possible for them, so their initiators were immortals who were just a little older than them."

That wasn't good. No one knew what a god's venom would do to a male Dormant. But if Toven had successfully induced Mia's transition, a fragile girl with a lot of health problems, he should be able to do that for Eric as well.

Still, it was more prudent to wait for Orion's return. Gilbert would just have to come back to the village for the ceremony on Sunday.

Looking at Eric, Darlene waited until he felt her gaze and turned to look at her. "We should wait for Orion to return or ask Kian," she said.

"What do you need to ask of Kian?" Toven asked as if he didn't know.

"Eric is obviously not transitioning, and we need to find a new initiator for him. I suggested that we find someone closer to the source. I thought that Orion would be the best choice. He's as close to the source as it gets, and he's not too intimidating, but he's not here, so we will have to wait for him."

Toven smiled knowingly. "Do you want me to do it?"

"Yes, please," Eric said.

"No." Darlene shook her head. "We don't know what your venom can do when you get aggressive. It might be too potent and kill Eric instead of initiating his transition."

"It won't. That's not how the venom works, and I have excellent control over the amount of venom I inject. The moment Eric's heart starts to slow down, I'll stop."

"Are you sure?" Darlene asked.

"I'm positive." He leaned and kissed Mia's temple. "I was very careful with Mia, injecting her with only a minimal amount of venom at a time. If I could do that while aroused, I can do that while aggressing on a male." He smiled at her. "I wouldn't do that for anyone else, but you are my granddaughter, and your happiness is important to me. I still regret not being around to help your mother and you. If I hadn't been such a jaded wreck, I wouldn't have turned Orion away, and we could have found your mother much sooner. Perhaps even before she met her husband."

Darlene chuckled. "Then I wouldn't have been born. I should be thankful to you that you threw Orion out, but at the same time, I regret all the years we all missed as a family."

They still weren't as close as she would have liked, but things didn't happen overnight, and she needed to give it time.

Her mother was doing her best to bring everyone together, but with Orion gone, everything had been put on hold, awaiting his return.

"When do you want me to induce you?" Toven asked Eric.

"As soon as possible. My brother is taking his family back home tomorrow, and I hoped that they would get to watch my second initiation ceremony." He grinned. "As the middle child, I'm always hungry for attention."

"We can do it tonight." Toven leaned back and crossed his feet at the ankles. "But there is no time to arrange for another ceremony and no need. We can meet up at the gym, Kian can say the ceremonial words again, and if you want, your family can witness the match."

Mia lifted her hand. "Before you rush off to do that, did you check with Bridget whether it's okay to try again after such a short time?"

Darlene looked at Eric. "We didn't, and we should."

"Call her now," Toven suggested.

"Can it wait for after lunch?" Rosalyn asked. "My casserole is getting dry sitting in the warming drawer."

"It can wait." Eric rose to his feet and offered a hand up to Darlene.

She didn't agree, but since everyone had gotten up and headed to the dining table, she couldn't voice her objection without sounding rude.

"So, Eric." Toven draped a napkin over his slacks. "Tell us about yourself."

"What would you like to know?"

"Everything. My granddaughter chose you as her mate, and you are about to become part of our family. I would like to get to know you better."

57

ERIC

*A*fter lunch was over and Toven had learned everything there was to know about Eric aside from his shoe size, they all returned to the living room, and Eric texted Bridget.

A quick question, if I may. How soon after the first initiation can I have another?

Instead of replying to his text, she called. "First of all, tell me, how are you feeling?"

"I feel the same as I did before Max bit me. There is absolutely no change."

"Do you feel well overall?"

"I do." He chuckled. "As you've seen, according to the results of my latest physical, I'm in perfect health."

"Is Max going to initiate you again?"

"Nope. This time I'm getting the highest and purest octane available. Darlene's grandfather agreed to induce me. In fact, he is here with me, and I'm going to switch the speaker on, so he can join the conversation."

Toven smiled. "I don't need that to hear perfectly well, but thank you for the consideration."

After a long moment of stunned silence, the physician said, "Good afternoon, Toven."

"Hello, Bridget."

"When is the event going to take place?" she asked.

"Tonight at the gym, but without all the fanfare," Eric said. "Toven hinted that one ceremony was enough for a schlump like me."

His attempt at self-deprecating humor didn't garner even a chuckle.

Tough crowd.

"I'll be there," Bridget said. "Seeing a god in action should be a sight to behold. In fact, I want to film the event."

Toven laughed. "Now you're giving me performance anxiety. Gods and immortals are not that different as far as brute strength goes. In fact, I've never needed to engage in hand-to-hand combat, and I'm so untrained that Eric might best me. I've always relied on my mental powers to defend myself."

"I have no doubt that you will be spectacular," Bridget said. "If that's okay with you, I will bring a professional camera."

"Be my guest," Toven said.

"Thank you. I'll meet you at the gym tonight at eleven-thirty." She ended the call.

Eric lifted a brow. "You've never fought with your hands? Not even as a boy?"

Toven shook his head. "My upbringing was very formal, and I spent most of my time studying. My mother would have disowned me if I was caught fighting with other boys."

"That's sad." Eric made a face. "You missed out on male bonding. Gilbert is seven years older than me, so we didn't get to fight much, but I found plenty of partners in crime at school."

Toven smiled. "It sounds like you had a great childhood. I'm happy for you."

"I did." Eric smiled as the memories flashed through his head.

Suddenly, it occurred to him that the ceremony was about more than just getting bitten, and that he and Toven would also exchange vows of friendship and loyalty. Would he be bound to both his initiators?

"I have a question. Since Max failed to induce me, am I still bound to him for eternity?"

Toven laughed softly. "The promise is not as binding as the ceremonial words make it sound. If you don't like Max, you don't have to be friends with him."

"What about loyalty?" Darlene asked. "Will Eric have to protect Max if the need arises?"

"If Eric transitions and becomes a member of the clan, he will owe loyalty to everyone in his new family, and if we are attacked, he will be expected to join our defense efforts."

"How do you know that?" Mia asked. "You are not even an official member of the clan."

"I am not, but I pledged my loyalty to Annani and her descendants. Do you think Kian would have allowed me to live in the village without that? I'm not subordinate to him or his mother, but I will stand with them if the need arises."

"Got it." Eric leaned back and wrapped his arm around Darlene's shoulders. "I have no problem with that. I like the idea of being part of a community of people who look out for each other. It's just that I feel uncomfortable asking a god to be my buddy."

Toven chuckled. "If you transition, you will be mated to my granddaughter. We will be more than buddies. We will be a family."

"Awesome." Eric grinned. "Wait until Gilbert hears about that. He always wanted us to have a big family, and now that he can have it, he's playing chicken."

"What do you mean?" Curtis asked.

"He and Karen are afraid of attempting transition because they have three little kids they don't want to orphan. They are seriously considering giving up on the opportunity to become immortal."

"I'll talk to them after the ceremony tonight," Toven said. "They have nothing to fear."

Eric wondered why Toven sounded so sure when everyone else kept warning them about the dangers to older Dormants. Was it because he'd managed to successfully induce a sick young woman? Or was he just cocky because he was a god?

"What makes you so sure that they will make it?" Darlene asked.

Toven smiled. "I'm sure you've heard about the blessings Annani gives to transitioning Dormants." When they nodded, he continued, "She's coming back to the village this Thursday, and I'm here to assist her. If your brother and his wife need help transitioning, they will get blessings from two gods, not just one. They are practically guaranteed to come out immortal on the other side."

"Forgive me." Eric dipped his head. "I don't want to sound disrespectful, but isn't that putting too much faith in blessings?"

Toven smiled indulgently. "Not when they are coming from a god." He snapped his fingers, and suddenly, his skin was glowing. "We command energy that we don't understand." He snapped his fingers again, and his skin stopped glowing.

"How did you do that?" Darlene asked. "I thought that you lost your glow."

"I did, but Mia helped me find it again." He leaned toward his mate and kissed her cheek.

Eric was impressed but not convinced. The glow was a neat trick, but it didn't prove anything. Nevertheless, it might be enough to convince Gilbert and Karen to stop fretting and embrace the incredible opportunity they were being given.

58

WILLIAM

$\mathcal{A}$ s William opened the door to his house, he was greeted by a happy-looking Kaia and the aromas of cooked food.

Both made him salivate.

"Welcome home, my darling." Kaia wrapped her arms around his neck and pulled him to her for a kiss.

As his hands roamed over the curve of her bottom, he was conflicted about what he wanted to do first, make love to Kaia or eat what she'd made.

Somewhere in the back of his mind, an annoying thought floated to the surface. Kaia was doing a great impression of a 1950s wife, and it was so uncharacteristic of her that it had gotten his attention despite the haze of lust and hunger clouding his brain.

Letting go of his mouth, Kaia took his hand. "I made dinner." She led him to the kitchen.

"I can smell it."

He had no idea what she could have possibly found in his refrigerator to cook with.

William made sandwiches, but he never cooked, so he didn't buy groceries to prepare meals with. Other than cold cuts, cheeses, and frozen buns, whatever was in his kitchen had been brought over by Darlene weeks ago. After she'd visited him, she'd gone to the supermarket and gotten him a load of dry and frozen goods that he could prepare quick meals from. With the exception of the occasional frozen pizza that they popped in the oven, he and Kaia had been eating mostly in the café and other people's houses.

"Sit." Kaia motioned to the kitchen bistro table. "I'm going to serve you."

He shook his head. "I will do that. You cooked, I'll serve."

"Not today." She shoved him toward the chair. "I want to do something nice for you, so don't argue."

William stifled a chuckle.

CHAPTER 58

That was the Kaia he knew and loved. Bossy and assertive even when she was playing housewife.

The baking dish she put on the table had a roasted chicken resting on top of rice pilaf and was decorated with baby carrots and green beans.

William's mouth watered. "Where did you get the ingredients to make this?"

"From Geraldine. She came over to check on me, and when I told her that there was nothing to make dinner from, she asked what I wanted to make and brought everything I needed from her house." Kaia handed him the chicken shears. "Can you do the cutting?"

"Of course." He got to work on the bird. "It smells so good."

"I hope you like it." She sat across from him.

"Did you get any rest at all?" he asked.

He'd been texting every thirty minutes to ask Kaia how she felt, and she'd answered right away, but she hadn't told him that she was making dinner.

"My mother and Gilbert came over with Cheryl and the little ones, and they made a mess, I mean the little ones. I cleaned the house after they left, and then Geraldine came, and then I cooked dinner, and here we are. I feel great."

Maybe giving her brain a rest and doing simple physical work was just what she'd needed.

Some claimed that it was therapeutic, and others claimed that exercise was great for mood improvement, but he'd never experienced either. Everything that took time away from his work annoyed him and made him anxious.

Well, not everything.

Time spent with Kaia was wonderful.

"I'm glad." He put half of the chicken on her plate and half on his.

She looked at the portion and laughed. "I can't eat all that."

"Eat as much as you can, and I'll finish the rest." He put rice pilaf on her plate and then on his and finished with the baby carrots and green beans.

"I don't have Coke." Kaia pouted. "And I can't drink that horrible beer you have in the fridge. It's the same one you had in Safe Haven."

"How about wine?" He got to his feet. "I should have a couple of bottles somewhere."

They were there when he'd moved into the house, part of a welcome basket that Ingrid had prepared.

"Found it." He pulled a bottle from the top shelf. "Now I just need to find a bottle opener." He started rummaging through the kitchen drawers until he found it.

"I'll get the glasses." Kaia pushed away from the table. "I know where they are."

After William uncorked the wine and poured it into two glasses, he raised his glass to Kaia's. "Cheers, my love. To your immortality."

59

KAIA

"To immortality." Kaia clinked her glass with William's and leaned over the table to meet him halfway for a kiss.

She still enjoyed kissing him, still felt desire for him, but it was tainted by the other part of her that had lain dormant along with her immortal genes and had been awakened alongside them.

She'd hoped that fussing with her looks and playing house would make her feel more like a woman, but Edgar was still there in the background, and she couldn't keep pretending that she was alright when she was nothing but.

But how could she tell William that the transition had brought the male side of her to the forefront and that she was no longer the woman he'd fallen in love with?

Would it be a deal breaker for him?

Even if it was, she couldn't continue like this. She had to tell him and get it off her chest. Maybe he could even help her.

Kaia put her glass down. "Something strange happened to me during my transition. I hoped it would go away, but it's still here, and it's driving me crazy."

His eyes clouding with worry, William put his glass down as well. "What is it?"

"Remember what I told you about remembering my past life?"

"Vividly."

"For some reason, the transition awakened way too many of those memories. I dreamt about being Edgar, and I found much more about who I used to be than I ever wanted to know. He wasn't a nice man." She shook her head. "I mean, I wasn't a nice man. I was a misogynistic jerk who hated women, put them down, and believed that they were good only for pleasuring men and bearing children."

"You shouldn't beat yourself up over that. Many men of that generation held the same beliefs. Changing those attitudes was one of the clan's missions, and it's been extremely difficult to undo hundreds of years of patriarchal indoctrination. We are still not where the Clan Mother would like us to be. Large portions of the

590

world are still stuck in the Dark Ages in that regard, and even the West still has a long way to go before true equality can be achieved."

"Don't try to make light of it. I was much worse than the average chauvinist. But my deplorable attitudes toward women are not the worst of it." She picked up the glass and emptied the rest of the wine down her throat. "Suddenly being attracted to women is."

William chuckled. "I don't think that's so bad. After all, I'm attracted to a woman as well."

Kaia could have throttled him.

He was usually so understanding, so willing to listen, but now he was belittling a very serious problem.

There was a good reason why the vast majority of people didn't remember their past lives. It was a curse, an affliction, and she wanted those memories and their influence gone.

"You don't get it. I found myself lusting after Bridget and thinking how perfect her ass and her boobs were. And then I lusted after Hildegard, thinking that her husky voice was so damn sexy. Those thoughts weren't kind, though, like an appreciation of their feminine beauty. They were nasty and lewd, and they weren't Kaia's. They were all Edgar's. I don't know what to do."

William's smile faded away. "I'll call Nathalie. She knows how to deal with invading spirits and how to prevent them from taking over."

"Edgar is not an invading spirit, and I don't need an exorcist. I need someone to erase those memories, but now that I'm immortal, I can't be thralled."

But she could still be compelled.

"That's why I want to go back to Safe Haven as soon as possible. Emmett and Eleanor might be able to compel me to forget Edgar's life."

"I'm not sure they can do that. Those are not your own memories, not as Kaia, and you have no control over them. Compulsion forces you to do or not to do things, but you need to be able to do them in the first place for it to work."

"What do you mean?"

"Emmett can compel you to sing opera, but he can't compel you to do it well if you don't have the ability to do that. Or he can try to compel you to shoot a bullseye on a target that's two miles away. You won't be able to do that no matter what. Do you get what I'm saying?"

"I think so. How about thralling? Would that work?"

"If you were still human, perhaps someone very skilled and very powerful could do it. But since those are very old memories, even then it might not be possible. Thralling works best on recent memories."

Slumping in her chair, Kaia groaned. "Then I'm screwed. I don't want to live forever with Edgar in my head. I'll go insane."

William leaned forward and put his hand over hers. "A god or a goddess can thrall other immortals, and Annani is an excellent thraller. She might be able to thrall away even old memories. But first, you need to meet with Nathalie, if only to eliminate the possibility that Edgar is not you in a prior life, but someone who hitched a ride on your brain."

"Fine. I'll talk to her, but I know it's not an invading spirit regardless of what that aura guy said."

60

DARLENE

"*A*re you excited?" Darlene asked as she and Eric got out of the elevator on the gym level.

After their lunch meeting with Toven, they'd gone back to her office, and Eric had gone back to working on a lease deal with his buddies. He'd seemed calm, and when they'd gone home, they'd made love and had fallen asleep.

It had been a good day, and hopefully, it would end well too.

"I am enthusiastic and, for some reason, less apprehensive than I was with Max." He chuckled. "Toven's claim about his lack of training is giving me hope."

"I wouldn't count on it. He's still a god with strength and speed you can't match."

"I know." He stopped and pulled her against him. "This time, it's going to work." He smiled. "It has to because there is nowhere to go from here. I jumped from the bottom of the ladder all the way to the top rung."

"Max wasn't the bottom rung, but I get what you're saying." She stretched on her toes and kissed his lips. "Ready?"

"Ready." He took her hand and pushed the gym doors open.

The place hadn't been rearranged this time, and only the family and a few others were there to witness Eric's second initiation attempt. It was underwhelming for such a monumental event, and Darlene regretted listening to Toven and not arranging another grand ceremony.

There were no tables, not even chairs to sit on, and they were all standing around the mat like spectators in an underground fight club.

Then again, if Toven's preference was to keep it low-key, she couldn't repay his kindness by disregarding his wishes.

"Good evening," Eric greeted their guests. "Thank you for coming to cheer me on." He smiled at Toven. "And thank you for agreeing to bite me."

"You're welcome." The god turned to Kian. "Shall we begin?"

"Bridget is not here yet," Kian said. "We also need the ceremonial wine, and Okidu is not done."

Kian's butler was using one of the treadmills as his table. He'd put the tray with small wine glasses on the track and was filling them from the two bottles he'd brought with him.

Gilbert patted Eric's back. "It's going to work this time. I feel it in my gut."

"Of course, it's going to work." Eric glanced at Toven. "I have a god inducing me. No other male Dormant has gotten induced by him before. I'm making history."

Toven put his hand on his shoulder. "First, you need to spur my aggression, and that's not going to be easy. I don't remember the last time my fangs elongated in response to a challenge by another male. I think it was when Mortdh irritated me. Since then, I have only used them to bring pleasure. But I have to admit that every time I think of him, which I try not to do too often, my fangs itch with the need to kill him, and I have to remind myself that he's already dead."

"Did you ever fight Mortdh?" Kian asked.

Toven chuckled. "I was too smart for that. He would have won, and he would have killed me." He sighed. "If I provoked him, and he *accidentally* killed me in the heat of the fight, it wouldn't have counted as murder. He was insane, but he wasn't stupid. In fact, he was very smart and calculating."

"I would love to hear more about him one day." Kian leaned against an elliptical machine. "It might provide me with a better understanding of his son." He smiled. "The more I know about my enemy, the better I'll be prepared to fight him if needed. Maybe we can meet and talk about Mortdh and your history with him over cigars."

Toven shook his head. "I don't like talking about him, or the other gods for that matter. Even after five thousand years, it's still painful."

"I thought that you'd grown numb," Darlene blurted. "That's what you told Orion."

"Guilty," he admitted. "When the pain and disappointment become intolerable, the only way to carry on is to become numb. But the moment I allowed myself to feel again, the pain returned along with the joy."

"Was it because of me?" Mia asked in a small voice.

"It was thanks to you. You brought me back to life."

The doors to the gym flew open, and Bridget rushed in with a big movie camera hoisted on her shoulder. "I'm sorry I'm late, but I was waiting for this." She patted the camera. "Brandon promised to get it for me, but he was stuck in traffic."

Syssi tilted her head. "At eleven-thirty at night? That's unusual even for Los Angeles."

"There was an accident on the 405." Bridget smiled at Toven. "I hope you're still okay with starring in this historical document."

"As long as no one outside the clan ever sees the recording, I don't mind." He looked at the camera. "Do you know how to use it?'

"It's not complicated." She patted the sleek device. "This thing does everything automatically. I just need to point the lens in the right direction and shoot."

Toven cast the camera another skeptical glance before turning to Kian. "Can we begin now that Bridget is here?"

"In a moment. I'm just waiting for Okidu to distribute the wine."

From the corner of her eye, Darlene saw the gym door open and then Max walked in. She nodded at him, and he nodded back, then leaned against the wall and crossed his arms over his chest.

61

ERIC

*K*ian and Toven's conversation about the god's rivalry with his dead brother had given Eric an idea for how to spur Toven's aggression.

He could taunt him by mentioning Mortdh and how he had been stronger and smarter than Toven. But what if the mention of the hated brother got the god so enraged that he accidentally killed him?

Nah. Toven claimed to have excellent control over his fangs and venom glands. Besides, he was too calm and collected to lose control, especially in front of his mate.

Mia looked up to him like the god he was, and Toven basked in her adoration. He wouldn't want to lose that by killing his granddaughter's mate.

Potential mate.

If, for some reason, this induction failed as well, there would be no point in trying again.

Who knew? Maybe he and Gilbert weren't related to Syssi after all? Those tests weren't always reliable.

When Okidu was done distributing the wine, Kian lifted his glass. "Eric is ready to attempt his transformation for the second time, and we are gathered here to witness his initiation. He's incredibly fortunate to have Toven as his initiator, which will probably earn him the envy of many. Having a god as your initiator is not only an honor and a privilege, it also dramatically increases your chances of transitioning quickly. In addition, you are gaining a powerful friend."

Eric bowed his head to Toven. "I'm honored and grateful beyond words, and naturally, I accept you as my mentor, initiator, and protector. I was told that after the ceremony, the role of the initiator is similar to that of a godfather, so I'm pleased to pledge my loyalty and eternal friendship to my god-brother." He offered his hand to Toven. "Shall we shake on it?"

Taking his hand, Toven smiled without a hint of fang in sight. "I accept your pledge and intend to hold you to it, my young god-brother." He turned to Kian. "Let's conclude the ceremony and get it done."

Kian nodded. "Is there anyone here who objects to Eric becoming Toven's protégé?"

Eric glanced at the small crowd and was surprised to see Max. The Guardian stood apart from everyone else, leaning against the gym wall with his arms crossed over his chest.

Max lifted a thumbs up and mouthed something that Eric didn't understand but assumed was good luck.

When no one voiced an objection, Kian nodded. "As everyone here agrees that it's a good match, let's seal it with a toast. To Toven and Eric."

Gilbert hooted, Karen and William said good luck, and Kaia gave him the thumbs up. Cheryl, who'd stayed just outside the door with Idina and the twins asleep in their strollers, blew him a kiss.

Eric blew one back.

"Let's do it." Toven toed off his shoes and turned to Eric. "Ready?"

"As ready as I'll ever be to challenge a god."

As they took their positions on the mat, Eric reconsidered his idea of taunting Toven with talk about Mortdh.

Having a god as his god-brother was a cherished privilege, and he didn't want to tarnish it from the get-go by saying something hurtful.

The god might hold a grudge.

"Well?" Toven beckoned him with his hand. "Unless you attack me, my fangs won't come out."

"What if I insult your mother instead? Will that work?"

Eric had intended it as a joke, but Toven tilted his head in contemplation. "You can try, but I can't think of an insult that would be relevant to a goddess. My mother was very beautiful, regal, and proper."

Toven's sense of humor needed some work, and Eric was just the guy the god needed to sharpen his funny bone.

"Right. So that's a no-go." Eric shook out his arms to loosen them.

He was well-trained, and he was in good shape. He might be able to get the god to punch back.

Lurching forward, Eric threw a roundhouse kick at Toven, but his foot never made contact with the god's chest. With lightning-fast reflexes, Toven caught it and held on.

Eric lost his balance and fell on his ass, but his foot remained in Toven's clasp.

"You will have to try harder," the god said.

"How? I move in slow motion compared to you."

Toven let go of his foot. "Maybe insulting my mother will work after all."

"It's worth a try." Eric got to his feet and thought of something that was insulting but not vulgar. "Why did your mother play hard to get when she was so hard to want?"

For a moment, Toven just gaped at him, and Eric was sure that an assault was imminent, but then the god burst out laughing. "That's so true. How did you know?"

Great. So, he managed to make Toven laugh, but he failed to spur his aggression.

That insult was as vanilla as they got, but Eric didn't want to go overboard and dip into vulgarity. There were too many witnesses to the show who he wanted to impress with his wit and charm rather than his ability to use crass language.

"Well, looking at you, it wasn't hard to guess." Eric waved a hand in Toven's direction. "You are stiffer than a broomstick and have no sense of humor. No wonder you had to resort to virtual match-making."

That was such a blatant untruth that it shouldn't have worked to rile Toven, but when he smiled, his fangs were a little longer than they had been before.

"Go on," Toven said.

"Mortdh should be thankful that he was born to a different mother, but given how he turned out, your entire family's tainted gene pool could use a disinfectant."

Hopefully, Toven would accept his apology when this was over. Darlene belonged to the same gene pool, and she was wonderful.

His eyes blazing, the god advanced on him unhurriedly but with menacing intent.

Fear slithering down his spine, Eric lifted his fists in self-defense, but Toven swiped them aside as if they belonged to a newborn baby, grabbed Eric by the back of his neck, and struck with his fangs.

The bite was brutal, and it burned, but a moment later, a cooling sensation washed over Eric, along with the kind of calm he'd only experienced once when his friends had tricked him into eating a muffin baked with psychedelic mushrooms.

In the back of his mind, Eric was aware of the cool venom being pumped into his veins and that it was dangerous if it went on for too long, but he couldn't bring himself to care.

62

KIAN

ian had to admit that Toven's control was admirable. The god hadn't hurt a hair on Eric's head, and he retracted his fangs after thirty seconds, which was probably long enough for a god's potent venom to activate Eric's dormant genes.

He hadn't needed a full minute like Max had, and no one had to tell him.

Bridget kept filming as Toven laid Eric gently on the mat and turned to Darlene. "He's all yours."

"Thank you." She rushed to her mate, sat on the mat, and lifted his head to rest in her lap.

Toven pushed his feet into his shoes and glanced at the camera. "This concludes tonight's festivities. Goodnight, everyone."

Getting the hint, Bridget turned the camera off and handed the device to Kian. "I should check on Eric."

"He's fine." Toven walked over to stand beside Mia, who was congratulating Gilbert and Karen. "I heard that you are hesitant to attempt transition."

Gilbert nodded. "But before we talk about that, I just wanted to say that Eric didn't mean any of the nasty things he said. He was just trying to rile you."

"I know." Toven smiled. "He loves my granddaughter, who comes from the same gene pool, so he couldn't have meant what he said about disinfecting it." He rubbed his chin with his thumb and finger. "Mortdh inherited his insanity from his mother, not our father, so Darlene doesn't carry it. Your brother shouldn't fear that his children will be predisposed to mental health issues."

"It never even crossed my mind," Gilbert said. "Or Eric's. Darlene is a wonderful lady, and I'm happy that she and my brother clicked. I wish them all the best." He looked at the mat where Darlene was cradling Eric's head in her lap and murmuring words of love and encouragement to him. "How long is he supposed to be out? Is it going to be like last time?"

CHAPTER 62

Toven shrugged. "I don't know. That was my first time inducing a male Dormant."

Kian glanced to where Max had been standing only minutes ago, but the Guardian was no longer there. He must have slipped out when everyone's attention was on Darlene and Eric.

"I saw the whole thing." Kaia's sister appeared right beside them, then looked at the god and blushed. "Good evening, your Excellence."

Chuckling, he gently patted the girl's back. "I'm no one's excellence. I'm just Toven."

"You are incredibly strong." She looked up at him as if he was a movie star. "Are you stronger than the immortals?"

"I might be slightly stronger and a tad faster, but don't worry. I've had thousands of years to practice moderating my strength. I didn't hurt your uncle."

"I know. It's just that it was scary to watch you bat away his hands as if he was a puppet on a string. Eric is strong."

"You should go back," her mother said. "You can't leave the babies alone in the vestibule."

"They are not alone. Max is watching them."

Kian wasn't sure whether Max knew what to do with a crying baby, but if either of them woke up, he could just open the door and call their parents.

Karen didn't look comfortable with the guy watching her children either, but she was too polite to say that. Instead, she glared at her daughter. "The match is over, and there is nothing more to see. Please, go back and let Max go home. He has work tomorrow."

"Fine." Cheryl glanced at the mat. "Is Eric going to be okay?"

Bridget was busy taking Eric's vitals, but she didn't seem worried.

"I'm sure he will be," Kian said. "Our doctor is with him."

When Cheryl left, Toven turned his attention back to Karen and Gilbert. "If you're not too tired, we can find a place to sit, and I'll try to convince you not to go home."

"We have to," Karen said. "Even if we decide to go for it, we can't just stay here. We need to figure out what to do with our house, my work, Gilbert's business, Cheryl's school, Idina's preschool, and the list goes on."

Toven just smiled. "I understand. It was much easier for me because I led the life of a nomad, but it was much more difficult for Mia, even though she's a freelancer and works from home. We've just recently moved into the village, and it's an adjustment, but we love it here."

"The village is lovely." Karen sighed. "But we have children to think of."

"I have a daughter," Kian said. "And I wouldn't want her to be anywhere else. This is the safest place for her." He put his arm around Syssi's shoulders. "There is a saying that it takes a village to raise a child, and it's never been truer than right here right now."

Syssi cast him one of her indulgent looks, communicating that he should let her take over. "The only way to address so many challenges is one at a time." She looked at Toven. "Can you meet with Karen and Gilbert tomorrow? We can all have a nice lunch in our backyard and discuss their options at leisure."

"I can, but you work in the morning, and they plan to leave in the afternoon."

"About that." She looked at Karen. "Aren't you curious to meet the goddess? She returns to the village on Thursday. Besides, Eric's transition might start as early as tomorrow. He was induced by a god."

Karen gave Syssi an apologetic look. "I wish we could stay, but we really need to go back. If it's okay with you, we can come back for another visit during the weekend."

Syssi let out a breath. "I want us to have a clear plan of action before you leave, and I also want us to have a proper goodbye lunch. I'll take a day off tomorrow." She looked up at Kian. "Our place at one in the afternoon. Does that work for you?"

"I'll make it work."

63

WILLIAM

*K*aia had talked a mile a minute on the way home from Eric's second initiation ceremony, and William hadn't interrupted her. He'd limited his responses to the occasional nod or a word here and there, and she hadn't even noticed that he was quieter than usual.

He wanted her so badly that his body ached all over, but she was in a funk, disturbed by urges she didn't welcome, and he wasn't sure she still desired him.

What should he do?

Should he let her take control and get her male urges out?

Or should he do the opposite, assume the dominant role, and hope that it would make her feel more feminine, more like her old self?

When they got to the house, he reached for her, sliding his arm around her waist. "Are you tired?"

It was after one o'clock in the morning, and she was still in the initial stages of her transition, but since her transition wasn't following the traditional path, he didn't know what to expect.

Kaia shook her head. "I'm immortal now."

"You're not over the initial stage of your transition yet. You don't have the energy of an immortal."

She looked at him with defiance in her eyes. "If you've already decided that I'm tired, why did you ask?"

He cupped her cheek and smiled. "There are degrees of tiredness. Do you want to sleep, or do you want to play?"

A smirk lifted the left corner of her lush lips, and she lifted her arms to his shoulders. "I want to play."

"That was the correct answer." He turned her around, pressing his erection to her backside. "Hands on the wall, Kaia."

She looked at him over her shoulder. "What kind of game are we playing?"

Caging her against the wall, he slipped his hand under her T-shirt and caressed her stomach. "The kind you're going to like." He added his other hand to the play, sliding it down between her thighs.

"How do you know that I'm going to like it?" She let her head drop back against his shoulder.

"Because I can smell your arousal." He nuzzled the side of her neck.

He could also feel the heat coming off her center, and as he rubbed her through the fabrics of her tights and panties, her thighs shivered deliciously.

"I think you like this game very much." He nipped her ear as he pulled her flimsy bra down and under her breasts. "Let's up the ante." He pinched her nipple.

Moaning, she bucked against him, rubbing her ass over his aching shaft in a blatant demand.

"Not yet, love." He left the heat of her center and added his other hand to the assault on her breasts.

Teasing her mercilessly, he caressed one breast while pinching the other and then switching it up. When he grazed her neck with his fangs, she lifted up on her toes.

Kaia was close to the edge, but he wasn't about to let her reach climax yet.

He took a moment to caress her tormented breasts and then slid his hands down her ribcage to her stomach and pushed them under the elastic of her tights to cup her center.

"William," she breathed. "Please." She pressed her core to his palm.

"Since you ask so nicely." He nipped her neck and pushed two fingers inside her, rubbing her clit with his thumb at the same time.

As the climax tore through her, Kaia gasped and arched back, her legs trembling from the force of it.

William pulled his fingers out and brought them to her mouth. "Open."

She obeyed, and as he thrust them between her lips, another tremor shook her body.

Evidently his gamble had paid off, and this was precisely what Kaia had needed to forget all about the male side of her.

When she was done sucking on his fingers, he hooked them under her chin, tilted her head, and kissed her.

As the taste of her exploded over his tongue, his eyes rolled back in his head, and he kissed her like a man possessed, sucking on her tongue and licking inside her mouth until he got it all.

64

KAIA

*K*aia was still boneless from her climax when William went down to his knees and started peeling her leggings off. If not for the wall her hands and forehead were pressed against, she would have collapsed in a heap on the floor.

As her pants and panties cleared her bottom, he nipped one buttock and then the other and then lifted one leg at a time to tug the garments off.

When she was naked from the waist down, William gripped her hips and reached with his tongue between her legs, lapping up her juices as if they were the most delicious thing he'd ever tasted.

A shiver ran through her, but it wasn't one of arousal.

Suddenly Kaia was Edgar again, and the thought of licking a woman down there was repulsive to him.

Her.

Him.

Them.

No, it was only repulsive to the jerk she used to be. She was Kaia now, and Kaia loved cunnilingus.

Except, that nasty invading tone had ruined her fun, and it didn't take William long to realize that she wasn't enjoying his tongue as much as she usually did.

After pressing two soft kisses to her butt cheeks, he pushed up to his feet, enveloped her from behind with his big body, and ground his erection against her backside.

As he nuzzled and kissed her neck, Kaia shut her eyes tightly, stifling the frustrated groan that threatened to leave her throat.

William would misinterpret it, thinking that she didn't want him inside of her, when the opposite was true. She was just angry at those damn memories that had ruined their fun.

Her defenses had been momentarily down when Edgar had intruded on her pleasure, but she'd gotten rid of him quickly enough and could have continued enjoying William's talented tongue, but he was so attuned to her that he'd caught that one moment and decided that she didn't want him to continue.

Turning her head, she offered him her lips. "Kiss me."

William kissed her gently and yet ardently, and when he let go of her mouth, he turned her around, lifted her into his arms, and kissed her again.

Kaia wound her legs around his torso as he walked back to the couch and dropped down.

When they came up for air once again, they looked at each other as if they were reconnecting after being lost, or maybe it was just her. His face was so familiar, so precious to her, and the love shining in his glowing eyes nourished her battered soul.

He was beautiful to her, fangs and all.

As love for William swelled in Kaia's chest, a tear slid out of the corner of her eye. "I love you so much." She shifted up to her knees, unbuckled his belt, and lowered his zipper.

He whipped his shirt over his head, buttons flying as they were ripped off, and tossed it behind him. In the next moment, he arched up between her spread knees and pushed his pants and boxers down his thighs.

Kaia didn't wait for him to get rid of them all the way. Gripping his hard length, she sank down on it until they were merged.

William groaned, and as his shaft swelled inside of her, it filled her so deliciously that it was almost too much, but he didn't move, and his hands were gentle on her back. "I love you, Kaia, in any shape or form. You are mine, and I'm yours, and there is no obstacle we can't overcome together."

His words were like a gentle balm on her frayed nerves, and if not for the hard length pulsing inside of her and demanding her attention, Kaia could have melted with all the emotions he was evoking in her, but sex wasn't about soft and cuddly, at least not this time. She needed it rough and wild to chase away the last vestiges of those unwelcome urges and ugly thoughts.

Bracing her hands on William's shoulders, Kaia lifted and then sank back down, and when she did it again, he gripped her hips and took over.

Driving into her, he was no longer the gentle lover she was used to. He was a ferocious beast, his thrusts so powerful that the couch groaned under the force of them.

Kaia hung on for dear life, her fingers digging into William's shoulders, and as he hissed and sank his fangs into her neck, a climax erupted out of her with a magnitude of eight on the Richter scale.

65

DARLENE

*W*hen Darlene's alarm went off at five in the morning, she groaned, found her phone, and shut it up.

There would be no swimming for her this morning.

The ceremony had ended late last night, and it had taken Eric nearly an hour to float down from his cloud of bliss and open his eyes.

He'd smiled up at her and said groggily, "I love you."

She still felt all warm and fuzzy as she thought about that. Regrettably, Bridget hadn't recorded that part of the event, so she would have to replay it over and over in her head until it was etched forever in her memory.

No one had ever looked at her like that. There had been more than love in Eric's eyes, there had also been fondness and warmth, and those were just as important.

When she and Leo had dated, he'd told her that he loved her, but there had been no warmth in his eyes when he had. Only lust. She should have known that it wasn't the real thing, but she'd wanted it to be, so she'd silenced the small voice in her head that had told her to walk away.

Turning to her side, she looked at the man sleeping soundly beside her. His stubble had grown overnight, darkening his jaw and making him look even more sexy and roguish.

Darlene used her finger to move aside a lock of dark hair that had fallen over Eric's forehead and cupped his cheek before pressing a kiss to his parted lips.

She'd done it several times during the night to check up on him, and each time he'd sleepily kissed her back. But this time, he didn't return her kiss, and when she kissed him again, and he didn't respond, Darlene's heartbeat went into overdrive mode.

"Oh, my God. You're transitioning." She shook his shoulder to make sure. "If you are just pretending to be asleep to mess with me, I will never forgive you."

He kept on sleeping, his rising and falling chest reassuring her that he was still alive and there was no need to panic.

"Yeah, right." She reached for the phone with trembling hands and searched for Bridget's contact.

The doctor answered on the fourth ring. "What happened?"

"Eric is not responding. He's breathing, so I'm not freaking out yet. What should I do?"

"If you are still in bed, get dressed. I'm sending a couple of Guardians with a gurney to bring him to the clinic."

"Thank you." Darlene let out a breath.

It was such a relief to let someone who knew what to do take charge of the situation.

Rushing into the bathroom, she left the door open so she could keep an eye on Eric while she took care of the morning necessities. It occurred to her that it was futile since she was still human and couldn't see whether his chest was rising and falling from even a few feet away, and she couldn't hear his heartbeat like any immortal could either, but that was all she could do, and logic was in low supply at the moment.

The knock on the door came when Darlene was pulling her pants on, and she nearly fell on her face when she tried to run to the door while tugging them over her ass.

Throwing the door open, she waved Max and the other Guardian in. "Thank you for coming so quickly. Eric is in the bedroom."

As the Guardians pushed the gurney through the door and rolled it to the bedroom, it suddenly occurred to her that Eric slept in the nude. In her rush, she hadn't thought to put at least underwear on him, and now that the Guardians were there, she felt embarrassed for the both of them.

"Can you put some clothes on him?" Darlene asked Max.

"No need." He and the other Guardian picked Eric up together with the blanket and transferred him to the gurney. "Bridget will need to get him naked anyway to hook him up to the monitors."

Darlene nodded. "I'll pack a bag for him and follow you."

"See you there." Max gave her a reassuring smile. "Don't worry. Eric is a fighter. He's going to make it."

"Thanks," she murmured.

When they rushed out, she went looking for her phone.

Gilbert would want to know that his brother was transitioning, and so would Kaia. She needed to call them, but she also needed to pack a bag for Eric and get to the clinic.

"Pack a bag first. I can make the phone calls on the way."

Talking herself through the packing helped keep her mind from panicking, and she reminded herself to put Eric's phone and laptop into the duffle bag. It might be a bit of wishful thinking that he would need them any time soon, but Darlene had to stay hopeful, or she would lose it.

66

KAIA

"*P*lease." Bridget shooed Kaia and William out the door. "As I said before, you should all go home or to the lab and continue with whatever you had planned for today. Eric is doing well, and he's not going anywhere anytime soon. Darlene can keep you updated."

Kaia opened her mouth to argue, but William took her hand and gave it a gentle squeeze. "Your family is at the café. Let's join them and get some breakfast."

What she needed was coffee. After the phone call from Darlene had woken them up, Kaia and William had gotten dressed in a hurry and rushed to the clinic without having anything to drink.

She let out a breath. "Fine."

Arguing wouldn't have helped anyway. Bridget hadn't let her family loiter in the waiting room when Kaia had been staying in the clinic, so there was no way the doctor would soften up now.

Besides, Eric didn't even know they were there for him.

That being said, if he remained unconscious, they should take turns sitting with him and talking to him. Supposedly, it was helpful.

Gilbert waved them over. "I got a mountain of sandwiches. There is enough for everyone."

The café wasn't open yet, but nearly everything that was served during the day could be bought in the vending machines. Someone must be refilling them several times a day for them to always be so well stocked.

William pulled out a chair for Kaia. "I'll get us coffees."

"Thank you." She sat down and smiled up at him. "Don't forget a packet of sugar for me."

"I won't." He leaned down and kissed her forehead.

She felt much better after making love last night, more like herself and less like Edgar. Her entire mood had improved, and it wasn't just thanks to the orgasm and the venom-induced euphoric trip.

Last night had shown her that there was hope, and that as long as she dug her heels in as Kaia and made love to the man she loved, Edgar could be shoved back to the small corner of her brain he'd occupied before.

Perhaps she should cancel the meeting with Nathalie that had been scheduled for later today and use Eric's transition as an excuse.

Kaia wasn't looking forward to sharing with a stranger all the sordid details she remembered from her life as Edgar, and if she was getting better at suppressing that part of herself, maybe she didn't need to.

"I'm amazed that Eric started transitioning right away," her mother said. "I was sure it would take at least a couple of days."

"He had a god induce him." Gilbert put his arm on the back of her chair. "That's some potent mojo."

"Are you going to stay longer now?" Kaia asked.

Her mother sighed. "We don't know how long it will take Eric to go through the initial stage of his transition. Bridget said that it might take two days or two weeks, and given that he's unconscious, she thinks it will most likely be closer to the two weeks than two days."

"She says that his vitals are good." Gilbert unwrapped a sandwich and handed it to Kaia. "But I don't know why she says that. He is running a fever of 102, and his blood pressure is 180 over 90. Even I know that is high."

"His heart is strong." Karen put a hand on Gilbert's arm. "He might be forty-two, but he's in such good shape that his biological markers are of a guy ten years younger."

"I don't know if that's true." Gilbert motioned to Kaia to eat her sandwich. "Eric likes to boast, and he might have made that up."

"Eric is not a liar," Kaia said. "He might sometimes exaggerate, mostly to make a joke or to tease, but I've never caught him lying."

As a good liar herself, Kaia knew how to spot the telltale signs, and Eric was mostly honest. If he lied, it was by omission.

"In any case, Gilbert has to stay for sure." Her mother cradled her coffee cup between her palms. "But I should take the kids home. Cheryl needs to go back to school, and I need to go back to work." She smiled. "You have no idea how much I miss Berta. Cheryl has been a great help, but I feel bad about asking her to babysit so many times."

Gilbert snorted. "You shouldn't feel bad. The girl's eyes sparkle with glee every time you ask her to take care of the little ones, and then they spark with even more glee when I pull out the twenties and pay her. The little capitalist loves seeing her wallet swell."

"You shouldn't pay her in cash. We should deposit the money into her savings account."

He laughed. "That would be a poor incentive for our young businesswoman, if at all. She likes to get paid right away and see her money grow. I think it's a good lesson for her. It feels more visceral to her when she gets the money she earns without delay and holds it in her hands."

William returned with two paper cups and handed one to Kaia. "Here is your cappuccino, my love. One packet of sugar already mixed in."

"Thank you."

Kaia loved it when William called her his love. She wished she had a great term

608

of endearment for him, but so far, she'd only come up with my prince, which was a little lame and unoriginal. She liked honey bear, but William would hate it. Maybe hunky bear?

"What are you smiling about?" William asked.

"Nothing important. Are we still meeting with Toven at Syssi and Kian's?"

"Maybe we can move the meeting to the café," her mother suggested. "That way, we can be close to the clinic and discuss our options at the same time."

"I would advise against it." William removed the lid from his coffee cup. "Toven might want privacy for what he has to tell you, and the café is usually overcrowded at lunchtime. Besides, Syssi took a day off to prepare a goodbye luncheon for you."

Karen nodded. "You are right. It's just that their part of the village is the farthest from the clinic. In case of an emergency, we won't be able to get here fast enough."

"Fast enough for what?" Gilbert asked.

"You know." Karen waved a hand. "Toven's blessing. If he's with us at Syssi and Kian's, it will take him fifteen minutes to get here."

"Maybe we should ask him to give Eric a preemptive blessing." Kaia looked at William. "Can you text Darlene and suggest it to her? She should be the one to ask Toven to do it now instead of waiting for Eric to get worse."

"I'll text her right away."

609

DARLENE

*D*arlene sat on a chair next to Eric's bed and read on her phone to distract herself from worrying. Around her, the medical equipment hummed and occasionally beeped, the blood pressure cuff inflated and deflated, and Eric breathed on his own, which according to Bridget was a good sign.

William had texted her, suggesting that she ask her grandfather to bless Eric preemptively, but she didn't. Toven might get upset with her for asking him to do that while Eric was doing well, and she needed to remain in his good graces.

Eric's family and William were meeting Toven later for lunch, so they might hint at it casually and let him decide for himself.

If only William could come in and sit with her for a little while.

Heck, she wouldn't have minded her mother or sister coming over, either. Sitting there with nothing to do and no way to help Eric, Darlene felt small and useless, and she could have used the support of someone who cared about her.

She'd left the door to Eric's room slightly ajar, so she could hear what was going on in the waiting room, but so far the doctor had done an excellent job of keeping everyone out of the clinic.

It was unnecessarily cruel, and Darlene wished Bridget would allow at least one additional person in Eric's patient room to keep her company. When the doctor came in again, she was going to ask her to relax the restrictions, and then she would call her mother and Cassandra.

It was early in the morning, so her mother was probably still sleeping. Despite never having been human, Geraldine kept to a human sleep schedule. In a way, it was like Toven's missing glow. After a lifetime of hiding their abnormalities, they had a hard time letting go of the restrictions they'd put on themselves.

Darlene had read an article about the plasticity of the brain and how areas that were used extensively grew more neural synapses, while those in neglected areas shriveled and died. Maybe it was true for immortal abilities as well.

As the clinic's front door opened, she tilted her chair back to get a look and was surprised to see Max come in with a cardboard tray and a paper bag.

"I brought you a coffee and a sandwich." He stood in the doorway. "Do you want to come out to the waiting room?"

That was so nice of him. No one else had thought that she might be thirsty or hungry, and the truth was that she'd been so stressed out that she hadn't felt it until Max showed up.

She cast a quick glance at Eric, expecting what? That he would wake up and invite Max to sit in the room with them?

He hadn't even twitched in the past couple of hours, and his face was frozen in a peaceful expression. He looked like he was sleeping, but that was sadly deceptive.

If she left the door open, she could still hear the monitoring equipment from the waiting room. Besides, Bridget was in her office, and she could see all the readouts on her computer screen.

"I'll come out." Darlene pushed to her feet.

When she stepped out, he handed her the coffee.

"Thank you." She took the paper cup. "How come you were on duty this early today? I thought you'd get half a day off after attending the ceremony last night."

He chuckled. "I'm immortal. I don't need eight hours of sleep. My shift started at four in the morning."

As she sat on one of the chairs in the waiting room, Max sat right beside her. "How are you doing?"

"I'm not the one transitioning." She removed the lid and took a sip.

"You must be worried."

"Of course, I'm worried. He's unconscious."

"That's not unusual for a transitioning Dormant. Kaia was the anomaly, not the norm." He shook his head. "She's going through the strangest transition to date. I wonder what makes her different."

"It's not a question for us mere mortals to ponder." Darlene chuckled. "But wait, you are not a mere mortal."

"Neither are you, but I'm glad that you still have your sense of humor. And just as an aside, you should have transitioned by now, and you certainly shouldn't wait."

He hadn't added that she shouldn't wait for Eric to complete his transition in six months, but that was what he'd meant by his comment.

"Yeah, that's what everyone keeps telling me, including Eric."

That got his brows dipping into a deep V. "What is he suggesting you do about it? Leave him and find another male to induce you?"

She hadn't missed the hopeful tone in his voice.

"No, that's not what he's suggesting."

"Then what other option is there?"

If Max couldn't figure it out, she wasn't going to spell it out for him.

"Something creative, I guess." Darlene looked at the white paper bag. "What do you have in there?"

"A couple of chocolate croissants."

Her mouth watered. "Those are my favorite."

"I know." He handed her the bag.

"How do you know that? We've never shared croissants."

"I've seen you ordering them a couple of times. I figured you liked them."

That was such a lie. There had been no chocolate croissants in Safe Haven, and the two of them hadn't even exchanged helloes before being stationed there.

He must have noticed what she'd been ordering in the café since they had returned, but she'd never seen him there.

What was Max's deal?

Was he stalking her?

It made no sense.

She was with Eric, and Max couldn't know about Eric's idea for a threesome with him. If he knew, he wouldn't have asked how she was supposed to get induced while still being with Eric.

Maybe he hoped that Eric wouldn't make it.

It didn't seem like that. The Guardian seemed to genuinely care about him.

Whatever.

Shrugging, Darlene bit into the croissant.

When Eric woke up, they would sort it out. Right now, she didn't have the mental bandwidth to deal with Max, his peculiarities, or what Eric had in mind for the three of them.

68

KIAN

*E*ver since Syssi had returned to work, she and Kian had rarely enjoyed lunch together during the workweek. She'd taken a day off to organize the goodbye luncheon for Kaia's family, and even though he didn't expect them to actually leave now that Eric was transitioning, he was still glad for the excuse to go home in the middle of the day and enjoy time with Syssi and Allegra again.

Perhaps he could take the rest of the day off and spend it with his wife and daughter?

It was tempting but impractical. If he did that, he would have to spend more hours in the office the following day. He and Shai had already planned on staying in the office later than usual today because of the long break he was taking.

Walking into the dining room, Kian gave the nicely set table a cursory look, but as the number of place settings registered, he looked again.

Had Syssi forgotten that Eric and Darlene weren't joining them?

He counted the guests he knew had been invited. Kaia and William were two, adding six members of Kaia's family, including the babies was eight, together with Toven and Mia, him and Syssi, that was twelve.

Kian counted again to make sure, but he'd been right the first time. There were fourteen place settings.

Perhaps Syssi had invited Mia's grandparents. Curtis didn't like late dinners, but he wouldn't mind a lunch invitation.

As Syssi walked into the dining room, he asked, "Did you invite Rosalyn and Curtis?"

Her eyes widened. "I didn't. Do you think I should have?"

"Not really. This lunch is dedicated to Kaia's family, and she's of no interest to them. Who are the extra two seats for?"

He'd seen Amanda leave for work this morning, so it couldn't be her and Dalhu.

"I invited Nathalie and Phoenix. Idina and Phoenix became best friends from day one, and I thought that having Phoenix with her would keep Idina occupied while we talked. Some of what needs to be said is not for her young ears."

"Good thinking." He pulled her into his arms. "My brilliant wife." He dipped his head to kiss her.

The doorbell ringing cut the kiss short, and a moment later, a loud demanding 'Da-da' sounded from Allegra's bedroom.

He chuckled. "I'll get our daughter while you get the door."

Their little one must have inherited her mother's foresight. How else could she have known that he was in the house?

Maybe she overheard him?

They never closed the door to her room so they could hear her, so it was possible that she'd heard him.

He found his daughter standing in her crib and holding on to the bars like a little prisoner.

"Da-da!" She started bouncing on the mattress, demanding to be picked up— her little tush going up and down.

"Come to Daddy, sweetness." He lifted her by the waist and started peppering her soft cheeks with kisses until she grabbed his nose and yanked. "Okay, I get it. No more kisses."

She was very good at communicating her wishes clearly and directly, which was an excellent trait for a future leader.

Ambiguity served no one's best interest, and the smell coming off her diaper didn't leave room for misinterpretation either.

"Let's clean you up." He carried her to the changing table in her bathroom. As Kian disposed of the dirty diaper in the special pail that blocked the odors from spreading, cleaned her up, and put a fresh diaper on her, Allegra was quiet and didn't look into his eyes as if she was embarrassed about having to be changed.

Once he was done, though, she leveled her intense gaze at him and said, "Da-da," in a tone that sounded a lot like a thank-you.

"You're welcome, my little princess."

When he returned with her to the dining room, all of their guests were seated around the table, including the twins who sat on boosters that were strapped to the dining chairs.

"Good afternoon, everyone."

Kian walked over to the head of the table where Okidu had put Allegra's high-chair between his and Syssi's seats, but Allegra refused to be seated in it.

When he tried to sit down with her, she twisted around, pointed at the boys, and commanded, "Da-da!"

Syssi laughed. "Oh, boy. We are going to have our hands full with this one. She's already interested in boys."

"We can make a match right now," Gilbert said. "Let's see which of my boys she fancies."

Okidu bowed. "Shall I move the highchair, master?"

"Yes, please. I'm curious to see if that's what she wants."

The twins were sitting between their parents, and it took a few moments to move everyone's chairs a few inches to the side to make room for Allegra's high-chair to be placed between the twins.

When her throne was ready, she happily agreed to be seated and grinned triumphantly at Evan and then at Ryan.

"Your daughter is assertive," Karen observed.

"Thank you. I've noticed." He patted her blond curls. "Daddy is going to sit in his chair. Will you be okay here by yourself?"

"Da-da."

Since this da-da sounded like an affirmation, Kian smiled at his daughter, kissed her cheek one more time, and walked to the head of the table to sit next to Syssi.

Allegra preferred to eat unaided, and she was a good eater. There was no need to feed her. She made a mess, but thankfully, they had Okidu to clean after her, as well as cook and do everything else around the house.

"Shall I serve lunch now, mistress?" Okidu asked.

"Yes, please." Syssi smiled at him and then turned to her guests. "I suggest that we eat first and keep the discussion for later." She glanced at the two little girls that were seated next to each other and totally absorbed in a conversation about a cartoon character. "After lunch, Okidu can keep an eye on the little ones in the den while we talk."

"I can watch them," Cheryl offered.

"You should stay," Kaia said. "Today's decisions are going to affect you as well."

Cheryl shrugged. "I can live with whatever as long as I have a good internet connection."

"Any news on Eric?" Syssi asked.

Kian knew that there had been no change, and so did Syssi, but he assumed she wanted to express her concern and let the family know that she was worried along with them.

Gilbert shook his head. "No news is good news, right?" He looked at Toven. "Eric is currently stable, but maybe a preemptive blessing could prevent him from deteriorating?"

Toven nodded graciously. "I will stop by the clinic this evening. After all, I'm Eric's mentor and protector now. I need to take care of my protégé."

"Thank you," Gilbert said. "I'm forever in your debt."

"I appreciate your gratitude, but I'm doing this for my granddaughter as much as I'm doing it for you. She chose Eric as her mate, and he seems to make her happy." The god smiled. "I also like your brother. I would have given Eric my blessing even if he wasn't Darlene's chosen and my protégé."

69

WILLIAM

$\mathcal{A}$fter they were done with lunch, Okidu cleaned up the table along with the disaster area created by the three babies, and then Syssi and Karen took the little ones to the den.

As Nathalie followed with Phoenix and Idina, holding one little hand in each of hers, William leaned closer to Kaia and whispered in her ear, "Maybe later you can talk to Nathalie."

She shook her head. "Not in front of everyone," she whispered. "No one knows, and I want it to stay that way."

He nodded. "I meant if you get a chance to be alone with her."

For some reason, Kaia viewed Edgar's resurfacing as a personal failure, and she hadn't even told her mother or Cheryl about it.

After serving coffee and desserts, Okidu bowed to Kian, turned on his heel, and headed to the den.

When Syssi and Karen returned with Nathalie, Karen didn't look happy.

"Are you sure the cyborg butler can take care of all the babies?" she said quietly to Syssi.

"We can see the den from here," Nathalie said. "Besides, Okidu raised Kian, so I'm sure he can handle a bunch of human children and one immortal girl who is very mature for her age."

"Idina is also mature." Karen sat next to Gilbert, shifted her chair a few inches to the side, and let out a breath. "I can see them from here."

"Then let's begin," Kian said.

When all eyes turned to Toven, he put his coffee cup down. "I probably don't have anything new to tell you, but I can emphasize what you already know and clarify things."

Karen nodded. "I would appreciate some clarity. Usually, I have no problem making decisions, but this time there are so many factors to consider, all of them life-altering, and I find myself vacillating between two extremes. One moment I

616

decide that Gilbert and I should do it, and the next, I decide that it's not worth the risk." She looked at Cheryl. "When you are ready, I'll encourage you to seek an immortal mate and transition at a young age, and I'll do the same for Idina and the boys. It's enough for me to know that my children will never die. My own life is less important."

Cheryl turned red as a beet. "Don't talk like that. I want you and Gilbert to always be part of my life, so don't you dare give up on immortality because you are scared. If you need more time to reorganize everything, that's fine, but don't decide to never try." She said it so quickly that she ran out of air and had to suck in a breath. "And on another note, I was told that the age of consent is seventeen in the clan, and I know that it is sixteen in most countries around the world, not just the backward ones. So, if I want, I can turn immortal now."

Karen glared back at Cheryl. "You know my opinion on that, so I will not repeat it here and waste everyone's time." She forced an apologetic smile at Toven. "Forgive me for my long-winded speech and for my daughter's outburst."

"That's okay." He gave her a reassuring smile. "Your daughter said some of the things I intended to say. What I want to add is that your fears are uncalled for. I know that Syssi and Andrew had a hard time transitioning, but they both made it with the help of Annani's blessings. Now that there are two gods in the village to bless you, you are practically guaranteed to make it. The other issue is Idina. She's still young enough to transition just from being around Annani. Don't you want the peace of mind of knowing that your child is indestructible? And by the way, the same goes for Cheryl. She's right about the age of consent. If she were my daughter, and if she was mature enough to engage in sexual relations, I would rather she turned immortal as soon as possible."

"Not happening," Gilbert grumbled. "She's not mature enough, and that's the end of this discussion."

William tensed.

Gilbert might be entitled to his indignation, but that was not how he should talk to a god.

Toven smiled, in that part indulgent, part condescending way of his. "Cheryl might be too young to engage in sexual activity by American standards, but let's be practical. Most young women do not concern themselves with the age of consent when they feel ready to explore their sexuality. Besides, eighteen is an arbitrary number, and it is much lower in many countries."

"It's thirteen in Japan," Cheryl murmured under her breath.

"That's terrible," Karen said. "They are still kids, and so is Cheryl. I don't care what the age of consent is in Japan or in Germany."

"It's fourteen in Germany," Cheryl grumbled. "Provided that both partners are under eighteen."

William stifled a chuckle.

It seemed that Cheryl had investigated the issue thoroughly, and the question was whether she'd done it before or after learning what was required for her to transition.

Kian lifted his hand. "This is not constructive. Karen and Cheryl can argue about it when they get home. We need to address the bigger issues."

KAIA

*K*aia had been trying to catch Cheryl's attention and signal her sister to shut up, but she'd been avoiding Kaia's eyes on purpose.

Cheryl might talk a big talk, and she liked to push their mother's buttons, but she wasn't ready for sex, so the entire argument was for naught.

Toven reached for the carafe and refilled his and Mia's cups. "So now that we've removed the fear of death from the equation, let's address the issues of gainful employment and business endeavors."

"I'm not sure that the fear of death is a done issue," Karen said. "Eric is unconscious, and he's younger than Gilbert and me."

Toven leaned forward. "You have my word that your successful transitions are 99.9% guaranteed. Take the odds of a fatal accident or a terminal disease and factor those in for your age, and you get much worse odds than that."

Once again, Kaia was struck by the differences in opinions between Kian and Toven and the rest of the immortals, including the doctor who was an expert on the subject. Those two knew something that the others didn't, and she was going to find out what it was.

Obviously, it was a big secret if Kian was keeping it even from his wife, but with the help of the journals, she might find the answer.

"You are right if the number you're citing is accurate," Gilbert said. "Why is everyone else so concerned while you are not?"

Go, Gilbert. He had noticed the same thing she had.

Toven leaned back in his chair. "I am new to the village, and they don't realize yet what an asset I am for transitioning Dormants. Mia, Kaia, and Eric are the first Dormants to transition since my arrival at the village." He cast Kian a challenging smile.

Kian didn't smile back. "We are all aware of you being a tremendous asset. Now let's keep going."

Interesting. Maybe Toven didn't want to keep guarding the secret he shared only with Kian. If Kaia didn't find the answer in the journals, Toven might be a good candidate to coerce the information from.

Right. As if she stood a chance of manipulating a seven-thousand-year-old being.

"Let's talk about your job." Toven turned to Karen. "I understand that you enjoy it. Could you find a similar job in Los Angeles?"

"Easily."

"Problem solved." He turned to Gilbert. "I understand that you are a builder. How many projects do you currently have running?"

"Only two, but they are big. I'm building two gated communities. I have about five months to completion on one and seven on the other, and then I need to sell them."

"I'm sure you have people working for you that can handle most of it without you looking over their shoulders."

Gilbert shook his head. "They need constant hand-holding. I can't leave all the decisions to employees. It would be a disaster."

"I can help you with that," Kian said. "We run multiple building projects here and in other states and even abroad, and I rarely see any of them. I have systems in place that allow me to run all of those projects with human contractors with practically no in-person supervision. The architect is a clan member, and so is the interior designer, and we have one member who launches new hotels and another who inspects the building projects. I can teach you our system so you can do everything from the village and only inspect your properties from time to time."

"I know that it's possible to run projects that way." Gilbert crossed his arms over his chest. "But my margins are slim, and I can't afford to hire big honchos who will do everything for me. I would have no profit left."

"Trust me," Kian said. "You'll make more profit than you do now because you will be able to run more projects simultaneously."

That had been the right thing to say to Gilbert.

He uncrossed his arms and put his hands on the table. "If you can show me how and convince me that I can make more money, we are moving into the village."

"What about me?" Cheryl said. "Where am I going to go to school?"

Kaia snorted. "Only minutes ago, you were arguing with Mom about hooking up with an immortal, and now you are concerned about school?"

"That was a hypothetical discussion about a principle, and I have no intention of hooking up with anyone anytime soon." Cheryl let out a breath. "I'm going to miss my friends, but this is more important. I guess I can finish high school online."

"Our young ones go to an excellent private school in Los Angeles," Syssi said. "I can introduce you to Lisa and Parker, who are about your age. They can tell you about the school."

"Thank you." Cheryl clutched her phone like a lifeline, and Kaia was sure she would check her Instatock stats under the tablecloth the moment she was no longer the center of attention.

"Any other objections?" Toven asked.

"Our house and our nanny." Gilbert took Karen's hand. "We are a big family, and we love our house. We also love our nanny. I'm not saying that those are reasons for refusing immortality, but I need help coming up with appropriate solutions. We need a bigger house than what you have available in the village, and we need help with the little ones so Karen can work." He looked at her. "Unless you want to take a sabbatical for a few years."

"I don't. You know that I need to work. It's not about the money."

"I know, love."

SYSSI

Syssi hadn't contributed to the discussion yet, but maybe she should suggest that Karen and Gilbert be given a house in the newest section of the village where the houses were bigger. Gilbert and Eric were her family, so maybe Kian wouldn't mind.

Andrew and Nathalie had gotten one just because Andrew was her brother and not for any strategic reasons, and there were still a few new houses that weren't occupied.

"I might have a solution," Kian said. "If you are willing to be a little cramped for a couple of weeks, I can build an extension to one of the existing homes."

Gilbert's eyes widened. "How can you do that so fast?"

Kian smirked. "No time wasted on pulling permits and waiting on inspections, and a 3D printer."

"Can I build a custom house in the village?" Gilbert glanced at Karen. "I prefer to start from scratch and design a house I like rather than add patches to an existing structure, and so does Karen. Our current house was as much her design as mine and the architect's."

Kian shook his head. "We have a plot of land we didn't build on yet, but the plans for it are done, and I don't intend to put in the utilities for just one home. When that section goes up, I might allow some customization, but as it stands now, we have so many vacant houses that there is no reason to build more."

"I get it." Gilbert rubbed his jaw. "If I may ask, why did you build so many if you didn't need them?"

"I hoped that clan members who currently live in Europe would join us, and I also wanted to have homes ready for future couples and their families." Kian smiled. "The Fates have been good to our clan lately, and we've been blessed with many new Dormants." He waved a hand. "Just look how fortunate we were to find your family."

Syssi cleared her throat. "The houses in the newest section are a little bigger. Maybe Kaia's family can stay in one of the remaining ones."

"They are bigger, but they also have only three bedrooms each." Kian frowned. "I have an idea." He looked at Cheryl. "What do you think about having your own guesthouse?"

"I'd love it."

Kian looked at Syssi. "They can have Amanda's old place, and Cheryl can use Onidu's guesthouse. The house originally had three bedrooms, but Amanda converted one into a closet for her wardrobe and another one for Dalhu's studio. We just need to convert them back into bedrooms."

"That's a great idea." Syssi could imagine how it would look with an extension in the back that connected the main structure to the guest house. "It sits on a larger plot, so it has room for an addition."

"Can we see it?" Cheryl asked.

"Sure." Syssi grinned. "It's been empty since Amanda moved into the new section."

"That leaves the nanny problem." Gilbert let out a breath. "I understand that you don't have any available in the village."

"We don't." Syssi sighed. "Many of the ladies are willing to babysit when needed, but they don't want to do it full time. To be able to work, I have to take Allegra with me to the university. Amanda converted her office into a nursery, and we hired a human nanny who takes care of Evie and Allegra there."

"Maybe your university needs a system administrator?" Karen asked jokingly. "Then I could add my boys to your nursery. Idina can go to the same preschool Phoenix goes to."

Syssi pursed her lips. "I can ask. Maybe we will get lucky, and the university needs a new system administrator. It's not as exciting a job as your current one, but there are advantages to working for an academic institution. The environment is much more relaxed."

Karen nodded. "That would be wonderful, but I can't just quit my job without training a replacement. I still need to go back home." She sighed. "I'm going to miss Berta so much. Do you have any idea how hard it was to find a great nanny who could also cook?"

"I'll cook," Gilbert said. "If Kian's system works as smoothly as he claims, I'll have a lot of free time on my hands. I can get into cooking." He patted his stomach. "A man who loves to eat should know how to cook."

Karen rolled her eyes. "We will live on things off the grill."

"What's wrong with that?"

"Nothing." She smiled at her mate. "It's a small price to pay considering all the benefits." She cupped his cheek. "You'll be home when I return from work, and we will spend more time together as a family. That alone is worth the price of admission."

"Let's sum up," Toven said. "All the objections have been addressed, and solutions for them were found. The last thing we need to discuss is the timeline." He turned to Karen. "How long do you need to train a replacement?"

"Ideally, a couple of months, but contractually, I'm only obligated to give it two weeks."

"Excellent." Toven leaned back in his chair. "Here is the plan. Gilbert needs to stay until Eric wakes up, and Karen needs to go back and give her notice. But instead of going today, I suggest that you leave Sunday. What's the worst that could happen? They'd fire you?"

"I still need them to give me a letter of recommendation. Why do I need to stay until Sunday?"

"Annani is arriving on Thursday, and I'm sure you want to meet the head of the clan you are about to join. The next day is Friday, so there is no point in you leaving before the weekend. And who knows, maybe Eric will wake up by then."

Karen looked at Gilbert. "What do you think?"

"I think you should do what Toven is suggesting. In the meantime, Syssi can check if they need a system admin at the university, we can check out the house and decide what we want to do with it, and I'll spend some time with Kian learning his hands-off building method. If Eric wakes up by Sunday, I'll go home with you, and we will spend a couple of weeks getting everything ready for the move. If he takes longer, I'll join you as soon as I can."

72

KAIA

$\mathcal{L}$ unch had ended over an hour ago, Gilbert and Karen had taken the boys back to the house, and William had gone back to the lab, but Kaia had volunteered to stay with Idina and walk her home when she was done playing.

Her objective had been to have a word alone with Nathalie, but so far, it hadn't been possible.

Kian headed back to his office, but Syssi had the day off, and Allegra was enjoying the company of the two little girls, so Syssi joined Nathalie and Kaia in the den, and the three of them had been chatting about this and that.

She considered asking both women for their advice.

Nathalie and Syssi were both super nice, and neither would look down their nose at her because of what she was going through, even if it was ugly.

It wasn't as if she'd invited those damn memories and unwanted urges. Her transition had somehow unlocked them, and although she'd managed to shove them back into their little corner in her mind, they were still floating up at random times and making her feel contaminated.

Eric's analogy of using a disinfectant on Toven's gene pool came to mind, only in her case, it wasn't a gene pool. It was a soul pool.

Ugh. Why me?

"I'd better head home and start on dinner." Nathalie offered Phoenix her hand.

The girl shook her head and hid her hands behind her back so her mother couldn't grip them. "I don't want to go home. I want to play with Idina."

Idina looked up at Kaia. "Can I stay to play with Phoenix?"

"You've already got to play for a long time. It's time to go."

Syssi regarded the two little girls with a fond smile. "You don't have to go yet. They can play for a little while longer. Allegra is so happy to have friends over who talk and do interesting things."

Allegra was sitting on a baby mat, surrounded by a mountain of toys, but she found Idina and Phoenix much more interesting than the inanimate objects.

"I have a better idea." Nathalie started collecting Phoenix's toys and putting them into her Disney princess backpack. "We can invite Idina and Kaia to our house, and the two of you can keep playing while I make dinner."

"No!" Phoenix shook her head, her beautiful long curls bouncing from side to side. "I want to stay at Syssi's house and eat waffles. Okidu's are the best."

The butler suddenly appeared in the den as if summoned by a magic wand. "I shall get to it right away, mistress." He dipped his head.

Syssi laughed. "Now you have to stay. I'll make us cappuccinos."

That was the opportunity Kaia had been waiting for to be alone with Nathalie, but with Syssi's immortal hearing and the house's open floor plan, Syssi might hear them talking and feel left out.

Besides, there was no harm in sharing her problems with both. Syssi was a seer, so maybe she would have a vision that would provide a solution to Kaia's problem.

When Syssi returned with a tray loaded with cappuccinos and snacks for the girls, Kaia sat down on the couch between the two women and picked up one of the cups. "I need your advice on something that has been bothering me since my transition started."

Syssi frowned. "What is it?"

"Well, the truth is that it didn't start with the transition, but it certainly intensified to an uncomfortable level. Since I was about six or seven, I've been able to access memories of my prior life."

Neither of the women looked shocked.

"That's awesome," Syssi said. "What do you remember?"

"It's not awesome. Well, it used to be, but it no longer is."

The two women listened intently as she told them about Edgar, using words that were appropriate for the young ears in the room and only hinting at what the problem was, but Nathalie and Syssi were both intelligent ladies, and she didn't need to spell anything out for them.

Kaia turned to Nathalie. "Because of what Spencer said about my double auras, William thinks that they are not memories from a prior life but an invading spirit, and he suggested that I talk to you because you have experience dealing with ghosts and blocking them from taking over your mind."

Nathalie shook her head. "I don't think Edgar is a ghost. He doesn't talk to you, and he doesn't take over and block you. You are fully aware of him at all times, but you don't converse with him. The way you understand mathematics is also an indication that it's not a foreign entity. I didn't know what my invading spirit knew, and he told me things only when I asked." She snorted. "More often than not, he refused to answer my questions."

"That's what I thought." Kaia let out a breath. "One last question. You keep referring to the ghost who lived in your head as he. Did you ever have a female ghost?"

"I had many trying to get in, and some might have been females, but the two who spent the most time in my head were both males."

"Did they make you feel more masculine in any way?"

Nathalie shook her head. "Never. It was like having an annoying friend squatting in my head. We talked, and we argued, but we never merged."

Kaia slumped against the back of the couch. "I sometimes catch myself thinking as Edgar, and it's terrible because he's a jerk." She sighed. "I loved remembering the mathematics he was so good at, but I hate everything else I remember about him."

It was easier to think of Edgar as him and not as who she used to be.

"Sari's mate remembers his past life," Syssi said. "I can put you on a call with him. Maybe he can help you."

Kaia turned to Syssi. "Was he a horrible person in his past life as well?"

Syssi tilted her head. "He wasn't horrible, but he did a horrible thing, and he certainly wasn't the wonderful man that he is now. I think that's the whole point of reincarnation. You are supposed to fix the bad things."

"Yeah, I get it, but I want to forget being him. Do you think the goddess will agree to thrall me? William said that she's the only one who can do that."

Syssi smiled. "Of course, she would. When Annani heard that William found his truelove mate, she was overjoyed. You are one of the reasons she's cutting her trip a little short. She wants to meet you."

"Awesome." Kaia felt a weight lift off her chest.

If the goddess was happy for William, she wouldn't deny his request to help his mate.

73

KIAN

*A*s Okidu eased the limousine into the parking spot, Kian and Syssi walked over, and Kian opened the back door for Annani.

Amanda had tasked them with keeping their mother and sister in the parking garage for a few minutes, so she could finish putting the last decorating touches on the Welcome Home sign she'd bought on the way back from the university.

It wasn't necessary to receive Annani and Alena with much fanfare, but Amanda had insisted.

"Welcome home, Mother." Kian bent nearly in half to embrace her.

Annani kissed both his cheeks and then gave him a gentle nudge to signal that she wanted him to let go. When he did, she turned to hug Syssi, who had finished embracing Alena and was waiting patiently for her turn.

"Welcome home, sister." Kian wrapped Alena in his arms, careful of her growing belly. "You look rested."

Alena also looked much more pregnant than she had been when she'd left, but he knew better than to comment on it.

"I had lots of fun," Alena said. "I enjoyed spending time with my children. It had been such a long time since we made an effort to be together as a family." She looked lovingly at her mate. "Thanks to Orion's insistence on getting to know them, I got to reconnect with them as well. I would have stayed longer, but Mother was impatient because she wanted to meet William's mate."

"Whatever the reason, I'm glad to have you back." Kian turned to Orion and clasped his hand in greeting. "Welcome home, brother-in-law."

Orion pulled him into a one-armed bro hug and clapped him on the back. "Not yet, but soon. How is the cruise ship renovation going?"

"It's on schedule despite all the shipment delays and worker shortages. I'm doing my best to have it ready on time."

"As long as it's on schedule, I have no problem waiting for its completion. Any longer than that, and we will need to wheel Alena to the altar. I think we are having twins."

"We are not." She slapped his arm playfully. "He's just a big baby."

"Do you know that the baby is a boy?" Syssi asked.

"Not for sure, but I think so."

"Didn't you get an ultrasound?"

"I did, and everything is fine, but I asked not to be told. I like the suspense of not knowing ahead of time." She patted her rounded belly. "Just like back in the day when there was no way to know."

"I bet they were correct fifty percent of the time," Kian murmured. "Shall we get out of here and head to your new homes?"

Okidu had finished unloading their luggage from the limo, and there was a lot of it.

Alena frowned. "What new homes?"

"I moved you and Mother to the new secure section of the village. Your things are already there."

"You should have asked if we wanted to move," Alena grumbled. "Orion enjoyed being close to Toven and Geraldine, and so did I."

"If you want, I can move you back, but I think you are going to like your new homes better. They are more upscale, and they are closer to Syssi and me."

His plan had been to lure his sister and mother into staying in the village by providing them with nicer homes, but apparently he'd been mistaken.

"I do not mind where I stay." Annani threaded her arms through his as they walked into the elevator. "My home is the sanctuary. I am just a guest here."

"We hope to change your mind about that," Syssi said from behind them. "And I want Alena to stay as well. We have a new family moving into the village that has twin boys who just recently turned one year old and an adorable toddler girl."

Kian snorted. "Idina is adorable in a devilish kind of way." He pressed the button for the elevator.

"She's just a feisty little girl," Syssi said. "Which, in my opinion, makes her even more adorable. They also have a sixteen-year-old who shows potential as a future businesswoman."

"I have heard all about the new family of Dormants." Annani floated into the elevator. "I also heard that Kaia's transition was unusual and that Eric is unconscious. Has there been any change in that?"

"No, but he's doing fine." Kian put his hand on the small of his mother's back. "Toven has been giving Eric his blessing, and it seems to be helpful." He tapped her back twice, letting her know that Toven had given Eric two transfusions.

Annani nodded sagely. "I am glad. I wonder what would happen if I added my blessing to Toven's. Do you think Eric would wake up sooner?"

Kian smiled at his mother's attempt at innocence. "It's worth a try."

As the elevator doors opened and Annani beheld Amanda and the banner, her glow doubled in its intensity. "I am so touched." She walked into Amanda's outstretched arms. "What is the occasion?"

"I'm just glad to have you back."

"I hope you are aware that Eve is still too young to turn immortal."

Amanda cast her a mock glare. "That's not why I'm happy. I just missed my mom and my sister." She hugged Alena and then Orion. "I missed you too."

CHAPTER 73

"Right." He chuckled. "I'm just an accessory to Alena, and I'm fine with that. I miss my sister and nieces too. How is Darlene holding up? I bet she's stressing over her mate."

"She is, but Eric is doing really well with the help of your father's blessings."

"When can I meet the rest of the family?" Annani asked.

"This evening, if you wish." Kian took Allegra out of her stroller. "They extended their stay so they could meet you."

"I will be delighted to meet them, and especially William's mate." Annani smiled at Allegra. "Now, let me have my granddaughter."

"Na-na." Allegra reached for her grandmother.

"That was a new word," Kian marveled. "My daughter is a genius."

74

KAIA

*K*aia had thought that no one could impress her as much as Toven had, but Annani was in a league of her own.

Toven was a gorgeous male, but the goddess was so beautiful that it was painful to look at her and yet impossible not to, and while Toven tried to subdue his natural sense of superiority, Annani flaunted it like a queen.

There was nothing apologetic about her.

And yet, despite the diva attitude, the otherworldly beauty, and the power that emanated from her in waves, she wasn't scary or even intimidating. Annani was warm, kind, and full of good humor, a real benevolent goddess who aimed to do good but didn't shy away from using her power when needed.

Not that Kaia knew that for a fact, but that was her impression of the goddess.

After the introductions had been made and Idina had charmed the goddess with her cute little curtsey, Annani turned her attention to Kaia.

"Come sit with me outside for a few moments, child." The goddess threaded her arm through Kaia's. Annani was tiny, more than half a foot shorter than her, and yet Kaia felt small and insignificant next to the powerhouse seemingly gliding on air beside her.

How did she walk like that?

She stole a glance at the bottom of the Clan Mother's gown. It was floor length, but it didn't actually touch the floor, and her feet were hidden under it. She couldn't really float, could she?

As Annani got to the glass doors leading to Syssi and Kian's backyard, one of her Odus rushed to her with a shawl and a pair of sunglasses.

"It is still sunny outside, Clan Mother."

"Yes, it is." She took the sunglasses and put them on her tiny nose.

They were huge and shaped like goggles, dwarfing her small face.

Unable to help herself, Kaia snorted and immediately slapped a hand over her mouth. "I'm sorry. I had something in my nose."

CHAPTER 74

Annani laughed, the sound raising goose bumps all over Kaia's arms. It was the most beautiful sound she'd ever heard, and she made a mental note to keep amusing the goddess so she would laugh again.

Was it Edgar's thought, though, or hers?

It was so confusing.

"I know these glasses look funny." Annani allowed the Odu to wrap the shawl around her shoulders. "My eyes are sensitive to the sun, and if I do not wear these ugly sunglasses, they get red." She threaded her arm through Kaia's again. "But I am a fast healer, and as soon as I get back inside, my eyes return to normal, so I only wear them not to scare people away." She leaned against Kaia's arm. "I have a feeling that a god's red eyes was how the vampire stories started."

As the Odu opened the sliding door and Annani stepped out, Kaia caught sight of a tiny foot. It was clad in a soft ballet-style shoe, the fabric the same emerald green color as the goddess's gown. Annani's feet were so small that she could probably wear Idina's shoes.

"I didn't see Toven wearing sunglasses," Kaia said, to distract herself from hunting for another peek at the goddess's tiny feet.

It was the oddest thing to get fixated on, and Kaia had a feeling that it was Edgar's fault. Heck, lately she was blaming everything that bothered her on him, but maybe some of the weird thoughts she had belonged to Kaia herself.

"Did you get to see Toven during the day?" Annani asked as she led Kaia to a comfortable-looking outdoor couch.

"I did, but it must have been indoors."

"That is the most likely explanation. His eyes should be as sensitive as mine, but then he is a male, and you know how they are. They have to be macho even if it means suffering."

"I know all too well how men are." Kaia winced. "I was one in my prior life."

It felt odd to confess her secret to the goddess mere minutes after meeting her, but she needed the Clan Mother's help to banish Edgar, so there was no point in dragging it out.

Who knew if she would get another chance to ask?

"How very interesting. It is more common to reincarnate as the same gender." Annani rearranged the folds of her gown, making sure that they were all even. "My son-in-law is an expert on the subject, and during my visit, we spent many fascinating hours talking about his research."

"I heard that he remembers his previous life as well."

"He does, but not the one that came right before this one. He remembers an older version of himself, a much cruder one that needed a lot of polishing." Annani lifted her head and smiled in the direction of the house. "Come join us, William."

"Thank you, Clan Mother." He came out holding a tray with a pitcher of lemonade and three glasses. "I thought you might get thirsty out here."

"I am a little thirsty." She took the tall glass he poured for her. "But you did not need to use an excuse to come out and join us. I am always glad of your company."

631

75

ANNANI

*Y*oung love was so sweet.

Annani sipped on her lemonade and observed the loving glances between William and Kaia.

It was about time the Fates found a truelove mate for William, and she could not be happier with their choice despite the little hitch in the form of disturbing memories.

Annani could sense Kaia's distress, the male urges she was fighting against, and the desperation with which she was clinging to her femininity.

The girl needed help, and she had come to the one person who could do that.

"Kaia was telling me about her past life as a man." Annani put her glass down. "That must be very confusing for you, child."

"It is." Kaia sighed. "Before my transition, it wasn't as bad. I only remembered the math skills and Edgar's self-image, which wasn't great. He was a big man, both in height and build, and he felt self-conscious about his size. I always thought that he was this gentle giant who did his best not to intimidate people, but it turned out that those were selective memories. After my transition, more of them surfaced, and I found out that he was a misogynist." She sighed and looked at William. "But the worst part is that I feel tainted by the combination of lust and hate he felt for females. I want things to return to the way they were before or eliminate those memories altogether. Is there a chance the Clan Mother could thrall them out of existence?"

Annani laughed. "Please, there is no need to refer to me in the third person. It is so contrived. And yes, I might be able to help you." She looked at William. "I will need you to go back to the house. I cannot have any distractions while I am doing this."

"Of course." He pushed to his feet, dipped his head, and turned on his heel.

When he closed the sliding doors behind him, Annani smiled to reassure Kaia.

The girl's eyes were darting nervously, and her breathing was shallow. She was too anxious to allow a deep thrall.

"Give me your hands, Kaia, and close your eyes." Annani clasped the girl's clammy hands. "I am going to look through your memories and try to push them back below the barrier of your subconscious mind. Hopefully, they will stay there, but if not, I can do it again until I succeed in keeping them there. Not everything needs to be achieved in one go."

Kaia let out a breath and opened her eyes. "Edgar was a nasty man. I don't want to remember anything of his personal life. But he was a gifted mathematician, and if possible, I would like to retain the memories of his craft. They've helped me a lot over the years, and I wouldn't have been nearly as successful without them."

Annani smiled. "As with everything else in life, things are rarely black and white, and most gifts come with a price. I hope I can allow you to retain the gift while freeing you from the burden of having to endure the less pleasant aspects of it."

"That would be awesome. Thank you." Kaia closed her eyes again, took a deep breath, and let it out slowly. "I'm ready."

As Annani gently entered the girl's mind, she did not encounter any resistance at first, but as she dove deeper, the male aspect hiding in the recesses of Kaia's mind tried to resist the invasion. It was as if her soul had split into two fragments.

Could that be the explanation for the split personality disorder? Nowadays, it was called dissociative identity disorder, and it was believed to be caused by trauma. Back in the day, it was called possession and was believed to be caused by invading demons or evil spirits. But perhaps a splintered soul was the real cause.

The question was how to banish the less desirable fragment and fill up the void that its absence would create so that what was left would be whole and not broken.

Perhaps instead of banishing it, she could mold it into something positive.

What if she could change Edgar's experiences of rejection and let him see them in a different light? If she eliminated that pain, or at least diminished it, the memories of his other emotions would lose their intensity, and Kaia would be able to push them back into the recesses of her mind.

It would be a long and difficult process. Annani could not do it in one sitting, and Kaia could not endure it all at once either. But since she intended to stay in the village for a while, she and Kaia could meet as many times as it took to remove Edgar's disturbing presence from Kaia's mind.

WILLIAM

*W*illiam shouldn't have felt anxious about leaving Kaia in Annani's hands. The goddess was gentle and caring and she was very skilled at thralling. She wouldn't damage Kaia's beautiful mind.

Furthermore, Kaia needed help.

She wasn't the type who admitted weakness easily, and the fact that she'd asked Annani to thrall away the memories plaguing her meant that she was desperate for relief.

He stood next to the bar, which was located in a convenient spot near the sliding glass door, allowing himself to watch Kaia and Annani without being obvious. The goddess had her back to him, so he couldn't see her expression, but he could see Kaia's, and she looked pained.

It doubled the size of the ball of stress in his gut.

What was Annani seeing inside Kaia's head?

Was Kaia trying to block the invasive probe?

If he'd had time to prepare her, he would have coached Kaia on how to relax and lower her mental shields. The less she resisted, the less damage her mind would sustain. But he hadn't been prepared for Annani to jump into action so quickly.

Gilbert walked up to him and looked at Kaia and Annani through the glass. "What's going on? What are they doing out there?"

Kaia hadn't shared her concerns with her family, so he couldn't tell Gilbert that the goddess was performing a sort of exorcism to free Kaia from her past life.

"The Clan Mother likes to get to know new members of her clan. She wants to talk with Kaia in private." William forced a smile. "She even kicked me out."

That had probably been the initial purpose of the talk, but when Kaia told Annani about Edgar, the Clan Mother had gone straight to work.

"So, it's not a test of some sort to see if Kaia is worthy of becoming a member of her clan?"

CHAPTER 76

"Not at all. Kaia is my mate, so as soon as she transitioned, she became a member of Annani's clan."

"I see." Gilbert turned to Kian. "So, Karen and I will not become members when we transition."

"That only affects the profit-sharing in the clan's holdings. Those who are not Annani's descendants, or are not mated to them, don't get the same cut as those who are, but they are residents of the village and members of our community with all the other rights and privileges as well as duties and obligations."

"What about Toven?" Gilbert asked.

"He doesn't need a share in the profits," Kian said as he joined them. "He's richer than King Midas." He chuckled. "Toven could buy the village and all of the clan holdings and still have plenty left to spare."

Gilbert's eyes sparkled with interest. "How did he become so rich?"

"Toven is seven thousand years old." Orion walked over to the bar. "He lived at a time when humans gave gold in tribute to the gods, or the one remaining god. My father hoarded it like a dragon hoards his treasure."

As Dalhu joined their group and the conversation turned to gold and the accumulation of valuables, including artwork, William shifted his gaze to look at Alena and Karen, who were each bouncing one of the twins on their knees.

On the couch, Amanda was showing Syssi Evie's new dress, and on the floor, Idina was telling Allegra a story about a princess who was looking for her lost golden slipper.

In another corner of the room, Cheryl had commandeered an armchair and was absorbed in her phone, probably checking her Instatock feed.

It was such a homey picture, and it loosened the tension that had taken hold of his shoulders.

That was why Kaia wanted a big family, and Fates willing, she would have one.

They would have it together.

"Do you still have the expensive jewelry you bought while serving Navuh?" Orion asked Dalhu.

"I had no reason to sell it." Dalhu accepted a glass of whiskey from Kian. "But if I ever need cash in an emergency, I will. I'm not emotionally attached to those trinkets. To me, they are just inflation-proof assets."

William hadn't listened to the entire conversation, so he didn't know how Dalhu had become the owner of expensive jewelry, and he didn't particularly care.

All he cared about was Kaia and whether what Annani was doing would help free her from her demons without causing permanent damage to her incredible mind.

635

KAIA

$\mathcal{W}$ hen Annani released Kaia's mind and then her hands, Kaia kept her eyes closed and looked inward. Edgar was still there, but his presence was muted. It was as if he had faded into the background, or rather the intensity of his feelings and his persona had, but he was still casting a shadow over her.

It was a marked improvement, but it wasn't the complete cure she'd hoped for.

Opening her eyes, she sighed. "I feel more like myself. Thank you."

"You are welcome." Annani patted her hand. "I was careful, and I did not go as deep as I would have had to go in order to submerge the memories of your past life. Instead, I just manipulated them." The goddess smiled mischievously. "I gave them a different spin."

Kaia frowned. "Forgive me, but I don't follow. What do you mean by spin?"

"Can you still sense the traces of Edgar's resentment of women?"

Kaia closed her eyes and dove inside. She still had fragments of those memories, but the emotions they evoked were much calmer. "I don't. It's like I can remember the rejection, but I'm no longer angry about it."

The goddess clapped her tiny hands. "That is precisely what I did. I changed those memories and made them much less painful and humiliating, and on the other hand, I magnified the feelings of satisfaction Edgar had from his academic achievements. That took care of the resulting anger and resentment."

Kaia wasn't a therapist, and she couldn't understand how the goddess had erased the hatred without erasing the memories of it, but the end result was that she felt calmer and more like herself, and that was all that mattered.

What about the male urges, though? Were they still there?

It was hard to tell. Annani was beautiful, but she was so otherworldly that even Edgar couldn't have fantasized about her, and anyone with eyes could see and admire her perfection regardless of their gender or sexual orientation.

"Thank you." Kaia dipped her head, wondering whether she should get up first or wait to be dismissed. "May I join William now?" She glanced at the sliding doors, but the glass was reflective, and she couldn't see inside.

"You may, but we are not done, my dear child." Annani refilled her glass with lemonade and took a sip. "We should meet again next week and the one after that so I can continue refining those memories until there is no sting left to them."

Kaia hadn't planned on staying in the village longer than the week that Bridget had demanded, but refusing the goddess's offer would be rude.

Perhaps she could phrase it in a nonoffending way?

"I'm sure you are aware of the secret project that William and I are working on. We need to return to Safe Haven to complete the work."

Annani nodded. "Then we shall continue our sessions when you are done. How long do you expect it will take?"

"It depends. Once we are done with the initial deciphering, William can dismiss the team, and we can continue working on the journals here in the village."

"So, the main reason for returning to Safe Haven is the team members you left behind?"

Kaia nodded.

"Then the solution is simple. William should pay them what he promised them and send them home. Your uncle is transitioning, and the rest of your family is planning to move into the village in a week or two. It makes no sense for you to be over there while they are over here."

Kaia's main impetus for wanting to return to Safe Haven hadn't been the research but the two compellers who she'd hoped could help her forget her life as Edgar. But what they could do was no way near as amazing as what Annani had done and still intended to do.

Kaia inclined her head in deference to the goddess. "I couldn't agree more."

78

WILLIAM

*W*hen Kaia and Annani walked back in, the smile on Kaia's face melted away the ball of stress that had been wreaking havoc on William's stomach.

He hadn't touched any of the fancy hors d'oeuvres that Okidu had been circulating, and he'd drunk way too much of the whiskey Kian had been pouring.

"Are you okay?" he whispered as he pulled her into a quick embrace.

"I'm great. The Clan Mother convinced me that we should stay in the village and not return to Safe Haven."

He arched a brow. "What about the research?"

"We can do it here. The team can keep working with Marcel on tasks that we assign to them, Marcel will send their results here, and you and I will assemble the puzzle pieces in your lab."

"What about the geneticist and the ethicist you wanted to hire, and the genetics lab you wanted to build there, and the people you wanted to hire for that?"

"Marcel can stay in Safe Haven and supervise a new team of humans who will build a genetics lab." She put her hands on his chest. "And you know what the best part of staying here is?"

"What?"

"No more goop for breakfast, lunch, and dinner."

He smirked. "I thought the best part was my comfortable four-poster bed."

Behind them, Gilbert groaned. "I really didn't need to hear that."

"What do you mean by goop?" Kian asked.

William turned around. "The so-called healthy food leaves a lot to be desired."

"Why didn't you say something before?"

"It wasn't important, and I didn't want to bother you with minutiae."

"I thought that you didn't want the guests to return for another retreat," Kaia added. "If they didn't like the food, they wouldn't come back."

"Why would I want that? I'll have a talk with the chef."

638

Annani sat on the couch between Karen and Alena, her face alight with pleasure as she looked at the children.

"What a lovely sight this is." She reached for one of the boys. "Can I hold him?" Looking apprehensive, Karen nodded. "Of course, Clan Mother."

As Annani pulled the child onto her lap, he looked up at her with doe eyes.

"He's fascinated with your glow," Karen said. "Are you sure that it's not harmful?"

Annani laughed. "If anything, it's beneficial, right, Evan?"

How did she know who was who?

William still couldn't tell them apart.

The boy lifted his hand and touched her face. "Na-ni."

"He said my name." The goddess grinned. "Such a smart boy." She kissed his cheek. "And so sweet."

Karen relaxed. "They are both very good boys. They eat well, sleep well, and are not fussy."

Annani nodded sagely. "I think boys are easier to raise when they are little. Kian was my easiest child, but then as a young man, he went through a rebellious stage." She leaned toward Karen and whispered loudly, "He ran off and got married against my explicit wishes."

"Mother," Kian said in a warning tone. "No one wants to hear that story."

"I would love to hear it sometime," Karen said.

Annani leaned back with Evan in her arms. "I am going to stay in the village for a while this time, so we can meet for tea or lunch and share stories." Her expression turned serious. "Stay here, Karen. This is your home now. The house in the Bay Area is just a place you used to live in."

Karen swallowed and looked to Alena for help.

"My mother is right. For the longest time, I thought of the sanctuary as my home, but I realized that I feel just as much at home in the village and in Scotland as I do there. I have people I love here, in Scotland, and in the sanctuary, so as long as I have a room or a house where I can keep my things and add personal touches, I feel at home in all three places."

"Isn't it confusing?" Karen asked. "I think that we need one place to be our anchor. I can't imagine having several and feeling equally connected to each one."

Alena smiled. "You don't know until you try. You haven't stayed in the village long enough for it to feel like home, but give it another week or two, and it will."

"I need to go back and train my replacement. They have been good to me, and I don't want to repay them by quitting without notice and without ensuring a smooth transition." She chuckled. "I think that word is going to haunt me."

"You can quit if you want," Cheryl said. "You can call and say that you have a family emergency that you need to take care of, and that you don't know how long it will take to resolve. It wouldn't even be a lie. Eric is unconscious, and we don't know how long he will stay like that. You can tell your boss that you're profoundly sorry and you understand if she needs to replace you with someone else. What are they going to do? Send the cops after you and force you to go back to work? We are not in China, and this is still a free country."

"Cheryl is right." Gilbert sighed. "And we should listen to the Clan Mother's wisdom. Let's just stay."

"What about Berta?" Karen turned a pair of pleading eyes to Kian. "Is there any way we can bring her here with us?"

He shook his head. "I'm sorry. You will have to find a different solution."

As the discussion about caretakers continued, William tuned it out and began running in his head the details of conducting the research in two locations. They'd already had a system that they'd employed before Kaia started transitioning, but it had been designed as a temporary solution, and they needed to refine it.

Kaia leaned her head on his shoulder and whispered, "What are you thinking so hard about?"

"How to make it all work."

A smirk lifting her lovely lips, she turned into him and whispered directly into his ear. "I hoped that you were thinking of ways to use that four-poster bed of yours."

His mind immediately went to where she'd directed it, and as scenarios of what they could do with that bed flashed through his mind, he couldn't wait to enact them.

The problem was that with Annani there, leaving right away wasn't an option. They had to wait for her to take her leave first.

"Hold that thought," he whispered in Kaia's ear, and as his hand migrated to her bottom, he quickly scanned the room to see if anyone was watching them.

Someone was, and Annani smiled knowingly as if she'd heard their exchange, which she might have. Her hearing must be superior even to that of the immortals.

"You make such a beautiful couple and you are so well matched." Annani's eyes glowed with mischief, and William wondered what was on her mind. "The Fates have rewarded you both magnificently, and I cannot wait to preside over your mating ceremony." Annani turned to Karen. "We are going to have so much fun planning their wedding."

Gilbert opened his mouth, probably to protest, but then closed it and released a sigh. "The Clan Mother knows best."

It was nearly midnight when Annani left with Orion, Alena, and her Odus.

William and Kaia said their thanks to the hosts, escorted her family to the bridge, and then they were finally alone.

Standing on the threshold of their home, William swung Kaia into his arms, and when she laughed and wound her arms around his neck, he walked in and kicked the door closed behind him.

"Let's see what we can do with that four-poster bed, shall we?"

"Definitely. But before you carry me off to your man cave and have your way with me, I have a question."

"What is it?"

"Is McLean going to be my last name when we get married? Or can I choose any last name I want? I would like to keep Locke, but I assume that at some point I will have to fake my own death and get a new fake identity."

William smiled.

Kaia's mind never took a break. "When the time comes, you can have any name you want, and I'll adopt it as well. We can be Mr. and Mrs. $E=mc^2$."

Kaia threw her head back and laughed. "I love it." She pulled herself up and smashed her lips over his. "I love you, my prince."

"And I love you, my princess. Forever and beyond."

CHAPTER 78

**COMING UP NEXT
DARK GAMBIT TRILOGY**
The Children of the Gods Series
Books 65-67

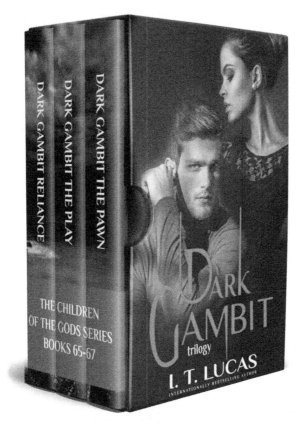

TEMPORARILY ASSIGNED to supervise a team of bioinformaticians, Marcel expects to spend a couple of weeks in the peaceful retreat of Safe Haven, enjoying Oregon Coast's cool weather and rugged beauty.

Things quickly turn chaotic when the retreat's director receives an email with an encoded message about a potential new threat to the clan.

While those in charge of security debate what to do next, Safe Haven's first ever paranormal retreat is about to begin, and one of the attendees is a mysterious woman who makes Marcel's heart beat faster whenever she's near.

Is the beautiful mortal his one truelove?

Or is she the harbinger of more bad news?

DEAR READER,

641

Thank you for reading the *Children of the Gods*.

As an independent author, I rely on your support to spread the word. So if you enjoyed the story, please share your experience with others, and if it isn't too much trouble, I would greatly appreciate a brief review on Amazon.

Love & happy reading,

Isabell

DARK GAMBIT TRILOGY

EXCERPT

SOIFA

"*Y*ou know who I am." Sofia handed the guard her identification card. "Why do you stop me every time I come home?"

"It's the protocol." Pioter smiled apologetically as he scanned her card and handed it back to her. "Are you here just for the weekend? Or are you going to stay longer this time?"

"I don't know. It's up to Igor."

Everything was up to Igor, but she shouldn't complain. At least she was allowed to leave the compound and attend university. Most of his subjects weren't as fortunate.

The founding group of pureblooded Kra-ell males were the elite of the compound and had more freedom and privileges than anyone else, but they couldn't come and go as they pleased either. Igor was a control freak who kept even his nearest and dearest on a tight leash.

Not that anyone was dear to him.

The male was cold and calculating, and if he were human, he probably would be classified as a sociopath. The Kra-ell might have a similar opinion of him, but no one was stupid enough to voice it.

He was ruthless and cruel to the purebloods and the hybrids, but surprisingly, he wasn't a monster to the human inhabitants of his compound. Perhaps he thought of them as pets, or maybe he pitied them for their short lifespans.

Supposedly, the pureblooded Kra-ell could live for a thousand years, but no one knew how long the hybrids would live. The oldest one was in his eighties, and he looked like he was in his twenties, so they might live just as long as the purebloods.

DARK GAMBIT TRILOGY

It was frustrating how little she knew.

Igor and his cohort of close pureblooded males didn't share what they knew with anyone. Not even their children and grandchildren.

One would think that being related to Igor's second-in-command would allow Sofia access to more information or get her preferential treatment, but it didn't. It might have elevated her status just a little over the humans with no Kra-ell blood in them, but most importantly, it provided her with a little more protection from unwanted advances.

Valstar might barely acknowledge her existence, but she was thankful for whatever advantage having him as a grandfather provided her.

Her relation to a high-ranking Kra-ell was most likely the reason she'd been selected to pursue higher education in the human world. Like the other fortunate young humans who'd been granted the opportunity, Sofia was under Igor's heavy-handed compulsion to keep the compound and the existence of the Kra-ell people on Earth a secret. She had to call once a week and report her progress to him, and she also had to make the long drive from the university to the compound for a monthly face-to-face meeting with her dear leader to reinforce the compulsion. But all of that was a small price to pay for her slice of freedom.

What was Igor afraid of, though? That she or one of the other students would reveal that they were the human descendants of aliens who drank blood? Or that their leader was most likely conspiring to take over the human world?

First of all, no one would believe them, and they would be subjected to a mental health evaluation. Secondly, none of them would do that willingly and endanger their families.

Well, she wouldn't, but in truth, she couldn't speak for the others.

Her mother was a piece-of-work Kra-ell hybrid who resented her human daughter, but she wasn't horrible enough for Sofia to want her dead, and her human father was great. Sofia loved him and her two aunts. She also had friends who were dear to her. Most were human, but there were a couple of Kra-ell hybrids who she considered friends as well.

Both were males who were interested in her as more than a friend, but Sofia had no intentions of hooking up with anyone from the compound, human, hybrid, or pureblooded Kra-ell.

She might never escape Igor's rule and live a normal life in the human world, but she could stretch out her studies for many more years and enjoy her freedom. He wanted her to learn foreign languages and master them, and that took time. Thankfully, the linguistics department of the University of Helsinki offered enough variety to keep her studying for many years to come.

After parking her ten-year-old Honda in the underground garage of the administrative building, Sofia climbed the stairs to the first floor, where she was stopped by a guard and her backpack was searched, and when she reached the second floor, she was stopped again by one of Igor's personal guards.

"Good evening, Gordi." She handed him her backpack for inspection. "Do you need to search me?"

She was wearing leggings and a form-fitting long-sleeved shirt that clung to her slim frame like a second skin. She couldn't hide a pin under that outfit, which was why she'd chosen to put it on. She'd hoped it would spare her a pat down.

"You know that I do." He motioned for her to lift her arms.

644

"Where do you think I can hide anything?" She did as he asked.

"Your hair." He motioned for her to release her tresses from the bun she had it gathered in. "You could hide a small firearm in that thing."

She rolled her eyes. "As if I would do something as stupid as that." She pulled out the pins holding the bun up, shook her long hair out, and let it cascade down her back. "Better?" She handed him the pins for inspection.

Gordi's eyes lit up with arousal. "You have such beautiful hair. Why do you always put it on top of your head like that?" He returned the pins to her.

It wasn't a style any of the Kra-ell pureblooded or hybrid females would ever adopt, which was precisely why she had.

It pissed her mother off.

"That's how I like it." She pretended not to notice the gleam in his eyes as she gathered her hair, twisted it on top of her head, and secured it with the pins. "Can I go now?"

Regrettably, the hybrids found her attractive for some reason.

Her dark hair, her height, and her slimness were traits she'd inherited from her Kra-ell grandfather, and her blue eyes and her gentle nature came from her Finn father. She was too thin to be considered attractive by human standards, and wasn't exotic enough to be attractive to the purebloods, but the hybrids found her features pleasing.

"Wait here." Gordi returned the backpack to her. "I'll check if Igor is ready to see you."

Slinging a strap over her shoulder, Sofia let out a silent breath and thanked the Mother that she was Valstar's granddaughter. If she were any other female, human or hybrid, Gordi could have commanded her into his bed, and there would have been very little she could have done to refuse him without courting severe retaliation.

Technically, it wasn't regarded as a command but as an invitation, and technically she could refuse, but in reality, no one dared to. To refuse a hybrid or pureblooded Kra-ell was to offend him, and since they held all the power in the compound, they could and would make her life and the lives of her family hell.

Gordi came out of Igor's office. "You can go in now."

"Thank you." She ducked into the room and immediately bowed her head. "Good evening, sir."

"Good evening, Sofia." Igor regarded her with his cold, calculating eyes. "How are your studies progressing?"

"Very well, sir. I receive top grades in all my classes."

It was the same exchange they had every month, and she often wondered whether Igor checked her grades by having them emailed to him.

Perhaps he had done it in the beginning, when he hadn't been sure she was up to the task, but after eight years of proven success, it would have been a waste of his time to keep checking on her.

Sofia was fluent in six languages and could converse in seven more, and she had no intentions of stopping unless Igor commanded her to quit.

He nodded. "I am satisfied with your progress. Keep up the good work."

She bowed again. "Yes, sir."

"Let's take care of your compliance with the compound's security rules, shall we?"

Sofia swallowed. Despite having gone through that once-a-month process for years, she still hated how it felt to have her will re-squashed with a ten-ton anvil. "Yes, sir."

EMMETT

"HERE ARE ALL THE CONTEST ENTRIES." Riley dropped a pile of printed papers on Emmett's desk. "I'm surprised that we only got forty-two." She glanced at the stack. "Are you sure you don't want me to read through them first? I can rate them and save you some time."

"Thank you for the offer." He smiled at her. "But I will enjoy reading them myself. I'm curious to find out what we caught in our net."

It wasn't a writing competition, and Emmett didn't care how well or how badly the essays were written. All he cared about was whether they hinted at the author's paranormal talent.

The contest had been Eleanor's idea. Those who couldn't afford to participate in a paranormal retreat could submit an essay to win a free subscription to Safe Haven's newsletter. They would also get unlimited access to its extensive library of self-improvement seminars and motivational materials. It was a good way to collect the names and email addresses of potential paranormal talents. Later, they could invite those who showed promise to participate for free and continue testing their abilities.

"As you wish." Riley cast another disapproving look at the stack. "It's such a waste of paper to have them printed. You could've read the emails on your computer screen."

"You know that I'm old-fashioned." Emmett lifted the first page. "I don't like staring at screens."

Shrugging, his office manager turned on her short, sensible heel and walked out the door.

Riley, who had taken over the management of the community and the retreats in his absence, was still adjusting to his return and her perceived demotion. She didn't like it, but she needed to get over it, or he would have to replace her with someone with a more subservient attitude.

Safe Haven was Emmett's baby, his creation, and even though he was sharing it now with Kian and the clan, he had close to full autonomy to do with it as he pleased.

Eleanor was running the paranormal enclave with the government talents that she'd recruited in her former job. Marcel had replaced William at the lab the clan had built on the premises and was temporarily supervising a team of scientists. Leon was in charge of security for the entire complex, and Anastasia was helping create content for the new paranormal retreats. That left Emmett to do what he did best, which was promoting the spiritual and paranormal retreats with his guru persona and giving the place its spiritual spin.

Leaning back in his chair, he got comfortable and started reading the first essay. He found nothing of interest and put it in the *no* pile. The next five landed on top of it, and the next two formed the *maybe* pile.

The tenth one was titled: *How the Lions and the Rats became allies. A fable.*

That should be interesting.

Emmett leaned back in his executive chair, lifted his feet onto the desk, and began reading.

A long time ago, in a far, faraway land, there lived a ferocious lioness named Viva who led a very large pride. Many different animals lived in that land, some big, some small, but the lions ruled over them all.

Viva was a proud female, and she paid little regard to the animals living in her territory who were too small for a lioness to eat. But there was one rat named Crafty, whose shenanigans were so outrageous that they had reached even Viva's ears. As his name implied, Crafty was cunning and smart, and he got away with mischief that other animals would never dare to try.

Emmett's heart thundered in his chest.

His father had named him Veskar after an animal from their home world that was similar to a rat and was known for being crafty. Only members of Jade's tribe knew him as Veskar, and Emmett knew of only two who were still alive and free, both residing in the immortals' village. The rest of their tribe had been either murdered or captured, so if this was written by one of them, it must have been submitted from captivity. Given that the first part of the fable was written from the pride leader's perspective, Jade must be the author.

The next part was written from the rat's perspective.

Crafty had a healthy respect for the lions, and he stayed away from them whenever he could. Those big cats normally didn't eat rats, but they might eat a rat who was prone to mischief.

Wishing to find a place where there were no lions and where rats were treated with respect, Crafty left the lions' territory and never looked back.

He traveled across the lake to where the humans lived, and he found a community of village rats who were all very well fed.

With his cunning and his smarts, it didn't take Crafty long to take over as the leader of the pack. Those spoiled village rats who never had to work hard for their scraps were now his to command.

He was the king of the rats.

Happy and contented, Crafty basked in his success, and the only thing missing from his perfect life was the satisfaction of showing his fellow wilderness rats how well he had done for himself. From time to time, he thought about swimming back across the lake to tell his family and friends about his wonderful new life in the human village, but it was too risky.

What if, while he was gone, another rat took over as the leader of the pack?

What if, on the way, Crafty encountered one of those ferocious cats and got eaten?

He stayed where he was and forgot all about those he had left behind.

This part did not give Emmett any new clues, and he was starting to doubt that the email had been sent by Jade. There were probably many fables featuring rats and other animals. If he searched the internet, he would probably find many more that had nothing to do with him.

The next part reverted to the lioness.

One day, when the big cats were all asleep, a massive earthquake shook the ground, collapsing the pride's home, killing some, and trapping the rest under a pile of stone. Not just the lions suffered. Many of the small cave dwellers were squashed under the avalanche of rocks. Those who survived fled through passages and openings that were too small for the big cats to fit through. The lions' size, the foundation of their superiority, was now a hindrance.

They were doomed.

"How many survived?" Viva asked once the count was done.

"Thirty adults and sixty cubs," answered the lion who had counted the live ones. Viva's heart sank. "How many died?"

"One adult female and her four cubs," the one who'd counted the dead said mournfully. "And if we don't find a way out of the collapsed caves soon, we will all die here as well."

"Who could save us?" a lioness cried out. "Does anyone even know that we are trapped?"

"Maybe the little critters who escaped through the nooks and crannies will tell someone who will be willing to help us," another lion said.

The only ones who could help were the humans, and they didn't understand animal language.

Despondent, Viva did not say a thing. She lay down and put her head on her paws.

Emmett was done with only the first one out of the three printed pages when he straightened in his chair, snatched the phone off his desk, and called Eleanor. "Come to my office right away. It's urgent."

"On my way." She ended the call.

MARCEL

MARCEL DIDN'T APPRECIATE BEING CALLED mid-morning by Eleanor and asked to come immediately to Emmett's office. If it were anyone else, he would have demanded explanations before rushing over, but Eleanor wasn't the type to get worked up over nothing.

The door to Emmett's office opened before he had a chance to knock. "Thanks for coming." Eleanor smiled apologetically. "I would have come to you, but I'm not allowed in the lab."

Normally, she would have been correct, but he would have allowed her in if she'd called and explained her problem. As long as he was there with her and made sure that she didn't see what he and the team were working on, it would have been okay.

"What's the emergency?" Marcel closed the door behind him.

"This." Emmett waved a stack of papers. "The email arrived two days ago, but I only read it today." He handed him a three-page document. "I need Kian to see it, but I don't want to send it from here in case it's encoded, and someone can follow the email to the village. I don't know the protocol for sending secure emails, but I assume that you have a safe channel of communication in your lab, and I need you to send it to him along with a note from me explaining what's going on."

Marcel read the title. "How the Lions and the Rats become allies. A fable." He lifted a brow. "It's a children's tale. Why does it need encryption, and what does it have to do with Kian?"

"It's from Jade," Eleanor said, cutting straight to the chase. "She wrote it in such a way that only Emmett would know it's from her. It's a call for help."

"Did you read it?"

Emmett might have seen in the story what wasn't there, but Eleanor was not prone to flights of fancy.

"I did. Without Emmett's explanation, I would have thought nothing of it, but with his input, the fable becomes a coded cry for help."

"How do you know it's from her?" Marcel asked Emmett.

The guy grimaced. "My Kra-ell name is Veskar. My father wasn't happy about the birth of a hybrid son who looked too human for his taste, so he gave me an insulting name. Veskar can be loosely translated as a crafty rat." Emmett pointed to the pages in Marcel's hands. "The fable's hero is called Crafty, and he's a rat."

"I see."

Marcel sat down and read the first page. "Do those numbers mean anything to you?"

Emmett shook his head. "They don't, but I'm sure that they are not random. I just don't know what she's trying to communicate."

"How many members did her tribe have?"

"None of those numbers add up to anything that makes sense," Eleanor said. "Emmett and I already tried to figure it out, but the numbers don't match the total number of the tribe's population, not the number of males or females, and not the number of humans. Not during Emmett's time in the tribe, and not right before the attack."

Marcel nodded. "That's what I thought. The sixty-four and thirty-one or the sixty and thirty could be latitude and longitude coordinates." He read the passage. "Thirty adults and sixty cubs lived. One female and her four cubs died." He lifted his head and looked at Emmet. "Longitude is also called meridian, and the synonyms for meridian are the greatest, the uppermost, and so on. Therefore, the number of adults could represent longitude. Latitude lines are also called parallels, and some of the synonyms for parallels are secondary and kin, which means that the number of cubs could represent the number for latitude."

"Oh, that's so clever of her." Eleanor crossed her arms over her chest. "And it's even cleverer of you to figure it out."

Marcel wasn't sure that it was. If Jade was trying to communicate a secret message in an email that she knew was monitored, that wasn't clever at all. He wasn't the only one who could figure out that those numbers were coordinates. Not that he was convinced that they were. It was just a hypothesis.

"Let's check those coordinates." Marcel pulled out his phone, opened the map application, and typed in the numbers. "Sixty longitude and thirty latitude point to

St. Petersburg. Let's check sixty-four and thirty-one." His brows lifted. "Interesting. It's probably a coincidence, but this set of coordinates is smack in the middle of a place called Karelia, which sounds a lot like Kra-ell. The area straddles northwest Russia and the eastern portion of Finland. The coordinates fall on the Russian side."

Eleanor turned to Emmett. "Mey said that the enemy Kra-ell male's echo she'd heard had a Russian accent."

They could be reading into the fable things that weren't there, and combining mismatched pieces of a puzzle, but Marcel was willing to suspend disbelief.

"Let's see if there are any more clues hiding in the story." He continued reading.

One day as Crafty was sitting on his throne and conducting pack business, a rabbit he had known from the wilderness hopped over. "Crafty, how good it is to see you. Did you hear what happened to the lions' pride?"

"I did not."

After the rabbit told Crafty about the earthquake that had trapped all the big cats underground, he sighed. "Even the cubs are too big to fit through the crevices that my family and I used to escape. They will all die in there." The rabbit shook his head. "I wish I could help, but I'm just a small rabbit, and all I can do is run."

Crafty might have disliked the lions' haughty attitudes, but they had never been his enemy, and he did not wish to see them all dead. He wouldn't leave the cubs to die of starvation.

The rabbit might be helpless, but a smart rat with a large pack could do what even the powerful lions could not.

He could dig an escape tunnel and prove the real value of rats. They weren't just parasites who lived off human scraps. They could be powerful and respected allies. Crafty summoned his followers and told them his plan. "The pride will forever be in our debt, and we will never hunger for meat again." He stretched to his full height and lifted his paws. "We will prove to everyone that rats are not at the bottom of the food chain and that we deserve as much respect as the lions. With our smarts, determination, and cooperation, we can do what none of the other animals can."

One of the bigger rats lifted his paw. "How do we know that they won't eat us once we get to them? Lions don't usually eat rats, but they will be hungry, and they have cubs that they will be desperate to feed."

"I will tunnel through the last couple of feet alone and talk to their leader. If she swears not to let anyone of her subjects eat us, I will come back, and we will enlarge the tunnel so they will be able to get out."

"She might promise you that and then eat us after we free her," a female said. "Or she might just eat you before giving you a chance to explain."

Crafty laughed. "I would not be much of a meal, and the pride's leader is too smart to eat her only hope of survival. She's a mother, and she'll do anything to save the cubs, even if it means making an alliance with rats. She's also proud, and if she gives me her word, she will stand by it."

"What about the other cats?" the big male asked. "They will eat us for sure."

It was possible. The leader might have lost her hold on the pride, or she might be injured and weakened, and they might not listen to her, but Crafty couldn't just do nothing and let them all die.

"She won't let them. Let's go!" He singsonged that special tune that would ensure the

pack's compliance. "We will prove to the world that rats are not to be sneered at."
It took the pack three days to swim through the lake and then another seven days to
burrow underground, and when Crafty smelled the lions, the live ones and the dead,
he made the signal for his pack to stop. "I shall continue alone from here."
As he dug through the last three feet, he didn't bother to make the tunnel more than
two inches wide, compressing his body and squeezing through.
When he emerged from the tunnel the lions were asleep, and as he scurried as fast
as his paws could carry him to the largest lioness, the others lifted their massive
heads and bared their teeth.
He slid between her outstretched paws. "Don't eat me! I came to save you!"
Her big feline eyes widened. "How?"
He stood up and stretched to his full height of seven and a half inches. "My name is
Crafty, and I am the leader of a big rat pack. I promised my subjects that you and
yours would forever be in our debt if we dug a tunnel and got you out. But you and
your subjects must swear alliance to me and mine. You also need to swear that you
will not eat any members of my pack and that once you are free, you will share
your kills with us."
Hope surging in her heart, the leader nodded her massive head.
To save her family, she would kiss the rat on his little whiskers if that was what he
demanded in payment, but all he was asking for was assurance for the safety of his
pack and future scraps. It was a very small price to pay to save the weakening cubs.
They wouldn't last much longer.
"I have heard of you, Crafty, and I know that you are a very smart rat. I swear it
on my life and the lives of everyone in my pride that if you and your pack save us,
you will never go hungry for meat for as long as we live. My pride and I will share
our kills with you and yours, and we will never eat any of your subjects or any
other rats." She grimaced. "Rats were never a food source for us and never will be."
Weakened from hunger, she lifted herself with effort and turned to the others.
"Swear it, and let's get out of here."
After the lions repeated the vow that their leader had made, Crafty returned
through the tiny tunnel he had dug for himself and told the others what was
promised.
When the rats had finished digging the rest of the tunnel and freed all the lions, the
leader of the pride and her subjects kept their promise. From that day on, the pride
of lions and the pack of rats lived in harmony and mutual respect, and no one in
that part of the world dared to look down their noses or whiskers at Crafty or any
other rat.

Marcel shifted his gaze to Emmett. "Does seven or three mean anything to you
or seven and a half inches?"

Emmett shook his head. "They don't. The only thing I got from the fable was
that Jade and the other females were trapped, that they had children with them,
and that they needed me to save them in a stealthy manner, maybe literally by
digging a tunnel. Without your input, I would have never suspected that the
numbers of the adults and cubs could represent coordinates."

Dark Gambit Trilogy

Also by I. T. Lucas

THE CHILDREN OF THE GODS ORIGINS
THE CHILDREN OF THE GODS

ALSO BY I. T. LUCAS

66: DARK GAMBIT THE PLAY

PERFECT MATCH
PERFECT MATCH 1: VAMPIRE'S CONSORT
PERFECT MATCH 2: KING'S CHOSEN
PERFECT MATCH 3: CAPTAIN'S CONQUEST

THE CHILDREN OF THE GODS SERIES SETS

BOOKS 1-3: DARK STRANGER TRILOGY—INCLUDES A BONUS SHORT STORY: THE
FATES TAKE A VACATION
BOOKS 4-6: DARK ENEMY TRILOGY —INCLUDES A BONUS SHORT STORY—THE
FATES' POST-WEDDING CELEBRATION
BOOKS 7-10: DARK WARRIOR TETRALOGY
BOOKS 11-13: DARK GUARDIAN TRILOGY
BOOKS 14-16: DARK ANGEL TRILOGY
BOOKS 17-19: DARK OPERATIVE TRILOGY
BOOKS 20-22: DARK SURVIVOR TRILOGY
BOOKS 23-25: DARK WIDOW TRILOGY
BOOKS 26-28: DARK DREAM TRILOGY
BOOKS 29-31: DARK PRINCE TRILOGY
BOOKS 32-34: DARK QUEEN TRILOGY
BOOKS 35-37: DARK SPY TRILOGY
BOOKS 38-40: DARK OVERLORD TRILOGY
BOOKS 41-43: DARK CHOICES TRILOGY
BOOKS 44-46: DARK SECRETS TRILOGY
BOOKS 47-49: DARK HAVEN TRILOGY
BOOKS 50-52: DARK POWER TRILOGY
BOOKS 53-55: DARK MEMORIES TRILOGY
BOOKS 56-58: DARK HUNTER TRILOGY
BOOKS 59-61:DARK GOD TRILOGY

MEGA SETS
INCLUDE CHARACTER LISTS

THE CHILDREN OF THE GODS: BOOKS 1-6
THE CHILDREN OF THE GODS: BOOKS 6.5-10

TRY THE CHILDREN OF THE GODS SERIES ON
AUDIBLE
2 FREE audiobooks with your new Audible subscription!

FOR EXCLUSIVE PEEKS AT UPCOMING RELEASES & A FREE COMPANION BOOK

Made in the USA
Las Vegas, NV
02 February 2023

66745587R00364